NANCY NICOLSON
MEG HAMILTON
THE STEPMOTHER

BY
ANNIE S. SWAN

SUNDAY MAIL EDITION
1933

NANCY NICOLSON

BY

ANNIE S. SWAN

SUNDAY MAIL EDITION
1933

CONTENTS

CHAPTER I

THE LAST HOPE

THE great room was empty and still, and in the far corners shadows lurked. The absence of light and laughter, of warm family life made it, with all its faded magnificence, a place which was not a home. Braidwood sighed as he came up the long outer room and swept the curtains of the inner recess aside. He was only a manservant, but his heart was heavy as lead for the fortunes of the house he served. He was a middle-aged man, of spare build, with a kind, shrewd and very Scotch face. One to trust, albeit his tongue might be sharp and his ways lack the polish which is supposed to be the lackey's most valuable quality.

" It's a place of ghosts," he muttered to himself, as he stirred the fire to a brighter blaze. " I wonder what took him all of a sudden to wait for him here ? "

A huge fire blazed in the wide dog grate of highly polished steel, but the place lacked the warm, kindly atmosphere of a room that is lived in, and where people spend happy hours. Braidwood's face perceptibly saddened as he retraced his steps whither he had come. He paused just at the further door and took a long look at the portrait of a woman which hung in an obscure place, half hidden by the portière curtain.

" Eh, I wonder where you are, my bonnie lamb ? " he said, and drew his hand quickly across his eyes. Now, moments of emotion were extremely rare in the order of Braidwood's quiet, self-restrained life, and certainly betokened some unusual atmosphere in the house.

He was not long gone, and when he returned he was guiding the feeble, tottering steps of an old man.

A tall figure, sadly bent, a shrivelled parchment-like face, white hair straggling under a black velvet skull cap, shaking hands, gripping nervously at his servant's arm. Such was Francis Riddell Learmonth, laird of Penninghame and Whitekirk, in the fair Lothians. He looked round him with an almost childish interest as he tottered up the long room to the inner recess, where he was carefully placed in an easy chair, and wheeled near to the dancing logs.

" How many years since I sat in this room, eh, Braidwood ? "

" A guid twenty, laird, if it's a day, an' ye wadna be here the nicht if I could prevent it," was the dry retort.

" I took the thought all of a sudden. We are going to restore the glory of Penninghame, Braidwood. The young blood will put fresh life into the old place."

" Maybe ay, an' maybe no," was the enigmatical reply.

Braidwood's face wore an expression of the deepest gloom. He was not so old as his master, but old enough to hate changes, and there were changes impending, ay, great changes, for Francis Learmonth the greatest change of all. Braidwood had served the house for forty years, and to his mind there had been no sadder page in all its history than that which was about to have " finis " written across it.

He saw death, if no one else did, in his master's face ; he knew him only fit for the bed from which he would never rise again. Yet he was attired in full evening dress, with amethyst studs in his frilled shirt bosom, and his gold fob dangling at his side. He had been living for weeks in a dressing-gown, and until Braidwood had put him in his dress clothes that evening he had no idea how emaciated his poor thin figure actually was.

" It's cold here, Braidwood," said the old man querulously. " Pile on the logs ; surely there are plenty in the cellar."

" Ay, plenty, but it wad take a hale wud to warm this place. Ye'd better come doon the stair to your auld bit."

" No, I have the fancy to receive Anthony Weir's boy here. Do you remember Anthony, Braidwood ? "

" As muckle o' him as I want, laird," replied Braidwood, as he lifted an old-fashioned twofold screen and set it carefully behind his master's chair.

" Dear me, Braidwood, you are in a very ill mood to-night ! Anthony was a ne'er-do-well himself, but I hear his son is a different breed. Everything depends on the mother. I should like to have seen Anthony's wife."

" Humph ! " said Braidwood. " I'll get your plaid for your knees, I think. Thae breeks are very thin."

" Hush, Braidwood, there's the carriage wheels."

" It's impossible ; the train's no' due at Penninghame for a quarter o' an 'oor."

" From South Africa all the way, poor lad. He deserves a kindly welcome. Lord, how the Learmonths are scatterèd ! Some of them could be found in every quarter of the globe."

" There's only wan Learmonth wha's whereaboots I wad like to discover," said Braidwood, greatly daring.

The old man frowned, and shook a warning fore-finger.

" No forbidden names here, Braidwood. You and I agreed long ago to differ on that point."

" I am richt and you are wrong," said Braidwood, stolidly. " An' I wad gi'e ten, ay, twenty, years o' my life, supposin' they were mine to gi'e, if it were Miss Isabel's son we were waitin' for the nicht instead o' Anthony Weir's."

The old man, still frowning, raised his hand again.

" It was wheels, and they are stopping at the door. Go down, Braidwood, and bid him kindly welcome, and bring him quickly, for the old know not how to wait."

Braidwood straightened his back and hastened from the room. As he reached the stairs the great bell at the front door awoke all the sleeping echoes of the quiet house. He hastened to throw wide the door and bid welcome to Penninghame its expected heir. His hands were nervous as they handled the heavy bolts, and he was trembling when the cold night air met him, and he saw the light stream upon a tall, broad figure wrapped in a fur coat.

" Good evening, sir, and welcome to Penninghame," he said as one who repeats the lesson he has conned. " The laird awaits you upstairs."

" Ah, that's all right. Who are you, may I ask ? "

" Andrew Braidwood, at your service, sir, that has been ain man to Mr. Learmonth for thirty years."

" Ah ! "

The new-comer took a long breath, and for one brief moment the two regarded one another with a kind of inquiring scrutiny.

The grey serving man, with his impassive face and shrewd eye, took stock of the youth from over sea, and his heart sank to the lowest ebb of hope. He looked in vain in that figure for any sign of breeding or grace, and the face, in spite of certain good looks which could not be gainsaid, repelled him. There was little look of the Anthony Weir he remembered about him, though he imagined in his voice a familiar tone. There was no kindliness in the penetrating eye, no diffidence in the demeanour, none of that gracious deference the young should be ready to pay to the old. Anthony Weir looked like one who had arrived for the purpose of grasping rights of which he had been too long defrauded.

"His father's son," said Braidwood, under his breath, with something like a groan. Outwardly he remained calm, and did his duty in the way of helping the newcomer off with his coat.

"How is my uncle now?" he asked, and the very use of the title Braidwood in his secret soul resented.

"Jist the same, neither better nor waur," he answered, with a touch of sullenness. "Wull ye mind no' to excite him, sir, for he is weaker than he thinks."

"All right, old cock. Don't look so glum. I'll let him down gently," he said, and thrusting his hands in his pockets, took a long critical look round the fine old hall, which was one of the chief features of Penninghame House. It had a floor of tesselated marble, oak panelled walls, and in every niche an armoured figure, which struck Anthony Weir strangely.

"What are they for?" he asked curiously. "Dummy bodyguard, eh? Looks a bit off. I should like to give 'em the right-about march."

Braidwood made no reply except to ask him to walk upstairs. As he followed, Anthony Weir used his eyes well, and felt himself deeply impressed. He came from a mean, sordid little colonial house where money and things money can buy were conspicuous by their absence. The rich subdued colourings, the unostentatious comfort, the spacious solidity of Penninghame were a revelation to him. And he swore a great oath, though under his breath, that this magnificent place should be his, that nothing should intervene to rob him of it. And from that vow Anthony Weir never departed.

Outside the door Braidwood paused. His honest heart was sore for the eager old man within. He would have softened his disappointment, taken the edge off the pain which must ensue. That being impossible all he could do was to speak another word of warning to him who, all unconscious to himself, was about to inflict a blow.

"The laird is very old, sir, and frail. Treat him as ye would treat your father were he alive and like him."

Braidwood was not good at expressing himself, nor was Anthony Weir quick at comprehension. Being colonial born he did not, however, resent the liberty taken by a servant as another might have done.

"All right, boss," he said, and Braidwood opened the door.

"Mr. Anthony Weir, sir," he announced, and, under pretence of seeing to the fire, made bold to follow the guest into the room.

The old man came eagerly forward, tottering, with his frail white hands folded above his ebony stick. His appearance almost that of a ghost, and rendered more striking by his clothes, gave Anthony Weir a sudden shock. He was unable to appreciate the compliment intended to be conveyed by his attire. At the very moment of greeting he struck a false note.

"How do you do, Uncle Francis; sorry to see you looking so jolly bad," he said, with the frankness upon which he prided himself.

The old man took the young man by the hand, turned his face to the full light, and regarded him with a pathetic eagerness.

"You are not very like your father, but you are welcome to Penninghame, Anthony Weir. It is long since one of my own kin set foot within it. What kind of a journey had you?"

"Pretty fair. An old chap on the train gave me the tip about getting out at Porth Junction. That's how I happen to be here so early."

"Come forward to the fire and sit down and tell me about yourself. You need not wait, Braidwood; I'll ring if I want you, and just tell them to hasten dinner."

"Yes, sir," answered Braidwood, but his voice had a slightly aggressive ring, and he did not hurry himself about leaving the room.

"He seems at home," said Anthony Weir suggestively, as the door closed.

"You must excuse him; he's a faithful servant, one of the old school, and I daresay he feels a bit jealous to-night. He and I have been alone here for well-nigh thirty years."

"Mighty slow business, eh?" said Weir lightly. "What a room! Why, it would hold our little bit of a place in it like an island in an ocean."

"Tell me about your life in South Africa. I am afraid your father had a hard time."

"He had, was down on his luck all the time, and the family's not much better."

"How many are there?"

"Only my sister Letty and yours truly."

"Mother dead, too?"

"Dead too, this time last year, enteric. We had a terrific summer with the heat, and, unfortunately, had not the needful to get her away to the hills."

"Letty is your sister, I suppose. What does she do?"

"She serves in a shop, Uncle Francis. I daresay you think that rather awful. Couldn't help ourselves. It don't matter out there either where Jack's as good as his master. Letty might have improved the situation if she had not been too jolly selfish for us all."

"How?"

"Might have married a little German Jew out there, by name Frankelstein. Awful little beast, but rolling in gold, simply rolling, and he was mad about Letty. He was her governor, you know. She was typewriter in his place. But she wouldn't even look at him. As I said to her, it was her duty to sacrifice herself for the sake of the family; that was before the mater died. She was of my mind, and Letty had a hottish time, but she stood it out."

"She must have pluck this sister of yours."

"She's jolly pig-headed in her own interests if you like, and she's jolly pretty, too. Oh, she'll do all right. A pretty woman always can do for herself. It's different with poor beggars like us that have to live by their wits, never even been taught a decent trade, Uncle Francis."

The old man kept his eye fixed on him oddly fascinated. To him he seemed the embodiment of all that was vulgar and impossible. His fastidious eyes noted his careless dress, his ill-kept hands, his slovenly, common air, and he could have laughed aloud. Was it for this he had waited so long? Was this the heir, soon to be the Laird of Penninghame?

Nay, God forbid!

CHAPTER II

THE LIMIT TO HIS LIFE

THE smooth resonant beat of the dinner-gong awoke the echoes afresh. Weir started, slightly inquiring.

" It's only the dressing-gong. Ring the bell, Anthony, and Braidwood will show you to your room."

" What for ? I'm jolly hungry ; I can see the room afterwards. I won't keep you waiting."

" You must dress, or at least wash," said the old man, a trifle hastily, and reaching to the bell rope, pulled it himself.

Braidwood, hovering about the passage outside, was on the instant in the room.

" Take Mr. Weir to his room, Braidwood, and see that he has everything he wants."

Braidwood nodded and led the way. He was bursting with curiosity to discover what effect the new arrival had upon the laird, but had been unable to gather anything from the expression of his face, which had never been more inscrutable.

" Looks like a galvanised corpse, doesn't he ? " said Weir suggestively, when they found themselves outside the door. " Can't last above a couple of weeks, I should think."

" He has looked like that for years," said Braidwood witheringly, stretching a point for his own satisfaction. " This way, if you please."

" I say, what a great barracks of a place. I'll get lost in it. How ghastly for one old man to have all this at his disposal, ghastly and unfair."

Braidwood resented his familiarity, and thought unutterable things. The laird was familiar with him, and allowed him great licence of speech, but never for a moment was the gulf between master and man forgotten. Braidwood knew to a nicety just how far a servant might go, and what he called afterwards to Susan, his wife, " impident upsettin'," filled him with disgust.

He led him along the long corridor to a room at the further end, a wide, pleasant chamber, lit by a cheerful fire, and having a commodious dressing-room opening off it.

" If ye want onything, ye can ring, sir, an' some o' the weemin'll come. I must go back to my master."

Anthony Weir was surprised to find his trunk there, all the straps undone, ready for his keys.

" They do you jolly well," he said. " Lap of luxury, and no mistake. Gad, I'm the boy to appreciate it."

He took a walk round the room, examined the furniture, the rich brocade bed hangings, the fine ornaments on the mantelshelf, with the eye of an appraiser rather than that of a connoisseur. To Weir's mind these things represented just so much hard cash, which was his present god.

Braidwood hastened to the drawing-room, and was not surprised to find his master crouching over the fire in an attitude of dejection.

" Ony warmer, sir ? I think the room is warmer, isn't it ? " he asked, anxiously.

" No, it's very cold. Take me down to the library, Braidwood, and don't let me leave it again. This is a place of shadows and of ghosts."

" Jist what I said, but ye wadna be putten past it," said Braidwood grimly. " Ye'd better bide noo or efter denner, or Nancy sees till the library fire. Ye'll be gettin' yer daith if we dinna tak' care."

" I've got it, Braidwood, long since, and this night is the finishing stroke."

" Do ye think him like his faither ? " asked Braidwood reflectively.

" Like and yet unlike. It was a mistake, Braidwood, and how am I to get out of it ? "

" It's early days yet, sir, and maybe the young man hasna had a chance," said Braidwood, rather to comfort his master than to voice any conviction of his own.

" You can't make a silken purse out of a sow's ear, Braidwood, and very well you know it," retorted the old man, with an unusual touch of spirit. " He can make a visit here. I will make it worth his while ; but I will look elsewhere for an heir to Penninghame."

An hour ago these words would have afforded Braidwood the liveliest satisfaction, but something told him that Anthony Weir's son would not be so easily set aside or ousted from the position he coveted and now expected. For his whole bearing indicated that he believed he had been summoned for one object only—to take his place as his uncle's heir.

The meal served in the small dining-room that evening was an odd little bit of unconscious comedy, bordering, however, on the edge of tragedy. In his high-backed chair sat the old laird, his pallid face showing ever more ghastly against the dark oak, his nervous hands playing with the food he scarcely touched.

Opposite to him the young man from the colony, alert, vigorous, with ruddy face and keen eye, the very embodiment of the modern spirit, the new age. Entirely satisfied with himself likewise, and talking incessantly, putting his foot in it so often that Braidwood grew hot and cold by turns, and wondered whether his master would not take an apopletic shock before the evening was over.

Immediately dinner was over the laird asked to be excused, and retired to his apartments. Anthony Weir, quite pleased to be left alone to take his bearings, as he expressed it, wandered about the ground floor until he found his way to the library. There Nancy Nicolson, the housemaid, niece to Braidwood, was attending to the fire. Nancy was a pretty girl, with a fresh-coloured rosy face, bright dark eyes, and a wealth of golden brown hair. Nor was her expression wanting in the promise of better and higher things. Much might be expected in life from Nancy Nicolson. In her neat housemaid's garb, with her becoming apron, cap and cuffs, she made a pleasing object in the eyes of Anthony Weir.

She rose in a hurry of confusion, being disturbed at her work, but as she essayed to leave the room she stole a glance at the youth whom some of them were already calling the young laird. And she decided that he would make a very presentable young laird indeed.

Weir smiled at her reassuringly. He came from a land where class distinctions are not so strongly marked and upheld, and the sight of a pretty face never failed to please him. In that big, desolate house it seemed a welcome and very unexpected bit of brightness.

" Don't be in such a hurry ; I won't eat you," he said pleasantly. " How long have you been here, eh ? "

" Oh, ever since I was wee," said Nancy blushing all over. " I came when my mither dee'd, and Aunt Susan cam' to Glesca and brocht me wi' her."

" I see, and do you like it in this dull old house ? It's hardly the place for a pretty creature like you."

" Yes, I like it. I've never kent onything else."

" That's the rub, you see. It's easy to be content if you've never seen anything. Never mind, perhaps it'll be a little livelier now I've come."

Nancy picked up her coal scuttle and departed, much mystified and no little confused. Pleased, of course, by the notice taken of her, she had yet intuition sufficient to know that it was unusual and not quite the thing. For that reason she said nothing to her aunt or to any of her fellow-servants. But the seeds were sown. From that night henceforth Nancy Nicolson began to harbour thoughts and dreams to which she had been a stranger.

Anthony Weir slept late next morning, and no one came to disturb him. As he was leisurely dressing about half-past ten he espied a hooded gig coming rapidly up the avenue. In it sat a middle-aged man with a slouch hat over his brows, and his arms folded across his breast. As the trap came rapidly up through the long stately lines of the beech trees, Weir got a better look at his face. It was a fine, strong, clever face, clean-shaven. He even observed that the hair at the temples was a little grey.

" The doctor, I suppose ; you can tell 'em. Well, if he can do anything for the old man he's smarter than the usual run. He looks like a living skeleton. I must try and interview Master Doctor this morning, and see how the land lies."

By the time Weir got downstairs, the doctor had already come to the laird's room. Weir found his way to the room in which they had dined the previous evening, and, seeing no sign of breakfast there, rang the bell. Nancy answered the bell, and her colour rose at sight of him.

" Oh, good-morning, my dear, do you happen to know if there's any breakfast going for a late-comer ? Or are the laws of the Medes and Persians observed, eh ? "

" Breakfast's laid in the mornin' room, sir ; I'll get it up," replied Nancy, and precipitately fled, for the open admiration in his bold eyes somewhat disconcerted her.

" The morning room ! In the Lord's name how many different places have they ? It's a perfect palace, but I'll soon accommodate myself."

He wandered out again, and searching in the hall found the comfortable cosy breakfast room, where the table was laid and the cheerful firelight glowing on the warm red walls and the gleaming silver on the table. The newspaper, neatly folded, lay on his plate, and the whole place presented such a comfortable home-like look that Weir's whole being seemed to expand with satisfaction. Each moment the place became more desirable, the idea of becoming its master caused his heart to swell with pride.

Meantime a different scene was being enacted upstairs. Doctor Jeffrey, admitted to his patient's room, found him in a state of extreme nervous prostration.

" Never sleepit a wink a' nicht, doctor," said Braidwood mournfully in the background.

" Go outside, Braidwood, I want to speak to the doctor. See that they are looking after Mr. Weir."

Dr. Jeffrey unbuttoned his overcoat, and finally took it off. The room was very warm, though the old man was sitting before the fire with his hands outspread as if he felt chilled to the heart.

"Well, well, we don't look up to much this morning, laird," he said cheerfully, as he took one of the feeble hands, and began to count the pulse.

"He came last night, doctor, Anthony Weir's son, and he won't do," said the old man, looking upward into the doctor's strong kind face as if finding some comfort in its contemplation.

"I didn't think he would, laird, from what I remember of Anthony Weir, but you would have your own way," said the doctor good-humouredly. "But you're not committed, are you? You can let him stop awhile, give him a present, and send him away."

"That's exactly what I said to Braidwood," said the laird eagerly. "I'll do something for him—yes, certainly, after bringing him so far; but give him Penninghame, no. Say, doctor, how long do you give me?"

"Not long if you keep your pulse like this, my man," said the doctor drily.

"I don't want an answer of that kind. I want to know as near as you can tell me how long I have to live, so that I may know what time I have to make arrangements."

The doctor put back his watch and turned away. These two were old friends, between whom there had never fallen the slightest shadow of doubt or misunderstanding. To give him his death sentence was no easy task either for the patient or for himself.

"You needn't be afraid. It isn't Death I'm afraid of. Why should I be? We've hobnobbed, he and I, many a time. Say the word, then I'll know where I am."

"I should say about the end of April would see you through, laird." said the doctor, but his voice sounded thick and unsteady.

"This is the fourteenth of November, four or five months. A lot can be done in that time. Thank you, doctor, for giving me a longer lease than I expected."

Francis Riddell Learmonth, Laird of Penninghame, was done with the things of time, but the love of the old place was in his blood, part of his body's life. He would preserve its honour, leave it in worthier hands than Anthony Weir's. But he was very old and frail, too frail to reckon with the new virile force that had arrived at his bidding to disturb the even tenor of his life.

CHAPTER III

IN HIS GRIP

" BRAIDWOOD," said the laird feebly, " send somebody to the village to telegraph for Mr. Shepherd."

Braidwood glanced at the clock. It was just ten minutes past seven, and, by the time a horse could be got and a messenger sent, the office might be closed. But the news was welcome news to Braidwood, and he determined that the message should go at all cost.

" I'll gang myself," he said quickly. " Is't the morn's morning ye want him to come."

" Yes ; as soon as he can get here, by the first train if possible. Send the telegram to him at Upper Dean House, Dean Bridge."

" Very well, sir," said Braidwood, but still lingered as if something weighed upon his mind. " Sir, may I mak' bold to speir something ? " he queried anxiously.

" What is it, Braidwood ? You are aye speiring something," said the laird languidly, yet with no trace of irritation in his voice.

" If it's the will, ye'll be cautious, sir ? Ye're no deid yet, an' them ye think weel o' will bring only wae to Penninghame."

" You mean my nephew ? "

" I mean Mr. Anthony Weir," replied Braidwood, with a touch of grimness. " He's no what ye think."

" You have never been just to him, Braidwood. He has been a great comfort to me ; why would he not make a good laird of Penninghame ? "

" Have ye forgotten the nicht he cam', hoo your he'rt wadna welcome him. Thon was the true speerit speakin'. He's as wily as a serpent. Ask ony o' them in the hoose, an' ye'll get his true character."

" You think very little of my judgment, Braidwood. I've got all my wits about me, though it may be the eleventh hour."

" Ask the doctor," said Braidwood desperately. " Him an' me's agreed."

" Go away and do my bidding, and keep your tongue between your teeth," said the laird.

Braidwood bit his lip, and silently withdrew. It was the first direct rebuke he had received in all the years of his faithful service ; his master had never before addressed him in such tone or words. His heart was sore as he made his way down the stairs to write the telegram, thinking he would send one of the stable lads with it on his bicycle. To save time he went bareheaded through the door at the far end of the hall, which opened on the terrace behind the house, and from which there was a path through the shrubbery to the stables.

He knew he should find the lad busy there ; there was plenty of work in the stables now since Anthony Weir had come. Beggars on horseback were words often on the tip of Braidwood's tongue.

It was a very dark night, the last night of January. But the air was warm, with a hint of spring, and a few drops of mild rain filtered through the still air. Sounds carried a long distance, and the moment Braidwood turned down the shrubbery path he heard the murmur of voices. Curious to know who could be talking there in the dark, he turned the small lantern he carried in the direction whence the voices proceeded, and the flash fell full on two faces, that of Anthony Weir and his own wife's niece, Nancy Nicolson. Nancy gave a little scream and fled. Braidwood turned the lantern round again and proceeded towards the stable, his errand being one that could not wait. But his mouth set in a long, grim, stern curve, and there was that in his soul which almost affrighted him. It was dark hate of the man who had destroyed the fair placid tenor of life in the old house of Penninghame.

He gave the lad his instructions, helped him to light his lamp, and then took his way into the house. In twenty minutes' time it would be his duty to wait on Anthony Weir at his solitary dinner, a duty from which the laird had never absolved him, though he had tried every stratagem in his power to get himself relieved. Day by day this ordeal had become more galling, and Anthony Weir, fully conscious of the man's antagonistic attitude towards him, took pleasure in reminding him that he was only a servant.

That night, however, Braidwood determined that no power on earth should induce him to play the servant's part. He would leave the house first. His face was curiously white as he re-entered the house and carefully bolted the terrace door. Then he set his little lantern in his own corner of the cloakroom, and proceeded to the small dining-room to see whether the table was all right.

Some one had laid the table. Braidwood, with the force of habit, put a few finishing touches to it, and then glided from the room. Just outside the door he met Anthony Weir face to face. For a moment the two looked at one another in silence, then Weir swore, and bade him get out of his sight.

"Ye needna swear," said Braidwood coolly; "come in here or I speak to you."

"If you have anything to say, say it here," replied Weir, with a faint smile of aggravating quality. The two months of idleness and ease, and good living at others' expense, had not improved his appearance, nay, his face had a coarse look, as of one who has few thoughts beyond creature comforts and personal ease. Braidwood's honest eyes betrayed the contempt he felt.

"That was my niece ye were speakin' till," said Braidwood steadily. "Understand that whaever puts ill thochts intil her head has me to answer till."

Anthony Weir smiled.

"I'll speak to her just as often as I please," he answered coolly.

"Ye ocht to be ashamed o' yersel', but it shows your low breeding," said Braidwood, his slow passion not easily aroused, like to get the better of him. "Nae leddy wad look at ye, so ye hae to speak your silly nonsense to a puir servant lass."

The taunt went home and Anthony Weir clenched his fist.

"Listen," he hissed, "you are trying to blacken me in every way to my uncle, and it is because you have not succeeded that you forget who you are. This impertinence shall be reported to him, and understand that if I can manage it you shall leave Penninghame without a character. You have feathered your own nest long enough. You and your tribe are the masters of Penninghame, and my arrival was none to timely. But there's going to be an end of it."

" Blacken my character if ye can, ye hae nane yersel'," said Braidwood, witheringly. " But I'll be even with ye yet, Anthony Weir."

" Mr. Weir, if you please. To your servant's duties now, and see that you have my dinner on the table a little more punctually than you have done of late. I will have you understand that I am master here."

" Oh, ye are, are ye ? Well, we'll see," said Braidwood, turning on his heel.

His hands were shaking, his whole frame, indeed, trembling with excitement and the strain of evil passions. He was a peaceable man who had striven hard to do his duty by God and man, and whose conscience was free from any reproach. This was a strange new element that had come into his life, and he did not know how to meet it. He had spoken unpardonable words, he knew, to his master's relative, who was also a guest in the house.

" If only the doctor pays a nicht veesit I'll tell him every mortal thing," he said, as he wiped his brow and proceeded with a heavier foot than usual to his wife's room.

Braidwood's wife had been housekeeper at Penninghame for thirty years. She was very frail now, and unable for active duty, but still kept the reins of government in her hands. She had a good staff of her own training under her, and the work of the house, laid down on methodical lines, went on like clockwork. It was not only a well-managed house, but an economically managed one. The laird owed more than he knew to that honest pair who, though invested with much power, had never abused even in thought the confidence reposed in them.

Susan Braidwood was a small, thin, wiry person with a pale, somewhat refined-looking face, and a pair of extraordinarily keen, restless dark eyes. In comparison with her Braidwood was a slow heavy person, phlegmatic even in thought. Never idle, she had a pile of household linen on the table before her, while a black cat, her special favourite, sat blinking on the corner. A very cosy place was the housekeeper's room at Penninghame. It had always been Braidwood's haven of rest, but of late his leisure to enjoy it had been very rare.

He closed the door with an impatient hand, and sank somewhat heavily into a chair. His wife glanced up in surprise. It was just on the stroke of half-past seven, when he was supposed to be on duty in the dining-room.

" Mercy me, Andra," she said. " What's the maitter wi' ye ? Are ye feelin' no weel ? "

" I'm quite weel, Shusan, but it's that bleckguard Weir. Oh, what wad I gie if I could fell him to the grund ? "

" What's he been daein' noo, my man ? Dinna fash aboot him, he's an impident upstart."

" But he'll maybe be maister here, Shusan, then whaur wull we be ? "

" Dinna meet the trouble afore it comes, Andra," she said in gentle reproof, as she held up her needle's eye to the light, at the same time puckering her brows over it.

" Ye'll maybe no say that when you hear what has happent," he said darkly. " I had to gang oot to the stable to send Dod wi' a telegram for the laird, and what do ye think I saw. Nancy an' that il skin stannin' thegither in the shrubbery."

Susan let her seam drop and stared aghast.

" Never, Andra ! Ye must hae made some mistake," she said in a voice of keen apprehension.

"Nae mistake, was it likely, dae I no ken Nancy's face when I see it? She's been a sicht ower saucy lately. This is the explanation o't noo; what's to be dune?"

Susan looked genuinely distressed.

"Leave it to me, I'll speak to Nancy. She's a glaiket craitur, but there's nae ill in her."

"She's ower bonnie for a servant when there's rascals like Anthony Weir aboot. As I said till him he canna get a leddy to look at him, so he has to be poorin' his silly claptrap intil the ears o' a servant lass."

"Andra, ye never telt him that!" she cried, regarding him incredulously, yet with a sudden access of respect.

"Ay did I, an' I'll tell him mair or I'm dune wi' him."

"But he's very thick wi' the laird, Andra. I doot we'll get into trouble. Had I been you noo, I would never hae said a word. Leave it to me, I'll settle Nancy."

"That'll maybe be easier said nor dune. Eh, it was an ill day when he cam' to Penninghame. He's just like the Bible's serpent worming himself in a'gate," said Braidwood, getting his metaphors slightly mixed, but leaving his wife in no doubt as to his meaning. "He's gotten the laird completely under his thoomb. Even he'll no listen till a word frae me noo. But I'll tell the doctor everything the nicht, ay wull I."

Susan looked into the fire and sighed, an expression of anxiety deepening on her face. Hitherto, the lines had fallen for them in pleasant places and they had not been ungrateful; could it be that the Lord would forget them in their old age and suffer them to be turned adrift. She looked at her husband's grey hairs and bent shoulders with a sudden pity. They were no longer able for hard toil, and though they had been paid good wages they had taken joy in helping the needy, and had not been able to lay by much. The laird had promised that they should be provided for, but how could anything be sure? She did not, however, express all these thoughts. She knew her husband's slightly melancholy tendency, and how prone he was to make and meet trouble half-way. She would wait and watch, and, perhaps, quietly in the background do something to mend matters. In the meantime there was Nancy. The door opened suddenly, and her round rosy face appeared in the doorway, apparently in no way disconcerted. She even smiled as she saw their concerned looks.

Very sternly Braidwood rose to his feet.

"Come here, ye hizzie! If I catch ye at ony cantrips wi' Anthony Weir, my wummin, I'll warm ye."

Susan held up a deprecating hand.

"Ye'd better gang to the laird, Andra, I'll speak to Nancy."

Even as she spoke, a bell evidently rung with impatient hand resounded through the house. It was the dining-room bell, and though inwardly chafing Braidwood had no choice but to obey.

CHAPTER IV

THE RIGHTFUL HEIR

HENRY AITKEN, office boy, in the employment of Maitland & Shepherd, Writers to the Signet, in Charlotte Street, Edinburgh, had just arrived. The discreet elderly caretaker, whose duty it was to clean the offices and light the fires, stood broom in hand ready to reprove him as usual for being late. Henry was an impish youth, extremely ready of tongue. He merely grinned as he beheld her in her favourite attitude.

"Ten minutes past nine, Hairry. If I dinna tell the maister the day I'm no' a leevin' sinner."

Henry had a small hard ball of paper ready, which he shied at her, and then went whistling into the office. His duty was to look to the ink bottles and pen holders, and he was thus engaged, enjoying himself immensely, and bestowing a considerable quantity of ink on his fingers, when the bell of the outer office rang. Henry flew to open it, much amazed. None of the clerks had yet arrived, though through the upper pane above the obscure glass he could see two approaching in a leisurely fashion from the direction of Princes Street. When he opened the door he was surprised to behold a lady outside.

"Mr. Maitland in? I wish to see him," she said, and though her voice was gentle it had an imperious ring which duly impressed Henry, who was a student of human nature in a small way, and could now discriminate with surprising exactness between what he called "the gentry an' the common."

The lady, though not exactly in her first youth, was yet surprisingly attractive to look at, albeit she was in no way grandly dressed. It was mourning she wore, and she put her veil back as she addressed Henry, so that he had an excellent view of her face. It was somewhat thin and careworn, but the small neat head was proudly carried, and there was a suggestion of haughtiness in her whole bearing.

"He hasna come yet, ma'am. He generally gets here about half-past nine."

"I will wait," she said, and walked passed the astonished Henry like one who has been accustomed to enter as she pleased.

Now Henry was in a quandary, being under strict orders not to admit any stranger—man or woman—to the private rooms, yet certain that she was not one to be asked to wait on the bench in the outer office. To get himself out of the dilemma he left her to make her way in, and, rushing to the outside steps, gesticulated wildly to the two clerks now approaching him.

The head of the firm, a tall, spare, elderly man with a thin, intellectual, ascetic-looking face, arrived on foot precisely at half-past nine. Almost immediately thereafter, a smart brougham drove up, and the junior partner, a pompous, well-dressed, slightly aggressive figure, also alighted. By the time he had given his coachman certain instructions for the afternoon his colleague had passed to his own room, and the door was shut.

"Any one with Mr. Maitland, Henderson?" asked Mr. Shepherd casually, as he hung up his hat.

" Yes, sir ; a lady been waiting about half an hour."

" Early visitor," he remarked, as he took his letters and proceeded to his own desk. Meanwhile, hat in hand, his partner had entered the room to interview the unexpected caller. She was standing at the fire apparently warming her hands. Her black gown in sweeping folds lay about her feet, giving height and dignity to a somewhat slight, slender figure. A thin veil hung from the back of her close-fitting bonnet, causing Mr. Maitland to decide before he saw her face that she was a widow. When she turned, smiling slightly and somewhat sadly, he gave a great start.

" Bless my heart and soul, Miss Isabel, is it you ? "

" Yes, it is ; come back, as they all predicted, in sackcloth and ashes."

She offered her hand, and the old lawyer took it in both his own. He was a still, silent, austere man, but the sight of her sweet face moved him mightily. He remembered her in her beautiful babyhood and in the gracious years of her young womanhood. And all the tragedy which had wrought such desolation and woe in her father's house came back poignantly to his mind.

" You are, pardon me, am I right, a widow, Madame de Castro ? "

" I am a widow, thank God."

The simple bald words, spoken without effort and with such a passion of emphasis, told their own long tale of the unspeakable years. James Maitland did not need to ask a single question, nor did he.

" Sit down," he said, with a great gentleness. " There is much to say. Where shall we begin ? "

" Oh, anywhere. Tell me first, is my father alive ? "

" Yes ; but very low. I have not seen him for a good many weeks now. He and I did not agree the last time I was at Penninghame. and my partner, Mr. Shepherd, has been going out to Penninghame. I felt it, of course, but I could not withdraw what I said. It concerned you and your future, Miss Isabel."

" You were always good to me," she murmured. " And my father is unwise to turn his back upon you, who were ever his friend. What was the cause ? "

He set her a chair, and took a contemplative turn across the room. The tidings he must give her could not be pleasant hearing. While he was wondering in what words he could best convey them she surprised him with another question.

" I know a good deal, Mr. Maitland. I have come from Bilbao. There, at the house of my very good friends, the Mortons, I met your son, David."

" My son David ? But may I ask what took you to Bilbao of all places in the world ? It is not a resort."

She smiled a faint ironical smile.

" It happened to be my husband's native place, Mr. Maitland, and we were there when he died."

" Pardon me, but I am afraid your marriage was not a success, Madame de Castro."

" It was not ; you and my father were right. But we need not pursue the subject. I have paid the price."

" Have you any children ? "

" Two, my daughter Sybil and my son Francis Riddell, the heir to Penninghame."

She was quick to note the changing expression on the lawyer's face.

" I know something, sufficient to alarm me, Mr. Maitland. Your son told me of Anthony Weir's arrival from the Cape, and that he was openly spoken of as the heir. Can my father actually give him Penninghame?"

"Yes; the only part of the estate entailed is Fintry. He has even wished to break the entail that Mr. Weir might have it all, but he has not succeeded."

She grew a little white, and nervously clasped her trembling hands.

"Mr. Maitland, my boy ought to have Penninghame. Tell me what to do. Shall I go out and throw myself on my father's mercy? If only he would see the boy, he would forgive all. He is a true Learmonth, and his face is like the morning. Oh, I have dreamed such dreams, and built such castles. He would love him, he would be proud of him. Let us go."

"It might be well, and no time ought to be lost. Anthony Weir is in the field, Miss Isabel, and he has got such an influence over your father that the will has actually been made, leaving Penninghame to him."

"But it would not stand!" she cried wildly. "Anthony Weir is only very distant kin. I am his daughter. I offended him terribly, I know, but I had hoped that the years would have softened his heart, as it has softened mine. So long as my husband lived I could not write or come, because I knew that any reconciliation would be impossible, and I would not have asked my father to receive him."

Again the words told. The compassion deepened in James Maitland's eyes. Truly she had paid the price.

"I have brought him up, keeping his future in view. He is a gentleman, I can tell my father that," she said proudly. "Shall we go out to-day?"

Maitland pondered a moment.

"Perhaps it would be as well for me to go alone, and then I can find out just how matters are. Remember, I have not been to Penninghame for a long time, and I refused to draw out the will in favour of Anthony Weir."

"Then, who did it?"

"My partner, Mr. Shepherd. Don't blame him; he never saw you. He was only concerned to keep the Penninghame affairs in the firm."

"But he would know that a man's daughter is his legal heir?"

He could have smiled at her ingenuous reasoning.

"Unfortunately half the business of firms like ours consists of attempts to refute such reasoning. If it were not for family troubles our occupation would be gone."

"I feel as if I could not wait," she said, beginning to pace the floor restlessly. "We only arrived in Edinburgh last night."

"Where are you staying?"

She mentioned the name of a third-rate hotel in an obscure street, and he saw her wince.

"I am very poor, Mr. Maitland; there is no use to hide it," she said frankly, and even with a certain pride in the admission. "We had to go to a place whose charges would be within the limit of our means. Yes, it is a sad change. The Learmonth pride, I have had to bury that, except when I needed it to uphold my self-respect."

James Maitland's face grew graver, and more compassionate than before. Remembering her bright girlhood, her high unbroken spirit, her indomitable will, he marvelled more and more. She must have drunk of bitter waters indeed during the intervening years to bring her to such a pass.

"It is impossible you can stay there," he said gently. "My house and all it contains is at your disposal. It is a large house, and there is no one in it, but my daughter Helen. She will make you welcome. You will go back at once, gather your things together, and I will take you there myself."

Her eyes filled with sudden tears.

"I should like it for my children," she said simply. "They do not complain; but it is hard for them, for the girl especially. She is a gentle, frail creature. My God, what would I not give to see her at home at Penninghame?"

Maitland sat still, gazing meditatively into space. His whole heart and sympathies were with the daughter of the old house, whose interests had been so long in his hands. Headstrong, erring she might have been in her stormy youth, but the good old blood ran in her veins. She was no alien like Anthony Weir, whom the old lawyer could not abide.

"Your father sent me about my business, Miss Isabel, because I told him the truth concerning Anthony Weir, but I will go out to Penninghame to-day and tell him the truth concerning you. You will wait at my house, and, if necessary, I will telegraph for you to come."

"Thank you; I will do exactly as you bid me, Mr. Maitland," she said, with a proud humility which once more brought the moisture to his eyes. Born to command, with a regal beauty he had never seen excelled, fit to mate with the highest in the land, what shipwreck had Isabel Learmonth made of her life!

"I shall have to see my partner at once, Madame de Castro; but, believe me, I will not keep you in suspense a moment longer than is necessary."

She drew down her veil and turned to go. Her look was wistful as it dwelt on his somewhat severe thoughtful face. Once she had flouted his advice, yet now only he could intervene and smooth the way home for her penitent feet. How kind he had been, never casting at her one word of reproach, simply accepting the situation, and anxious even as she was herself to find the best way out.

At the door he held out his hand.

"Miss Isabel, if it can be done, if any earthly power can accomplish it, your boy shall have Penninghame." As he spoke, all the softness died out of his face, and once more he was the man of iron who saw obstacles only to overcome them. It was as if he took a vow upon himself.

She wrung his hand, and hastened out with bent head, fearful lest any should be witness to her tears.

Maitland only waited until she should have left the office then he crossed the passage and knocked at his partner's door.

CHAPTER V

SHADOWS BEFORE

THAT Maitland should have chosen William Shepherd for a partner in his business was one of the anomalies which we see constantly exemplified in life. By nature they differed as widely as the poles. You could read it in the contrast presented even by their appearance.

Shepherd was a large man with a florid, not unhandsome face, and a slightly aggressive air, suggestive of prosperity and power. Raised from small beginnings, having in the far past indeed occupied Henry Aitken's post in the office of which he was now one of the heads, he had a good deal of the self-made man's conscious assurance. Although he lacked Maitland's finer perceptions, and had none of his intellectual culture, he had brought to the firm a share of ability and foresight which had been of immense benefit to it, regarded from the mere commercial standpoint.

It was one of the oldest Edinburgh legal firms ; the long row of deed boxes on the shelves, bearing distinguished names, indicated that it had been entrusted with the private affairs of many a great house.

But other days, other methods, and the old order sadly changes.

The somewhat narrow, stiff, unrelaxing method of business pursued by the old firm brought so little grist to the professional mill that Maitland had been obliged to cast about for some means to extend his connection. And a chance word heard outside decided him to raise William Shepherd from the post of confidential clerk to that of junior partner.

That had happened twenty years before, and the result had justified all his expectations. Shepherd had thrown himself heart and soul into the work of building up what was really a declining concern, and from the beginning his efforts told. He brought an influx of modern and lucrative business to the firm, and, though Maitland did not approve of all his methods, nay, stood aghast at some of them, he scrupulously allowed him a free hand. In ten years their business and income had well nigh trebled. But all the time there had been a dividing line somewhat sharply drawn between them. Maitland adhered to the old clientele, and was even jealous of his dealing with them. He left Shepherd to his own domain. Oddly enough, this method, though it paid from a commercial point of view, did not altogether please Shepherd, who was an ambitious man. He had a large and clever family, and his wife shared with him the ambition and desire to gain for them entrance to Society, which had never received their parents. And to that end, all their efforts had been directed of late years. Maitland looked on rather amused, a little contemptuous, wholly wondering. He was himself singularly free from all ambition of that kind. He was a scholar and a recluse, and his son and daughter shared his tastes. They had many friends, some few among the great houses that closed their doors rigidly against the Shepherds. So do things seem to be unevenly balanced here ; what one man strives for, and would give his life blood to obtain, lies unheeded at another's feet.

It had been a secret gratification to Shepherd when the difference of opinion between Francis Learmonth and his legal adviser summoned him to Penninghame. And there he had walked carefully, doing his best, yet failing absolutely to make the impression he desired. The old man even chafed at his coming, and continually longed for the lifelong friend he had driven from his side. But pride prevented his acknowledging it.

Shepherd was by no means blind to the situation. He could see through Anthony Weir, though his soul did not revolt from him as Maitland's had done. Beholding in him, however, the probable future laird of Penninghame, he managed to keep the right side of him, which, in Shepherd's parlance, was merely good business.

Shepherd was still busy with his letters, and the telegram that had come to his house late the previous evening lay on his desk. He rose at his partner's entrance, and gave him good-morning, at the same time handing him the telegram.

Maitland read it in silence, and laid it down.

"If you don't mind, I'll go out myself this morning," he said quietly.

Shepherd looked slightly put out.

"Well, you see, it is addressed personally to me. Mr. Learmonth might take it in the light of personal carelessness."

"I'll take the brunt of it. Something has happened this morning that slightly alters the complexion of affairs. I have just had a visit from Madame de Castro, Miss Learmonth that was."

"His daughter, do you mean?" asked Shepherd aghast.

"Yes, she has just come from Bilbao, of all the places in the world. What she was doing there heaven only knows. Her husband died there. It was David who told her of Anthony Weir's arrival at Penninghame. She met him at my brother-in-law's house there; she called them her good friends. I guess they were kind to her in her hour of need."

Shepherd thoughtfully stroked his chin. The news upset and annoyed him. It opened up many vexing possibilities.

"I suppose her object is to be reconciled to her father?"

"Precisely."

"And she wishes you to be the medium?"

"Yes."

"Do you think it would be wise to undertake such a mission at this time. You have had the misfortune to offend Mr. Learmonth. In her interests it might be wiser to keep out of it. I will tell him if you like."

Maitland slightly smiled. It was an inscrutable smile which Shepherd failed to read.

"You don't know her," he said quietly. "She used to ride on my shoulder more than thirty years ago. Poor, poor thing."

Shepherd never mixed sentiment with business, indeed he despised sentiment as a quality, though as a family man he was seen at his best. He was, indeed, sincerely attached to his wife and children, and seriously concerned regarding their advancement in life.

"I would do my best, but, of course, you know your own mind about it. Has she any children?"

"Two—a girl and a boy. Her son ought to have Penninghame, Shepherd, and will if I can manage it. That upstart would make ducks and drakes of it."

"It is his hard and fast enough at present. It would be rather hard lines on him, don't you think, to be disappointed now. After all, he came at his uncle's bidding."

" He could be paid for what he has done. It was work undertaken for an object anyhow," said Maitland drily. " No sane man would seek to uphold his claim against Isabel Learmonth's for her son."

" It will take some manœuvring," said Shepherd, and his face was troubled.

It was a grievous disappointment. The old laird could not last long, and all the business resulting from the transfer of the property would have swelled the coffers of the old Charlotte Street house.

" Perhaps, in the circumstances, it would be well for us both to go out. Can you be ready for the eleven-thirty ? "

" Quite. I have to send a message to my daughter and attend to my own letters, that is all."

He went back to his own desk, looked casually at his letters, and absently locked them up. He was in no mood for the daily round. His thoughts were entirely engrossed with the past and its bearing on the events of the moment. After a moment's meditation, he put on his coat and hat, and leaving the office wended his way, still in a brown study, towards his own house in Great King Street. It was an old family house, once the acme of James Maitland's ambition, the crown of his professional life. His wife only lived a year to enjoy it, and at times he felt very lonely in its great rooms. But memory bound them to it, and they had stayed to grow more and more attached to it as the years rolled by.

He let himself in with his latchkey. The sound of the pianoforte guided him to the drawing-room where Helen was at her daily practice. She was fond of music, a good player, and possessed a sweet, well-trained voice. Maitland loved music too ; he even paused on the stairs before disturbing her to hear the words of her song. She was practising for a sacred concert, and these were the words which floated in compelling sweetness to her father's ears :—

" Trust in the Lord ! Wait patiently for Him, and He will give thee thy heart's desire."

They awoke some tender chord in his heart, and he passed his hand across his eyes. Partly ashamed of his momentary and inexplicable weakness he ascended the remainder of the steps and hastily entered the room.

" Are you there, Helen ? "

" Why, father ! " she cried, jumping up in unmixed surprise. " Whatever brings you back at this hour ? "

She was a very fair, winsome woman, with a graceful figure, a well-poised head, an air of dignity and repose. But she had to be known to be loved. Her intimates were few, but these clung to her with a wonderful devotion. Perhaps it was the limited area of her life, the responsibility of a household laid upon her in her early girlhood that had made her at three and twenty a self-reliant, capable, dignified woman, who looked able to meet and cope with any vicissitude.

Maitland looked at her with sudden tenderness. She looked her best in the morning, the rose-leaf bloom on her cheek was like the down on a peach. She was so near, so winning, so gracious, pleasant to the eye and dear to the heart, that a sudden sense of his riches in her possession smote him. But he did not know how to express himself.

" A strange thing has happened, Helen. I don't often talk business with you, but I daresay you remember the story of how Isabel Learmonth eloped with her music master nearly twenty years ago ? "

" Oh, yes, I remember it perfectly. It was an awful thing. How could she do it? And I have heard since that he was not a good man."

"He was not; as she herself expressed it, she has paid the price. He is dead, however, and she has come back to Edinburgh. She was at the office this morning."

"And she will go back to Penninghame and that impossible person will have to go," said Helen, in tones of lively satisfaction.

"That is what one would like, but unfortunately it is not so easy a business as it looks. I am going out to Penninghame this morning to see what can be done. But that is not what I came to tell you, but to ask you to go to Lorimer's Hotel in Leith Walk and bring Madame de Castro and her children here."

"Leith Walk!" echoed Helen, in a perplexed voice. "What kind of a place can a hotel be there?"

"Not first-rate you may be sure. She is very poor and sad, poor thing. I can leave her with you. You will be kind to her, Helen, and make her comfortable here till I return."

"Why yes, certainly, I should like to do that. I will order fires in the spare rooms. Will she be proud and difficult, papa, I wonder?"

"Oh, poor thing, no! Her spirit is broken. She only wants kindness. She has had precious little of it these twenty years. Make her comfortable, Helen, never mind the cost. My heart warmed to the poor thing. As a child she was the sweetest creature God ever made. And what a mess she has made of her life."

Helen looked deeply interested, and her eyes glowed.

"I'll do my best, papa, to please you, and to be kind to her. I suppose you will get back in time for dinner?"

"For tea, if I can manage it. Good-bye, my dear. You are a great comfort to me."

Helen flushed with surprise and pleasure. Such words were rare between them. They fell like wine upon her heart. She put her hands on his shoulders and kissed him suddenly.

"I am a very happy girl to have a father like you," she said, and with these words ringing in his ears, James Maitland went his way. Once at the end of the street, oddly drawn, he looked back, not knowing that it was the last time he should cross that threshold to his home of peace.

CHAPTER VI

THE FRIEND IN NEED

THE two young creatures, who in their few years of life had been no strangers to its sorrows, stood disconsolate in the window of the dingy hotel sitting-room, looking out upon the sluggish traffic of a wide thoroughfare which disappointed all their ideas of Edinburgh. Often had their mother painted the city of her love to them in glowing colours. But they had arrived amid drenching rain late the previous evening, and had risen to grey skies and threatening airs. Troubles they had had in plenty; they had grown accustomed, though never reconciled to their mother's sad looks, but somehow that still, grey February morning things looked their blackest. Their mother had gone out early, bidding them remain strictly in their own sitting-room until her return.

" I ought to have gone with mamma, Syb," said the lad discontentedly. " She ought to have some one to take care of her, and she looked so horribly tired this morning."

He was a handsome boy of tall, slender figure, with a noble head and a winning face. His abundant hair lay heavy on a brow which indicated high gifts. It had been no mean part of Isabel Learmonth's griefs that he had never had his due of education. It had been picked up in desultory fashion at the various foreign places whither his father's precarious occupation had taken them. He could speak French and Spanish as fluently as his native tongue, and they both possessed that indefinable ease of manner and bearing which foreign travel more than anything else imparts.

It had been Isabel Learmonth's solace in many weary hours that her boy was so truly, in looks and in all else, of her own blood and race. What pride the old man in happier circumstances might have taken in that gallant boy!

The girl was a vision of beauty. She had the blue eyes of her Scotch ancestry, and the rich dark hair and colouring of the south. And she seemed to unite in her personality all the charms of both. She was winsome unexpected, wholly charming. Often her mother regarded her with mournful forebodings. What could beauty be for one so forlorn but a fatal dower.

For the sake of these two, whom she loved, and who loved her with a passion rarely seen, she had buried all her pride and determined to come a suppliant to her father's door.

" She did not want us, Frank; she said so quite plainly," said Sybil, flattening her straight little nose against the window pane. " What skies they have here! The sun has no place in Scotland. How shall we live without it? "

" Oh, it can't be always like this," said the boy listlessly, keeping his eyes fixed on the street whence he expected to behold his mother reappear. " If I were only sure of finding the place, I should go out after her even now."

" She has been gone nearly an hour, she can't be long now," said the girl. " Why, there she is! "

She came round an unexpected corner. Who knew all the byways of Edinburgh better than Isabel Learmonth? Had she not learnt them by heart during the first stormy year of her married life?

Seeing them at the window, she smiled gaily and waved her hand.

"I believe she has got what she wants," said Sybil, smiling in return. "She looks so much brighter, don't you think so, Frank?"

But he was gone, flying down the stairs to meet her at the door. To his surprise she leaned forward and kissed him with tears in her eyes.

"Come upstairs, darling, I have great news for Sybil and you."

When the door was closed, she laid her gloves on the table, and smoothing them out, began to tell them the substance of her interview with the lawyer.

"He is such a kind good friend, darlings, we ought to have come to him long ago, and to-day he will do all he can. Perhaps to-morrow, who knows, we shall all be at dear Penninghame."

"Does grandpapa know about us?" asked the boy.

"Not yet, but he will. Mr. Maitland is going out this very morning to tell him all about us, and he fully expects to be able to send for us to-morrow, perhaps even to-day."

"I don't want to see grandpapa very much," said the boy gloomily. "He has not been kind to you."

"Oh, my son, never say that! He loved me very much, and I broke his heart. I was all he had, and I left him cruelly. Think if one morning we should wake up and find that Sybil had run away, had left us without a word of explanation or farewell, how terrible we should feel! It would be bad, Frank, but not so bad as the thing I did to grandpapa, for he was an old man and had nobody in the world but me. And he was the best father that girl could have."

So anxious was she to soften their hearts towards their grandfather that she drew aside the veil of the past, and even debased herself before them. Nothing could poison their hearts against her, and, even if she should fall in their estimation, it was as nothing in comparison with the importance of the reconciliation which she hoped was now near at hand.

Upon that, indeed, must everything depend; she was at the end of her resources, and knew not where to turn for aid.

"Grandpapa is very old now, old and ill. And, if he will allow us to go back to the beautiful old home I have so often told you about, you and Sybil must try and make up to him for all your mother has made him suffer. I am sure he will love you very much."

But there was rebellion in the boy's eyes. His mother was passing dear to him, and often he had been witness to her tears. Even if she had done all she said, he need not have been so hard-hearted, so unforgiving. Of their own father they never spoke. When death relieved them from an incubus of terror and misery they seemed to agree tacitly that his name should be forgotten. His memory was a nightmare, nothing more. An adventurer without principles, baulked of his ambition, and finding that he had not married the rich wife he expected, he had speedily thrown off the mask. For well-nigh twenty years Isabel Learmonth had borne that long martyrdom, taking it as the punishment for her sin. Whatever struggle or misfortune the future might hold, it could never be as dark as the past. While they talked, a knock came at the door, and the untidy little maidservant announced Miss Maitland.

Helen came a little timidly into the room, and they all looked at her with wondering interest. Her pleasant face, her sweet smile, her kindly eyes seemed to warm their hearts. Hers was the first friendly face the children had seen in their mother's native land.

" I come on my father's behalf, as well as my own," she said, looking at Isabel Learmonth with a wonder of admiration at her youth and beauty, still so marvellously preserved. " I am to take you to our house. The carriage is below. Can you be ready soon ? "

" It is most kind of you. For the children's sakes I will come gratefully. Let me introduce you. This is Sybil and this is Francis Riddell, otherwise Frank. Do you know who this is, Frank ? David's sister. Your brother and he became inseparable in Bilbao, Miss Maitland, so we cannot be quite strangers."

No one noticed the quick colour that rose in Sybil's face, nor that she turned away as if to hide it.

" It is strange that David has not written about you," said Helen, as she took the boy's hand, but it was at Sybil she looked with the strange stirring of the heart. A creature so fair ought to be born to some brighter destiny ; her winsome looks crept into Helen's heart, and from that hour they loved one another with that deep affection which takes no account of time or circumstance or space, but is love till eternity. There was something like a vow in Helen's heart that so far as lay in her power she would shield and befriend her, and try to brighten the life that had been so dark.

" I am afraid you are not very comfortable here," she said quickly to the children's mother. " We have plenty of room, and only papa and I alone in that big house. It will be sweet to have you there."

Isabel Learmonth bent forward suddenly and kissed the girl with wet eyes.

" There are kind hearts still in the world. To find them one must come home."

The pathos of these words remained in Helen's mind for long, recurring again and again when her own burden seemed too intolerable to be borne.

" Let us go, then," she said cheerfully. " Papa thought you would probably not have unpacked your things. Can you get them now ? Let me help you."

" We have not much ; we can be ready in a few moments. Sybil will help me while Frank talks to you."

They left the room, and Helen turned to the boy.

" So you met my brother in Bilbao ? He is a good brother. You would like him, did you not ? "

" I did rather," said the boy, and his eyes glowed. " He is splendid ; he was so kind to my mother. I shall never forget it as long as I live."

" He is kind to every one, it is his nature," said Helen. " It was terrible for us to let him go away. Papa missed him so much. But he will not stay there for ever."

" I should hope not, it is not a nice place," said the boy, in a tone of frank detestation ; " but he likes the place where he works, and he told me he could learn things there he couldn't learn anywhere else."

" That is like David ; he does not mind how hard he works, or how uncomfortable he is, so long as he learns what he wants to know. I wish I were like him."

" So do I. He was always telling me that one should do things thoroughly or not at all. Beside him, I wanted to work, but whenever I got away from him again I felt idle. I am not like him."

" You have not had the same chance, dear," said Helen kindly. " My father has always been a hard worker, and David has been taught thoroughness almost from his boyhood. Now, perhaps that you have come back to Scotland, you will work in earnest at your studies first. You must have a great deal to learn yet. How old are you?"

"I shall be sixteen next month."

"How tall you are for your age! I can't understand how it is my brother has not written about you."

"Well, you see, I think it was like this—he did not know anything about us really that my mother's people lived near yours, until just the day before we left Bilbao. We only left then because of what he told my mother about my grandfather, and he even gave my mother money to help us. You should hear Sybil talk about him. She thinks that he is the nicest chap we have ever seen."

"I agree with you and Sybil," said Helen smiling, well pleased.

The sun filtered through the grey mists as they drove away from the door of the place that had been so poor a substitute for home to those who were now wanderers on the face of the earth.

Helen Maitland felt that glow at her heart which flows from the doing of genuine kindness. She had not been so happy for many a day. When they reached the door of the tall old house in Great King Street, and Isabel felt the gracious peace and comfort and homeliness sink into her heart, she suddenly gave way.

"Pray forgive me. I have seen no English home since I left Penninghame. To me this looks like heaven."

"I hope at least that it will be a real haven for a time, dear madame," said Helen sincerely, as she laid her kind hand on her arm and so guided her to the spacious chamber at the back, with two long windows overlooking the sea, where she had hurriedly made some extra preparations for the comfort of her unexpected guests. A fire burned cheerfully in the low grate, sending its comforting glow over all the dainty appurtenances of a lady's room, two easy chairs stood invitingly by the hearth, the table in readiness with writing material upon it, and a glass of early spring flowers.

"I made ready the dressing-room across the passage for your son. I thought you would like to have him near. It is large and pleasant, though only looking into the street."

"God bless you, my dear; you have warmed a desolate heart," was the low reply.

Little did either guess what was hid in the womb of the immediate future, and what an early opportunity would be afforded Isabel Learmonth of acknowledging the kindness she felt at that moment it would be impossible to repay.

CHAPTER VII

THE OLD HOUSE

It was not a long journey to Penninghame, but the train belonged to the order known in railway parlance as "stopping trains," and managed to accomplish the sixteen miles in an hour.

The station was merely a little country platform on the edge of a typical Lothian village. The pale February sun gleamed kindly on the handful of red roofs, and struck with a shaft of light the vane on the spire of the village church. It seemed a lifeless place, the centre of a scattered agricultural parish, with no special industry to stir its lethargy. The two lawyers were the only passengers to alight. The stationmaster, who knew them both by sight, touched his cap, and informed them that the dogcart from Penninghame waited without.

It was a relief to Maitland at least to see it in charge of a groom instead of Anthony Weir. It was half an hour's drive, and soon they left the village behind, and came within the shadow of the Penninghame woods, which were famous along the Lothian seaboard. The house itself was not conspicuously beautiful, being solid rather than picturesque, but set in a noble park, through whose spreading vistas could be caught the gleam of water and the graceful outlines of the browsing deer. It was a heritage any man might be proud to possess.

"How shall we arrange about seeing Mr. Learmonth ?" asked Shepherd, as they alighted at the door. "He will not wish to see us both at the same time."

"You had better go up, as he has sent for you, but you need not say anything about my business, which I prefer to explain in my own way."

"All right," said Shepherd, and they were at once admitted by Braidwood, who looked surprised and gratified to see Mr. Maitland. They were old friends ; together they had watched and in a manner shared the chequered fortunes of the house of Penninghame. They were surprised that Anthony Weir did not appear, but his name was not mentioned.

"The laird is expeckin' ye, sir," Braidwood said to Shepherd. "He's in his room ; it's seevin weeks since he left it, seevin weeks the morn."

This was information intended for Maitland's benefit.

"You need not trouble to announce me, Braidwood," said Shepherd. "I can find my way."

Braidwood suffered him to go, nothing loth. He was eager for a word with Mr. Maitland, and had that very day discussed with Susan the wisdom of taking a special journey to Edinburgh for the purpose of seeing him. For things were all at sixes and sevens in the old house, and Braidwood was in dire mental straits.

"Eh, michty me, sir, but I'm gled to see ye," he said, wiping the moisture of excitement from his brow. "The ongauns in this hoose wad gar a peaceable body rise in his grave. He's awa' to Whitekirk this mornin' to kick up a row wi' the doctor, but he'll be ready for him, never fear."

" Come in here, Braidwood. I have something wonderful for your ear," said Maitland, opening the door of the morning-room. He was almost as familiar with the old house as with his own. Many a happy day, ay, and night had he spent under its roof.

" Yes, I'm glad to see ye, sir. It wasna fair o' ye to desert him at the last."

" Desert him ! I had no choice, Braidwood ; he ordered me out of the house. There are some things a man can't stand, you know."

" It didna matter. It's my opeenion, he disna ken what he's daein' noo hauf the time, since that ill skin cam'. But what's yer great news ? "

Braidwood was familiar, yet entirely respectful. There was no man except his master for whom he had a greater regard than the old lawyer, who had always a kind word for him and an interested query for his welfare.

" Braidwood," said the lawyer solemnly, " Miss Isabel's come back."

Braidwood grew pale and red by turns, and his eyes began to glow.

" The Lord be thankit !—but when, and whaur is she ; what way no here ? "

" I came out to smooth the way. It will be a little difficult now, on account of the laird's weak state, and his perverted mind. And then the complication of Anthony Weir."

" Miss Isabel'll sune settle him," cried Braidwood in a low ecstasy. " But tell me aboot her, a' aboot her, my bonnie lamb, that has sat sae often on my knee. Eh ! I could greet, silly, auld man that I am, Maister Maitland, and Shusan'll no be whit better."

" I feel a little that way myself," admitted Maitland, in a curiously soft voice. " She is sadly changed. She has had a hard experience, and has come back a widow and penniless, with her two children, a boy and a girl."

" Never mind," said Braidwood, in a full, satisfied voice. " A son that'll be heir to Penninghame and Whitekirk ! Eh ! whaur are ye noo, Anthony Weir, my man ? The Lord disna a'thegither forget, Maister Maitland. He only bides a wee."

" How is the laird this morning ; pretty strong, I hope ? Have you any idea what he wanted with Mr. Shepherd ? "

" It's something aboot Fintry, for I heard Weir an' him discussin' it last nicht. They didna think I heard, but I did. Eh ! he's a perfeck horse-leech. It's no a bit he'll tak', but everything he can lay his hands on. Wait or he gets Miss Isabel's een on his ill face an' her tongue in his ears. He'll wonder what's the matter wi' him. Eh ! the fling she used to gie her prood heid an' the witchery o' her een ! An' we'll see them again in Penninghame, the Lord be praised ! "

" You're a faithful soul, Braidwood ! The laird is well off to have one like you near him in these times."

" Ay, but he disna think it ; his mind's pushioned by that serpent, an' whether he lives or dees there'll be michty cheenges here, sir. Shusan an' me'll hae to fend for oorsels, that thocht to end oor days in Penninghame."

" Oh, we will hope not. It is just possible that this may change the whole colour of events. Tell me, Braidwood, has the laird ever spoken of his daughter lately—I mean, while he has been so ill ? "

Braidwood shook his head.

" I wish I could say yes, sir, but it wad be a lee. No a fortnight syne he bade me gang to the drawin'-room, an' turn her picter wi' its face to the wa', an' I did it for an hoor or sae, so's I needna lee till him, but there it is a richt noo. Ye can see it if yet step up."

" I'll take a walk round the house for old times' sake, Braidwood. Take charge of my bag, and you can call me when Mr. Shepherd comes downstairs."

Braidwood nodded, and ran to acquaint Susan with the new and unexpected turn of affairs. It was a beautiful February morning, the first day of the month, and it seemed as if spring had suddenly resolved to begin in earnest. The soft air had wooed and tempted the birds, who were chirping on every bough, and the smell of the fresh earth was good in the nostrils. Maitland vaguely wondered as he strolled to the far end of the terrace whether it might not be a good thing now to retire from business, and find a little house somewhere in the country, where Helen and he could be happy together with their books and a few simple pleasures. His thoughts flew to Whitekirk, where his old friend Jeffrey had been a doctor so long. Many a good holiday had James Maitland spent in the rambling old house on the edge of Whitekirk Green.

They had not met for a long time ; both were busy men ; but that day Jeffrey was oddly present in his thoughts ; he even wondered whether he might call on him before his return to town.

He was pacing slowly to and fro in a pensive and reminiscent mood, when he beheld Braidwood gesticulating wildly to him from the hall door. He turned, and went towards it, and was met in the outer hall by his partner.

" I have finished my business with Mr. Learmonth, and he will see you now. He declined at first, but I assured him it was something of extreme importance."

" Very good of you," said Maitland, with a sudden note of dryness in his voice.

The irony of the situation struck him, and he gave a slight laugh. Once the tried friend and privileged adviser of Francis Learmonth, his dealings with him had now to be arranged by a comparative stranger. Shepherd saw that he had slightly overstepped the mark, and bit his lip. As Maitland entered the house Shepherd was relieved to behold Anthony Weir on horseback riding up the drive. The greeting was cordial on both sides. To Shepherd Anthony Weir had been able to speak with great freedom regarding his position and prospects, and he had rejoiced sincerely over the rupture between the laird and James Maitland.

" Good morning, have you seen my uncle ? " he asked, as he swung himself from the saddle and threw the reins loosely over his arm. " I thought him very poorly this morning. I don't think Jeffrey is doing his duty ; not been here this morning yet. I've just given him a piece of my mind. Nice lot of fossils have been fattening themselves off the old man."

Shepherd slightly smiled at the curious mixed metaphor, the absurdity of which, however, Weir did not observe.

" Seen him, eh ! and settled the Fintry business," he repeated keenly, as he kept his eyes on the lawyer's face.

" Yes, it's all settled as far as I can settle it, but there's something else to be reckoned with. My partner came out with me this morning, Weir."

" The deuce he did. In Heaven's name what for ? I thought he got the tip straight enough and was shown pretty clearly that his room would be better than his company."

" Yes ; but unfortunately there's a new development. Hadn't you better get rid of your horse, and let's get inside and talk it over ? "

Weir glanced round, and, espying a gardener in the shrubbery, whistled to him to take the animal away. Then he led the way into the house to the very room where James Maitland and the faithful Braidwood had held their friendly little conference.

" His daughter has come back," said Shepherd bluntly, the moment the door was closed.

" The deuce ! " Anthony Weir's face became a livid hue, and his brows knit ominously. " Honest Indian, no fake, his daughter, really ? "

" Unfortunately, yes, a widow, two children, girl and boy. I'm afraid the outlook's bad."

" But she was disinherited, wasn't she ? My uncle has gone over the tale to me again and again. Lately he has always been speaking about it. I could almost swear there is not the ghost of a chance that he would see her, and he can't last. Where and how did she turn up ? "

" This morning at our office. I did not see her. Maitland did. He is here to see what he can do for her."

" And you let him up, Shepherd ; a devilish bad move surely from our point of view."

" Well, you see," said Shepherd confusedly, " what could I do ? Maitland is my senior partner ; he is more at home in this house than I am ; you were not on the spot. I couldn't help myself."

" How long has he been up ? "

" Only while we have been speaking."

" What do you think of the old boy this morning ? "

" His mind seems clear enough, but he is frightfully weak. As you say, he can't last."

" And at the present moment I am right enough."

" As right as it is possible to be, unless another will is made."

" She can't have the place unless another will is made ? "

" Absolutely no. She might contest it, of course, plead undue influence, anything you like ; but in the circumstances, legally speaking, she would not have a leg to stand on."

" Then the only thing that stands between me and the place is a possible will which that old weasel may even now be ferreting out of him."

Shepherd nodded. He did not like the terms, nor at the moment the man, but could not deny that he stated the case.

" That will shall not be made," he said, in a thick unsteady voice. " I am going upstairs."

CHAPTER VIII

THE UNFORESEEN

JAMES MAITLAND entered the room prepared to find his old friend perceptibly weaker. But it was a shock to behold him so like death. He was now in his bed, sitting partly up, resting against high pillows, a quilted dressing-gown about his shoulders. Each day he seemed to slip a little further down in the bed, to become less akin to the mortal world.

"There's a great change, sir," whispered Braidwood at his elbow, as he crossed the threshold. "I doot he's no' lang for this world."

They advanced together to the bedside, and the laird watched them with eyes which, though curiously bright, seemed to have no recognition in them. He did not smile when Maitland held out his hand nor did he offer to take it.

"Get a chair, Braidwood," he said in a listless whisper, "and keep within call."

Braidwood first administered to his master the necessary stimulant, put something more over his knees, laid a log on the fire and withdrew. It was something to be able to leave him in such safe company. Of late Braidwood had suffered many tortured hours, knowing that things were going on in the background, but unable to stretch out a hand to prevent what he called to Susan "wholesale robbery and corruption."

"What do you want?" asked the laird. "I thought we agreed to have no more dealing in this world, Maitland."

"We did, and I have regretted that I took my dismissal so simply. I know now that I was wrong, Mr. Learmonth," said the lawyer quietly.

"It was your own fault, you overstepped the bounds; you know after all I was my own master, not a puppet in your hands."

It was on the tip of Maitland's tongue to say that he had only changed masters and that hardly for the better, but reflecting that his business was to inform the laird of his daughter's return, and that the time was too short and too precarious to be wasted on personalities concerning their relations, he refrained.

"I would hardly have intruded on you even to-day, believing that you are entirely satisfied with your present advisers, but unfortunately I had no choice. I am here on behalf of another, whose interest in you and in Penninghame must come before all others. I am speaking of your daughter, Madame de Castro."

The laird gave a great start forward, and tried to sit up, but his strength failed.

"I forbade her name twenty years ago. I have never had occasion to go back on that decision arrived at after treatment the most shameful and ungrateful," he said indignantly.

"She was young, she had no mother. You did not understand her," said the lawyer quietly. "Anyhow it is time that old wound was healed. She has two children, one a boy who ought to be Laird of Penninghame.

He is a Learmonth, every inch of him. You will not defraud him of his rights for a stranger?"

"His rights! the son of a low-bred foreigner, one of the tribe that bring all their vices here to batten on honest folk," cried the laird, with a flash of the old passion. "You may keep your breath to cool your porridge, Maitland. Even if this story were true, and how am I to know even that he is her son, it will make no difference now."

Maitland kept silent a moment. The refusal was no more than he expected, and he did not despair yet of touching the right chord.

"She is greatly changed. I should not have known her. She is widowed, without means, desolate, broken-hearted. If she sinned, she has paid the price. Those are her own words."

"Words, words!" said the laird, tossing his head uneasily on the pillow. "It is deeds that tell."

"She would have come with me to-day, but I over-persuaded her. I could see her tired, anxious, distraught. And fearing what reception she might have, I offered to come in her stead. If you will see her and her children I can bring them back to-morrow, or even this afternoon. She is at my house in Helen's care."

"At your house! then you have played me false in more ways than one, Maitland," said the laird, with another flash of passion.

"Not at all," was the calm response. "She came to me in distress. She has money only to pay the poorest lodging. Remembering what she was, I could not bear that; so I took her home. And she is welcome to it as long as she likes to stay. Indeed, I would consider it no burden to give her a home for the rest of her life."

"But why should you do this? She is nothing to you."

"Nothing, it is true, but we all loved her. I am a foolish old man, but it is better to grow soft of heart as we grow older, than to become as the nether millstone."

"You are not afraid to speak out, Maitland. I will say that of you," said the laird, compelled to an unwilling admiration.

"I have no reason to be afraid. I owe no man anything, am under obligation to none. So far as you are concerned, laird, I have in the past faithfully done the work for which I was paid. It was a great deal more to me than that of course, but, in self-defence, I must say that I have never hesitated to speak the truth, even when I knew it went against my own interests. I am no time-server, even my enemies could say that of me."

"You spoke unwarrantable words against my heir, Mr. Anthony Weir."

"I spoke what I believed to be the truth at the time, and which now has been proved. He is a time-server if you like. God help Penninghame when he has it in his grip."

"You are prejudiced against him unreasonably. He has been kindness, consideration, forbearance, personified to me. I could not prove myself ungrateful."

"Well, that must be as you please," said Maitland, a trifle coldly, at the same time rising to his feet. "Well, we need not prolong this unprofitable discussion. I can only tell Madame de Castro that I have failed. I will do my best for her. There will always be a place in my office for the boy, who ought to be Laird of Penninghame."

"Your presumption is colossal, Maitland, but you can sit down again. I am not done with you yet. What have you got in that bag?"

"My bag! Oh, various things. I carry it always. It is part of myself."

" Sit down and tell me more about my daughter. How long has she been in Scotland ? "

" About twenty-four hours."

" Where did she come from ? "

" From Bilbao."

" Bilbao ! Where's that ? Never heard of it."

" You have forgotten. It is in Spain. My son David is there in his uncle's engineering firm. It was he who told Madame de Castro something about what is happening here."

" Your son, David ! So you got your finger into the pie after all. How old is that son of hers ? " " About sixteen ; he is the younger of the two."

" I might see him, but not her, never again. I swore never to look upon her face after her disgrace, and I will keep my vow. If he is a likely lad I might do something for him. Anthony Weir, who will succeed me here, would be the first to say it was my duty."

" I beg leave to doubt that. I will go back to Edinburgh now, Mr. Learmonth, and bring them here this afternoon."

" Is there any need for such fell haste ? You're getting fussy in your old age, Maitland, and begin to belie your reputation as a cautious, slow-going person."

" It is a matter which presses," was Maitland's ready reply.

" On my account, eh ? but perhaps I'll cheat you all yet. Jeffrey gave me till the end of March. We're hardly in February yet," he said, with a note of triumph in his voice.

" To-morrow then," said Maitland, as he rose to go. He was blaming himself at the moment for his caution. Isabel Learmonth had been right after all. It would have been better to have trusted to the inspiration of a sudden meeting. He decided not to lose a moment longer, all unconscious of the tragic events laid in the womb of the future.

Little did he know that his plea for mercy and justice for Isabel Learmonth was the last he should make on earth.

" Sit down," said the laird querulously. " You're in a fell hurry. I'm willing to pay you for the time you seem to grudge so meanly. Many an hour you've wasted here and thought nothing of it."

" The business for which I came is ended, laird," said the lawyer quietly. " We are less agreed at this moment than we have ever been, and it would be better for us to part."

" Sit down and dry up," was the irritable reply. " You're too mighty sharp in the tongue, and your pride is enough to turn anybody sick. It must have cost you a goodish bit in your time. Why don't you take a leaf from your partner's book. He only disagrees when he is paid for it."

In spite of himself, Maitland smiled. Never had the character and aim of William Shepherd been more shrewdly summed up. He gathered from the remark that he had failed to impress the laird as deeply as he had imagined.

" I'm not built that way, laird."

" Evidently not. If you had been, we needn't have quarrelled. I've missed you, though it's bad for you to hear it. Since you're on duty's high horse, supposing you tell me just what you consider my duty in the circumstances."

" It will not be palatable, laird. We'd better let sleeping dogs lie."

" Speak out, I'll pay you for it, man, and you can't possibly offend me more than you have done."

"Well, I've told you your duty already. It is to bring Miss Isabel back to make her home here with her children. Let her son grow up as Penninghame's heir, which he is, though you may take the place from him. You would die a happier man, laird, more likely to live a happier one. She's your own flesh and blood and bonnie! Gad, all the tears she's wept haven't washed the witchery from her eyes."

"You've a guileful tongue for your years, Maitland. And what about the honest, good-hearted chap that has waited on me hand and foot for weeks, that came across the sea at my bidding? He has a right to his expectations and their fulfilment."

"He can be paid for what he has done," said the lawyer coolly. "If needs be, give him Fintry. Miss Isabel would let you break the entail for that purpose."

"Give him Fintry! Gad, I like that. We've just been trying to break the entail so that Anthony might have it all. The hussy would not be ill off if she had Fintry."

"No; but this is her home, and will always be."

"The lad has ill blood in his veins. It would break out and be the undoing of Penninghame."

"He is his mother's son, and unless I am mistaken he will be cured of what faults he may have before he grows to man's estate. Her experience will be of service to him."

"You have an answer pat to everything. Open you bag, Maitland, and take out a piece of paper."

Maitland did as he was bid, not having the remotest idea what he should be called upon to write.

"Now, see, write what I tell you, and don't interrupt me by a single word."

The lawyer took his pen from his pocket-case and dated the sheet of foolscap he took from the roll within. His hand trembled as he waited for the words he must write, whatever their purport.

"I, Francis Riddell Learmonth, being in my sound mind and judgment, make this my last will and testament in favour of my only daughter and child, Isabel Learmonth or de Castro, and her children. What do they call the boy, Maitland?"

"Francis Riddell," was the reply, which caused a faint glow of satisfaction to flit across the drawn parchment-like face.

"Francis Riddell de Castro I declare to be my heir, to be Laird of Penninghame and Whitekirk on condition that he takes the name of Learmonth. His mother and sister to come here and live during his minority and afterwards to be life-rented in a sum to be hereafter agreed upon. That'll do. In the meantime send for Braidwood and Susan to witness."

"What about Anthony Weir?" asked Maitland hardly believing his ears.

"Oh ay, add that he shall have Fintry and five hundred a year as long as he lives. It will never be missed from the estate. Get Braidwood, will you, quick. Who's that at the door?"

It opened, and Anthony Weir, trying to look unconcerned, stepped across the threshold. Seeing the paper on the lawyer's knee a mighty terror shook him.

"I came up, certain that you are exerting yourself too much, Uncle Francis. You had better withdraw now, sir," he added to Maitland, "you can see for yourself how exhausted my uncle is."

"Leave us a moment, Anthony," said the laird tranquilly. "And tell

Braidwood as you go down that I want him here at once."

He had no choice but to obey. Braidwood was not far from the door; he entered speedily, and called Susan from her room. She came by way of the back corridor and through the laird's dressing-room, so that Weir, watching on the stairs, did not see her.

They signed as they were bid, having no idea what it was, but assured because the thing was in Mr. Maitland's keeping that all must be right.

Left alone again Maitland carefuly dried the signatures of which the laird's was only just decipherable. When he entered the room he had no expectation that his interview would have such favourable issue. Truly every hour we meet the unforeseen. Did some voice from the spirit world waft a message to Francis Learmonth's soul warning him that the night was at hand?

"You have done a good day's work, laird; God bless you. I would offer my hand in gratitude if I dared. To-morrow Miss Isabel and her children will thank you for themselves."

"Bring them to-morrow early, before I am tired," said the old man drowsily. "Thank you, Maitland. After all you were right, it ought not to be put past one's own flesh and blood. Give her my love."

He turned on his pillow as if to sleep. Maitland called to Braidwood outside the door, and softly slipped away downstairs.

CHAPTER IX

CONFLICTING INTERESTS

NOTHING was to be gathered from the expression of James Maitland's face when he joined the two waiting in the room below.

Anthony Weir looked sullenly defiant and very mistrustful of the grave, silent man who, perhaps, for aught he knew, carried in that little unpretentious bag the document which might be his undoing.

Shepherd looked intensely uncomfortable ; he had had a bad half-hour.

" We shall not catch a train just now, I think." said Maitland, glancing beyond Anthony Weir to his partner.

" No ; there is not one for a couple of hours."

" You had better wait for luncheon," Weir forced himself to say ungraciously enough, though fully conscious of the importance of detaining them as long as possible. " It will be served in about ten minutes, or should be, but servants are their own masters here."

Maitland looked undecided.

" I am in no hurry. What do you say ? " he said, addressing himself to Shepherd.

" There seems no sense in hurrying to the station to wait there when Mr. Weir is good enough to offer us hospitality," he answered gloomily.

" I'll hurry 'em up," said Anthony Weir, and left the room.

Shepherd took an eager step forward.

" How did he take it ? Have you done any good for Madame de Castro by coming here ? "

" I will tell you later," said Maitland quietly. " I'd rather not remain to lunch ; a bit of bread and cheese at the Old Bell would be preferable to Anthony Weir's black looks. They make sour enough sauce."

Shepherd had no time to reply. Almost immediately Weir returned and the gong was sounded. They went into the small dining-room and sat down in silence. Seldom had a more uncomfortable meal been eaten in that room. Maitland felt glad of Braidwood's silent presence, feeling the sympathy which had no voice.

" Has Doctor Jeffrey been here to-day ? I should like to see him," he said, with an inquiring glance at Weir's face. That worthy's grim silence in no way disconcerted him. In fact Weir, inflated as he was with a sense of his own importance, would have been surprised had he known how little he disturbed the even tenor of the old lawyer's thoughts.

" He has been here, yes, this morning, at some unholy hour, before seven wasn't it, Braidwood ? "

" Yes, sir, just afore seven."

" He has taken to that of late, to avoid me, perhaps. I rode to Whitekirk this morning to ask an explanation."

" Did you get it ? " asked Maitland, with a slightly amused elevation of his brows.

" I didn't see him ; he's as slippery as an eel, but I will see him. He has a sight too much side for his position, but I'll be even with him."

"His position is his own, it can't be assailed from without," observed Maitland tranquilly.

"He's another who has battened on the bounty of Penninghame," said Weir sourly.

"I would advise you to tell him that," said Maitland, smiling slightly again; "his answer might refresh you."

Weir was conscious of some hidden irony, and. while chafing under it, he was powerless to meet it with any shaft that would tell.

It was a dreary meal, not prolonged a moment beyond the time absolutely necessary for its consumption.

"We have an hour to spare," said Maitland easily. "I think I'll walk as far as Whitekirk. I'll just catch the doctor at his midday meal, eaten usually about three o'clock. I can get the four-thirty train, if he'll drive me down."

"The dogcart is at your disposal," said Weir sourly. "Why walk? The roads are muddy enough in all conscience."

"I should like the walk, and I know every foot of the way. I think I'll go now. What will you do?" he asked, turning to Shepherd.

"I? Oh, I might pay a visit to my wife's cousin, Jane Allen, who lives in Penninghame, and meet you at the four-thirty. It's the only fast train in the day, and we should be home in time for the evening mail."

"Very well; good afternoon, Mr. Weir."

He did not offer his hand, but Shepherd did, and it was warmly shaken. In the hall Weir observed Braidwood hand the bag to Mr. Maitland, and cursed his own lack of foresight that he had not been clever enough to acquaint himself with, if not actually possess, himself of its contents during the half-hour it had been out of the lawyer's keeping. He felt that it might contain what would be a death-knell to him and his high hopes, and all the evil of his passionate nature was roused.

As he watched the two go down the avenue he cursed aloud. Braidwood heard him and chuckled to himself as he cleared the table.

"We've been one ower mony for ye, my man," was his inward thought.

Before he had finished his work in the dining-room, he observed Weir leave the house and proceed with a couple of dogs at his heels across the park. Glancing casually at the clock, he observed that it was twenty minutes past two.

"How did you get on with the laird?" inquired Shepherd, when they were beyond range of the windows, and Maitland seemed in no way inclined for speech. "Did he seem inclined to forgive Madame de Castro?"

"He will see her and her children to-morrow," answered Maitland, with an absent air.

"Then probably it will be all up with Anthony Weir."

"I should say probably yes."

"Hard lines for him, don't you think?"

"No, he will be paid for what he has done. He is an alien here. It would have been a shame and a sin to see him its master."

"You are severe. He is not a bad fellow at bottom. Unfortunately you rub one another the wrong way, and you see the worst of him."

"I have seen all I want, thank you," said Maitland tranquilly. Then suddenly he went off at a tangent. "I like a day like this in the country. It soothes one's nerves. There's something in the spring that stirs even old blood."

" It looks dreary enough in all conscience," said Shepherd, with an indifferent glance across the sodden park. " But then I'm town-bred. I suppose it makes a difference."

" Undoubtedly. Something draws a man born on the land back to it. I may even invest in a little place of my own one of these days, when we get that worrying bit of business settled."

" I suppose I have gotten my *congé* now ? " said Shepherd, with slightly wounded air. " It's a game of battledore and shuttlecock."

" What's the odds, we'll get the business to do, and it will be a more satisfactory thing to settle a real Learmonth in Penninghame than that underbred upstart."

" They walked on a few steps in silence, and presently came to the lodge gates which had been left open in expectation of the dogcart coming through. The lodge keeper, a decent woman, who had been in the Learmonth employment for many years, observed them on foot and wondered.

" I may as well walk a little way with you," said Shepherd, when Maitland paused outside the gates, expecting that they would go different ways. " Two hours of Jane Allen's company would be rather too much of a good thing, but I promised my wife I would call if I had a chance."

" Very well," said Maitland, and they turned eastwards together.

Just there the trees grew very thickly, making even in winter a kind of twilight in a solitary place. And from Penninghame north lodge there was no house for nearly two miles.

" It's a fine old place," observed Maitland, looking up at the great bare branches interlacing overhead. " The timber itself in the hands of an unscrupulous person would bring a fortune."

" You can't wonder if Weir feels sore at being done out of it. Most men would put their best foot foremost to secure it," said Shepherd.

" Granted, but he's not fit. Man, you've never seen her. Come down to-night after dinner and you'll pipe to a different tune. She's one of the sweetest creatures God ever made."

" Thank you, I'll come. I should like to see her, after all that's been said and done."

" I haven't tramped this road since my boyhood, I verily believe," said Maitland, who seemed to be in a reminiscent mood. " There used to be a curious freak of nature in the woods yonder, called the Penninghame Pool. The water comes from nobody knows where. It has never been fathomed or been known to dry up except twice, when the family were in dire trouble ; curious bit of folk-lore, eh ? "

" An auld wife's tale," said Shepherd, with a slight touch of contempt. " It's a wonder somebody hasn't drained or filled it up long ago."

" It's been tried," said Maitland drily. " Twice I believe, without success. Auld wife's tale maybe, the country is full of them ; they help to give spice to life. God knows we are prosaic and material enough in towns fighting for our daily bread. I think I'll explore a bit, being in a reminiscent mood ; perhaps you wouldn't care."

" No, I shouldn't ; it's too wet for one thing."

" Not in the woods, the pine needles are feet deep. I remember them yet."

" I'll be toddling on to Jane Allen's," said Shepherd, pausing in the road. " Can I take your bag and keep it till train time ? You have a good walk before you, and don't want to be hampered with any superfluous goods."

" No, thank you ; it has no weight. Good-bye just now then, we'll meet at the four-thirty. If I shouldn't happen to find Jeffrey, I may turn up at Miss Allen's for a cup of tea."

"She would be glad to see you, I am sure," said Shepherd cordially enough, and they parted with a smile and a nod. As he slowly retraced his steps, Shepherd's thoughts were curiously reminiscent too. He went back, bit by bit, over the ground of the last twenty years, and he owned to himself that he was no nearer a full understanding of his partner's nature than he had been at the beginning. It would have been a better thing for both, perhaps, had they been able to see eye to eye regarding the conduct of business; but on the whole, they had managed to sail amicably in different boats, and Shepherd remembered several instances in which he had been treated with conspicuous generosity.

After all, he told himself it might be better for them as a united firm to act in the interests of Francis Learmonth's daughter than to be troubled with Anthony Weir's affairs. He would be a hard taskmaster and a less generous one than those of the old blood that are accustomed to pay with both hands without asking a question.

He became more cheerful, and as he lit a cigar, one of the best brand in the Penninghame cabinet, he even whistled to himself.

The day had turned out better than he expected. It seemed even as if the spring had touched his blood.

As he passed the lodge gates again on his way to the village some one slipped out, a young girl with a sweet, winsome face under the brim of a red Tam o' Shanter cap. He gave her good-afternoon, recognising her as one of the Penninghame maids. He did not know, however, that it was Nancy Nicolson away to the woods to keep tryst with Anthony Weir.

CHAPTER X

MURDER DONE

JAMES MAITLAND was surprised at his own mood. An hour ago his mind had been alert, vigorous, keen to grasp the pressing affairs in which he had intervened. He had succeeded in his mission beyond his expectation; safe in the bag lay the paper he had taken every precaution to make valid and indisputable, and which would secure to Isabel Learmonth and her children their rights for ever. He had no qualms concerning Anthony Weir, but rather felt the calm assurance that justice would be done. He would receive that which would pay him over and above his deserts. Fintry was a snug little property, and when its modest rent-roll would be supplemented by the sum to be paid out of the estate, he ought to be a happy and a grateful man. That he would be neither, Maitland knew.

And now his thoughts would go back across the misty vista of the years to the sunny mornings of his boyhood. The Jeffreys, who had been surgeons in Whitekirk from time immemorial, were old friends of his family, and though there were ten years' difference in age between the present doctor and himself they were intimate friends. They did not meet often—both being busy men; but in long and unavoidable intervals of silence their friendship suffered no hurt. They could meet after a year's absence as they had met but yesterday. So it is with the few and rare friends whom we are permitted to cherish through the whole of life, and upon whose attachment falls never a slur or a cloud. Surely there can be no man so forlorn in that widespread country men call life that he cannot claim one such as his own.

In the old incomparable days of school and college, which are too rapid in their passing, and have no marrow in the days which supervene, the old house on the edge of Whitekirk Green had been a second home to James Maitland. Then it had been a merry household, ringing with the laughter and glee of happy boys and girls, who were now scattered to the four winds of heaven. The eldest son, a man of brilliant parts, contemporary in age with Maitland, had become a diplomatist, and was now Governor of one of the British possessions oversea. Two daughters had married well. The third was matron of a great English hospital. And in the old house, alone with his memories and his work, the youngest of all, who had been the Benjamin of the family, lived alone.

He was now in his forty-sixth year, and had never married. He was a silent man who kept close counsel regarding his own affairs, and none guessed the romance which had condemned to the solitary life one obviously created for the joy and the inwardness of warm family communion. His secret, however, had been guessed by James Maitland, and, as he climbed the steep path through the woods, his feet on the thick carpet of pine needles giving forth no sound, he casually wondered whether Isabel Learmonth's return to Penninghame would make any difference.

" She might do worse, and, of course, now the case is altered. She will only be the mother of Penninghame's heir, and, though her jointure will be handsome, she would sacrifice nothing. And so she might be happy at the last."

The thought brought a smile to his lips, and so he came enveloped, as it were, in a halo of memory and of hope to the pool that had been the burden of many an old wife's tale. To this spot Maitland had come often from Whitekirk, drawn as boys will be drawn by the uncanny and the forbidden. The place was held in disrepute by some, and shunned by most, but it is to such places boys most do congregate, and Maitland remembered many an expedition, many a peering gaze into its fearsome depths, many a tale of imaginary hairbreadth escapes. As it had looked then, so it looked now; whatever change might fret the minds of men here was no change, here nature remained dark, inscrutable, immovable as of yore. Into the thicknesses of these fragrant pinewoods the sun seldom penetrated; on still days the air was heavy with the pungent penetrating odour. From a rough cart road in the valley used by the foresters and labourers on the estate, the path rose with sudden and surprising steepness. On the crest of the ascent you came without warning upon the pool set like a dark gem in a hollow basin which looked like a chasm rent by nature in one of her most painful throes. The sides of the chasm were steep and jagged, reminding one of a disused quarry, and, though vegetation grew rank everywhere around, there was not a blade or a branch from the summit to the water's edge.

It seemed as if some blight, some poisonous breath, came up from the still depths to destroy nature's kindly impulses.

Maitland set his bag on the ground, and, bending down, peered into the depths, feeling the old fascination of his boyhood returning. He admitted to himself with a half smile that he had come to see whether the pool had anything to say regarding the fortunes of the Learmonths. It is the finer, the more reverent nature that is most prone to superstition; the man who lives a wholly material or gross life must in self-defence reject it. In the course of his long experience which had brought him behind the scenes in many a family, Maitland had encountered numerous strange things which all the vaunted philosophy of men could not explain away. This was one. In one of the drawers of his desk in the King Street house he had kept a record of his experiences that had come under the category of the unexplainable, and only the previous evening he had been dipping into it. And there he had found an entry regarding the Penninghame Pool recording how in the 18th of November, 1862, it had dried up mysteriously. On the opposite page was an entry to the effect that on the morning of the 19th, the father of the present laird had blown his brains out in the gunroom at the house.

To-day, however, the pool seemed to have no pronouncement regarding the fortunes of Penninghame.

"I must bring Helen here one day," he said, as he rose from his stooping posture. "It would interest her."

A sudden creaking of the underbrush and the echo of a soft footfall caused him to start. Looking quickly down the path he beheld to his immense surprise the figure of Anthony Weir approaching.

It was a mutual surprise. Weir's face flushed, and he glanced quickly behind him, looking indeed for the girl he had trysted to meet him here. He had chosen this spot because it was seldom or never frequented. He felt annoyed. It would not help to raise him in his opponent's estimation if he were detected in an adventure with a servant girl whom Maitland of course knew quite well by sight.

Maitland concluded on the moment that Weir had followed him and desired some speech with him regarding the position of affairs, and he was equally determined that he would not accord it.

He simply nodded, and would have passed him by to descend by the path he had come, but Weir stopped in front of him.

"A curious place to find you, Mr. Maitland," said Weir, and as his eye fell on the bag held tightly in the lawyer's hand, the desire to possess himself of the contents again swept over him almost uncontrollably.

"It is hardly less surprising to meet you here, Mr. Weir," said Maitland, with a slight shrug of the shoulders.

"Not at all; I am in my own domain. You are a trespasser. What brings you up here? It does not lead to anywhere?"

Maitland glanced backward to the pool.

"I was renewing an old acquaintance," he said lightly. "I daresay, you have heard all the legends of the pool?"

"I have no truck with superstition. I leave that to them that's fit for nothing else," he said, with amazing rudeness, which, however, Maitland took tranquilly.

"I will bid you good-day, sir," he said, and would have passed, but Weir still barred the way.

"In a moment; as we have met in this extraordinary and unlooked-for place and way, I may as well take some advantage of it. Tell me before you go what kind of a spoke you have put in my wheel to-day. I know you hate me, possibly because you know that once I am master your pottering ways and confounded side will get a sudden awakening. You belong to the tribe that have lined their own nets at the old man's expense."

"Let me pass," said Maitland, in no way disturbed. "I decline the honour of conversation with you."

Perhaps he could not help the inflection of contempt on the word honour delicately conveying an opinion which raised all the bad blood in one who had never been taught to control it.

"Take care; don't rouse me too far. I have you here; you are an old man. If you don't choose to tell me what I want to know, perhaps I may take means to discover it for myself."

"What is it you wish to know?" asked Maitland, quite coolly. He was not abashed by the threatening tone. It was not the first time he had been face to face with, and got the better of a bully.

"I don't need to ask the object of your unwarrantable intrusion to-day. Your partner has acquainted me with it, and he agreed with me that it was not only unwarrantable but underhand, even criminal. My uncle is no longer able to transact business, and if you succeeded in getting him to agree to any of your nefarious schemes, you were making use of undue influence."

"Had the business concerned you, I suppose it would have been all right," observed Maitland coolly. "We need not prolong this needless, and to me most disagreeable interview. I will wish you good-day, Mr. Weir."

"I will hear first what was your business with my uncle. I warn you that though you may think you have succeeded in getting the better of me you don't know who you have to deal with. I will not be baulked of my rights. I will stick at nothing to obtain them."

"That I could very well believe; so far as your rights are concerned, you have obtained, in my estimation, far more than you are entitled to."

"You must be more explicit. What do you mean by these libellous words?"

"What I say. If you press me I will be more explicit, but perhaps it would be unwise on your part," said the lawyer significantly.

"Unwise or not, I'll make you disgorge your suspicions, whatever they are. What do you mean?"

"I don't believe that you are the son of Anthony Weir, and, if necessary, I can obtain the proof."

Weir's face grew livid, and he was for a moment speechless.

Then there gathered in his eyes a slow consuming fire, which had murder in its depths.

"I'll trouble you to let me know the contents of that bag, and if there is a will in it, which you wrested from my uncle by your own machination. when he was incapable of comprehending what was wanted, I shall see it."

Maitland's answer was to grip the bag more tightly in his hand, and endeavour to push past on the narrow path.

The next moment they were in grips. Maitland was fifty-seven, but in his youth he had been a wrestler, and had not altogether forgotten the art. Something told him it might be for dear life that he fought, the man before him being unscrupulous and evidently in desperate straits. For a moment their heavy breathing and laboured movements were the only sounds upon the still air. Maitland was old, and he quickly failed; back step by step he was forced, then suddenly, without warning and with one faint gurgling cry, he went down the precipitous bank into the depths of the mysterious pool. For a moment Weir stared aghast, with eyes starting from their sockets, to see him rise again, but after the first eddies died away the smooth surface remained unbroken, telling no tale. A mighty horror held him. He was bold, unscrupulous, playing a dangerous game, but he had not intended to have James Maitland's life.

When, shaking like an aspen, he turned from the edge of the pool, he saw in the path before him Nancy Nicolson with a frozen look of horror on her face.

CHAPTER XI

PARTNERS IN GUILT

For a moment man and maid looked at one another in a ghastly silence. How much did she know? What had she seen? These were the questions Weir asked himself even while he cursed the folly that had made him notice her pretty face. Upon the issue of the next moments much depended, even perhaps his liberty and life.

"Awful thing, isn't it, Nancy?" he said, trying to speak in a voice duly impressive without betraying the horror of his own soul. "I was just in time to see him tipple in, not in time to hold him back unfortunately. A clear case of suicide apparently. Queer old chap. Must have had something on his mind."

Then Nancy, shaking like a leaf, found her voice.

"But I saw ye fechtin', I heard ye, an' saw ye push him in." she said faintly.

Then, knowing the worst, Weir's manner changed.

He stepped forward, and gripped her roughly by the arm.

"So you saw that, did you; and who's to believe you; who's to prevent me pushing you in after him if you persist in believing such a lie?"

Nancy stared, her eyes starting with terror, dumb before the man's evil face. Hitherto it had been wreathed only in smiles for her, and she had dreamed her silly dreams of a grand future in which she would walk a lady by his side, perhaps even be Lady of Penninghame, and rule where she now served. But this was not the smooth-voiced lover that had poisoned an inoffensive nature with words of guile, that had changed her from an innocent country girl into a vain, boasting, ambitious woman, with ideas far beyond the simple order of life that had hitherto contented her! His beetling brows bent threateningly upon her, his evil eyes, his low hissing voice terrified her. For the moment Nancy expected nothing but to be pushed over the bank after the poor old man, who undoubtedly had been done to death. She felt paralysed, and did not even utter a word. She fluttered like a trapped bird in his rough grasp, her face pale as the linen collar at her throat.

Once more, and as suddenly, his manner changed.

"Look here, Nancy, you and I have got to sail now in the same boat. We'd better go on a bit and talk things over."

"I want to go home. Oh! let me go home," she said, in a pleading whisper.

"To blab out the whole thing? Not if I know it. I must get you under proper control first, explain the thing to you, see. Come along; let's get away from this accursed place."

"An' leave him?" she said, with a terrified yet pitying backward glance at the dark pool. "We micht hae tried to save him. He hadna a chance."

"Has anybody a chance that once gets in there? It's the devil's cauldron, I believe. They say it has no bottom. It was his own fault. I never harmed him, but he managed to-day to poison my uncle's mind against me, so that he has robbed me of Penninghame."

"And who will get it?" asked Nancy, momentarily interested. The probable succession was the constant topic of conversation in the servants' hall, where Anthony Weir was no favourite.

"Himself, most likely. I tell you, Nancy, these lawyers are fit for anything. Shepherd is the decentest one I've come across yet, but he's only a puppet in the other one's hands."

Nancy was quick enough to understand.

"My uncle Braidwood thinks the very opposite; he says Maister Maitland was one o' the best o' men. Oh! what will he say when he kens?" she wailed, and began to tremble again.

"Nancy, look at me."

She lifted her terrified eyes, and was at once held by his compelling gaze.

"When I said we were to sail in the same boat, I don't think you quite comprehended my meaning. If anything is discovered we should both be put in gaol, perhaps hanged for it. It was all on your account I was so anxious about getting the place, and it's not likely I would suffer alone."

"But they will discover it," said Nancy faintly. "I've aye heard that murder will out."

It was an ugly word, and it made Anthony Weir wince.

"You'd better be more careful about your words, my dear, he said grimly. "There was no murder about it; the thing was a pure accident. I wanted him to let me see the papers he had in his bag, and I had the right to see them since they were the instrument to rob me of my rights. He refused, and it was in trying to get the bag from him that we got into grips. Do you follow me?"

"Oh, yes," said Nancy, but her tone lacked conviction.

"What followed was a pure accident that might have happened anywhere. That's our line, Nancy, when the hue and cry is out, and if they discover anything. But my own opinion is that they won't, and that this is not the first secret the pool has determined to keep to all eternity."

"But hoo can we pretend to ken naething when we ken everything?" asked Nancy, voicing the doubts natural in one who all her life long had been accustomed to babble of small affairs as well as great.

"It'll come easy enough when the fear of the hangman's rope is at the back," he said suggestively.

"But hoo could they hang me?" she persisted. "I did naething, only saw what you did."

"But I would take care that you should share my fate," he said grimly. "And who would take your word? You are nobody, and the fact that you were on the spot would condemn you at the first."

Nancy's reasoning powers were not highly developed, and there was black terror in her soul.

"Ye wad never dae that. Of course, I'll no tell, no even my Aunt Susan."

"If you told her, my dear, you might as well go to the nearest policeman. Much better, in fact. You might find some bowels of mercy in him; there would be none in her. No, no; mum's the word. It'll soon blow over, and when my uncle's away out of this troubled world, and I'm the Laird of Penninghame, your reward will come. You would like to be Lady of Penninghame, wouldn't you, Nancy?"

"I thocht I would this morning," she said ingenuously, which enlightened

Weir as to the trend of her imagination. " But I wad be feared to live so near the pool. It micht dry up ony day, and then whaur wad we be ? "

" The chances are unlikely."

" I've heard my Uncle Braidwood tell aboot it. He minds it dryin' up once after the auld laird killed himself. It's a queer place, an' no canny."

" I would need to see it to believe it," he said lightly. " Anyhow, we've got to take our chance, and we'll keep an eye on the thing. If it's likely to give trouble we'll take care to clear out with plenty of money in our pockets before that. But even then, we wouldn't need, if only you could learn to play the part well."

" It'll be awful the day, an' the morn, and the next day to gang aboot as if ye ken naething, when ye ken a'thing," she said, shuddering afresh. " An' in the nicht-time I'll see the place, an' you fechtin', an syne him fa'in in. I hear his cry at this meenit."

Weir bit his lip. His unpremeditated crime was very new, and his own composure hard to sustain. As he looked at the cowering creature in his grip, and reflected on her scanty intelligence, her probable inability to keep a secret he felt such a loathing for her that he could almost have killed her on the spot. But for the cursed folly that had caused him to wile away the dull hours with her all might have been well. His own burden of a guilty secret he could have borne successfully, but when there was added to it the weight of keeping her up to the mark, he foresaw that it must soon become intolerable. He resolved to get her away from Penninghame without delay. In the meantime, and until he could make the necessary arrangements, he could only work upon her imagination, and put the fear of death upon her for herself. Which he did in language which lacked nothing in force or vividness. While he was speaking, Nancy could almost feel the rope about her neck.

" You needn't be so frightened, I'll stand by you," he said, with assumed tenderness. " So long as you trust me, and do as I bid you, all will go well. The moment you go back, even a hair's-breadth from what I have told you you must do, it's all up. And it won't be for long. How would it be to go to Edinburgh one day and get married quietly ? That would settle everything, wouldn't it ? "

" Oh, I dinna ken," said Nancy. " I wad like to get away, of course. It'll no be easy wi' my Uncle Braidwood and Aunt Susan ; they're aye at me as it is ; I havna the life o' a cat wi' them."

" Well, we'll put an end to all that, Nancy. Just you leave it to me, and when you're Lady of Penninghame you can snap your fingers at the whole tribe."

" An' I'll be mistress ower my Uncle Braidwood and my Aunt Susan ? "

" They'd need to clear, my dear," said Weir, weary of the discussion, but seeing that the girl was growing calmer and more reasonable as her thoughts dwelt on the subject. To make her Lady of Penninghame had never suggested itself to him even in his most lover-like moments. Poor Nancy, with the sweet face and the winsome ways, was but the plaything of an hour. Even now he had no serious intention of linking his future life with her. He knew too well that such a step would ruin his position for ever. But he must assiduously foster the idea, must let her grasp the fact that she was indissolubly bound to him, that his interests must be hers, that with him she must stand or fall. Only so could he buy the silence that would give him the time he needed.

So they came to the outer fringe of the wood where they must part, lest any should see them together. In the last kindly shadow Weir stood still, and took her two cold hands in his firm grip once more.

"Now, Nancy, look at me again."

"I am lookin'," she said faintly.

"You understand the situation perfectly? The thing was an accident, a deplorable accident, to which we unfortunately were unwilling witnesses. In the circumstances, and it being known that he and I were for the time being, and for business reasons only, enemies, if anything should be discovered it will go hard with us. Everything would be against us, see, and practically nothing could save us."

"Oh, I see it!" said Nancy desperately. "I see it quite weel."

"If we keep quiet, live our ordinary lives, and say nothing, the thing will blow over. There is only about one chance in a hundred, hardly that, even, that the secret of the pool will ever be discovered. And if we find that we are not as happy as we would like to be in Penninghame, we can sell the place, and go abroad. You've often said you'd like to see the world. I'll take you to South Africa, Nancy, for a honeymoon trip if only you are the brave good girl you can be."

"Oh, I will be," she sobbed. "Only let it be sune, for it'll be terrible hard to live on here, pretendin' I ken naething."

"I will put an end to that for you at once. To-morrow I will go to Edinburgh, Nancy, and arrange that we shall be married quietly. And you will have a comfortable little home, where I can come and see you as often as I could get away, but only until things are settled."

"Yes, yes," said Nancy eagerly. "I'll dae a' ye want till then, an' I'll never tell a soul."

"If you do, you know what to expect, and I warn you that if you should betray us I'll get away, and leave you to bear the brunt yourself; nothing will be easier."

She shrank from him; a little wounded by his tone, but he hastened to reassure her, and when they parted her face had resumed its ordinary expression, though it certainly looked whiter than usual. As she sped across the park she looked hurriedly at the little watch, one of his gifts, hid in the bosom of her dress, and saw that it was past her aunt's tea-time. One of Nancy's duties was to lay tea for her aunt and uncle in the housekeeper's room at four o'clock each day.

But when she came to the house there was no rebuke and no questioning, only a great commotion, servants running to and fro, the doctor's gig standing before the door.

The laird was dead.

CHAPTER XII

GATHERING FEARS

Katie Niven, the housmaid at the old King Street house, knocked lightly at the drawing-room door. When her mistress bade her enter, she found them gathered in a little circle about the fire, apparently enjoying a cosy chat. In reality there was a good deal of anxiety, at least in the minds of Helen and her elder guest, regarding the non-arrival of her father. They had waited in vain for him at tea-time. The message he had promised Madame de Castro had failed to arrive. It was now eight o'clock, and there was still no sign of his return. An open time-table rested suggestively on Helen's knee.

"Yes, Katie," she said, looking round at the opening of the door.

"Please, miss, cook's askin' will she not serve dinner. The vegetables is spoilin', and everything getting quite cold."

"Just wait another ten minutes, Katie; that gives your master time to get here from the eight o'clock train."

Katie withdrew, and Helen exchanged glances with Madame de Castro.

"He is quite certain to come by this train," she said cheerfully. "We must not worry."

"But is it not strange that he has not telegraphed?" asked Isabel, almost feverishly. "He promised to do so."

"But it is sometimes difficult to get a telegraph message sent in the country when one wants it. Let us take his silence rather as a sign that all is going well. Mr. Learmonth is very ill, and the news of which papa was the bearer was exciting. The whole matter would have to be proceeded with quietly."

Thus spoke the lawyer's daughter in low, quiet, judicial tones. But even while she sought to reassure her guest, her own mind was full of uneasiness. The piano was open, they had been having some music, and Helen asked Sybil to sing again. She possessed a sweet, tuneful voice which had not been trained. When Helen thought of all these young creatures had missed already in life, she felt still more sad for them. Their mother interested her intensely, and the few hours of intimacy had served to knit their hearts together in such affection as is usually the slow product of years. Isabel de Castro was in a grateful and receptive mood. Long buffeted by the sea of life, bereft of friends and fortune, devoid of hope for the future, she was prone to exaggerate even a simple kindness. The minutes passed, half-past eight sounded on the silver gong of the drawing-room clock and pealed from the deeper bell of a neighbouring church. Then Helen rose. She still strove, however, to hide an anxiety momentarily deepening.

"Dear Madame de Castro, if you will excuse my leaving you to take dinner alone, I will take a cab round to the house of my father's partner. It is not far. I shall not be gone many minutes. They went out together, and if Mrs. Shepherd has heard nothing of her husband either, we may conclude that affairs are very pressing at Penninghame, and that it augurs well for you."

Even at the last she dropped a crumb of comfort for the woman to whom the issue of that day meant so much. She ran downstairs, bade Katie call her a cab, and then serve dinner for the guests at once.

"You're not afraid anything has happened, Miss Helen?" said the girl anxiously, as she wrapped her mistress's cloak about her.

"I think I am a little afraid, Katie. It is so unlike papa—but there, what could have happened? Why, nothing, of course. It is only that there have been things happening at Penninghame. See that they have all they want, Katie, and I will hurry back as quickly as possible."

The cab in response to the whistle drew up noisily at the door, and Helen got in, bidding the man drive as quickly as possible to Upper Dean House, which was the somewhat pretentious name of the West End mansion William Shepherd in his prosperous days had built for himself.

The house was as pretentious as its name. It had a pillared gateway to the public highway, and an avenue sweeping up to the imposing portico, which had sometimes been the butt of ribald jest on the part of those who remembered him as office boy and lawyer's clerk. A flag waved from the square tower, and no sign of importance or prosperity was lacking. The moment the cab drew up at the door Helen ran lightly up the steps and rang the bell. It was answered at once by the man-servant, who knew her well by sight, and looked surprised to see her at that hour.

"Good evening, Nicoll; is Mr. Shepherd at home?"

"Yes, ma'am, just risen from dinner, all the rest savin' missus have gone to a ball at the Music Hall."

"When did he come back from Penninghame?" she asked, with blanching cheek, as she stepped into the warm, well-lighted hall.

"About tea-time; the missus drove him from the station. Here is master."

Hearing the voices Shepherd came out of the library, where he and his wife had gone to drink their after-dinner coffee.

"Oh, Mr. Shepherd, what has become of papa? I am so anxious about him. Why did he not return with you?"

"I can't say, Miss Helen. We parted at Penninghame gate early in the afternoon, agreeing to meet at the four-thirty train. I was very late for it myself, having stayed too long at my wife's cousin's. I had only time to jump into the last carriage as it was steaming out of the station. But I got out at Porth, and looked through the train for your father. Didn't he come with the seven-ten?"

"No; I am getting horribly anxious, and so is Madame de Castro. We have them at our house," she added, observing his look of surprise. "My father came home before he went to the train this forenoon and asked me to go and fetch them, as they were living in quite a miserable place. Did he say where he was going when you left him?"

"Yes, he did; but come inside to Mrs. Shepherd and let us take the thing quietly. There is not the smallest occasion for alarm, I assure you."

She followed him into the library, and was there warmly greeted by Mrs. Shepherd, a largè, comfortable handsome person, always well dressed, and looking satisfied with herself. But beneath all the pretentiousness which an altered position had thrust upon her, there beat a truly kind and motherly heart. She was sincerely fond of Helen Maitland, and it was not her fault that the intimacy between the two families did not make much progress. It was rather Helen's fault. The gay, pleasure-loving life pursued by the Shepherds did not appeal to her, and she came to their house but seldom. Some of the younger members thought her very proud and stand-offish when in reality she was only shy.

The moment the fresh greeting was over, she turned eagerly to Mr. Shepherd.

"Where did papa go when he left you?"

"He went off intending to walk to Whitekirk for the purpose of seeing Dr. Jeffrey."

Helen's face instantly cleared.

"Oh, then, perhaps he has been detained there, or missed his train. When is the next one?"

"The next gets in something after nine; here we are," he said, reaching Murray from the writing-table. "Nine twenty-seven, not long to wait, it's just about nine now."

"I'll drive round to the station and get him. Don't you think it odd that he did not telegraph? It is so unlike him. You know how methodical he is. And he promised Madame de Castro to let her know how matters progressed at Penninghame. Do you know whether he had a satisfactory interview with Mr. Learmonth regarding her?"

Shepherd's face momentarily hardened, which did not escape Helen's discerning eye. She could only surmise the cause, since her father had made it one of the rules of his life to leave business outside the door of his home. In all the years she had been his intimate and close companion, Helen had never known him to depart from this rule.

"Mr. Maitland did not say much to me, but I gathered from his few words that the interview had been satisfactory from his point of view. I should say that Madame de Castro may keep her mind quite easy on that score."

His tone was exceedingly dry, and informed Helen quite as convincingly as was necessary that her father and his partner had had some difference of opinion on that particular matter.

"I suppose Whitekirk is a good distance from the station?" she said, in order to change the subject.

"It is almost five miles from Penninghame Station, so you see even if he failed to get home to-night you need not be unduly anxious."

"Oh, but that would be so unlike papa!" repeated Helen. "He will certainly let me know if he can't get back. He would know I should be anxious. But surely there must be a telegraph office nearer than Penninghame?"

"That I am unable to say," said Shepherd. Then Helen turned to go.

"I will drive round by the station. Good-night, Mrs. Shepherd."

Shepherd rang the bell for his boots.

"Yes, yes, of course I will come. I should like to come, and we have plenty of time. Sit down quietly and talk to my wife until I get ready."

Helen took a chair, but she looked, as she felt, uneasy.

"They have all gone to the Lanark Hunt Ball, Helen," said Mrs. Shepherd, "chaperoned by Mrs. Mackenzie-Seton."

"Mrs. Mackenzie-Seton!" repeated Helen, momentarily interested. She knew the lady mentioned as one of the most exclusive Edinburgh hostesses, and wondered what her sudden change of front towards the Shepherds might portend.

It is curious how even in the midst of corroding anxiety we are able at times to give our minds to trifles, and to pursue them even to their conclusion. Knowing the Setons to be poor, Helen casually wondered whether some matrimonial alliance could be in contemplation, or whether it was only a little attention paid for business purposes. She was not, however, enlightened. She could see how pleased the proud mother was to have her brood under such irreproachable care, and smiled a little inwardly, even while she seemed to sympathise. Helen was quick to see the humorous side, and managed to extract a great deal of quiet enjoyment from the standpoint of the looker-on.

" You will be making a great match for Kitty one of these days," she said, as she rose again, too restless to be still longer than a moment. " She is a dear little girl ; she deserves it."

Genuine pleasure beamed on Mrs. Shepherd's comely face at these spontaneous words, and she bade the girl good-night rather more affectionately than usual.

During the drive to the station Helen and Mr. Shepherd talked of ordinary affairs, but the minds of both were filled with that vague uneasiness which cannot be put into words. In spite of his reasuring words to Helen, Shepherd thought it strange and inexplicable that Maitland had not come home, or at least that he had not sent some word of explanation to his daughter. As she had said, it was altogether unlike one whose habits were methodical to a degree.

When they came to the station Helen was arrested by its quiet, deserted appearance. There was no bustle of arrival or departure, the clean swept platforms and empty sidings had an unfamiliar look.

" The train is signalled, Miss Helen ; our anxiety will soon be at an end," said her companion quickly.

She nodded with evident relief, and pressed forward as it came lumbering up to the platform.

A mere handful of passengers alighted, and quickly dispersed. Among them she did not discern the tall, stooping figure for which she longed. Her face blanched again, and she betrayed signs of keen nervous distress.

" What must we do now ? Something must have happened to him ? Can I go out to Whitekirk to-night ? "

" You can't ; the last train went half an hour ago. Try to be calm, Miss Helen. Go quietly home, and if no word comes I will meet you here in time for the first train in the morning, which leaves at six-twenty."

" Six-twenty, and it is not yet ten. More than eight hours ! Oh, is there no way of telegraphing to Doctor Jeffrey ? "

" Not to-night ; we must just thole, Miss Helen, and try to comfort ourselves with the thought that probably your father is smoking his pipe of peace by his old friend's fireside."

" He would never do such a thing, knowing how anxious I should be at home," cried Helen indignantly. " Tell me, Mr. Shepherd, is it a lonely dark road between Penninghame and Whitekirk ? "

" It is not a nice road, certainly, though your father to-day seemed to be regarding the whole place with an extraordinary affection," he answered. But though his own mind was full of what his partner had said about the mysterious Penninghame Pool, he did not think it wise to repeat it to Helen.

He took her gently by the arm, and helped her to the waiting cab, in which they drove across the quietened city almost in silence.

CHAPTER XIII

TOO LATE

HELEN passed a sleepless night. In the grey dawn she was astir, moving quietly about the house, so as to disturb no one. About five o'clock there came a light tap at her door, and when she opened it she was surprised to see Madame de Castro fully dressed standing outside.

"Good-morning. I am going with you; yes, my dear. It is surely the least I can do for you," she said, with a look of indescribable sweetness. "And, if you fear your dear father has met with harm in the public highway, no one could guide you better there than I. I could walk between Penninghame and Whitekirk blindfold."

Helen's eyes filled. She had felt terribly alone all the long night; a sudden sense of security and strength seemed to come to her.

"It will tire you so much, and even perhaps I am foolish to be so anxious. But something must have happened. My father would never act like this. If you knew him you would understand. If he is even to be an hour later than usual at the office, he never fails to send me a message."

"Your anxiety is quite natural; and it would make me happy to go even on my own account. There is so much at stake."

"They are preparing an early breakfast. Are the children asleep?"

"Soundly; they will be all right. I told Sybil before she fell asleep that I would accompany you, and they will go out together and explore Edinburgh."

Helen said no more. A little later they ate a very slender breakfast and left the house, the anxious maidservant who served the house for love hovering about them to the last.

"Miss Helen, you'll telegraph as soon as you can, we are so anxious," she pleaded, as she opened the door.

"Yes, yes, thank you, Katie. Look after Miss and Master de Castro until we come happily back."

The sweet breath of the spring morning, freshened by the salt wind of the sea, met them on the threshold. Helen stood still and drew a long breath.

"It is good," she said involuntarily. "We don't get the freshness of the new day often enough."

They were almost silent as they made the steep ascent to Princes Street, feeling the charm and stillness which lay upon the newly awakened city like a spell. The air was crystal clear, the vapours of the day had not yet tarnished its heavenly freshness. Helen long remembered that early walk. It was one of the experiences that are photographed on the memory, and remain clear and finished in every detail to the end of life itself. At the station there was the same air of repose. Early journeys are undertaken through necessity rather than for pleasure, and the few passengers moving about had an alert look, as if fully realising the importance of their own business. As they descended the stairs Helen saw Shepherd waiting for them under the clock. He guessed the identity of her companion as he came forward, raising his hat.

" Mr. Shepherd, my father's partner, Madame de Castro," said Helen.

Isabel scarcely looked at him. He in no way interested her. He felt the careless glance, and imagined undue hauteur in the slight, cool inclination of the head.

" Does Madame accompany us ? " he asked politely. " If so I will get her ticket."

" Thanks," she replied curtly, and Helen looked at her in surprise. It was as if another side of her nature had been unexpectedly revealed.

" I do not like that man, dear ; he is not sincere," was all the explanation vouchsafed.

There was little time to spare. Immediately they were seated in the train it moved out. Shepherd, after a moment's reflection, inwardly conscious of Madame de Castro's antagonism, wisely put them alone into a carriage, and took the adjoining one himself, promising to meet them at their journey's end.

" Good," said Isabel, when the door closed upon them. " I did not think he would have had the tact."

" He can be very kind ; he has been most kind about this," said Helen staunchly. " And my father thinks highly of his business abilities."

" Doubtless, but there is a something. He is not quite a gentleman. Ah, how quick one is to know and feel the true ring ! There are so many counterfeits. But who am I to sit in judgment, a poor derelict in the sea of life ? I cannot help it. It is a matter of temperament. It has been an obstacle in my path all my life."

Helen remained silent, and turning her eyes to the window, tried to discern the landscape through which they were passing. It was still dark, and the stars were gleaming in the clear, soft sky, but as they left the environs of Edinburgh behind, a long yellow line stretching out to sea indicated the dawn of the new day. A strange unreal feeling held both in thrall, which as they sped through the wintry fields deepened in Helen's mind at least to a certainty of evil. But what that evil was she could not define ; it was but a corroding shadow which pursued her with a sickening dread.

At Porth Junction, where the trains from the South were due, there was a brief stoppage, and Shepherd joined them in their carriage.

He felt himself by no means easy in mind, and the sight of these two forlorn women, whose faces bore traces of their anxiety, touched him oddly.

So subtle is the essence of the human spirit, Isabel de Castro became at once conscious of his unspoken sympathy, and bestowed upon him a more cordial glance. The grey light was now stealing across the country; in the long furrows could be seen the patient team addressing itself to the day's work, the pleasant smell of the fresh brown earth was in the air, and here and there could be caught the faint green of the winter wheat. Upon these things Isabel de Castro gazed with untold depths of yearning tenderness in her eyes. She was country bred, and had spent the incomparable years of childhood among them, and they awakened in her heart a passion of memory that would not be stilled. They saw her mood and uttered nothing to disturb it ; they came in perfect silence to the little station in the Lothian plain. They were the only passengers to alight, and the stationmaster regarded them curiously, recognising only one. He was not a Penninghame man, but a South country official transferred to Penninghame a few years before.

" It was very sudden at the end, sir," he remarked, as he took the tickets from Shepherd's hand.

" What ? " asked Shepherd, with a great start.

" The laird's death. He died suddenly afore the doctor could get to him yesterday afternoon aboot fower o'clock," he said, with the air which distinguishes the man able to convey important news.

The ladies had already moved out of hearing, for which Shepherd felt thankful. He had received an unexpected shock. This untoward happening must considerably complicate affairs. He moved forward a little unsteadily, his face wearing a bewildered look. But he managed to recover himself before he passed through the booking-office to the little enclosure where his fellow-travellers waited for him.

A lumbering old brake called by courtesy the post-gig, stood in the roadway. He opened the door and helped them in. He was wondering in what words he should convey to Isable de Castro the news of her father's death. As it happened, however, he was spared the necessity. Post Jamie, the garrulous old man who drove them, turned on his seat brimming with information.

" The laird gaed oot like a wisp o' strae on a windy nicht at the last, sir, efter a' their waitin'."

He also spoke in ignorance of the identity of Madame de Castro, though he had driven her often in the bygone days, but he was now old and his sight waxing dim. Also the light was still grey about them, and she was closely veiled. She leaned forward with a sudden start.

The broad Scotch sounded unfamiliar in her ears, but she just managed to grasp the significance of the words.

" What does he say ? Is my father dead, Mr. Shepherd ? "

At these words Post Jamie turned full round on his seat and stared at the strange lady almost aghast.

" It's Miss Isabel, as I'm a leevin' man ! Eh, but ye're ower late, my leddy. He dee'd yestreen about fower o'clock."

For a moment they feared she would succumb to the shock ; her face grew ghastly pale, and a violent fit of trembling shook her slender figure from head to foot. Helen passed her arm about her waist and tried to comfort her. Shepherd sat by miserable, not knowing what to say or do. It was a pathetic picture of desolation and sorrow. What was such sad hearing for her, however, relieved the tension of their own anxiety regarding Mr. Maitland. Doubtless he had been met on the road by Doctor Jeffrey in his gig, and taken back to Penninghame. Such was the conclusion immediately arrived at by both Helen and Mr. Shepherd.

The post gig only took them as far as the old Bell Inn, in Penninghame Street, where, however, they were quickly transferred to a vehicle more comfortable and seemly. While it was being got ready, Helen persuaded Madame de Castro to drink a cup of tea. Her hopeless and wretched look went to her heart.

" Too late ! " she moaned ; " and what will become of me and of my children, Helen ? Tell me that."

" The way will open up, my friend," said Helen gently. " Wait until you have seen my father, and all will be well. He always knows the way out."

" Shall we find him at Penninghame ? " she asked, with the wistfulness of a child. It was as if the spirit had gone clean out of her, and despair taken the place of hope.

"Surely, it is what we all expect; of course this explains his absence and his silence. There would be so much to do he would not have time to think of us."

"But I am surprised that he did not telegraph to me. Four o'clock yesterday afternoon. It was quite early. There was plenty of time."

She admitted it, but pointed out what a shock death coming unexpectedly is to a household, and what a multitude of things can intervene to occupy the time.

Shortly they were driven through the open gates of Penninghame. Now Isabel put back her veil, and suffered her eyes to roam across each familiar landmark. Oh, how often she had seen it all, both in her dreams and in the haunting memories of her waking hours, and how incomparably beautiful and more dear it seemed than any! Yet now, perhaps, it had passed into the hands of a stranger. Eight o'clock pealed from the stable tower as they drove up to the door.

Braidwood, laying breakfast for the new master, who was still asleep, heard the wheels and ran out.

When he saw who occupied the back seat of the Bell dogcart, the old man put his two hands before his face, and burst into tears.

CHAPTER XIV

HER CHILDHOOD'S HOME

ISABEL sprang lightly to the ground, and laid her hand on Braidwood's arm.

"So we meet again, my old friend," she said trembling. "You seem the only one unchanged. Shall I find Susan, too, just as she was when I went away?"

"Shusan's here, Miss Isabel, gettin' a wee auld an' frail like mysel'; but oh, my lamb, this is a black ill day for Penninghame! What way—what way did ye no come yesterday?"

"How could I? I did not know. Tell me about my father. How did he die? Did he speak of me at all?"

Braidwood shook his head.

"He dee'd in his sleep, Miss Isabel, as easy an' sweet as a bairn fa's ower. He was terrible tired after the lawyers were dune wi' him, and I gied him some brandy an' some soup, and covered him up. In three meenits he was alseep. I jist slipped up to Shusan's room to drink my cup o' tea, and when I gaed back no fifteen meenits efter, I couldna wauken him. It was a' ower."

"Will it be possible for me to see him?" she asked, in a curious calm voice, which indicated how great was the strain she was putting on herself.

"Yes, for certain; him that thinks himsel' the laird is in his bed, an' wull be or ten o'clock, maybe eleeven. Come in, and I'll get ye a' some breakfast!"

"I suppose my father slept here last night," said Helen suddenly. "Or did he go back to Whitekirk with Doctor Jeffrey?"

Braidwood looked puzzled, and scratched his head.

"Mr. Maitland you're meanin', miss, I suppose? I've never seen him since you an' he left yesterday after luncheon," he said, looking towards Shepherd.

"What! you've never seen him!" exclaimed Shepherd, dumbfoundered. "Do you mean to say he did not come back here after the laird's death?"

"If he did, I never saw him."

"He went off to Whitekirk; did the doctor say nothing about having seen him?"

"No' a word; I'm sure he didna see him either, for he said to me it was a peety Mr. Maitland hadna bidden a' day."

Once more a wave of fear swept over Helen's heart, and she looked round helplessly. Shepherd felt at his wits' end. The mystery whose solution they imagined they had found was only deepening each moment.

"We had better drive to Whitekirk, Miss Helen, and see the doctor ourselves," he suggested; and Helen turned to the trap at once.

"What will you do, Madame de Castro? Miss Maitland is naturally anxious to discover the meaning of this apparently inexplicable occurrence. Will you remain here?"

"I will remain here; you will drive back this way and tell me if you find him at Whitekirk."

" Certainly, but it may be painful for you to meet Mr. Anthony Weir when he comes downstairs," he suggested, with a touch of hesitation. " It will not take us long to drive to Whitekirk."

" It is my father's house, and, I hope, mine, Mr. Shepherd," said Isabel steadily. " Why should it be painful to me to meet Anthony Weir? I am not afraid of him. Probably he has cause to be afraid of me. If Miss Maitland does not mind, I will await your return here."

Helen shook her head drearily. The sickening return of suspense and dread after a cheerful gleam of hope seemed more than she could bear.

Shepherd felt himself in an odd and difficult position, but decided that his first duty was to accompany Helen. They mounted to their seat and drove away, while Isabel preceded Braidwood into the house she had left under cover of the darkness on a wild March morning twenty years before. There was no hesitation or faltering in her gait or mien; a new resolve had been born with the hour in her heart.

Although too late to receive the forgiveness for which her penitent and contrite heart had craved for her children's sakes, she must bear herself courageously. The place was hers and theirs by right, even the law should not wrest it from them. She hoped that the outcome of Mr. Maitland's visit yesterday would be to make any contest unnecessary. With that thought in her mind she turned to Braidwood in the hall.

" Do you happen to know if anything of importance transpired between my father and Mr. Maitland the lawyer yesterday? " she asked eagerly.

Braidwood held open the door of the morning-room, where the fire burned invitingly, and following her in, shut the door.

" Maister Maitland was wi' him a long time, Miss Isabel, the better pairt o' an 'oor, and he was writing something on a long blue paper. Syne me an' Shusan had to pit oor names till it, and Maister Maitland lookit weel pleased. He says to me doon the stair, says he, when he gied me his bag to tak' care o', when they were at luncheon, ' Look after that bag, Braidwood; it'll bring Miss Isabel an' her bairns back to Penninghame '."

" Where is that bag, Braidwood, and Mr. Maitland? "

Braidwood helplessly shook his head. Events were crowding too thickly upon him, and his intelligence was scarcely sufficient to grasp them all.

" Is Maister Maitland lost? That was his dochter, wasn't it? What did she mean by askin' me if he sleepit here? Maister Shepherd kent that they left thegither on the back o' twa o'clock."

" They parted, it seems, outside the gates soon after, and he has never been seen since," Isabel answered. " Can anything have happened to him, any foul play? "

" O, I dinna think it. Dootless he'll turn up," said Braidwood rather vaguely. What was happening immediately under his own observation sufficed for him at the moment. He was wondering what would happen if the door should suddenly open to admit Anthony Weir. Braidwood looked forward with much inward exultation to his discomfiture.

" Ye arena that muckle cheenged, Miss Isabel. An' twa fine bairns, hae ye? " he asked affectionately; " a son that'll be Laird o' Penninghame and Whitekirk, as it should be."

" He would have pleased his grandfather, Braidwood. It is cruel hard that death has cheated us of that satisfaction," she said, in a low painful voice.
what crumbs of comfort he could to a heart evidently riven with its own
" Maybe he kens whaur he is," said Braidwood simply, administering
bitterness.

She shook her head with a faint sad smile.

"We want him here, Braidwood. If only I had written sooner to tell him of my grief and regret for what I did; but now it is too late!"

Ah, the common universal cry! Too late for the tardy reparation of awakened love, too late for the kind word, the word that would have made all the difference between day and night to those passed within the veil. How is it that the cry goes on, is never stilled, that we who are left learn nothing from its bitterness?

"Tell me about Anthony Weir," she said suddenly. "Will he feel it very much if he has to leave Penninghame?"

Braidwood could have laughed aloud.

"Miss Isabel, he'll never leave it till he is driven oot, an' that you'll see."

"Does he know that I am so near?"

"He kent ye were in Edinburgh yesterday, for Maister Maitland telt him."

"And what did he say?"

"Naething to me; we dinna sail in the same boat. I have watched him a' the time he's been here as oor Tibbie watches the mice in Shusan's store-room. They're no mair eager on the sugar an' the meal than he is for Penninghame, an' he'll keep it in spite o' ye, I doot, unless Maister Maitland has it that hard and fast that it canna be set aside."

"Well, that belongs to the future; meantime, Braidwood, you can rest assured that I'll do my best for my children's sakes. In what room shall I find my father? I should like to go up to him now."

"Ye'd better see Shusan first, Miss Isabel. She'll jist be aboot at her breakfast. Come."

He opened the door and stood aside to let her pass, his glance falling upon her with adoration. She was the good old stock, the poise of her head, the proud sweep of her gown, her sweet, pure face, all proclaimed it. Braidwood's faith in the Almighty was unassailable; he did not believe that claims so righteous, so indisputable, could possibly be set aside. But Braidwood had lived in a manner an irresponsible life, and he knew little of the guile and injustice of which the world is full. Others had thought for him, had provided him with all his comforts; he had but given in return a faithful service.

She went slowly up the wide staircase, pausing often with breath that came and went a little quickly as she recognised each familiar object. Here was no change; save for the stress and storm of the intervening years she might have imagined herself a gay girl as she had been on the wild March morning of her flight. Braidwood did not follow her; he stood still before the hall fireplace wiping his eyes and shaking his head. These things were too much for Braidwood, who was no longer the man he had been. He felt bewildered, out of his reckoning, helpless under the floodtide of events.

Susan was just about to pour the water upon her fragrant spoonful of tea in the brown teapot when her door opened.

"Come, Andra, I'm tired waitin'. What was a' that noise doon the stair?"

She looked up and saw before her in the flesh the bairn she had nursed at her breast, and whose image had never faded from her faithful heart. The next moment she was locked in her arms; then, indeed, did Isabel's tears fall without restraint upon the breast that had mothered her in the days of her motherless babyhood. She wept out all the aching sorrow which lay so heavily on her heart, that had robbed her cheek of its bloom, and her eyes of their lustre, and made her an old woman before her time.

As for Susan, she was too happy to weep.

" There, there, my lammie, never mind ! That's you ; greet it a' oot on nursie's hert. I aye kent ye wad come back ; the peety o'd, that ye are jist a day ower late."

" Perhaps even it is better, Susan. He might have been too ill to know me, or perhaps my heart would have been wrung by his harsh looks. Tell me, did he never speak my name in your hearing ? "

" No lately. Eh, if only ye had come three months ago. Your place has been usurpit an' nae mistake ; but Braidwood thinks that yesterday Maister Maitland put it a'richt for you an' yours. An' to think ye hae twa bonnie bairns o' yer ain ! Hae ye brocht them wi' ye ? "

" No, I left them at Mr. Maitland's house in Edinburgh. How homely it all looks, and you are but little changed. To think how calmly and quietly the years have rolled on here, while I have been so storm-tossed."

" Ye lived to rue it, my dear, I dinna doot," said Susan tenderly, as she stroked her soft hair.

" Rue it ! It is a thing which will not bear to be spoken of now, and I will never speak of it again as long as I live. God took pity on me and released me from my fetters nearly a year ago. At least now I am a free woman, and can do as I would for myself and my children."

" Ay, ay," said Susan, with a deep breath, impressed by the intense bitterness with which she spoke.

" Now, I think I will go and look at my father, Susan. Is he in his old room ? "

" Ay, he has never left it. He hasna been doon the stair for seven weeks noo."

" You need not come, Susan. I know my way, and would be alone with him. He is past hearing or knowledge of my penitent tears, but it will ease my heart if I can but whisper my sorrow even in his dead ears."

" I wadna say he is beyond it, Miss Isabel. Ye never ken. Them that's awa' are nearer than we think."

Isabel smiled faintly, shook her head, and passed out into the long, narrow corridor which opened upon the wide landing at the head of the stairs. Just then a step sounded from the opposite direction, and the next moment she was face to face with Anthony Weir.

CHAPTER XV

UNDER ONE ROOF

THERE was no doubt in Anthony Weir's mind as to the identity of the strange lady, but for the moment he was at a loss how to act. A night of broken sleep, pursued by a thousand hideous phantoms, had unstrung his nerves; he was on his way then to seek the solace of a stiff brandy and soda. Isabel, seeing his indecision, put an end to it by sweeping past him with a slight inclination of the head in which there was no cordiality, scarcely recognition. The next moment he heard the door of the death-chamber shut. He had not been there himself yet, and had no intention of going. He had the true coward's dread of the mysterious and the infinite, and already the old house was to him a place of shadows. He only suffered existence under its roof because in the circumstances it would not be seemly to depart, and because there were such tremendous issues at stake. His step was unsteady as he gripped the stair rail to descend to the library. He was at least an hour before his usual time of getting down, and he found Nancy where he had seen her first, busy about her work. He closed the door, and turned the key in the lock. Here he might talk. Here was one towards whom he need exercise no restraint. She rose slowly, and he noted with satisfaction that though she was pale, there were no other signs of mental disturbance about her. One curious incident again indicated the trend of her thoughts. When he spoke to her, she untied her apron, and laid it on a chair.

"How are you this morning, Nancy? I've had a beastly bad night myself. Glad to get up even at an unearthly hour. I don't like death in the house. There ought to be some way of preventing it. Who was the lady I met on the landing just now?"

"Madame de Castro, the laird's daughter. She cam' this mornin' wi' Mr. Shepherd and Miss Maitland."

"And where are they?"

"They are gane to Whitekirk to see whether he sleepit at the Doctor's," said Nancy, and gave a shrill little mirthless laugh which Weir did not like.

"You said nothing, of course?"

"Me, no; I never saw them bar frae a windy. Naebody has said onything to me. They're a' ower busy."

"It was a mercy for us in a way that my uncle's death took place as it did. It divided the interest as it were. They won't stop long at Whitekirk, I'm afraid."

"No, they winna; when am I to gang to Edinburgh?"

"To-day, if you like. Don't you think you had better?"

"Yes; I'll no be answerable if they speir onything at me. It's awfu' to hae sic a thing on yer mind."

"When could you get away, and how would it be possible to escape questioning even then?"

"I've planned it oot. I've gotten the maist o' the things I need hidden ootside doon by the burn at the back. I can gang that way to Porth. It's only a seevin-mile walk an' naebody kens me there."

Weir regarded the girl with surprise and a kind of admiration. She had been part of his heavy burden. But lo ! she was developing qualities which might be invaluable to them both.

"You're a clever girl, Nancy, and when could you propose to start ?"

"This efternune aboot half-past twa. My aunt aye lies doon on the sofa, an' disna rise till teatime. I'm supposed to be mendin' linen, or I micht hae an errand to Penninghame for her. She often sends me, like yesterday when I met you."

"Admirable. Well, I'll meet you at the little gate, other side of the Birks Wood, at ten minutes past three. You should get the train about four-thirty. There's some money in case I should be detained at the moment, and here's an envelope for you to send me your address."

He bent over the writing-table, and scribbled his name and address on two envelopes. Nancy glanced at them in surprise.

"It's no the least like your writin'," she said. "Naebody wad ken it."

"We have to watch that uncle of yours as a cat watches a mouse, Nancy. He's an old ferret."

Nancy slipped the envelope and the five-pound note into her pocket, and picked up her broom and dustpan. She was being initiated in guileful ways, and proving herself an apt pupil. But it was the instinct of self-preservation that was at the bottom of it rather than any feeling of affection for the man who had led her into such a frightful dilemma. He had succeeded in frightening her thoroughly, and she had not yet had time to think over the matter quietly and arrive at any conclusion of her own regarding it. Also, she was thoroughly tired of the monotony of her life at Penninghame and much excited at the prospect of having such an adventure. To be a lady at large in Edinburgh, with money in her pocket, and some one with plenty more responsible for her future, pleased her mightily. Poor Nancy was destined to prove that the way of transgressors is hard.

Weir, relieved at the quick and apparently easy solution of the difficulty regarding Nancy, fortified himself with a stiff glass of brandy, and then proceeded in search of his breakfast. When Braidwood appeared he bade him a more civil good-morning than usual, and, after a moment's hesitation, said quietly :—

"I hear that Madame de Castro has arrived, Braidwood. Please convey my compliments to her, and ask her if she will honour me with her company at breakfast."

Braidwood could hardly believe his ears.

"She's wi' the laird, sir ; an' my wife was gettin' her breakfast in the hoosekeeper's room."

"Be good enough to take her my message," repeated Weir, and Braidwood departed forthwith. He was not many minutes gone.

"Madame de Castro bade me say she is much obleedged, sir ; but she needs nae mair breakfast. But she would like to speak with you when ye are disengaged."

"All right ; tell her I'll see her here or in the library in half an hour."

While he made a pretence of eating breakfast, for which he had no appetite, Weir went over carefully the whole ground of his position, and decided upon his course of action. To adopt a conciliatory, rather regretful attitude towards Madame de Castro he imagined might be best, to deplore with her the fact that she had arrived too late, and even to discuss what compromise might be made ; such was his programme. He wished, however, that he had been able to see Shepherd first.

He was standing before the library fireplace when Madame de Castro swept into the room. Never had she borne herself more haughtily or with such distinction. Weir, while admiring her carriage and her beautiful face, felt himself shrink, and concluded that, whatever might be the issue of their interview, she would have the best of it. He had a good deal of experience among women, but one like this had never come across his path. He stepped forward to place a chair for her, which she declined with a slight shake of her head.

" I hope I need not say how sorry I am that you arrived just a day too late," he said, in smooth well-modulated tones. Again she slightly shook her head.

" It is of business we must talk, Mr. Weir," she said quickly, and her sweet voice took a somewhat hard ring. " I understand that my father sent for you to come home from the Cape ? "

" To make me his heir, madam ; he said so from the first, and Mr. Shepherd will tell you that my uncle's wishes have been carried out to the letter."

" Yes, but at that time my father was unaware that I had a son. Though I had offended him he never would have put the place past him. That I know. Mr. Maitland came here yesterday to acquaint him with my whole history in the past twenty years. I have reason to believe that he was received most favourably. But where is Mr. Maitland ? he has most unaccountably disappeared."

She fixed her eyes keenly on Weir's face ; not for a moment accusing him even in thought of any complicity in the strange disappearance, only curious to see what effect the first part of her speech would have on him.

Weir managed to preserve an admirable composure.

" I am in total ignorance of what transpired during Mr. Maitland's interview with my uncle," he said suavely. " Had we not better wait Mr. Shepherd's return from Whitekirk ? My affairs are entirely in his hands."

" Perhaps," she said doubtfully. " But in the event of nothing having been altered yesterday during Mr. Maitland's interview with my father, I suppose you would claim all your rights."

" It would be ungracious and ungrateful in me to set aside the last wishes of one who bestowed so much kindness upon me."

She gave her hand an impatient wave.

" Mere words, Mr. Weir ; they mean nothing. I warn you that I will contest the will in my son's interest, if the matter can be arranged in no other way. Mr. Maitland was of opinion that if Fintry were given to you and a sum of money you would be "—" well paid," she was about to add, but managed to keep back the words, and to substitute for them the milder phrase—" You would have no occasion to complain."

" These are purely technical and business matters, Madame de Castro," said Weir, smiling a little. " It would be futile for us to attempt to discuss them. We have really no choice but to wait until they are taken up by those whose business it will be to settle them."

Isabel de Castro turned away and there was the bitterness of death in her soul. She saw this man, unscrupulous, cruel, and clever too. From him she need expect, need hope for, nothing.

" May I beg you to remain here as long as it suits your convenience," he began, but she turned upon him, her fine eyes blazing, her figure drawn to its full height.

" Sir, have a care ! This is my father's house ; he is lying dead upstairs. It is you who are the usurper here."

Her fine scorn, the curl of her lip, the quivering nostril drove the words home. Weir flushed uneasily. Once more he felt that he was not sure of his ground. He had no previous knowledge of such a nature to guide him now. But he admired her exceedingly. It even flashed through his mind that if it could have been arranged they might have married, and so have settled the whole difficulty. But it never once occurred to him that it might be a manly and a generous course for him to retire from the field, for a time at least, and leave this sad woman alone in that house of memories with her dead.

" I shall wait here just so long as it suits my convenience, you may be certain," she said more quietly. " And that without considering you."

So saying she swept from the room. He had driven her too far, forgetting that the thoroughbred cannot bear the spur.

At that moment, smarting under her contempt, Weir almost thought that the position he so much coveted might be too dearly bought.

CHAPTER XVI

THE QUENCHING OF HOPE

MEANWHILE the dogcart from the Bell was conveying Shepherd and Helen Maitland by the highroad to Whitekirk.

She sat behind by her own request. She wished to be quiet, and also have an uninterrupted view of the road along which her father was supposed to have passed yesterday.

It was a beautiful landscape through which they passed ; once clear of the deep shadow of Penninghame woods, the veritable garden of Scottish farming industry, large well-tilled fields, bounded by trim hedges, and well-kept cart-roads, proclaiming the supervision of the expert no less loudly than his handsome dwelling-house testified to his success as a tiller of the soil. Here nothing was left to chance ; there was no wastage. The soil royally treated gave back a royal return.

Towards Whitekirk the outlook slightly changed. Ascending all the time, the landscape assumed certain Highland characteristics, a wildness and picturesqueness most pleasing to the eye. But the value of the land correspondingly decreased. Nature will not be lavish with both hands. She distributes equally, with strict adhesion to the law of compensation. Whitekirk was one of the few really picturesque villages of which the Lothians could boast. It stood high on a bare plateau, but beyond the undulating country sloped to the sea. Helen could catch the shimmering line clearly in the opal morning light.

The village was built in English fashion on three sides of a square, with a green open space in the middle. The doctor's house, a landmark in a wide and scattered parish, was easily found. He was sitting at his breakfast, with his red visiting list open on the table beside him, when the shadow of the stopping vehicle fell athwart his window.

The house stood close on the pavement without a garden or railing before it to give that privacy which is sometimes desirable.

He drank his last mouthful of coffee rather hastily, and went out into the hall just as the callers were being admitted. Shepherd he had never seen ; Helen he did not for the moment recognise, she being the last person he might expect to pay an early morning call in Whitekirk. Helen approached, holding out her hand.

" I see you don't remember me, Doctor Jeffrey ; I am Helen Maitland. Is my father here ? "

" Your father here ! No, why ? certainly not ! "

Helen looked aghast, and sank into the nearest chair. It was to Shepherd the doctor looked for explanation of what seemed to him an extraordinary question.

" My name is Shepherd ; I am Mr. Maitland's partner, doctor ; a strange thing has happened. Mr. Maitland and I came to Penninghame yesterday to see Mr. Learmonth. We left the house just after luncheon, and parted outside the gates, Mr. Maitland intending to walk to Whitekirk to see you."

" I have not seen him," said the doctor. " Do you mean to say nothing has been seen or heard of him since ? "

" Nothing ; strange, is it not ? "

" Very." The doctor glanced at Helen. In her presence it was necessary to be careful what was said.

" What opinion have you ? " he asked her, and his voice took that tender, kind note which made him such a favourite with women.

" Either he has been taken ill and crawled behind a hedge, or into the wood, or some one has attacked, perhaps killed him," she answered, in a low clear voice. " He had a most valuable watch on, and always, I know, carried a considerable sum of money. We will not wait here, Mr. Shepherd. As the doctor has seen or heard nothing of him, we need not trouble him any further."

She rose as she spoke, but the doctor motioned her to be seated.

" There is no great haste. Let us consider calmly all the possibilities. I admit that either of those you mention might be the right one. Will it not be better for me to put the matter into the hands of our sergeant of police here ? He is a very clever fellow, quite above the average, and would certainly help us greatly."

Shepherd glanced doubtfully at Helen.

" Would you like it put in the hands of the police now ? "

" Yes," she answered feverishly, " I should. Everything must be done. It is impossible to bear this suspense longer. We had better go back the way we have come, Mr. Shepherd, and explore the road."

She opened the door, and, stepping out, climbed to her seat.

The doctor lingered just a moment behind to put a question to the lawyer.

" I have not seen my old friend for a couple of years. Was he quite all right—nothing to account for this strange occurrence ? "

" He was perfectly all right ; as sane as you or me."

" And there was absolutely no reason why he should disappear ? "

"Absolutely none. We have not time now, or I would explain matters to you."

" No, there is no time. Miss Maitland is working herself into a fever. I am sorry for her. I'll go and see the sergeant before I follow you. If any one can unravel the mystery he will."

He stepped bare-headed into the pleasant air of the morning, and went up to Helen.

" Try and keep calm, my dear Miss Maitland. It is even possible that there may be some quite simple explanation of the matter. People don't disappear forever and in the full light of day. We shall soon be at the bottom of it."

" I hope so," she replied, but there was no hope in her voice. She thought of her brother David as she spoke, and wondered dismally how long it would be before he could be at her side. None could be so strong, so sympathetic, so helpful as he. Why was he so far away ?

The horse started forward, and they began the descent of the Penninghame road once more. Before they had gone far, Helen looked round.

" I must get down," she said desperately. " It is no use to drive. We might miss him."

Shepherd, with a compassionate look on his face, swung himself to the ground, and helped her to alight. He did not entertain her idea for a moment, but saw that it would be unwise to thwart her. He understood that in her state of mind some action was absolutely necessary.

The driver regarded them with a mild surprise. Ignorant of the circumstances, he could only suspect in them some silent aberration of mind. Shepherd bade him drive on slowly to Penninghame gate and wait for them there. Then he joined Helen where she stood looking over the hedge into a field.

" Do you see that man ploughing ? " she said eagerly. " He must have been here yesterday. I will cross the field and ask him whether he saw any one like my father on the road."

" Wait until he comes to this side. Don't you see he has turned, and will be here in a few minutes ? "

She acquiesced, but her face wore the restless eager look of the seeker. They moved a few yards further down the road to the five-barred gate where the furrow ended. The ploughman came towards them, addressing his horses in that strange jargon which cannot be put into words, but which horses and men seem to understand. The man was young, his slouching gait and round somewhat vacant face proclaiming him a true son of the soil, but he comprehended at once what they wished to know.

" Ay, I was plooin' here a' day yesterday, an' naebody came by in the afternune that I saw bar the minister an' twa tinks. I spoke to the tinks and gied the wummin a licht till her pipe."

" What time was that ? " asked Helen quickly.

" Jist turned three. The minister gaed by at ten to fower, for I speirt him the time to see if my ain watch was richt."

" Thank you," said Helen, as they turned to go. They came by slow degrees towards the Penninghame woods, and as they neared the gap in the trees where they had parted yesterday Shepherd felt a strange kind of horror laying hold upon him. Some one must be told about the Penninghame Pool, but at the present moment he did not think it was wise to mention his fears to Helen. He decided to speak to the doctor or the sergeant at the earliest opportunity. Helen took a casual glance at the gap, and stepped just inside it. She could see the path winding up the hill, but seemed to have no suspicions regarding it.

" It is very dark in there," was all she said, with a little shiver. Shepherd heard her in silence. At the gates the trap stood motionless in the roadway, and when Shepherd offered to help her up she made no demur. Before they had gone many yards up the avenue the hoofs of the doctor's horse sounded behind, and he presently rode up beside them.

Jeffrey looked his best on horseback, his fine well-built figure showing there to great advantage. And he always rode a good horse, being a first-rate judge and fastidious to a fault.

" No luck, I suppose ? I did not think you would have," he said cheerily. " I have seen the sergeant, and he will be after us presently on his bicycle. He thought it would be well to investigate the matter from the beginning, which would be from the moment Mr. Maitland left Penninghame.

Helen scarcely acknowledged the words. Already her face wore the hopeless look of one who expects nothing.

" Don't give up yet ! " he pleaded again, " and please believe that we will do everything to make the mystery clear. Even yet it may be capable of some very simple explanation."

She shook her head, and they continued their approach to the house. As the trap drove up to the front door, Madame de Castro appeared at the door, eager to welcome them back. At the moment Helen happened to turn her head, and saw the expression on Doctor Jeffrey's face. It was only fleeting. In a second it disappeared, leaving him impassive as before.

But in that instant the veil had been drawn back. Helen knew that that was the woman Wallace Jeffrey had loved all his life. All the elements of pathos and tragedy and comedy were present at that little scene. Of such is composed the woof of life.

CHAPTER XVII

AT PENNINGHAME POOL

DOCTOR JEFFREY alighted, and, hat in hand, approached her whom he had only known as Isabel Learmonth. Her face wore a soft and lovely look as she greeted him. He was associated with the happiest and the best part of her life. In the old days there had been many comings and goings between Whitekirk and Penninghame, and his sister Agnes, now matron of a London hospital, had been the dear friend of her girlhood.

" So we meet again," she said, with difficulty. " These are sad days for me, but at least it is good to find one or two unchanged."

" Need I say that it is good to me to see you in your father's house once more," he said, and his voice had a ring of strain in it. " Though where or how you have come is all a mystery. I had no idea you were even in Scotland until this moment."

" You did not see Mr. Maitland yesterday, then ? Is it not strange how he has disappeared, strange and inexplicable ? I must go now to Helen. We can talk another day."

Her glance was lingering kind, and seemed to find some comfort in his face. Here at least was one good man, in whose hands justice and truth would be safe, no less than the interests of a lonely woman. Some such words might have voiced her unspoken thought. She did not know what was in that solitary man's heart concerning her. In her stormy girlhood she had ridden rough-shod over many a heart. But she would be gentler now. Suffering had levelled her to a quick understanding of the world's pain.

As Jeffrey watched her tender ministrations to Helen Maitland, never had she appeared more beautiful in his sight. Ten years seemed to have but lightly passed her by, the soft hair ruffled by the whispering breeze that had sprung up had not a dull or grey thread among its gold, and she carried herself with a dignity which could not be surpassed. She appeared to be doing the honours of the house, and Anthony Weir was nowhere to be seen. Jeffrey was not surprised. He could understand how a nature like his would shrink away from Isabel Learmonth, awed no less by her womanliness than her dignity.

She took Helen by the arm, and led her in, then the two men were left to discuss the matter freely. Almost before they had uttered a word they were joined by the sergeant of police, who rode up the avenue on his bicycle. He dismounted at once, and, giving them good-morning, took out a fat note-book, in which he jotted down the particulars. He had a stolid, rather unexpressive face. Anthony Weir, watching the scene from an unobserved window, concluded that such a country bumpkin would probably make ducks and drakes of the whole affair, and with his stupid pottering prove himself Weir's best friend. In this, however, he was woefully mistaken.

The sergeant spoke never a word until he had taken from Shepherd's lips the oft-told tale of how he and Maitland had left Penninghame and parted on the road outside the gates. The time was carefully noted, then Shepherd thought it his duty to acquaint him with that odd little bit of conversation regarding the Penninghame Pool.

The sergeant pricked up his ears.

" You think he went there, eh ? "

" He intended to go, I think. He asked me to accompany him, but I declined. I have no fancy for that kind of exploration."

" Nobody has been there, I suppose ? " said the sergeant, looking round inquiringly.

" There has been no opportunity," answered Shepherd. " I've been with Miss Maitland all the morning, and I did not think it my duty to put that idea into her head, at least until every other possibility had been exhausted."

" No, no, of course not. Well, we'd better get to the pool with the necessary ropes and things. If he has fallen in there, it's all up with him, poor chap ; question even if we will find the body. I suppose we can go round to the stables and get some ropes. There's one of my chaps waiting at the gate."

At that moment Anthony Weir, hands in pockets, sauntered out of the house. His face wore a set look of unconcern. Shepherd glanced at him with a curious expression. Something had occurred to him that made his blood run cold. But he dared not put it into words, even to his own mind.

" Good-morning, gentlemen, what's all this fuss about ? " he asked, with a slightly ironical note in his voice.

He could very well plead entire ignorance of the object of their search, since nobody had acquainted him with the fact of James Maitland's disappearance.

" Good-morning, sir," said the sergeant, seeing that none of them seemed disposed to be spokesman. " We are glad to see you, as you will help us in this difficult bit of business. We are looking for Mr. Maitland, who has mysteriously disappeared since yesterday between this and Whitekirk, and we have just decided, on Mr. Shepherd's recommendation, to drag the Penninghame Pool."

Anthony Weir was undoubtedly a clever man, and skilled in the art of deceiving. Even Shepherd, watching him with unrelenting keenness, failed to detect in him any sign of perturbation. And it really gave him a sense of immediate and great relief.

" The pool, why certainly ; but why think of that ? It is a good half-mile out of his way supposing that he actually started to walk to Whitekirk."

The sergeant, meditatively stroking his beard, made no reply, and Shepherd felt himself obliged to repeat his information he had just given.

" Mr. Maitland spoke of the pool and its mysteries just before we parted. He said, indeed, that he should walk that way and have a look at it. He connected it in some way with the fortunes of Penninghame, and, thinking over it after I left him, I believed that he wanted to see whether it would make any pronouncement at the present crisis."

Anthony Weir shrugged his shoulders and significantly tapped his forehead.

" Not quite right here—evidently suicide, eh ? "

Doctor Jeffrey turned upon him indignantly.

" Sir, I knew Mr. Maitland well ; he was one of my oldest friends. There was no man in the world I should say less likely to take his own life."

" And I would say the same thing," put in Shepherd hastily. " He seemed in a somewhat sad mood, and talked a good deal of the past, but he was as sane as any one of us here at this moment discussing his probable fate."

More notes went down in the sergeant's book, then he turned to Weir.

"I suppose we may go round to the stables, sir, and get what we want for the dragging operations?"

"Why, certainly. I'll come with you," said Weir, but his voice though steady had a slight thickness in it. It, however, passed unnoticed. "While it is right and necessary to take every means," he observed to the sergeant, as they began to move round the gable end of the house, "it might be well not to lose sight of other possibilities. I have a theory now."

"What is that, sir?" asked the sergeant interestedly.

"Men have often found it expedient to disappear without apparent rhyme or reason. How are we to be certain that Mr. Maitland was not in the thick of business or private difficulties, out of which there seemed no visible means of escape?"

"There's his partner," suggested the sergeant, who did not think much of the suggestion. "Ask him. Mr. Shepherd, do you hear what Mr. Weir suggests?—that Mr. Maitland might have had some reason for disappearing?"

"He had none," was the immediate response. "That theory won't hold water for a moment. He was a rich man for his position; he had no worries except those connected with this estate, and being deeply interested in Madame de Castro it was his interest not to disappear, but to be very much in evidence. We may dismiss that idea as absurd."

Shepherd spoke with more heat than the occasion seemed to demand, and Weir regarded him with ill-concealed disappointment. Somehow he had expected some backing there. But, truth to tell, a sudden inexplicable distrust of Weir had taken possession of the lawyer's mind, and he could not altogether hide it. It was now high noon, and there being some delay in getting the necessary appliances it was almost one o'clock before they reached the suspected spot. All the while Weir's restless mind was occupied by every possibility. Certain that they would find the body, the idea of suicide or accident must be carefully fostered. Also he must walk with great wariness, lest a breath of suspicion should fall on him. No one appeared more eager or anxious for a thorough search. When they had occasion to discuss afterwards his conduct that day, they could not say that he had shown the slightest nervousness or disinclination to have the search prosecuted, or that he had thrown any obstacle in their path. But none of them noticed that he added a little to the delay, or that he took a longer time than was necessary to procure the ropes and hooks. This was on Nancy Nicolson's account. He desired above all things that she should get clean away from the house before they should return. If they should bring the body with them, he believed that she would blurt out the whole truth, and then his fate would be sealed.

Forgetful for once of his professional duties, Doctor Jeffrey joined the melancholy train that set out for the Penninghame Pool. They took a byway through the park at his suggestion, lest Helen might be watching from any of the windows. The great house seemed to have swallowed her. As a matter of fact she had abandoned all hope with a rapidity singular in a woman of her calm temperament, and was even then in a state of collapse, being ministered unto by the skilled hands of Susan Braidwood.

Grimly, and saying little, they marched on to the scene of yesterday's tragedy. From the moment they entered the gap in the wood the sergeant kept his eyes about him, keenly alert for the faintest mark or footstep, but a path of pine needles is kindly, and leaves no trace. Then some heavy showers in the night had soddened them, and made any outward or visible sign of traffic or struggles impossible. None knew that, in the silent night watches and accompanied only by a terrier that had come with him from the Cape, Weir had visited the place, and carefully removed every trace of the struggle. When they came to the brow of the ascent to the very spot where the two men had been in grips, they looked about them in silence. The stablemen, easily frightened, both wore an apprehensive air. Weir was the coolest of the company. But his face was a curious colour, and if any had happened to touch his hand they would have been struck by its icy coldness.

"No sign of anything here," said the sergeant deliberately. "Looks as if there hadn't been a human foot on the path for years."

He stepped forward and glanced down the declivity into the pool. It was not an inviting spot. All felt a strange reluctance to see the operations begin. But the sergeant did not linger long. With the assistance of the Penninghame policeman, who had joined them on the way, he adjusted the rope, attached the pole and hook, and prepared to lower it.

It was a weird impressive scene. The little group of men, with varying expressions on their faces, the shadowy light, the absolute stillness, the weird look of these inscrutable waters left an indelible impression on the minds of all who took part in that morning's work. Down went the rope and the grapnel, but almost immediately was drawn up again, not being long enough to touch the bottom. Another length of rope was attached and down went the hook again. This time bottom seemed to be reached, and the two men carefully groped about. Three times was it brought to the surface entangled with a mass of undergrowth. In this way several hours were easily passed. Weir stood the ordeal remarkably well, and remained throughout the whole of the operations.

"The apparatus is faulty, sergeant," he said once. "If we are unsuccessful to-day we must get something better—a diver, eh?"

"I don't think it would be easy to get a diver to tackle Penninghame Pool, sir," said the sergeant grimly. "I begin to think that we have made a mistake."

That was not the last time they tried to wrest from the pool its dread secret, but all their efforts proved unavailing. So passed James Maitland from mortal ken, and the place which knew him once knew him no more forever.

CHAPTER XVIII

WHERE IS NANCY?

DOCTOR JEFFREY was the first to go back to the house. Braidwood, hovering with suppressed excitement about the hall, had the door set wide before he reached it.

" Oh doctor, have they found anything ? "

" Nothing, Braidwood, and it is time I went about my business. I had better see Miss Maitland ; where is she ? "

" Lyin' doon in Susan's room. She has had a faint turn. Miss Isabel is beside her."

" Ask Madame de Castro if she will be good enough to speak to me."

Braidwood nodded and ran off. In spite of the untoward events which seemed to be crowding so thick and fast upon one another, Braidwood's spirits were rising. The sight of Miss Isabel moving about the house as of yore seemed in his estimation to settle everything. In face of that, how could Anthony Weir be Laird of Penninghame ? Braidwood's process of reasoning was simple. He believed that possession is nine points of the law.

Madame de Castro came at once, her face wearing a look of eager inquiry.

" Has anything been discovered ? "

" Nothing. We are forced to the conclusion that, whatever the solution of the mystery, it will not be found in the pool."

" It is very mysterious. Have you any theory, Doctor Jeffrey ? "

" I cannot say I have. If a shadow theory has crossed my brain, I should not be justified in uttering it."

She did not ask for further explanation. Perhaps she understood.

" What is to become of his poor daughter ? She is quite distraught. We gave her a draught, and she is sleeping presently. One is relieved to see her quiet. She was awake the whole of last night, and this horrible kind of suspense is most exhausting. I feel it myself. Meantime, I have taken it upon myself to telegraph to her brother in Bilbao ; he ought to be here at such a crisis."

" You are right ; you have been thinking of others better than many of us, Madame de Castro."

Her colour rose slightly as she shook her head.

" Would you mind calling me ' Miss Isabel,' as Braidwood does, and as I would wish all my friends to do ? I intend to relinquish my married name, and take my own again."

" It is the name all who care for you would wish to know you by," he said involuntarily.

Her face assumed a pensive look.

" I cannot believe that I am here actually in Penninghame House, and talking to you, Doctor Jeffrey. And to find you so little changed ! "

" Nay, I am an old man ; see my grey hairs," he said, half playfully.

" I don't see them. Tell me about Agnes and Flora. And Kit ? where is he ? "

" Kit is a great man now, Miss Isabel, a sort of little king in his own right out there. Flora is the mother of six sons, and doesn't look a day older. Agnes is still at St. Barnabas Hospital, and I haven't seen her for over a year."

Suddenly she changed the theme, and put one straight question to him.

" Doctor, what do you think of Anthony Weir ? "

" Very little ; he is a cad of the first water. How your father has suffered him so long, how he was ever taken in by him at the beginning, has always been to me inexplicable. But it showed the deplorable weakness of your father's health. What a pity you did not get here two months ago ! "

" You were always my father's friend, even when you were young he liked you, Doctor Jeffrey. Of late you have seen more of him than any one else. What do you think of it all ? Did he ever say positively to you that he intended to leave Penninghame and Whitekirk to Anthony Weir ? "

" Unfortunately, yes, he said so many a time. I expostulated with him, pointing out how monstrous it would be when you were alive. Then none of us knew that you had any children. I can't help thinking it was a pity you did not try to communicate with your father from time to time. If he had known of your son's existence, I am sure it would have made a difference. He was mortally afraid lest your husband should come here after he had gone."

" Of that he need not have been afraid," she said, with a proud wounded ring in her voice. " I suffered myself, but I was left with some sense of the fitness of things. I should never have brought De Castro here."

" There is no use going back on the painful past now," he said gently. " There is a great deal to do for the present and the future. Am I justified in inquiring what plans you have ? "

She turned and looked at him in wonder.

" I believe," she said simply, " that now I am bereft of Mr. Maitland, you are the only friend I have here, save for poor Braidwood and his wife, who are powerless."

" Anything I can do you may be sure will be done," he said, with unexpected haste, oddly moved by her words. " I fear that the future will be full of difficulty for you and your children."

" You believe then that Anthony Weir will uphold his claim to Penninghame ? "

" Most certainly I do. Shepherd is now the only man possessing the key to the situation. I believe he drew out the will in favour of Weir after Mr. Maitland was dismissed. Nothing can now be done until after the funeral. Are you going to make the arrangements ? "

" Yes, I will stay here until all is over at least."

" And Anthony in the house ? "

" If he chooses to stay as my guest he may do so. I will make no attempt to hide that he will be unwelcome."

" And will you bring your children ? "

" Most certainly. Braidwood or Susan will go to Edinburgh for them this afternoon."

" I admire your courage, and yes, it is the right thing to do. I wonder how he will take it ? "

" That does not concern me at all. If, when the will is read, he is left Laird of Penninghame and Whitekirk, I will contest the will in my son's interests. I have told him so already."

"It will cost a great deal of money, and you might be defeated," he felt himself obliged to say.

She flashed her fine eyes upon him in a sudden passion.

"Oh, Doctor Jeffrey, surely my father would not cast me and my children into the outer darkness, and leave us nothing? Even if he thought to punish me by giving Penninghame and Whitekirk to Anthony Weir, he would remember his own flesh and blood. If not, is there any law in the land iniquitous enough to uphold such a will?"

The doctor shook his head.

"It is beyond me. I can only pray that it may not be as you say," he said. "Now I must go. I will call on my way back from my round, and see Miss Maitland. Will she remain here?"

"Certainly. She will wish to be on the spot where her father so mysteriously disappeared," was the answer.

She smiled as she offered her hand; a ghost of the smile that had once such witchery in it.

"I cannot remember the years between, when I see and speak with you, Doctor Jeffrey. I thank God, you at least are left to me."

He was unable to answer, lest haply he might betray himself. In silence he went his solitary way, to ponder on the strange workings of fate that had brought Isabel Learmonth back to disturb his peace and the even tenor of his life. He had imagined himself cured, deluded himself with the idea that his work sufficed, that the old memory had grown too dim to sting, and, lo! all his specious self-deception was scattered like chaff before the wind.

That afternoon Susan Braidwood waited in vain for Nancy to set the stillroom tea. Of late Nancy had caused her a great deal of honest concern; she had grown so saucy, so careless, so defiant when rebuked or admonished for work badly done that Susan had been seriously contemplating finding another situation for her far removed from Penninghame and the scene of her temptation. But already Nancy had sought and found a situation for herself.

A fire had been hastily lighted in the smaller portion of the great drawing-room where the laird had had the whim to wait for Anthony Weir on the night of his arrival from the Cape. When the folding doors were shut, it made a very cosy, snug sitting-room, which Isabel intended for the occupation of herself and Helen Maitland.

Thither, when Helen awoke, she led her, bestowing on her every possible care and kindness, her heart full of infinite compassion for her evident misery. Nothing had been done, nothing been discovered outside, though the sergeant and his helpers were still at work. Having with her own hands carried in the drawing-room tea, Susan descended to the kitchen to make inquiries for Nancy. The women there shook their heads. None of them had seen her since the servants' one o'clock dinner, when she had scarcely eaten anything. Braidwood had departed to Edinburgh by the half-past three train to bring out "Miss Isabel's bairns," as he fondly called them. Almost at her wits' end Susan climbed the weary flights of stairs to the little room occupied by Nancy, and, shutting the door, took a thorough survey of its whole contents. In the hanging-cupboard hung all Nancy's cotton dresses; the others were gone.

Susan stood aghast. This extraordinary occurrence could in her estimation have but one meaning. There must be some reason for Nancy's flight. She was no longer the innocent girl who had grown up to bonnie young womanhood under her care, her dead sister's child! Such a passion of anger surged in her honest soul that had Anthony Weir appeared before her at that moment he would have felt the weight of her scathing tongue. She wrung her hands helplessly as she turned from the nest from whence the bird had flown.

Oh, what sorrows had come upon that house! Surely for some reason or another the Lord must be angered against it! The laird was lying dead in his own room, Miss Isabel come back a lone widow, penniless, to fight for her children's bread, Mr. Maitland, kind friend and adviser, apparently gone from mortal ken, Anthony Weir undisputed Laird of Penninghame, Nancy gone none knew whither. It was a long, black, dismal list.

Trembling mightily, she slipped back to the drawing-room door, craving for sympathy, yet afraid to disturb the two within who had their own troubles to bear. It was a relief when she heard the bell which she was only too thankful to answer herself.

" We don't want to keep you running after us, Susan; it is only a little hot water that we need," said Madame de Castro kindly. " Where are all the girls? "

" I like to come; I want to come, Miss Isabel," cried Susan, and began to cry helplessly.

" Why, what is it now—a fresh trouble, you poor dear old woman? Tell your own bairn all about it."

" It's Nancy, my niece Nancy, maybe ye've never seen her," she said brokenly. " She's been here eleeven year come Martinmas. I brocht her mysel', when her mither dee'd, frae Glesca. She was a guid lassie, an' a comfort to Andra an' me, till—till him I canna name entered the hoose."

" You mean Anthony Weir, Susan? "

She nodded.

" He started pittin' silly nonsense intil her heid the first day. Braidwood's gi'en him it strecht mair nor aince, an' has very near gotten his leave ower't Noo, I find she's awa, an' us that's been honest God-fearin' folk will be brocht to shame through her."

For a moment Isabel could not speak. Wheels within wheels there were indeed, and what a complexity of affairs were at war under one roof!

CHAPTER XIX

CLOSING IN

WEIR's face wore a gloomy, almost threatening, look as he came across the park with Shepherd in the fading light of the February afternoon. The search at the pool, for the time being at least, was ended, and the sergeant, admittedly baffled, had departed to put other machinery in motion for the finding of a clue to James Maitland's disappearance. For the moment Anthony Weir was master of the situation, and he meant to make the most of it.

" I am not getting the support from you I am entitled to, Shepherd," he said, casting a glance full of meaning at Shepherd's face.

" I don't understand you, Mr. Weir ; pray explain yourself. What support have I withheld ? "

The question slightly nonplussed Weir, for he would have found it difficult to state his inward grievance in explicit detail. It was rather in the withdrawal of moral support, if the term may be used to indicate a position with which morals had very little to do. Weir, however, had partly mistaken his man. Because, for purely business and selfish reasons, Shepherd had differed from his partner regarding their attitude as a firm towards Anthony Weir, that gentleman had imagined him as unscrupulous as himself. Of that idea his mind was now to be disabused. It was only legitimate business that Shepherd would undertake ; he would be no party to any nefarious scheme whatever, and his point of view had changed, as Maitland had predicted, since his introduction to Madame de Castro.

Then he could not rid himself of an uneasy feeling that Weir knew more about James Maitland's disappearance than he chose to tell. The idea that he had foully murdered him did not indeed crystallise into a conviction ; it was rather a suggestion, a vague suspicion, which, while it could certainly not be put into words, sufficed to make his manner towards the suspected person cold. Also he foresaw that all whose opinion was worth having or preserving would be in full sympathy with the daughter of the dead man.

Observing that Shepherd would not be bullied, Weir met the difficulty by another question, suggested by the sudden apparition of a fully lighted window in the drawing-room, which seemed to indicate that Madame de Castro had taken possession.

" I shall be obliged if you would tell me what is the legal aspect of the position at the present moment, and until my uncle's will is declared."

" That is easy enough. The house and all it contains belongs to his daughter."

" Indeed ! What constitutes her right, may I ask ? She had forfeited it by her infamous behaviour to a good old man. It is rather too late in the day to assume injured innocence."

" I don't think Madame de Castro assumes anything of the sort. She is here in her capacity as Mr. Learmonth's daughter, prepared to fight, if need be, for her own and her children's rights, especially for those of her son, who in the ordinary way would be next-of-kin."

"But doesn't the will alter anything? I thought you assured me, almost on your bended knees, that nothing could stand in my way? Didn't that precious document there was such an infernal lot of trouble about getting properly attested give me the property absolutely?"

"Unfortunately, yes," said Shepherd, on the spur of the moment, incensed and repelled by the true nature of the man, now expressed without any attempt to hide it, on a most forbidding face.

"Why unfortunately, eh? Are you going to dance to a different tune now, eh? Sell yourself to the other side?"

"Unfortunately," repeated Shepherd, with emphasis on the word, "legally speaking, there is no other side, but it would be to your credit, Mr. Weir, to be generous. I have known men behave with conspicuous generosity in circumstances as trying."

"You are pleased to be vague," sneered Weir. "Do you mean that I should walk out, and leave that proud beetle-browed woman mistress?"

"She is the daughter of the dead man, the place is hers by right. I do not, however, suggest that you should do that. But it would be graceful to retire at least until the funeral day is over."

"Pretty cool request. The house is big enough. The same roof can cover us. We need not meet."

"That is true, but it would not be pleasant, hardly even decent."

Weir took a few steps in silence, tugging severely at his moustache.

"If there should be a fight, I'm afraid you'll play into the hands of the other side, though you may take my money. Perhaps it would be better to own up to it now."

Shepherd's face flushed.

"I am not aware that I have given you the right to insult me, sir, and I will not stand it. I am ready to withdraw at any moment since that is your opinion of me."

Weir was compelled to an unwilling respect, the respect that he had been obliged to accord, though grudgingly, to another man, who had had the calm courage of his convictions.

He foresaw endless difficulties, and, rapidly reviewing his own position and prospects, decided that it would be unwise in his own interests to quarrel with Shepherd. He tried to clear his face, and turned to him in a more conciliatory manner.

"I didn't mean to be rude, Shepherd, but you must own that the lines are pretty hard for me. Am I going to sit down tamely, and let the whole thing pass from me? Not likely. I've earned it, Lord knows, burying myself in this God-forsaken hole at the mercy of an old man's whim, night and day, for months."

"I did not mean to suggest that you should withdraw. The place being willed to you by a man who was in his sound judgment no man could expect that of you. But I do say that you should be generous. If Madame de Castro had Fintry and its rent-roll, she and her children would not be so badly off. And you know that Mr. Learmonth intended her to have Fintry, though he was then unaware that she had any children."

Weir thoughtfully stroked his chin. The idea of posing as a generous benefactor towards Isabel Learmonth rather pleased him. She should partake of his offered bounty. How it would gall her proud spirit, yet being utterly penniless, how dared she refuse it?

He took the limited view natural to a person of his outlook upon life. He knew nothing of an honourable pride, high enough to reach the heavens, capable of any sacrifice, of enduring poverty, obscurity, starvation even, rather than of eating the bread of a despised charity.

" How soon can we bury him ? " Weir asked, as they stepped from the sward to the smooth rolled gravel before the doorway.

" This is Tuesday—I should think Friday or Saturday a suitable day."

" Saturday ! Gad, what a piling up of the agony ! What's the use of keeping a corpse so long ? We don't do it on the Rand, wouldn't be allowed."

" It is a matter entirely for Madame de Castro to settle," said Shepherd, and the expression of disgust deepened on his face. " I have just time to catch the four-thirty train, but I should like to see Miss Maitland, if I may, to inquire what she means to do."

" Stay here probably, as she seems to be a pal of Madame's," said Weir. Then, as they were on the steps he paused and looked Shepherd full in the face.

" Then you won't play me false ? You're acting for me in this thing, whatever the issue may be."

" I'm pledged to that, sir ; it is sufficient assurance. The name of my firm is a guarantee of honest dealing."

Weir accepted the assurance, but he was by no means comfortable in his mind. He rang the hall bell when they had passed within, but for once Braidwood did not answer. He rang again with the same result.

Then suddenly he remembered Nancy.

" I think the ladies are in the drawing room. It looks as if Madame de Castro had instructed Braidwood not to pay any attention to me. Do you know your way ? I don't suppose it would be wise for me to venture up."

Shepherd looked at his watch, and made haste to ascend the stairs. He had just time for a word with Helen to assure her of his sympathy, and to get to the station in time. Indeed, he was weary of the house and all it contained. It had been an exciting, exhausting day, and the mystery of his partner's end lay heavy on his soul. He wished to be at home. Never had he felt more keenly the need of his wife's sympathy and counsel.

" The next item on the programme ?—Nancy ! " said Weir to himself, as he mixed a brandy and soda. " What a day we're having. Wonder if the little vixen got away ! "

He sat down quietly, and took out his pipe. He had been without a smoke all day, and his nerves felt the need of it. On the whole, the day had passed better than he had expected. There had been no discovery, no need for the exercise of an almost superhuman self-control. Each hour strengthened his position, no less than gave him time to clear the ground beneath his feet.

" If only the whole infernal business could be settled, then I'd put the place in the market to the highest bidder, and make myself scarce. Monte Carlo, Paris, Berlin ! Lord, what a time I'd have ! "

He gave himself up to a brief vision of what might be termed the rogues' paradise. He had succeeded beyond his dreams, and success began to render him arrogant.

" Now, Nancy ! she's too near, I'll have to go and see her to-morrow. I suppose her mouth's got to be shut. Mock marriage—only way out."

The door opened suddenly without knock or preliminary, and Braidwood appeared. Weir turned on his chair and surveyed him with a fine air of resentful anger.

"Doing missus' bidding, eh? Be good enought to get out of this room, and when you want to come in again, knock at it civilly."

"I'll dae neither for you," replied Braidwood sullenly. "Whaur's my niece, Nancy?"

"Do I keep your niece, Nancy, eh? She's a chip of the old block; give 'em an inch and they'll take an ell. Because I spoke a civil word to her, she thought she would be Lady of Penninghame. Part the place among you, ey? Get out of my sight, you whining blackguard, your day's just about over."

"Whaur is my niece, Nancy?" repeated Braidwood, with a stolid calm, which gave small indication of the fire beneath. "If ye've ruined and enticed her awa', I'll thresh ye within an inch o' your ill-kindet life."

For the moment Braidwood, in spite of his grey hairs, looked equal to the task.

"Gone to join the old man, perhaps," said Weir, with a sneer. "Never know that pious, long-faced species. Find the lawyer, friend Braidwood, and you'll doubtless find the bird."

The words, uttered on the spur of the moment, staggered Braidwood with their enormity. In no way desirous of a scene with a servant, Weir rose rather wearily to his feet, and spoke in a more conciliatory tone.

"Look here, my good man, try not to be a full-grown idiot. Is it likely that at a time like this I should trouble about a servant girl? I have said very little to her since the last time you were pleased to address me, not very civilly, on the subject. If she's cleared out, it's for some end of her own. I know nothing about her, and care less. Go away and don't trouble me. I have enough on my hands at the present moment without any assistance from you."

So saying he opened the French window, and stepped out to the terrace, leaving Braidwood dumfoundered in the middle of the room.

He had spoken with an ease and carelessness which carried conviction with them. Braidwood, simple old man, did not know where to turn next.

CHAPTER XX

AN ARRIVAL AT PENNINGHAME

TRAVELLING overland, without a break or rest on the journey, David Maitland reached Edinburgh on Friday morning. He drove home to the King Street ouse, only to find the servants alone. They were unfeignedly glad to see m. For them life had seemed almost intolerable in the last few days. They could add nothing, however, to the meagre intelligence he already essed. He consulted a time-table, and found he had just time to call e office in Charlotte Street before getting the half-past ten train for nghame. When he had breakfasted and refreshed himself with a e looked and felt more able to cope with the calamity which had ned him home. The women hovered about him, anxious to be of d feeling that things must mend now Mr. David had come home. ted that atmosphere wherever he went. His pleasant strong face, r and absolute unconsciousness of self made him the ideal friend. rs of his absence in the South had changed him from a beardless to a well-developed and most capable-looking man. He was Helen's r by two years, but that morning he certainly looked older. His eyes careworn, and no sleep had visited them since he set out on that sad rney. That his father was actually dead he would not permit himself to ieve. He was devotedly attached to him. For three and twenty years ere had never been the faintest shadow of misunderstanding between hem. Even when Maitland's keen disappointment over his boy's choice of a career had threatened their pleasant relations, David's sunny temper swept every barrier away. That lovely disposition which blesses all it touches he had inherited from his mother, for which reason, perhaps, recalling her as he did at every turn, he had been very dear to his father, and when he had departed to Bilbao to work in the engineering shop of his mother's brother, the old King Street house had been empty indeed.

He took a cab to Charlotte Street, arriving just on the stroke of ten. Shepherd had arrived for the morning's business before proceeding to Penninghame for the laird's funeral, arranged for that afternoon. He rose when David Maitland entered and grasped his hand in silence.

" My lad, this is a sad homecoming for you," he said, with sincere sympathy. " I wish we had better news for you."

" Has anything been heard or discovered ?—the servants at home said not."

Shepherd shook his head.

" Nothing ; we are still groping in the dark. The police seem baffled. It is the most extraordinary case they have ever had through their hands."

" Has the search been abandoned then ? " asked young Maitland, with a curious tremor of the lips.

" By no means ; they are still at it."

" Believing he is out there, I suppose. What is Helen doing at Penninghame ? Remember I have had no letters. Is she living in the house with Anthony Weir ? "

In a few words Shepherd explained the situation, and surprise deepened in the young man's eyes.

"They are all there! Will Madame de Castro have Penninghame, then?"

Shepherd shook his head.

"I could wish myself well out of what will be a ghastly business, David. The laird is to be buried this afternoon at three o'clock. I'm trying to get through to catch the one o'clock train. Everything but Fintry goes to Weir. There will probably be a scene this afternoon at the house."

"Madame de Castro did not arrive in time to see her father in life, I suppose?"

"No; just missed him by a few hours. But your father was able to inform him of her return to Scotland, and also of the fact that she had two children. It is certain some arrangement was made in her behalf, and that the papers relating to it were in the bag he carried with him when he disappeared. I felt certain of it during my last conversation with him, though he did not give me any definite information."

Maitland started and looked straight into the lawyer's face.

"What kind of a man is this Weir?" he asked suddenly. "Would he be capable of any treacherous dealing to serve his own ends?"

"I would rather not say, David; you will see him to-day, and can judge for yourself."

David Maitland clenched his strong right hand.

"I will solve this mystery, and if it is true that my father is really dead, his death will not only be elucidated, but avenged. My God! I can't realise it! My dear old father, and only last Sunday I had his letter! I have it here yet. It was a sad kind of letter, Mr. Shepherd, and for the first time he asked whether I could not break my engagement in the middle, and seek a berth nearer home. It made me a bit uncomfortable, for he knew how happy I was in my work at Morton's yard."

His face worked with the emotion he could scarcely control, and he dashed his hands across his eyes.

"I'm going out to Penninghame by this train. You are coming later, you say?"

"Carriages are to meet the Edinburgh mourners at one forty-five. Madame de Castro has arranged it all, but there will not be many. By the bye, I hear that Weir left her in possession of the house since Wednesday morning. I suggested it to him. It was certainly the most seemly course. Where he has been in the interval I don't know, but he will probably turn up to-day."

"Are they to go through that dreary business of reading the will at the old house in the old style?"

"Yes, and it is Madame de Castro's desire that all even remotely connected with the family shall hear it. That is why I said there would be a scene."

He opened the door, and accompanied the young man through the outer office. Many a sympathetic glance followed him, and he nodded to one or two, but dared not trust himself to speak. Most of them were old trusted employees of his father, who would mourn his loss as sincerely as that of a personal friend.

Once more David Maitland drove the familiar way of Princes Street, his eyes roaming about seeing little. He loved the city of his birth with no common love, and easy hoped to fulfil his manhood's day at least within call. But to-day there was little pleasure in his return.

Somehow the hopelessness of the whole affair sank into his soul. If in three days those skilled in such matters had failed to discover the slightest clue, how could he expect success? But he told himself again, and the very thought was a vow, that he would leave no stone unturned to elucidate the mystery, and bring the whole facts of his father's inexplicable disappearance to light.

He took a first-class ticket for Penninghame, and got into a smoking carriage. Just as the train was moving off, the door opened suddenly, and another passenger flung himself into a corner.

Maitland glanced casually at him from behind his paper, and gave him good-morning. The stranger answered him affably, and offered his cigar-case; after a moment's hesitation and another look David helped himself.

"Nice spring morning," he said, in his pleasant voice. His innate kindliness and unselfishness made it easy for him to push self into the background, and make himself agreeable to a fellow-traveller. Little did he know or guess who that fellow-traveller was.

"New to these parts, eh?" asked the stranger, as he bent forward, and gave Maitland the benefit of his own light.

Their faces were close together at the moment, and they looked into one another's eyes. There was nothing sinister or suspicious about Anthony Weir's appearance at that moment, however. He was a good-looking, well-dressed, prosperous-looking man, with perhaps a slightly sporting air. Maitland was in no way unfavourably impressed by his looks.

"No; I am a native of Edinburgh," answered David. "You are not, judging by your tongue."

"No; I'm a bit of a cosmopolitan, knocked about a goodish bit. Scotland seems a bit slow to me, I must confess."

Maitland faintly smiled as he leaned back and enjoyed the first whiff of what was really a most excellent cigar.

"Going far, eh?" asked the stranger. "Nobody would need to be in a hurry in these parts. The trains want resurrecting a bit."

"People are not generally in a hurry in country places," answered Maitland absently. They were gliding along slowly by the sea line, and the sun was glittering like gold on the placid waters of the firth.

Many a happy day had he and Helen spent on the yellow sands, every foot of which was familiar to them. Memories began to crowd upon him, and his face perceptibly saddened.

"I am going to a place called Penninghame," he answered. "Do you know it?"

"Yes, I'm going there myself."

"Do you know it well?" asked Maitland.

"Fairly so; I've been living there for the last three months."

"Ah!" said Maitland reflectively. "Then perhaps you are aware of certain events that have happened there within the last week?"

"I've been out of it for a week," said Weir, with the air of a man on his guard. It suddenly occurred to him that this might be a plain-clothes man interested in the Maitland case.

He was unaware that the man who had disappeared had a son grown to man's estate. During the past three days Weir had been entirely occupied with Nancy Nicolson, with whom he had gone through a mock marriage. At least, in that light he regarded it. Unfortunately for himself he had not taken the trouble to make himself acquainted with the rather comprehensive and elastic Scotch marriage laws. Nancy imagined herself in reality Mrs. Anthony Weir, and, as it happened, she was right.

Weir, however, believing otherwise, had no intention of burdening himself permanently with the pretty country girl that had taken his fancy and helped to while away many idle and what would have been otherwise dreary hours at Penninghame.

Weir adroitly changed the subject, and managed to steer clear of Penninghame themes until they stopped at Porth Junction, where they had to wait for a north-going train. Then he got out and transferred himself to another compartment. The last five miles of the journey David was alone, and he felt glad of it. He felt as if a dead weight of misery bore him to the very dust. When he alighted at the little dreary station he saw his some time companion at the further end of the platform. Passing through the booking office, he beheld a dogcart waiting in charge of a man in livery. An unusual curiosity caused him to wait to see whether it belonged to the stranger. Weir came out unwillingly, wishing his fellow traveller, towards whom he now felt an unaccountable aversion, would get out of the way. Finding him still standing, he was obliged to acknowledge him.

" What direction do you take ? " he asked civilly, but without cordiality.

" I am going to Penninghame House," answered Maitland. " I suppose I must walk the distance. Perhaps you will be good enough to direct me.

" I can drive you. I am going there myself," replied Weir, with the manner of a man forced into an uncomfortable situation.

" Oh, thank you." A sudden light dawned on Maitland's face, and he took a step forward. " Perhaps I address Mr. Weir ? " he added.

" I am Anthony Weir. And you—— ? "

" David Maitland, at your service. My errand you can guess. I have returned from Bilbao on account of my father's extraordinary disappearance. Can you enlighten me ? "

" You had better get up," said Anthony Weir, in a low thick voice ; but he kept his head up and his face fairly impassive under the keen scrutiny bestowed on him. " Get down, Simpson," he added to the groom, " this gentleman and I will take the front seat."

CHAPTER XXI

THE TRUE FRIEND

THE delight and pride of Sybil de Castro and her brother over their mother's old home was at once a lovely and a painful thing. Again and again she blamed herself for her haste in bringing them. Now they had seen and known it for themselves the pang of parting must be rendered keen indeed. They had enjoyed two days of perfect serenity.

After Anthony Weir's departure from Penninghame, the whole house rallied round them, anxious only to serve those of the old stock, and the issue of the funeral day was waited with a kind of subdued apprehension. The search for James Maitland had been prosecuted with unavailing vigour ; to that had been added also inquiry for Nancy. It had only been ascertained that she took a train at Porth on Tuesday afternoon, going south, however, instead of to Edinburgh as expected. Nevertheless, in Edinburgh she was hidden safely enough, in a small obscure house in an unlikely suburb, of which she knew something herself, having once visited a fellow-servant there, who had married an Edinburgh tradesman.

Braidwood, after the first burst of indignation, had agreed to take the thing philosophically and merely remarked that, as " she had made her bed, so she maun lie on it." But Susan could not take that view. She was a woman, and she knew full well how much such a step means for a woman, also Nancy was her own sister's child, and though she had been wayward and often trying, her heart yearned over her. There was no real ill in her ; only she had been foolish and easily led. She had no doubt at all in her mind but that Weir was at the bottom of it, and only bided her time until the laird's funeral was decently over before she took more active steps.

Sybil and Frank spent most of their time out of doors. They never tired of the beautiful park, with its noble trees and browsing deer, which they now saw in their own haunts for the first time. The woods also, even in their winter dress, drew them with a magnet. And they had not failed to explore the environs of the mysterious pool, of which so many strange and gruesome tales were told.

The whole place interested and enchanted them, and they understood, as they had never yet done, how their mother's heart must have cleaved to it in all the years of her absence from it. They only partly understood the situation, though she had tried to explain to them that they were only there for a little time, and would have to leave after their grandfather was buried. That her boy should take his rightful place there sooner or later, Isabel de Castro was determined. She superintended all the arrangements for the funeral herself, not the smallest detail escaping her attention and observation. Sybil was in the park with the dogs bounding about her feet when the dogcart from the station drove through the gates. Weir had sent a telegram from the station to the stables ordering it to meet the train, and that order had been obeyed. Penninghame presented the strange spectacle of being possessed by two masters. Surely such an anomaly had never before in its history been seen.

It was not at Anthony Weir, however, that the girl looked as the trap came swiftly towards her. Her exquisite face flushed, her eyes brightened, she even trembled a little, as she recognised one who had befriended them in Bilbao, who had endeared himself to them all by his manly consideration, his unfailing kindness. In a moment the world became a fairer, brighter place for Sybil de Castro. As for David—but we shall see.

He took off his hat, and as they drew nearer the girl he asked Weir to be good enough to stop.

" It is Miss de Castro. I must speak to her."

" Miss de Castro is it ? And how do you happen to know her ? "

" They came from Bilbao, where I have been for the last two years," he answered, and even as he spoke he swung himself to the ground, and began to stride across the sward to where she stood. Weir bit his lip, and passed on. Things were even more complicated than he imagined. To find a son of Maitland's hand in glove with the De Castros was bad. And already he saw that David Maitland was not a man to be trifled with. His keen, straight look, his square determined jaw and firm mouth indicated courage, fearlessness and exceptional business ability.

Meanwhile there was nothing but tenderness on Maitland's face as he approached the girl, hat in hand. He had not hidden from himself that he loved her, and though he had no hope of a successful issue to his love, she being far removed from him, he could not altogether hide it. And because he was so modest in his estimate of himself, he did not read aright the sweet wavering light in her eyes, or the flush upon her face.

" Oh, David ! " she cried, giving him two hands outstretched. " I am so very glad to see you. Now, perhaps your poor sister will hold up her head. It is all so sad and inexplicable ; we don't know what to think."

Her warm sympathy beamed in her looks, and was expressed in every note of her voice. For the moment Maitland was at a loss what to say. Plenty of words burned on his lips, but these words he dared not utter.

" You are very kind," he answered lamely, when he had touched her hand. " To have my sister here is the truest kindness of all. I shall never be able to thank your mother enough. How is she, and where is Frank ? "

" They are quite well. Isn't this a lovely place, David ? Shall we have to leave it, do you think ? " she added wistfully. " It will break all our hearts."

It almost broke his to contemplate it, and as he glanced after the retreating dogcart rolling rapidly towards the house, his brow darkened.

" It will be an iniquitous and a horrible thing, Miss Sybil, and I pray God that something may intervene to prevent it."

" Frank cannot sleep at night for thinking of it. His heart seems to be joined to Penninghame. Of course, it is because mamma has talked so much about it. She taught us to love it from our very babyhood, but we never knew it could be so beautiful or so dear."

" Justice is still on the earth, Miss Sybil," he said, with difficulty, for her words moved in him a mighty passion. " It will come home yet ; we must just wait, and be brave and patient."

" It is for mamma most of all. I wish we could stay. She has suffered so much, and these days you can't think how different she is. She carries herself so differently ; the very tones of her voice seem to have changed. And yet, when none are looking, her heart is more sad, I think, than it has ever been. Always when she is alone her eyes are full of tears, though she tries to hide them from us."

"We must do what we can to comfort her, Miss Sybil," he said, putting his own biting anxiety in the background in order that he might speak words of cheer to her. Suddenly she looked up at his strong kind face timidly.

"Why do you call me Miss Sybil all of a sudden David? It was not so in Bilbao."

His face flushed at the question.

"It is very different here; you are a great lady. My father was only your grandfather's legal adviser, paid for what he did. Our positions are not the same."

She looked puzzled and slightly rebellious, shaking her bright head to and fro.

"In Bilbao I was Sybil de Castro; here I am the same girl. I will not answer you, David, unless you call me Sybil."

He laughed, but there was a restraint in his voice. He felt relieved that they came almost immediately to the door of the house. Such moments, though dangerously sweet, must not for his peace of mind be much prolonged.

The next moment they were within, and the real business of life called him. He was taken at once to the library, and there he found Helen looking very white and woe-begone, like one out of whom both hope and life had gone."

"Oh, David," she moaned, as she tottered forward and was clasped in his arms.

So these two, who mourned together so irreparable a loss, tried to comfort one another, and, after the first strain of the meeting was over, tried to look at the affair from a clear standpoint. But all their efforts only brought them back to the one melancholy fact, that their father had now been out of mortal ken for four days, and that the passing of every fresh hour not only deepened the mystery, but rendered it more difficult, if not impossible, of solution. But for David Maitland the word impossible did not exist.

"Look here, Helen, before God I will leave no stone unturned to find our father's murderer and bring him to justice."

"You believe that he has been murdered, David?"

"I do. My suspicions I must keep to myself meanwhile, until this day is over at least. Where is Madame de Castro? You like her, Helen; I am sure you feel that she is in her rightful place here."

"Oh, yes; the whole thing is a most pitiful tragedy: and to think that papa, who was her only friend, and who undoubtedly possessed the papers which would have established her rights, has gone none knows whither. Dead, of course, he must be now. It makes one not only question the goodness of God, but ask whether God really does exist."

"Justice will come home," repeated Maitland solemnly. Then they sat down together, and went over the whole ground until Madame de Castro came to call them to luncheon. As Maitland sprang to greet her he was struck by the nobility of her looks. The long straight folds of her black gown, with the soft white at the throat, seemed to give unusual height and dignity to her figure. Her face was set in unutterable sadness, as one from whom hope is slowly ebbing, but her composure did not give way.

"We are thankful to see you, David; now, indeed, I have a friend," she said, and pressed his hand. "We are companions in misfortune; we must try and comfort one another. It was a bad day for you, David, when you befriended me and mine. I feel that it is through me your own terrible grief has come."

"No, no; it was a trouble none could foresee, Madame. I will not listen to such words."

"They are true words," she repeated. "Oh, if this day were only over, and yet I grudge its moments as they pass. Anthony Weir has arrived, but he will not lunch with us. I have not seen him, but Braidwood will wait on him in the morning-room; we will wait on ourselves. Have you seen Frank? The boy is beside himself at the thought of seeing you again."

He bounded in at the moment, and again a greeting of the most affectionate kind took place between Maitland and one bearing the name of De Castro. Adoration and unfeigned joy was on the lad's face as he grasped the hand of the friend who had given him lessons in true manhood, and was himself the embodiment of it.

Clinging to his hand, looking up into his face with a perfect confidence and love, the sight caused a sudden moisture to dim Isabel de Castro's eyes.

"Look at them, Helen. Did I exaggerate? I thank God my boy has such a friend. With you and him we cannot be altogether forlorn."

Helen could not speak. She was conscious of the uplifting sense of her brother's presence, yet so human and faulty are we, she was also conscious of faint pang of jealousy. He no longer belonged exclusively to her. Others had discovered his worth. Her pride in him was somewhat marred by that jealous pang, but David of the sunny heart and the generous outlook was entirely unconscious of it all.

He put his arm about the lad whom he loved, and thus they crossed the hall to the dining-room. And Anthony Weir saw them through an open door, and cursed them in his heart.

CHAPTER XXII

HIS LAST WILL AND TESTAMENT

IT was a great burying, for though Francis Learmonth, Laird of Penninghame, had in the latter years of his life pursued the habits of the hermit and the recluse, he was much respected in the place where he had ruled so long. They came from far and near to pay the last tribute of respect to his remains, and the old grey churchyard of Whitekirk, where the family burying-ground was situate, was thronged to its utmost capacity, while the road for a mile at least was black with waiting vehicles. It was verily an event in the countryside.

A good deal of interest of a special kind was attached to the ceremonial, and report had been busy for many days regarding the affairs of Penninghame. The fact of Madame de Castro's return with her children was now public property. Contrary to expectation, all three were present in the churchyard. Interest was almost equally divided between the tall figure in widow's weeds and a slim, fair-faced boy who stood bareheaded by her side. There was not one heart present that did not pray God bless him, and hope he would stand among them as the new Laird of Penninghame.

In this sympathetic crowd Anthony Weir had but a sorry place. But he stood among the mourners at the graveside, though Isabel had arranged that no hand of his should touch the coffin. The cords were taken by her own son, Dr. Jeffrey, David Maitland, and Braidwood. Thus only hands that were kindly and truly sympathetic were about the old laird at the last.

Shepherd, the lawyer, was also present, looking as uncomfortable as he felt; the shadow of the approaching ordeal at Penninghame was upon him.

The service, after the manner of the Scotch Church, was very brief, and immediately thereafter the mourners dispersed, and the carriages rolled rapidly back to Penninghame.

At four o'clock there gathered in the library a small company to hear the last will and testament of the deceased man. It consisted of Madame de Castro and her two children, the Maitlands, Dr. Jeffrey, Mr. Clephane, the minister of the parish, and William Shepherd, the lawyer. Acting on the advice of the latter, Isabel had abstained from inviting any outsiders, as she had at first intended.

It was a mild grey February afternoon, very still and quiet, without a breath of wind or a gleam of sunshine—a gentle, melancholy day—a fit day for the burial of earthly hopes. The light in the fine old room was softly subdued, and the bright glow of the firelight fell athwart the warm red of the walls above the bookshelves. They entered almost simultaneously. Shepherd, obviously considerably perturbed, busied himself with the papers, which he took from his brief bag. He glanced keenly at Madame de Castro as she entered, and observed her paleness, but she seemed very calm.

Weir stood at the window away from the rest, his hands in his pockets, apparently self-possessed. He was in no way nervous about his own immediate prospects; he had been assured by Shepherd that his position was entirely unassailable. He did not care for the scene which would probably ensue, but, shrugging his shoulders lightly, he prepared to go through with it.

Isabel moved quickly up to the table, and requested Shepherd to make no delay. With this request he was only too glad to comply. His was a task he could wish well over, one which no man need envy him. The woman before him, and her two fair children, were the true heirs to Penninghame, and the deed which took it from them was both iniquitous and unjust. He smoothed out the sheet of foolscap, and with a little nervous sound cleared his voice.

"Madame de Castro," he said, glancing towards her with a slightly apologetic air, "this is your father's last will and testament, dated the 13th day of January. It was drawn up by myself and witnessed by Alexander Corbett, my confidential clerk, and by Walter Baillie, the factor, who was called in for the purpose."

"Be good enough to read it," she said, in a clear curt tone.

"Presently. I would explain that this will was drawn up and signed under considerable protest. My late partner, Mr. Maitland, absolutely declined to touch it, and it was only because I foresaw that the whole matter would be lifted out of the hands of my firm that I obeyed his directions. I would absolve myself, Madame, of any complicity in the matter."

"We will dispense with your explanations, Mr. Shepherd," she said, with a touch of coldness, which caused Weir much satisfaction. "Be good enough to read on."

He cleared his voice again, and proceeded :—

"I, Francis Riddell Learmonth of Penninghame House and Whitekirk, in the county of Midlothian, being in my sound judgment, do hereby will and bequeath my whole estates, saving and excepting such portions of the same as shall be hereafter mentioned, to my well-beloved nephew, Anthony Gordon Weir, who, in response to my request, came from Cape Colony to Scotland, and has in the last three months been my constant companion and comfort. I hereby desire and enjoin that he shall take the name of Anthony Riddell Learmonth, and as such shall be called. And that the whole furnishings, pictures and silver plate, except such articles as shall be hereafter mentioned, shall be his absolutely so long as he shall remain resident at Penninghame. And he shall not be at liberty to sell any part of the estate or to become non-resident thereon. If he wishes to do this he must forfeit all his rights as my sole legatee, and accept in lieu thereof the sum of ten thousand pounds, the estates to be thereafter sold by my executors, and the money distributed among Edinburgh charities to be hereafter named.

"To my daughter, Isabel Riddell Learmonth, now Madame de Castro, the property of Fintry, together with all its furnishings and appurtenances, and the sum of five hundred pounds per annum, to be paid out of the revenues of Penninghame. Also to her her mother's jewellery in the strong box under Braidwood's care, also such articles of silver and certain pictures, to be mentioned on a separate slip of paper. And I desire and enjoin her to be friendly towards Anthony Gordon Weir, and to take my assurance that I have proven him worthy that which he is to receive, he having paid me that filial duty in which she has so woefully lacked.

"To Andrew Braidwood and his wife Susan, who have been my faithful servants for thirty years, to be paid the sum of seventy-five pounds per annum as long as they both shall live. And it would please me to think that they would remove to Fintry with my daughter if she comes to the place."

Then followed sundry small bequests, over which Shepherd hastened, fully conscious that no word of them was comprehended by those who listened. He laid the paper down, folded his pince-nez from his nose, and looked round the room. The boy Frank had covered his face with his hands. Sybil was quietly weeping with her face on Helen's shoulder. By the table stood their mother erect, immovable as carved out of stone. She had turned her back on Anthony Weir. He, however, moved by an immense fascination, took a step round where he could see her face.

She pointed straight at the document lying on the table.

"Sir," she said to Shepherd, and her very voice seemed to have changed, "I give you notice here and now that in my son's interests I will contest this will. That not a moment shall be lost, that every penny I possess or may possess, or can gather by fair means or foul, shall be expended on getting back for my son his just rights."

"Madame, I am in sympathy with you," said Shepherd, forgetting Anthony Weir; "but it is my duty to warn you that only failure would attend your efforts. Mr. Learmonth was in sound judgment when he made this will; there is no ground whatever why any court should seek to set it aside."

"It shall be set aside," she answered quietly; then suddenly she turned a lightning glance full upon Weir.

"Sir," she said, and never had she looked more majestic, "I know not who you are or by what means you have wormed yourself into my father's confidence, but I swear before God that I will leave no stone unturned to put you out of Penninghame. Here you will eat the bread of the widow and the fatherless, and sleep on the bed of the usurper, and no blessing but a curse will follow you all the days of your life. Children, come, we are driven from Penninghame, and are homeless on the face of the earth."

The boy suddenly flung up his head and ran to her, flinging his eager, loving young arm about her waist.

"No, no, mother, I will make a home for you. All will be well. Although we may not have Penninghame, we can be happy together elsewhere. Don't look like that, darling mother, we can't bear it."

Maitland, watching her closely, saw that the strain had told. Springing forward, he took her on his arm, and the melancholy train passed out of the room, and the door was shut. Weir took a long breath. He was not made of stone; the scene had been even more trying than he had anticipated. Shepherd's hands were a trifle unsteady as he essayed to gather his papers together. He did not look at Anthony Weir. Nothing was further from his thoughts than the congratulations he could once have offered freely. The events of the last few days had considerably altered his view of things, and he regretted from the bottom of his heart that he had had any hand in the parting of Penninghame. Even the knowledge that if he had kept out of if, some one else would have reaped the harvest, did not tend to raise his spirits.

"Well, you look mighty sick, Shepherd; gone over to the enemy entirely, I suppose," said Weir, a trifle sourly.

Shepherd raised his eyes, and looked him full in the face. "It was a painful scene, the most painful, I think, I have ever witnessed in the whole course of my professional career. I will be honest with you, Mr. Weir; I cannot offer the congratulations fitting to the occasion."

" Oh, I don't want them, thank you," he answered lightly. " I grant you that it is rough on her, but if she would learn to be less high and mighty, things might be better for her. Is a man going to lick the dust before her? She looks at me as if it contaminated her to breathe the same air with me. In Heaven's name, what have I done to her? The place came to me fair and square; you know it. The old man had his mind made up that she wouldn't have it; he was afraid, and rightly so, of that foreign scum she had married. And if I hadn't stepped into the breach it would have been parted among a lot of hungry charities. What better off would that have left her? It might pay Madame de Castro to be a little bit civil to me."

Shepherd could not repress a faint smile. " You don't know what mettle she is made of when you suggest it," he replied. " I am glad that she has Fintry. Even that you would have had, I believe, if the laird had lived a little longer."

" It's a nice little place, the pick of the batch," he replied, " but I don't grudge her it. That condition that I must live here and on no account sell takes the gilt off the gingerbread. Shepherd, I own to you frankly, I intended to clear out at once, and put the place up for sale."

" It can't be done then," said Shepherd, and there was a distinct note of satisfaction in his voice. He closed the bag with a click, and prepared to go. His thoughts were entirely of the little company that had just left the room.

" Surely they'll have the grace to clear out, or, if they prefer it, I can leave them in possession for a week or so."

" I should think they would return to Edinburgh with the Maitlands to-night," said Shepherd. " Happily, Fintry is untenanted at present, and can soon be got ready for them."

Shepherd was right in his surmise. That night Weir slept in undisturbed possession of his fine heritage, and those he had defrauded were beholden for the time being to the charity of strangers.

CHAPTER XXIII

MISTRESS OF PENNINGHAME

IT was a wet afternoon, and the dingy little suburban street looked its dreariest. It was very narrow, and the tall houses overlooked each other's windows so successfully that there could be no privacy except when the blinds were drawn. From that narrow way little of the sky could be seen, and the sun did not care to linger even when it rioted elsewhere. It was a busy neighbourhood, the centre of an immense working-class population, the pavements swarming with children, who played in the gutters all day long. One of a dozen streets as characteristically dull, it was a good place in which to hide—a place where one might live undiscovered for years, simply because it was so drearily commonplace.

The noise of the children's play ascended through the still air, and seemed to fill the comfortable sitting-room on the top floor where Nancy Nicolson sat with a bit of sewing on her lap, to which, however, she was paying but a listless attention. Her face wore a discontented look. The life of a lady, or rather the life without occupation, which had represented Nancy's idea of ladyhood, had soon palled. A week had passed since she left Penninghame, an interminable week, which she felt rebelliously she could not possibly prolong. By nature a garrulous, happy person, the enforced silence regarding affairs of such absorbing interest was a strain almost beyond her endurance. She had found a lodging with a decent woman, the wife of a railway signalman, who had accepted her statement that her husband was absent on business, and would presently rejoin her, when they would go abroad. She not only accepted the information in good faith, but congratulated herself on having secured a lodger who gave so little trouble. Forbidden to write to Penninghame, instructed to wait patiently and in absolute silence until she should hear from Anthony Weir, Nancy was at the moment feeling that the limit of her endurance had been reached.

Had he not turned up it is certain that she would have taken some step on her own account. She had made a daily study of the newspapers, and had obtained from them the story of the laird's funeral, which had been given in full detail as an event of considerable importance in the neighbourhood. She had also come across sundry paragraphs relating to the disposition of the estates. She knew that the man she believed to be her husband was now Laird of Penninghame, and she chafed at the narrow groove of her own life, and resented his delay in coming to take her away to share his new estate. These thoughts gave to her pretty face a somewhat sullen look, which had not left it when the door opened, and he came in, carefully closing it after him, and even turning the key in the lock. She smiled then, as she turned somewhat shyly to greet him.

" What are you feared for ? There's nobody in but Mrs. Dalrymple, and she'll no come in."

" Or listen at the keyhole, eh ? I wouldn't like to trust her too far," he said jocularly. " Well, how are you, Nancy ? Looking a bit pale and off colour. You don't go out enough."

" It's very dull wandering the streets wi' no a soul to speak to. I very near socht oot my auld neeber, Teenie Leadbetter, yesterday. I got desperate."

" But you didn't do anything so foolish, Nancy, surely?" he said, and his voice grew stern at once.

" No, I thocht better of it. When are you going to tak' me away?"

" Sit down and we'll talk about that presently. I've a great deal to tell you, Nancy. We got the laird buried all right, and had a fine scene afterwards. And Madame de Castro is going to make a court case of it, so I'll be tied to the place indefinitely. Ugh, I'm sick of it!"

" D'ye mean that she's gaun to try whether the law will tak' Penninghame frae you and gi'e it to her?"

" Precisely. I've been very busy these two days with law business, I can tell you. I've given Shepherd the go-by."

" Oh, what for? I thocht he helped you a lot, and got the laird to mak' the will ye wanted? Ye telt me that a while syne."

" True enough, but he's backed out since then, and his conduct on the funeral day was scandalous, considering what he was paid for. Yesterday I had him out, and gave him my opinion pretty freely, and now I've placed my affairs in the hands of a new firm."

" Oh!" said Nancy reflectively. " I hope it'll be a' richt. An' when am I to leave here? I canna bide ony longer."

He looked at her steadily, and saw that the limit of her endurance had been reached. She was a person without much resource, and the enforced idleness had been too much for her.

" What would you like to do?" he asked experimentally.

" Gang back to Penninghame. You promised that. If you are laird, I am lady, am I not?"

" Yes, of course, but just at present there are difficulties in the way. With this case hanging over me, and Madame de Castro is sparing no effort to make her claim a strong one, it would not do to spring our marriage on them. It would damage my case from the outset."

" I dinna see it. Efter a', it has naething to dae wi' onybody but us," said Nancy stolidly.

" That's true, my dear, so far as it goes, but you don't understand. Of course, a man who is perfectly free and has an assured position can do as he likes, but when his position is assailed as mine is, he has to walk warily. It would be disastrous, positively disastrous, to spring our marriage on them just now. You have no idea what the law is like, Nancy; they might take Penninghame from me for it."

Nancy listened, duly impressed. Her knowledge of the law was indeed scanty, the only representative of it she personally knew being John Woodhead, the Penninghame policeman, an expert in pursuing boys for poaching and other depredations on the laird's lands. To her the law was a vast mysterious machine, possessed of unlimited power.

" But I canna bide here," she said forlornly. " I'll dae something desperate."

" Of course I never intended that you should stop here. What would you say to a trip to London, Nancy, for a week or so, while they are getting ready for the fight?"

Her face brightened, and her eyes shone.

" I'd like that," she said. " I've never been faurer nor Edinburgh or Glesca in my life."

"Well, get your hat on, and let's go out and buy some things for you to wear."

"But we micht meet ony o' them—Maister Shepherd, for instance."

"It's not likely; besides I heard this morning that he had gone to the country with his wife. I called there at his office before I came out here, and that was the message I got."

Nancy rose, all her listlessness gone.

"When are we gaun—to London, I mean?"

"To-morrow if you like. On second thoughts, perhaps we'd better not venture near Princes Street or the West End shops. Any of the De Castro tribe might see us, and, though they don't know you, they might put two and two together."

"What did Uncle Braidwood say, an' Aunt Susan?" she asked, with a slight faltering note in her voice.

Weir shrugged his shoulders.

"Oh, your uncle tried to bully me as usual, but I was able for him, and I don't think he'll try the same game again. They've cleared out from Penninghame, bag and baggage."

"Oh!" said Nancy, betraying the keenest interest. "Whaur have they gane?"

"To serve their new mistress, Madame de Castro, at Fintry. The whole tribe will be settled there to-day or to-morrow, and it's my belief that that's where Shepherd and his wife have gone. You can't trust any of them any further than you can see them," he added, with a virtuous air.

Nancy's colour changed, and the look of terror, which sometimes crept to her eyes when she was alone, came back.

"Hae they discovered onything aboot—aboot ye ken what?"

Weir laughed what sounded like a big, easy laugh.

"No, my dear, they haven't. So far as we are concerned, the pool is as safe as the Bank of England. They've been at it several times, and tried all the new fangled apparatus, but it's no good. It means to keep its own secrets evidently, ours among others."

Nancy looked relieved.

"But I'm never quite easy in my mind," she murmured. "They aye say that murder wull oot."

"Hush!" he said reprovingly. "You must never say such a thing again. It was nothing of the kind, but an accident, a mere accident, which I was powerless to prevent. Supposing I told them the whole truth, would I be believed? Not likely; there's too many knives in me already. Got a fresh one lately—that son of Maitland's that has come home from Bilbao; he haunts Penninghame like a shadow. I heard this morning that he and his sister are to stop indefinitely at Fintry to prosecute the search. Much good may it do them."

"I'll be glad to see London," said Nancy, with the same apprehensive air. "An' when we get settled doon at Penninghame I hope I'll be able to forget a' aboot it."

Weir looked at the little maid with considerable surprise. The cool way in which she spoke of becoming the mistress of Penninghame rather staggered him. Long familiarity with the idea had shorn it of all its awe and terror for Nancy, and most of her lonely hours were spent in anticipating her new life. She also wondered what it would be like to be served instead of to serve, to ring bells when she wanted anything, and scold the servants when they did not come quick enough. She had tried the experiment on her landlady once or twice, but that otherwise agreeable person had indicated that she would not answer bells, so Nancy's little attempts at authority had been nipped in the bud.

Weir, even while he smiled indulgently at her, casually wondered how he would get rid of her when the time came. After the law case was over, and he was fully established as Laird of Penninghame, he would probably wish to marry and settle down. Nancy would have to be scored off; put out of his life's reckoning altogether. He had no doubt that the way would follow hard upon the need. Meanwhile her naïveté amused him; then she was the only person to whom he could talk without restraint, and she was pretty enough to disarm anything. When properly dressed, as he meant she should be when they got to London, she would pass muster anywhere, until she opened her mouth. Probably he would leave her in London; all would depend. Nancy, believing herself to be his wife, had no suspicion of the true nature of his thoughts and intentions. He was always kind and considerate, and she had no reason to complain. She did not think it unreasonable that he should wish to keep their marriage quiet for a time; nay, she quite saw the wisdom and necessity for it.

Next day they met at the Caledonian Railway Station, and took their seats in the London train. Nancy, in a neatly-fitting black coat and skirt, and an inoffensive hat, looked very pretty, and as happy as a queen. As they steamed out of the station, it was as if some incubus had fallen from her companion's shoulders. He had money in his pocket, an attractive companion, nothing apparently to stand in the way of his enjoyment of the next few days. He became as lover-like as the heart of the most exacting woman could desire.

Poor Nancy was not exacting. Her fool's paradise seemed to her to lack nothing. She had reached the height of her ambition, and felt herself to be a lady indeed.

CHAPTER XXIV

IN COUNCIL

DAVID MAITLAND was sitting on a wooden stool in the Police Office at Whitekirk Green waiting on the sergeant coming in. It was a little, bare, common, place, which had become familiar to him during the last few days. Also his respect for the sergeant was a sentiment likely to last through life. While he waited he occupied himself in studying the calendar which hung on the wall. It was now the 14th of February, exactly thirteen days since his father's disappearance. And the mystery still remained unsolved. Personally he had given up all hope, and was now at his wits' end what to do next. He had still fifteen months of his engagement to fulfil with his uncle in Bilbao, who could ill spare him. He felt that he and his sister ought now to face and accept the inevitable, and order their future precisely as they must have done had they laid their father in the grave in the ordinary way. But the only time he had spoken of dismantling the house in Edinburgh Helen had showed such signs of distress that he had hastily changed the subject. What to do with her was a serious problem ; but he had determined that very morning to suggest that she should return to Spain with him on a visit to the relatives she had never seen. While these things were taking shape in his mind the door opened, and the sergeant came in. A hearty greeting passed between them, their regard was indeed mutual. Maitland's sound common sense, shrewdness of judgment and restraint, had greatly impressed the sergeant, who, when occasion offered, was loud in his praises.

" Good-morning sergeant. I came out to Fintry yesterday with Madame de Castro and my sister, and I thought I should like to see you to-day. I can't live this sort of life much longer. I'll have to get back to Spain to my work."

" Humph ! "

The sergeant leaned against the high desk which stood against the wall, and looked somewhat vaguely into space.

" I suppose," said David slowly, " you are no further forward ? "

The sergeant shook his head.

" No, actually, Maister David, but this thing winna get the better o' me, an' if ye maun gang, ye can leave the matter in my hands."

" I have no choice. What good can I do loafing about here or in Edinburgh ? You and the Edinburgh men can follow up any possible clues far better than I could possibly do. And in any case now it will only be the mere finding of a body, and will be horrible when it comes. For my sister's sake, sergeant, I could even wish that the matter might end here."

" It canna," observed the sergeant, in his slow quiet voice, which gave no indication of the swift working of his mind. " The thing wull mairch on withoot let or hinder frae us until the day comes. It aye comes sune or late ; I've never kent it to fail. I could tell ye things, Maister David, that ye widna believe. We'll get at the bottom o' this, sir, and when we dae, there'll be nae surprise for me."

Maitland looked at the grave inscrutable face with a sudden wonder.

"Sergeant, we are alone here; I am safe; you know me no babbler, carried by every wind that blows; what do you believe?"

"I believe, Maister David, that your father's at the bottom o' Penninghame Pool, and I mean to be at the bottom o't too. Three times we've been maistered, but my time wull come."

"And do you believe he got there by accident?" asked Maitland, and his eyes gleamed a little with the inner excitement that began to rise in spite of him.

"Nae accident, Maister David, he was pitten there by ill hands, wha's I could name, only I winna. In my mind it's as clear as a pikestaff. But unfortunately ye canna convict on mere imagination, nor arrest a man on sic slender suspicion. That is to say, there maun be some ground to go upon. If only I could get a haud o' that lass o' Braidwood's she could tell something. Whaur is she, do ye suppose?"

Maitland shook his head. Hitherto he had not connected her in any way with the tragedy; he had heard some talk about her disappearance, but had put it down to a love affair of the common kind.

"What can she have to do with it?" he asked in surprise.

"She's awa' wi' Anthony Weir. I'm as sure as I stand here. She's been seen in Edinburgh, but them that saw her werena quick enough. It's like that in oor business, sir, unless the nail is knockit on the heid at wance the whole thing's lost. If only a man had twa pair o' een an' could be in five or six places at wance we'd get at the bottom o' things quicker."

"Is Anthony Weir at Penninghame just now?"

"No, they say he's gane to London. Faith, I dinna wonder. For him Penninghame should be a haunted hoose. I heard frae Sandy Turnbull, the gardener, that he was very ill because the wull disna let him sell the place. Certy, if it did, it wad be in the market the morn. Is the laird's dochter pleased wi' Fintry, d'ye think?"

Maitland shrugged his shoulders.

"It's a cold, dreary place, sergeant, but she is thankful for a shelter she can call her own. It's hard, in fact it won't bear thinking of. Have you seen young De Castro? He's a fine manly fellow, and would make a capital laird of Penninghame."

"We'll maybe live to see him that yet, Maister David," said the sergeant enigmatically. "Meanwhile we maun bide oor time."

Maitland sat a moment in silence.

"If only we could get at the bottom of that pool." he said. "It's an extraordinary thing that everything has failed; stranger than all that the body never came up."

"Well, ye see, the bottom's thick wi' weeds o' every kind, and guid kens hoo mony holes there are intilt. It's a queer place, an' has aye been, but as I'm a leevin' man I'll be at the bottom o'd yet, Maister David; ye can leave the maitter wi' me. It's no likely I'll rest. It's to my ain credit that I shouldna', an' as for Anthony Weir, I'll watch him, ye can tak' my word for it. He disna think muckle o' me, but we'll may be see wha's the cleverest yet. It pays to appear stupit; whiles I've foun it no a bad move, an' this is the first job I've had in the Lothians that has baffled me. D'ye mind that case wi' the tinks, when a wummin was killed at the back o' Bennin Wud, and naebody could find the body. If I were to tell ye the tale bit by bit, an' show you hoo the hale thing hung on tae trifles, ye wad wonder. There's naething ower sma'. In my notebook there's things wrote doon that wad gar a man think me dottled. No me; every wan o' them has a meanin', a connection wi' something else. I'll be at the bottom o'd yet, an' I say that we'll see the richt laird in Penninghame afore we dee."

"Is your theory so far advanced that you can state it specifically?"

The sergeant nodded, and went to look at the fastening of the door.

"You're a safe chap, Maister David, an' I'll piece it oot to ye as faur as I've gotten mysel'. That day your father was at Penninghame Shepherd an' he left thegither, an' pairted at the gates, Mr. Maitland meanin' to walk to Whitekirk to see the doctor. He had been speakin' aboot the pool, an' there's nae doot at a' that he gaed there. Weel, as Shepherd was gaun the ither way, he meets Nancy Nicolson, Braidwood's niece. Whaur was she gaun, d'ye think? Awa' to the wud to meet Weir. Braidwood telt me that they were coortin' or something o' that kind, an' that he had had words wi' Weir aboot it. Weel, they suppose that Weir was in the wud near the pool, no expeckin, very likely to see your faither, but when he did, kennin' perfectly weel that there was something in his bag that micht dae him damage, they began to speak aboot it. I never saw your faither, Maister David, but I hear on a' hands that he was a silent, prood man that couldna bide idle clashes. Very likely he telt Weir to mind his ain business, then Weir, bein' beside himsel' wi' anger an' ither things, an' determined to see what was in the bag, tried to get it frae him. Syne your faither gaed back to the pool, an' either fell in or was pushed in. Then the lassie comes on the scene. Maybe she saw or heard something that made it necessary for her to disappear. Onyway, she did disappear that very day. What do ye think o' that?"

"It's as plain as daylight; you've a wonderful mind, sergeant."

"No me; that's my business, an' that's the lines I'm gaun upon. Twa things I've got to dae as sune as it's possible; lay my hands on Nancy Nicolson an' get to the bottom o' Penninghame Pool. The first'll no be that difficult; the second——"

The sergeant stopped and shrugged his shoulders. He was not the first the pool had baffled. As fast as they drained it, it filled up again as if some mysterious spring from the nether world supplied it, and no man had ever seen its bottom or its source.

"There needna' be ony backgaun, Maister David," said the sergeant kindly, observing the painful look on the young man's face. "I mean we needna be blamin' oorsels for no gettin' on fast enough. Ye see if it happened as I think, an' I could very near tak, my oath on it, naething could hae saved him. He wad be deid five meenits efter he fell in. An' the mair leisurely we are aboot it the better oor chance. As long as a man kens he is watched he's on his guard. My cue is to let Weir think me a born eediot, that has bungled the business, and let it drap as sune as I decently could. Then he'll be off guard, as it were, an' me in the back grund, ay, an' whiles in the foregrund, watchin' like the fox at the rabbit hole."

"Well, I may leave it, sergeant, and if you succeed in bringing justice home it will not be forgotten to you."

"It's to my ain credit, sir, forby bein' the wark I'm paid to do," said the said the sergeant, as he unlocked the door. Maitland stepped out into the pleasant sunshine and held out his hand.

"Good-bye in the meantime, sergeant; I'll go back to Fintry and explain matters to my sister."

"But mum's the word aboot what I hae telt you," said the sergeant hastily. " If it gets aboot I may as weel gie up the ghaist ; besides, till we can prove something, Anthony Weir's innocent."

" Precisely, I did not mean that ; I only meant that I must try and get things into shape somehow, and go back to my work. Good-day, and a thousand thanks."

The sergeant nodded, warmly gripped the offered hand, and they parted. Maitland walked across the Green and knocked at the doctor's door. It was just half-past two, possibly he might find him at his lunch.

As he stood on the step the rattle of wheels from the opposite side of the square brought the doctor's gig quickly to the door.

" Hulloa, Maitland ; glad to see you," said the doctor cheerily. " Curiously enough I was thinking of you not long ago. Spirit wave, eh ? Well, we're made of queerer stuff than we know. Where have you come from ? "

" Fintry."

" Fintry ! Oh, are they there ? "

" We came out last night. Madame de Castro, her son and daughter, and my sister. Braidwood and his wife have been there since last Saturday, and the place is wonderfully home-like."

The doctor opened the door with his latch key and motioned him in.

" I'm just going to have my midday dinner. Will you share it ? "

" No thank you. I had lunch at Fintry before leaving. I walked in to see the sergeant and leave a message for you from Madame de Castro."

" Ah, does she want to see me ? "

" Yes, this afternoon if possible."

" I'll walk across with you presently. Well, what's the sergeant about ; seemingly not much perhaps, but you may take my word for it he is covering the whole ground."

" I'm fully convinced of that," said Maitland heartily. " But all the same it's a sorry business, as well as a slow one."

All at once, in the presence, perhaps, of a stronger, and, at the same time, more sympathetic nature, his own strength and courage seemed to give way. It had been a terrible week. He had not dared for others' sake to think of himself, and now the strain was beginning to tell. The doctor, catching the inflection of his voice, wheeled round suddenly and laid his kind firm hand on his shoulder.

" All right, my lad, I see how it is. Don't mind me. You've borne up nobly, and thought only of others. You'll get your reward. Don't fight against it now. Sometimes it's a relief to let the womanish tears have their way."

David Maitland sat down and burying his face in his hands sobbed as if his heart would break. Somehow for the first time hope seemed to have absolutely fled, and the longing for his father, who had filled so large a part of his life, who had loved him, and whom he had loved with no common devotion, would not longer be stilled.

CHAPTER XXV

PRIDE OF RACE

In the soft sweet air of the spring afternoon they walked across the fields to Fintry, talking as they went.

They had seen very little of one another, but both felt that bond of mutual attraction which is the base of true friendship. Jeffrey was young for his years, and had the power of attracting young spirits towards him. Their talk turned naturally upon the subject which was uppermost in their thoughts. In spite of the sergeant's admonition to Maitland to keep silence, the theory he had himself advanced was already in most of its details in possession of the public mind. The interest taken in the case was extraordinary, and the Penninghame Pool had become a place of resort on Sundays and other leisure hours, so that one of the foresters had been told off to prevent wholesale trespassing through the woods. The usually quiet, rather lethargic, neighbourhood became all at once instinct with life, and every boy and man assumed the role of amateur detective. But the pool kept its secret well, and seemed likely to keep it until the excitement passed away or something else happened to fret the minds of men.

" I suppose," said the doctor kindly, " you have now no hope of seeing your father in life again, and must order your lives accordingly. What do you propose to do ? "

He put the question rather to divert the painful current of Maitland's thoughts than out of any mere personal curiosity.

" I am trying to bring my mind to it. To-day I have resolved to return to Bilbao not later than Monday. I was bound to my uncle for a term of three years, scarcely two of which have passed. Only my sister's future troubles me. She will be very much alone. You see my father and she were all in all to one another, and inseparable companions. She had really very few friends."

" Couldn't you take her with you ? "

" That is what I thought. There is a great deal to do, of course ; the house, for instance. It must be let or sold. Were you ever in it, Doctor Jeffrey ? "

" Once, several years ago ; I remember it quite well. It seemed to me then a large house for so small a family."

" My father often talked of leaving it, but I believe he clung to it because my mother liked it so much. If I could let it furnished that would be the simplest way out of the difficulty. But, unfortunately, the letting season is over. In October I should have had no difficulty."

" One never knows ; it is an excellent idea. Tell me, how long have you known Madame de Castro ? "

" About a year ; she came to Bilbao soon after I did, and my aunt, Mrs. Morton, showed her some kindness. Her husband was in ill health, and they were frightfully poor. Madame de Castro was giving music lessons to the handful of English children there, and was contemplating starting a school with her daughter to help her, when she decided suddenly to come home."

"Did you ever see De Castro?"

"Never; but he was a brute. I have heard my aunt say so, though not exactly in these terms, and his wife's patience with him was marvellous, she said, almost divine."

"It is inexplicable. What had a man like that to commend him to Isabel Learmonth?" he asked, as if the subject pursued and fascinated him.

Maitland shrugged his shoulders.

"He was very handsome they said, and seemed to have some sort of fascination for women. He belonged to quite poor people. I have often seen his mother, an old Spanish witch, and one of his sisters danced in the Casino. They were quite impossible in every way."

Jeffrey turned his head away, and looked across the spreading fields with bitterness in his eyes. Was it for this he had kept silence, thinking himself no mate for a daughter of Penninghame? Better life with him in the old house on Whitekirk Green; at least there she would have had decent comfort, and been spared such depth of degradation.

"Penninghame has had a good many vicissitudes," he said musingly. "I hear that Madame de Castro will contest her father's will. For the sake of that fine boy of hers, we must wish her success."

"It is a shame for a man like Anthony Weir to have it. I shall never forget him that day of the funeral. It made one's blood boil. But Mr. Shepherd does not think she has a ghost of a chance; that she will only spend her money, and break her heart. Who is to testify to undue influence? Only old Braidwood, and he is so frightfully prejudiced that his word would carry no weight. Did you ever see anything of him while you were in attendance?"

"I did not like the man, and he knew it; therefore he kept pretty much out of the way when I happened to be about," replied the doctor. "Honestly speaking, I never saw anything that could be taken exception to. He behaved very well to the laird. Madame de Castro's friends would do well to advise her not to take the thing into Court. If she loses, with costs, see what it would mean for her. Meanwhile she ought to be very comfortable at Fintry. Having been so poor as you say, her present income must seem like untold riches to her."

"Where are her friends?" asked Maitland.

"She has none that I know of, unless yourself and Mr. Shepherd. Do you know that he has had a rupture with Weir, and that the whole of the Penninghame affairs have been removed from that firm?"

"No; that's a pity, I think. I suppose Weir has found a more unscrupulous firm, who will see eye to eye with him."

"Mr. Shepherd now regrets having been the instrument of preparing the will in direct opposition to my father's opinion. I am sure that is why he has withdrawn so easily. He is frightfully cut up about it, and each day seems to get worse."

"There's Fintry. It lies very bonnily to the sea," said the doctor suddenly, as they ascended the slope of a little hill, and saw the whole panorama before them. "I havent been over this way for a long time."

As the doctor said, Fintry lay bonnily to the sea. In a landscape more sparsely wooded than the richer breadths of Penninghame, it stood on a gentle eminence, a handful of fine old trees dotting the slopes of its tiny green park. It was a square rambling old house, not large, but exceedingly picturesque, being entirely covered with ivy of a century's growth. Behind it the ground sloped gradually backward to the Moorfoot Hills, while before there was the long level seaboard, washed by the sparkling waters of the firth, and intersected by many cunning bays and inlets fringed with the living green of the golf links, just then springing into fresh fame. A most desirable place for a person of modest taste and means, it did not satisfy the proud heart of Isabel Learmonth. There was scarcely a window from which she could not see some part of Penninghame, and she had strangely chosen for her own occupation a bedroom from which she could see the square towers of her old home peeping out among its sheltering trees. Already Isabel Learmonth had spent some sad and rebellious hours there, and the resolve to fight, and if possible win, the day for her boy became still more deeply rooted in her mind.

The interior of the house was shabby to a degree. It had been left furnished since the days when it was used as a dower house for Penninghame, and had been occasionally let for a period to some approved tenant. But though shabby, it was by no means poor or mean in its arrangements. The furniture, though belonging to a bygone day, was of considerable value. There was nothing modern or aggressive; everything was sober, old-fashioned, fitting to an old house, and part of its very existence. It was a place of quiet tones and neutral tints. The few pictures were good, and the china in the cabinets a delight to the eye. Isabel had herself been at once surprised and pleased with the interior, and while longing for her other home, of which she considered herself unjustly defrauded, she accepted Fintry thankfully as a place of refuge, as a home of her own, where at least she and her children might never know the sordid misery of the intervening years. She was in this mood when the two gentlemen entered the house. Her face brightened as her eyes fell on Jeffrey's face, and again that odd comforting sense of strength came to her.

"I am glad to see you," she said simply, as she held out her hand.

"And I to see you, Miss Isabel, in this house."

She smiled as her name fell from his lips.

"I am glad that you remembered," she said graciously. "They have all gone for a walk down to the sea, David," she added, "by way of Rosford village. I said that if you were not too tired, you might go to meet them when you came back. But you must be tired with your walk to Whitekirk," she said, when he seemed eager to go.

"Tired, no, it is only a couple of miles. I will go and meet them," he said, understanding that she wished for an opportunity of private talk with the doctor.

Isabel watched him go with a kindly eye.

"That is a heart of gold, Doctor Jeffrey," she said in warm tones. "I can never repay him for his kindness and consideration for us in Bilbao."

"I like him very much; he is manly, simple and sincere. It is a hard blow that has fallen on him and his sister."

"Very," she gave a little shudder as she spoke. "He told me this morning he must soon return to Spain. I have been thinking about it a good deal to-day, and I mean to ask his sister to stay the whole summer here. She will not be happy away from this neighbourhood, at least until something throws light on her father's strange disappearance. Isn't it the most inexplicable thing, doctor?"

Jeffrey agreed, but his thoughts were further afield. He was thinking of the contrast between the Isabel Learmonth of twenty years ago, and this quiet sad woman whom sorrow had made so sympathetic towards others, and he admitted to himself that never had she seemed fairer in his sight.

"It is about my daughter I wish to consult you," she said suddenly. "She is not at all strong. I am afraid that the seeds of the disease of which her father died are in her constitution. She gives me many anxious moments. Then she is so excitable, and difficult to control. My son is very different. Sybil has the temperament of the South. Often I am afraid, looking forward, wondering whether she will make shipwreck of her life, as I did, and praying God forbid."

"She will not have the same temptation," he hastened to say, scarcely knowing how to comfort her.

She shook her head.

"Temptation! what is it? So often it comes from within. The best thing for Sybil would be to marry while she is yet quite young, some good, steady, reliable man, preferably older than herself. He would guide her, and help to balance her character. Often I find myself at a loss."

She looked at him straightly and in spite of himself he reddened. Could it be possible that she had such a thought in her mind even for an instant. He hastened to banish it from his own by making a suggestion for which there was perhaps no justification.

"I thought young Maitland admired her very much. Was there anything between them?"

She started slightly, and he imagined that she drew herself up in some offence.

"I think nothing," she said quite coldly. "He was very kind to us, yes; but I don't think he would have presumed."

In spite of himself Jeffrey smiled. The old pride would out, even after it had been trailed through the mire. Yet it was of this woman, whose pride unabashed was still high enough to reach the heavens, that he had even a moment ago permitted himself to dream! For the first time he felt himself repelled. She felt the change in his looks, her fine spirit was quick to detect in him the jarring note.

Her eyes filled with sudden tears.

"Oh, who am I?" she cried, "to set myself up so high! God knows I have suffered enough. My pride might have been quenched. Pray forgive me, friend, and help me to take better views of life—your views, which are always the truest and best."

All that was most womanly and most winning sprang to the surface again, and his face softened.

"Oh, I was wrong and unjest to David. I believe he cares for Sybil. If it should be that she cares for him, I will never stand in the way. Is to be happy, after all, not the chief end of life? What do other things matter? Not at all. I am distraught. But, whatever I do or say, promise that you will never leave me or be estranged. I cannot do without my friend."

"Let us talk of other things," he said gently, but there was that in his face which forbade her to go on. "You are making mountains where none exist; let us forget it, and think only of what will be best for you and yours. I can assure you you need not be too much troubled about Miss Sybil; a few weeks of Fintry air will soon revive her, and when she begins to interest herself in the life of the place, and perhaps to make a few friends of her own age, your anxiety will be at an end."

CHAPTER XXVI

A NEW POINT OF VIEW

ANTHONY WEIR rode across the fields to Fintry on a windy March afternoon. He looked his best on horseback, and took a pride in his horseflesh. The stables indeed were his hobby ; on them he would spend freely, while he was niggardly in the affairs of the house.

His face wore a curious expression as he approached the house, for it was a bold thing he had in contemplation. After much thought and deliberation he had resolved to offer a compromise to Madame de Castro. What was known in legal circles as the Learmonth Succession Case was to come on in a fortnight, and in the minds of most people the verdict was already a foregone conclusion. Sympathy might be with the widowed daughter of Penninghame, who had fully restored herself to her old place in the affections of the neighbourhood, but it was impossible to get away from the fact that she had been by her own act estranged from her father for twenty years, and that he had made no secret of his intention to keep her out of Penninghame. Even William Shepherd, who was now acting for her throughout, felt the deplorable weakness of her case. But she was determined to fight it out for her son's sake. He, poor lad, was very well content with the home provided for him ; in all his sixteen years of life he had never lived in one so much to his liking.

There was a fine entrance gate but no lodge at Fintry, and Weir had to dismount to open it for himself. As he did so he saw a figure approaching on the Whitekirk Road, which he recognised as that of Sybil de Castro. Now, during the six weeks he had been in residence as Laird of Penninghame, Weir had striven with all his might to ingratiate himself with the neighbourhood, had made himself gracious and affable to both rich and poor, had given money freely, and announced his intention of trying to live up to the best traditions of Penninghame. He was indeed a man in desperate case, living betwixt two fires, scarcely knowing which way to turn, and this course had recommended itself to him as pre-eminently the most expedient. His efforts had been by no means lost. He could make himself very agreeable when he chose, and already he had won a good many golden opinions in the parish. There were even those who said it would be a good thing if he won his case, for he was likely to make a better Laird of Penninghame than any Learmonth of the last generation. But his life was burdensome to him ; there was that in the background that would not let him enjoy the splendid inheritance that had come to him. But for the impending case in the Law Courts, he would have left it in charge of a bailiff, and taken himself off to the other ends of the earth.

But circumstances compelled him to wait, and while he waited, Nemesis was on his track. He stood in the roadway beside his beautiful horse with the reins over his arm, no ignoble figure. Even Sybil unwillingly admitted that his looks were in his favour. She knew him sufficiently to make it impossible for her to pass him unnoticed, especially when he was avowedly waiting for the purpose of having some speech with her.

He raised his cap, and advanced to meet her, holding out his hand. From a distance he had admired her exceedingly, and a very bold project had taken root in his mind.

"Good afternoon, Miss de Castro," he said politely. "I am on my way to Fintry, to pay my respects to your mother. Do you think she will see me?"

An immense surprise gathered in the girl's eyes.

"I cannot tell. One never knows what my mother will do, Mr. Weir."

"May I walk beside you up to the house then, to discover for myself?"

Sybil's sweet face flushed slightly, and she smiled.

"I suppose you may, there is nothing to prevent you, Mr. Weir."

The prospect in no way appalled her. His manner was entirely respectful and pleasant, and speech with him partook of the nature of forbidden fruit. She had tired somewhat of the monotony of life at Fintry; even Bilbao, with its sordid memories, seemed lively in comparison. She was sufficiently a daughter of the South to long at times for the sunny skies, the movement and life of her native land. The two dull women, her mother and Helen Maitland, entirely occupied with their own grey thoughts, sometimes forgot the young life about them which needed fostering care. To Isabel herself the rest of the new life was still sweet, and she had taken of it to the full. Thankful to have bread for herself and her children, to be removed from actual sordid care, she was apt to be careless of other things. The boy needed no anxious watching, and Sybil's apparent contentment had deceived her. Also David Maitland was far away.

Weir eyed the beautiful fresh face beside him, and wondered what would be the proper cue to take. Everything might depend on the impression made in the next few minutes.

"I hope you have got comfortably settled at Fintry," he said kindly. "I have often wished to ride over and inquire, but, truth to tell, I am afraid even now. Mine is not a particularly enviable position, Miss de Castro."

"Are you, then, not happy at Penninghame? We have thought you had everything in the world you could desire. My mothers thinks that to live at Penninghame is sufficient to make any one happy. She would be surprised if she could hear you now."

"Does she still look upon me as an unprincipled villain, who came from the Cape for the sole purpose of stealing that place?" he asked, with an admirable assumption of humility. "I have not got bare justice, Miss Sybil, and I am glad of this opportunity of trying to clear myself in your eyes at least."

"Well, what is it you would say?" she asked, in a voice of the liveliest interest.

"You have doubtless heard only one side of the story. Let me tell you the other," he continued. "I was working in an obscure position, it is true, but honourably enough, in Cape Town, when your grandfather wrote to ask me to come home for an indefinite period. He told me even in that letter that his idea was, if I was fortunate enough to please him, that he would make me his heir. Naturally I accepted such an offer, and came off at once."

"Naturally you would," she assented, struck by this fresh presentation of facts whose outline was not only familiar to her, but the burden of every day's tale.

"I gave up a certainty, a poor certainty of course, but still in my employment I might have risen to a fairly good position, and I came here to wait upon the whims and vagaries of an ailing old man."

" It could not have been very pleasant," said Sybil unexpectedly. " I don't like sick people. I must be dreadfully unsympathetic, but I can't help it."

" You are too bright and—and beautiful," he said, with a slight hesitation, not certain how this broad compliment might be received. " And I don't wonder at it at all."

" Had you no people out there in South Africa ? " she asked suddenly.

His face flushed at the question, only she was not a particularly observant person, nor at the moment on the outlook for tokens of confusion.

" I have a brother and sister. They will be coming home presently I expect. The truth is, I am waiting till this horrible lawsuit is settled, and then I thought I'd go out and fetch them."

" A brother and a sister ! How very curious ! Does my mother know you have a brother and sister ? "

" I don't know I am sure. I fancy not. Your grandfather knew, and we often talked about them ; he knew that I would bring them home."

Sybil gazed contemplatively into space.

" Everything sounds quite different when you are talking, and even I begin to think you might be badly used," she said unexpectedly. " Anyhow, I think it quite stupid to have this law case. Everybody is certain mamma will lose, and we are really very comfortable where we are. It doesn't matter a fig to me who has Penninghame, only mamma and Frank are mad about it."

" It is because I, too, am certain that your mother will lose her case that I am here to-day, Miss Sybil."

" Are you going to talk to her about it ? " asked Sybil, almost in awe. " Aren't you afraid ? She thinks you are quite a dreadful person."

" I know that. I saw it in her face last Sunday in church, and I know she thought I had no business there."

" She was certainly surprised to see you ; we all were. We thought you a very different kind of person."

" Perhaps I may be less black than I am painted, Miss Sybil," he said, with a side glance at her face. The witchery of the girl was cast about him like a spell, he who had seldom given a thought to another was being forced to his knees. That hour made a revolution in the whole tenor of Anthony's Weir's life.

" I am going to try to justify myself to your mother," he said steadily. " After all we are kin to one another, and ought to be friends. I would rather give up the whole affair than that we should live as we do. In the same parish, a stone's throw from one another, and not even on speaking terms, it is a world's wonder."

" Will you say all this to my mother ? " she asked, her bright eyes wide with the excitement of the moment. There was something in the courage of the idea which pleased her. She regarded Weir with an increasing favour.

" That is my errand to-day, but if you would stand by me, or at least be as amiable, and as just as you are now," he hastened to add, seeing the slight pucker in her brow, " it would be a tremendous help ; you see, I am only one against three—or four, rather ; I suppose Miss Maitland is still with you ? "

" Oh, yes, she will stay always I think, at least until David comes back."

" David ! Surely he has the privilege of unusual intimacy when you call him by his Christian name so familiarly," he said involuntarily, trespassing once more the bounds justified by his very slight acquaintance with her he addressed and those of whom he spoke.

"We all love David," she said, as if surprised at his question. "Sometimes I am afraid of mamma. You see, she has suffered so much, and Penninghame is the whole passion of her life. Penninghame and Frank; sometimes even I feel myself on the outside."

"I have seen it before," he said, trying to hide his satisfaction at this unexpected bit of confidence. "It is the failing of many mothers. I suffered it myself. Although I was the elder, my sister was always preferred. It makes one bitter at times."

"Oh, I am not bitter. I understand, you see, why it is, and even I am not a Learmonth. I am like my father, and because of it sometimes I think my mother will never love me as she loves Frank."

"It is a horrible injustice. We can sympathise with one another, Miss Sybil," he said, so sincerely and kindly that her heart suddenly warmed to him. She had a heart quick to feel for injustice, perhaps because she had seen so much of it in her short life.

"I hope mamma will be kind to you," she said simply. "As for Miss Maitland, she is so changed. It was a most terrible thing, and for her it seems to grow more terrible. Have you ever known a mystery so strange, and do you believe that the poor old man is really at the bottom of the pool? Sometimes Frank and I walk that way and peer into it. Mamma has forbidden us to go into Penninghame woods, but sometimes we cut across the corner just there; it fascinates us."

"You are welcome to the whole of Penninghame grounds, Miss Sybil, but why choose that particular place? I am thinking of making drastic changes, destroying that part of the wood and abolishing the pool," he said, and his voice had scarce a tremor. He had schooled himself so long in the part that he was well-nigh perfect.

"Oh, we hope you won't do that; it is such a mysterious place, it would take away half the charm of Penninghame woods, and every time we go that way, Frank and I are hoping that we shall see the thing that happened long ago; that it will have dried up suddenly, and we shall see its mysterious depths uncovered."

"It was only a superstition, Miss Sybil; such a thing never actually happened."

"Miss Maitland says it did; she read a little account of it to us from a diary her father used to keep, and if it happened once it will surely happen again. That is what we hope. Here we are; mamma sees us from the drawing-room window. How astonished she looks!"

CHAPTER XXVII

A CLEVER ACTOR

"For Heaven's sake, Helen, come and look here," cried Madame de Castro. "Can I believe the evidence of my own eyes?"

Helen made haste to the long window, and together they looked down upon the straight part of the avenue on which could be seen Anthony Weir leading his horse by Sybil's side.

"The colossal presumption of the man, and Sybil must be mad," cried the indignant mother. "What do you think of that picture?"

"It is extraordimary," Helen admitted, but her tone was absent. Her eyes were fixed with keenest scrutiny on Weir's face. Believing in her inmost soul that he only in the wide world possessed the key to the mystery of her father's disappearance, she felt a sudden and mad desire to charge him with it, to try and tear off the mask an bring justice home.

She had become so absolutely a person of one idea, her mind solely concentrated on all the unhappy and apparently unsolvable details of her father's death, that it dwarfed her conception of everything else. Isabel de Castro was a daily witness to the change in the girl who at the first moment of their meeting had been so different, so human, so capable and sympathetic.

"I will go down and see what this means," said Madame de Castro, and swept from the room. "I will teach Anthony Weir that there are some things he may not do in this world."

Helen did not follow. The man's face fascinated her; she continued to stand motionless by the windwow until the figures had been swallowed by the overhanging eaves of the porch. Then she began to pace to and fro the long, low room, with her hands folded before her, nervously interlacing, feeling some hidden excitement rising in her soul.

Madame de Castro swept down the stairs, and was at the inner door when the pair appeared outside. Anthony Weir, with a composure that was admirable, took off his cap once more and bent to the ground.

"I apologise for this intrustion, which, doubtless, you consider unwarrantable," he said, in his best manner. "I came for the purpose of asking a brief interview with you, and I was fortunate enough to meet Miss Sybil at the gate, and to have the privilege of walking with her to the house. May I beg that you will grant me a little of the courtesy she has extended to me?"

Madame de Castro was for the moment entirely taken aback. The man spoke with a dignity that could not be gainsaid. How could she tell that it was only part of his desperate game, one more ruse on the part of a clever and quite unscrupulous person to strengthen a position that had become intolerable? She had suffered indeed, and seen a good deal of human cupidity, but she was a very woman after all.

She looked at Sybil before she answered him.

"Go upstairs, Sybil. I will talk to you afterwards. Stay, first send some one to take the horse. Where is Braidwood?"

A page boy appeared through the baize-covered door, which shut off the servants' quarters, and at a motion from his mistress went out and led the horse away. Not until they were quite alone did she address herself to Weir.

Then her tone was cold as ice, her manner sufficient to freeze even the most cheerful assurance.

"I am at a loss to know what you can have to say to me, Mr. Weir," she said, "but since you are here, I will listen to you. Pray, come in here."

She opened the door of a small business room, into which she might have invited a tradesman or her bailiff for consultation, but where no friend would be asked to sit down. She did not invite Weir to sit, however. Closing the door she looked at him steadily, and will ill-concealed dislike.

"I hardly know how to begin, Madame de Castro," he said, confused by the steady gaze of the haughtiest eyes he had ever seen. "It seemed quite easy to explain the position to Miss Sybil."

"We will leave my daughter's name out of the question, if you please," she said stiffly. "You had no right even to address her. She is a total stranger to you, and incapable of judging. But go on."

He shifted from one foot to another and finally met her gaze once more.

"Madame de Castro, I have been thinking that before this case comes on next week, we ought to talk things over, and see whether we can't make any compromise."

She stared at him almost aghast, and her proud mouth trembled. For the moment she felt that she could have slain him with her tongue. But what she considered his colossal presumption fascinated her. She would hear what he had to say.

She was not altogether able, however, to command her voice. "I had better not speak out all that is in my mind," she said with difficulty. "I daresay you can guess part of it. I will pass over your presumption in coming here to offer me a compromise, and ask you what that compromise can possibly be."

"It has hardly taken shape," he answered, gaining confidence since he had her permission to speak. "But, as I said to your daughter, the spectacle of members of the same family living at daggers drawn, as we are, is not an edifying one, and something might be done to put things on a better footing."

"Members of one family; but we are not that!" she said, in quick resentment.

"Well, perhaps not exactly of one family, but, after all, my father was your father's cousin; we can't get away from that fact," he said steadily. "And the connection is no fault of mine. I can assure you, Madame de Castro, I have often regretted coming to Scotland. Had I known all I know now I should certainly have remained at the Cape."

"But you are not anxious to go back now?" she said, with suggestive emphasis on the adverb.

"That is as you think. As I explained to Miss Sybil, I left a certainty for an uncertainty at your father's request. I did not even ask a single question, but when his letter came, packed up and took the first boat. I submit that for that I'm am entitled to some consideration."

"You have had it," she said drily. "If you gave up a certainty, you have at least been well paid for it."

It was a rude speech, of which she was entirely conscious, but his manner somehow irritated her. And she felt vaguely that somehow he had the best of it.

"That may be, Madame de Castro," he answered cooly. "I came to Scotland knowing nothing about you or your children, and I would point out to you that the existence of these children seemed to be known to no one. Doubtless if your father had been aware of their existence, he might have acted differently. For his ignorance you alone are to blame."

"You would presume to censure my attitude towards my father, sir," she cried indignantly. "Have a care, you have no right to come here to insult me."

"Nothing could be further from my thoughts," he made answer quietly. "But plain speech seems to be the order of the day, and indeed it is better, since it will not leave us in the dark. Are you willing to listen to me any further?"

"You spoke of a compromise. This is a most extraordinary interview, but perhaps it would be better to understand one another before we part. What compromise can you have to suggest that I could entertain or accept for a moment?"

"It needs talking over," he said, in a lower voice. "The whole ground of our relationship might advantageously be gone over before we arrive at any conclusion. First, I would wish you to know that for Penninghame as a place I care nothing; in fact, the sooner I am out of it the better I shall be pleased. I suppose there is a good deal in being born on the land. My environment up to now has been very different, and I don't feel at home here. In these circumstances, why should we not discuss the matter, and see whether we can't arrange for you or your son, if you prefer it, to have the place?"

She stared, not believing that she could hear aright.

"Well, you see, next week this case is to come on. As far as you are concerned, it is no earthly good. Even Shepherd, who acts for you, because he was too weak-minded to refuse, knows that the verdict is a foregone conclusion. And when you are made liable for the costs of the other side, as well as your own, where will you be?"

"It is a question for me entirely," she said, with a return of her first hauteur.

"That is beside the question," he said, with increasing boldness. "Look here, Madame, why should we let the lawyers part our substance among them, as they will do? Let us withdraw the whole thing from their hands."

"But what have you to offer me instead?" she asked breathlessly.

"Can't we divide the spoil in some way? Come to an arrangement. I don't want to stop here. I want to travel. If you are willing to pay me a substantial sum, I'll hand over Penninghame to your son, and not trouble you any more."

"But I have no money," she answered faintly, for the suggestion opened up an almost overwhelming prospect. "There is nothing but the revenue of this small place and the income that comes from my father's estate."

"Precisely; that's why I say you are very ill-advised to let the case go into Court. It'll cripple you for life, and, besides, it is not a very edifying spectacle this family squabbling laid before an admiring world. I don't pretend to very fine feelings, but, honestly, I'd rather forgo something than lend a hand at providing it. That's why I'm here to-day."

Isabel de Castro regarded him with a narrow scrutiny. The immensity of her surprise almost banished the former doubts. He spoke with every evidence of sincerity. The plea he urged was a perfectly reasonable one. He had little to gain by it. Perhaps, after all, in her wrath she had misjudged the man ; he might be less obnoxious than he had seemed.

Beholding in her wavering looks some guarantee of his success, he sought to press the matter home.

" If we could come to some arrangement, as I say, and you could have the place as a home, I should be the last person to grumble. The details could easily be settled later, between ourselves, for the less one has to do with the law tribe the better for all concerned. If we could agree upon a certain sum to be paid out of the estate, no difficult matter in your son's minority, the funds would accumulate. I should then clear out."

She continued to regard him with a steadfast, wondering look.

" I am trying to grasp this proposition that you have made and to understand your motive."

" My motive ! I thought I had explained it," he said, with a slight weariness such as one might adopt towards an uncomprehending child. " I am not beloved in this place, but regarded as the proud usurper or something of that sort. So far as the usurping business is concerned, my conscience is quite easy, but I don't care for the atmosphere ; do you understand ? And for that reason I have pocketed the insults you heaped on me the last time we met, and have come to see whether we couldn't come to some more amicable arrangement. What do you say ? "

" It would need some thinking over," she said quietly. " Meantime I apologise for what I have said about you and for the insults of which you speak. Perhaps, had you been in my place, you would not have been more restrained."

" I shouldn't," he said frankly. " I would have gone much further. Believe me, Madame de Castro, that though I appeared a monster to you, I did not feel like one. But it was obviously impossible to attempt any justification or explanation then ; you were in no mood to receive it. I want to avoid this lawsuit, convinced that after it is over you at least will be left practically penniless."

" How long will you give me to consider this extraordinary and unlooked-for proposal, and to take advice upon it."

At the latter part of her sentence he winced.

" As long as you wish to think over it, as long as time will permit with the Law Courts in view ; but as to advice—" He shrugged his shoulders. " To whom, may I ask, would you go for this advice ? "

CHAPTER XXVIII

OUTSIDE THE PALE

SHE hesitated a moment before she answered him.

"My advisers would naturally be my lawyer, Mr. Shepherd, my old friend Doctor Jeffrey, and Mr. David Maitland."

"Exactly; these men are all hostile to me, Jeffrey and Maitland specially so, doubtless on your account. Tell me, Madame de Castro, has Doctor Jeffrey ever in conversation with you accused me of using undue pressure to your father? Did he see anything at Penninghame during his attendance while he was ill to justify him in accusing me of coercion?"

"No," she answered candidly. "He does not like you, but he has never said anything of the kind, because I have repeatedly asked him. The one who is most bitter against you is my father's old servant, Braidwood."

"Precisely," said Weir, with a careful inflection in his voice. "And the explanation of that is so simple that a child might read it. Braidwood was jealous of his own influence and power. I found him paramount, a law to himself and the rest of the household. Naturally, seeing how poorly your father's interests were being looked after—the waste in the house, the thousand and one discrepancies which none would have detected and resented quicker than you would have done—I tried to remedy them. And because in some few minor matters I got my uncle's ear, Braidwood resented it, and abused me accordingly."

Isabel de Castro remained silent; these were facts she could not deny.

"Then in some extraordinary way," said Weir, with conspicuous boldness, "he has chosen to connect me with his niece's disappearance. For ought I know he may even accuse me of Mr. Maitland's disappearance likewise. There is no limit to Braidwood's imagination, or to my enormity in his sight."

Bit by bit the ground seemed to slip beneath the feet of the woman listening to him. The frankness with which he recognised the charges that had been brought against him was staggering. Surely only an honest man could dare to stand up with such words on his lips.

"I will not deny," she said at last, "that all these things have been laid to your charge."

"Madame, I have been perfectly aware of it, but, secure in my own innocence, I only waited to live them down. I begin to think that the public eye is open—at least, I am no longer so utterly ostracised. This village tittle-tattle and provincial amenity are very amusing and instructive to one who has lived a cosmopolitan life as I have done."

Never was his consumate cleverness more strikingly demonstrated than in this skilful touch. To be called provincial by the man she had despised and hated lowered Isabel de Castro in her own self-esteem.

"You have entirely altered my point of view, Mr. Weir," she said, looking beyond him across the sunny breadth of the park. "But as I said, I must have time to think over the matter carefully. Can you come here again to-morrow or next day?"

" At any time you may appoint. I am an idle man, and while in no special haste to rush the thing, it would ease my mind to feel certain that it would be settled out of Court."

" I thank you for the consideration you have shown to me to-day," she said, with the unwilling air of one forced to an unexpected admission. " I will expect you unless you hear from me further to-morrow about the same hour."

" Thank you. I shall await your commands."

He did not offer his hand, but held open the door for her to pass out before him. Instead of leaving him in the hall she walked with him to the outer door, then suddenly she remembered his horse.

" Let me ring for your horse. I had forgotten," she said quickly.

" Pray don't trouble," he said politely. " I can doubtless find my way to the stable."

" Certainly not; it shall be brought to you. Won't you sit down till then? It is comfortable here. We use the hall a great deal; it is very roomy for a small house."

Her tone had entirely changed; she spoke to him now with the friendliness of one who would make amends for some past injustice. Looking on her beautiful face, on which was set the seal of eternal sadness, he felt a passing qualm. She was not of his order or his world. Never had he felt himself more aloof than at that moment, when her friendly look would have bridged the impassable gulf. He had succeeded beyond his wildest dreams, but after all what had he profited? Only complicated an affair which was already beyond his power to unravel or control. Almost he could have wished she had received him differently or not at all. Then he could have pursued his relentless way without one pitying pang to deter him.

" Tell me," she said suddenly, as she leaned her arm on the mantelshelf, with the point of her dainty shoe on the polished steel of the fender, where the firelight cast its ruddy glow, " what do you think of this inexplicable affair of Mr. Maitland?"

" I have held the same theory from the first," he answered, with admirable coolness. " I think that for some reason or another he found it expedient to disappear. Such occurrences are by no means uncommon in these modern days; we are constantly hearing of them."

" But all who knew him, both intimately and otherwise, say it is impossible. His son and daughter say there was nothing to conceal. It is a theory difficult to accept. I believe myself he is at the bottom of the pool."

" Then the mystery must remain hidden with the other mysteries for which the place has been responsible," he said, with a slight shrug of the shoulders. " Do you believe these superstitions about it, Madame?"

" I do, but then I am, as you say, native to the soil. Almost every old house in Scotland has some such superstition attached. Some day perhaps, when we least expect it, the pool will lay bare its secret to the world."

At the moment the sound of approaching hoofs relieved what was for Weir an undoubted strain. The horse appeared at the steps, and he took his switch and gloves from the hall table and prepared to depart. She crossed to the outer door, and there, to his surprise, offered her hand. At this his face flushed with what was really an honest shame. She took it for modesty, and still further reproached herself.

" I repeat I regret that I have misjudged you, Mr. Weir," she said kindly.

"I shall give your suggestion the most serious consideration, and look forward to our next meeting."

He murmured a word of almost inarticulate thanks, and made haste to get into the open air. He saw that she was beginning to trust him, and trust from the woman he had so cruelly wronged was more intolerable than her dislike and contempt. He mounted, took off his cap in farewell, and rode quickly away. His face wore a strange expression when he was relieved from the scrutiny of her eyes. It was the expression of a man who had had a somewhat painful awakening. He had acted that day upon a sudden impulse, which had come whence he knew not. And after the first moment of doubt he had been received frankly on the ground of common honesty and fair dealing. She with all her pride had even stooped to apologise for having misjudged him. He could have laughed aloud.

Mingling with the irony of his thoughts was a thread of inextinguishable and keen regret. He knew himself in truth to be outside the pale of decent folk. Had Isabel de Castro been able to obtain even one glimpse into his innermost being she would have fled from him as from a plague. But she had accepted him for what he had that day pretended to be, not for what he was. For absolutely the first time in his life he was overwhelmed with a sense of honest shame. For their sakes he could have wished himself all he pretended to be.

He was conscious of a sense of relief that he had not seen Braidwood. That shrewd old man had never once departed from his first expressed opinion regarding the interloper from over the sea. To him he traced all the ill that had fallen in the latter days upon the old house he loved. Braidwood was told by the page boy who had been with his mistress, and just as he rode away he came into the hall looking dumbfoundered. Madame de Castro saw him as she was ascending the stairs, and turned back for a word with him.

"I have had Mr. Weir here this afternoon for quite half an hour, Braidwood."

"What did he want, ma'am?" asked Braidwood, and his face wore a look of actual alarm.

"I can't give you the particulars just yet, Braidwood, but I believe that we have been painting him blacker than we need have done. He behaved to me to-day with conspicuous generosity and consideration."

"Eh, michty, it's for his ain ends, Miss Isabel!" said the old man tremblingly. "Dinna you believe a word he says."

"You are too prejudiced, Braidwood. By and by, perhaps, you will change your mind, as I have been obliged to do. After all, actions speak more convincingly than words."

"Ay, they dae that, Miss Isabel; and what has Anthony Weir ever dune that could gie folk confidence or win their respect?"

"I am not at liberty to speak to-day, Braidwood; but perhaps this horrible lawsuit may be averted, and we might even get back to Penninghame," she said, and so passed on, leaving the old man in a state of abject bewilderment.

Uppermost in his mind were terror and anxiety regarding any dealings his mistress might have with Anthony Weir. His distrust and aversion to him were qualities too deeply rooted to be swept aside by every wind that blew.

When Madame de Castro entered the drawing-room Sybil ran to meet her.

"You did not ask Mr. Weir up to tea, mamma. I was hoping you would; but look at Helen! she is perfectly horrified at the suggestion."

Helen had been very uneasy throughout the interview, and had been puzzling herself as to its purport. She turned to her friend with ill-concealed anxiety.

"How could you see him, Isabel; what could he possibly have to say that you could wish to hear?"

Madame de Castro closed the door, and came forward to the fireplace. A little bright spot was burning on either cheek, and her eyes had an unusual light in them.

"I have had a most extraordinary interview," she said, in a musing voice. "Even yet I can't quite believe that it has actually taken place."

"Mamma, did you like him better?" asked Sybil eagerly. "I have been telling Helen that he talked quite nicely to me, but she refuses to believe me."

"The child is right, Helen. Let me tell you what he said."

She went over the chief points of the interview quietly, and they listened in silence. But no change came upon Helen's face. She had greatly altered in the last month. Her face now wore a set, hard expression, her eyes had a glitter in them which told something of the unrest within.

"You were not taken in with this specious talk, Madame?" she said quietly. "Nothing, not even an angel from heaven would convince me that Anthony Weir could be capable of such generosity. He has some end of his own to serve."

"No, no, Helen. If only you could hear him talk. I felt quite sorry for him to-day," cried Sybil. "I only wish you could hear him. I am sure he would convince even you."

Helen, only unbelieving, shook her head.

"I must try and see Doctor Jeffrey between this and to-morrow afternoon," said Isabel. "If only David could be got as easily I should like to have had his advice. But David is so far away."

"Is Mr. Weir coming back to-morrow afternoon, mamma?" asked Sybil, with the liveliest interest. "I shall be quite pleased to see him again."

Helen looked at the girl's bright face with a sudden dull resentment. Yes, David was very far away.

CHAPTER XXIX

THE TRUSTED FRIEND

TEA over, Madame de Castro ordered the unambitious cart, which was the only vehicle in the Fintry stableyard, and drove alone to Whitekirk.

The grey dark was beginning to fall when she stopped at the doctor's house. He had not long come in from his round, and after a belated dinner was enjoying a pipe by his fireside. When her name was brought to him he was on his feet in a moment, all his weariness forgotten. These were not very good days for Wallace Jeffrey; raking the ashes of a dead past is but sorry work. The family at Fintry was a distinctly disturbing element in his life.

He wondered what her errand could be since Sybil had much improved under his care, and he was no longer in attendance. He had resolved to limit his visits to Fintry strictly to professional attendance, deeming that best for his comfort.

She was standing by the pony's head at the kerb, and at once he took the reins.

"Pray step inside, Madame, and I will send some one to take charge of your trap. Why did you drive alone?"

"There was nobody convenient. I did not want to bring Frank, and I was in a hurry."

"Nothing wrong, I hope?"

"Oh, no, nothing. I want your advice, that's all."

She crossed the threshold of the old house for the first time since the great changes. As she did so a sigh fell from her lips. Its orderly silence smote her with a reminiscent pain.

Once it had been a happy family house ringing with the stir and movement of gay young life. Now where were they? All gone, scattered to the four winds of heaven. Some grown grey and sad with the sorrows of life, even as she. She needed none to guide her. She was in the little room, which had been a doctor's sanctum from time immemorial, when Jeffrey joined her.

"The atmosphere is bad here. I was at my pipe, you see, the only one I now permit myself in the day. Come to the other room."

"No, I will stay here if you don't mind. Oh, how this house is changed, or is the change in me? Don't you feel oppressed by its stillness?"

"Sometimes, but it has come upon me gradually, and perhaps also I am getting to that stage in life when quiet is the natural environment."

"Nonsense, you look younger than ever," she said, with a slightly playful touch. "Yes, thank you, I will sit down. It was your father's chair. How he used to lecture me from it! Will you lecture me, I wonder, too?"

"I should not presume," he answered smiling, and entering slightly into her gayer mood.

"Coming in here one is instantly taken back over the melancholy bridge of the years, but perhaps you are busy; I must not take up your time too much. Tell me, why have you left off coming to Fintry, making it necessary for me to seek you here?"

" Miss Sybil is better," he answered a trifle formally. " It is needless to multiply visits."

" Professional ones, perhaps, but that sin was never laid to the charge of any Jeffrey. We need you as a friend at Fintry. Why is it that you will not come ? "

" I will come when you want me gladly," he answered, not looking at her. " But I am a busy man with little leisure, and often when it comes, too tired to enjoy it or to inflict my weariness on others. But you will find me ready always when you need me. What can I do for you to-day ? "

She looked him straight in the face, and was silent a moment. Somehow she felt the difference between him and the man who had called on her that afternoon. Here was right thinking, just dealing, true friendship, love of all that was honest and of good report ; what a tower of strength to any woman, most of all to one so forlorn as she !

" I had a visit this afternoon, doctor, from Anthony Weir."

" No ! Almost impossible I should say. What did he want ? "

" Exactly what my good friend Helen asked after he had gone. He came to offer what he called a compromise."

Jeffrey sat down opposite to her, and looked straight at her face, betraying the keenest interest.

" What kind of a compromise ? "

" Well, he is anxious to prevent the case coming on next week."

" Why ? The general opinion is that he will win."

" Yes, and he thinks so himself. It is on my account that he would prevent it."

The doctor shook his head.

" I should very much doubt the sincerity of his motive, Madame ; but what did he say ? "

She told him the substance of their talk, and he listened attentively without making a single remark.

" It sounds all right, and coming from any one except Anthony Weir I should call it a most generous and considerate offer. You must see Shepherd before you decide anything."

" Yes, I will go to Edinburgh in the morning ; but what do you say about it ? "

" I prefer not to say. I am prejudiced. I don't like the man. Why I can't tell you. He is no gentleman to begin with, and—and well really I have no ground except general suspicion and distrust," he added frankly.

" Precisely where we all are. It is just possible, however, that we may be misjudging him."

" It may be, but do you remember that painful scene on the day of your father's funeral. I consider that his behaviour that day was most callous."

" He was in a trying position too," she reminded him. " Every man's hand against him. Perhaps it was all a bit of bravado."

" It was certainly not in keeping with his present offer. He has favourably impressed you evidently, and you are inclined to consider his proposal."

" I am. I expressed my regret even for having treated him so badly. He struck me as being perfectly sincere. Indeed, he must have been. What had he to gain by such a proposal ? Nothing, but something to lose."

" That's true," said the doctor, stroking his chin reflectively. " I am obliged to treat it as a conundrum, and give it up."

" Then you won't advise me ? "

"Whether to accept or reject? No, you must consult Shepherd. If Weir can satisfy him regarding the legal aspect of things, I should then say accept by all means."

"It would make a wonderful difference to me," she said frankly. "Especially since every one, even Shepherd, seems convinced that we shall lose our case."

He looked at her with a sudden touch of compassion. She was so much a woman, so incapable, after all her hard experience, of dealing with hard facts. His own opinion was that Weir for some end of his own had succeeded in working on her feelings. But he could not say so in plain words.

"Why do you look at me so oddly?" she asked, struck by his expression.

"Did I look oddly? A man may think many things he dare not express," he answered lightly. "If you like, I will go to Penninghame this evening, and see whether any light can be thrown on the matter."

"Will you? That would be truly kind. I was afraid to suggest it, but it was in my mind. Did you guess it?"

"Perhaps," he answered, smiling a little. "Your eyes have a wonderful compelling power about them. But don't for a moment imagine that he will talk with any frankness to me. Still it is my business to dissect," he added, faintly ironical. "I have not spoken to him since the funeral day. Dunn, of Rosford, now attends to the Penninghame ailments. But I am not afraid of being ill received, and as a human document he would seriously interest me."

"How oddly you put things! And when can I see you to hear the result of your interview?"

"Provided always he grants me one; well, if it is not too late, I'll come round by Fintry afterwards. If I don't turn up by nine, you will know either that I have not seen Mr. Weir, or that there is nothing to relate."

She thanked him and rose to go.

"You always help me somehow," she said gratefully. "Even when your tongue is declining to advise, your heart is planning some comfort."

"Hush!" he said, and his voice had a somewhat stern ring in it. "Miss Sybil keeps better I hope," he added hurriedly, and with a suspicion of confusion.

"Oh, yes, quite well and brighter too. I wish I could say the same of Helen. What is to become of her, Doctor Jeffrey, if she goes on as she is doing? There seems to be such a strain. She is getting to look like it now; sometimes her eyes are positively alarming to look at, and she sleeps so little. I hear her pacing her room at all hours of the night."

"I expect there will be a breakdown. It was a thousand pities that she did not go to Spain with her brother. Perhaps it is bad for your young people to have her always there. It is an atmosphere of tragedy, of course."

"Oh, they don't mind that, and they are very fond of her, Frank especially. Besides, can we ever forget her kindness to us when we came friendless to Edinburgh? Never. And now that the house is let she has no home. She must remain at Fintry as long as she chooses."

He could not gainsay the reasonableness of her view, and as he walked out with her to the street he wondered casually what the next three months would bring forth.

Immediately she had gone, he had his horse round, and rode off to Penninghame, arriving just as the laird had risen from the dinner-table. He dined at half-past six always, having upset most of the household arrangements, and ordered new ones to suit himself. A young smart butler had taken the place of Braidwood, one who believed implicitly in his master, and had no hesitation in calling him a good one.

The doctor was ushered into the library, and there Weir, slightly apprehensive, came to him at once. But there was no sign of hesitation or anxiety about him as he entered the room, and gave him a quite courteous good-evening.

"Good evening, Mr. Weir, I can see you are at a loss to understand this visit. I can soon enlighten you. I am here on behalf of Madame de Castro. I have just seen her, and heard of your visit to Fintry this afternoon."

"She has lost no time. She told me she would consult you, though I pointed out to her that I would be unlikely to receive just consideration from any of the advisers she named. But that is by the way. Well, what have you to say?"

"The proposal you made to her is a generous one. Her advisers would all be anxious for her to accept it if they could be satisfied as to the motive."

"The motive! What has that to do with it? And, anyhow, it is between Madame de Castro and myself. I explained my motive to her, and she understood."

The doctor looked round vaguely, distinctly nonplussed. He was dealing with shadowy unrealities, with phrases he could not substantiate or even justify. But the place seemed full of shadows; never had he distrusted Anthony Weir more thoroughly than at that moment.

"Madame de Castro is quite alone in the world, and she has already suffered beyond the common. Those who are interested in her future are anxious to safeguard her as much as possible. Unfortunately, the qualities which induced her to make shipwreck of her life before are still to the fore. She is impulsive, and apt to form hasty judgment, also very determined on any certain course of action which commends itself to her at the moment. The whole situation is bristling with difficulty of the most acute kind. Are you really willing to forgo your rights in this place for her sake, and if so, what do you gain by it?"

CHAPTER XXX

THE FACE IN THE NIGHT

"I DON'T admit your right to question me, Doctor Jeffrey. You have been no friend of mine since I had the misfortune to come to Penninghame," Weir said slowly. "But supposing you are right, and that I do want to forgo my rights for Madame de Castro, what then?"

Jeffrey hesitated a moment.

"It would be a generous act," he said at last, "and totally unexpected. Nothing you have done has prepared us for it."

Weir shrugged his shoulders, and gave a short laugh.

"You may be very wise, Doctor Jeffrey—you are so, I believe, in your own estimation—but you don't know everything. Since we are on the subject, will you tell me what I have gained by coming here? The place, yes, but of what use is it to me? No one has called upon me; they have put me outside the pale, most unjustly and iniquitously, and yet this has the reputation of being the most religious country in the world. What have I done? As I explained to Madame de Castro and her daughter, I gave up a certainty at the Cape, and came here to please the whim of an old man. I did not force myself on him. I came by request, and did my best. He made no secret of his intention from the first to leave me the estate; you have yourself heard him repeatedly say his daughter should not have it, that he would part it first among strangers. Now he is gone, she is here, seeking to usurp my place. You don't like that point of view, but it is the true one. My character has been torn to shreds among you; I am accused of taking away Braidwood's niece, of killing old Maitland, of Heaven knows what. It's a nice, virtuous, charitable community. Can you wonder I am in haste to leave it? If you will have the truth, I may tell you for your delectation that if I had the power to sell the place outside, I should certainly not trouble Madame de Castro. You were present at the reading of the will; there was no clause in it forbidding an arrangement with her. I have already consulted my lawyers, and while they advise me strongly against it—in fact, I could see that they thought me a little touched in the head to think of forgoing my rights in such a manner—they admitted that it might be arranged."

Jeffrey listened in silence to this long speech.

"I see your point of view," he said coolly. "Well, I suppose there is no more to be said."

"Except that you are still hostile to me," suggested Weir. "As I said to Madame de Castro, so far as I am concerned, she is not happy in her advisers."

Jeffrey shrugged his shoulders.

"I do not presume to advise her. I am simply an old friend of the family. It is to Shepherd she must look for advice. It is a most complicated and difficult business. I don't envy any of those concerned in it."

"But at least you will not advise her against dealing with me, or against any arrangement which might have an issue such as I have indicated?"

Again the doctor's face wore that slightly incredulous look.

"I have said I will not advise. It would be too much responsibility, even too much danger; besides, Madame de Castro is not easily advised."

Weir slightly smiled.

"I agree with you. From the little I have seen of her, I should say she was a headstrong woman."

"Impulsive rather, that is why at such a crisis her interests will have to be carefully safeguarded."

"I see you don't trust me, but you may take my assurance that whatever else I may or may not have done, in this I am at least perfectly sincere."

"I will take your word for it," said the doctor unexpectedly. "And I hope for the sake of all concerned it may be possible to carry such an arrangement through. Affairs as they now are don't present an edifying spectacle to the world, and it is always a pity for a neighbourhood when one of its great houses is in trouble."

"A country where there are no 'great houses,' as you call them, is infinitely preferable in my estimation," said Weir drily.

"Perhaps from one point of view, but they will be established as the new countries go on. I could swear that even now there is an aristocracy, or rather a plutocracy, in South Africa, as exclusive, and ten times more conservative than anything we have here, and, shall I add, with a conspicuous lack of that sense of responsibility which establishes life on such a solid basis here."

"Perhaps you're right. Won't you sit down now, and take a cigar?"

Jeffrey shook his head.

Feeling as he did towards this man, he would not break his bread nor accept any hospitality whatever from his hands. Weir, not lacking in perception, comprehended his attitude perfectly, and again a strange wave of regret passed over him, and he longed with a passionate longing to be received freely in that inner circle which he affected to despise and belittle, but which had begun to represent the forbidden land for him. As for Jeffrey himself, he had been compelled to respect him. Since the first time they had met at Penninghame, he had pursued the same unwavering course, had come and gone quietly to the house, done his duty, and bowed his head to none. Also he had taken his dismissal as the medical attendant of the old house without so much as a backward glance.

"I wish you'd come back to your old post," Weir said suddenly, as they walked towards the door.

"Why?" asked Jeffrey, with a faint inscrutable smile.

"Oh, it would be the right thing. I find from the old books that your firm, or forebears, or whatever you call them, have always been medical attendants here. It seems a pity in a conservative country to make any change. I did so in a moment of pique. Won't you take my apology and come back?"

"It would not be fair to the other man," replied Jeffrey. "No, thank you: we'd better leave things as they are."

"You won't meet me then even a quarter of the way? Well, well: perhaps you, too, may live to change your mind."

He did not offer his hand at the door, fearful lest it should be refused, but Jeffrey would not have been guilty of such an insult without some more serious cause.

As he pondered the thing going out between the dark lines of trees he even wondered whether after all he had not been unduly prejudiced. He had never heard a man speak with more show of sincerity, and he was forced to admit that his point of view was an entirely reasonable one. He had certainly nothing to gain from the course of action he had apparently marked out for himself. Jeffrey, if a trifle hard and set in his own opinion, was a singularly just man, and the idea of having seriously misjudged a fellow-creature was not a particularly comforting one. "I must see Madame de Castro and talk it over—but not to-night. I'll sleep on it first," he said to himself, and, pausing, he fumbled for his pipe and matches. As he struck a light something brushed passed him in the darkness, and he heard the swish of a woman's skirts. He fancied something familiar in the outline of the figure and uttered a name aloud on chance.

"Is that you, Nancy?"

But there was no response, and, listening intently, he could not even hear the light tread of a retreating foot.

He must have made a mistake; doubtless it was one of the maids returning to the house after an evening out. And yet that odd sense of familiar nearness did not leave him, and his thoughts persistently returned to the girl whose disappearance was part of the mystery in which Penninghame continued to be enveloped.

Meanwhile the slight figure pursued its way towards the house. As she approached it more nearly she swerved a little, and cut through the shrubbery which grew thickly at the gable end. A little path which only familiar feet could have found so unerringly on a night of such inky darkness, led her to the back of the house. The inner portion of the library only was lighted, three long shafts of brightness lay athwart the broad terrace, and cast reflecting shadows on the grass beyond.

There were many double rooms in Penninghame, the idea having been a craze with one of the lairds, who had a mania for light and air, and had knocked down many partitions to obtain it. In the late laird's time, however, all these double rooms had been divided by heavy curtains. He hated large rooms, and in his later years never used them, complaining bitterly of their draughts and shadows.

The figure stood a little back on the terrace for a moment, as if undecided how to act. Presently, however, some courage seemed to come to her, and she drew nearer somewhat boldly.

The blinds were only partially drawn, and through the parting of the long lace curtains she could obtain a pretty fair view of the interior. It was indeed quite sufficient for her purpose, which was to learn whether the new laird was within and alone.

He was sitting at the table with his face towards the window, a large volume open before him. It seemed to be a book of plans, and she could see him trace some lines with a silver pencil on the margin of the pages.

She pressed her face against the pane where the open space was widest, and with her finger made that peculiar squeaking sound on the glass which can break so alarmingly upon a perfect solitude.

He rose with a nervous start, and came forward, with quick decision sweeping aside the intervening curtains. And there he saw a face, the one he least desired to see, the face of Nancy Nicolson!

CHAPTER XXXI

AT BAY

He dropped the curtain, and with one stride towards the door turned the key in the lock. Then he came back, opened the side of the French window and motioned her in. She stepped across the threshold quite quietly, evidently appreciating his desire for silence and secrecy. He drew the curtains close, so that no one could see him from without, and then faced her.

" In God's name ! " he said hoarsely, " what are you doing here ? "

" I came," she answered doggedly, " because I couldna bide in London ony longer."

" But how did you get here ? Where did you get the money ? "

" I had some. I dinna spend much, and my landlady gied me the rest."

" Your landlady ! Then you have been speaking to her ? "

" Yes. Hoo could I live speaking to naebody ? Ye dinna ken what ye are sayin'. I'm no gaun to dae it ony longer."

She sat down, and for the first time he observed the whiteness of her face. Poor Nancy was no longer the rosy-cheeked, bright-eyed girl she had been. Experience of life was beginning to tell. Weir, though angry beyond expression, and at his wits' end, could not bear to see her so spent. He stepped across to one of the cabinet doors and took from thence some whisky and a box of biscuits.

" Drink this. Not a word till you have taken something. You have acted in a way I can hardly forgive, but there, you need something before we can talk."

She did not feel hungry, but only faint and ill. Something told her she had better eat and drink before they spoke another word. For she had come to assert her rights as mistress of Penninghame, and the battle might be long.

" Where did you come from just now ? How long have you been in Scotland ? "

" I left London this morning," she answered, the colour beginning to return to her pale cheek. " I got out at Porth Junction. The train stopped there for Lord Kilravock. Syne I walked."

" You look dead beat. You are mad, Nancy ; you should do as you are bid. Nothing but misery results when you take the law into your own hands."

He tried to speak kindly. He had perception enough to see that Nancy was for him in a somewhat dangerous mood. She had arrived at a moment the most inopportune, but she would require very careful dealing unless he wished disaster to ensue.

" I'm tired of doing as I'm bid," she answered dully. " What way should I live in dingy lodgings whaur I ken naebody an' you here ? Mrs. Laurence telt me I should show mair spunk, and stand up for my richts. I'm o' that mind too."

" Nancy, I suppose you told this woman the whole story ? "

" No me ; no even oor names. I'm no a perfeck fule," she answered equably. " I telt her jist as muckle as I thocht fit, and askit her what she wad dae if she was me. She disna even ken it's Scotland where you live. So I'm here."

" And, now you're here, what are you going to do ? "

" Stop," she answered laconically.

" It's impossible, Nancy, quite impossible. You are mad to suggest it ! " he said, and his face flushed, his eyes glittered ominously.

Never in the whole course of his scheming life had he been in such a desperate fix. She was only a little woman, an insignificant, ignorant country wench, but in her and through her he beheld his whole undoing. How he could have cursed, not only her, but the whole unspeakable folly that had led up to it. Her very ignorance and trustfulness were her strongest weapons. Had she possessed more knowledge of the world she would have guessed at the truth. But there she sat, quiet, apparently unobtrusive, but determined to have her rights.

It was a ghastly situation, requiring all his powers to cope with it.

" Have you forgotten what I said about the law case ? It comes on next week. It is certain that if it is known that I—I have married you the whole thing will go against me."

" I'm sure I'm no carin'," she replied. " Ye can work for me, I suppose, as ither men work for their wives."

Her assurance was colossal. Evidently she had gone over the whole ground, and fully made up her mind.

" It will be a horrible situation, even to-night for instance, if you insist on staying here. Think of the scandal in the house ! There are some of your old fellow-servants here."

" I'm no carin'. I'll shut their mooths if they say onything to me," she said stolidly, like one who had faced every contingency.

" They won't believe it, Nancy—that you are married to me. How can you expect it ? "

" They're no needin' to believe it unless they like. If they dinna like their new mistress they can gang."

She smiled a little, as if the prospect of a wholesale scatter of the household rather pleased her. That smile maddened Weir, and the old evil passions which for some weeks had been in abeyance began to clamour for the mastery. For less men had laid crime upon their souls.

When he thought of how completely he was in this creature's power he could in a frenzy of wrath have crushed the life out of her.

There was only one way out—the way of flattery and persuasion was the only course open to him, if he would gain a little time to make further arrangements. He rapidly reviewed the whole matter in his mind, and decided to take her so far at least into his confidence.

" Look here, Nancy, will you listen to me for a few moments and give me your whole attention ? "

" Oh, yes," she replied, " as long as ye like. I'm in nae hurry."

" We are trying to make a new arrangement. The issue of the case in the Courts next week is so uncertain that we have thought it might be better to make a private compromise."

" What's that ? "

" A sort of private arrangement to settle it all among ourselves. I have seen Madame de Castro to-day."

" But what has that to dae wi' me ? " asked Nancy, with a slight air of fatigue.

" Everything, since what concerns me must concern you," he replied, setting his teeth to prevent his temper getting the better of him.

" I'm trying to dispose of Penninghame privately to Madame de Castro. Then, when we get the money, you and I will be free to clear out from the place, from Scotland, in fact, and make a tour round the world to see everything worth seeing."

" I'd rather stop here," she answered stolidly. " I've seen enough of the world. I dinna think much o' it."

" You have seen nothing of it, my dear girl ; there speaks your ignorance again. Of course, I understand it's a little rough on you, but, after all, you are your own mistress, and have nobody to order you about."

" Bar you," she said somewhat tartly. " Eh, but there are worse things than Aunt Susan's sharp tongue."

He saw that her bravado was dying down, and that tears were perilously near her eyes. It relieved him ; he could work on that side of her feeling with more likelihood of success. Of the other Nancy he felt less sure.

" Look here, my dear," he said, with studied gentleness. " I know it is hard for you, but it's no bed of roses for me. They hate me, every man Jack of them, and woman too. I haven't the life of a dog among them. And neither would you. Nobody would come to see you here. This big dreary house would be nothing but a gaol."

" A gey an' comfortable gaol ! " she said, with a glance round. " I'll hae a shot at it, onyway."

" Well, you shall have, later, when things are arranged. To-morrow I am to see Madame de Castro again. Won't you wait quietly and say nothing for my sake until this little matter is settled ? "

" Oh, I can wait, but I'll wait here," she said, with the same stolid air.

" But you can't," he cried desperately. " I don't know what would happen if it were known, if it came suddenly on them like this. The whole matter would fall through."

" It wadna maitter. I'm here, and I'm gaun to bide. I cam' for the purpose."

" Then I'll go, this very night, too, Nancy, and I'll never come back. I swear it. I'll leave you to make a kirk or a mill of it, as they say here. They'll make short work of you in Penninghame, my lass. You had much better let me manage the thing in my own way."

She made no answer. Her blue eyes wandered round the room with a straight, somewhat vacant stare.

" Nancy," he said suddenly, " haven't I been kind to you ? "

" Oh, yes," she answered. " Naething to compleen o'."

" Won't you trust me a little further ? "

" No," she answered, a little unexpectedly, " I dinna think I wull."

" But why ? What have you to gain by behaving like this ? "

" I am your wife. I want to come here an' bide wi' you. I have come, and I'm gaun to stay."

" A wife promises to obey her husband. I say you can't stay here, Nancy, until things are settled."

" Then I'll gang to Fintry," she said drearily. " I canna live ony langer away from folks. Even my Uncle Braidwood and his sour looks wad be better."

" Braidwood would shut the door on you, Nancy ; he believes no good of you."

" Aunt Susan wadna. Besides, I'm Mrs. Anthony Weir. They canna kick me aboot as they like."

" They hate me so much that that plea wouldn't serve you, Nancy. I'd advise you not to try it."

"Well, I can bide here. I'm feelin' tired noo. It's a long walk frae Porth."

Weir took a turn across the floor. He was entirely at a loss what to do next. She sat there, aggravatingly quiet and determined, and the night was wearing late. Absently, he lifted a time-table from the further table, and turned to the trains, only to find that the last for Edinburgh left Porth in an hour and twenty minutes. Nancy must catch that train at all costs, if he should have to get her there by main force.

"Nancy, if you'll go to Edinburgh to-night, I'll promise you to come and fetch you home properly to-morrow or next day at the latest, when I've arranged and explained things."

"Ye're aye speaking aboot arranging and explainin'. I'm here. This is my hoose. I'm gaun to bide."

"Then I'll leave it never to come back. I'm sick of it anyhow. I'll go now, and you'll never see my face again."

He turned to the door. She rose up, and called him to come back.

"Look here, Anthony," she sat quietly still, but with an odd inflection in her voice that he had never heard before; "let me gang to Fintry, and bide quietly there or ye are ready. If I show Uncle Braidwood and Aunt Susan my marriage lines they'll be quite pleased to tak' me in and stand by me."

He shook his head.

"I won't do that. If you choose to act in complete opposition to me you can, but I swear to you that I will leave you to bear the whole brunt of everything, and that you'll never see my face again either in Scotland or anywhere else. They can take the place and burn it to the ground if they like for me; I don't want it, I don't need it, and I'm beastly sick of the whole ghastly business."

Nancy looked at him in affright, and began to waver. She knew him determined, and if he persisted in the course laid down where would she be? A wife, and yet no wife, left to the tender mercies of a censorious world, it was a black enough prospect.

"Well, I'm gang to Edinburgh for twa days, but nae longer," she said unwillingly. "But hoo am I to get there the nicht?"

His face cleared.

"That's my own reasonable, sensible girl. There's nothing I won't do for you when you are like that. It's your nature to be sweet and gentle, and when you are different it's been put into you by somebody else. Tell me, would you like to go back to the life of a servant again?"

"I never wull," she replied, with her head in the air.

"You would have no choice if I left you. I would go where you would never see or hear from me again. But I don't want to do that. It's as hard for me as for you this beastly secrecy, and all that. But it's nearly at an end. A few more days, a week at the outside, and you'll be up-sides with the best of them."

"Hoo am I to get to Edinburgh then?" she asked, cutting short his lover-like words.

"I'll drive you to Porth or even to Westerlea, which would be better still. Slip out the way you came, cut across the park, and meet me at the stile just beyond Lauder's old cottage. I won't be more than ten minutes."

He opened the long window, and Nancy once more stepped out into the darkness of the night.

CHAPTER XXXII

ADRIFT ONCE MORE

ANTHONY WEIR himself went to the stables, and, finding a lad there looking after a sick horse, helped him to get a light dogcart ready for the road.

"Where's Bill?" he asked, in a displeased tone of voice.

"Gane to Whitekirk, sir, for the vet.; he said you gied him leave."

"Never heard of it till this moment. Give the beast a bran mash, and tell them to leave her alone till I come back. I'm only going as far as Rosford. I shan't be gone more than an hour."

"Want me to come, sir, to haud the horse? I can be ready in a meenit," asked the lad, who had no fault to find with his master, but rather the reverse. The new laird was friendly disposed towards his servants, and seemed anxious even to stand well with them.

"No, I shan't need you. There will be no stopping. Light both the lamps; it's very dark."

The lad did as he was bid, and in a few seconds more the turn-out was quite ready.

"Don't let them touch the mare till I come back. If Bill brings the vet. with him, let him wait. I'll be back by half-past nine."

He jumped to his seat, took the reins, and went off like an arrow through the darkness. The soft wind caressed his cheek as he drove against it, and the sweet smell of spring seemed to rise up from the teeming earth. It was so dark that he could not see anything beyond the little circle cast by the carriage lamps, for which he felt thankful. There would be less chance of his companion being recognised. He felt by no means certain that he would find her at Lauder's cottage. A cold sweat broke over him at the thought that she might even then be speeding across the fields towards Fintry. But, before he came within sight of the ruined cottage where he had bidden her wait, he saw the movement of her figure in the roadway. He drew up without a word; she swung herself up to the high seat beside him.

"I haven't been long, have I? Meet any one, eh?"

"The minister, but I crept into the hedge, and he didna see me. If we're no in time, what then?"

"I'll drive you all the way in; but there's no fear, she'll get us there in time."

He gave the whip a suggestive flick about the mare's ears, and she gave a plunge forward.

"She's very fresh. Where would you like to go in Edinburgh? There's a quiet hotel in Cockburn Street, near the station. You'd better drop into that for the few days. It would be too late anyhow to go out to your old landlady."

"Oh, yes," said Nancy, "I wadna gang there."

"You may take my word for it, Nancy, I won't keep you waiting long," he said reassuringly. "I'll see Madame de Castro to-morrow, and then probably I may come on to Edinburgh, and tell you the result of the interview."

"Will you tell her about me?" asked Nancy stolidly.

"I'll see, probably I will," he answered, with admirable carelessness, though the suggestion appalled him. Suddenly Nancy turned to him with a little shiver.

"Eh, michty! It's dark here aboot! I never used to think aboot it. Have ye ever been in the wud since thon day?"

"Yes, often; they're always hovering about there—the police I mean. Only the other day I warned them that they were trespassing."

"They've never seen onything though?"

"No, but any day they may, one never knows, Nancy; that's why it would be better for us to get clear away from this neighbourhood. We're really not safe, even for a single day."

He spoke thus of a set purpose, to impress upon her the danger she was in, and also the fact that she would be most imprudent to attempt to act apart from him in any way. Nancy heard him in silence, but he felt her shiver at his side.

"I rue the day I ever came here," he said as he flicked the mare, and set her plunging forward again. "You have no idea what a pleasant life it is out there at the Cape—plenty of sunshine and liberty, everything people want; that's the country for my money."

"I wadna care for it," said Nancy stolidly. "I've seen England, an' Scotland's the country for me."

He understood the motive perfectly. It was a woman's natural vanity that was at the bottom of everything. To be a lady in her own right, to queen it where she had once served, was the acme of Nancy's ambition, the feverish dream with which she had tried to comfort many a dark hour. For now in her heart of hearts she bitterly rued the step she had taken; she longed, ay, with many tears, for the old sweet peaceful life, the very monotony of which now seemed the most desirable thing on earth. For it was a thorny way on which her faltering feet now sped, and none knew what a day might bring forth. Also she thought at times of a certain honest lad, who used to meet her when she went her errands to the village, and who, she felt, must be mourning her loss.

A silence fell upon them both then, and the only sound was the ring of the hoofs on the hard road. Soon the lights of Westerlea appeared twinkling in the near distance, and Weir, at least, heaved a sigh of inward relief.

"Here we are, and in good time," he said, as he drew out his watch and bent to the lamp to see the hour. "Have you any money, Nancy?"

"Seevin and sixpence."

"Dear me, I had no idea that you were so near the wind! I thought I had left you plenty. You must always write before you get so low."

"I had enough. I've nae way o' spendin' money."

"How much did you borrow from the landlady?"

"Thirty shillings."

"Well, first thing to-morrow morning send her a postal order, and, mind you say nothing about where you are, or give her any address. It is most important that she shouldn't know."

"I'll say naething; I'll jist send the money."

He handed her five sovereigns, which she slipped into the old-fashioned pocket under her skirt.

In two minutes more they were close to the lights of the tiny wayside station, and Weir drew up the mare rather sharply to let Nancy alight.

"I won't come any nearer; it's just possible some one may see me. Now, you know exactly what you're to do, Nancy?"

"Yes, I'm to gang to the Lennox Hotel in Cockburn Street, and bide there or you come or send."

"And say nothing to anybody."

"An' say naething to onybody," repeated Nancy, like a child conning a lesson.

"Good-night, then. I'm sorry, my dear, to let you go in the darkness like a thief, but there's no use putting the rope round our necks, is there? Keep your pecker up, and things will soon come right."

She nodded, and, without even a good-night, she darted across the little yard, and entered the dingy booking office.

Weir did not wait, but, turning the mare's head, at once drove off. By the time an inquisitive porter had sauntered out to see whence the sound of wheels came, he was lost in the darkness. He looked curiously at the girl, as she stood before the little window of the booking office, but she was a stranger, and not interesting. He went back to yawn over his copy of a newspaper, which had done duty as reading matter so long that he knew every line of it.

Nancy was a solitary passenger. She remained out on the platform, walking slowly up and down, pondering many things. She had alighted at Porth that night with the glad, almost triumphant, feeling that her wanderings would soon be over, and, lo! she was cast on the world again without a friend. Though dominated by the stronger will, whenever its influence was removed, distrust and dull resentment struggled for the mastery. It is certain that had the train been long delayed Nancy would have headed across the fields for Fintry, and the tale must have had a different end. But the signal was down, and in a moment the train came lumbering in, and Nancy climbed into a first-class compartment. In a sudden fit of extravagance, and feeling that it was due to her altered position, she had taken a first-class ticket, but the luxury did not afford her the smallest gratification. She sat down on the soft cushion listlessly, and, pressing her hot face against the cold glass, peered out to the platform to see whether any passengers had alighted.

Only one man, Sergeant Gunn, of Whitekirk, searching for a man concerned in a drunken brawl, and who was reported in lodging at Westerlea. He was in the rear end of the train, and had paused for a word with the stationmaster regarding his prey. The train was moving out rather quickly as he turned to walk forward. As it glided past him he caught a glimpse of Nancy's face. The next moment speed was up, and the train was through the tunnel with a shriek. He stood still a second in puzzled silence; then her identity flashed upon him all of a sudden. He ran back, and gripped the inoffensive stationmaster by the arm.

"You couldn't stop the train, I suppose, Sandy?"

Sandy was a slow person, and scratched his head.

"What for?"

"I've seen somebody I want particularly to get a word with."

"I canna noo or it gets to Penninghame; that wad be ower late."

"Rather. Did you observe anybody get on here?"

"A lassie. Looked like a dressmaker or something o' that sort; but she took a first-class ticket."

"Did you see her come?"

" To the station ? No one did. She was driven, Jamie said, but the machine didna wait."

" Did he recognise whose machine it was ? "

" No, it was doon the brae afore he gaed oot. It didna drive close up. Who are ye speirin' for noo ? "

" Oh, nobody," said the sergeant, with a disappointed look. An incomparable opportunity had passed him by, and he blamed himself prodigiously. If only he had not spoken to the stationmaster he would have seen her before the train started and had speech with her. And, after all, he could hardly have stopped the train and commanded her to alight. Against Nancy Nicolson he had no charge to bring. And if she were only going to Edinburgh she would come speedily within his grip. That very night he would write to headquarters and put them on her track. Meanwhile he tried to give his mind to the matter immediately in hand, but found it very difficult. The disappearance of Mr. Maitland was still lying heavily on the sergeant's mind, and he suffered from fits of depression over his defeat. But he had never altogether lost hope.

In ten minutes the train stopped at Penninghame Station, and quite regardless of consequences Nancy got up and stood at the window, and looked out upon the familiar place. It was now near ten, and the station consequently almost deserted. She did not see a single familiar face. For a moment the desire to get out was so strong that she could scarcely resist it. It was a long way to Fintry, but not so long that her willing feet could not bridge the distance. But would it bring her home ? Or would she only meet sour looks and harsh words, perhaps be turned adrift again in worse plight than she now was in ?

There was no delay with the late train. Anxiety for the day's work to be over sharpened the wits and hastened the steps of everybody concerned. It scarcely awaited for scheduled time, but with a little warning whistle was up and away again. Nancy sank back among her cushions once more, and, as the train passed under the old bridge, gave way to a burst of miserable tears.

CHAPTER XXXIII

THE JUDICIAL MIND

WILLIAM SHEPHERD, the lawyer, alighted at Penninghame Station next morning at half-past ten in obedience to a summons he had received from Madame de Castro. To his surprise the first person he observed on the platform was Helen Maitland. She came forward eagerly to meet him, and her greeting was most cordial.

"Madame de Castro does not really expect you before twelve. I came down on chance, hoping I might see you. There are so many things I want to say to you."

"I am more glad to see you than I can say," he answered, with a perfect sincerity. "And I am glad to see you looking so well."

She smiled a trifle sadly.

"Do I look well? I suppose I am well, though Doctor Jeffrey seems to think not; but I have walked across the fields from Fintry, and the air is very fresh. How are you all at home?"

"Well. They sent their love, and my wife bade me ask when you were coming to pay us a visit."

Helen shook her head.

"Not just yet, thank you. Do you mind walking? The trap will come down at twelve, but we shall get there before it leaves. It won't take us an hour. But if you prefer it we can hire from the Bell. I know Madame de Castro would wish it; indeed, she said to me I was to do so if you came by this train."

"I would rather walk; there is a good deal to speak about," he said, as they passed out into the roadway. "It is a good while since I was here. The country is looking very pretty. How do you like life at Fintry?"

"Very well. I am beginning to understand my father's love for the country. I feel so sorry now I stood in the way of his getting a little country house. I thought I should not care for it; but he was right."

"Are you going to stay indefinitely?" he asked, with a curious look at her still pale face.

"Meantime, yes," she answered, in a low voice. "Madame de Castro sets no limit. We are very happy together, and I am always hoping that something will happen. That we shall ultimately clear up the mystery here I feel certain."

"Do you? Have you any grounds to go upon?"

She shook her head, and her eyes assumed a far-away look.

"We are waiting on the vagaries of the pool," she said, in a perfectly serious voice. "It will reveal its secret in its own time and way."

He looked at her again, wondering even whether much brooding had unhinged her sane judgment, but detecting no sign of aberration anywhere.

"Do you really believe that such a thing could possibly happen, Helen?"

"I do, and papa believed it too. I read his diary often, and he refers to such things again and again—not only to Penninghame Pool, but to other things of the same sort that had come under his observation."

"I suppose the police have quite given up?"

"Not quite. I met Sergeant Gunn as I came down this morning, and we had a talk. He feels humiliated that he has been baffled, but won't own to it. He says something will be discovered yet."

"That may be. I don't doubt it. But it will be by perfectly natural means. How is David?"

"David is quite well. He wants to leave Bilbao, Mr. Shepherd, and I think my uncle will relieve him at midsummer. He has not been able to settle to his work at all since he was here, and I don't wonder at it."

Shepherd reflected a moment.

"Do you think Miss de Castro has anything to do with his unrest?" he asked experimentally.

"Sybil? Oh, no, I don't think David has any thought of that kind, and if he had it would be no good. Her mother is very kind and good, but she is also proud. Such a marriage would not please her, I am sure."

"Perhaps she will have less pride after next week," he said reflectively. "I wish the whole sorry business were over. She's bound to lose, Helen. Nothing can save her. Do you happen to know what she wants me for to-day?"

"Yes; that is why I came. We had a visit from Mr. Weir yesterday at Fintry."

"What did he want?"

"What do you think? To lay an extraordinary proposition before Madame de Castro. He appears very anxious to avert the lawsuit, and offers to sell Penninghame to her at a reasonable rate."

"Oh!"

The lawyer took a long breath. Helen enjoyed his surprise.

"You stare. I don't wonder at it. But the strangest part is to come. He managed to impress Sybil favourably first and then to commend himself entirely to her mother. Before he left she even apologised for having misjudged him. What are we to make of that?"

"Did you see him?"

"No; I had no wish. He is coming back this afternoon to hear her decision. That is why she sent for you to talk the thing over. Probably you will have to interview him as well."

"Now, what can the motive be?"

"He made no secret of it. He owns himself miserable here, and that he has no position or standing. He would be happier to return to the place whence he came, and a very reasonable sum would buy him off. What Isabel is anxious about is whether the terms of the laird's will will permit such an exchange. It was expressly stated that the place was not to be sold, wasn't it?"

"Expressly. It certainly raises a very nice point. But you surprise me. It is the very last thing I should have expected from Anthony Weir."

"Yes; but it is the unexpected that happens always. For me it is not so difficult to follow the whole course of his reasoning."

"Would you enlighten me?" said Shepherd suggestively.

"Presently, perhaps. Would you mind walking through Penninghame woods to Fintry? I came by the road, but I should like to pass by the pool. Will you come; it is not longer?"

"I should like to come. I have not been there since that horrible day after it happened. Have you?"

"I! Oh, yes. I could not count the times. I am watching the pool. I promise you one day I shall come and find what I desire."

Again Shepherd looked at her askance. His own cast of mind forbade the reception of such a weird superstition, and he began to feel certain that much brooding had weakened Helen's mind in one particular point at least.

"What do you think the sergeant told me this morning?" she asked, as they struck off the road by the gates into the woodland path.

"I could not guess."

"That last night, at Westerlea Station, he saw Nancy Nicolson—that's Braidwood's neice—who has been missing since the day after papa disappeared. She got in at Westerlea. The sergeant is certain that she had been at Penninghame, and that Mr. Weir drove her over."

"He persists in thinking that Weir was responsible for that too."

"He is certain of it. He is piecing the thing together bit by bit, he says; he is going to Edinburgh this morning to try and find Nancy. He thinks she has the key to the whole situation."

"What was the deduction you promised me?" he asked, with a deepening interest.

"It is so plain, to my mind and to the sergeant's, that it wants no elucidation," she said calmly. "It was Anthony Weir who pushed father into the pool, either because they quarrelled and his temper got the better of him, or it was an accident through his trying to get possession of the bag. Do you remember that you met Nancy at the gates after you left papa? You mentioned it at the time."

"I met a girl whose face I knew through seeing her about the house. I did not know her name, or that she was Braidwood's niece."

"Well, she was away to keep an appointment with Weir. She came to the place in time either to see the struggle or its terrible result. Then it became absolutely necessary for her to disappear. Don't you see the whole fabric?"

"It sounds plausible enough," he admitted, marvelling at the ingenuity that had pieced the whole story together.

"The position is becoming daily more intolerable for Weir; perhaps even Nancy is insistent. Weir will sell Penninghame, don't you see, and get away abroad with her before anything else transpires."

"I see you ought to have been a man and a lawyer, Helen; you have the judicial mind."

"But does it not sound reasonable?"

"Not only reasonable, but convincing," he admitted.

"Well, I wonder which will be the cleverer of the two."

"If there is any justice in heaven, Mr. Shepherd, Anthony Weir will not succeed with his scheme. You can hinder him if you will."

"How can I? Once the legal objections are removed Madame de Castro can please herself. She is never undecided, Helen."

"Never; but she is very impulsive, and often difficult. If she takes up a defensive attitude towards Anthony Weir she will be as prejudiced in his favour as she was formerly against him."

The lawyer walked on a few steps in contemplative silence.

"I am glad I have seen you, Helen. All this is very useful and prepares me for to-day's work."

"I told Isabel I should lay the facts before you. She made no objection, but only said it would save her the trouble of explaining. I can't tell you how often I wish David were here. She does listen to what he says, and for one so young he has wonderful tact, and even experience. When he was here he constantly surprised me."

"Perhaps we may get him here sooner; we must try. How do you propose that I shall prevent the consummation you do not desire?"

"Oh, well, I have no objection to the consummation, so far as Isabel is concerned. It would be excellent for them, especially for Frank, if it could be settled. He is a delightful boy, the most lovable I have ever met, and his heart is sore about the old place, though he would not vex his mother's heart by saying it. Sybil is less unselfish and more difficult in every way. About preventing it, that might be impossible, but at least there need not be any haste. Weir will want it pushed through as quickly as possible; I could gather that from what Isabel said. You can dally a little, can't you?"

"It will be impossible to push such a matter through quickly; it is full of technical difficulties, and will probably require a counsel's opinion to be taken on it. And the collapse of the case for next week will itself involve a lot of work and delay."

"I thought so," said Helen. "They don't know so much about the law as I do. Here we are again. What a strange fascination this place has for me. I could come to it blindfold, and without a tremor. I am never afraid here."

"Familiarity, I suppose," he answered, and looked round with a slight shiver. He had not seen it since that memorable morning when the search had been first prosecuted, and the scene rose up before his memory, upon which every detail seemed to have been photographed. It seemed less deary a place that bright sunny spring morning. The sun was filtering through the fresh green of the whispering leaves, and the woodland ways were ablow with the delicate and lovely blossoms of the spring.

But the steep sides sloping to the mysterious waters were bare as before; there was no change, or ever would be. None had ever seen a green blade or a kindly bloom on the yawning chasm.

Helen got down upon her knees and leaned over the steep bank, her eyes fixed with intolerable yearning on the unruffled bosom of the dark water, which hid its secret so well. Suddenly she rose with flushing face and nervously clasped her hands.

"I was here yesterday, Mr. Shepherd, and since then the waters have gone down quite three inches. Perhaps it will dry up gradually."

"Perhaps; as the season gets drier, of course, there must be less body of water everywhere," he said vaguely.

"Not here; it does not depend on ordinary supplies," she said, with the conviction of one who had studied the matter from every possible standpoint. "Its source is part of its mystery, but one of these days we shall have it laid bare to us. Then this horrible long-drawn suspense will be at an end."

CHAPTER XXXIV

ANOTHER WAY OUT

ANTHONY WEIR arrived at Fintry punctually at half-past three. Braidwood's face wore a curious expression as he admitted him. The old man stood in the hall mute and motionless while the guest removed his coat and laid it down. He had sworn that no hands of his should render service, however slight, to Anthony Weir, and that vow would be kept.

Weir did not seem to notice it. He said good-day to the old man, and then ignored his presence. He was unconscious apparently of any studied insult.

" This way," said Braidwood, when he was ready, without the prefix of the " sir."

There was a small library at Fintry, where the surplus books of Penninghame had been stored in the lifetime of Isabel's grandfather, who, with all his faults, had been a bookish man, spending on rare editions and sumptuous bindings money his successors were not slow to say should have been sunk in the land or in estate improvements.

It was a cold room, however, facing north ; a room where little sunlight came, and was seldom used by the present inmates of Fintry. But it was the proper place for the interview about to take place.

When Weir entered, Madame de Castro and Shepherd were already there, and Frank, with his hands in his pockets, stood at the window. The boy looked round at the opening of the door, and fixed his clear gaze on the face of the man who entered, and whose action, if consummated, would make so great a difference to his future. Curiously enough, it was that clear, straight look that disconcerted Weir several times throughout that interview. Madame de Castro advanced with cordially extended hand. Shepherd and Frank were thus obliged to follow suit.

The kindliness of the greeting reassured Weir, and his face cleared.

" I hope I have not kept you waiting ; I thought I was punctual," he said politely.

" You are quite in time. Mr. Shepherd was rather anxious to get away by the four-thirty. Even yet it may be managed."

" I did not expect to see him to-day," said Weir pointedly.

" I thought it better," Madame de Castro hastened to explain. " It is a matter of grave importance. Mr. Shepherd thinks well of your proposal, and has to-day been going into the whole matter with me. The financial part is the chief difficulty. But he assures me that it will be easy to raise a mortgage, especially during the period of my son's minority. There would be five years, you see, in which to pay it off. Won't you sit down, Mr. Weir ? "

" No, thank you," he replied, and advancing to the table, where the lawyer stood, he addressed himself to him.

" Madame de Castro has explained to you in full, I suppose, what I wish to do. I don't like the place. Even if I am compelled to keep it, I shall be a perpetual absentee, which is bad for any estate. Do you not agree that it would be better to dispose of it as I propose ? "

" Certainly, if you feel so, and Madame de Castro seems pleased with the idea," replied Shepherd. " It will be necessary to take counsel's opinion, but I don't anticipate any difficulty that it will not be possible to dispose of. But I must add that I cannot recall a single precedent."

" Well, the circumstances are a little out of the common, it is true," said Weir. " How soon can you get the opinion you speak of ? I am anxious that the matter should be pushed through as quickly as possible."

" There is bound to be some delay. The first step must be to withdraw the case from the Court of Session."

" Madame will be as pleased as I shall be to see that done, I suppose ? " said Weir, turning to her interrogatively.

" I shall be pleased, of course," she answered. " Personally, I have no love for Law Courts, and, as I was to enter this particular one in full opposition to all my advisers, possibly the result would have made me like them less," she answered, with a slight tinge of bitterness in her tone. Though fully cognisant of what she believed to be Weir's generosity, her pride chafed against the whole affair. To buy back for her boy what was his by right seemed an intolerable injustice.

" Mr. Shepherd and I have been discussing the probable sum you would require," she said presently, feeling that it would be better to confine themselves strictly to the matter in hand.

Weir turned to the lawyer.

" How much, roughly speaking, is the place worth ? "

" I have not the exact figures, but, roughly speaking, without Fintry, about fifty thousand pounds."

" Fifty thousand ! " He elevated his eyebrows as if astonished at the sum. " Shall we say half then. Twenty-five thousand would content me, if it would be possible to raise the sum. I am a poor man, of course, and it would be necessary to have it paid down."

Shepherd looked surprised. Isabel's face flushed.

" You're more than generous, Mr. Weir. We did not think you would accept so little."

" It would be enough for my needs," he replied drily.

Shepherd eyed him keenly again, and wished with all his heart he could sweep aside the outer veil, and behold the inner workings of his mind ; that he could, in a word, be face to face with the real man. He had always had that feeling with Weir, especially of late, and he was even yet not free from suspicion of an ulterior motive.

For this he blamed himself, since what motive could possibly be the mainspring except the frankly expressed one that he did not care for the place, and would prefer to let it go at a sacrifice rather than be bound to live upon it.

" There would be absolutely no difficulty in raising the necessary mortgages," he said. " As Madame de Castro says, you are indeed generous, Mr. Weir. You part with a fine property at a conspicuous sacrifice."

" I give it back to those who have the best right, and because I need money I cannot give it as a free gift," was the unexpected answer. Suddenly he paused and looked across the room where the boy stood listening intently with open wondering eyes.

" What does the young laird say ? " he asked, with a faint mysterious smile. " Will it please you to go and live at Penninghame, Mr. Frank ? "

"Yes, but——"

"But what?"

"There is something about it I—I can't get over," replied the boy, flushing too.

"What is it, Frank? Don't be afraid to speak out openly," said his mother kindly, arrested by his words.

But the boy only shook his head.

"I couldn't explain it," he answered, a trifle confusedly. "It's only something I think, that's all."

CHAPTER XXXV

LUCK FOR THE SERGEANT

NANCY NICOLSON was sauntering along Princes Street, looking in at the shop windows. Now that she had determined to assert her rights she felt no need for secrecy. She walked Princes Street like one who had every right to hold up her head. Nancy had some of the instincts of a lady; she loved pretty things, and her tastes were quiet. Therefore it was at the best shops she fixed her gaze.

It was a sunny afternoon, and fashion was abroad. About five o'clock the throng of carriages was at its height, and all the fashionable tea shops were full. Nancy, having nothing to hurry her, took delight in watching everything. A slightly uplifted feeling was in he heart because she felt assured that soon she would be able to mix with that fashionable crowd as one of its units.

The Lady of Penninghame would have the right to drive in a fine carriage and wear some of the elegant creations set forth in the windows for the delectation of female eyes. Having money in her pocket, she entered one of the tea shops and refreshed herself. As she stepped out about a quarter-past five a victoria containing two persons drove slowly up the steep slope from the Waverley Station. In it sat Shepherd and his wife who had just driven in to fetch him from the train. As they waited at the busy corner to turn into Princes Street he saw Nancy, and Nancy saw him. Without a moment's hesitation or explanation to his wife he jumped out and crossed the street. Nancy stood paralysed for the moment, not knowing where to go or what to say.

"You are Nancy Nicolson, Braidwood's niece?" he said, keeping his keen eyes fixed on her somewhat flushed face. "Do you know what trouble and anxiety you have caused them by running away as you did?"

She made no answer, but used the moment to recover herself, and even to rapidly review the situation. And she decided that she need not be in the least afraid of the lawyer.

"What are you doing here? Have you been in Edinburgh long?" he asked sternly.

She stared at him straight, still without speaking.

"Won't you speak to me, Nancy? I have just come from Fintry, where I saw your uncle and aunt, both looking very miserable because they have heard nothing about you."

In this he drew upon his imagination, the thought of Nancy never having once occurred to him while he was at Fintry, but it was necessary to draw her out somehow.

"Are they quite well?" she asked, with the same imperturbable stare.

"How can they be well, my girl, after the way you have treated them?" he asked, with a touch of severity. "At least when you are so near you might let them know that no harm has befallen you."

" You can tell them that," she said, rather pertly.

He looked at her straight, inwardly annoyed, yet reflecting that it was not worth his while to lose his temper with such a creature. Besides, if he did he would learn nothing.

" Are you married ? " he asked, trusting to the suddenness of the question to bring the true answer.

She had come out with her gloves in her hand. She manœuvred so that he saw the plain circlet on her finger.

It did not impress him greatly, however ; he had often known it to be worn without any right. But at least it gave him some clue.

" If you are happily married, and certainly you look it," he said, with a slight smile, " what sense is there in hiding yourself like this, and making a good many people anxious and miserable, besides, perhaps, directing unfounded suspicions, to certain quarters ? "

He never for a moment suffered his eyes to leave her face ; but in these few weeks of double life Nancy had learned to mask her features, and to be mistress of a good many difficult situations.

" I'll tell them what I think fit," she answered quietly. " If ye see them again ye can tell them I'm a' richt, an' that they'll hear o' me yet."

He hesitated for a moment, wondering what step to take next. He felt that he ought not to let her go without making one attempt to solve the mystery to which the sergeant had attached so much importance.

" Do I address Mrs. Anthony Weir ? " he asked suddenly.

But Nancy was ready for him. Her face assumed an air of unmixed surprise. Had Weir seen her admirable nonchalance he would have been proud of his pupil.

" Mrs. Anthony Weir ! " she repeated, in a puzzled voice. " Don't I wish I was. D'ye see that carriage there ; yours is it ? Well, I'd ride in one like that, only it wad hae twa horses instead o' wan, see ? "

Shepherd nodded, conscious of an odd sense of relief. He was a clever man, but the country girl had circumvented him. He absolved Anthony Weir on the instant of any complicity in her escapade, and inwardly reproached himself for his readiness to cast a stone.

Convinced that so far as Weir was concerned she was innocent, his interest in her proportionately declined.

" Well, my good girl, Mrs.——, whatever your name is, take my advice and write to these kind relations of yours and relieve their minds. If it is true that you are respectably married and comfortably off, there is no sense whatever in the way you are behaving. What you may consider romantic is only foolish after all."

So saying, he touched his hat, and crossed to his wife's carriage where it stood on the opposite kerb.

" Who on earth was that, William ? " she asked, in surprise.

" The girl that disappeared from Penninghame the day after Mr. Maitland. Everybody had been thinking Anthony Weir was at the bottom of that little escapade, and everybody has been wrong, Mary ; give a dog a bad name and hang him."

" She's a pretty creature. Where has she been ? "

" She didn't inform me ; but whoever took her away, it isn't Weir. Poor thing, there's a screw loose somewhere, and she has the assurance of twice her age. What a complicated business it has been, to be sure ! Poor old Maitland ! "

She saw the cloud steal over his face again, and her wifely hand went out and touched his. They were deeply attached to one another, and no dispeace had ever jarred the happiness of their married life.

"If only he could come back for an hour. I often misjudged him, Mary; and sometimes didn't treat him well," he said, in a somewhat painful voice. "And he was quite right in a lot of things I didn't agree with him about. The way we live, for instance, Mary; what do we get out of it? Doesn't it taste like ashes in the mouth to-day?"

She looked ahead and her comely mouth trembled. Tears were very near her eyes.

"We spend too much, you think?" she said, in a low voice.

"It's not so much the spending, but what do we get out of it? Precious little! Here's Kitty engaged to young Mackenzie, of course, but they're expecting me to set them up in a good establishment, and finance them generally. We've made a mistake with the children, Mary; I wish I had a son like David Maitland. See, he had only one, and he never spared him; and Maitland was a richer man than I am, or shall ever be."

"Let us live differently then, dear," she said gently, and stole an anxious glance at him, hating to see him thus, and observing for the first time the many lines on his face, the fast thinning grey hair at the temples.

He turned to her eagerly.

"Would you, Mary? I'd like to sell the house, and go into something plainer and simpler, even to the country—I shouldn't mind. We'll talk it over, and decide something before the summer comes, and after we get this curious bit of business off our hands."

They continued to discuss it as they drove, and Nancy Nicolson was banished from their minds. Shepherd determined to write to the sergeant, however, that very night, and tell him he had been entirely wrong in his surmise. Also he would send a line to Braidwood or to Madame de Castro so that she might tell him that his niece was well and apparently quite happy, spending her leisure like a lady at the windows of the Princes Street shops. But the sergeant, as it happened, was before him.

Instead of sending word to headquarters, he had taken a run in to tell that he had seen Nancy in the train, and also to have a little look round on his own account. And as he walked leisurely down the Mound from the head office of the police he beheld the very person for whom he sought crossing the road in the most commonplace way. He drew back so that she might not see him, and keeping his eye on her, followed her from afar. His blood began to flow a little faster and his heart to beat with pleasurable excitement. This was absolutely the first bit of light that had been shed on a particularly dark and baffling case which the sergeant had confided to his wife would sooner or later send him to his grave.

Nancy entered the gardens and sat down upon a seat. Evidently she was in no hurry. From a safe distance the sergeant watched her, and was able to obtain a good view of her face. She certainly looked well, and by no means unhappy. He stood a little behind the monument, keeping his eye on her lest she should vanish from his sight, and pondering what would be his best course of action.

He was exceedingly anxious to speak to her, but it might defeat the very end he had in view. Upon reflection he decided that it would be better to move quietly, to watch whither she went, and try and discover what manner of life she was living. The sun had now set, and the soft gloaming, surely the pleasantest hour of the day, was stealing over the beautiful city, enveloping it like a bridal veil. Westward the sky was a wonder of pink and gold, and the glow of the sunset seemed to linger as if loth to die away.

Did Nancy notice these things? Her face wore a somewhat sad look as she rose to go, and had the sergeant been near enough he would have heard a sigh. Her eyes wandered across to the towers and ancient roofs of the old town and back again to the blow of spring flowers at her feet. Once she bent towards them as if with a sudden yearning. The day had been very long, she was surely the loneliest creature in that great city, and her heart was longing for home. In this mood she came out upon the stony street once more, all unconscious that some one was following her. The throng behind was pressing homewards at the close of the working day. She even looked at the faces of the passing workmen, at the eager, busy women with envy. How often had she in these long days of enforced idleness envied those who had work to do.

She turned up Cockburn Street, the sergeant following at a discreet distance. Presently he was rewarded by seeing her disappear within the doorway of a small hotel which he did not know even by name.

He waited until she would have had time to go upstairs, and then followed her in. A small boy, who acted as hall porter, came forward to inquire his business.

"Is there a lady stopping here, by name Mrs. Weir?" he asked.

"Weir? No: there's only wan lady. She cam' frae London last nicht. Her name's Mrs. Colville, but she's no English. Want to see her?"

"No, thank you. Is she quite alone?"

"Yes, but she's expeckin' her man the nicht, for I heard her tellin' the chambermaid."

At that moment the landlord came forward and reproved the boy for his garrulity with a look which said unutterable things.

"Pardon me, I am expecting a friend, a Mrs. Weir, to come here from the south, but possibly she may not arrive till to-morrow; when she comes tell her John Graham called, and asked her to write as soon as she can."

With which mythical message the sergeant disappeared. But not wholly. Later in the evening from a dark entry opposite he had the satisfaction of beholding Anthony Weir enter the hotel.

CHAPTER XXXVI

NEMESIS

ANTHONY WEIR had driven over from Penninghame, and his trap waited in the Fintry stableyard in charge of Bob Aitken, the young groom who regarded him with unbounded admiration. He saw when his master approached that his face wore an air of the deepest gloom.

"Home, sir?" he said solicitously, as he stood at the mare's head, while his master prepared to swing himself up to his seat.

Weir looked round vaguely.

"Home!" he repeated, and took out his watch. "No, drive me to Porth Junction. I shall just catch the mail train. I have some business to do in Edinburgh to-night."

"Back to-night, sir?"

"Yes, meet the nine-fifteen and if I am not there, come on to Porth for the ten-ten. If I'm not coming, I'll telegraph to Bill."

He took the reins and turned the mare's head down the short wide avenue. As they bowled rapidly away from the house he turned round and took a long look at the windows. But no one was visible there. Madame de Castro had made no reply to his unpremeditated speech, but neither had she exhibited any signs of anger. He felt as if he had seen through the half-open door, as if one chance had come to him to leave the old life and enter upon the new. To be the husband of Sybil, connected honourably with those he had wronged, to be allowed such an incomparable chance of reparation, to quit forever if he liked the broad and precarious road of evil doing—he longed for it as a man longs for water in a dry land. Here was no sudden conversion, but rather a gradual process, born of the intolerable conditions under which his present life was lived. He had proved to his bitter satisfaction that there are many things money will not buy; that even a great position, if wrongly acquired, will not cover a man's sins, or set him high in the estimation of his fellow-men. He had been accustomed to a different code of life, he had learned that in a simple Scotch village a man is estimated for what he is rather than for what he has, and the lesson had been good for him. And now, apparently, the incomparable chance was his. Honest eyes had met his kindly, even with gratitude in their depths. He had been welcomed to a home and asked to come again. Nay, his presumption in even seeming to aspire to Sybil de Castro had not been spurned. But now where was he? Journeying to see her who hung like a millstone about his neck.

When he recalled the expression on her face only a few hours before, her air of quiet determination, her assumption of rights she believed to be hers, he could see no loophole of escape. Even she was a product of the life he would fain enter now. She had refused to be satisfied with less than marriage. She carried what she believed to be her marriage lines in the bosom of her dress night and day. It would be impossible to shake her off. He thought of a thousand plans, each one less feasible than the other, and finally arrived where he had been at the beginning, face towards a blank impenetrable wall. If even she got the smallest hints as to his intention or desire to leave her, she would out with the whole truth. The secret of the pool would be a secret no longer, and though so long as these mysterious waters maintained their reputation for secrecy nothing could actually be proven against him, he had seen men hanged on evidence more slender and less convincing.

Looking back upon the events of the past months he cursed himself for his own unspeakable folly. If only he had been content to let things drift, to bide his time, to wait patiently the development of events, he would not only have been a free man, he might also have been a happy one. But now he was in the meshes of a toil it seemed a superhuman task to unravel or unwind. Feeling himself completely baffled, he gave up the struggle and told himself he would now let things drift with a vengeance, and simply wait the development of events. He would not even trouble to plan his next step with Nancy, but leave her to decide. Perhaps even since yesterday she might have changed her mind. During the drive he never opened his mouth. The lad by his side concluded that he had had a stormy interview at Fintry, and discreetly held his tongue.

" How old are you, Bob ? " his master asked him suddenly, as they came within sight of the Junction station. The question was so sudden and so irrelevant that the lad's face flushed with surprise.

" Auld ! Seventeen, sir," he replied, after a moment's hesitation.

" Ever had a sweetheart, Bob ? "

" Not yet, sir," he replied, growing redder than ever.

" Then don't be in a hurry or you'll rue it. Wait till you're in a position to marry, and then stick to her through thick and thin. That'll be the happiest life for you."

" Yes, sir," answered Bob, and the words sank into his soul, and remained there through the whole of his after-life. He could not understand their hidden significance then, only the touch of human sympathy appealed to his honest, unsophisticated heart, and bound his master to him with hooks of steel.

" Am I a bad master, Bob ? "

" No, no, sir ; a guid ane. I aye say that, whatever they may say," he answered impulsively, and then furiously reddened again, feeling that he had given himself away.

" They do say then, even yet ? " asked Weir, with a quietly bitter smile. " When will they get to the end of my misdeeds I wonder."

" They are a pack o' clashes, sir. I wadna mind them," said Bob sympathetically. " As I telt Tam Galbraith, the jiner, that was Nancy's sweetheart, ye ken, he should be sure o' his grund afore he opens his mooth."

This speech considerably enlightened Weir, and his face wore an interested look.

" So Nancy had a sweetheart, had she ? "

" Oh yes, Tom Galbraith ; they were to be cried, folk said, at Christmas. Hae ye never seen him, sir ? He's often workin' at the hoose ? He does a' the odd jobs for his faither."

" I don't know him, but I'll look out for him next time he comes. Is he much cut up about Nancy, eh ? "

" So he lets on. He's jist a big mooth, sir, an' as saft as butter. I dinna believe Nancy wad hae married him ; she was aye makin' fun o' him."

They dipped down into the hollow and up again to the station, where

Weir alighted, leaving Bob with a friendly nod. The lad did not immediately drive away. He felt an odd sense of nearness to his master, and stood still to watch him stride along the platform, where he was lost to sight. Bob did not know that he had seen him for the last time.

The train was twenty minutes late. Weir paced impatiently to and fro chafing at the delay. He had promised to see Nancy that night, and though it was little to his liking, he feared to disappoint her. For the time being she was master, he the obedient slave.

Presently with a great hiss and din the London train came tearing in. No one looked out or got out, and Weir was the only passenger to take his seat. Consequently there was scarcely a moment's delay.

It was the last stoppage till Edinburgh was reached at half-past six. There Weir alighted leisurely, and, not knowing what tempted him, lingered a moment to watch the throng which never fails to alight from the London train. Suddenly his face went white and rigid, and he stretched out his hand to grip a friendly lamp-post, while his eyes, somewhat wildly staring, fixed themselves on two figures moving together towards the luggage van, round which there was the usual bustle and confusion.

There was nothing either striking or alarming about the two figures—a man and a woman, both young, quietly dressed, pleasant featured, and apparently happy. They might have been brother and sister or a newly-married couple coming back from a quiet honeymoon. Of the two the woman had the stronger, more interesting face. And there was undoubtedly an air of breeding about them which singled them out even among that cosmopolitan crowd.

" Are you ill, sir ? " said the kindly voice of an elderly woman at Anthony Weir's side, as he stood stock still, staring after the retreating figures as if they had been apparitions arisen from the dead.

The voice brought him to his senses.

" Oh, no, thank you ; a sudden faintness, that's all," he said bluntly, and walked away not once looking back.

" The game's up," he said with a groan, as he mounted the steps and turned towards the narrow approach to Cockburn Street. Suddenly he stopped a railway porter coming towards him to put a single question.

" Any train for London to-night ? " he asked, with feverish eagerness.

" Ay, twa ; the Midland at nine-fifteen, and the East Coast at ten forty-five."

" Right ; thank you," he muttered, and moved on.

It was grey dark in the streets now, and the sunset glow had faded from the towers and turrets and picturesque roofs of the old town. Weir took small heed of these things ; at the moment he was a person of one idea. Just at the foot of the street he hesitated, and looked first one way and then the other. Should he leave Nancy there and then, see her no more, let her go back when she got tired of waiting, and reveal the whole story, by which time he would be far away. Something told him it would be the better, perhaps the manlier course. And yet something drew him to her—after all she was a woman and kindly, and he was in desperate need. Believing herself to be his wife she would perhaps stick to him, and at least he would not go forth into the outer darkness alone. A little thing decided him. A pair of lovers coming arm in arm together across the bridge—she looking up into his face with a look of adoring trust. He turned towards the steep incline, and walked up to the door of the hotel. Seven pealed from the town as he crossed the threshold and asked the hall boy whether

Mrs. Colville was within. He did not glance across the street or he might have seen Sergeant Gunn standing in the shadow, a look of grim satisfaction on his face.

"Now," said that worthy to himself, "what's the next move on the board?"

He stood still, gazing across at the open doorway that had swallowed Weir, for the moment entirely at a loss.

"Gang in an' confront him, or wait a wee or things ripen a bit. Waitin's the game. I've proved that he and Nance are in league, the rest'll be easy; the thing's to get a haud o' her by hersel'. Wull I bide here a' nicht, or gang hame, an' come back the morn?"

He took a turn down the dusky street, keeping to the side where the hotel was situated in order that he might not be seen from any of the windows, and pondered the whole situation in his mind. Also he consulted the little time-table in his pocket, and found that he could just catch the seven-thirty train.

"They're safe or the morn's mornin' onywey, an' my day hasna been lost after a'."

He chuckled to himself as he ran down the station steps, not knowing that his procrastination, although seemingly justified by the circumstances, would have to be written down later on as one of the fatal mistakes of his professional career.

CHAPTER XXXVII

HER METTLE

MRS. COLVILLE had engaged a large, pleasant room, with windows to the back of the house, and there was comfortably ensconced, toasting her toes at the cheery fire, when the door opened to admit Weir. She sprang up well pleased, not having expected him so soon.

"I wasna thinking ye would come or nine maybe," she said, as she held out her hand. "Hoo did ye get on? Mercy me, ye dinna look weel! Has onything happened?"

He locked the door, laid down his coat and hat, and approached the fire-place, holding out his hands, as if they were chilled, towards the cheerful blaze.

Should he tell her nor not? That was the question agitating his mind. Were there any resources behind that pretty rosy face? How far might a man trust her in his desperate need? Would she play him false and think only of her own safety, or would she prove herself a comrade willing to stick to him through thick and thin? He must walk warily in order to discover of what mettle she was made.

"I'm all right; sat in a draught in that beastly train, and feel a bit shivery, that's all. Got any whisky or brandy?"

"I have the flask you gied me in London," she answered. "I've never touched it."

She walked over to the wardrobe and unlocked the little bag which contained the few belongings she had brought with her from London. The rest she had left with the landlady who had advised her to follow her husband to Scotland. He took it eagerly, swallowed a long draught, and said he felt better immediately. He drew a chair opposite to her and sat down, staring fixedly into the fire.

"Ye havena been successful wi' Madame de Castro, I doot?" said Nancy anxiously.

"Oh yes, I was; found her most amenable, and the whole thing was likely to be amicably arranged, but——"

"Something else happened; the pool maybe?" and her cheek blanched.

"Oh, no, that's safe enough. Look here, Nancy, I'll give you a chance. I'm a wrong 'un; you'd better leave me to-night; go back to these decent folk who brought you up, and forget all about me."

She stared at him steadily without flinching.

"I winna," she answered quietly. "Ye'd better tell me what has happened."

"If I tell you anything it must be all," he said, with a slight note of warning in his voice. "You don't know what you are doing, my dear; you'd better take my advice and go back before it's quite too late. I am sorry that you ever met me, sorry for the wrong I've done you. I was a scoundrel. If I knew how to atone for it I would."

" I'm your wife, and whatever you've done, it can make nae difference," she said, and her tone lost nothing of its quiet decision. " I'm no gaun back there by mysel' to be pinted at, no likely. Besides, I've nae faut to you. You've been guid enough to me. The only cross word ye ever spoke was that day in Penninghame Wud, when it happened. I've never thocht ye meant to kill him, though I saw it a', an' I was stand up in ony Coort an' sweir it."

He looked at her with a sudden sense of wonder, not unmixed with gratitude. After all, such testimony was something to a man in such an hour, when he felt and knew himself to be outside the pale of all decent folk. When he remembered how that very day he had been planning how best to get rid of her a keen sense of shame smote him.

There was something pathetic in her clinging to her idea of wifehood, and yet it was absolutely necessary that on that point she should be undeceived. He cast about for words in which to tell her, and could find none.

" Tell me what has happened ? " she repeated. " I suppose they've found oot something."

" Not what you think," he answered. " Something has happened certainly, but it is in connection with my life before I came here at all, in fact before I left the Cape."

" Did ye kill somebody else ? " she asked in a low voice, and at the simple naïveté of the question he could almost have laughed aloud.

" No, no, I'm not a wholesale slaughterer," he answered, trying to speak lightly. " Nothing so bad as that, but it's bad enough. It is no longer safe for me to remain in this country, and I'm thinking of going off to London to-night ; and abroad again at the earliest possible moment."

Nancy stared at him a trifle wildly, and her face was seriously troubled.

" To London again ; the nicht ; an' for hoo lang ? There's nae rest whaur you are."

" God, you're right, my girl," he said, with a sudden touch of passion. " I'm feeling that way myself. It was a black day for you when you first set eyes on my face."

" When does the train gang ? " she asked, glancing at the cheap little clock ticking unconcernedly on the mantelshelf.

" Plenty of time yet, but—but, Nancy, I don't think I can take you."

Her eyes met his in a straight keen glance.

" What for no ? If, as ye say, ye are to leave the country, what way would ye leave me behind ? "

" There's no prospect, nothing," he said desperately. " I'll never come back to Penninghame or be its laird. Your dream of reigning there is shattered for ever, my poor girl."

" An' what d'ye propose to dae wi' me then ? " she asked quietly. " Throw me aside like an auld boot, eh ? "

" Not exactly that ; it's because I have nothing to offer you that I would leave you."

" But you are a strong young man," she said, with a single touch of scorn. " As I said before, ye can work for me as ither men work for their wives. What's to hinder ? I'm no feart for wark ; I've dune plenty in my time."

Her faculty of reducing the situation to the simplest possible plane was immensely disconcerting. She had a simple, clear mind incapable of following the tortuous windings of a scheming brain perhaps, but quick enough to grasp the salient points of any case, and the salient points for her at the moment were that she was this man's wife, that for some reason or another he wished to leave her, and that she had no intention of being left. Anthony Weir did not know yet what depths of determination were hidden in the heart of the country girl.

"It would be a hard life," he repeated vaguely. "You would be infinitely better to remain here, at least until I could send for you when things get brighter."

"No, thank you; I've heard o' them that went to furrin' pairts to send for folk, and never sent. I'm gaun wi' ye, my man, wherever ye gang. As I said afore, catch me gaun back to Penninghame or Fintry for them to wipe their boots on me. I ken what they are oot there."

"But, Nancy, I don't even know whether I have the right to take you," he said, then driven into a corner and forced to tell part, at least, of the truth. "That marriage of ours was very irregular, you know, and can't possibly stand."

Her face flushed a little, and her lips parted in a half-smile.

"That's whaur ye're wrang, Anthony. I made sure o' that pairt o' it. It wasna likely I was gaun to leave it to chance. Twa days efter I gaed to a lawyer in Edinburgh and telt him a' aboot the mairrage, and showed him the lines, and he telt me that in Scotland it's a mairrage legal and binding if ye declare yersels man and wife afore twa witnesses. An' oors was mair than that, for there was a kind o' minister there. See, here's the lawyer's letter. I made him write it doon, and I keep it beside the lines."

She undid the bosom of her dress, and took from a little linen bag the two precious documents which were strong to make and keep her an honest woman in the eyes of the world. Weir looked at her with a sudden access of admiration for her cleverness and foresight.

He took the lawyer's letter and read it through, then handed it back.

"You've got the better of me, Nancy; not that I wanted to play you false altogether. Well, lass, we've got to sink or swim together, I suppose, at all costs, so I'll tell you what has happened, the whole truth, and hear your verdict on it. I'm beginning to think a man might do worse than consult you when his back is to the wall."

He sat down before her and began to talk eagerly, Nancy listening as eagerly, though with slightly blanching face.

"My, you're in a michty ticht place!" she said, interrupting him only once. "The suner we get away the better."

"You think that? But what about the money, Nancy, unless I wait until to-morrow? I have barely enough to take us as far as London."

"Supposin' we wait for the morn; can ye get ony?"

"Why, yes; I have a few hundreds lying to my account in the bank. I could draw it at ten o'clock, and we could get away immediately after."

"Then we must dae that. It's no your money either; but a's fair in war, they say," said Nancy, with an unexpectedly shrewd touch. "An' if they get Penninghame and Fintry an' a' they're no bad. Eh, me, what a business, an' whaever thocht I wad be mixed up in it!"

"You don't seem much shocked, Nancy," said Weir, faintly amused at her point of view. "I should have thought now that, brought up as you were, you would never have looked at or spoken to me again."

"It's geyan bad, but the hale thing seems to me raither comical at this meenit," said Nancy, shrugging her shoulders. "What a fecht it has been atween you an' them, an' a' the time ye had nae mair richt to onything than me, maybe less, for I was on the premises. My, ye are clever! But if ye get awa' this time, ye maun promise me that ye'll meddle nae mair wi' ither folk's money or property, but live a decent life. Hae ye been learned a trade ? "

Anthony Weir laughed aloud. Her simplicity was most refreshing. There was no beating about the bush with Nancy. She drove to the seat of things straight as an arrow to the mark. At least with her one need never be at a loss. She was not only a staunch and true little woman, but amazingly pretty at the moment. Weir suddenly decided that he might have been much worse off, and that with such a companion and standby, the future need not be so dark as it had seemed an hour ago.

" I played a bold game, Nancy ; wicked, yes, I know, but I wonder how many men situated as I was would not have succumbed to the temptation ? I don't regret any of it except the poor old man's death, and I didn't mean that. I'm bad, but I didn't deliberately plan his end. I wish it were possible to bring him back before we clear out."

Nancy looked at him with an odd wondering light in her eyes. Her intelligence was limited perhaps, but she had some vague consciousness of the warring elements in conflict in the man's soul. There was much good among the evil there. Perhaps in happier circumstances he might even have been a good man.

" I've aye heard my Aunt Susan say that we wad only be punished for oor sins o' intention," she said, in a low voice. " So maybe ye'll get aff Scot free."

" You are a good little comforter, Nancy, and I beg your pardon if I have not always acted straightly towards you. Now, we'd better get to business. What's the programme then ? "

" Get the money in the morning, an' off to London as quick as we can."

" Not to London, direct, at least ; that's where they seek everybody. And things will not begin to move at Penninghame, I should think, until the day after to-morrow at least. They've got to get their bearings and find out the lawyers and do a multitude of things. I believe we'll get two days clear advantage."

" Well, so much the better. An' efter we get to London, what then ? "

" We'll go to America, Nancy—Canada perhaps. This is just the season of the year. You see, they'll seek me at the Cape, likely, where I came from. There's a steamer for America every Saturday. We must get to Liverpool in time for that."

" Very well," said Nancy. " I'm no carin' much so long as it's guid-bye to Scotland for ever."

" And you're not afraid, Nancy, to trust yourself with me ? I came here to-night intending to leave you behind. Aren't you afraid that the same thing might happen again ? "

She shook her head and gave a little sob.

" No," she said. " I'm no feared. Ye've never said an ill word to me, an' ye're no as black as they wad seek to pent ye. Onyway, ye're guid enough for me."

A strange, softened look came upon the face of Anthony Weir. A woman's trust brought to the surface all the manliness of which he was capable.

" I'll take care, my girl, that you never rue it," he said, with a sudden and real tenderness. " If we get clean away from this awful mess, who knows but what we may be happy yet ? "

CHAPTER XXXVIII

THE UNINVITED GUESTS

THAT night Bob Aitken, the Penninghame groom, waited in vain at Porth Junction for his master. The train came and went without discharging a single passenger, and there was nothing for it but to drive back, and await the next orders. But he did so disconsolately, being deeply disappointed. There was no alarm felt, however, and the household retired to rest undisturbed, being well accustomed to the vagaries of the new laird. He was a restless being, given to sudden resolves and unpremeditated acts.

Morning broke, and the day wore on, but no word came nor any sign of the returning laird. Twice Bob on his own responsibility drove in to the station at train time, only to be disappointed. The second time, at the noon train, two passengers, a lady and gentleman, came out and stood irresolute in the roadway, evidently not knowing where to turn. Finally the gentleman spoke to the groom on the box of the dogcart as a likely person to direct a stranger.

" Can you tell me how far it is to Penninghame House, and how long it will take us to get there ? "

" It's just on three miles, sir, and it'll take bout an hour. I'm going there, and could drive you if you have business with the maister."

" We have. Is he at home ? "

" No, I came to meet him, but apparently he hasna come," answered Bob. " But he'll be hame some time the day. Will you get into the trap, sir, and I'll drive you up ? "

The stranger looked at the lady inquiringly.

" Shall we, Letty ? It seems a good chance, and we could have a look round before he comes back."

" Very well, Anthony."

Bob pricked up his ears, struck by the name, which was not common in these parts. In fact, until the new laird had come to Penninghame, he had never heard it.

He sprang to the ground and held the horse's head while the lady was helped up to the front seat. Bob thought no ill, and only imagined he did his duty by his master's visitors. Also, he hoped he would return soon.

" Has Mr. Weir been long away ? " asked the lady, as he turned the animal's head from the station.

" No, he only went to Edinburgh last nicht, ma'am, and we expeckit him hame last nicht too. He'll be here sune, or there'll be a telegram."

She nodded, and, holding on her hat in the high wind, looked about her interestedly. Bob stole a side glance at her, and admired her, though why he could not have told.

" It seems a fine country here," she said at length. " Is this the village we are coming to ? "

" Ay, Penninghame village, it's a quarter o' a mile frae the station. D'ye see the trees yonder at the back, that's Penninghame woods."

" And where is the house ? "

" Among the trees ; ye canna see it except frae Whitekirk Brae. In summer it's quite hidden, even from there."

" What an odd little village. This is the church I suppose ? "

" Ay, the Auld Kirk, the Free's in ahint, an' the U.P. along the Vennel."

She did not comprehend him altogether, but suffered the remark to pass. She was interested in the general features rather than in details.

" I understand the old laird of Penninghame is dead ? " she said presently, after they had left the straggling village street behind.

" Ay, twa-three month syne, afore I came to Penninghame stable."

" You have not been long there then ? "

" No, six weeks. I was at the Bell Inn afore, and aften drove the laird, the new laird I mean, when he cam' unexpected-like frae Edinburgh. He's been a guid freen to me."

" You like him then ? Is he well liked in the neighbourhood ? "

" Middlin', ma'am," said the lad with caution. " But that's because folk dinna ken him, and because o' the clashes."

" The what ? "

" The ill stories that's been fleein' aboot, but they're gaun to dee doon noo. He was at Fintry yesterday, an' I wadna wonder."

" Wonder what ? "

" I'm speakin' ower free, ma'am," said Bob, with a sudden qualm. " Unless you're a freen o' the laird's ? " he added inquiringly.

" We know him very well, and we are immensely interested," she said, with an admirable coolness. " We knew him at the Cape before he came here. We come from the Cape ourselves.

" Oh, I see. Eh, michty, the things they've said aboot him. Mony a man's been hanged for less," said the lad, chattering guilelessly. " They even said that he killed Maister Maitland, the lawyer, because he had made anither will in favour o' Madame, that's the laird's daughter that bides at Fintry."

" Oh, where is Fintry ? In this neighbourhood ? "

" Ay, awa doon near the sea. If ye stand up ye'll see a little clump of trees awa' richt ower there. That's Fintry."

" And is she there now ? "

" Yes, an' I believe the laird an' she's to mak' it up ; he's been twice there this week, an' yesterday he stoppit to his tea."

" I see, and is he a good laird—as good as the old one ? "

" Oh, better ; no near sae nairry ahint," said Bob in the dark phraseology of the countryside. " He's very free wi' servants, an' grudges them naething. We're a' pleased bar Braidwood, an' he gaed to Fintry wi' Madame de Castro. He believes oor laird to be perfect Satan's sel'."

So did the guileless Bob prattle on, meaning no ill, and making clear and plain much that had been dark and mysterious to these two strangers an hour ago.

They came without delay to the Penninghame gates, and the lodge-keeper ran out, regarding with interest the passengers, of whose arrival she had heard no word. Seeing her face, Bob began to wonder whether perhaps he had not taken too much upon himself.

" Ye're seekin' the laird, are ye no ? Ye want to see him ? " he asked doubtfully.

" Yes, we have come a long way to see him, and can wait until he comes back," the lady answered, with a faint inscrutable smile.

She raised herself slightly on her seat as they swept round the curve in the long avenue and came within sight of the house.

It stood out again the clear March sky, an immense and imposing pile.

" Oh, Anthony, look," she cried suddenly. " Isn't it beautiful and far, far grander than anything we have expected to see."

" It's very fine," answered the young man, speaking for the first time.

His face wore a somewhat sad expression, like one who at some cost puts a curb upon himself.

Bob drove up to the front door, and the butler made his appearance, looking surprised at the sight of strange visitors without his master.

" A leddy and gentleman for the laird, Maister Swanston, said Bob grandly. " An' they'll wait or he comes hame."

" Certainly, certainly. What name, sir ? " he asked, as he stood respectfully aside while the lady was helped to alight.

" Name ? Oh, Weir," he replied, and the instant conclusion of the servants was that they must be some relatives of their master.

" Nice-lookin' folk," was Bob's verdict to his colleagues in the stableyard, and he was right.

Swanston escorted them into the house, and, having left them in the library, went to see what could be obtained in the way of luncheon for the unexpected guests, of whose arrival his master had given no warning.

Left alone, brother and sister looked at one another in a silence too eloquent for words.

" What a lovely place, Anthony ? Can it be possible that we might even have the smallest claim to it ? "

The true Anthony Weir shook his head. He was a tall, pale, delicate-looking man, with slightly stooping shoulders and thoughtful, intellectual face. His sister resembled him not at all. She had a short, rather plump figure, with a fine, open, regular face, striking by reason of its intelligence as well as beauty. It was beauty of a kind, the beauty that lasts and is enhanced by the wear and tear of life. Her bright, clear eyes could look unafraid into the reality of things. Already Lettice Weir had had to solve the problem of mere existence for herself and others, and, while the struggle had told perhaps in giving to her that self-reliance and calm assurance which is won in no other arena, it had in no way detracted from her womanly qualities. " A perfect woman, nobly planned, to warn, to comfort, and command." These words might fittingly have been applied to her. And it was easy to see that her brother, though the elder of the two, had been accustomed to lean upon her sound judgment, and to be guided by her in most of the affairs of life.

He walked to the bookshelves, and stood there devouring their contents with the hungry air of the man who had never before been filled.

She crossed the room and looked through the terrace window, finally opened it and passed out. The whole house interested her. She could have opened every door and wandered through the rooms, only she must wait. The time was not yet. It had often been described to her, but the reality far surpassed the fabric her imagination had built. Accustomed to small means, a narrow way of life, the dignity and greatness of this old family house, which seemd to represent untold wealth and inexhaustible leisure, laid a strange hush on the spirit. She was standing on the terrace looking westwards through the green vistas of the park, when the servant came to summon them to the luncheon that had been prepared for his master.

They looked at one another slightly askance at the invitation.

"Should we break his bread, Anthony?" she whispered.

"Why, certainly. It is our bread, not his. Come along," he answered, for once courageous where she would have drawn back.

So they sat together in the small dining-room, with the portraits of their father's forebears looking down upon them, feeling themselves enveloped in unreality, as if they were puppets in a play. Swanston waited upon them decorously, at the same time watching intently, and favourably impressed both by their looks and manners.

"They're quality," he reported in the kitchen; "and the laird has no reason to be ashamed of his relations." Whereat Bob delivered it as his opinion that they "wad help to shut mooths that were ower wide open."

When the door was closed Lettice Weir leaned her arms on the table and looked across at her brother.

"Anthony, I wonder how long he will be, and what will he say? Do you feel nervous?"

"No, do you?"

"I feel excited rather. It will be the strangest scene. How will he take it, I wonder?"

"There is only one way. We can punish him, and he knows it; but for his mother's sake we'll let him go free."

"I suppose it would be best. Can you believe that we are really here in Penninghame House, eating under its roof?"

"It's real enough. It took a clever man, Letty, to do it. We needn't grudge him that much."

She sighed ever so slightly.

"It was a terrible thing to do, but somehow I feel sorry for him. Don't let us forget, Anthony, that he never had a chance."

The sound of wheels on the gravel disturbed them, and Lettice sprang up. A small country cart, driven by a lady, wheeled round and stopped at the door. It was Madame de Castro driving alone to seek an interview with Anthony Weir.

CHAPTER XXXIX

COMPLICATIONS

THE butler stepped out to speak to Madame de Castro. She looked disappointed to hear that his master was absent from home.

" I hope he'll come by the next train, ma'am, for there are visitors in the house."

" Oh," she said interestedly. " Have they been here some time ? "

" No, ma'am ; arrived this morning, unexpected. The groom went to the station expectin' to meet the master at twelve, and they came. Their name is Weir—a lady and gentleman."

" Weir ; they must be his relatives from the Cape. I think I will see them."

She did not know what prompted her to such an unusual action. But the butler looked relieved rather than anything else.

" They've just had their lunch, ma'am, and if you'll come into the library I'll tell them."

He stepped back into the hall, and rang for some one to look after the trap, and presently ushered Madame de Castro along the familiar corridor to the library door. A slightly bitter smile tinged her lips as she entered the house under such auspices as a chance caller, who had less right there than the servant who admitted her.

Left alone in the room, she took a sharp glance round as if eager to assure herself that no desecrating hand had been laid on any of its treasures, and was relieved to find that everything, even to the smallest detail, remained as she remembered it. She was not aware, of course, that this was a room the new laird seldom entered. It was even more redolent of reproachful memory than any other part of the house, seeing the old man in his lifetime had spent all his time there, when able to come downstairs.

She was not long left alone. When the door opened she turned towards it, slightly at a loss and fully conscious that she had taken rather an unusual step. When the brother and sister entered, she looked at them with a swift and keen curiosity, and the first thing that struck her was the entire lack of resemblance to Anthony Weir. They looked like beings of some different order. The gentle, bookish man, and keen, alert, pleasant-faced woman, with the quiet air of breeding and self-possession, presented a sharp contrast to the somewhat imposing and always slightly aggressive personality of Anthony Weir.

" I must apologise for what must seem extraordinary, even unwarrantable," she said, with that winning grace of manner which none could assume more easily or more successfully. " I am Madame de Castro, daughter of the late Mr. Learmonth. I came over to see Mr. Weir, and, hearing of your arrival, thought I might bid you welcome in his absence. Surely your arrival has been somewhat unexpected. I saw him only yesterday, and he did not mention it."

The strangers looked at one another in mute bewilderment. It was an extremely awkward moment.

" He would not expect us, naturally, Madame," replied the man at once. " Nor can our arrival be at all in the nature of a pleasant surprise."

" But why ? " she asked, in a perplexed voice. " He has several times spoken of your probable coming. I feel sure he can only be too pleased. He has felt the isolation of the life here, and often regretted the old one, I think."

Perplexity deepened on both their faces, and it was the lady who spoke next.

" We had better speak quite frankly to this lady, Anthony, as she seems to know about his affairs."

He nodded, and Lettice Weir proceeded to address herself to Madame de Castro.

" There is some strange misunderstanding evidently, Madame. Since the man calling himself Anthony Weir is not here, I had better try to explain matters a little."

" The man calling himself Anthony Weir ! " repeated Isabel in blank amazement.

Lettice Weir inclined her head, and after a moment's hesitation pointed to her brother.

" This is Anthony Weir, Madame, the son of the late Anthony Gordon Weir, of Cape Town, and I am Lettice, his only sister."

" Who, then, is the man who has been here all this time, who came at my father's bidding, who has been personating your brother so successfully that he is now the master of this place, while I and my children are on the outside ? "

" It is soon explained and very simply, Madame. His real name is George Boothroyd. He was a clerk in a somewhat confidential capacity to my father in his lifetime, and on very intimate terms at our house. In fact, after my father's death he practically managed the business until my mother retired from it, in her last illness."

" But how did he ever come here as he did ? That is not explained," said Isabel, and the red flamed in her cheek as she thought of how she had been fooled by a nameless adventurer, who had even aspired to the hand of Sybil.

" He had my mother's full confidence, and he knew of the letter which came inviting my brother to Scotland. It was impossible for him then to accept, for our mother was in the last stages of a fatal illness, and could not be left. The further explanation is quite simple. This man, in full possession of the facts, and knowing our family history to the uttermost detail, simply came on chance. Apparently he has succeeded only too well."

Madame de Castro continued to gaze aghast, scarcely comprehending this new, and to her appalling turn in events. Looking at the two standing before her, not a doubt of their sincerity could cross her mind. Nay, there were certain family characteristics which she found in them strongly marked, and which she knew now had been entirely missing in the false Anthony Weir.

" I have never heard anything so terrible," she said " When did you come to Scotland ? Have you seen any lawyers regarding your claim ? "

The true Anthony Weir shook his head.

" No, Madame ; we only arrived in London two days ago ; in Edinburgh last night. Our idea was to come here first, and confront Boothroyd with his duplicity. We do not anticipate any difficulty when he sees us."

" But he ought to be punished. It is an awful thing he has done," she said hotly. " I should like to punish him myself. Why, only yesterday he was received at my house on the terms of equal friendship. And even he had the presumption "—here her voice broke—" the presumption to aspire to the hand of my daughter. It is just possible that you have arrived in time to prevent what would have been the most deplorable catastrophe."

" We are glad to be in time," said Lettice eagerly. " As for his presumption, it has no limit. He possessed our father's confidence, and to some extent our mother's. But on her dying bed she seemed very uneasy about him, and repeatedly entreated us to try and find out what had become of him."

" But he brought proofs of his identity home with him ; proofs sufficient to satisfy the most astute lawyers in Edinburgh."

" Whatever proofs he possessed must have been forgeries, since we have all the necessary documents. He had access, especially at the time of our father's death, to all his private papers, and must have made copies. He was an extraordinarily clever person, and most unscrupulous."

Madame de Castro turned with a kind of sudden quiet fury to the silent, studious-looking man who stood meekly by while his sister laid the whole case before her so clearly.

" What were you about, sir, to allow a person of that kind so much opportunity ? You have been most culpable, and have involved many innocent persons in untold trouble."

His face flushed.

" You are quite right, Madame. I feel that I have deserved your strictures, but I was never a business man. My tastes lie in other directions. I am a teacher and a student."

She continued to look at him with scarcely disguised contempt. In spite of his air of breeding, she wondered for the moment whether she did not prefer the virile force, the handsome face and figure of the man who had stepped in and made such rich capital out of his incapacity and lack of foresight. Lettice was quite conscious of the inwardness of the scrutiny, and resented it.

" Madame, all men are not similarly gifted," she said, a trifle stiffly. " My brother is a student, as he says, and has had great success in his own domain."

" That may be, but there never has been a student in Penninghame," she said good-humouredly. " If this fresh claim should be substantiated, it is you, my dear, who will be Laird of Penninghame."

Lettice Weir looked at the beautiful proud face with a sudden understanding of the bitterness hidden under her apparently calm exterior.

" It does not seem fair," she said quickly. " If you have children, their place is surely here. We are aliens, only in a less degree than the man who has kept you out."

Isabel's face softened, and involuntarily she held out her hand.

" My heart warms to you, as it never did to him. After all, we are kindred, and it may be possible for us to arrange matters amicably together. But in the meantime a great deal has to be done. The thing must be placed on a firm, substantial basis. We must take advice, and that at once. I question whether it will be wise for you to remain here until the pretended Anthony Weir returns. It gives him a chance he does not deserve."

" What can we do otherwise, Madame ? "

" I would suggest that you come to my house of Fintry. It is not far distant. Together there, we can go into the whole matter, and descend upon him when we have got our plans matured. We can also have the very best advice. This will alter the whole complexion of affairs for all concerned."

The brother and sister exchanged glances.

"We have already given our name to the servants. Directly Boothroyd returns and hears that we have been here, he will know what has happened, and can then escape much more easily than if we were here."

"That is true. I wonder where he is, and whether they have any idea of the time when he will return."

"Madame, they have none. They expected him last night, and have been meeting several trains to-day. That is how we chanced to be driven directly here."

Madame de Castro pondered a moment. Her mind was a whirl of conflicting thought, and she longed for some solid judgment to direct her.

"If you remain here," she said, "I will drive on a few miles further, and consult one who has the interests of Penninghame at heart. You will let me know what transpires here. The case really ought to be put in the hands of the police. Shall I send the sergeant of police here as I go through? I can easily see him as I pass through Whitekirk where he lives."

"The police! Would it not be better to settle this matter privately, and not give a fresh scandal to the world?" asked Lettice, with a touch of worldly wisdom and foresight which surprised Isabel.

"Good, so far as it goes; but is such a wholesale criminal to be allowed to go off scot free? It is not justice, Miss Weir. See what he has made innocent persons suffer. And even in the public interest and safety he ought to be prosecuted in spite of sentimental reasons."

Lettice sighed. She thought of the fair-faced boy that had been the playmate of their youth, and her reluctance grew.

"At present we can decide nothing," she said. "We can only wait here until he returns."

"Then I will wait too," said Isabel decidedly. "This unexpected development has changed everything. It may be even that Penninghame is actually mine now. Oh, was there ever so extraordinary an entanglement known since the world began?"

She rang the bell, and asked whether any one could drive or ride to Fintry with a note. Being answered in the affirmative, she wrote two—one to Sybil and one for Doctor Jeffrey.

Then she took off her bonnet and prepared to wait. But the waiting was destined to be a much more lengthy matter than any of them dreamed.

CHAPTER XL

FRIENDLY FACES

DAVID MAITLAND had been quietly making his arrangements to leave Bilbao. He realised that it was impossible for his sister to remain indefinitely at Fintry. Something in her letters warned him that it was time for him to come home, but he said nothing to any one in Scotland, preferring to come quietly, and perhaps by his sudden appearance learn that he most desired to know. His father had left him a competency, but he had no intention of relinquishing his calling, or even of relaxing his efforts to succeed in it. He did not even leave Bilbao until he had set in train other matters which would secure him an appointment when he wished it. But he needed and desired a little leisure first to put the affairs of his house in order.

He arrived in Edinburgh on an evening at the end of March, nearly three months after his father's death. Alighting at the station somewhat at a loss, he suddenly resolved to go straight out to Upper Dean House, and throw himself on the hospitality of Mrs. Shepherd. This for two reasons—he hated hotel life, being by nature and habit a social person, and secondly, because he was without immediate news of affairs at Penninghame. The law case would have been concluded that week, he had been unable to hear anything, or even to see a single paragraph alluding to it in any newspaper. Helen's letter containing the news of Anthony Weir's unlooked-for change of front had not reached him when he left Spain. Of later developments he was, of course, in total ignorance.

Getting into a cab he gave the address of the lawyer's house. Never had Edinburgh looked more fair as he drove along the incomparable sweep of Princes Street. The living green of an early and unusually genial spring clothed the grassy slopes, and made a wonder of beauty out of every tree. The sky had that tender opal hue so often seen in April, and the air was soft and balmy as a child's kiss. But the lad's heart was sore as he drove, for, while he loved it all with a surpassing love, it had become partly for him a place of painful memory. For the old man who had made it home for him and for his sister was not, and never would come again. In this mood he came to the imposing dwelling of the Shepherds, just beyond the Dean Bridge. It was just seven o'clock, and they were preparing for dinner when he was announced. Mr. Shepherd came to him first, and there was no doubt of the warmth of his greeting. It sent a glow into the boy's empty heart.

"David! David! I'm more glad to see you than I can say. We need you here. I suppose you have come on account of Helen's letter. I would have telegraphed, but she thought there was no haste, and in a foreign cable one can say so little, that it is apt to be a little alarming."

"Has anything happened then, or been discovered?" he asked eagerly. "I have had no letter out of the common, only the ordinary weekly one, full of nothing in particular."

"Nothing has been discovered about your father, my boy," said the lawyer sadly. "But a great deal has happened. Anthony Weir was an impostor altogether, David ; no more right to the name or what accompanied it than you or I ; in fact much less right."

"An impostor!" A number of varying expressions mingled on the young man's face. "How has it been discovered then?"

"Oh, quite in the usual way ; in fact, it differs not at all from the most approved three-decker novel ; the real Weirs came back—brother and sister—and they're installed at Penninghame in the meantime at least."

"And where's the other one?"

"They're hunting for him, but so far unsuccessfully. They've traced him and Nancy Nicolson as far as Liverpool, and there the clue is lost. What baffles us all is why he ran away at all, since it is certain he had no expectation of the Weirs turning up. My own private theory, David, is that the other thing has got on his nerves. Sergeant Gunn thinks so too. He's been in England several days hunting for him—feels his own reputation to be at stake. I must say, lad, that in spite of Jeffrey's high opinion of the sergeant, he has behaved throughout this case like an idiot. Why, any baby could have managed it better."

"Yet he seemed a shrewd man, and the last talk I had with him in his own office at Whitekirk impressed me with his ability."

"He can't apply it ; he's so busy piecing things together, as he calls it, that the prey slips through his fingers."

"The law case is off, then?"

"Yes, meanwhile. We are waiting counsel's opinion on the whole affair. It's the queerest complication I've ever seen ; but don't let's talk any more about it now. Come upstairs ; my wife will be glad to see you, and I take it very kindly, David, that you have come straight out to us at once, as if you felt that we were your friends."

"I felt a bit lonely as I came off the train. It's a poor business to have no home, Mr. Shepherd, and I'll set about getting one as fast as I can get things arranged. Helen has been long enough at Fintry."

"That's what I think. Indeed, I have said so to Mary, and she agrees ; but your sister has some idea of remaining there until the mystery is solved. She might stop there long enough, but she doesn't seem to realise that. She wants somebody to take rather a high hand with her in the matter."

David spent a very happy evening in that pleasant household, where all tried to make him feel at home. And when he went to bed he slept soundly, rocked by the music of the wind that cradled his babyhood. He could hear it sweep across the deep gullies, and almost at times fancied the beat of the grey waves mingling with it. He was in that sensitive, reminiscent mood which is apt to exaggerate and accentuate everything.

It was a gentle grey morning when David Maitland alighted at the now familiar station of Penninghame. A soft mist was creeping in from the hills, but there was no rain, and an occasional lightening of the filmy veil indicated the near proximity of the sun. It was a day when the fresh earth seemed to teem with life, what the farmers called a "grand growin' day". Maitland felt its sweet breath in his nostrils, and after the arid heat of the little Spanish city called it good.

He had learned many of the byroads of the neighbourhood during his short visit to Fintry, and, purposely avoiding the village, he came to the Penninghame gates by a field path little frequented. Then, crossing the road slantwise, he entered the woods by the gap in the hedge that had now become famous ; or, to speak correctly, he vaulted the fence that had been erected there by Anthony Weir to forbid the hordes who had begun to frequent the neighbourhood of the pool and generally to infest the Penninghame woods. It was a long way round in spite of what Helen had said to Shepherd, but David was in no hurry.

The Penninghame woods were looking their loveliest. More than once he picked a leaf and held it to his nostrils and inhaled its sweetness, and the chorus of the birds was indescribably beautiful. It was a fair spot indeed to have been darkened by any hint of tragedy.

Suddenly the perfect solitude was broken by the tread of a light footfall, and, looking down the little green alleys through the trees, he saw a woman's figure coming towards him. Just for a moment his heart beat, hoping it might be Sybil. But the next moment he was assured that he beheld a stranger. He waited until she came forward, and, guessing that she must be one of the new inmates of Penninghame, probably the sister of its laird, he raised his cap as she approached.

"I must apologise for what is an intrusion, madam," he said, with that fine courtesy of manner he had inherited from his father, and which foreign life had undoubtedly helped to perfect. "My name is Maitland. I am on my way to Fintry to see Madame de Castro."

To his surprise she at once extended a frank hand.

"I have met your sister. My name is Lettice Weir. Perhaps you have heard that my brother and I have just recently come to Penninghame from the Cape."

"I heard it only last night from my old friend, Mr. Shepherd. My sister has written, I believe, but the letter had not reached Bilbao when I left. May I congratulate you, Miss Weir, and Penninghame too, after its many vicissitudes on finding its true heirs at last."

She sighed, and her bright face clouded slightly. Suddenly she looked at David Maitland with a faint smile.

"I should like to talk to you if I may. I have heard of your goodness from every one, but chiefly from Frank, who adores you. Let us walk a little way together."

Maitland's face flushed with sincere pleasure.

"You say too much, Miss Weir. I feel a trifle overwhelmed. But it is pleasant to meet a friend in an unexpected place. I daresay, now you have heard the whole story of the past months, you can guess my errand."

Her face flushed a little too, and her eyes had an odd light in them.

"You mean the pool! I am going there myself. I come every day, sometimes twice. It is not very far now. Let us walk that way together."

"You are interested in the pool?" he said interrogatively, as they turned to climb the steep incline.

"Very much. I was born in South Africa, where there are no superstitions—I suppose I must call them—but there must be a Scotch strain in me somewhere, they interest me so deeply."

"Already, then, you have heard of the pool's mysterious qualities. I wish I could believe in them myself, Miss Weir. I suppose you know the melancholy interest I take in it?"

"Oh, yes," she answered sympathetically. "I often meet your sister here."

"You have seen her recently?"

"Yesterday in this very spot. We had a long talk about it."

"I am afraid poor Helen has grown morbid dwelling too much on one painful idea. I have come home to take her away as soon as arrangements can be made."

"Morbid is hardly the word. She is wonderfully cheerful, and she is perfectly assured that one day the secret will be revealed."

"It is a theory I can't accept, although I admit that it is strange how all ordinary methods have failed."

They entered the deep shadow of the trees, and a little hush seemed to fall naturally upon them. For David Maitland it was a painful moment, recalling all the misery of his last visit to the place.

He fell a step or two behind, inclined to silence, and so it came to pass that Lettice Weir came first to the edge of the pool.

Behind in the shadow he was disturbed and startled by a sudden sharp cry.

CHAPTER XLI

GIVES UP ITS DEAD

He hurried forward expecting he knew not what. Lettice Weir was standing on the path by the steep declivity looking into the depths with an expression of terror on her face. For a moment he stood quite motionless, half appalled, by her side. The water was all gone, and there was nothing left but the slimy bed of the pool forty feet below. Strange undergrowth and long green weeds were there twisted in inextricable confusion. And in the middle was the gnarled and twisted trunk of a tree, which looked as if it had been blasted by unseen force and snapped in twain in the middle of its happy growth. In the crevices of the trunk he saw a friendly little newt hopping about as if feeling quite at home. It was ten times more horrible now than it had been when the water covered it, and also more fascinating. David Maitland felt his face blanch, and something laid hold of him akin to the fear which is said to whiten a man's hair in a single night. He turned to his companion and laid his hand upon her arm.

"You had better come back; it is no place for you. I will go and get some help."

"Help for what?" she asked, as she turned to do his bidding, moved by the commanding note in his voice.

"Don't you see it will be possible now to make some search. And may I entreat you to say nothing. I would not have a gaping crowd here until —until we have made sure."

She shivered slightly in the warm soft air.

"How terrible for you! Is it not strange? Yesterday there must have been thirty or forty feet of water, and your sister said it had gone down several inches each day for more than a week. I am so thankful she is not here, but she will certainly come at some period of the day."

He turned and looked at her a moment, wondering whether he might ask her to befriend him. She was so calm and self-reliant, so frankly willing to be friendly, he felt the courage to do so.

"Is your brother in the house, and could you, do you think, get sufficient volunteers to come and help in the search? The men I would most wish to get, I am afraid will not be available—Doctor Jeffrey and Sergeant Gunn, who is out of Scotland."

"Doctor Jeffrey is coming to Penninghame this morning to see my brother, who is confined to his room. He is never very strong, and was very ill on the voyage. Let us go back together to the house, and see what we can do. We might be even fortunate enough to meet him."

Maitland glanced back towards the empty basin where many secrets might yet be hid, and where the one which had darkened life for him might even that day be discovered. Outwardly calm, he was inwardly disturbed, and his face was as pale as death.

"There are plenty of men at the stables and all about the place," she added quickly, when he did not speak.

"We ought to get the police first. Perhaps we had better go on to the house, and see whether the doctor has come. I sincerely hope he has. He will take the lead. I don't know what has come to me. I am as weak as water."

"It is natural; yours is the saddest interest," she said sympathetically, and, straining a last backward glance in the direction of the pool, shivered again.

They began to walk rather quickly down the incline, and, as they stepped out upon the road, the sound of wheels met their ears, and the doctor's gig came in sight.

His surprise at sight of David Maitland in company with the lady from Penninghame could not have been expressed in words. Before he came within speaking distance he saw that something unusual had occurred. The gig drew up in the roadway, and he bent down to hear what had happened. Maitland whispered something in his ear, which he fancied he had not heard aright. He leaped to the ground, and stood aside so that the groom could not hear.

"Dried up! Not a drop of water!" he repeated blankly. "It's impossible! Anything else to be seen?"

Maitland shook his head.

"Drive Miss Weir up to the house, Gentles," said the doctor to the groom. "We'll follow in foot." She made no demur, guessing perhaps that they wished some private speech together.

"What does it look like? How is it to be explained?" asked Jeffrey, with visible excitement. Maitland explained the situation as best he could.

"We can do nothing until the police come, David. You see, the circumstances make it a police case. I have to see Weir at Penninghame—the new Anthony Weir, I mean—and when we get up to the house I can send the gig on to Penninghame to bring the police up. Unfortunately for us the sergeant is absent in England on what I believe to be a wild-goose chase."

"Seeking the other Weir, I suppose. What a curious complication it has been, and what a tragedy of events crowded into a short space of time."

The doctor walked along in silence, swinging his arms behind his back.

"You're right. The countryside has had enough of Penninghame and its affairs to serve it for the next generation. Nice young woman that Miss Weir—worth two of her brother, but it is Frank de Castro that ought to have the place."

"Who knows? If all rumours come true, it may be his yet. The pool may now have its say in the matter," said Maitland suggestively.

"True! I didn't think of that. Do you really believe your poor father will be found to-day?"

"I do."

"It's most extraordinary. Now, how is such a thing to be accounted for; obviously there is no explanation. It comes into the region of the occult and the unsolvable. After all, we are obliged to come back to the old truism—'There are more things in heaven and earth. . . .'"

"Perhaps there may be some more feasible explanation. I would be loth to believe in such strange superstition," said Maitland. "Everything around and within us seems to forbid it."

The doctor shrugged his shoulders.

"I don't agree with you, but I shall be glad for your sister's sake if the matter could be cleared up. She has clung faithfully to her first conviction, but it has been a great strain. She will have to be very carefully told if anything is found. Strung up as she has been so long, I could not be answerable for the result of any shock."

"She has wonderful reserves of strength," said Maitland briefly. "I am not afraid of any such thing myself, but it is time she left Fintry for various reasons."

Jeffrey pondered on this speech later, but they arrived at the house at the moment, and the subject had to be abruptly changed.

He stepped up to the groom and bade him drive as rapidly as possible to the village, and bring back the policeman with him. Then he went indoors to his patient. He did not spend many minutes there, and when he again joined Maitland he suggested that they should proceed together on foot to the pool. Lettice Weir promised to send on the police and the necessary appliances whenever the trap returned from Penninghame. Maitland and his companion came in silence to the strange spot about which there had been so much supposition, so many strange assertions and beliefs. And there Jeffrey found it even as he had been told. He took off his hat, and the sweat drops of excitement stood upon his brow as he hung over the edge and looked into the yawning chasm.

"It's a ghastly place, and it will be a ghastly business recovering anything from these unknown depths. Do you think you should stay? It will be horrible for you."

Maitland looked at him in wonder and even faintly smiled.

"Stay! Why, of course. It is my duty. I should not shrink from it, and I am certain that it will be less difficult than you imagine."

As he spoke he clambered down the bare sides until he came within reach of the tree stump in the middle, to which he swung himself without difficulty. Grasping his stick firmly in his hand he stuck it into the soft mud and quickly found bottom.

"Not more than a foot. Shall we go ahead?"

Jeffrey's reply was to roll his trousers to his knees, throw off his coat, and follow. The excitement grew with every moment, but both kept cool enough to attend most thoroughly to the business in hand.

Maitland stepped ankle deep in the mud, and began to search among the high, slimy undergrowth with which the edges of the pool had been clothed. Jeffrey followed suit from the other side, so that they should meet in the middle. They worked silently with bated breath, bringing to the surface many things that had been carelessly thrown into the unknown depths. Once Jeffrey fished up a shining piece of jewellery and laid it flat on his hand. It was a long chain studded with sparkling stones that looked like diamonds, and, save, for the green ooze clinging to it, seemed intact.

"Look here, David, here's one of the secrets, a bauble that might tell a tale." But David never spoke. He was at the further side of the chasm bending towards a large thick tuft of weed and rushes.

"There's a hole here, doctor; come over; this is the spot!" he said hoarsely.

As he spoke he made a sudden gesture, and turned round with something on the end of his stick, the soft remnant of a silk hat which there was difficulty in recognising. Jeffrey never forgot the sickening horror of that moment. He had had many a strange experience behind the scenes, by dying beds in the silent night watches, but this far surpassed them all. He felt his nerve shaken as he made his way with faltering steps across to where Maitland stood. He was perfectly calm, though deadly pale, his eyes glowing in his head. They stood side by side a moment looking into the centre of the reeds where there was evidently a hole in which the water still stood.

"In there," said Maitland. "Will you search, doctor? God, I can't!"

"Perhaps we'd better wait," said the doctor, looking round a trifle desperately. "It would be better for you to go up. It won't be pleasant for you, but horrible, I warn you. I know what I'm talking about."

But the momentary shrinking passed. Maitland grasped his stout stick more firmly in his hand, and bent to his task once more. He stooped down, and there was a careful tenderness in his movements, which the doctor fully understood. He feared to hurt or to mark what he might find there—all that was left of the father he had adored.

So the horrible sickening moments passed. Then Maitland looked up and said simply—"The body is there. I can feel it quite distinctly. Can we manage to lift it ourselves?"

"Is the water deep?"

"No, only a few inches, but it is a curious hole, almost like the bed of a stream lower than the rest. Put your hand in. You will feel it as I say."

Before the doctor could make any movement the sound of voices clave the still air, and, looking up, they saw the policeman with two others looking down upon them in open-mouthed wonder.

"Come down as quickly as you can, men," said the doctor peremptorily. "There is something here."

The policeman grasped the long hook he had taken the precaution to bring with him, and clambered hastily down the side, the others following hard upon his heels. They were both young, however, and their hair almost stood on end. A few moments later what they had come to seek was revealed to their gaze. The body of James Maitland, long hidden from mortal ken, was once more restored to the light of human day. The bag which had been the cause of his death was still firmly gripped in his hand.

But the greatest wonder of all was that from his looks he might have died but yesterday. The body was wholly intact, the face swollen and discoloured, it is true, but easily recognisable.

Doctor Jeffrey took his hat from off his head, and looked round upon the stricken company.

"It is beyond our ken," was all he said.

CHAPTER XLII

THE MYSTERY

THEY looked from one another askance. David Maitland walked a little apart, and stood behind a tree, where they could not see him. He felt completely overcome, and only realised now that he had never really parted with hope, but that there had lurked in the far background of his mind a faint belief that there might be truth in the supposition made at the time, that his father for some reason known best to himself had deemed it expedient to disappear. But now the simplest explanation had been the true one after all ; it had happened in every detail just as the sergeant and others had supposed. The doctor and the policeman held a hurried conference. It was the sound of their voices that brought Maitland to himself. They were discussing what to do with the body, and the policeman had just announced that he should have it conveyed to the village mortuary. Then he stepped forward to put in his word. At the same time a fresh figure appeared upon the scene, to the surprise and dismay of all, the figure of Lettice Weir, who had quickly followed upon the footsteps of the men from the stable. The doctor stepped back, lifted his overcoat from the tree branch where it had been suspended during the searching operations, and covered the prostrate form lying on the soft green sward. She stepped forward, and though a little plea did not look disturbed.

" You have found him ? " she said hurriedly. " Oh, I am so sorry for poor Mr. Maitland."

Maitland inclined his head at this expression of sympathy, and for a moment there was an awkward silence which Lettice broke, addressing herself to the doctor.

" You are wondering, I think, what to do with the body. Please have him carried to Penninghame. I come direct from my brother with that message. He would have come himself had he been able."

The doctor looked round. It was the simplest way out of the difficulty, also there was something fitting about it.

" Thank you, Miss Weir. Believe me, I shall not soon forgot this extraordinary consideration," said Maitland huskily. " But it will be a trying experience for you, most painful in fact ; it ought not to be inflicted upon you."

" We don't mind in the least ; why should we ? " she asked quietly. " I understand from your sister that your own home in Edinburgh is occupied at present, and it would be difficult for you to arrange the matter."

" It would only be for a day," he said eagerly. " We should certainly bury him to-morrow or next day in our own vault at Greyfriars at Edinburgh. If you will do me this great kindness, it will be deeply appreciated."

She nodded and bade the stablemen go back to the house and prepare a stretcher. All turned to her and waited. It was as if some guiding spirit had suddenly descended in their midst, to end all their perplexity and doubt.

" I will go round by the village and send the carpenter to the house at once," said the doctor. " And you, David, I suppose your sad errand will take you to Fintry."

" Presently ; I will see everything done first," he replied.

At the same time he approached the prostrate figure and kneeled down beside it. With one dexterous stroke of his pocket knife he severed the handle of the brief bag from it and lifted it aside.

" This must be taken care of," he said, with a significant glance towards Doctor Jeffrey, who nodded in reply.

" I can't leave you here alone, David," said the doctor, when all the others had disappeared, the police to report the occurrence to headquarters, and the stablemen to bring the stretcher. Lettice had gone on also to prepare a room for the reception of the sad burden.

Maitland smiled faintly, and shook his head.

" Why not ? I should like it. The poor old man who never harmed a soul, or harboured an evil thought ! It's a cruel end, doctor, and, if there's justice in heaven, it ought to come home to his murderer."

" Oh, it will, never fear, though it's a poor enough satisfaction. I'll wait here with you. They can't be long."

" It really is not necessary. Do you think I'm afraid to be left with the old man ? " he asked, with a touch of pathos which brought a swift moisture to Jeffrey's eyes.

" Not afraid exactly ; but to me it's a most unholy place. I could take a stiff glass, David, and that's the solemn truth. Will you open the bag while we wait ? "

Maitland undid the clasp without difficulty, and looked within. A few sodden papers lay at the bottom. That was all. He took them carefully between his fingers and lifted them out.

" I think we had better not touch them, doctor. They must be dried first. I sincerely hope they will then be decipherable, so that all doubt regarding the Learmonth Succession Case may be at an end."

He replaced them in the bag, closed it, and sat down on a fallen tree trunk. Conversation did not flourish between them in that silent, gloomy place upon which the sweet clatter of nest-building birds seemed to fall with an alien sound.

They had not long to wait. Within half an hour the little procession with its sad burden moved through the green alleys towards the old house of Penninghame, and so within. Not knowing, Lettice had caused the old laird's room to be prepared, and so it came to pass that for the second time the dead lay there. There was much whispering and consternation in the servants' hall, a little horror likewise, and a momentary desire to flee the place, but, seeing their new mistress so brave and unconcerned, they gathered courage likewise, and began to regard the occurrence with more fortitude.

The policeman called in at the carpenter's on his way down, and early in the afternoon he drove up with an oaken coffin, which had lain in his attic above his workshop for a long time, having been prematurely ordered for a person who was now walking about hale and hearty, and as likely to live as any one in the parish.

When all was over, David Maitland walked away quietly across the fields to Fintry. He was not afraid that the news would be before him. Fintry was an out-of-the-way place, to which news travelled slowly. He had to pass through the Penninghame woods again, and, as he ascended the path that had now become so familiar, he descried a figure in the distance easily recognisable as Helen. He hastened on, and they met just on the ridge very near the edge of the pool. She was too much surprised for the moment to speak.

"David, David ! is it really you ?" she cried shrilly. "Where have you come from ? Did you know I could not bear my life another moment at Fintry. Oh, I am so very glad to see you !"

She threw her arms about his neck, and for a moment he held her close, and wondered in what words he should tell her of the extraordinary thing that had happened.

"You got on my nerves, Helen. I felt that it was time something was done," he said tenderly. "Dear me, how thin you have grown, and how pale and anxious-looking ! Why did you not write to me, my dear, if you were unhappy, and wanted a change ? You know we have only each other left now, and must stick together."

"Yes, yes. I know ; I ought to have gone to Spain with you, but I waited on, always hoping something would be discovered. But I have quite given up hope now, and I will be glad to go, dear David. In the wide world I know I have only you. They are tired of me at Fintry. A sad face is not long welcome, and since there has been so many changes I shall be glad to get away."

"You have seen the new people, Helen ; they seem to be very kind," he said, still putting off his telling, though why he could not have explained even to himself.

"Oh, yes, they are very kind, especially Lettice, she is so wholesome and sound-hearted. Doubtless they are the true Weirs, but I am so tired of it all. I want to get quite away where I shall never here the words Learmonth or Weir or Penninghame again. Madame de Castro is so changeable, so full of caprice, no one can manage her except Doctor Jeffrey. She really stands in awe of him. And she acts on such ridiculous impulses. Why, before this strange new development, Anthony Weir was on visiting terms at Fintry, and had even aspired to the hand of Sybil."

"The hand of Sybil !"

"Oh, don't look like that, David. I don't want you to care for Sybil de Castro ; she is not good enough, and her mother would never allow you to marry her. She is much too proud."

He put her a little away from him, and kept hold of her hands. It was time to change the subject, time to tell her the truth.

"Helen have you heard nothing to-day ?" he asked with a sudden hoarse note in his voice.

She shook her head, regarding him with a fixed surprise. She had been talking so much that she only now noticed for the first time the strangeness of his looks.

"Heard what ?" she gasped, in a faltering whisper. "Has anything happened ?"

"Everything has happened, Helen. We have found him to-day."

"Found father ?"

"Yes."

"But where, and where is he now ?" she cried wildly. "Oh, why have I been kept in the dark so long ? I, who have suffered so much, and waited and watched so long, never relaxing even for a moment."

"Hush, hush, Helen. These things are above and beyond any of us. Did you notice nothing yonder as you came by ? We found him in the pool in the very spot where you always said he would be found."

"But how have they managed it? Have they been trying some new apparatus? Everything has failed. The sergeant and I have had many long talks about it, but nothing ever came of our efforts. And what have you done with him?" she added wildly. "I want to see him. Who has dared to take him away from me? You ought not to have allowed it, David."

"He is only at Penninghame, dear. Miss Weir was here soon after we found him, and she offered us the shelter of Penninghame. Come back with me now, and you will see him lying in the laird's own room. Strange, is it not, that he would be laid there in the last room he was in before he disappeared."

Her face wore an awe-stricken look, and she lingered, holding him by the arm, and glancing backwards towards the pool.

"How did you say you had found him, David?"

"That is the strangest part of it, Helen. When I came here this morning the water was dried up to the very bottom, and it was only a question of a very few moments to do the rest."

"Dried up!"

She spoke the words in a voiceless whisper. "Come back with me, David, and look again. Are you sure of what you say?"

"Quite sure. I was down in the very depths on the muddy bottom and I found him myself in a hole which I will show you among the reeds."

They took some steps forward, and then stood still, open-mouthed, before the wonder they beheld.

They might have dreamed the occurrence of the morning, for the pool was as it had been for many a day; the water still, motionless, deep and inscrutable, up to its former level, and not showing a single ripple on its breast.

CHAPTER XLIII

IN THE QUEEN'S NAME

George Boothroyd, otherwise Anthony Weir, had no difficulty in lifting three hundred and fifty pounds from the Commercial Bank in George Street next morning. The cashier expressed no surprise at the amount of the sum, which comprised the whole balance of the current account; but Weir volunteered the information that it was for the payment of some extensive work being carried out on the steading of the home farm. They exchanged a few remarks on the weather and things in general, and Weir departed thankfully with the notes safely in his pocket. He had asked the cashier to give him Bank of England notes and sovereigns rather than Scotch notes, but even that did not arouse his suspicion; he had frequently heard dislike, and even distrust, of Scotch notes expressed by clients who had come from England or abroad.

Nancy was waiting for him at a shop window opposite, and when he assured her he had the money, her face assumed a more satisfied look. Nancy was becoming initiated into the mysteries of living by one's wits and proving herself quite an apt pupil. She was now feverishly anxious to be gone, to shake the dust of Scotland from off her feet forever. Having once put her hand to the plough, she had no intention of looking back. Woman-like, being thrown entirely on the mercy of the man who had won her from the old peaceful life, she had given to him the whole depth of affection of which she was capable. What self-sacrificing depths they were he was yet to prove. At noon they took their seats in a south-going train which carried them as far as Carlisle. Later in the day they reached Crewe, where they waited for the night mail for Liverpool. Nancy never forgot that arrival in the chill grey dawn. Tired, cold and disconsolate, she waited while her husband collected their scanty luggage and put it into a cab, afterwards directing the man to drive them to a quiet respectable hotel.

"Not too dear," he added, and the cabby nodded comprehensively.

He took them a long way round, and brought them to a small obscure house near the docks kept by a relative of his own. It did not look a very inviting place, but they had not choice; they only needed and asked a few hours' sleep, expecting to sail in the American boat the next afternoon. Nancy was dead tired, and slept without waking until ten o'clock.

When she rose she found that her husband had already left, and for one moment only a feeling of sick horror overcame her. She dressed herself unsteadily, and rang the bell to ask where he had gone, and whether he had left any message. She was reassured by the sight of sundry belongings of his scattered about the room, but it was long before she recovered from the shock of the fear lest he had gone off and left her stranded, penniless among strangers. The message the slatternly chambermaid brought was quite reassuring.

"Genelman went out at nine, ma'am, said he would be back in an hour, gone to the shipping office, ma'am, that's all. He said he was very seedy, an' had a brandy and soda before he went out."

Much relieved, Nancy finished her toilet and went down to the coffee-room for her breakfast, and before she had begun to eat he came in. She was struck by his strange look.

"Ye're no feeling weel, Anthony," she cried, springing up.

He held up a warning forefinger.

"You must forget the old name, lass," he said, not unkindly. "I do feel beastly bad, suppose it's the excitement. I'll have a cup of strong coffee. No, I couldn't eat anything, every morsel would choke me. Well, the news is bad this morning. The *Cambria* we wanted to get off on this afternoon got knocked coming out of the dry dock yesterday, and the Board of Trade won't pass her. They don't think she's seaworthy."

"But is there no anither boat?" cried Nancy, looking genuinely alarmed.

"Yes, the big White Star liner, but she's full up. I've spent twenty minutes trying to get them to take us on; even offered to pay for first-class berths. But they won't. What do they care; got more business at this season than they know how to manage, and got swelled head in consequence. I gave the chap in the office a bit of my mind, he was too high and mighty altogether."

"What are we to dae then?" asked Nancy blankly, laying down her knife and fork.

"Wait till next Wednesday, but I don't think it good enough. Think we'll go to Southampton to-night and catch a North German Lloyd; we'd be safer there anyhow than here. Liverpool's their happy hunting-ground, you see. Everybody clears out from Liverpool. It would have been all right if we could have got away to-day, because the *Cambria* doesn't stop till she gets to Quebec."

"I'm feared," said Nancy, in a low voice. "I dinna like the look of things."

"Oh, there isn't much in that, if I felt better, but I do feel beastly bad, Nancy, and no mistake. I think I'll have a good hot bath and get to bed. I've got a chill or something. Wish we were in a better place. After Penninghame this seems a bit low down."

"Oh, what does that matter?" said Nancy feverishly. "If only we could get away. I hope you're no gaun to be ill here. It would be terrible."

"I'll be all right when I've had a sleep; you can go out and get a few things we need. I'll write out the list. Have you finished your breakfast? Try and make a good one, it puts pluck into one. Here, waiter, bring me a cup of strong black coffee, and a liqueur brandy, and tell the chambermaid to put a rousing fire in the room we had last night."

They lingered by the little table in the dingy window, until they thought the fire would have burned up. But Nancy did not like the look of her husband. She had to give him her arm on the stairs, and when they got into the room he sank as if exhausted on the bed.

"I believe I'm in for an illness of some sort. If I don't mend in time to get off to-night, promise me you won't send for a doctor, but doctor me yourself, and keep quiet about where we came from, and where we mean to go."

"It's no likely I wad say onything, I'm ower feared," said Nancy. "But I'll no promise aboot the doctor. If I think ye need one, I'll bring him."

"Don't, unless it's desperate. I think I'll be better when I've had a good sleep. It's a mercy we came to this hole after all. It's in such an obscure street nobody could ever find it, and it's very handy to the docks and the shipping offices. I feel drowsy. I think I'll get a good sleep."

His eyes were closing as he spoke; the coffee, which at another time would have acted as a strong stimulant in conjunction with the brandy, produced a very deep sound sleep.

As Nancy sat limp and miserable by the fire, listening to his heavy breathing, she was not to be envied. She hated to be alone. In the enforced silence all sorts of terrors took practical shape. She pictured the opening of the door, the entrance of the police, she and Boothroyd sitting on the north-going train perhaps with handcuffs on their wrists. There was no horror possible to their situation that Nancy did not go through in imagination that dreary interminable day. It wore to evening, however, as will the longest day, and when her husband awoke, though feverish, he seemed better. But he agreed with her that it would be unwise to try and leave Liverpool that night. When the Sunday dawned he was obviously worse and rambling in his talk, which alarmed Nancy to such an extent that immediately after breakfast she left the house in search of a doctor.

She had not far to go. A few doors further down the street she came upon one of the open surgeries with which the poorer parts of Liverpool abound. The name on the brown painted window arrested her—Doctor Galbraith.

Feeling that she would be more at home with a countryman of her own she opened the door boldly, and walked in. The little waiting-room, with its bare floor and table strewn with magazines, had already its full complement of patients, and she had to wait quite twenty minutes before her turn came to slip into the inner room. The doctor, a young fresh-coloured man, with sandy hair and a pair of kindly blue eyes, looked at her interestedly as she sat down. She was rather better dressed than the majority of his poor clients, and had not altogether lost the fresh colour that had been one of her chief attractions.

"Good-morning, what can I do for you?" he asked politely.

"I want you to come and see my husband," she said quickly and nervously. "We're living at Marsham's Hotel, jist up the street."

"Oh, you're not long from Scotland, perhaps."

"No long, we were on our way abroad," she said, impelled to a certain amount of confidence. "We were to have sailed yesterday, but he wasna able. He seems to hae some kind o' a fever and disna' ken me the day."

"I'm sorry to hear that. I'll come in when I close at twelve, Mrs.—Mrs.——"

"Boothroyd," she answered, with a momentary hesitation.

"English husband?" he remarked, with a smile. "You're Scotch enough."

"Oh, yes, I'm Scotch," she answered, a trifle confusedly; "like yersel'," she added, trying to recover herself.

"Ay, my name betrays me. We do well here, and the Scotcher the name the better. Good-morning, just now, Mrs. Boothroyd—I'll be round to Marsham's inside of an hour."

The sound of his voice, his quiet cheery way, somehow reassured her, and she departed to wait his coming with what patience she might. After all it would be better to have a countryman of her own, he would at least understand what she said. In London Nancy had had great and continual difficulty in making herself understood.

He was as good as his word. At ten minutes past twelve he was in the room where Boothroyd lay staring straight before him, murmuring unintelligible words that filled Nancy's heart with untold alarm. He made a brief examination and then turned to the poor young wife, smiling to reassure her.

"Only a very bad attack of influenza—be all right in a day or two. Don't worry about him, Mrs. Boothroyd. I'll send round something that'll take down this high temperature and stop the rambling. It's that that alarms you, I can see."

Nancy did not say what she feared, that in his slight delirium he might say things to arouse suspicion. For that reason she was anxious to cut the doctor's visit as short as possible, though he was evidently inclined to sit down and have a good talk. The pair interested him, and he would have liked to learn a little more about them. But he found her reticent and distant to a degree, and had to depart unenlightened. He called again next day to find his patient considerably better, but there was no encouragement given to him to prolong his visit, or to sit down for a friendly talk, as he felt inclined.

"We'll get out of here whatever happens to-morrow, Nancy," said Boothroyd, the moment the door closed. "It was a pity you sent for him. He seems inquisitive, and it's always widening the area, don't you see?"

Nancy only partially comprehended him.

"You seemed awfu' ill, an' I'm no sorry I sent, for he's made ye better very quick. By the morn ye'll maybe be able to gang oot an' see what we're to dae next."

"Well, well, have your own way. I'm surprised even that you're so anxious about my worthless life, Nancy. It's a poor plight you're in now."

Nancy turned away suddenly, her eyes filling with tears. She could not gainsay the truth of what he said, yet how contradictory is the nature of woman. She had very few regrets, and would not have exchanged her present estate for any that could have been offered to her. Its very elements of uncertainty and excitement helped to make it more interesting than the common lot.

Doctor Galbraith looked in early next morning as he proceeded down to open his surgery. He found the couple at breakfast, the room all tidy, and the fire burning cheerily. It was impossible for Nancy to live among untidiness or dirt; her aunt had trained her too well. So she had got the necessary utensils from the chambermaid, and before her husband was awake cleaned the room to her own satisfaction. He was sitting up in bed, looking a trifle weak and pale after his sharp attack, but more like himself than he had been since they had left Scotland. The doctor rubbed his hands in satisfaction at sight of him.

"There, what did I tell you?" he asked cheerily. "He'll be as right as a trivet in a day or two, but you must be careful not to run any risks."

"We must go on to-day, doctor, so if you tell us what we owe you my wife will pay," said Boothroyd formally.

"But my dear fellow you can't," cried the doctor in dismay. "I shan't take the responsibility of permitting it."

"I don't want you to. I have no choice. We've got to get to the steamer in time or we forfeit our passage money."

"Never heard anything so idiotic, it'll end in a burial at sea," he said warningly.

"Well, it wouldn't matter much. Get the purse, Nancy, and pay the doctor, and let him go."

"Grand excitement in the papers this morning," said Galbraith, while he waited for Nancy to get the purse from the wardrobe drawer. "I don't suppose you ever heard of that queer case in the Lothians. I'm interested myself, for all my people live in Roxburgh. An old lawyer disappeared, and they thought he had been murdered, pushed into a pool in the woods there. Queer story altogether; said the pool couldn't be fathomed, and all that sort of thing; they were never able to search it in the ordinary way. Country folk believed that it dried up of its own accord when it wanted to make things hum, and by Jove, it has just done it, dried up, and they've found the body, of course. . . . Why, what's this?"

There was the sound of heavy feet outside on the landing, and the door was suddenly pushed open with no gentle hand. Nancy gave a faint scream, as her eyes fell on the quite familiar face of Sergeant Gunn, of Whitekirk. She guessed his errand even before his dread words fell on her ears.

Marching up to the bed, he laid his heavy hand on her husband's shoulder. "Anthony Weir, alias George Boothroyd, I arrest you in the Queen's name for the murder of James Maitland at Penninghame, Midlothian, on the thirteenth day of January last."

CHAPTER XLIV

IN THE PUBLIC WAY

At nine o'clock that evening the little party arrived at the Caledonian Station in Edinburgh. Nancy would never forget to her life's end the shame of that experience. But she never flinched.

" Whaur will ye tak' us, sergeant ? " she asked, as they steamed past the familiar environs of the city and approached the great terminus.

" Us," repeated the sergeant. " I havena apprehended you, my lass ; though maybe," he added with caution, " that'll come later."

" Then whaur'll I gang ? " she asked dismally. " I'll no leave my man."

Boothroyd, who had sat for the most part staring moodily out of the window or with his head sunk on his breast, looked up at this and partially smiled.

" You should leave the sinking ship, Nancy ; that's the way of the world."

She shook her head.

" That I'll never dae," was all she said.

" I can tak ye oot to Penninghame the morn if ye like," said the sergeant. " If naebody'll tak' ye I will. My mistress is no that parteecular, an she's used to a' kinds."

It was meant kindly, but somehow sounded a particularly brutal speech. Nancy drew herself up, and a few inches further away from the sergeant.

" No, thank ye, I'm no needin' charity, an' I dinna happen to be ' a sorts,' Sergeant Gunn ; I'm a respectable married wummin, and please dinna you forget it."

" Bravo ! " said Boothroyd heartily, but the sergeant only grinned broadly, and at the moment the train steamed into the station.

Nancy alighted first, and immediately, as if acting on a sudden impulse, stood straight in front of the carriage door with her skirts spread out in a vain endeavour to shield the handcuffed man from the public gaze. It was a wholly womanly and pathetic picture, which moved even the stolid sergeant, though he made no sign. It is certain that in that moment of acute anguish Nancy fully expiated her sin.

" You had better give your wife some money, my man," he said mildly. " It will all be taken from you presently, and till the trial comes on she must live."

Boothroyd dived into his breastpocket and gave Nancy his pocket-book, also a handful of loose coin from his outer one. The sergeant discreetly looked the other way. This was his way of sympathising with the poor, forlorn creature who was finding the way of transgressors so hard.

" Where will you go, Nancy ? Back to the hotel in Cockburn Street ? " whispered Boothroyd. " As long as they don't know who you are it'll be all right, and it is conveniently near—that is, if they'll allow you to see me. Good-bye, my dear. I won't say I'm sorry. Between you and me that would be a mockery now."

Nancy wrung his hand and stepped back into the throng, so that none noticed that she had actually made one of the little party in the reserved compartment. The next moment the sergeant had hurried his prisoner into the nearest cab, the door was shut with a bang, and they drove away through the gaping crowd. Nancy glanced round the brilliantly-lighted station, and half staggered against the wall. She was once more cast desolate and forsaken on the sea of life, uncertain where to turn, without comfort for the present or hope for the future.

But it was growing late, and some shelter for the night she must have, since she was weak and far spent. The strain of the last few trying days had told more than she imagined. She was very strong, certainly, with the fine, sound strength which country life can give, but she had been hitherto quite unaccustomed to mental strain. Oh, if only she could lie down and sleep, sleep for ever ! That was the burden of her desire. She called a cab at length, and gave the hotel address. Arrived there, she was admitted without comment, and after drinking a cup of tea and eating a morsel of bread and butter she locked her door and crept miserably to her bed. She had little knowledge of the slow procedure of the law, and fully expected that the trial would begin probably to-morrow morning. Had she foreseen the dreary weeks of suspense she would have to endure before the case came on for hearing she might have slept less soundly than she did.

Next morning she read in the newspapers a full and detailed and slightly embroidered account of the capture of George Boothroyd, evidently a hardened criminal, in Liverpool, together with some description of herself as his female companion. She laid down the wretched, lying sheet, as she described it inwardly, and, laying her head on her hands, sat in dumb misery. She was in the coffee-room at the breakfast-table, but had apparently forgotten. She was aroused by some one uttering her name, the old alias, Mrs. Colville, which she had given on the happy spur of the moment when she came in the previous night.

She looked up and beheld the landlady before her, a portly, important-looking person in a shabby gown of black silk and a large bunch of keys jingling at her side.

" Excuse me, ma'am, but I—must ask you a painful question, which I hope you will understand. I wouldn't ask if I weren't in a public way."

" What is it ? " asked Nancy listlessly, yet feeling her face redden.

" It's not very easy, but you see, in the public way as I am, and a widow woman, I have to be very particular."

" Oh, yes," murmured Nancy. " Say away."

" If you can only assure me that you are in no way connected with—with that terrible person the police got a hold of yesterday in Liverpool, I'd be much relieved. I couldn't help suspecting something when you came in last night just after the train they came by must have arrived, and the papers mention that there was a lady with them. If it's a mistake I beg your pardon, ma'am, but you see, being a widow in the public way, I've got to be very careful. It's so easy to get a house a bad name, and there's always folks ready to throw stones."

" Yes, indeed, there are," said Nancy, as she rose to her feet. " I'm his wife, ma'am, and what's more I'm not ashamed of it. He's a better man than plenty that's walkin' free, and as for your hoose, it's nae treat for onybody. If ye could keep it a wee cleaner ye micht get mair customers."

Poor Nancy may be forgiven that last arrow of revenge. The first part of her speech had been delivered with a quiet, pathetic dignity which almost melted the good-natured landlady's heart; the last put her into a fury past expression. In less than ten minutes Nancy was out of the house. She took her luggage down to the station cloakroom, and there left it until she should fall upon some plan for the future. It was now only eleven o'clock. As she wandered aimlessly along the platform her eye was suddenly arrested by one of the boards directing passengers to the trains.

"Next train, Porth Junction, Penninghame, and Rosford, 11.20."

She hesitated a moment only, the next she was rapidly walking towards the booking-office, where she took a ticket for Penninghame.

"A'body seems to be gaun to Penninghame," said the clerk jocularly. "That's the fifteenth ticket I've selt this mornin'."

Contrary to his expectation the fresh passenger made no comment on his remark, and he went back to revel in the exciting details of the crime and its late unravelling, of which all the newspapers were full.

Nancy took her seat in a corner with a newspaper, too, which she studied diligently, holding it up well before her face. A curious and searching kind of martyrdom was hers during that brief hour which the stopping train took to get to its destination. She was in a third-class carriage, where there is usually to be found a general disposition to talk. Every man had a newspaper, and every woman was gasping to hear what was in it. And they talked entirely and continuously of the crime in all its bearings. The little woman shrinking in the corner heard her own character and behaviour discussed in an entirely new light, and got a fresh baptism of the tender mercies of the world.

A "limmer," a "hizzie," a "thorough bad lot"—such were the epithets freely bestowed, and one large complacent female gave it forth as her opinion "that dootless she was at the bottom o' a'thing, an' had led the puir chap awa'".

What wonder that, driven almost to the verge of desperation, having but one desire—to throw back their lies in their teeth, and hurl defiance at the whole world—the tortured creature was thankful to alight at Porth Junction pursued by the desire to escape from such merciless tongues. She did not know what she was doing there even, nor what she intended to do. She had acted on an impulse for which there was no accounting, and which seemed likely to lead her only to more suffering. If she were to present herself at Fintry now that the whole facts of the case had been laid bare, what could she expect but cold looks and a shut door? The attitude of her fellow-travellers was doubtless the attitude of the whole world. So said Nancy in her haste, but before the day closed she was to prove that there were still kind hearts left and brave souls not afraid to wander a little out of the beaten track in order to show kindness to a sister in distress.

She needed none to guide her footsteps when she passed without the little booking-office and found herself on the open road. She tried to count how many days had passed since she had been driven there before, but no order would come out of the chaos of her thoughts. She felt like one dazed and bewildered, unable to grasp the simplest fact.

She made no mistake in the direction, however, but turned to the Penninghame road when she got to the foot of the station brae.

It was a fine bright spring morning, with a fresh breath in the air, and the wonder and joy of the opening year seemed scattered everywhere. Never had hedge, and tree, and smiling fields seemed more fair in the eyes of the girl as she walked along what was to her a desolate highway, leading she knew not whither. Its very familiarity was almost a pain. Once she bent forward and took a sprig of early hawthorn from a sheltered nook at the hedge and stuck it in her breast. It had a festive look little in keeping with her actual mood.

For about two miles she followed the boundary hedge of the estate which marched with Penninghame. The moment she crossed that she climbed the fence and entered the Penninghame woods. She had an odd sense of right to them which she could not have substantiated in words, only it was strong enough even to comfort her slightly. At that early hour ordinary strollers were not about, and she did not even meet a forester or a gamekeeper to question her right to wander on restricted ground. All the by-paths and woodland ways were familiar to Nancy. Had she not in the days which now seemed centuries away wandered there with the lads who had sought her favour, and whom she had mostly laughed at for their pains? So she came unerringly, and with considerable speed, to the part of the woods that had witnessed the tragedy mainly responsible for the secondary tragedy of her life. And yet was it secondary? At least the old man who had died after a useful life, full of honour and deeply mourned, was now at peace. Whereas she——

The newspapers had not failed to give prominence to the more superstitious and mysterious side of the discovery at Penninghame Pool, and Nancy was curious to see how it looked now after having, as it were, revenged itself for its long silence.

She came upon the top of the cliff from the other side, and waited a moment on the brow of the descent, all the details of that fateful afternoon coming sweeping back upon her in a great flood, and she suddenly became aware that she was not alone.

A lady was standing motionless by the brim of the pool, a stranger lady whom Nancy had never seen in these parts before. It was not Helen Maitland, whom she knew quite well by sight. Her first impulse was to flee, but the lady turned towards her, smiled slightly, and bade her a pleasant good-morning.

CHAPTER XLV

THE TRUE CHRISTIAN

"GOOD-MORNING," said Nancy, somewhat confusedly. "I didn't think I would meet onybody here."

"Don't look so alarmed, there is no crime in walking through the woods; but I rather suspect from your looks you were bent on something more than a mere stroll on a pleasant spring morning. We have had a very large number of visitors here of late."

Nancy did not fail to notice the proprietary pronoun "we," and a sudden fear smote her. For, if she were really face to face with one of those whom her husband had so shamefully defrauded, where would she look or what could she say? She felt as if it would be the very last straw added to an already almost intolerable load.

"I hae nae business here, I ken; but I will go on again."

Lettice Weir, who had somehow an intuition regarding the identity of the girl to whom she spoke, sought to detain her in order to make sure.

"Have you any special interest in this place?" she asked casually.

But Nancy did not respond.

"I'll say guid-mornin'," she said, rather quickly, and would have passed on, but Lettice Weir stood straight in front of her.

"Do I speak to the girl of whom I have heard a good deal since I came to Penninghame, Nancy Nicolson?"

"Yes," answered the girl, and a dull red flush mounted to her face. "I was Nancy Nicolson."

"You poor creature, how forlorn you must feel! When did you come here? We have all thought you far enough away."

"We came from Liverpool last night," she answered, in a low voice, and suddenly sinking on the trunk of the fallen tree close by the edge of the pool, covered her face with her hands. She was so forlorn indeed that she did not know where to turn next, and the kind notes of a woman's voice, the first she had heard for long, almost broke her down.

Lettice Weir moved to her side and laid a kind hand on her shoulder.

"Look up and listen to me, my dear. I am older than you, and I would befriend you if I could."

"Ye canna be her I thocht, the sister of the real Anthony Weir," said Nancy, in a low voice, and without looking up.

"But your surmise was quite right. I am Lettice Weir, and I still say I would befriend you if I could."

"But I'm his wife," she said, suddenly throwing up her head. "And I'm no ashamed o' it; I wad gang to the ends o' the earth for him, and now they'll hang him, and what'll become o' me?"

She moaned a little, and rocked herself to and fro on her rough seat.

"Perhaps it will not be so bad as that. I am glad to hear you speak even as you do, my dear, for we knew him, too, across the seas, and we can never believe him such a hardened criminal as they seek here to make out."

" He didna kill the old man for sheer love o' it," said Nancy, with a straight glance at the waters gleaming under the sun rays which penetrated through the spring leaves. " I was here and I saw it. It was a struggle, and in the middle o' it he fell ower. My man says it was an accident, and I believe he speaks the truth."

" If you can tell them that in the Court, Nancy, it may save your husband's life, perhaps even get him off."

Nancy hopelessly shook her head.

" I hae heard," she said slowly, " that a wife canna gie evidence either for or against her ain man, an' it disna seem just or richt."

" We shall see. Meanwhile I want to know what you are going to do and where you are living ? "

" Living ! " A wintry smile wandered across her face. " I'm livin' nae place. They set me oot o' the hotel this mornin', kennin' wha I was, an I'm feared to seek intil anither ane."

" Perhaps you are on your way to Fintry to your own folk ? "

" No, I dinna think I am. I happened to be at the station an' saw that a train was gaun oot for Porth. I got into it, no thinkin' much aboot it, and I've walked ower."

" And where will you go when you leave this ? "

She shook her head again.

" I dinna ken," she said. " I asked the sergeant to tak' me to the Calton too, but he wadna', but it's whaur I'd like to be."

Lettice Weir saw that the girl was in a dangerous mood, that she and hope had parted company, and she forthwith decided to act on her own account.

" You will come home with me, Nancy. I'll take care of you till something is settled."

Nancy, not believing that she heard aright, rose slowly to her feet.

" What are ye sayin' ? " she asked. " Hame to Penninghame ? Are ye sure ye understand everything ; wha I am, what has happened, and everything ? "

" I think I know everything," replied Lettice, with that bright smile of hers that made sunlight wherever it shone.

" An' what aboot the real Mr. Anthony Weir—him that my man has tried to cheat ? I'm no seekin' to gloss ower that, it was awfu', but he needna be made oot ony waur than he is."

" I quite agree with you. Oh, the real Anthony Weir will not say much He is happy amongst his books. He is quite ready to forgive what has been done, and if there has been any talk or thought of punishment it has been on my side."

" You punish ! " repeated Nancy, and her look spoke volumes.

" Well, will you come to Penninghame ? You must be hungry for one thing, after that long walk, and I don't suppose you will wish to go into the village."

" No, I wad probably walk back to Porth or to Westerlea, an' I wasna' thinkin' aboot eatin'. My thochts are meat enough for me, miss."

" Come then." Nancy still hesitated, unable to believe what she heard.

" D'ye mean what ye say, that I am to come to Penninghame, to get shelter frae you ? "

" I mean what I say, Nancy ; I will shelter you and look after you, at least until this painful business is over, and you can be as quiet as you like. No one shall throw a stone at you, or say what you would not wish to hear. You shall have a little room to yourself, and need not mix with the household.

You shall be my guest. I have been very poor, a working girl in sore straits myself, Nancy, and my heart can feel for you. No doubt you have done wrong, but you are suffering for it now."

Nancy, without a moment's notice or warning, suddenly dropped on her knees and pressed her lips to the hem of Lettice Weir's dress.

"I dinna care what ye hae been or what they ca' ye," she sobbed. "But ye hae been sent an angel frae heaven to save me. D'ye see that water? Anither wad hae gane doon in its depths the nicht if ye hadna met me."

"Then you'll come, Nancy; get up, it is absurd to kneel to me; I can't permit it."

"Ye canna prevent it, an' I can kneel to ye in speerit if no in reality," said Nancy, and her looks did not belie her words.

So they turned away from that place of ill omen together.

Thus did Lettice Weir, setting entirely aside the opinion of the world, act upon a truly Christian impulse. She did more that day than save the body of Nancy Nicolson from the cruel water, she lifted her soul also from the lower depths, and sowed a harvest whose richness she was destined to reap in years to come.

Fortunately for Nancy, most of the household servants had left at the time of the old laird's death. The domestic affairs of Penninghame were naturally in a strange unsettled state. Anthony Weir and his sister were living in the house unaware even whether they had the right to it. The recent development of events had complicated everything, and the law did not move rapidly enough to cope with them.

Lettice was as good as her word. She found a room for Nancy, and wrote to the goods department at Edinburgh station for her luggage to be forwarded. She had no difficulty with her brother, he was only too pleased to acquiesce in any arrangement which commended itself to his sister.

To say that Nancy was grateful for the haven and for the extraordinary kindness and consideration that had prompted these truly good people to offer it, but feebly expresses her state of mind. She tried to efface herself as much as possible, never left her own apartments except when desired to do so, and her presence was scarcely noticed in the house. But one of the gardeners saw her at a window, and speedily the news spread. Sergeant Gunn, eager for new laurels, heard it on the Whitekirk road and promptly made it his business to call at Penninghame. He had a new project in contemplation which did more credit to his head than his heart.

He went round to the back door of the house and leisurely interviewed the kitchenmaid, who answered his knock.

"I've come to see Nancy Nicolson; I hear she's here; is it true, my lass?"

"Yes, but she's ca'd Mrs. Boothroyd here."

"Oh, very weel, Mrs. Boothroyd, if she likes it better. Is she in the kitchen?"

The girl laughed.

"No, she's a guest wi' the missus; she disna veesit wi' us," she answered pertly.

"Oh," said the sergeant contemplatively. "It's a sight more than she deserves. Is Miss Weir in?"

"No, they've baith gaen to Edinburgh."

"So much the better for me. Gang to Mrs. Boothroyd then, lass, and tell her the sergeant wants to see her on particular business concerning her husband."

" Ye'd better gang roond to the front door, and Swanston'll let ye in," said the girl, and the sergeant acted on this suggestion.

He was surprised to find Swanston quite friendly, and not at all inclined to resent taking a message for Mrs. Boothroyd. Nancy had by her quiet unobtrusive ways and visible gratitude for every kindness disarmed them all; they even took a certain pride in her because she had achieved such distinction.

The sergeant was ushered into the morning-room and presently Nancy entered. She was looking well, and bonnier than ever. The sergeant could not altogether hide his admiration for her, but her face wore a sad anxious look.

" Well, lassie, you've found guid quarters," he said pleasantly. " I wanted a word wi' ye, an' it was a mere chance that I heard ye were here this very day. I mentioned it to your Uncle Braidwood; I met him driving into Whitekirk for the doctor."

" Oh," said Nancy, and her parched tongue could not utter a word.

" I've just come to offer you a little bit of advice, friendly way like, that'll maybe be of service to ye when the time comes."

" What is it ? " she asked, and already there was a faint note of suspicion in her voice.

" Nancy, hae ye ever heard o' what they ca' Queen's evidence ? "

Nancy shook her head.

" It means that when twa hae been concerned in a thing, like—like this ye ken, that sometimes the yin, oot o' remorse, tells the hale story. It's aye a guid thing, for it prevents ony suspicion bein' attached to innocent folk. Noo I mair than suspect that ye were there that day, an' it wad be a great help to a'body an' a guid thing for yoursel' if ye were to speak oot. I'm no at a' sure but that ye'll maybe be had up yersel' yet, ye see, charged wi' complicity, an' if ye turn Queen's evidence ye would certainly be a' richt."

The sergeant had a very limited knowledge of woman's nature, and a very poor opinion of the quality of which this particular one was made. The colour which had risen at sight of him faded, and she drew herself up, till her slight figure seemed to look tall and commanding.

" Ye can clear oot, sergeant," she said clearly. " I'm no' for sale, nor I'm no' seekin' to save my ain neck. If the law ye represent wants to pit a rope aboot it, ye can tell that to them that sent ye."

She left him forthwith with her head in the air. To say that he was surprised does not do justice to his state of mind. He prepared to depart ruefully. Nancy walked with steady unfaltering feet out into the hall and there she saw sitting on one of the old settles, unless she dreamed it, the figure of her Aunt Susan. And there was on her face the yearning mother look that had dwelt continuously upon it during those old far-away days when she had been cast orphaned on the world.

Nancy staggered forward blindly, with hands piteously outstretched.

" Oh, auntie, auntie ! " she cried, and next moment her head was pillowed on the heart that had never turned against her, that had wept its secret tears, and never ceased to pray for a moment such as this.

CHAPTER XLVI

CLEAR LIGHT

ONCE more a family conclave was held in the library of the old house of Penninghame for the reading of a will. James Maitland had been reverently gathered to his forefathers in the family vault in old Greyfriars; buried from his own house in Great King Street, which those who had rented it for a few months had vacated for the purpose. All felt it to be a decent and fitting conclusion to one of the greatest mysteries of modern times. And the day after this burying, which was attended by an immense throng of both gentle and simple, the conference was held in the library at Penninghame. At this one, however, the Maitlands were not present. Already the contents of the bag had been restored so far as was possible, and submitted to the skill of an expert in handwriting, and the testimony was at once clear and final.

About the issue of the new will that had been found, Anthony Weir and his sister concerned themselves not at all. During the few days that they had lived in undisputed possession of the place their unworldliness and unconventionality had astonished, while it endeared them to all who came in contact with them. The hand extended to Nancy Nicolson in her hour of most bitter need was the crowning act.

Madame de Castro had shrugged her shoulders when she heard it, and wondered what Lettice Weir would do next. It was an act of which she would have been incapable. Perhaps the one who, next to Nancy herself, appreciated this deed of Christian kindness most keenly was Doctor Jeffrey. It was a deed after his own heart, similar to many a one he had performed in secret, never letting his right hand know what his left did. He was often at Penninghame in these days, and a daily witness to Lettice Weir's goodness of heart. She had been through the stress of life, it is true, in its working ranks from her earliest years, and experience had doubtless helped to widen her sympathies, and give her generous views of life; but her sweet high nature was what appealed to Jeffrey, and interested him beyond the telling. Also he could not help drawing comparisons between her and the other woman, whom he had enshrined in his heart so long. So far as she was concerned, these had been disillusioning days for him as well. There are some whom sorrow and the stress of life embitters and sours. Such was Isabel Learmonth. She had suffered much, and pride of race had still complaint in her; now, however, pride reasserted itself in every act and purpose of her life. She was possessed by one idea, to get back Penninghame for her son; nor did it greatly concern her by what means. Her eager excitement was visible on her face that morning when they gathered, a little company, in the library to hear the secret the pool had so long hidden in its mysterious depths.

The only stranger present besides the lawyer that represented the Weirs was Doctor Jeffrey, by Madame de Castro's express desire. The whole matter interested him mightily. To the keen student of human nature the little drama served to bring into play many of the dominant characteristics of the human race.

Mr. Shepherd looked older and more careworn, for the stress of these days had moved him greatly, and the funeral of his old friend had been no common ordeal for him. He was for the moment the central and most important person in that little company, and all eyes were fixed upon him as he adjusted his gold eyeglasses, and opened his bag with precisely the same gesture and look as on another morning which was prominent in the memory of most of those present. His voice was a little unsteady, and his hand visibly shook as he took out the poor, shrunken, discoloured paper, which was James Maitland's message from the dead, to adjust that strange tangle of human affairs.

" We are assembled under somewhat strange and painful circumstances, and I am sure it is the desire of all present to get this business over as quickly as possible," he said. " Fortunately for us all, for me specially, perhaps, it is an entirely simple matter which admits of no dispute or a word of protest. This document has been proven and accepted by counsel and others concerned in it to be absolutely the last will and testament of the late Francis Riddell Learmonth of Penninghame and Whitekirk. I will now proceed to make its contents known.

" ' I, Francis Riddell Learmonth, being in my sound mind and judgment, make this my last will and testament in favour of my only daughter and child, Isabel Learmonth or De Castro, and her children for ever.

" ' Her son, Francis Riddell de Castro, I hereby declare to be my heir, to be Laird of Penninghame and Whitekirk, on condition that he takes the name of Riddell Learmonth. His mother and sister to come here and live during his minority, and afterwards to be life-rented in a sum to be hereafterwards named.

" ' To Anthony Weir the estate and house of Fintry, and five hundred a year, to mark my sense of gratitude for his kind attention to me at the present time'."

" Here the document somewhat abruptly ends," added Shepherd, as he laid down his glasses. " It must be remembered that the laird was very ill while this document was under discussion and preparation, and that he died the same afternoon."

He glanced round the company, and there was a moment's silence.

" The positions are simply reversed," he added, lest any apprehension might exist. " I congratulate you, Madame de Castro, on your son's accession ; he will make an excellent and promising Laird of Penninghame."

Lettice Weir crossed the room, and held out both her hands to the boy.

" I am glad, Frank ; you were made for this place. May God bless you in it, dear, and give you every happiness."

As usual, it was the mission of this sweet woman to smooth away every element of discord. Even Madame de Castro seemed touched.

" I am sorry for your sakes," she said sincerely, and at the same time glancing expressively at Anthony, who did not seem to be concerning himself at all. Nay, the uppermost element in his thoughts was that of relief. Already the magnitude of the place and its heavy responsibilities had begun to weigh upon him. He was honestly glad to be rid of it.

" You need not be sorry on our account, Madame," he said cheerfully. " For my sister and myself great estate has few charms. Believe me, we shall be happier at Fintry, and we are grateful to God that so much we have little earned or deserved has fallen to our share."

These words lifted what might easily have been a sordid moment to the high platform of all that was best in human nature. Shepherd closed the bag, contrasting in his mind that last scene at which he had officiated in that very room. And there flitted through his mind a feeling of deep compassion for the solitary and miserable man lying in the Calton waiting trial for his life. It was a feeling shared by at least one other. Having paid his congratulations, a little forced, perhaps, Doctor Jeffrey left the room. Lettice Weir quickly followed him.

" It is all as it should be now," she said, with a smile. " But I feel for the one who has yet to be judged."

" Boothroyd, do you mean ? "

She nodded. " I am going now to his poor wife. Such devotion as hers might redeem any man. I have been talking over the possibilities of the trial with Mr. Shepherd this morning, and he tells me that you have a verdict here in Scotland called ' Not proven,' a verdict which may possibly be brought in in this case, all the evidence being so entirely circumstantial."

" It is a consummation you would wish, I can see," he said, with an odd tenderness in his eyes.

" Yes I would, for his sake, as well as his wife's. As I say, she would redeem him. We knew him well, Doctor Jeffrey, and, believe me, he is not wholly bad. He got himself into a desperate strait by one desperate act, you see, and so was gradually led further and further astray. But where would any of us be if God harshly judged us ? "

" Where indeed ? Good-bye, Miss Weir ; you have lifted this matter out of its sordid groove. I could pray that you might get your heart's desire, which would be to bless all humanity."

She smiled, shook her finger at him, and glided away to see Nancy.

Before Jeffrey could quit the house, Madame de Castro's voice called him.

" You are so hurried, Doctor Jeffrey, I don't feel that you have congratulated me properly even yet."

" I am sincerely glad for the boy's sake. It is undoubtedly what should be."

" They have behaved sweetly about it, the Weirs I mean ; but you see for yourself how unsuited they would have been for the position. I cannot tell you how thankful I am."

Her eyes shone with elation, her whole bearing seemed to strike a note of triumph.

" Now, when the trial is over, and that scoundrel fitly punished for all his crimes, we shall be able to settle down quietly, and take up all the old threads."

" Some of us," he said involuntarily.

" What do you mean ? " she asked, struck by his obscure words.

" Miss Weir has just been expressing a different opinion, the desire even that he might be pardoned," he said experimentally.

Her lips pressed together in a harsher curve.

" She is an excellent creature, doctor, but all sentiment, the sort of person who would disintegrate society in a week. It is a mercy for poor old Penninghame that it has at last escaped the extraordinary administration which has such a colonial flavour. Good-bye again, if you must go. Come soon again, and often. You will always be welcome at Penninghame."

She spoke with the regal grace of a queen, and Jeffrey smiled slowly to himself as he went out by the great door. As she passed across the tesselated hall out of sight, so she passed out of his life.

He had cherished an ideal all these years, and for a brief space, when she returned, he had imagined her that ideal still. But now it was shattered for ever.

That evening David Maitland and his sister sat alone by their desolate hearth, realising to the full the emptiness and sorrow of life. Their solitude was disturbed by the entrance of an unexpected guest.

When Maitland went out to the hall and saw Jeffrey there his heart seemed to warm and his face to glow.

" I am more glad to see you than I can say, and Helen will feel just the same. We have been expecting Mr. Shepherd to come and tell us what transpired at Penninghame."

" Everything went well. It was quiet, even uninteresting. Madame de Castro is jubilant, the Weirs equally pleased, so things have come to a happy ending."

There was a note of thin sarcasm, however, in the tone, which did not escape Maitland's quick ear.

" Something struck a false note, then ? I am sure it was not the Weirs. From the little I have seen of them they seemed people above the common."

" It was Madame. Yon's a high proud nature, David, that will stoop to none. Pity the heart that leans on her. She has disappointed me, yes, bitterly. She will be all for the advancement of the Learmonths now, lad ; her ambition is high enough to reach the heavens."

" It's the emptiest and least satisfying of all the human passions," was the unexpected answer. " And in the face of some things it shrivels into nothingness. I have been to the Calton this afternoon."

The doctor started, and looked straight at Maitland's fine face.

" Do you mean that you have seen Weir, or rather Boothroyd I should call him ? "

Maitland nodded.

" I had a long interview with him. He has told me what I believe to be the truth. It was no premeditated murder, doctor, but rather the fatal result of blind fury. He swore to me that my father's actual falling into the pool was purely accidental. The struggle was for the bag, you see, and Weir's passion got the better of him for the moment."

" Is he penitent ? "

" He sincerely regrets it. Curious as it may seem, that little servant girl, who, by the bye, is undoubtedly his lawful wife, has got the right side of him. I hope for both their sakes he may get off, and that they may be able to start a new life together in another country."

For the second time that day Jeffrey's soul was refreshed by witnessing a conspicuous instance of human generosity.

He held out his hand.

" You're a thoroughly good chap, Maitland, and I honour you for it. I am sure your father where he is to-day is pleased. It is an act after his own heart, and would have pleased him well."

Maitland's eyes filled as they silently gripped hands.

" How is your poor sister ? "

" Not well. I am most anxious about her, doctor, and I am sure I have made a mistake in leaving Bilbao. She is willing even now to return with me, and I have just been writing my uncle that we will come back next week. Whether I stay or not will depend, but at least it is imperative that Helen should have an immediate change. With my aunt and cousins she will have a delightful one. They are a very happy household. I am only sorry I did not insist on it before. You would approve of the idea ? "

" Most certainly, I think it is very wise."

" Everything is made easy for us, for our kind tenants here are willing to take the house for another year, so that we need not trouble about anything. By the end of that time we shall be able perhaps to make some more permanent arrangement."

" Then you mean to leave Scotland indefinitely ? "

" Indefinitely, yes, in the meantime."

" Will you go out to Penninghame ? "

" No."

" There is some one there who will miss you, I am afraid."

Maitland flushed slightly, and suddenly looked Jeffrey straight in the eyes.

" Once I had my dreams perhaps, but that particular one is over. Doctor, I have well considered the whole matter, believe me, and while it might have been possible through course of time to reconcile Madame de Castro partly to it, she never would have been satisfied. And I am not the man to walk contentedly behind my wife, or to be patronised by her relations. It is better as it is. She is very young, and will soon forget. As for me, well, I've heard my father say often that happiness is not, after all, the chief or only end in life."

" It is what most men seek nevertheless," said Jeffrey, smiling a little.

" You are the exception yourself," said Maitland quickly. " You have lived the solitary life and seem none the worse."

" Right, but it is better all the same for a man to marry in his youth."

" You are not too old yet," suggested Maitland, almost affectionately.

" I, too, have been pursuing a shadow through those empty years," the doctor said, somewhat sadly.

Perhaps Maitland understood, but he made no comment.

" Let us go to Helen," he said, and they went silently up the stairs.

CHAPTER XLVII

THE QUALITY OF MERCY

DURING the two days of the trial of George Boothroyd the Court was crowded. Public interest had been wrought up to the highest pitch beforehand, and sensational developments were freely talked about and fully expected. But none came. Contrary to all expectation, the case dragged from the beginning, and the interest was only feebly sustained.

The evidence, wholly circumstantial, was far less exciting than the public had expected, and from the first there seemed a disposition on all hands to favour the prisoner. Even the case for the Crown was conducted in a somewhat lukewarm fashion, and the verdict among those who had any knowledge of legal procedure was a foregone conclusion. It was not publicly known, of course, that powerful private interest had been brought to bear from without, and those most interested in the proper carriage of justice had intimated that what would please them best would be to see the prisoner set free.

He had no expectation of such a happy issue himself, not perhaps did he greatly desire it. A changed man in many respects was George Boothroyd in these days, and those who saw him oftenest could make very little of him. He spoke scarcely at all, and seemed indifferent to his fate. He had only once seen Nancy. That experience was too bitter to be repeated, and he had begged her not to come again.

Maitland he had seen many times, and always welcomed, albeit with a strange shyness, which showed that he acutely felt his position. The Weirs he had not seen, nor was he aware that in the background they also were doing their utmost for his cause.

The Advocate-Depute took a lenient view, and, while he went mercilessly into every detail, he left on the mind of the jurors, as well as that of the general public, the impression that the capital verdict would neither be expected nor desired.

The speech for the defence occupied three hours in delivery, and was, from the prisoner's point of view, all that could be desired. Counsel for the defence dwelt upon the sudden temptation, the cause of provocation, the swift desire to undo what had been sincerely regretted. His strongest point undoubtedly was that, the act being entirely unpremeditated, the result of a sudden outbreak of passion, a verdict of guilty could not possibly be given, and when he sat down there was considerable applause in Court.

The Judge summed up in the same strain, and the jury did not take long to consider their verdict.

In less than twenty minutes they returned with a verdict of "Not proven." Boothroyd heard the words without understanding them. Certainly he did not comprehend that they restored to him his freedom—that he could leave the Court an unconvicted man.

He was listening dazedly to the judge thanking the jurymen for their services when some one tapped him on the elbow. It was his law agent, who whispered to him hurriedly that he was at liberty to leave the Court.

"Am I? Do you mean that there will be no sentence?" he said, staring vaguely before him as he staggered to his feet.

The lawyer nodded, and took him by the arm to get him beyond the gaze of the prying eyes.

"I don't understand it. I've not denied the thing," he said confusedly. "The only thing I did deny was intent to kill. And I was willing to bear the brunt. How is it they have not passed sentence?"

"Why, man, because the jury have agreed that the charge is 'Not proven' against you. Everybody knew what would happen after the speech for the Crown, but there is no doubt that the man you have to thank for it is Mr. David Maitland."

A curious tremor crossed Boothroyd's face as he stepped into the little bare room behind, and looked dazedly round. Suddenly Maitland ente .ed, and as the lawyer withdrew he closed the door and, approaching Boothroyd, laid his hand on his shoulder.

"You are a free man again. Do you understand all that that involves?"

"I don't realise it. Is there no mistake?" he asked feverishly.

"None. You leave the Court practically, in the eyes of the law at least, without any stain on your character. It is for you to see that none remains."

"It is you who has done this. They have told me so even if I did not know it. What does it mean? What are you made of? Not the common stuff like other men."

"I am my father's son," answered David simply. "It is exactly what he would have done. He never broke the bruised reed."

"Yet I killed him; yes, I will say it. He met his death through me, yet I go scot free. Gad! I'd rather bear the penalty after all than feel as I do at this moment."

"That will pass; the future remains. A new life is possible for you and for your wife."

"Where is she?"

"Where you will go presently. We brought her up yesterday, and she is lodging in the house of an old servant of ours, where you and she would be safe for a day or two, but you will leave Edinburgh as soon as possible."

"I have to see the Weirs first. Isn't there another case to be tried for fraud, or something of that kind?"

"There will be no further prosecution of any kind, and they will see you perhaps to-morrow. We have been in conference together concerning your uture."

"If this sort of treatment of the criminal is common in Scotland, do they not put a premium on crime?" asked Boothroyd, with a curious look.

Maitland very faintly smiled. "The circumstances are exceptional. You are going to justify them, Boothroyd."

"How?"

"By starting here and now that new life of which we have spoken. When you have seen your wife, and talked matters over with her, there will be a sum of money placed at your disposal, and you will be at liberty to take that voyage to Canada that was interrupted so untimely."

The man's face flushed, and the veins stood like cords on his brow.

"This is beyond me, I am afraid," he said hoarsely. "It isn't human nature. Is there anything behind?"

"Nothing. Come, be a man; let's out, and I'll drive you down to your wife. A brougham is waiting at one of the private doors; we can get in there, and escape while the crowd is still waiting."

He opened the door, and motioned him to follow, which he did, speaking no words. He was indeed far beyond speech. Maitland left him to his own thoughts as they drove rapidly across the city to an obscure, little-known street in Stockbridge, where his old nurse now lived alone. He stopped the carriage at the end and motioned Boothroyd to alight.

"It might create remark if we drove up to the door. We can walk the rest; it is only a few steps. I have only one other thing to say to you, Boothroyd, the last word. The wife who is waiting for you has been loyal to you through it all. It is of her you must think now, for her you must live. That is the payment I, nay, we all ask. Will it be made?"

Boothroyd lifted his hat momentarily from his head. "It will, so help me, God!"

They came in a silence that could be felt to the door of the little house, and there parted. When Maitland looked back he had gone in, and the door was shut.

* * * * * *

He walked back leisurely and quietly to the hotel where the whole party from Penninghame had been waiting for the issue of the case.

All was over, and though many had disapproved and even condemned the lenient attitude towards the prisoner, Maitland himself had the approval of his own conscience and something more. He was conscious as he walked through the sweet summer air of a strange nearness to the Unseen and the Eternal.

"After all, the veil is thin," he said, within his soul. "We are nearer than we dream."

When he reached the comfortable shelter of the Roxburghe Hotel he found the whole Penninghame party round a tea-table in a private sitting-room discussing the conduct of the case.

"A miscarriage of justice, I must call it, in spite of you all," said Madame de Castro, in her loftiest manner. "Here comes the chief delinquent. I am not afraid to repeat it, David, a gross miscarriage of justice."

"The future will prove it, Madame," he replied serenely.

"What does the doctor say?"

"My common sense agrees with Madame de Castro, my sentiments agree with you. After all, perhaps, we had better call it a matter of temperament."

Lettice Weir slipped across the room, and came close to Maitland's side. "Tell me," she said in a whisper, "how did he take it, and has he gone to Nancy?"

"He took it as I expected, and he has gone to Nancy, Miss Lettice. You and she together will make a man of him."

"Was it not better?" she said aloud, and addressing herself to Madame de Castro she repeated, "Was it not better to give him another chance? What was the use of adding to the criminal list? He would have come out a worse man than when he went in."

"True," said Jeffrey absently, as he looked at her sweet face. "After all, when we pull up stakes it won't be our mercy we regret, but the other thing."

* * * * * *

One more glimpse, and we have done.

Penninghame on a fair summer morning a year later. Jeffrey on his horse at the terrace steps, Madame de Castro leaning on the balustrade talking to him animatedly.

" So the Maitlands are coming back to Edinburgh for good. Well, well, and what about their proteges in Canada—still doing well, eh ? Lettice won't answer me seriously when I speak about them."

" She imagines you ironical and unsympathetic. They are doing well," replied Jeffrey, rather curtly.

" I heard it rumoured that Braidwood and his wife were actually going out on a vist."

" I haven't heard of it."

" Why do you come so little here, and go so much to Fintry, doctor ? You are not faithful to old friends."

" Wherein have I failed ? " he asked.

" You don't come, I say, and you are often at Fintry," she said, with a slight frown. " Is it true what they are saying, that Lettice is the attraction ? "

To her surprise he neither denied nor sought to laugh it off

He turned to her quite seriously, with slightly reddening face.

" Madame de Castro, I hope to marry Lettice Weir next October."

" Oh, indeed, has it gone so far ? Who can say now you are faithful to the old friends ? And you have kept your own counsel, shall we say, selfishly well ? "

" I did not know it would so greatly interest you."

" Neither perhaps does it, but I wish you well. She is very amiable, and for a bachelor of set habits that is a great point."

" Indeed it is. Good-day, Madame de Castro."

He raised his hat and rode away. As she watched the goodly figure and handsome head disappearing among the shadowing trees she tapped her foot impatiently, and turned away with a little sigh.

So far as the outward eye could discern she had much to be grateful for—nearly, if not all, a woman's heart could desire. And yet—— Some shadow had fallen athwart the summer sunshine—the shadow of the might-have-been.

THE END

MEG HAMILTON

BY

ANNIE S. SWAN

SUNDAY MAIL EDITION
1933

CONTENTS

CHAPTER I

SON AND HEIR

THE LAIRD OF BALLOCHEAN rode back to his house on the red roan with the evil eye, himself in a most cursed temper. The ill luck of the Hamiltons, which had pursued him all his life, seemed to have culminated that day on the race-course at Ayr, where he had dropped, in a couple of hours, seven hundred pounds.

Now racing like gambling debts must be paid, and the Laird did not know where to get the money with which to meet his debt of honour—save the mark! Another mortgage he could not raise upon Ballochean, for it was already burdened to the hilt. There was no treasure inside the old house he could sell, for all its treasures had been made away with by him and his father before him. A few old sticks of furniture, some family portraits of old Hamiltons of that ilk, and some shelves of books of no particular value will not realise much if brought under the hammer.

Gavin Hamilton was at his wit's end.

As he dismounted at the stable door and shouted in choleric voice for somebody to come and relieve him of his horse, it was seen that there was considerable stiffness in his figure, which was of full habit, accentuated by the extreme tightness of his riding breeches.

He wore an odd-shaped square bowler of a shabby brown colour and an old-fashioned stock with a hunting tie below it, and in consequence he looked not unlike one of his own ancestors.

Yet, though his dress was not modern, he possessed a certain dignity of bearing as well as some remnant of the handsome looks that had been many a woman's undoing, and that had broken the heart of at least one. He was of immense height and of powerful build, and his face was ruddy like a winter apple; his eye, in spite of his hard-drinking habits, was clear and piercing, and it fell with a glance of lightning on the diminutive stable-boy, who came trembling from the loft to wait upon his master's pleasure.

"Hulloa, Tomtit, are you the sole representative of the Ballochean stables, eh?"

"Yes, sir. Please, sir, they've a' gane to the races."

"Oh, they have—have they?—and without so much as by your leave! Well, and I don't blame them. The race-course is the devil's playground, but there's a something about it that stirs the blood. Can you take in the mare and rub her down, and see that she has what she needs?"

"Yes, sir, please, sir, I can. I dae it often."

"And without giving her enough water or oats to founder her?" continued the Laird, in his most threatening voice.

"Yes, sir, please, sir."

"All right. Take her in—and there's a sixpence to you. It's my last, lad, but you are welcome to it."

He tossed it on the rough cobbles of the stable-yard where it fell with a little tinkle.

Then he turned on his heel, waving his riding switch, and walked away towards the house. It was a respectful distance off, and the stables themselves were admirable, having been kept up by the sporting Lairds of Ballochean, while the house and its contents had been suffered to go to rack and ruin.

As he came to the gable-end of the house, on which was built a vast conservatory of a rounded shape, at present almost empty of plants or flowers, he entered by that door, and, taking off his hat just inside, wiped his brow.

He was needing a drink, and he proceeded at once to the library, where he usually sat, and where he kept a private cupboard.

It was a fine, even a noble, room, gallantly proportioned, and lined with book-shelves, many of them empty, for all the treasures they had once held had gone. A Turkey carpet, worn and shabby, covered the greater part of the parquet floor, and a large, round table, on which books and papers and pamphlets were scattered. stood in the centre of the room along with several armchairs covered in brown morocco set about it. A great settee, covered with Persian rugs, stood between the windows, and two large easy-chairs, one on each side of the fireplace.

The place was gloomy, for, though it was a day in the early autumn, and the sun was shining gloriously without, the house had a north front and little sun penetrated to the rooms at that side.

The room was occupied by one person—a young man, sitting at the table with a map spread before him, and with several books lying at his elbow. He looked about twenty-one, and, so far as could be discerned from his stooping position seemed to be tall and slender, and to have the bookish air of a student. A pair of spectacles—in his father's eyes the final degradation—shaded his eyes, and his expression was remote and a trifle melancholy, as one who felt himself out of place.

At his father's entrance he pushed back the chair with evident nervousness, and stood up, facing him.

"You're back earlier than you expected, surely, dad," he said, and his voice was musical and very pleasant to listen to. "Had a good day?"

"No, an infernal bad one! What are you doing, mewed up here on a day like this? Why aren't you down at the course with Guy, making a kirk or a mill o't? I hate the sight of you and your books! I'm damned sick of them. If you were half a man you'd be down at the course.

"I know nothing about horse-racing, and I care still less," answered the lad with a sudden dour note in his voice.

Somehow, the answer—or the manner of it—raised an unholy passion in his father's soul.

"You dare stand there, you whelp—you, a Hamilton of Ballochean!—and say you know nothing about a horse? Then, what do you know about? It's in a pulpit you should have been, with gown and bands—a Holy Willie, teaching ne'er-do-weels the way to repent! I'm damned sick of you, Ludo, and you're no son of mine! You're an ootlin or a foundling, and you have neither right nor business here."

"Very well, father," said Ludo, whitening a little about the gills. "Give me fifty pounds and let me go and I'll never bother you again."

"Fifty pounds! And where am I to get it—tell me that, lad? I haven't fifty pence to bless myself with, and I've lost seven hundred pounds the day at one fell coup. But I'd do it again to-morrow—and the next day—and if it were my last day; for horse-racing is a gentleman's sport, and I don't know why I should be cursed with a white-livered scholar like you for a son. It's Guy that shall have the place. If it's a scholar you call yourself, I'll take care no scholar shall be Laird of Ballochean."

"Guy is welcome to it for me," said Ludo dourly, "for I'm more than damned sick of my life here with you and him."

It was so unusual for his elder son to use a profane word that the father, mollified by its very sound, stopped and stared at him. Then he gave a little hard laugh, and strode up to the cupboard, which he unlocked with his master-key, and proceeded to help himself to a glass of whisky neat.

"I'll tell you what, Ludo; you should take a teaching job somewhere. Either that, or go to your mother's folk in the South. This is no place for the likes of you, and, forby, there's not room in Ballochean for the three of us."

"And that's the truest word you have spoken yet, father—and more the shame to you! For both Guy and I should have been taught to get a living for ourselves instead of being the useless wastrels we are. I'll take you at your word and go."

Ballochean merely laughed, not taking the lad's words seriously, for, indeed, where could he go? There was no money to back him in anything that he might undertake, and he was as helpless as a baby in all the affairs of life. In his father's eyes he was of no more account than a great, overgrown child.

Ludo left the room, and the old man sat down, with the decanter by his elbow, to make some calculations on a sheet of paper. But they did not concern the finding of the wherewithal to launch his elder son in any new way of doing. He was merely trying to find his own bearings and to prepare himself to face what was in front of him.

"A bit more of the land will have to go," he muttered at last. "Thank God, that can't run away."

Ludo stalked out into the hall, took a cap from a peg in the cloakroom, and left the house.

It was a beautiful old place, exquisitely situated on an eminence on one of the banks of the Doon, and at a distance of about four miles by road from the town of Ayr. From the wide sweep before the door a magnificent view could be obtained, embracing all the country right down to the sea, and taking in the frowning Heads of Ayr.

The land was smiling in the glow of the September sun, and, though most of the harvest was gathered in—that being one of the favoured breadths of Scotland—there was no hint of bareness or poverty anywhere. The meadows were green and lush, and the trees, here and there showing a tinge of yellow, bore testimony to the richness of the soil.

Ludovic Hamilton loved the place where he had been born; but, as he strode away from it that day, he was a person destitute of hope. All his ambitions and longings had been thwarted, or rather ignored. He had a thirst for intellectual attainment, and his heart's desire had been to take a University course. But his father had merely laughed at him when he had expressed his desire; and, when his public school life at Glenalmond was over, he had brought him home to drift about the place.

Many misfortunes had fallen of late years on Ballochean, but the greatest, surely, was the death of the wife of its laird, which had taken place when Ludovic, her elder son, was but nine years old. Two younger children, besides, she had left, to wit, Guy of the fiery temper and the wayward heart—a real Hamilton every inch of him—and Meg, who embodied in her adorable person all the gifts and graces of two families, both remarkable for their attainments in that direction.

But in her, too, the wayward strain prevailed, chiefly because she had had no guiding in her youth, as there were no women about Ballochean save hired ones—and these not of a very high order, seeing that the place had no great reputation.

Ludo's one idea as he strode through the gold of the September afternoon was how to get away honourably and with some prospect of a future, which would enable him to live away from his father's house.

Suddenly there came to him an inspiration which brightened his face.

Still keeping to the field paths, which brought him out close upon Alloway village—shrine of a world of Scottish hearts!—he presently left the high ground and plunged down to the low path which skirted the waters of the Doon.

Here was the sylvan loveliness which Burns had loved, here were the very birks and alders of which he had sung. The music of its waters—one of the sweetest sounds on earth—stole into the lad's suffering heart and helped to heal its bruises. Cast in the acutely sensitive mould of the poet, it would have been no marvel had Ludovic Hamilton sought relief for his overcharged feelings in song. But if he had ever done so, none knew of it.

To his father's way of thinking, such idle dalliance indeed would have been the last straw to break the back of a man already bending under the weight of his heir's incompetency and foolishness. The Laird of Ballochean imagined himself a person of no mean cleverness, yet his eyes were so completely holden that he was blind to the fact that all the ignorance and incompetence and foolishness were on his own side.

He had by his side a rare soul, whom his coarser clay was powerless to comprehend; therefore he behaved towards his elder son as a bully and a fool, and so increased his outward shrinking.

But the words he had spoken that day, more brutal than usual, were to be the last. Ludo had reached the end of his tether—the worm had turned! There are none so stranded and alone in the world of men as not to have a single friend. Ludo had one, and, though he was by no means sure that he would find him at home at that hour of the day in the middle of the week at Kildoon, he took his chance.

The house, once the home of a branch of the Montgomery family, lay low on a green plateau at one of the most enchanting bends of the Doon. It would not be considered a suitable site for a dwelling-house in these enlightened days of hygiene and highly-ordered living, but the beauty of the situation was beyond compare.

An old white house, many-gabled and pierced with little windows set, like so many bright eyes, in its bonnie face, with trees sheltering it on every side, save where the river swept past the terrace before its door, with the sighing of wind and water and woods for ever in its ears, and with the mystery of the seasons and all their lure so near that there was no escape—such was Kildoon, where abode David Sillars, whom Ludovic Hamilton considered his only friend in the world, and who was certainly the one that might help him now.

Upon the anguish of his spirit stole the spell and glamour of that enchanting spot, and even when he reached the iron-studded door he was in no haste to enter, but lingered outside, wondering that, in a world so fair, men could be so little in unison with it.

But presently an old serving-man, dozing on the monk's bench on the other side of the glass door, saw him and made haste to open.

"Guid-day, sir. It'll be Maister Sillars ye are seeking. He has just come in."

"Ah!" said Ludo. "Then I'm in luck, Dalrymple. When did he come?"

"Last nicht, sir. He has had a look at the races. Waur riff-raff than ever! Ech, sirs! it would be a guid thing for the toon if they could be done away with. He likes to be at hame on race nicht, for ye would be surprised, Maister Ludo, to ken hoo far the riff-raff will travel for what they micht get or tak'. He's up the stair but I'm takin' his tea to the library. So, if ye will please come this way."

Ludo followed gratefully, for the ordered quiet, the restfulness of the house, which offered the last word in comfort and homeliness, with a kind of indescribable beauty added, further consoled and soothed his spirit.

All the windows were open in the library, which was filled from ceiling to floor with books. In such a room Burns himself might have loved to spend a delightsome hour, turning from the pages of the books which men had made to the book which God had spread outside in a lovely world. Tradition had it that the Poet had actually often been a welcome guest in that old family house, and that there had dwelt some of his truest friends. But the Montgomeries had never been exploiters of their deeds of kindness or of their own distinction; and of many of their most precious records the world was in complete ignorance. There were treasures in that old house undreamed of either by virtuoso or Philistine.

David Sillars abode there alone—an eligible bachelor of thirty-five, who had inherited the place from his mother. It was not large enough to be entitled to be called an estate, consisting, as it did, of a single farm—which was let—and a very spacious park, surrounding the house and thereby ensuring its complete privacy. Sillars himself followed his father's calling—that of a sugar-refiner at Greenock—where he lived all the week, returning thence to his home on Friday or on Saturday, according to the state of his business affairs.

Ludo was not kept waiting long, and when Sillars entered the room his grave, somewhat dour face lightened at sight of the lad, and his smile robbed his features of all their sternness.

He did not smile often, but never did smile make such difference to a human face. It was as if all the windows of his soul and heart had been suddenly opened to the sun. His habitual expression was reserved, a little cold and unapproachable, and was due, perhaps, to the solitariness of the life he led.

Nobody professed to know why Sillars, one of the most eligible bachelors in the county, and one known to be a very rich man, should have remained unwed so long. His had been given up as a hopeless case by such as make the stalking of eligible bachelors their principal occupation. He was happy enough, and he appeared neither to need nor to desire any woman to disturb the even tenor of his life.

"Glad to see you.Ludo. I came over from Greenock last night. I like to have a look at the races. There's a bit of the boy left in me still, though I'm thirty-five to-day."

"Is it your birthday, David?" said Ludo, rising and greeting him with a somewhat awkward smile. "I wish you many happy returns. I wish I were seventy-five—then I should be near done with it."

"Done with what, lad?" asked Sillars, bending his deep, penetrating eyes on the lad's pale and rather sad face.

"With the thing folk call life—a pretty rotten business it has been all along for me, David. As I came up the Doon, the lure of the Kelpie's Pool was drawing me. At least, there would be peace down there."

"Wheest, lad," said Sillars in a reproving tone, yet with a sort of compassion born of his quick understanding.

He had noted before now the melancholy strain in Ludovic Hamilton, and, as he knew the order of life at Ballochean, it had awakened his deepest pity. Ludo was no more than an alien in that unruly house, in which his highly-strung spirit could never find a home.

"Come and get a cup of tea—that will do us both good. I saw your sister and Guy in the stand with the Kessocks. Surgeon Dove was there, too, with his wife and daughter, but I did not see your father at all. Hasn't he patronised the course to-day?"

"Oh, yes, and lost—Heaven knows what! He came back, blind with rage about something, and let out on me. I've left the house, David, and I'm not going back."

He spoke quite quietly, and, as Sillars poured the tea into the cups, he paused and eyed him steadily. He saw his nostrils quiver, his brow contract, his nervous hands tremble, and he divined the perturbation of spirit, which was deeper and even more searching than usual.

"You know what your father is, Ludo. Try and not take what he says or does to heart."

"It's because I know what he is that I do take it to heart, David," said the lad in a low, intense voice. "I hate him. I wish he was dead—and myself too!"

Sillars wisely did not seek to check this outburst, recognising the fact that when a flood is dammed too much disaster must ensue.

"Let out, Ludo, for all you are worth!" he said in a low, kindly voice. "It will do you good, and I am as safe as the Bank of England."

And Ludo "let out." The tale he told was in its way the strangest thing, the wildest story, that David Sillars had ever heard. But, above and beyond all, it was a terrible indictment of the hard-drinking, hard-swearing old rip of a father, who so poorly comprehended the duties he owed to the children whom he had begotten.

As Sillars listened to the miserable recital of misapprehension, bullying, daily strife and nagging, he took swift action and decision within himself. He was a man of the world and of business. He had great knowledge of men and things, and he had an understanding which much quiet study and thought had polished into something very fine and keen. And he realised that action must be taken—and that quickly—else some tragedy would inevitably ensue.

He could follow the workings of that sensitive soul, goaded and strung to something akin to madness. A blow in the dark had often been struck for less than the lad had borne, and even in the quiet depths of Ludovic's heart there was a spark of the flame, a hint of the old Adam, which had driven the fortunes of Ballochean into the dust, made the name a byword, and robbed the old house of both honour and repute.

"I had no idea that it was so bad as that. But doesn't your sister stand by you?" asked Sillars, with a curious note in his voice. "I have always imagined her as a champion of justice and fair play."

"Meg's all right. She stands up to him. But he is not so bad when she is there. I don't complain to Meg, however. Hang it all, to whine to a woman—that would be the limit, David! Give me half a chance!"

Sillars smiled, well pleased, since these words revealed the manhood still alive in the lad's soul. He only needed guiding, like the rest of Ballochean.

"I see that you are right, Ludo, and that it is high time you left your father's house. Well, I can help you, if you are not too particular as to what you will do when you leave it."

"Beggars can't be choosers," cried the lad, and an eager pulse beat in his voice.

"Well, I can make a place for you at Greenock as easy as ninepence. It would only be figures you would have to deal with, you know, Ludo, for there is nothing inside the refinery you could do. Or I could send you out to Jamaica. Perhaps in present circumstances that would be best. It would at least cut you clean away from this."

"Jamaica! Oh, David, if you only would! Work! I'm not afraid of it. It's because there's nothing to do at Ballochean that we're continually tearing at one another's throats. I told my father one day that it would have been a kinder thing if he had set us up as ninepins when we were little and had a successful pot at us."

"Did you tell him that? And what did the old sport say?"

"He smiled sort of queerly at me and never said a word. But do you think you could find me something to do in Jamaica?"

"I could. There's the plantation—you could try that. And there's the office, where you could get a stool, if you did not care for the overseer business. I'll write to Hislop, our manager, and tell him you're coming out. He's a good chap, Ludo, and would give you a fair chance. But it would have to be work, lad—real, honest, hard work, and no mooning or kidding."

He paused there, for the lad's face was buried in his hands, and one hard, bursting sob, wrung from his over-charged heart, broke painfully upon the air.

CHAPTER II

THE BOSOM OF THE FAMILY

" AND where, may we inquire, is Ludo ? " cried Meg Hamilton in her clear, ringing voice as, five minutes after the gong had sounded, she ran into the dining-room, where she found her father and her brother Guy already seated at the dinner-table.

She saw even as the words left her lips that her father was in a bad humour ; and, while she had no fear of him, she was wise enough to know that the less said the better when he was in such mood.

She had on a white frock, made very simply for a home dinner and showing a neck " like the snawdrift " for whiteness. Her lithe figure was fitted to perfection by the long straight lines of the gown, which made no attempt at fashion or style. But Meg could not disfigure herself—which was a happy thing, seeing that there was no money at Ballochean to pay for modish or expensive clothes, and that she had to get a clever housemaid to turn and twist and alter her things and otherwise keep her decent. Meg herself disdained the use of the needle, and she was more at home in handling a bridle rein, or in tramping through fields with a couple of dogs at her heels and a gun under her arm.

But all the indulgence of her propensity to mannish and outdoor sports had taken nothing from her beauty. She was a creature charmingly fair, her hair like red gold, her eyes as deep as the sea and as blue, while the smile of her was such as sends men headlong to their doom.

Both men, the old and the young, looked at her as she came darting into the room, and thought that they had never seen her look so fair as now. Her father, however, merely grunted, pointed to the chair, and ordered the soup to be served.

" Have you seen Ludo, Guy ? " she asked her younger brother—a tall, fair youth with reddish hair closely cropped, a handsome face of the coarser type, and a somewhat heavy, sullen-looking under jaw.

He shook his head.

" Not since breakfast. He'll be mooning with his book somewhere, I don't doubt," he answered. " Say, Meg, did you notice young Storrer beside the Scrymgeours in the stand ? I wonder which of them he's sweet on ? "

Meg shook her head, pushed her silver bangles well up her shapely arms, and broke some bread into her soup. She was healthily hungry, for tea at Surgeon-General Dove's had been very genteel and far from satisfying.

" Did you ever see such a skimpy tea as they gave us, Guy ? " said Meg rather disparagingly. " Why, I could have eaten the lot, and none the better, or worse ! I can't think why Mrs. Dove is so mean."

" They are not accustomed to our kind of appetites, Meg," answered Guy, with a sort of apologetic air, as if he did not like to hear such a stricture passed on their friends.

" It would do Ellison good if she would eat a hearty meal—and I believe she does eat it when there's nobody looking," she added viciously. " I don't like my dinner when Ludo is not here, and I do want to know where he is."

" Hold your tongue about Ludo. He knows the meal hours, and, if he doesn't choose to conform to them he can go without dinner. Do you hear that, Jean ? " said the Laird, turning to the tall, bouncing tablemaid who was carrying away the plates. " No dinner is to be kept for Mr. Ludovic. Some sort of discipline must be maintained in the house."

" Very well, sir," said Jean, but she inwardly resolved that if by any chance Ludo should come in late and be in need of a meal it should be forthcoming.

That was how it was in Ballochean. Each man and woman there was a law to himself or herself, and even the servants obeyed only under pressure.

Meg glanced steadily across the table at her father's glowering face and longed to ask him a question. She was shrewd enough to discern that something beyond the common betwixt him and Ludo had happened to account for his extreme irritation with her elder brother.

Mere bickerings were things of daily occurrence, and, though Meg was generally on her brother's side, there were moments when she lost patience with him and asked him why he didn't rise up and hit out.

" You don't like your dinner, father," she said presently, " but please don't take any more whisky."

She rose quite quietly and removed the decanter from her father's elbow. At the same time she coolly touched his left temple with her forefinger.

" Your tell-tale veins are beginning to stand out, old dear," she said calmly. " Not another drop this night, if I can prevent it."

" Bring back that bottle, my lass," her father called out threateningly.

But she paid no more heed to his threat than if he had not spoken.

Guy watched this little scene in surprise, admiring the courage of his sister, which he could not have emulated. His life consisted largely of ingenious and more or less successful attempts to hoodwink his father in various ways.

Meg never took the trouble of trying such indirect and crooked ways with him. She simply stood up to him, and she was apparently without fear of his tempers. But she did not like such scenes—nobody knew how little she liked them. She carried her head high before the world, and there were few—very few—who knew what sort of a girl Meg Hamilton really was. She went on her way, laughing, careless, and defiant, taking no pains to conciliate anyone. But her heart was often bruised and sore, and very often was at war with her strange, lonely destiny.

At the table all efforts at friendly discussion of the Ayr Races failed ; and, as the meal progressed, it was more and more borne in on the brother and sister that the day had not been a good one for their father, and that something altogether unusual must have happened to upset him so completely.

The Laird rose from the table when the sweets were brought in.

" I'm for nothing more. When you are finished, Meg, come to me in the library. I want to speak to you."

" All right, old dear," said Meg, and, when the door closed behind him, she leaned her elbows on the table and looked across at Guy's face.

" What's up ? " she asked laconically.

" Dropped a bit, I should say. I asked him what was the matter, but he swore my head off. I saw him go off the stand about three—just after Larrikin ran—so I guessed pretty well what had happened."

Meg shrugged her shoulders and bent her brows over her plate.

" Tell you what, Guy—we Hamilton's have no luck," she said.

" None—and what's to become of us in the long run, which of us knows ? "

Meg's bright, brave face became shadowy for the moment, and the change of expression brought out a brief resemblance to Ludo.

" Sometimes I wonder why any of us were ever born," she said bitterly. " We're no use, we can't make any money, we don't even live decently. That people continue to know us at all surprises me. But I thought some of them were fighting shy of the old man on the course to-day. That was my impression, at any rate. Think there's anything in it, Guy ? "

Guy forebore to say what he thought. Had he done so it would have necessitated an explanation that would have been too long and too complicated, he imagined, for his sister's comprehension.

" Most people fight shy of the party with no money, Meg ; and the old man has done a bit of sponging in his time."

The word " sponging " hurt Meg like the cut of a whip. A red streak sprang in her cheek, and she pushed back her chair rather noisily and rose to her feet.

" Sponging isn't a nice word," she said hotly. " I'll go and see whether I can get anything out of him. But I wish I knew where Ludo is. We are in the habit of laughing at him ; but I'm not sure that in the end he won't get the better of us. He's got a hold of the right end of the stick, at any rate."

With this cryptic and inelegant remark Meg glided through the doorway and crossed the hall to the library. This she entered without knock or other ceremony, for there was no such thing as respect for another's privacy or convenience in the whole house of Ballochean.

Her father had lit a very old and evil-smelling meerschaum, whose fumes filled the air, and his face had smoothed a little, and the knob had disappeared from his brows.

" That you, Meg ? Come and sit down. Have a cigarette, if there are any in the box," he said graciously.

" Not now," answered Meg soberly, though the sight of her sitting cross-legged between her father and Guy and sharing their evening smoke could be seen any day in Ballochean.

" What did you think of the races to-day ? Had a goodish time at them, eh ? " asked he presently.

The affable tone of his voice, the entire absence of ill-humour in the expression of his countenance surprised the girl not a little, and she regarded her father's weather-beaten face attentively.

" Fair to middling. Queer crowd the Kessocks had about them to-day. But didn't the little Dove preen her feathers ! " she said satirically.

" The old one or the young one ? " said the Laird, amused, as he seldom failed to be, by the flowers of his daughter's speech.

" Both—but it was ma I was thinking more particularly of at the moment. If I ever fall down before a title in the way that she does I shall be ready for another kind of shot, father, and I hope you won't hesitate to send it after me ! "

" Got your back up, eh, Meg ? Did Kessock pay the little Dove too much attention, then ? " asked the Laird with a chuckle.

A look of mighty scorn swept across the girl's face, and she threw up her head with that proud, somewhat arrogant, glance which alienated some who would fain have shown themselves friendly to her. Her temper was high and hasty, and none had ever taught her the lesson of self-control, or how true it is that the tongue is an unruly member which no man can tame.

" But Kessock is a rattling good sort, Meg, and shrewd as well. He'll see through their game."

She made no answer, but the colour seemed to linger in her cheek, and there was an odd brilliance in her eyes which betokened some disquiet of spirit.

" What did you want to talk to me about, dad ? " she asked after a moment's silence.

" Oh, things in general. You are not in a hurry, I suppose ? "

" No—I've got nothing to do, of course. But I do wonder where Ludo is. His absence is worrying me. Haven't you seen him to-day ? "

" Yes. He was here when I came back in the afternoon."

" Oh ! "

Meg began at last to understand. Earlier in the day—when her father's anger was hot upon him, and Ludo happened to get in the way—well, she could imagine what had occurred.

" It's time something was being done with or for Ludo, father. He's very unhappy here," she said pleadingly.

" The sooner something is done the better I shall be pleased, for he's not a bird of this nest, Meg, and I don't just know how he dropped into it."

" Ludo may easily prove the only bird worth counting, father," said Meg gravely. " It seems to me that that we're on the wrong tack altogether—all except Ludo."

" You got the megrims, too, then ? He did pay too much attention to the ring-dove, eh ? " he said banteringly.

" Don't be silly, father. I don't care where Hew Kessock looks, or what he says ! There's no dependence to be placed on him."

But a subtle thrill in her voice, a something in her eye, betokened that she was less indifferent than she wished her father to believe.

" Say, Meg, if you could become Lady Kessock it would mean a lot to this God-forsaken house."

The choice of the adjective sent a chill to the girl's heart.

It was used in the profane sense, but no one could deny that it expressed the unpalatable fact in a nutshell. In the old house of Ballochean fear of God or of man there was none. And what house run on these lines can prosper ? None. It marches straight as an arrow to the mark, which, in the end, is destruction.

"Tell me, Meg, hasn't Kessock said anything yet? A good many folks—me among the number—have been waiting to hear that you are going to Sangster," said he, in pursuance of the subject that he had asked her to the library to speak about.

Meg swallowed something in her throat.

"That is my business, dad," she said presently, in a high, clear voice, "and we'll talk no more about it, if you please."

But old Gavin Hamilton was not easily repulsed.

"But, hang it all, he was mad enough about you at one time. Why don't you bring him to the point? What more or better could you or any woman want? He's a fine-looking chap, he has plenty of money, he has a title, and he holds the first place in the county. I say, what more or better could you or any woman want? Don't be too high and mighty, lass, or you'll get left."

"I'm not talking about it, if you please," Meg repeated with dignity, and made as if she would go to the door.

"But listen, lass—think of your old father and of Ballochean! With Hew Kessock for my son-in-law all our troubles would be over. I'm deep in debt, Meg—smothered in it, drowned in it, if you prefer that expression. To-day I've added to it by seven hundred pounds and that has got to be paid in forty-eight hours—or something will happen. Get me out of it, lass—at least, out of some of it; for I've come to the end of my tether, and unless something's done, and that quickly, we'll be homeless before we know where we are."

The girl's face whitened, and her strong, virile, young hands made as if they itched to be at somebody's throat. What she had heard as to her father's desperate strait need not have been news to her, whose eyes had been open so long to the facts of the case. But such cold, measured words as her father had used had a horrible menacing sound.

"What can I do?" she asked shrilly. "I would marry Hew Kessock to-morrow, but I can't until he asks me properly!"

"Hasn't he said anything at all?"

"He has said oceans of things—the kind of things men say to women, taking care not to commit themselves too far, but to keep intact their own liberty. It's his mother who pulls the strings! She disapproves of me. I fancy she knows that if I was mistress of Sangster she would have to pipe a different tune."

"Old Gavin Hamilton forebore to chuckle—as he might have done at another time—at what he considered a proof of his daughter's high spirit.

Oh, the pity of it, that there were none to point out or to warn her how all this smirched the sweet flower of her opening womanhood, and made her less fit to be wife to any man worthy the name, much less to be the mother of his children!

The Laird sat forward, his eyes furtive and eager, his long mouth hard, even to the verge of cruelty. A man in desperate straits is none too particular as to what means of exit from them he will try. At that moment, so pitiable was his plight, Gavin Hamilton would have sacrificed his girl without a pang.

"But, Meg, couldn't you—couldn't you play the game with a little more skill, lass? It's like playing a difficult salmon. You've seen the thing done often up the Doon at the Kelpie's Leap? The angler who loses his temper, his patience, or his nerve is lost, so far as the capture of the salmon is concerned. Land him first, Meg, and pay the score after!"

The gross vulgarity of the suggestion somehow sickened the girl, and the fierce flame of her indignation blazed hot against her father.

"I'm not a creature of sale, father, and I refuse to play up to Hew Kessock. At this moment I hate him too much! If he asks me fair and square he'll get his answer—whatever answer comes pat at the moment. But that's all I will or can do, and you have not the right to ask me to do more. After all, who brought us here?—you did. And you have not the right to bully and bait either Ludo or me. Guy is the only one that you're afraid of—and he's the meanest worm among us!"

With these words she flung herself from the room, fearing lest the storm should wax fast and furious if she remained longer, and lest words should be spoken which would inflict a wound that could never be healed this side of the grave.

But her heart was hot to bursting, and she pressed her hand to her temples, as she ran through the long corridor, and, in her haste, almost fell into the arms of David Sillars, who had been admitted a moment before and was making his way to the library.

" Hullo, Meg ! What's happened now ? " he asked in surprise.

She stood still for half a moment, and fixed him with her stormy eyes.

The expression on his face was good. He represented strength, kindness, steadfastness of moral purpose—all the forces that were lacking in the house of Ballochean.

" Oh, David ! " she cried, " it's the deluge ! "

He dropped his hand on her shoulder, and in his eyes there were such depths of tenderness as those who knew Sillars only in his bleaker moods could not have credited him with possessing.

" But even the deluge passes, little woman," he said in his voice of kind cheerfulness.

" Oh, oh, this one won't ! " she said with a quick breath that was almost a sob. " What I wonder is—why God, if there is one, doesn't send down fire and brimstone from heaven and burn up Ballochean and all its ungodly crew ! Now, do you know where Ludo is ? " she added.

" Yes, my dear. He's at this moment in Kildoon."

" Oh ! "

She looked at him intently, trying to piece together the events of the day. Her intuition seldom failed her. It was almost like an extra sense.

" Father got a bit too much for him and he flew to you for comfort, King David !—as we all do," she said, with a sudden drop from her high rage and indignation to the charm of a womanhood soft enough to keep any man in thrall.

Sillars had been enthralled by it all his days—and, what was one pang more, he had long since decided that Meg Hamilton was not for him, and that Kessock was the man destined to carry off the prize. A lesser man, sure of this, would have sheered off, and so spared himself inevitable pangs. But Sillars was not built on these lines. " Faithful unto death " was the motto of his mother's family, and he embodied its high morality in every action and motive of his life.

Meg Hamilton leaned upon him mightily. He was ever the last refuge flung by fate, and as yet he had never been known to fail her.

" So Ludo is at Kildoon, David ? And you've come to talk to father about him ? "

Sillars nodded.

" Then go and give it to him hot and strong ! Oh, he's needing it badly, David ! I'll watch for you as you go out and I'll convoy you part of the way. Good luck ! Don't be afraid to slash out. The time has come—and the man ! "

She folded her hands on his arms, where she allowed them to remain a moment, and flashed the glory of her eyes upon him, all unwitting of the pang she gave. That a creature so vividly quick of apprehension and so clear-sighted as Meg Hamilton was should have travelled so far on the journey of life without being aware that Sillars loved her was one of the anomalies of which existence is full, and which there is no explaining away.

To her he was big brother, faithful friend, watchdog, final refuge from all the most evil happenings of life. Strange that it had never occurred to her to probe into the origin of all this devotion to her and her family, in themselves so unworthy of any devotion whatever. For they belonged to the order of the horse-leech—taking all and giving nothing in return.

Sillars passed into the library on the back of a slight knock, and he surprised the Laird in the act of filling his glass. Of late he was quite well aware that Ballochean had been drinking harder even than usual, and the fact troubled him, chiefly for Meg's sake.

" Good evening, Mr. Hamilton," he said with a brief nod.

" Oh, good evening, David," said the Laird, rather taken aback. " I'm glad to see you. Draw in and sit down. What will you have ? " he added, recovering himself.

" Nothing, thanks," Sillars answered briefly. " I've come to speak to you about Ludo. He's at Kildoon, and he says that nothing will induce him to come back to Ballochean."

" He is welcome to remain there for me, David, as long as you are minded to give him house-room," said the old man dourly.

" It's not a question of that, Mr. Hamilton. I've always liked the lad and been sorry for the ruin and waste of his life."

" Oh, indeed ! Who has wasted and ruined his life, may I ask ?—who, except his muling, puling self ? "

" You have, Mr. Hamilton. But we'll let that flea stick to the wa'," said Sillars, with the calm candour of the privileged and quite fearless intimate of the house. " I'm come to say what I'm prepared to do for Ludo, seeing that you will do nothing."

" Do nothing !—do nothing ! " cried the old man testily ; " pray, what can I do ? You know I am tied by the heels for lack of money—how I am on the verge of bankruptcy ? What can I do for a chap like Ludo, that ought to have been a girl—only he would have been a poor one ! Why, Meg has more in her little finger than he has in his whole carcase ! "

" I would beg leave to doubt it," said Sillars. " You don't know Ludo or what he is capable of. I am willing to put him in a way of doing. He is willing to go out to the West Indies to help my manager in Jamaica. I take it you have no objection ? "

" None in the world. And it's mighty good of you to give him such a chance. But I couldn't even raise enough money for his outfit or his passage, if that's what you've come about."

" No, I didn't come about that. I came merely to say that Ludo is ready to go next week. There is nothing to be gained by wasting time ; sufficient has been wasted already."

Old Gavin narrowed his brows and eyed the man standing opposite to him with a certain hawk-like look. The private query in his soul was how much more he could ask from this tried friend of so many years' standing, whose friendship stood many a searching test.

" David, you have much to be thankful for," he said presently. " A young man still, with money at your back and with no encumbrances—you are to be envied ! Take an old rip's advice and remain as you are, or you'll rue the day."

" What's this apropos of ? " inquired Sillars, quick enough to grasp the fact that the Laird, whom, in spite of his many sins, he liked, had some fresh trouble on his already burdened mind.

" Sit down and be sociable, and I'll make a clean breast of it, David. How can I speak to a man who is dodging about on his heel as if he were in a hurry to be off ? What did you say about Ludo ?—that he won't darken my door again ? Does that mean that you are to be saddled with him forthwith ? "

" It means that he is going to Greenock with me to-morrow morning, and that he will start for the Indies from there," said Sillars, and, drawing in his chair, he took out his pipe.

CHAPTER III

LOVER AND FRIEND

Meg Hamilton, like an unquiet spirit, haunted the upper landing and the gallery stair, watching for Sillars to come out of the library. She looked into the dining-room, only to find that Guy had left it.

In the intervals of Ellison Dove's coldness Guy had a small affair with a game-keeper's daughter to keep him occupied on dark nights. He had gone to keep tryst with her at the far side of the Howff Wood, and Meg, in his absence, had nothing with which to take up her attention while she waited.

She was, for some odd reason, intensely interested in what was going on on the other side of the library door, but something kept her from entering. Quite half an hour elapsed before the door at the end of the long corridor creaked, and she heard the voices of Sillars and her father as they came out.

By this time she was hiding in the little cloak-room, which opened at the right side of the hall-door, and, on hearing the sound, she flew out into the darkness of the terrace with an old tweed cape about her shoulders, and there she waited for the visitor to come out.

She observed that her father's farewell was unusually fervent, and she concluded therefrom either that he had been imbibing freely, or that he had something to be specially grateful for.

At last, however, Sillars, with an evident feeling of relief, got away from the Laird. But, directly the swing-doors closed, he caught a gleam of Meg's white skirt, and in a moment she was by his side, clasping two rather warm, impassioned hands on his arm.

"Oh, David, I thought you were never coming out! Whatever have you been talking about to the old man all this time?"

"Ludo, chiefly," answered Sillars laconically.

Half unconsciously he tried to free himself from her clinging hands. It was not because he did not like to feel them on his arm that he did so, but because he liked it too well.

"Tell me about Ludo," she said eagerly. "I'll convoy you to the Howff gate. Tell me every single thing that has happened this day!"

Her voice was imperious yet withal coaxing, and she did not dream of any refusal on the part of Sillars. Had he ever refused her anything in all the years she had known him?

"There isn't much to tell. Ludo and his father had a tussle this afternoon. I gather that these tussles have been rather frequent of late, and the lad is dead-sick of it all. He has run away from Ballochean, Madge."

By David Sillars alone was Meg Hamilton ever called Madge. It was his name for her, and she liked to hear it from his lips.

Her big eyes grew round with wonder in the darkness.

"Run away from Ballochean—how ripping! But where has he run to, David?"

"In the meantime he is no farther away than Kildoon."

"Oh, Kildoon!" she cried in scorn; "not much of a jaunt that! And have you brought him back, then, like a good little baa lamb to the bucht?"

"No, he won't come back any more, Madge. I am taking him to Greenock with me to-morrow."

"To Greenock? Whatever for?" she questioned in astonishment.

"As a preliminary to shipping him to the Indies, my dear. It is about time Ludo started out for himself, and, as it happens, an opening there fits in, and he is willing to go."

Meg was stormily silent for a moment—in this sense, that while her tongue made no sound, all her mental faculties were alert and working busily to find solution of the problem involved in this extraordinary combine between Sillars and her brother Ludovic.

" I want to get at the bottom of this, David. Please take me into your confidence," she said at last.

" The bottom is at the top," he said whimsically. " I've told you all there is to tell. Ludo can't stop beside your father any longer, and it is not advisable that he should. Why do you look at me so oddly, Madge ? I'm not making a present of anything to Ludo. He is going to work for his living."

" When, and where, and how ? " quoth Madge imperiously.

" In Jamaica, when he gets there, and the manner of his work will be in the hands of my manager—George Hislop—a demon for work himself, and a nailer at getting the most out of others."

" Oh ! " said Meg, and she pursed her lips up in utter disbelief. Then after a moment she continued : " And who, pray, is going to buy clothes for Ludo, and pay his passage, and give him something to land with ? "

" I will—as a loan, to be paid back. I've done it often before for protégés. It has worked out all right hitherto, and Hislop will see that it does so in Ludo's case."

" But why should you do it for Ludo ? " inquired Meg sturdily. " That's what I want to get at the bottom of. We are not related to you, though you've been better to us than any relations of ours that I've ever known or heard tell of."

" Why am I doing it for Ludo ? Well, because I like him and because I believe in him, and—what's more—because I'll live to see him come out on top ! "

Meg lifted wondering eyes to the grave, strong face of the man towering above her. So bright was the shining of the moon that it was almost like day about them as they crossed the open spaces of the park towards what was called the Howff gate, through which Sillars could pass to his own demesne.

A queer, warm, comforted feeling was at Meg's heart—a feeling which she could not have put into words, even if she had dared to try. Soft feelings, though not alien to her undisciplined heart, she found uncomfortable and disturbing, and to these she usually refused house-room. She wanted to thank Sillars—she felt that she ought to—but the words choked on her tongue.

" What did the old man say ? "

" The old man is easy, my dear. He cares for nobody but himself now. I wish it were possible to keep the whisky from him. Won't you try, Madge, to do so ? The love of it is getting a terrific hold on him."

" I do try, but I have no control over him. Oh, David ! I sometimes wish I had died when I was a little bairn, for when you grow up and are only a woman there is nothing but misery for you in this world ! "

The poignancy of that most unusual cry drove Sillars' prudence to the wind. He stood still in the middle of the path, and gripped her two hands, and held her eyes fast.

" Madge, give yourself to me, my dear ! I'm rich, I'm strong, and, by God ! I love you beyond everything on earth ! I don't want to bribe you—but I could smooth out all the tangles. I would look after your father, and I would try to get Ballochean affairs put on a solvent and solid basis, and, above all, I'd see that you never had an anxious hour."

He felt her tremble a moment in his strong grasp. Then she laughed.

She could never afterwards understand what hideous impulse made her laugh at the moment, for tears were not far away from her eyes.

" Are you asking me to marry you, David ? " she asked merrily.

" It is what I mean—yes, that's what I'm asking you," he said, and he let go her hands, for her tone cut him to the quick.

" Then I'm sorry, but I can't. I've known you too long, David, and you're too old. I could never cut myself to your pattern. I would as soon think of marrying Ludo or Guy. Whatever made you think of anything so impossible, and—and—so grotesque ? "

She floundered for the word, and at last brought it out with a brutal fervour which sounded like relief.

" All right. Let's say no more about it," he said, and his voice was so quiet that she had not the faintest idea of the tremendous curb he was putting on himself. " We'd better say good-night, now, hadn't we ? It's getting late and cold."

"It's neither late nor cold," she answered ruthlessly. "Would you mind telling me, David, what made you think of this all of a sudden? It is most awfully good of you to be willing to do all that for us. But what made you think of it?" she repeated.

"The same thing that makes other men propose to you, I suppose," he answered coldly. "You can't now be a novice at the game."

"Oh, but I am! Nobody has ever proposed to me except Bobbie Sanderson, when he was seventeen. I accepted him, too! But he's married now, so it was never serious!"

"Well, since you ask me, I'll tell you. I've cared about you since you were a small imp with two pigtails flying down your back; and I'll go on caring for you to the crack of doom! And, since we are at it, I may as well tell you that that's why I've never married, and why I never will marry now all my days. Good night, now. Having satisfied the Inquisition and been properly laughed at for my pains, may I go?"

"Oh, David!" cried the girl, and there was something dangerously like a sob in her voice.

She would have touched him again, but he fled from her. Merely lifting his cap, he vaulted the Howff gate and disappeared among the trees, leaving her to digest his last impassioned words.

He did not regret having spoken them, for though hope was quenched in his breast, at any rate she now knew his secret, and would, perhaps, understand some things in his conduct which had puzzled her before.

She walked across the moonlit spaces of the park, swinging her hands by her side and thinking, thinking deeply. Sillars in a new light—that of a lover—passed before her astonished vision; but the thought of it did not make her pulses beat one whit the faster.

If only Hew Kessock had spoken these words, with what joy she would have tossed back her gay answer!

"Queer business is life! Now, why can't David go and make love to Ellison Dove, who would marry anyone under heaven that could keep her in decent comfort?" she soliloquised. "I wish he hadn't told me, and yet—and yet——"

She never put into words the thought at the back of her mind. But it was one which comforted her with the assurance that she need never be homeless so long as Kildoon nestled by the side of its murmuring stream, nor friendless so long as David Sillars abode beneath its roof.

Next morning about seven o'clock, as Meg peeped over her window-blind to see the manner of the morning, she beheld Ludovic striding across the park from the Howff gate. By the time he was in the house and she had heard his foot on the stairs, she had got into a few clothes.

Very few of the dainty accessories of women's attire did Meg Hamilton possess, nor had she missed those she had had to do without. An old red satin kimono—relic of some loot from the East brought home by a marauding Hamilton of former days—made a slightly bizarre setting for her fresh young loveliness. The dew of sleep hung on her eyelids still, for Meg was a healthy young animal, who lived, and ate, and slept with all her might.

She popped her head round the door as Ludovic glided past in the direction of his own room, and beckoned to him mysteriously.

Not loth, he turned aside for a parting word with her.

"I didn't want to see any of you, Meg," he said briefly. "I'm done with Ballochean."

"Oh, but Ludo," she said with reproach in her voice, "I haven't been so bad to you as all that!"

"No. And, besides, you don't count—no woman does," said Ludo in a rather dull voice, and with the conviction of an ignorance that was superb. "I hope neither the old man nor Guy is up."

"No, it'll be ten at least before the old man turns out this morning after yesterday," she said significantly. "As for Guy, he keeps the hours that please himself, and I never saw him after dinner last night. But, I say, this is wonderful, Ludo, and I wish I was going with you."

"I'll tell you what I think, Meg; it's mighty good of Sillars, and he has done more for me than any blood relation," said Ludo fervently. "Can you tell me how the old man took it last night? David said 'well.' But I have my doubts, for I never saw a man so down as he was when he came back to Kildoon."

Meg said nothing, for her conscience smote her. She had witnessed the friendly parting between Sillars and her father at the door, and she knew well that she—and she alone—was at the bottom of the gloom of Sillars. But she did not propose to tell Ludo anything about it.

"It isn't easy talking sane common-sense to the old man or getting him to talk it after a race meeting, Ludo, and David ought to know that. At least, dad made no objection that I have heard of, but he was sound asleep on the sofa when I went to say good-night, and, for all I know, he may be there yet."

"It's an unholy house, and men ought to live like Sillars, Meg. It's the only possible way. Do you know that he reads out of the Bible to the servants every night? He says it's the band that keeps the house together, and that his mother, before she died, made him promise to keep it up."

Meg looked the surprise she felt.

The Bible as a book had no place in Ballochean. She was not even sure whether a copy existed in the house.

"David's queer, but he's a good sort. We have to take him all in all," she said briefly.

At the utterance of this casual word, which seemed to Ludo to convey contempt of the man whom he had set on the highest pinnacle of his regards, his eyes blazed.

"I tell you what—there are few David Sillarses in this world, Meg, and nobody need wonder; for people neither know how to appreciate nor how to treat them! But don't you dare to laugh at Sillars, Meg. Some day you'll know what he really is and be ready to bite your tongue out that you ever said a disparaging word about him. Till then try to keep that same tongue civil in your head. Now I must go and get a few things out of my drawers. They are of no use to anybody else, or I would leave them, for I'm owing nothing but my birth to Ballochean, Meg, and that I could have done without."

"Shall I come and help you?" she asked, and a sudden womanly desire to mother him swept over her irresistibly.

But Ludo shook his head.

"No. It would make too much noise next to Guy's room. Stop here, and I'll see you as I come down."

"And you won't even say good-bye to father?"

"No, and that I won't! He has shoved me out. He hates the sight of me."

"But surely you'll come back!" said Meg breathlessly. "For, after all, you are the elder son, and the place will be yours some day."

"Let them take it and keep it that want it—and it's Guy that I'm meaning, Meg. Here, I must go."

He fled with fleet but quite noiseless step to his own room, and in the shortest possible time returned with an old kit-bag, into which he had stuffed such of his belongings as might, he imagined, be useful to him. There was nothing of value, and poor Ludo, with his unshaven chin and dishevelled hair, looked cold and thin in the merciless morning light.

Meg had only pity for him; and in spite of the high words of encouragement that Sillars had spoken, she felt at the moment no belief whatever in the success of Ludo's future.

"Good-bye, then," he said, and after an awkward handshake she suddenly threw her arms about his neck and kissed him.

"Good-bye, old Ludo. I take back all the rotten things I've ever said to you! I never meant any of them, but now I wish I had never said one."

"It's all right, old girl. You've always been decent to me, and, when I get to the new place, I'll write and tell you how I am getting along."

"No message for dad?" she pursued, almost wistfully, for at the back of her mind was the womanly feeling that this sort of thing in a family could not be right.

"None. He wants no message from me. He'll be glad to hear he's seen the last of me."

But he lingered a moment, as if something was still unsaid.

"Say, Meg, if you get a chance to do anything for Sillars—and you never know, for life is a queer thing and we're all mixed up together—will you do it, not meanly or shiftingly, but with all your heart? You might have a chance to pay off a bit of the big score we owe."

In spite of her effort to steady herself up shot the hot flame in Meg's cheek.

"It's not likely that David Sillars will be wanting anything from me now," she said confusedly. "He'll probably drop us after you're gone. But I'll thank him, of course. Only, it is you who must pay back David, Ludo, and he expects that you are going to."

"I will—so help me God!" said Ludo with a solemn note, which was a vow, in his voice.

Then he gripped the handles of his bag, nodded to her, and sped down the stairs, to be stared at and commented on by such of the servants as had begun to creep about their tardy morning duty.

But to them he spoke not at all.

Meg stood by her open window with the cool autumn wind playing on the white snow of her breast, watching the lank figure as it strode across the open spaces of the park, and pondering on the pity and cruelty of it all. For it was not as it should be that the elder son of the house—the heir to Ballochean—should be striding away at daybreak—and apparently for ever—from the house that should be one day his.

All at once full realisation of the limitations and the absolute meagreness of their home-life smote on Meg with a sort of terror. Ludo had spoken of Sillars reading from the Bible to his servants, ordering his house on lines of decency and Christian forbearance and kindliness. How great, then, was the gulf fixed between Ballochean and Kildoon!

Poor Meg had small acquaintance with the Bible, and the only words from it which sprung up for her comfort at that unusual moment were ominous—"Vengeance is mine, I will repay, saith the Lord."

Of the other diviner message—"As one whom his mother comforteth, so I will comfort you"—no inner voice whispered.

Though conscious of an ache and a hunger at her heart, she did not know that her greatest need in the world at that moment was mothering.

Eight o'clock was the nominal breakfast hour at Ballochean; but when the Laird was in good fettle he would be bawling for porridge by half-past six in the morning. Meg dressed herself leisurely, took the dogs for a run across the park, and returned to the terrace just in time to hear the breakfast gong. To her surprise she found her father already seated at the table and looking fairly fresh and fit. He nodded curtly to her, and immediately the meal began.

"Where's the lads?" he asked, after he had taken a long draught of strong tea, and declined anything more solid.

"Guy isn't up yet, I suppose. Ludo is away, father," said Meg, eyeing him steadily.

"Ludo! Then he did not come home last night after all. He really slept at Kildoon!"

"Yes, but he has been here early this morning, and taken away his things; and now, I suppose, he is sitting at this moment in the Glasgow train with David. I remember he told me he was to leave by the eight-fifteen. Then he changes at Paisley and gets down to Greenock soon after nine."

The Laird pushed back his chair, and looked strangely at his daughter.

"Queer move this on Ludo's part, Meg! Do you know the meaning of it?"

"Oh! yes," she answered quietly.

"Well, tell me the meaning of it," he said irritably. "It's information I'm seeking, though you don't appear to know it."

"Why, it's as plain as a pikestaff," said Meg, not meaning to be rude, for speech was ever free and casual at Ballochean. "The worm has turned, and, according to David, it's going to grow up into a great, big, powerful serpent that will make folk get out of the way."

If the metaphor was a little mixed, it suggested possibilities to Gavin Hamilton's mind.

"What surprises me most of all is why Sillars should do this, Meg—that and other things. He's about the only man in the county who has befriended us." Then suddenly, struck perhaps by a certain radiance in Meg's looks, he added, with crass stupidity and complete lack of fine feeling, " If it's you he's after, Meg, I hope you'll know what side your bread is buttered on. He would be even better, from our point of view, than Kessock, for he has no relations to poke their fingers into the pie—eh, what ? "

For Meg had sprung to her feet and her eyes were blazing.

" Look here, father. Let me just say, once for all, that if there is any more of this kind of talk, I'm off, too, after Ludo to Jamaica—or to Timbuctoo ! If it's me you're looking to to pay your racing and your gambling debts—why, then, the deal's off. I didn't make them. I hate them, and I'm nearly as sick of my life as Ludo was before he cut the ropes. I've little enough, Heaven knows, of the things that most girls prize, and, though I've never asked them, I don't propose to stay here and be made to feel cheap and nasty at the same time. I'm not for sale, old man ! That's the one solid fact I want you to get firmly fixed in your mind—see ? "

The menace in her young, clear voice was terrible, and her father quailed before it.

" Hoity-toity ! The revolting daughter and no mistake ! Keep your wool on, my dear ! "

At that moment, perhaps, to the relief of both, certainly to the father's, the door opened and Guy, red-eyed and half-slept, slouched in.

" What's the racket ? " he asked with a casual nod across the table.

" Only Meg getting on her high horse ! " answered his father. " It only remains for you to follow suit, lad, and then we've a nice, comfortable kettle of fish all at boiling-point."

Meg pushed back her chair, and, with her head in the air, walked out of the room.

Then the two men, whose tastes, aims, and pursuits were similar, drew up to the table together to discuss the events of yesterday.

Guy got two items of information that surprised him mightily—first, that his brother had left the house for good ; and second, that somebody was going to pay the racing debt his father had incurred on yesterday's course.

So, for the moment, the immediate stress of Ballochean was removed once more. That was the curse of it, however. A strange kind of luck, which never visits better men, had constantly intervened to relieve Gavin Hamilton and to lift him out of tight corners.

At many a turning, where nothing had stared him in the face but total destruction, the cloud would suddenly lift, and he would be set on his feet again. Those who thus helped were not, however, always proving themselves his best friends.

CHAPTER IV

IN THE DOVECOTE

MEG HAMILTON had few women friends.

This will not surprise any who have made study of human nature and life. A woman is the most conservative creature on earth, and, were she entirely immersed in politics, would not go in for the wholesale reforms generally credited to her. She moves slowly, she attaches herself to places and to persons, but, without doubt and almost beyond relief, above all, to customs. She is a positive slave to custom. She does this or that because it has always been done; and this is specially so in all matters pertaining to convention and conduct.

Her laws are as the laws of the Medes and Persians—fixed, immutable as the stars in their courses. She has neither countenance nor quarter for those among her sisters brave enough to disregard these laws.

Meg Hamilton, dressing as she saw fit, and seldom well, though rarely unbecomingly, acting on whatever impulse the moment brought, caring for no man's blame and less for any woman's, alternately shocked and scandalised the strict matrons and maids among whom her lot was cast.

The county gradually dropped her, eligible sons were warned against her, anxious mothers sat in a watch-tower when she was by, and of course all her sayings, doings, and intentions were exaggerated, misrepresented, twisted out of all semblance to their actual shape.

Few guessed of the loving, passionate heart which beat beneath that gallant and ofttimes defiant front, of the wistful longing for love and womanly things lying behind that laughing face, of the tremulous accents that at times could move to gentleness her biting, fearless tongue. The few who knew her intimately loved her devotedly and beyond telling.

Sillars was the chief. But poor Meg, her eyes holden, pursued her flighty way and passed by the gold of that constant heart.

Feeling the world of home flat, stale, and unprofitable, and thoroughly out of tune with her own folk, she sallied forth on foot early next afternoon and walked into Ayr that she might pay a call on the Doves.

In a neat, double-fronted, but by no means imposing house which overlooked the old race-course at Ayr, abode Surgeon-General Dove of His Majesty's Navy, retired, along with his wife and daughter, Ellison, who was Meg Hamilton's only girl friend.

Mrs. Dove, a scheming Englishwoman, whose small nature had been still further narrowed and distorted by the petty jealousies of life among Service folk at Southsea, only permitted the intimacy because she saw in Meg the one stepping-stone by which she might reach county society.

With all her pranks and unladylike ways, Meg was in the county. Her name and lineage had nothing mushroom or doubtful about them, while the Doves were merely struggling for a foothold.

For herself, perhaps, Mrs. Dove might have been less ambitious, but for Ellison her ambition was without bounds. She beheld in that demure, kitten-faced creature, with the pretty bands of fair hair braided modestly about her soft pale cheeks, a possible countess, or, at least, "my lady."

For that end she lived, moved, and had her being, endured innumerable and unthinkable snubs, meekly made a door-mat of herself times out of number.

And Ellison aided and abetted her mother.

The father was cast in healthier mould. A breezy, outdoor person, devoted to golf and spending hours on the course and at the Ayr Club, he knew very little of the machinations of his womenkind. His chief grievance was the meagreness of his pension, which deprived him of many little luxuries that his soul loved and craved.

His wife was Spartan in her disbursement of the pension, for she had as great a horror of debt as the Laird of Ballochean had a love of it—an honourable feeling which was certainly something to the woman's credit.

Strange that Meg Hamilton should be able to suffer that environment; still more strange that she should make an intimate and confidante of Ellison Dove!

She felt special need of seeing her that day; and, arriving at Prospect House some time after half-past two, she was immediately admitted.

"It's Mrs. Dove's 'At Home' day, and they're up dressing, Miss Meg," said the general servant, who had just scrimmaged through her dish-washing and got into her black frock to be ready to admit early callers.

"If Miss Ellison is in her own room, Katie, I'll just go up," said Miss Hamilton, her words showing the terms of intimacy on which she was with the inmates of Prospect House.

"Very well, Miss Meg," said the girl, smiling kindly.

She adored Miss Hamilton, beholding combined and personified in her the essence of all the heroines of the penny novelettes with which she beguiled her scanty leisure. Miss Meg, in Katie's opinion, was the sort of person to whom anything in the way of adventure might happen. There was high romance in the glance of her eye, the poise of her head, and the clear tones of her bird-like voice. Even her workmanlike skirt of Harris tweed and the ill-cut Norfolk coat, thrown open to show the bare pillar of her stately young throat, could not destroy or even impair the vision of her as it presented itself to Katie. Hero-worship was in the girl's eye and mien as she watched her take the steps, covered with the worn Brussels carpet, two at a time.

She knocked lightly at Ellison's door and entered forthwith to find that damsel, attired in a white dressing-jacket trimmed with blue ribbons, in the act of coiling her abundant hair.

"Good-day, Ellie—sorry it's your 'At Home' day. What do you have it for?"

"I don't have it—it is mother who has it. Ask her. Don't imagine for a moment that I care about it. The tabbies who come are perfectly sickening," answered Ellison, looking round with some hairpins stuck between her lips. "Walked down, I suppose?" she added.

She eyed unfavourably the everyday dress of her friend, and Meg, catching the look, instantly took the hint.

"Oh! I'm not coming to the 'At Home.' You know how I loathe that sort of show. It should be stopped by Act of Parliament. I only wanted to walk off something that was troubling me, and to tell you things. I suppose I can sit here while you are getting into your clothes? With the first warning tinkle of the little tin pot at the door I'm off."

"Sit down, of course, Meg, and don't be silly. You'll have to stop to tea, now you're here," said Ellison, fitting the last coil deftly about her shapely head and then turning about before the mirror to observe the effect. "Like it, Meg? It's the latest coiffure from the Maison Nicol. Got it out of a fashion paper. Couldn't sleep last night till I got the style into my head."

"And now it's on!—yes, it's quite fetching. You've a goodish bit of hair, Ellie. I never thought you had so much."

"I haven't a mane like yours, but I know how to make the most of what I have," answered Ellison, as she poised the handglass to get the effect behind. "It'll do. Mother has given me a new frock. She's pleased with me over the head of something. I'm getting into it to-day."

Meg, half sitting on the front of the bed, fingered the soft blue stuff critically.

"It's pretty—the colour of your eyes. But what a lot of frocks you do get, Ellison! How you can stand to get them all fitted on I can't think! It would drive me clean wild. I should like to be a squaw in a blanket."

"Oh! I like being fitted on, and Miss Carrick has begun to understand my figure at last, and the value of the long straight line."

She threw off her dressing-jacket and began to get into the blue frock, Meg volunteering to do her up—a task she accomplished with fingers that were not conspicuously deft.

"It's gorgeous—but you don't look comfortable, Ellison. Isn't it a trifle fine, however, for the ordinary 'At Home'?"

"I don't think so. We may have extra callers to-day; there are so many people in town for the races. What did you think of yesterday, Meg?"

She leaned against the dressing-table—a very neat and quite pretty figure not unlike a Dresden shepherdess. Everything about her was dainty, well-considered, just what it ought to be.

Poor Meg, in her brogues and leather-bound skirt, struck an entirely different note.

Between the friends there was a great gulf fixed. Yet Meg Hamilton was a beautiful creature, with a woman's unawakened soul looking out from the depths of her sea-blue eyes.

" The racing was pretty rotten," said Meg briefly, " and, on the whole, I loathed it more than usual," she concluded, with a passing cloud on her level brows.

" Oh, the racing ! I don't know anything about that. I leave that to you. I'm not a sporting woman, Meg," remarked Ellison. " But we had a good time on the stand. Didn't you think the Kessocks and their friends very nice ? "

" No nicer than usual. When I see the Dowager something goes up my back, Ellison—something worse than a poker. It's a little demon that urges me to say the worst kind of things and to behave generally like an outsider."

" You succeeded," said Ellison primly. " I think it rather a pity, Meg—so does mother."

" When a woman puts up her lorgnette and glares at me she gets what she's looking for," quoth Meg ruthlessly. " Say, Ellison, Ludo has run away."

" Ludo ! "

Ellison paused in her work of nail-trimming and stared out of her round china-blue eyes.

Meg nodded violently.

" Really and truly run away ! He went off to Greenock with David this morning, and he's sailing for the West Indies next week."

" Whatever for ? "

" To be made a man of. It's David's doing, Ellison. I wish I could go too ! At this particular moment I'm violently sick of everything under heaven."

" I've heard you say that before, Meg, but nothing comes of it," answered Ellison tranquilly. " But I would like to know what Mr. Sillars has to do with Ludo ? It's the queerest thing I've ever heard."

She kept her eyes on Meg's face as she spoke these words, and she was rewarded by beholding its colour rise. Meg, with the need of sympathy, perhaps of counsel, at the moment, gave her heart away to a wholly unworthy confidante.

" I'll tell you, Ellie, if you don't tell a soul."

" Whom should I tell ? Besides, we're chums, aren't we ? "

" Well—I believe it's on account of me, chiefly, that David did it. He's—he's what people call in love with me, Ellie."

She spoke the words in a sort of awestricken whisper, which caused Ellison to smile inwardly. A very child in such affairs beside Ellison Dove was Meg, and the machinations of the match-makers were a sealed book to her. Her nature was pure and sound, and her life among men and boys at Ballochean had undoubtedly kept her free from some of the narrowness and pettiness of her sex.

" Oh, how interesting ! Did he tell you, Meg ? " said Ellison in a low, deeply interested voice, " or did you only guess it ? "

" Oh ! he told me. It was last night after he had been interviewing dad about Ludo. I waylaid him outside the library to hear about it ; and then he told me. Don't you think it the most amazing thing you've ever heard ? "

" It is a little surprising. We certainly, up till now, have all thought Mr. Sillars a confirmed bachelor. Well, and what did you say ? "

" I'm afraid I laughed, Ellison," said Meg ruefully. " David, of all the people in the world ! Why, he might be my father ! or, at least, my very oldest brother. I told him that."

" You told him that ! Oh, poor Mr. Sillars ! he wouldn't like it. Men are far more touchy about their ages than we are. You couldn't have said anything that would hurt him more."

" Are they ? " asked Meg, with a mystified air. " How do you know so much about men, Ellison, seeing that you've no brothers and only your father ? I might be supposed to know more about them than you."

" You might—only you don't, my dear. You are very young for your years.

Besides, I read a lot. You can learn a good deal from novels. If they are good novels they represent life."

"Can't stick them," said Meg flatly. "Life itself is a jolly sight more interesting. So I oughtn't to have said that to David about his age! I thought something gave him the hump!"

"Don't be so slangy, my dear. I'm sure Mr. Sillars would disapprove."

"Oh, no, he wouldn't. He likes me as I am—at least, I think so," said Meg ingenuously. "And, anyway, he has no business to criticise me. No man has, thank goodness!"

"But you're going to give him the right, aren't you?" asked Ellison, and her casual manner betrayed no hint of the intensity of her interest in the reply.

"Oh, not at all! I said 'No.' So it's all over and done with."

"Oh! but, Meg——"

"But what?"

"Weren't you a little bit hasty? Think of how well off he is, and what a lovely place he has at Kildoon! And he isn't really old, you know—only about thirty-five."

"If I ever marry a man, kid, it won't be for what he has. If I did, that would finish both him and me. Was that the bell?"

"Not yet; if something rang it was the kitchen bell. Probably the milk. So you refused him. And was he very much cut up?"

"He said very little after it except good-night. But he won't bear malice, Ellison. He isn't that kind of worm. You won't tell anyone, kid. I don't know why I told you, I'm sure. I don't suppose I ought, and I almost wish I hadn't."

"Oh! but we swore to tell each other our secrets. I only wish I had anything to tell," said Ellison, with a small sigh.

"Don't tell your mother, Ellison. Promise me you won't?" cried Meg, becoming more and more uneasy.

Perhaps the first hint of the shallowness and treachery emanating from the atmosphere of that house touched Meg's clear young soul—who knows?

At that moment the door opened, and Mrs. Dove appeared in a black satin gown, much trimmed with Maltese lace, which she had procured cheaply when stationed on the island with her husband.

She was a small, bird-like person with rather a high colour, which she sought to soften with liberal applications of Violette de Parme. She was like Ellison, but her mouth had developed hard lines; in repose it was even cruel in its outline. A long battle with narrow means and constant efforts to keep up appearances on them had doubtless done a good deal towards destroying the finer qualities of Mrs. Dove. Certainly she now belonged to the hawk species, and she lived for what she could get out of other folk.

She did not look at all pleased to see Meg just then, though she strove to disguise the fact.

"How do you do, Meg? I thought you would be too tired after yesterday to tramp into town to-day. I said to them at breakfast that I felt sure you would."

"I'm never tired, Mrs. Dove. But if I had remembered it was your 'At Home' day I wouldn't have come," answered Meg candidly. "But I'm going now."

Just then, however, there was the sound of wheels, and Mrs. Dove, hearing it, flew to the window.

"The Sangster carriage!" she said, preening her feathers, like a satisfied bird. "Come down quickly, Ellison. Good-bye, then, Meg, if you really are going. But we shall be pleased if you will stop to early tea."

Meg said neither yea nor nay; and Mrs. Dove closed the door and ran down to pose as appearing at ease in the drawing-room, when Lady Kessock should be announced.

"Won't you come down, Meg?" asked Ellison, turning once more to the mirror to have a last look at herself and to see whether she was fit for the inspection of the great lady.

"I don't want to see the old dame, Ellie. Whoever marries her precious Hew will have to keep her in her place and take the high hand, or her life won't be worth living."

Now, what possessed Meg Hamilton to make that injudicious speech to Ellison Dove no man, or woman either, could tell !

Ellison smiled demurely to herself and treasured the words in her heart.

" Oh ! she only wants a little managing, Meg. Diplomacy, my dear girl, is sadly lacking in your composition."

" Diplomacy ! Hypocrisy, you mean, Ellie. Call things by their right names. Well, I suppose I'd better be going, as no doubt you are anxious to go down and exercise your diplomacy."

" I'll come with you. But mother asked you to tea, you know," said Ellison, and, as she glanced at Meg, already in the doorway, it occurred to her that it would be no bad thing could she contrive that they should be seen together in the drawing-room. Meg's outdoor garb, her brogues, soiled with the field-clay, and her general disregard of all that pertains to womanly charm, would be an excellent foil to the new blue gown.

Meg continued to shake her head, and they went together downstairs. But, as it happened, the drawing-room door was open sufficiently wide to give the inmates of the room a full view of the narrow passage, and Lady Kessock saw them and called out.

" That is Miss Hamilton ! Won't you come and say ' how do you do ' ? " she inquired in her high, shrill, penetrating voice.

Meg made a little " moue " and stalked unwillingly into the room in the wake of Ellison.

Lady Kessock, sitting in Mrs. Dove's best easy-chair, extended a friendly, if rather patronising, hand to Gavin Hamilton's daughter. Fortunately she did not put up the lorgnette, which dangled from a massive chain above her velvet mantle, for scrutiny through the handled glasses never failed to rouse Meg's ire.

" I'm all right, thank you, Lady Kessock," she answered, with a touch of sullenness, extending an arm as stiff as a pump handle. " I am not paying calls. I came only because I had something to ask Ellison."

" Oh ! don't hurry away," said the Lady of Sangster graciously, and she even pulled forward a small chair for Meg to sit down upon. But Meg held aloof.

" Miss Hamilton is not much at home in drawing-rooms, Lady Kessock," said the Surgeon-General's wife with her simpering little smile. " She thinks them a frivolous waste of time."

Lady Kessock smiled slightly in response, and contrasted the two girls, much to Ellison's advantage.

She was herself a tall, commanding woman with high cheek bones and a hooked nose, indicative of her high lineage, but nevertheless giving a curious hawk-like expression to her face. She had the reputation of being one of the haughtiest women in the county, and of being the mother of its most eligible bachelor.

She was in no haste for her son Hew to marry, since that would mean that she would have to quit Sangster altogether or, at any rate, abdicate in favour of its new mistress. Much, therefore, depended on the woman he should choose to be his wife. That he had thought of Meg Hamilton Lady Kessock was perfectly well aware ; but her choice would have fallen on Ellison Dove, in whom she imagined she discerned a gentle, pliable creature, who would allow herself to retain the reins of government at Sangster.

Never, however, had a bigger mistake been made ! So far as her own comfort was concerned, she had far better have fixed her choice on Meg.

" Now, I wonder whether you two girls would come and spend a long day at Sangster ? " she said presently. " My son goes into camp on Monday, and I shall be very much alone. Shall we say Tuesday ?—and if Miss Hamilton could get down this length, the carriage would pick you both up."

" I'm sorry I can't come, Lady Kessock," answered Meg, in her most abrupt, uncompromising tones. " I have to take some children for a picnic to the Maidens. Will you excuse me, if I run away now, Mrs. Dove ? I really did not come meaning to stay."

Mrs. Dove was graciously pleased to excuse her, and, when she had closed the door upon the girls, she heaved a little regretful sigh.

" It is a pity, dear Lady Kessock—is it not ?—to see a young creature so sadly neglected. She has quite a nice disposition—at least, so my Ellison maintains—only she has had nobody to set her a proper example."

"She is not one who would meekly follow any example," said Lady Kessock severely. "That was a very rude answer she gave me after I had gone out of my way to be kind to her, even overcoming a certain prejudice, for I do not like the girl, Mrs. Dove, and I disapprove of all she does."

"Ah, yes! but your standard is much higher than mine, dear Lady Kessock," sighed the little woman. "Sometimes I tremble a little for Ellison. But it would not be quite kind to bring their friendship to an end, though, of course, it is only a slight affair. It would be rather a blow to Meg, for I believe I am right in saying that Ellison is her only friend."

"The two are very different. But then, Gavin Hamilton's girl has never had a chance. It is a pity her mother did not live. Did you see her father yesterday? It was a scandal to the county to see him in the company of that riff-raff on the race-course. I really don't know what is likely to be the end of Ballochean. My son says there will be a big burst up there one of these days."

At that moment Ellison re-entered the room, looking mysterious and important.

"Mother! Ludovic Hamilton has run away from Ballochean, and David Sillars is sending him to his sugar plantation in Jamaica!"

Instantly Lady Kessock's eyes flashed with interest and curiosity.

"You don't say so!" she said. "It is very good of Mr. Sillars. I am surprised that a man of his character and standing in the county should mix himself up with people like the Hamiltons. I wonder why he does so?"

"Oh! I can tell you," said Ellison glibly. "It is on account of Meg. She——"

But the telling of the secret was interrupted, for at the moment three more callers were announced, and for the next half-hour there was a steady stream, and Lady Kessock had not another opportunity of hearing more about the Sillars-Hamilton affair from Miss Dove.

At last she had to leave, but, as she shook hands with Ellison, she whispered, "You must come to lunch one day soon. Shall we say Monday, seeing that Miss Hamilton has declined? Then you can tell me the rest of the story."

"Thank you, dear Lady Kessock," said the girl, with her most demure and grateful air.

Mrs. Dove herself walked with her distinguished guest to the outer door, and when she returned to the less distinguished ones she was positively beaming!

"Such a dear, kind woman—Lady Kessock!" she said, "and so fond of Ellison. She came to arrange for her to spend a long day at Sangster. Quite charming of her, don't you think?"

The ladies agreed that it was quite charming; but, at the same time, they asked themselves and—a little later—one another how Mrs. Dove had managed to worm herself so far into the good graces of the proud Lady Kessock.

They concluded in the end that it was because she was English and would stick at nothing.

CHAPTER V

STORMY PETREL

As Meg passed Lady Kessock's prancing bays at the kerb she remembered that she had some shopping to do in the town, and accordingly she strode on, feeling a little uncomfortable when she thought of the occurrences of the last half-hour. Two things had surprised her—Lady Kessock's visit to Prospect House and something in Ellison Dove's manner which she could not define. It was really a kind of quiet triumph. But what was there to be triumphant about ?—the invitation to Sangster, perhaps, which Meg herself had declined.

It was not possible for Meg, whose own nature was clear and transparent as the day, to comprehend the eagerness of people like the Doves to be recognised by those whom they knew or imagined to be of higher station than themselves, or to realise of what subterfuges they could be guilty in order to attain their ends. To Meg Hamilton that would indeed have savoured of the under-world much more than the frank code of manners obtaining at Ballochean.

She had not arrived at any solution of the puzzle when she reached the shops and placed her orders. It may be said here that Ballochean was heavily in debt to almost every tradesman in Ayr, and that it was only the charm of Miss Hamilton's own personality which procured for the family even the necessaries of life. They had not paid their butcher a shilling for over three years, yet they lacked for nothing that he could supply them with. Nobody as yet blamed Meg for this state of matters, though one or two had suggested that she might now be expected to take a tighter grip of the domestic reins.

But, oddly enough, those who were the biggest were also the most long-suffering creditors. When she entered the shop of Mr. Macmichael, the butcher, he received her as if she had been the highest lady in the land and treated her with quite as much deference. As he made a note of what she required in a special book which, in his own mind, if not actually on the title-page, was labelled " Bad Debts," or " Doubtful," Meg was suddenly struck by an odd expression on his face.

" Mr. Macmichael," she said brusquely, " isn't it about time you sent us an account to Ballochean ? "

Macmichael regarded her for a moment over the rim of his spectacles.

He was a large, comfortable man with a jolly face, and he had daughters of his own whom he could afford to send to an expensive boarding-school and to keep a riding horse for all the year round. Perhaps that was why he always had a soft side to Miss Hamilton.

" I have been in the habit of sending the account in twice a year to Mr. Hamilton, miss."

" Oh ! " said Meg, with a little gasp, " and father has paid it, I suppose ? Then it is quite all right ? "

Macmichael hesitated for a moment, fingering the doubtful pages.

" As a matter of fact, Miss Hamilton, nothing has been paid for three years," he then said.

" Three years ! But that is quite terrible, Mr. Macmichael. Can you tell me how much is owing that I may recall it to my father's memory ? "

She spoke with a kind of pathetic dignity, poor child, which very nearly brought a lump into the kindly butcher's throat. He ran his finger and thumb over the pages and then eyed her again.

" A hundred and seventy-three pounds up to date, Miss Hamilton."

Meg started back in affright.

" A hundred and seventy-three pounds for meat alone, Mr. Macmichael ! Oh, surely there must be some mistake ! My father can't be aware of it ! If he had been, he never would have allowed it to go on so long."

Macmichael had his doubts.

" The account is as it stands, Miss Hamilton. It was last rendered on the first of July. It will be sent in again, I don't doubt, on the first of October. My son Tom keeps the books. He was speaking about it the other day and asking what I was going to do about it."

" I am not at all surprised," said Meg, with some dignity. " Please send it in at once without waiting until the first of October, and I will see that a cheque is sent."

Her heart was heavy as she stepped from the shop across the street to the Post Office to buy some stamps.

A hundred and seventy-three pounds for butcher's meat alone! Then what about the baker and the grocer and all the other tradesmen whose shops existed to supply necessaries to the household of town and country ?

Every shop window suddenly became a menacing eye to poor Meg, and life grew hideous.

Her face wore an expression of blank dismay as she left the Post Office, in the doorway of which she knocked up against a tall man in a grey tweed suit, who immediately lifted his cap in apology.

" Hulloa, Meg ! " said Bobbie Sanderson's pleasant voice ; then, " You are indeed a sicht for sair een ! "

Meg smiled, in spite of herself, at the hearty greeting and the expression of good-will on the plain, freckled face of Bobbie Sanderson—her first lover, and still her very good friend.

He was the only son of " the doctor," as old Dr. Sanderson was called in the town, while his son was variously dubbed " Dr. Robert," " Maister Bobbie," and " the young yin." All three appellations were terms of affection, however, for it would have been hard to say whether father or son was the more beloved in the place.

" You've never come to see the bairn, Meg, and I'm not sure that I'm forgiving you."

" The bairn ! Oh ! I forgot you had a bairn, Bobbie. It's ridiculous. But I'll come one of these days. Your wife isn't up yet, is she ? "

" Why, of course she is ! It's three weeks old to-day, and it's going to be christened next week. Come across now and see Edie and Aunt Ann and the baby and have a cup of tea."

Meg considered a moment, half-allured by the prospect. Anything that could divert her mind from the painful and almost terrifying thoughts that had taken possession of it was welcome at the moment.

" All right. Let me post this and I'll come. I've things to tell you anyway, Bobbie. Ludo has run away."

The young doctor whistled the astonishment he felt.

Meg nodded with vigour.

" To be more correct, Mr. Sillars has taken him away. He's going out to the West Indies to grow sugar, or herd black people, or something. Anyway, he's gone. I'm glad, I think, and yet I'm sorry."

" It'll be a jolly good thing for Ludo, Meg, and I'm glad Sillars thought of it. Awfully good chap, isn't he ? "

" Oh, yes ! I believe that he is actually too good for this world," said Meg ruthlessly. " Say, Bobbie, can you tell me what's the matter with us all at Ballochean ? "

They were in the middle of the street by this time, and Sanderson had suddenly to grasp the girl's arm to pull her away from before a passing carriage.

" You'll get run down one of these days, my dear. This isn't a hunting field or a race-course, remember," he said warningly. " What were you saying ? Oh ! I remember. Are things gone wrong at Ballochean, then ?"

" Wrong ? They've never been right. I'm going to tell you something awful, Bobbie. I've just discovered that we owe Macmichael, the butcher, a hundred and seventy-three pounds."

Bobbie did not appear in the least surprised. He expected it to have been more.

" Oh ! well, things must mend some day. Don't let it worry you, Meg. You're not responsible," he said soothingly.

" Am I not ? " she asked, with a sudden upward glance of wistfulness that made

Bobbie Sanderson's heart as suddenly melt. For Meg had been his first love, and, though he was now happily married to a gentle, sweet girl who had brought brightness to the old High Street house, yet he had never forgotten this creature of the wind and sunshine, who was so different from all other women whatsoever.

They had been partly brought up together in the days when Meg's mother had been delicate. The old doctor had been much at Ballochean at that time, and he had often taken his boy with him. Bonds like these are seldom broken altogether—they retain a kind, odd link and spell right through life.

"Well, I don't see how you can be responsible. It's your father's business, after all."

"Then it's hopeless," said Meg dejectedly, "for he doesn't seem to have any sense where money is concerned. I tell you what, Bobbie—I wish I had died when mother did or, at any rate, that I had never grown up. It's a hateful, horrible thing to be a woman, and I'm deadly sick of it! If you're a man you have a chance. A woman has none."

They had come to the great, wide, flat-fronted house with the innumerable windows and the low oak door which had been "the doctor's" house from time immemorial in the High Street.

It was a friendly, warm-hearted house, where generations of kindly folk had lived and whence the healer had gone forth—father and son—in direct descent for five generations.

The Sandersons belonged to the aristocracy of the medical profession, and their social position, as well as their influence, was unassailable.

The house, bare, but very dignified without, was beautiful within. There was nothing new or garish. Everything bore the hall-mark of solid worth and substantial, if not great, possessions. Much taste had guided the furnishing arrangements, and if the tone was a little sombre, it was fitting and quite in keeping with the dignity of an historic house.

"They'll be in Aunt Ann's sitting-room, I expect," said Bobbie, as he tossed off his cap. "I heard them say the drawing-room was not to be reoccupied till next week. Come up, it's just on tea-time."

The stairs of dark oak, carpeted in a sweet, soft, blue colour, invited them, and Meg followed with an odd feeling that here, in this house, though it was very simple, there were things which money cannot buy.

The landing, lit by a long window, in which there was some fine old coloured glass which one of the old doctors had picked up in some of his peregrinations through the county, showed innumerable doors, one of which Bobbie opened. It revealed a wide, low, cheerful room panelled in the same dark oak, but relieved by big patterned chintz and many water-colour paintings on the walls, and a cheerful fire at the far end.

The clink of cups and the warm smell of buttered toast proclaimed that tea was in progress.

"Are you there, Edie? I've brought a visitor. I found Miss Hamilton wandering in the wilds of the High Street, looking very hungry. Here she is!"

The young wife, looking a picture of sweetness in her pink wrapper, rose, holding the precious baby with a kind of shy awkwardness on her left arm. She had been the daughter of a country clergyman and had slipped into her place in the doctor's house with charm and adaptability.

The old doctor and his sister, who had rather feared the day of Bobbie's marriage, had already blessed it; for Edie had brought no discord, but only brightness, and joy, and sunshine. As for the bairn on her arm, what chance would it have of growing up unspoiled at the hands of four adoring worshippers, to say nothing of the doctor's "man," Scrymgeour, and the three house-servants, who had joined the worshipping throng?

Meg smiled into the sweet face of Bobbie's wife, shook hands with her and with Aunt Ann, who looked inordinately pleased to see the girl, then asked whether she might hold the baby.

"It won't break, will it?" she asked comically. "I'm not afraid of puppies, or foals, or any other kind of live stock, but——"

"She's calling it live stock, Edie!" interrupted Bobbie teasingly. "Can she be permitted to live?"

" You have said ' it ' Bobbie—and that is the unpardonable sin. Yes—a boy, Miss Hamilton. Another Robert Dalziel Sanderson, to prescribe pills and bring Ayrshire babies into the world after we've left it ! "

The happy girl had a pretty wit, and the laugh that followed these words set them all at their ease.

Meg lifted the little scrap of embroidered flannel from the sleeping head and gazed down on the crumpled roseleaf of a face with a very odd expression on her own.

" It's a heavenly thing, but I can't bear it," she said suddenly, holding out her arms. " I'm going to drop it ! I want to cry—why, Heaven alone knows, and I suppose it's unlucky to cry over a baby."

Her eyes were full of bright drops when Bobbie took the baby. She dashed them away in open shame.

" Must be going dotty ! And how are you, my dear, darling Miss Ann, and is your dear nose hopelessly out of joint now ? "

The little old lady, looking like a cameo picture in her black frock with the lace fichu, her soft cap, and her knitting, nodded and made a place on the sofa for Meg.

" I was saying only yesterday, Peggy, that you had never looked near us. How are you, my queen ? "

" Queen ! I'm a base-born subject now. There can't be two crowned heads in any house. He's the king now," she said, pointing to the baby's brown head, " and I predict that he will rule you all with a rod of iron so that you won't be able to call your souls your own ! I know what the Robert Dalziel Sandersons are—tyrants, every one of them, from the cradle to the grave ! "

" What, what ! " said a deep, good-humoured voice in the doorway. " Who is the Pride of Ballochean slating now ? "

Meg sprang up, laughing and flushing, to meet the old doctor, with whom she shook hands warmly.

An old man, he carried his seventy years well, and his kindly face, with its deep lines and firm but mobile mouth, inspired trust in every man, woman, and child who looked upon it.

" It's only my havering tongue, doctor ; but this time it happens to be the truth I'm speaking. I was only saying that this queer little red thing is going to be king in Ayr. How are you, dear doctor, and why do you never, never come now to see the Pride of Ballochean ? "

Long, long ago, when she was a leggy creature in short skirts with two thick pig-tails hanging down her back, the old doctor had dubbed her the Pride of Ballochean, and Meg had loved the name and cherished it simply because his lips had spoken it.

Here, in this house, where they loved and understood her, Meg Hamilton was at her best. Gay and tender by turns, she wove a spell over them which none could resist.

" I heard of you yesterday, and that you were distracting folks' attention from the legitimate business of the races," he said teasingly.

" Oh, doctor ! how can you—how could anybody say that ? I sat as mim as a mouse, hiding behind Mrs. Dove, and nobody heard me speak a word."

" It was not what you said, but how you looked ! And when is it going to come off ? When are we to behold the new mistress in Sangster, eh ? "

Hew Kessock's admiration for Meg Hamilton was well known in Ayr, as was also his mother's opposition to the affair. But of Meg's state of mind nobody had the least idea. It was perhaps with some hope of finding it out that the old doctor put these teasing questions, for he had heard that day of the Laird's doings on the race-course, and he was wondering what was to be the upshot.

He well knew that everything that could be turned into money at Ballochean had been sacrificed, and that, had it been possible to break the entail, the place itself would have been gone long ere this. But if Meg was to become Lady Kessock, it was within the bounds of possibility that Hew Kessock, who was a shrewd business man, as well as a keen landlord, would do what he could to restore part at least of the broken fortunes of Ballochean.

Many a good talking to had old Robert Sanderson given his lifelong acquaintance at Ballochean, but fruit of his counsel he had seen none, and he had long washed his hands of him. The books locked up in the surgery drawer showed a much bigger sum set down against the name of the Hamiltons than Macmichael's had shown, and "Bad Debt" had been written across it long ago.

It will be seen, therefore, that Ballochean credit was hopelessly gone; but there were few hearts that did not feel a pang of pity for the motherless girl who had been engulfed in that cataclysm, and there were many who hoped that by a suitable marriage she might secure her future.

Meg impatiently shook her head, while with her hand she tried to shade the red flush on her tell-tale face.

Bob Sanderson, seeing it, was conscious of a pang which had in it no disloyalty to his own wife. But Meg Hamilton turned into my Lady Kessock would occupy a different footing everywhere, and, in the very nature of things, all the old ties must slacken.

They spent a happy hour together, and Meg at parting kissed the baby, though she was not given to promiscuous kissing, especially of the few women friends she had. Indeed, she openly mocked at Ellison Dove for the little pecks she would give to her female acquaintances, even to those she hated most.

Again the queer softness stole to her eyes at sight of the helpless mite, and when she smiled into the young mother's eyes there was pathos in that smile.

"You're rich, Mrs. Bobbie—very, very rich! Don't forget the hungry poor."

It was one of the cryptic speeches which Meg often made, and which nobody took seriously, though to any close observer the words would have given hint of the heartache behind.

It was the old doctor himself who went down the stairs with her, and he detained her a moment in the hall.

"Your father has gotten in with a thoroughly bad set, my dear—a set that will never do him the least good. Can't you keep him at home more than you do?"

Meg shook her head.

"I can do less and less with him, doctor, and I'm tired trying. Is there any use in trying anything in this world? Things just happen—and there you are! Ludo has gone, and if I were Guy nothing would keep me a minute longer at Ballochean. There is nothing for a young man to do there but to get into mischief.

"Poor lass!—poor anxious, motherless lass!" said the doctor, and at these words, which stirred a hidden woe in the girl's heart, she opened the door suddenly and shot out without so much as a word of farewell.

"If people pity me, I'm done!" was her inward cry. "But what are we to do—owing money everywhere? We haven't the right even to the bread we eat!"

She was in no haste to get home, and the sea called her. She made her way down to the shore, and, finding the tide far out, crossed the level stretches of the sands, and soon she was a remote and solitary figure half hidden by the soft haze which was creeping in from the sea to the land.

One or two riders, tempted by the lovely reach of sand, were out, and presently one came galloping towards her, and drew rein so sharply that the horse was almost forced back on his haunches.

It was Hew Kessock, looking very smart in his riding kit—a fine figure of a man, with a fair, handsome face, yellow hair, closely cropped, and a pair of dashing grey eyes that could soften dangerously at sight of a pretty woman.

Meg was not looking particularly pretty at the moment, and already Hew Kessock's wandering fancy had roved from her who had given him the first-fruits of her girlish heart. She had been hard to win. All the pretty speeches he had made at first she had flouted and laughed at, and she had refused to take a single one of them seriously. This had piqued Kessock, who was unaccustomed to have his favours so casually treated.

Therefore he had persevered, making love in season and out of season, seeking her here, there, and everywhere, with the result that by the time he had succeeded in making the impression he desired his own ardour had cooled. Within the last month or two he had sheered off a bit, and he had even agreed with his mother that Meg would hardly be a suitable wife.

In common with most of the men of the neighbourhood, Kessock barred Gavin Hamilton and all his ways, and the idea of being related to him by marriage was not pleasant. Had he felt, or been capable of feeling, a great passion for Meg—or, for that matter, any woman—he would not have paused to reflect and weigh up things; but the one being whom Hew Kessock loved was himself.

He was by no means, however, indifferent to Meg Hamilton even yet, and the sauce of her tongue was refreshing after the sweet words that other girls were ready enough to speak to him.

Meg hated herself mortally because she could not restrain the high colour from mounting to her cheek, but her eyes were defiant as they met his.

"Don't get down. I'm in a hurry. I've been out all the afternoon and I'm getting home," she said in her most unfriendly voice.

Kessock's reply was to dismount leisurely, throw the reins over his arm, and turn to walk by her side.

"Queer that, if you are in a hurry, you should take the longest road home! Is this a short cut to Ballochean?"

"It suited me at the moment. I've been to tea at the doctor's. I saw Bobbie's new baby. Bobbie as a father!—funny idea, isn't it? It makes us all horribly, unaccountably old."

Kessock's lips under his fair moustache smiled provokingly.

He admired Meg Hamilton's face, and her high, proud carriage, and the gold of her hair, but he thought it a pity that she did not take a little more pains with her dress. The skirt she wore was frayed at the hem, and she had no gloves on her firm, virile hands, which, though of a beautiful shape, were neither white nor soft.

His present mood was to admire the small, and fine, and womanly in a girl, and his gaze in the race-stand yesterday had rested with considerable approval on Ellison Dove. Meg had noticed it, and it was that which was actually at the back of all her immediate disquiet.

"We haven't met for weeks, have we—eh, Megsie?"

"Yesterday," she answered laconically; "but perhaps that doesn't count."

"You wouldn't look at me. When are we to have another tryst? Is it all over, Meg?"

Something in his voice raised her inmost ire.

"Is what all over?" she asked, looking at him with one straight, defiant glance.

"You know—all the old, sweet fooling. Of course, we know it can never come to anything, but it embroidered life, which is sometimes mighty slow in these parts. Why have you thrown me over? Somebody else in the running—eh?"

Again his tone, a little hint of disrespect in his manner, went home like a barbed arrow to the mark.

"I don't know what you're talking about," she said in a voice of ice, "and I think that, instead of wasting my time here, you'd better go to Prospect House and call on Miss Dove. She's expecting you and has got her best frock on for the occasion."

With these wholly undignified words, which came from she knew not where, and which, in their very utterance, gave her anguish, Meg sped across the firm sand and up the narrow footpath by the tumbling Doon, not caring how or whither she went, if only she got away from the spell of Hew Kessock's eyes.

She knew that he no longer loved her, that he had no longer any intention of asking her to be his wife—if, indeed, he ever had had such intention—and for the moment life was impossible and the world an empty place to poor Meg Hamilton

CHAPTER VI

THE COOING OF THE DOVE

KESSOCK watched for a few moments the slim figure hurrying across the sands, his expression one of mingled chagrin and longing. To marry Meg Hamilton was certainly impossible owing to the disreputable character of her family, but certainly no man could have found a more adorable bride.

She would bore or weary none, since her moods were as varying and enchanting as those of an April day. Meg, even in her angriest mood, was to be preferred to more amenable creatures, who had nothing but smiles and kind looks for those who paid them court.

Hew Kessock was no saint, and perhaps, had he been left wholly to his own devices, he might have had the courage to brave public opinion and make Meg Hamilton lady of Sangster. But, though five-and-twenty, he was still in a measure under petticoat government. His mother, however, was far too diplomatic and clever a women to permit him to know it. A word dropped here and there, a mere suggestion, a lift of the eyebrows, a shrug of the shoulders judiciously timed had awakened in Hew Kessock a secret shame over his preference for Meg.

Lady Kessock was far too wary openly to belittle the girl; she had gone even so far as to " damn her with faint praise." Yet somehow, Hew Kessock felt that if he were to marry her whom they called in jest the Pride of Ballochean—because she was the only thing left for the old house to be proud of—his position in the county would be lowered, and he would be an object of compassion to his compeers.

But dallying with her had been mighty pleasant, and now that she had so drastically ended it, she had, like most of the things beyond our reach, become a lure. He was angry, too, for he had done nothing, he told himself, to draw upon him her sour looks and bitter words.

He had even gone out of his way that day to find her, having heard from a casual source that she was in the town, and, knowing her fondness for the beach, he had ridden in that direction in the hope of encountering her.

" What a spitfire she is ! " he muttered to himself. " I'm well rid of her."

As he rode over the bridge to take the high road to Sangster, he bethought himself of Ellison Dove. He wanted something to soothe his ruffled plumage. What more likely to do so than the cooing of the Dove ?

He pulled out his watch to find that it was now half-past five, and that probably any chance callers at Prospect House would have gone by this time.

With Hew Kessock to desire was, as a general thing, to attain, or at least make the attempt, generally successful, to attain, and so he rode by tortuous windings to the prim gate of Prospect House.

It stood just a few paces back from the pavement, and, in order to ensure as much privacy as is possible in a suburban house, it had a thick belt of shrubbery growing behind the railings. Everything about the little house proclaimed careful management, argus-eyed supervision on the part of its mistress. No soiled blinds drawn awry, no dim panes of glass, no brasses crying aloud for the polishing clout—everything was trig and neat and shining.

But very, very small houses unconsciously reflect the moods and temperament of their ruling spirits. They are demure, prim, aggressive, retiring, forbidding, or inviting, according to the nature of those who dwell within.

An air of ordered quiet, with a subtle suggestion of welcome to the visitor, descended on Kessock as he walked his horse up the wide path between the well-pruned shrubs and rang the bell with a mighty peal.

It at once brought the maid, weary and cross with much door-answering, and at the sight of Kessock she grinned a welcoming grin.

" Mrs. Dove at home ? "

"No, sir, but Miss Ellison is."

"I'll come in," he said, "as soon as I have found somebody to walk my horse. Please leave the door open. I can find my way."

The girl nodded and flew, with bated breath, to inform Miss Ellison, who was upstairs getting out of the blue frock.

By the time Hew Kessock had entered the drawing-room, with which he had become fairly familiar of late, Ellison, a little flushed, but contriving, nevertheless, to look natural and at home, was sitting demurely in the corner of the couch with a morsel of embroidery in her hands.

Of her complexion and her hands Ellison took the greatest care. She would never venture out without the protection of a veil; and to go out ungloved was unthinkable. Also, her mother, past-mistress in the art of make-up, had already initiated her into the use of creams and unguents and milk-washes, and such-like. And, beyond doubt, her skin was sweet and soft, and her clear pallor alluring, though most would have preferred the natural, clear glow of perfect health on Meg Hamilton's face.

"Oh, Sir Hew!" murmured the Dove, as she sat forward, not even attempting to rise, for her pose was just right, and the rose-coloured curtain behind her, drawn at the proper angle, formed a becoming setting for the picture she hoped she was making.

So far as Hew Kessock was concerned it was made, and he admired it mightily.

"How do you do, Miss Dove. I thought I might find my mother here. She said something about an 'At Home' day. Has she been here?"

"Yes—an hour and a half ago, quite. She was among the early callers. We have had such a lot! So many people are in town for the races. Father will be sorry when he hears that his old admiral was here with his wife. Mother was so very pleased! They are staying at Babbington for the races."

Hew Kessock was not interested in the tit-bit of information which the Dove rolled like a sweet morsel under her tongue.

"I see. And where's the mater now—eh?"

"Gone into town to tell father about the admiral. They are leaving Babbington to-morrow, and she wanted to drive out with him that he might see them at once. The admiral made quite a point of it. Father was a great favourite in the Navy, Sir Hew, and, of course, since we came here and everything has been so different, he has felt the change a good deal—we all have."

"I daresay you have," said Kessock, walking about the room, looking at this thing and that, and wondering how women could have the patience to collect so many queer and quite useless objects and crowd them together in such a small space.

"We had Miss Hamilton among our callers," said the Dove presently, and, though her eyes were again fixed on her work, there was a little gleam shot out from a corner that she might see how Kessock took the mention of Meg's name. He showed no outward sign of any particular interest.

"I thought I saw her down by the shore," he remarked casually. "She did not appear to me to be dressed for calling."

Ellison smiled her small, suggestive smile.

"Dear Meg thinks clothes don't matter. She railed a good half-hour at me about my frock. Such a simple little thing, too, costing hardly anything! I hope I am not too fond of dress, but I have been brought up to think that a women should take a little pains with her clothes—that she owes it to the people she lives with."

"Quite right. And you look ripping, Miss Ellison; 'pon my honour you do," drawled Kessock, and at that moment he certainly thought it.

She had made a little study of her pose, and, as she raised her work a little as if to catch a better light, the lace fell back from her elbow-sleeves and revealed the pretty rounded arm, as white as the linen it touched.

"I'm afraid poor Meg is in sad trouble. I'm so sorry for them all at Ballochean," said the Dove's cooing voice. "It must be rather terrible to have a father like Mr. Hamilton. I don't profess to understand what happened yesterday, but it seems to have been something rather terrible—at the races, I mean."

"Oh, at the races! I heard he had dropped something near a thousand. Old fool! He should be shut up, and his son Guy along with him. They're the worst pair of bounders in the county."

"Meg had heaps of things to tell me to-day, Sir Hew—oh, no! not exactly secrets, for soon everybody will know them. Perhaps you may have heard that Mr. Sillars has taken Ludovic in hand—given him something very lucrative to do on his sugar plantation in Jamaica."

"Well, if he is off it must be within the last twenty-four hours, then, Miss Ellison; for I saw Ludovic Hamilton with my own eyes yesterday morning, as I drove with my mother to the races."

"I believe that the offer was made only last night, and that a lot of other wonderful things happened. Anyhow, he has gone off to Greenock with Mr. Sillars this morning."

"What are the other things?" asked Kessock, leaning on his elbow against the chiffonier and eyeing Ellison with a deep interest awakened by her words. He did want to know what was going on at Ballochean, hoping perhaps to hear something that might explain Meg's very unchristian-like behaviour to him within the last hour.

Ellison kept her gaze fixed most demurely on her work, and a little mysterious smile hovered on the red of her lip.

"Well, I don't know that I ought to tell it, though, of course, it can't be a secret long," she said, and then, dropping her work, she crossed her dainty bronze-slippered feet and looked with an air of complete innocence into Kessock's sunburnt face. "I don't suppose," she went on, "that Mr. Sillars or any man would do such a big thing without some very sufficient reason, for, of course, everybody knows that Ludovic Hamilton is no good. My mother says he's degenerate—that they all are at Ballochean, though in different ways."

"Ludovic is certainly a queer chap. What reason could be at the back of Sillars' mind for doing it, do you suppose?" asked Kessock, and she was conscious of his quickened eagerness to hear the answer.

A little archness crept into the Dove's demure smile.

"Oh, Sir Hew! can't you guess? I thought men always knew these things; and it is not for me to say."

"I suppose you are meaning that there is a love-affair between Sillars and Miss Hamilton; but I'm sure that can't be the reason—he's more like a brother in the house."

"Maybe," was all that Ellison said, and her accent was provoking.

"Tell me what you mean by that. I'm interested, Miss Ellison, as I would be interested in any man who took a big jump, not knowing what was on the other side."

"Oh, how queerly and cleverly you put it, Sir Hew!" she said, with a little gasp of appreciation. "It's what I feel myself; only I could never put it so neatly."

"Then you think that Sillars is after Meg?"

"Oh, yes! I think he has always been in love with her. At least Meg has—has boasted a little about it to me now and again, just as she has spoken about other men—much in the same way as a Red Indian counting his scalps might speak, don't you know? I don't think it is quite nice; but then, as mother points out, Meg has never had a chance of learning what is nice."

Kessock chewed his moustache, and his lower lip drooped a little, and his brows were knit. The idea of Meg Hamilton hanging his scalp on her belt, like an Indian, was hurtful to his pride.

"Now I've said what I ought not, Sir Hew, and you are vexed with me! You can't think how sorry I am for poor Meg. I try to befriend her, and she comes here a great deal, though mother would rather I had a friend who would be more like her idea of what a girl ought to be. She says no girl can be too careful."

"And that's true, too," Kessock agreed a trifle heavily. "So you think a love-affair is at the bottom of Sillars' engineering of Ballochean affairs?"

Ellison nodded softly, with her pretty eyes demurely fastened on her work.

"Perhaps it's a dreadful breach of confidence," she went on, in her soft, cooing voice. "But you and Lady Kessock have always been so kind that you seem just like old friends. I heard it from Meg's own lips to-day."

"That—that Sillars had asked her?" said Kessock, with a kind of heavy eagerness, which sent a thrill of apprehension to the Dove's heart, for if he was going to mind so much as all that it would certainly have been better not to tell him.

The manner of the question, however, made it easy for Ellison to answer without telling an absolute lie. Afterwards, when her conduct came under review, she was able to be plaintively emphatic on that point.

"Yes—last night. He must have gone to Ballochean after the races, and then everything would be settled up."

Ellison grew a little cold in the silence that ensued.

Kessock strode over to the window and stood at the straight parting between the immaculate lace curtains, where he appeared to be chewing the cud of a most bitter reflection.

Presently he was brought to himself by the echo of a little sob in the room. He wheeled round, for if there was a thing on earth that Kessock feared and hated it was a women's tears. His mother never shed them and a man naturally shrinks from the thing of which he has no experience.

"Oh, come, Miss Ellison, don't cry! Why, what are you crying about?" he asked with a kind of clumsy tenderness, taking a few—but only a very few—steps towards her, for he was perfectly well aware that he was inside the danger zone.

Ellison was one of the few women whom tears do not disfigure. True, she took care not to shed them to excess. A pearly drop here and there, just trembling on her eyelid, and so poised that it did not roll down her pretty cheek, was rather an offset than otherwise to her particular kind of charm.

To Kessock, indeed, smarting under another woman's high-handed and indignant treatment, there was something at once soothing and alluring about the tear-filled eyes uplifted to his face.

"I'm afraid I have done wrong! I ought not to have told, but I have felt so glad about Meg, you can't think! She has had such a lonely, hard life, and now she will be rich and able to have everything she wants. But if I had known you would mind so much I would have cut my tongue out rather than have told you."

Kessock straightened his back at this and assumed a defiant air.

"Mind—why should I mind?" he said with a little hard laugh. "I was only pondering on the inscrutable ways of women. What you tell me accounts for the way she spoke to me this afternoon," he said, tripping into the admission.

"Oh, have you spoken to her to-day, Sir Hew?" asked Ellison, and a little note of apprehension crept into her voice.

"I met her as I was taking a gallop on the sands. She was very hoity-toity. Of course, that accounts for everything. Well, I wish poor Sillars joy!"

"Oh, but, dear Sir Hew, why do you say that? Don't you admire Meg Hamilton? Sometimes I think she looks so sweet! If only she would take a little more trouble about the things that matter so much in a woman's life! But, as mother so often says, she hasn't had a chance of learning these. But dear Meg is so set on her own way! You wouldn't believe the times we have tried to show her differently. Now, this very afternoon, we had a discussion about clothes. I was pointing out to her that a leather-bound skirt, all splashed with mud, is not drawing-room attire. And what do you think she said?—she said she would like to be a squaw in a blanket! Wasn't that awful?"

Kessock laughed bitterly. The idea of Meg in a blanket with her glorious mane tossing in the wind, was even more alluring at the moment than the ringdove's soft charm!

"She's a caution, but she has a knack of sweeping a fellow off his feet, and poor Sillars—confirmed bachelor and all as he is—will find that a deluge has descended on his life. When is it going to come off?"

Ellison dropped her sewing then in sheer terror.

"Oh, not for ages and ages! Not a soul except me knows yet. I'm sure that Meg hasn't even told her father. Promise, promise, dear Sir Hew, that you won't tell a living soul what I have told you. I should get into dreadful trouble with Meg; and you can't think how nasty she can be when she's angry!"

"Can't I! I've seen it—I saw it to-day," said Kessock savagely. "So, it's a secret? Perhaps it won't come off after all."

"Oh, but it will! You wait and see. Ludovic's trip to Jamaica at Mr. Sillars' expense is the proof of it. Please do forgive me for what I've done, won't you, Sir Hew? and promise not to say a word until I give you leave."

She covered him with her soft, imploring glance, and she looked so pretty at the moment that Kessock felt his power of resistance ebbing.

A sudden inspiration flashed through his brain. Why not ask Ellison Dove to marry him here and now, and thus get even with Meg Hamilton ? How dared she boast of having his scalp at her girdle ? The idea filled him with an unholy rage. And since he might not marry Meg, whom his inmost being craved—why, then, any woman would do, this woman better than most. And it would please his mother, who beheld in Ellison Dove the plastic, easily-managed young woman whose coming to Sangster would never endanger her own position there.

The air was filled with a tense silence, while Kessock, standing hard by the mantelpiece, surveyed the pretty head, so modestly downcast, and noted the clear outline of the soft cheek and the swift plying of the white hands about her womanly work. She was pretty, she was restful, she would fulfil most of the conditions a man asks in his wife, and she would make him a home. Better that than the tempest of Meg Hamilton's moods, her lightning glance, her tongue of fire !

" Oh, I say, Miss Dove, let us get even with them. Marrying seems to be in the air—let us even get ahead of them ! " he spluttered, finding it difficult to utter the fitting words.

When the heart is in thrall to a great passion, then the fount of being is opened and words rush forth like a torrent. But Kessock was only mildly stirred. He admired the ringdove and saw in her a peaceful and fitting mate, but she had no power to quicken his pulses or to give him one hungry heart-beat.

Her pretty colour rose, her nervous hands seemed to flutter, she turned the appealing eyes of a child to his face.

" Oh, Sir Hew, what is it you are saying to poor little me ? " she asked, and out went the little fluttering hands and they were presently held against his breast !

" It's all right, my little dear. Yes—I'm asking you to take pity on me and come to Sangster. I think we should be very happy together, for you are the right kind of woman—the kind with whom a man's happiness and honour would be safe."

" Oh, oh, it is too much happiness ! I never dared to hope—not even lately when you have been so kind. Yes—yes, dear Hew, I will give all my life and all my effort towards making you happy. To-day you have made me the happiest girl in the whole wide world."

That was perfectly true ; and Kessock felt a little glow of virtuous self-satisfaction as he clasped the yielding figure close and took his first lover's kiss.

As he did so he recalled how he had stolen a kiss from Meg Hamilton in one provocative moment, and how her eyes had flashed fire at him and her voice had vibrated as she bade him stand off. But the savour of that stolen sweet remained, and was destined to remain, coming between him and the imagined bliss through all the years that were before him.

He was a poor thing, afraid to take the plunge, to brave public opinion, and to assert his will in despite of his mother, and so the prize had slipped from his possible grasp.

Presently they were side by side on the couch, and the needlework was on the floor under Kessock's heel, and the ringdove was cooing on his breast.

And with such poor semblance of the real thing he had perforce to be content.

" Keep our secret, little woman, until I give you leave to speak. I must tell my mother first," he said when he rose to go.

" But you will not keep me waiting too long, dearest Hew, for I shall never be able to carry this burden of happiness all by my little self," she said archly, looking up into his handsome face.

" Oh, not long—just a few hours. I will most certainly tell my mother to-night. I am sure she will be pleased for she likes you, Ellison, and is always praising you up to me. It is outsiders that I mean you not to tell—Miss Hamilton, for instance. She may expect you to return the confidence she was so ready to bestow on you. We do want to have a little time to ourselves, don't we ? Good-bye, sweetheart. I must positively go. Heaven knows where ' Spitfire ' may have got to by now. The poor wretch who is holding her by the head may have been dragged to the Maidens by this time."

" Good-bye."

He got away, and from the open door Ellison waved her farewell as he rode off, not certain whether he was glad or sorry for himself, but assured that he had got even with Meg Hamilton. A heart caught in the rebound is not always to be depended on, and there was more regret than joy in his heart as he rode rather savagely across the bleak hills to Sangster.

But there was no regret in the ringdove's heart. Had she not attained the desire of her heart? And was not the pledge of it a plain gold ring with the Kessock badge on it, which Hew had taken from his own finger and slipped on hers?

She could hardly wait for her mother's return from Babbington. It was close on seven before she heard the sound of her father's key turning in the door, and even then she did not go down.

"Ellie, are you there—Ellie?" called out her mother's sharp, shrill voice.

"Yes, mother! Oh, please come up quickly."

Ellison's eager face on the landing had such a light on it that the mother paused half-way upstairs with a quick inquiry on her lips.

"Why, whatever has happened, child?"

"Come up, and I'll tell you," said Ellison excitedly, and the moment her mother had reached the landing she held up her left hand, on which hung loosely Hew Kessock's ring.

"Why, what's this? What does it mean?" asked her mother eagerly.

"It means, mother darling, that I'm to be Lady Kessock! Yes—he has been here, and—and it's all right. Lady Kessock, mother—and Sangster! Oh, isn't it wonderful?"

"Thank God!" said the Surgeon-General's wife; and, sinking on the nearest chair, she wept some real tears of genuine gratitude and joy.

None need blame her. She had had a long fight with poverty, in which she had borne herself with indomitable courage, in which she had displayed wonderful resource, bringing with her a certain dignity to uplift a small and narrow existence and making plaint to none. Her reward was higher than she had dared to hope for, but for the moment it made her a better woman.

She caught her child to her heart and blessed her fervently. But the embrace left the ringdove perfectly cold. She had very little heart, and only her pride and her ambition as yet were fired.

Before she slept that night, despite the embargo laid upon her by her lover, she wrote these words to Meg Hamilton, and she stole out herself at midnight to post them at the nearest pillar-box:—

"Dear old Girl,

"I can't sleep till I've told you. Hew has asked me to marry him, and soon I shall be signing myself, your ever devoted friend, Ellison Kessock.

"P.S.—It can never make the smallest difference to us, dear old girl. It never, never will. I'm most awfully happy. Please don't tell a living soul till I give you leave."

CHAPTER VII

BIRDS OF EVIL OMEN

As she sped half blindly by tortuous byways towards Ballochean, Meg Hamilton wondered what ailed herself and the world.

Up till now, though full of unnecessary care at times, life had never been a thing which irked her nor with which to quarrel. The *joie de vivre* had beat high and strong in her young pulses. Shortage of money there might be, but that did not stop the carol of the lark in the lift, the hum of the bee, or the sigh of the wind in the trees. Perhaps her home lacked qualities that other homes possessed, but there at least she was free to come and go as she liked, none making her afraid. Her father might storm and rage, but anon his face would clear, the twinkle would leap in his eye again, while he would try with clumsy kindness to make amends to his girl child for the churl in him that he had permitted her to see.

A good horse, a faithful dog, a friend or two—none of these had Meg Hamilton lacked, and so, according to her own thinking, she had fared not so ill in the inn that men call life. Ignorance of the largesse which life can hold for the specially-favoured, or even of the privileges to which her sex and beauty entitled her, had spared her much disquiet of spirit.

The only thing she had actually missed was a sordid thing, but she realised far back in her young girlhood that money can smooth the path of life and take the edge from care.

All at once, however, the face of things had changed, and in her inmost spirit she was conscious of treachery, disloyalty, cruelty of a refined and intolerable kind. Hew Kessock had sought her love for no end apparently save to amuse himself, and, having won it, he had smiled and ridden away!

She had heard and read of such things. That anything of the kind should happen to herself was unthinkable. The red burned in her cheek as she tried unflinchingly to recall, nay, more, to tabulate, any moments, in which by word or look or gesture, by a sudden flame in her cheek, by a glint of her eye, or by a faltering smile, she had betrayed her heart's secret to the man who had no use for it.

In these torturing moments it was natural that she should exaggerate and magnify every such trifle, being wholly unaware that even yet Kessock had not the remotest idea whether he had genuinely touched her heart.

And so she came, a young fighting creature at war with all things, even with the fair world about her, to the autumn splendour of the woods of Ballochean. She had no idea of the flight of time. It seemed days, even ages, since she had set out blithely to the old town on her quest for sympathy and comradeship.

As she came within sight of the house the bell from the stable tower rang six, which startled her not a little. She had been four hours away. But what were four hours, or four days, or millions of years, to one who was feeling as she did? Life had become hideous, humiliating, altogether impossible. The thought of days and days to come, each one of which would bear the burden of such humiliation, appalled her.

Poor Meg of the undisciplined heart took hold of all things mightily—even of suffering, which youth naturally resents and seeks to combat with both hands.

She knew now the meaning of the weight that had oppressed her all the previous day, of the envy that had surged in her heart when she heard of Ludo's escape from Ballochean, and of the sudden snapping of the slender tie which bound him to the house that had never been a home.

Swift upon that reflection came another—that David Sillars had made her the offer of a way out, and that, after the thoughtless, high-handed way of youth, she had flouted it. Doubtless that offer was open still. But it held no attractive invitation for her. The well-ordered life at Kildoon, the quiet, studious habits of Sillars, his grave outlook on everything, did not commend themselves to Meg Hamilton. She wanted ardently to live. To one like her Kildoon would be a cloister or a grave!

Jean, the tablemaid, sunning herself at the open door—a valued licence not permitted in houses where the reins are stiffly drawn—did not run away at sight of her young mistress, but, on the contrary, seemed to beckon mysteriously.

As Miss Meg approached, the girl suddenly thought that she looked very worn, and that she must have overtired herself.

" Are ye tired, Miss Meg ? " she asked kindly. " Ye look it. Would ye like a cup of tea ? "

" Tea ? Oh, no, thank you. Were you looking for me ? " she asked, somewhat anxiously.

" I was—and I wasn't, Miss Meg. I was hoping it would not be long till ye came. Two gentlemen have arrived from Glasgow to dine and sleep, and cook was asking what's for dinner ? "

" What a question to ask at six o'clock at night ! She must furbish up something," answered Meg indignantly. " But who are the gentlemen ? "

Jean shrugged her shoulders.

" I don't ken, Miss Meg. Between you and me, though, they are a queer-looking set—perfect Jews, I'm thinkin'. But the Laird wishes them to be made comfortable. He's ordered the Red Room and the big spare room to be got ready—with fires in them, too ! Tweeny is rinnin' off her legs."

Instantly Meg swept into the background of her mind the distress that had threatened to overwhelm her, and became for the moment a person of affairs.

" Where are they now, Jean—the gentlemen, I mean ? "

" In the library wi' the Laird and Maister Guy. He sent oot, no' five minutes syne, to ken whether ye had come hame. That was why I came out to look."

Meg passed into the house.

" Did my father say at what time he wanted dinner ? "

" No, Miss Meg."

" Well, I'll see cook. It must be half an hour or even an hour late if necessary. In the library the gentlemen are, did you say ? "

" Yes, Miss Meg. They arrived in a dogcart from the Station Hotel about three o'clock, and since then they have been driving round the place. The Laird went wi' them, but no' Mr. Guy."

A strange thrill clutched at the girl's heart.

Men who looked like Jews—arriving unexpectedly—driving round the place ! It had an ominous sound.

Meg stepped into the cloak-room, where she was accustomed to hang her outdoor things, put them on their usual pegs, took a glance in the mirror, and, observing the unusual greyness of her face, pinched it to bring back the colour.

Then she passed through the swing-door, preceding Jean, and so to the kitchen region, there to learn the actual state of affairs. Her colloquy with cook was sharp and decisive. On occasion Meg could exhibit housewifery qualities which would not have shamed an older devotee of the game. She met every objection of the irate Mrs. Greig either with flat contradiction or with prompt suggestion.

" I want less talk, Greig, and more action," she said presently, and those who heard were amazed at the clear incisiveness with which their young mistress spoke. " I've seen what there is in the larder. I've told you what to do—please do it. Dinner as near to half-past seven as you possibly can, but certainly not a moment later than a quarter to eight. And no more grumbling, if you please."

Old Greig, trained under a chef, and given to boasting, though in no house but Ballochean would her indolence and her indifference have been tolerated, was thus put on her mettle, and had no choice but to obey.

" It's clean ridiculous," she said sullenly, " to think a six-course dinner can be made ooten naething at an oor's notice."

Meg, overhearing the muttered words at the kitchen door, returned, her head high in the air.

" Didn't I say ' no more grumbling,' Greig ? If you can't do what is required of you, and do it pleasantly, you may go to-morrow morning."

This cowed Mrs. Greig, who was in no mind to leave Ballochean, knowing full well that she would find it difficult to get another suitable berth, and that she would certainly never find an easier one.

Once more on the right side of the green baize door Meg made pause and seemed to listen.

At the far end of the corridor was the library door, behind which some strange conference was being conducted—perhaps things of portent being said and done! But because she was a woman she must not intervene or seek to enter! It was her portion to wait until her menfolk should acquaint her with just as much—or as little—as seemed good in their sight.

Yet at the moment she felt more capable than either of them to deal with the problems of Ballochean, and a mighty yearning took possession of her to put that power into immediate action.

Work is ever the sheer cure for heartache. A big disaster never came yet but it brought balm to some hearts, even while it hurled others to the dust.

But when, after the lapse of five minutes, no sound came from the long corridor, she turned aside and began to ascend the stairs. Then she stepped back again and looked into the dining-room, where already Jean was laying a clean cloth. She glanced quickly at the flowers which stood on the sideboard, a handful of ruddy outdoor things such as come up year by year in the herbaceous border, and need neither care nor money to be expended on them. They were fresh enough.

"I'll just pop round to the shrubbery and gather a handful of berries and some of the yellow and brown leaves, Jean, and you must do the best you can with them."

Jean, who would have been more interested had the company been better, offered to attend to the table decoration, repeating her conviction that Miss Meg was tired.

"I'm not tired at all. But, if you think you can get them, do so. I'll go upstairs."

Once in her own room she was in no haste to survey her meagre wardrobe. The woman of few frocks is at least spared the quandary in which the woman of many frocks sometimes affects to find herself.

The old white cashmere and a faded blue soft silk, made in what is called the demi-toilette style, comprised Meg's wear for state occasions.

She supposed, as there were stranger guests present, she would need to wear the white.

She walked to the windows, of which there were three in the wide, long room that had been the old schoolroom. Meg had wheeled her iron bedstead into this room, where, in that great space, it looked for all the world like a camp-bed on a fighting plain!

Standing there, looking out upon one of the most enchanting prospects ever spread for the delectation of human eyes, she asked herself passionately why human beings were born. Like struggling little ants on an ant-heap, living out their little day and coming to an end, the futility of it all smote her strangely. Even the glint of the sea in the near distance, and the light shed by the red sunset, and looking like a path of flame stretching to the far hills of Arran, failed to fill her with the accustomed joy.

She began to disrobe slowly, and, in her old loose dressing-sacque, she was brushing out her glorious hair, when a tap came to the door.

"May I come in, Meg?" asked her father's voice, and she immediately answered, "Yes."

She thought that he entered furtively, and that there was an odd eagerness and apprehension in his looks.

"Where have you been all the afternoon?" he inquired.

"Down in the town. It was Mrs. Dove's 'At Home' day, and after staying there a little while I dropped in at the Sandersons', and that's all."

"It was a pity you stopped out so long. Is there a decent dinner in the house to-night?"

"I've done what I could with old Greig, but she's on the warpath. Who are the men that are here, father?"

"Mr. Leyden and Mr. Morris Bien, from Glasgow," he answered enigmatically.

"Strange-sounding names, dad!" was her comment. "Why have they come here?"

"On business pure and simple, my dear—something to do with my affairs. It is important that they should be made comfortable. I am sure you will do your best."

Meg looked doubtful and just a trifle suspicious. Her mood made her so. Like the thief who "fears each bush an officer," she imagined double-dealing and trouble everywhere, even in the simplest happenings.

"All right, father," she said, turning to her hair-dressing once more. "I'll be down in good time. The servants are attending to the guest-rooms. You ordered fires in them, I think, though it isn't at all cold."

"Mr. Leyden is not strong. Morris Bien is his nephew. They are quite nice gentlemen, otherwise I shouldn't ask you to come down. Guy is smoking with them now."

Meg made no reply, and, after hesitating for a moment, almost as if he had something else to say, but feared to say it, her father left the room.

About half an hour later Meg descended to the library. The drawing-room at Ballochean was so little used now that it was seldom taken into account as an apartment for social purposes. Few ladies came to Ballochean, and such a thing as an afternoon tea-party had never taken place in the house since its mistress died. The library was for all purposes the family living room, but Meg had a den of her own, on the topmost floor in the square tower, which, she said, overlooked the world!

She had not been much there of late, however; even the high-perched den had lost its charm.

When she entered the room, a slim figure in her white gown, she found a stranger occupying the Laird's chair. It was drawn quite near to the fire, across which a tremendous log had been laid. It was blazing royally, though the September night was quite mild.

She stepped lightly, and came within range of the stranger's vision only when she reached the edge of the big, old, threadbare Persian rug, which lay before the immense stone fireplace.

She then saw that the stranger was quite an old man, very stout, with a bald head and a snow-white moustache, which showed vividly against the sallow hue of his face.

He struggled from his chair, making an obvious effort to be polite and smiling in a quite friendly fashion.

"Ach," he said, with a strong gutteral accent, "is this Miss Hamilton—yees?"

"I am Miss Hamilton," answered Meg, but she did not offer him her hand, and, after a slight gesture, the old man withdrew his rather quickly, and with the air of a man who did not like to be slighted.

"I am Leyden—August Van Leyden, at your service, mademoiselle," he said, as if in doubt what was the best appellation to bestow on the radiant vision before him.

Never had Meg looked lovelier, more regal, or more unapproachable. A new dignity had come to her along with the dim realisation of the suffering that life can hold, and she bore herself no longer with girlish carelessness and glee, but with a certain hauteur, which certainly became her well.

"I am sorry my father is not here to introduce us, Mr. Leyden—or Mr. Van Leyden, is it?" she asked, showing her white, even teeth in a smile that enhanced her beauty It was a white loveliness which almost overwhelmed the old man, the milk and roses of her cheeks being things to marvel at.

"Since I came to Scotland, mademoiselle, I drop the Van, because the Scotch are a very simple people. Hein! they do not like to be confused. They call a spade a spade; therefore, I am plain Leyden, though in my own country the 'Van' stands for something, believe me."

"What is your country, Mr. Leyden?" asked Meg, interested in spite of herself.

"Mademoiselle, my country is Holland. I was born in Amsterdam. But originally the Leydens belonged to Frankfurt-am-Maine. Vill you be seated, if you please?"

"Oh! no, thank you, I prefer to stand. But do you sit down, Mr. Leyden. I am sure you are tired."

"I haf not been at all vell, mademoiselle. Ach, this Glasgow! It haf so mooch rain that von never sees the sun. And it is the sun that can heal, is it not, mademoiselle?"

"It certainly helps," assented Meg, wondering why she was at one and the same time repelled and attracted by this strange man, so unprepossessing to look at, and yet endowed with such a suggestion of power and personality.

But why, oh! why had he come to Ballochean? He was a bird of a feather that surely could have no place there! The visit was one of portent. She longed to sift the meaning and the purpose of it to the bottom.

"We get a good deal of sun here, and we are so near the sea that we have no fogs.

Don't you think it a pretty country ? " she said, feeling the need to make conversation, and wondering how long she would have to entertain him before anyone came to her aid.

" Ach, mademoiselle, it is lofely. I haf nefer seen any place I like so vell in the whole of Schottland. I vonder not that you lofe such a home as this."

Meg made no answer, but a sudden terror gathered in her eyes.

What if this old Dutch-German person had come to rob them of Ballochean ? What if her father was hopelessly in his clutches ? She had heard and read of money-lenders—she had even guessed that her father had had certain dealings with them. But a money-lender at the end of a comfortable postal journey is very different from a money-lender in the house.

" You have come to look at it, perhaps ? Have you known my father long ? " she asked desperately.

" For some time, mademoiselle. Yees—ve haf come to look at the place—at least, my nephew has. Ve no more like Glasgow to lif in. It is not possible for me to haf another vinter there. Hein ! It was too terrible the last von."

At the moment the sound of approaching voices interrupted the conversation, and the door opened to admit the other three men.

Ballochean himself was in his old brown velvet jacket, but Guy, out of courtesy to the guests, who had brought no evening clothes, wore a suit of blue serge, in which he looked very well.

At sight of his daughter Gavin Hamilton started forward a trifle nervously.

" Ah ! there you are, Meg. Have you and Mr. Leyden already made acquaintance ? This is Mr. Morris Bien, Meg—my daughter, Mr. Bien."

Once more Meg slightly inclined her head, at the same time taking anxious survey of the nephew, as she had already done of the uncle.

There was not a single point of resemblance between them, as she was quick to note. Morris Bien was tall and slender, handsome according to a very dark Jewish type, with thick black hair, a small moustache on his rather clearly-cut upper lip, and deep dark eyes. The face was a refined and a clever one.

The glance which he bestowed on Meg Hamilton's face at the moment of introduction was one of frank and even fervent admiration. Her fair beauty dazzled him, and Meg was conscious for the first time of the effect she was creating. But, instead of being pleased or flattered, she was assailed with such a sense of loneliness and helplessness that, had she obeyed her inward impulse, she would have fled from the place.

A solitary woman-creature among all these men, whose business with one another she could not pretend even to guess, of which, however, she was certain that it could not make for happiness and peace, she felt unutterably forlorn.

But so gallant was the creature, so fine and brave of fibre, that she suffered no hint of her shrinking to appear.

She laughed and smiled to Mr. Morris Bien during the few brief moments which elapsed before Jean, looking rather sullen and downcast, as if fresh from a wordy campaign in the regions beyond in which she had had the worst of it, came to announce that dinner was served.

Ballochean hesitated for a moment, as if he were about to ask one of the strangers to take Meg in to dinner, but she solved the problem by walking straight out of the room alone.

In the dining-room Meg noted once again the old Dutchman's quick, curious glance of appraisal, and her heart sank so that she was unable to respond to Mr. Morris Bien's very evident and very sincere efforts to entertain her.

There was a sauve courtesy in the young man's manner, and an impressiveness in his looks, that might have flattered a less discerning woman, and that contrasted strongly with his uncle's brusqueness, but Meg liked the younger man less.

She was disturbed, too, by her father's attitude and manner. He was eager, deferential, and even a trifle servile to these outsiders. As for Guy, his face wore an expression of unrelieved gloom, and he scarcely spoke a word. During the first part of the dinner Meg preserved a silence so complete that it could not but be marked ; then, in response to her father's somewhat imploring glance, she turned to Mr. Leyden and began to ask him some questions about Amsterdam, wholly ignoring his nephew.

On the whole, it was a ghastly, dreary meal, and the moment she could decently do so she left the men to their cigars.

That strange day, which to poor Meg seemed to be drawn out to the verge of eternity, passed at last, and about half-past nine she went to her own room to try to think things over.

But always the presence of these two strange men in the house would come between her and the thought of everything else. So superconscious was she of the intruders that once she even found herself on the landing, listening for some sound from below. Up the gallery stair there floated the sound of a deep, hearty laugh—a loud guffaw which seemed to indicate that they were enjoying themselves.

She unbound her hair, put it into two long plaits, preparatory to going to bed, threw on her old dressing-gown, and sat down to try to read. Never had sleep been further from her eyes. Every faculty was alert, and the tension on mind and heart was very great.

Soon after ten she heard some one coming heavily up the stairs.

As only Guy slept in that part of the house, she opened the door, and, holding her candle high, peered out.

"That you, Guy?" she asked very quietly, as if fearing that she might be overheard.

"Yes. I want to speak to you. May I come in?" he answered in an equally hushed voice.

"Yes. Come now. Have they all gone to bed?"

"The old man has—old Leyden, I mean," said Guy, and, shutting the door, he sat down on the edge of a chair and looked round him as though quite bewildered.

"I say, Meg," he said rather helplessly, "I believe it's all U.P. with us."

"What do you mean?" she tremblingly inquired.

"Can't you see? These beastly bounders are money-lenders, and they've got the governor in their clutches. What I want to know is: What are you going to do about it?"

"Do? What can I do, Guy? That's the misery of the whole business of being a woman—one can't do anything!"

"Oh! Tommy-rot," he said impatiently. "There are heaps of things a woman can do. The governor's afraid of you in his secret soul. You're the only one that stands up to him."

"Tell me how things are—that is, if you know. Tell me exactly what has happened? If I'm to do anything—though I don't know in the least what I can do—I must know everything."

Never had she seen Guy look so crushed and miserable. A mingling of pity and contempt was in her soul as she surveyed him. Oh, to be a man and to feel as she did at the moment! How in that case she would assert the prerogative of manhood, make of it some worthy and noble thing that would command the admiration of the world!

"They hold the whole of the mortgage on Ballochean now," said Guy, "and they've come down either to foreclose or to make some fresh arrangement. The old man applied to them for the racing money that he dropped yesterday, and that has to be paid to-morrow. If they clear him it's going to be at a tremendous cost—probably at the cost of the place itself!"

"Do you mean that they'll take it away from us?" she asked in a hollow whisper.

"Yes, unless you can do something to prevent it," he suggested.

"But can't you do anything, Guy? You're a man. That is what you are made for—to do things, and to solve problems like this. You have never done one useful thing in the whole of your life," she said in tones of reproach.

Her candour was brutal, but this was no moment for the ornamental courtesies of life.

Guy took her outburst well. The prospect really appalled him, for without Ballochean where would he be, or what would his future be like?

He had hoped a good deal from Ludo's going. He had expected that it would clear his feet, and he had in imagination even beheld himself Laird of Ballochean with a free course before him, and a chance of living a better life!

"I can do nothing," he said sullenly. "The governor will not even let me put in an oar! He as good as told me to shut up before the bally bounders! I couldn't stand that, so I came off. It's up to you to do something Meg, and you've simply got to do it ! " he said with a rather weak pretence to firmness and decision.

" Go away, Guy ! " said Meg, and the voice sounded quite unlike her own. " I can't talk any more about it to-night. Go away, if you please."

He went out and closed the door.

Meg had a sleepless night, and next morning, when she went down to the breakfast room, she found the note which Ellison Dove had posted at midnight lying upon her plate.

CHAPTER VIII

THE BLANK WALL

In the early days when the father of David Sillars had first gone into business he had occupied a modest dwelling in the immediate vicinity of the works, which had been a very small affair, covering a narrow space and employing only a few hands. But the close application of Robert Sillars, the founder, to business, to which he gave unwearied personal attention in every detail, had been rewarded by its steady and rapid increase.

The Langdyke Refinery was now one of the biggest commercial concerns in Greenock. It extended over two acres of ground, had splendid offices, and was equipped with every known modern improvement, together with all the latest inventions in machinery and plant.

David Sillars, the present head, was wed to the business, in that he loved every stick and stone about Langdyke and devoted all his energies and most of his time to its nurture and extension.

Very often the rich man despises or is ashamed of the humble ladder by which he has risen to eminence. There was nothing, however, of that false shame and scornful feeling in David Sillars. Had he been asked to preach a new gospel, he would merely have chosen an old text and declaimed in praise of work.

He took such pride in that splendidly equipped and managed affair that perhaps he had scarcely realised to what an extent he was developing his life and nature on only one side. He had a great gift for humanity in this sense, that he was skilled in the management of men, and had the knack of binding them to him by an odd sort of personal tie, which it took much to break. Discontent and labour unrest were unknown at Langdyke, partly because of this strong personal tie, and partly because of the quixotic ideas which Sillars held regarding profit-sharing.

Langdyke was really a vast co-operative concern.

Spending so much of his time at Greenock, Sillars might have been expected to have had some sort of a home there befitting his position, while he kept Kildoon for his recreation and pleasure.

He had often been twitted about this, and had been offered eligible sites as well as houses in the Esplanade and Lyle Road districts, but he had pursued his own way quietly, shaking his head and simply remarking that he was very comfortable as he was.

To the small two-storey, ugly-fronted house just within the gates of the works, in which his father and mother had started their married life, though his mother had been a daughter of Kildoon—Sillars clung with an odd affection. The rooms were small, but memory hallowed them, and in small rooms a man may get together countless treasures. There Sillars had a few from which no gold would have tempted him to part. An Ayrshire woman, an old servant in his mother's family, assisted by her neice who had likewise been cradled on the banks of the Doon, kept house for him at Langdyke.

He could not have had a more convenient residence elsewhere, and, though the outlook from the small house might have been more beautiful, the comfort of that bachelor establishment was beyond compare.

Ludovic Hamilton spent two days very happily there, occupying the time in getting a brief insight into the work of the great industry with which he hoped now to be identified. Sillars was extraordinarily kind to the lad, and, in these hours of close intimacy, got to know him better and to like him more.

The pity of it was that a young man of three-and-twenty should still be a loose end in the web of life ; and this feeling grew upon Sillars and made him sincerely glad that he had had the chance of helping him to a more useful and independent mode of life.

Sillars had many interests in commerce and many shares in certain shipping companies, and he decided to send Ludo out to Jamaica by a circuitous route, partly for the lad's own sake and partly in order that the letter to Hislop, his manager, which was to go by the mail-boat, might arrive there ahead of him.

The saving of time was at present no object to Ludo, and he left himself very gladly in the hands of Sillars.

On the third morning of Ludo's visit, as the two of them sat together at breakfast, Sillars received among his letters a brief note from Meg Hamilton which filled him with amazement and some disquiet.

"DEAR DAVID," it ran, "please come. There is nobody in the wide world who needs you more than

"MEG HAMILTON."

He glanced at Ludo, who was intent on his breakfast, and who, besides, was never either very observant or very suspicious, and, seeing that he seemed quite uninterested in his correspondence, Sillars decided to say nothing about it to him. Ludo was to sail at noon from the Tail of the Bank; and what would be gained by telling him that apparently his sister was in the throes of some fresh trouble? He simply thrust the letter into his pocket and began talking about something else.

"Make a good breakfast, Ludo, for you don't know whether you'll enjoy your next meal," he said encouragingly.

"Oh, shan't I?" said Ludo with a smile. "I'm going to enjoy them all, I hope."

"After you've found your sea-legs, I don't doubt that you will," answered Sillars kindly. "Had any letter from home this morning?"

"None," answered Ludo lightly. "They would only hear this morning that I'm sailing to-day. Probably they'll wire. If not, it doesn't matter."

Ludo was sending no regretful thoughts homeward, at any rate.

He exhibited a quite genuine emotion, however, when the moment came for him to part from his friend and benefactor. It was on the deck of the fine liner that was to take him by a circuitous route to the West Indies that the parting took place; and, when the lad saw all the arrangements that had been made for his comfort aboard, and realised the care and genuine foresight that had been called into action on his behalf, he was rather overwhelmed.

"Say, old chap, I don't know what to say! I can't say anything, but I'll work. By Heavens, how I'll work! You won't have any reason to be ashamed or sorry that you've done this."

"That's all right, my boy. Stick to that, and you'll come out on top," said Sillars kindly, and with that odd shyness with which men of his stamp receive personal tributes.

They shook hands warmly, and Sillars hastened away. Somehow the parting brought back to his memory other partings, when his mother used to journey to Greenock to see the last of him on the occasions of his making his Jamaica trips.

He went back to the works, had a little talk with the manager, and said he thought he would go back to Ayr that afternoon.

"As this is Thursday, probably I won't be back here till Monday again," he added. "If anything turns up you can wire."

Sillars had not established a telephone between Langdyke and Kildoon, because when he was at home he wanted complete privacy.

He reached Ayr between five and six o'clock in the evening and found the dogcart waiting for him outside the station. After taking brief counsel with himself, he decided to drive first to Ballochean, and, if he found that it was necessary for him to make a prolonged visit, to dismiss the cart and walk home by way of the Howff Wood.

He handled the reins himself, and he enjoyed the fresh, keen air as he rapidly covered the distance between the station and Ballochean.

As it happened, he had to drive up the road in which Prospect House stood, and there, before the door, he beheld a very smart ralli-car in charge of a groom, whom he recognised as one in service at Sangster.

Knowing very well that Lady Kessock never drove in an open trap, he naturally wondered who it was that was paying a call there. But the incident passed from his mind until a little later when his attention was called to Hew Kessock.

Six o'clock was ringing from the stable tower when he reached Ballochean; and Meg, who had left nothing to chance and had calculated to a nicety the probable hour of his arrival, was on the outlook for him. She had, in fact, gone half way down the avenue to meet him. Observe that it never occurred to her that Sillars would refuse to come or that he would allow anything to prevent him from coming!

He drew up sharply, and sprang from his seat, throwing the reins to the groom, and drawing off his gloves that he might shake hands.

"Thanks awfully for coming! I thought I should just catch you about here," said Meg quite naturally and pleasantly. "Send the groom away, David. You can walk home."

"All right, madam," he said with a little amused smile.

Sometimes when Meg was more than usually commanding he would so dub her, with a laugh at her majorful ways.

Though Meg had not forgotten that Sillars had so recently proposed and been rejected, she had not hesitated to summon him. She had no idea of the depth of his love for her, and so, after the selfish, inconsequent way of youth, she treated it all too lightly.

That Sillars placed himself still at her beck and call showed the fine, unselfish fibre of the man. But presently she was to find herself up against that other side of him which was revealed to very few.

She linked her hand in his arm and drew him on towards the green spaces of the park, and the young groom, much amused and edified, smiled as he drove swiftly away through the trees, wondering whether anything was likely to come of it.

"Well, Ludo's off, Madge," said Sillars, watching how the wind ruffled the gold of her hair.

She had no hat on—only a scarf thrown about her neck, and her right hand was thrust deep in the pocket of her knitted coat.

"Is he off?" she asked in a thrilled voice. "Why, surely his going was very sudden at the last!"

"Ludo might have been suffering from a lingering illness which had just cut him off, to hear you speak," said Sillars with a laugh.

"Well, perhaps he was. But why did you hustle him away so quickly? I quite thought he was going to stop in Greenock for a while to learn things, and that we might even have a chance of saying good-bye to him later on."

"There happened to be a boat sailing to-day, in which I thought he would be particularly comfortable and see a goodish bit of the world. The captain is an old pal of mine, and will look after him."

"I see. And was he cheerful when he went away?" she enquired with interest.

"He was pleased to go. There is more in Ludo than meets the eye, Madge. You'll hear of him yet at Ballochean and be proud of him."

"I'm sure I hope so. We're needing something there badly to lift us up. Oh David, I'm so miserable!"

"Are you, my dear?"

Her tone was so dismal, her face so woebegone that his tone insensibly became dangerously soft.

"I'm more than miserable—I'm mad, David," she said presently, pushing back a refractory lock that would stray into her eyes. "I want to kill somebody! Read that."

From the bosom of her frock she drew the mean, horrid little pæan of triumph in which Ellison Dove had announced to her bosom friend her engagement to Kessock.

"Um," said Sillars, looking the surprise he felt. "Surely nobody expected this."

"Nobody but Ellison. She's a cat, David—a horrid, mean little cat! All the time she was pretending to be my pal this was going on behind my back! This explains everything—but I don't care! I hate and loathe them both, and I want to get even with them."

Sillars folded up the note and returned it to Meg, who tore it into a hundred fragments and scattered them upon the breeze.

"Oh, no; you won't do anything of the sort, Madge. Dignity is your cue," he said, and he could have laughed aloud at the sublime comedy of it!

Here was he, the rejected lover, chosen as the confidante; and there was Meg who apparently saw nothing incongruous in the situation!

"A display of dignity would be lost on them," said she shortly. "They've got to have an object-lesson, and I'm going to give it to them presently. Tell me, David, are all women like Ellison Dove?"

"My dear, I've little acquaintance with women. I'm an elderly bachelor," he answered, with as much gravity as the circumstances would permit.

"Oh, but you surely know something about them! You meet heaps of them at dinners and things. Am I like that, David?"

"You best know that," he answered, smiling in spite of his efforts to maintain his gravity.

"I don't think I am. I should hate to go behind people's backs and give them a dig—but then, one never knows! I feel so wicked at the present moment that I could kill somebody. So you see, I might really be capable of anything."

"You might—but then, again, there's just the off-chance that you might not."

"Now you're laughing at me, David; and if there's anything I can't stand it's that," she protested indignantly.

"You are the only one to be allowed to laugh at people—eh? You reserve that privilege for yourself?" he suggested.

"I don't laugh at people when they really are wretched," she said huffily, and she walked about a hundred yards in silence, whereupon they immediately found themselves in the shadow of the Howff Wood.

The foresters had been cutting trees there all day, and, though by this time they had left, there still lingered the pleasant, pungent smell of freshly-cut wood, and there were some felled trunks here and there to suggest their recent occupation.

As Meg and Sillars passed through the wicket she suddenly changed the subject.

"Say, David, you know a lot of people in Glasgow, don't you?"

"A goodish few," he answered cautiously.

"Ever heard of anybody called Auguste Van Leyden?" she asked with an affectation of indifference.

Sillars appeared to reflect.

"Or Morris Bien?" she pursued.

He shook his head.

"I don't know them—but I don't like the sound of their heathen names, Madge."

"You'd like them a lot less if you saw them," she said shortly. "They have been here staying all night, David. The old man's in their clutches."

"Money-lenders?" enquired Sillars with a start. "Their names sound uncommonly like it."

"Money-lenders, of course! And it's my belief, David, that they're going to have Ballochean."

"Oh, no, my dear! Mr. Hamilton would never get so far as that," he remonstrated.

"He wouldn't, if he could help it, but he can't!"

"Tell me what has happened," he asked, rather glad on the whole to be relieved from discussion of the Kessock-Dove engagement, though he had by no means recovered from the mild shock it had caused him.

"Let's sit down here," she said, edging towards a newly-felled trunk, about whose stem the sweet-smelling sawdust lay. "I'm most awfully tired, somehow. I rode on Jerry to the Maidens to-day—and Heaven knows where else, and he isn't exactly an easy chair. Fact is, David, vulgarly speaking, I'm all to pot."

"Don't talk like that, dear," said Sillars gently and gravely, for somehow the slangy expression hurt him quite as much as the very evident fact that the girl was acutely miserable.

"Oh, don't lecture! Common language doesn't fit my case to-day, David, and if I can't let out to somebody I'm done!"

"You were going to tell me about the gentlemen with the Hebraic names," he suggested patiently.

"I'm coming to them. You must learn patience, David. Well, when I got home from Ayr last night"—she said with an odd little gasp, "Heavens! was it only last night? I think it must have been last century!—they were there hob-nobbing with the old man in the library, and there was Guy in the background, looking like a little dog that had got his tail trodden on. I didn't see them just at first, but Jean told me that they were to stay overnight and that fires had been ordered for them in the bedrooms, and that father was fussing about what there was to eat. So I had to go down and skirmish with old Grieg. Then, when I was getting into my clothes upstairs, up comes father to interview me and to tell me that everything must be absolutely up to the mark. No—he didn't tell me why, and I didn't ask. I got ready as quickly as I could and went down to the library, where I found the old one—Mr. Van Leyden—all by his little self. We had quite a pow-wow, and I rather liked him on the whole. He was quite gentle and nice; and I am sure he would be interesting, if one knew what subject to get him on to. We had started on Amsterdam when the rest of them came in—father, I mean, and Mr. Morris Bien, and Guy. Mr. Morris Bien, it appears, is the nephew of the other. He was the absolute limit!—Mr. Bien, I mean."

"In what way?" asked Sillars, deeply interested in Meg's graphic description of the incident.

"Well, he's good-looking in that smooth, polished foreign sort of way—tall and slim and as black as a sloe, with a kind of pale ivory face—don't you know?—and hair glued down on his sleek head, with brilliantine, I suppose. He certainly smelled of it! He was awfully well dressed and really quite gentlemanly. His politeness was prodigious."

"Well, and what else happened?"

"I don't think there is much more that I know of. This morning they left about eleven, driving all over the place again before they went, and thence to the station. And after lunch father took it in his head all of a sudden that he must go to Glasgow—and he did. Guy has gone to Stirling on some business connected with a horse, and I am the sole representative of the family at home."

"Your father didn't give you any more information?"

"No—but Guy did. He said that this Leyden person holds the mortgage on Ballochean, and that he meant either to foreclose or to take possession of the place."

"And what has the other man, Morris Bien, got to do with it?"

"He is the old Dutchman's nephew, as I have said, and the apple of his eye apparently. But don't let us talk about him. He paid me compliments, David—compliments to me, Meg Hamilton! And I had to suffer them in silence!"

"I'm very sorry for you, my dear, but I don't just see what I can do. Unless your father speaks to me, I can't put my oar in."

Meg sat still with her eyes fixed on the ground, the point of her shapely boot deep in the sawdust. There was a very odd expression on her face.

"I didn't send for you to talk about Ballochean and the money-lenders, David, though it has all made me fell pretty sick. Still, as you say, it is father's business."

"Then what is it?" he asked. "Is there something else?"

She looked up at him with the first hint of shyness he had ever observed in her.

"Well, it was chiefly about the other thing—the—the letter, don't you know? I want you to advise me what to do about it."

"I have advised you. There isn't anything in the world you can do but hold your tongue and hold your head higher than you've ever done."

"That isn't enough for worms and vipers like these!" quoth Meg wrathfully.

"Then what can you do?"

"I—I could get married myself, David, before them," she said quietly, regarding him from the tail of her eye demurely, yet with the most intense interest.

"You could, of course. Probably there would not be so very much difficulty about it, if you have really set your mind on it. But matrimony at best is a leap in the dark, Madge. I wouldn't advise you to try it."

"Wouldn't you? Yet you seemed rather keen on it the other night?"

His face reddened slightly and, just for a moment, his mouth hardened. He attempted no reply.

"I thought it would be quite easy, David," she went on. "But it isn't—you're so frightfully dense! I'll marry you, if you like—and the sooner the better. Couldn't you run away with me to-night? I'd just love it! Then I should get even with them."

Sillars laughed, not taking her seriously at all.

"That wouldn't mend matters, Madge—it would make them a lot worse. I'm sorry this has happened to you, and I'd like to kick Kessock. But he'll get his deserts. Miss Dove is not so meek as she looks."

"She isn't meek at all! That has all been pretence. I see through her now! I've often wanted to slap her, and I have done it once or twice. But I thought it was mostly fun. I know now she was in dead earnest all the time! But, David?"

"Yes, my dear?"

"Why don't you listen properly and understand? I've never known you so dull of comprehension before!"

"What do you want me to comprehend?"

"That I'm in earnest. I'm willing to marry you—even to run away with you, if you like—that's why I sent for you."

Sillars straightened his back and looked at her steadily, hardly even yet taking her seriously. But something in the expression of her face convinced him that she was in earnest.

Then a change swept over his face—a dark and terrible change. His slow anger, for the first time in Meg's remembrance, was roused.

"So that you may be revenged on Kessock and Miss Dove? No, thank you, my dear. Even if you are willing, I'm not taking on matrimony at that price. Let's forget what you've said. I promise not to remember it after this moment. I'm glad it was to me you've said it, and to nobody else."

She looked at him incredulously, not recognising in this cold, bleak, forbidding person the warm-hearted comrade who hitherto had been ready to obey her slightest behest.

"Oh, but, David—won't you?" she insisted, as a spoiled child might have cried for the moon. "Just think how lovely it would be, and how cheap they would feel?"

"So should we, my dear. Let's be done with this fooling. Shall I walk back with you to Ballochean?"

She rose and eyed him steadily for a moment. Then, reading inflexible purpose in his eye, she felt a sudden rush of shame and anger and ineffable disgust sweep over her.

"Oh, David Sillars! Is this all you amount to, after all? You are just like the rest. I positively hate you, and I'll never speak to you again as long as I live!"

She dashed away from him like a mad thing, her hair flying in the wind, and was soon lost to sight among the trees.

Sillars, a little paler than usual and more upset than he would have cared to own, pursued his way not towards Kildoon, but on foot back to the station, when he sent a special messenger to Kildoon to say that he had returned to Greenock and that he would not be down again until further notice.

He felt that the safest and best thing was to put some considerable distance between him and Meg Hamilton.

CHAPTER IX

CLOSING IN

Lady Kessock had had a shopping day in Glasgow and arrived at St. Enoch's station in time to catch the five o'clock train for Ayr. As she was buying some magazines at the bookstall the Laird of Ballochean came to her elbow.

Now, in the far-back days, there had been certain passages between Lady Kessock —then Miss Anne Dunlop of Stevenston—and Gavin Hamilton which neither had entirely forgotten. Even late in life a man and a woman who have once been something to each other cannot wholly forget.

Anne Dunlop had married in obedience to her parents, who had barred the wild, extravagant young Laird of Ballochean as a husband for her, and she had had no cause to regret the marriage thus arranged for her. If she had not tasted that passionate happiness in wedded life which, after all, is the lot of very few, she had at least had a life of ease and comfort and perfect peace.

But though she would not for the world have owned it, she had still a warm corner in her heart for Gavin Hamilton, and it gave her no pleasure to hear from the lips of others how low he had fallen.

Her sharp, keen eyes softened as they rested for a moment on the figure, once so gallant but now gross and undignified, the shabby clothes, the shifting eye, the general air of disrepute which characterised her once too handsome lover.

As soon as he recognised her, up went his hand to his head, and off came his hat with a touch of his old-time courtesy.

"Good-day to you, Lady Kessock," he said a trifle grimly, not at all sure whether she would care to recognise him.

To his surprise, she extended a well-gloved and perfectly friendly hand.

"I am well—and you, Mr. Hamilton? I have not seen you for a long time."

"No, my lady. Birds of your feather and mine fly—shall we say?—at different heights," he said with a touch of his old humour, which had once been as brilliant as the rest of him.

"But that need not hinder us from foregathering on occasion," she smiled back. "Ballochean and Sangster might be in different continents for all the commerce there is between them."

"That is my loss," said Hamilton quietly. "Our train, I think. I'll say good-day, my lady."

"Won't you even travel in my compartment for the sake of auld lang syne?" she asked with increased kindliness in her look.

He was unaware, had not indeed the slightest idea, that, because her mind was now relieved from the menace of any possible relationship between their children, she was prepared to be gracious to the utmost limit. Besides, she wished to have a talk with him and to discover, if that were possible, how things actually stood with him.

"I can at least see you to the door of your compartment," he answered. "But in these days I am no fit company for the rich and the great," he added.

"The more shame to you, Ballochean," she retorted quickly with a bright flash from her still beautiful eyes. "But you will come with me to-day, provided we can be alone? You and I ought to have something to say to each other."

Somewhat flattered, since, as a rule, he was shunned by Lady Kessock and all her set, Gavin Hamilton did not demur further, but helped her into the compartment with something of his old gallantry, and, following her, closed the door with the utmost care.

It was a first-class compartment, and Gavin Hamilton had his white ticket safely in his pocket, for, even in his most evil days, he had never descended to the practice of such small economies as are beloved of lesser or more conscientious folk. "If I have to go to the dogs," he would say, "then I will go like a gentleman."

His standard of what constituted a gentleman might have been interesting, could he have been persuaded to set it down in black and white.

He waited on her assiduously, arranged her small packages on the rack, asked whether she would like a foot-warmer, was anxious to consult her comfort about the opening of the windows, and was altogether so over-powering in his attentions that her patience at last came to an end.

"Sit down, Gavin," she said abruptly but kindly. "I'm not needing all that fuss made. I'm an old woman accustomed to wait on myself."

"Doubtful," he said with a shrug of his shoulders. "Old, did you say? I see no signs of old age. Look at my grey hairs; yet once there were not so many years between us!"

"Your own fault, my dear," she said quickly. "Don't, for my sake, let that woman get in here, Gavin! Scowl at her—anything to keep her out!"

Lady Kessock, recognising in the woman a very garrulous acquaintance whom she particularly disliked and wished to avoid, shrank into her corner lest she should be seen and pounced upon.

Ballochean stood up at the window so that his portly figure filled it, and, as he had fully expected, the lady passed on.

"They won't come where the ill bird is," he said grimly. "There's the whistle—now we're off."

He sank back in his corner, apparently both relieved and amused, took off his hat, and ran his fingers through his hair, once so rich and golden, now alas! both grey and scanty. The pity of it sank into Anne Kessock's heart.

"I'm rather pleased to see you to-day, Mr. Hamilton," she began more formally than she had yet spoken, "because, though circumstances have kept us a good deal apart—especially of late years—you are a very old friend, and, as you know, I liked your wife above any woman I knew in the county."

"Very good of you, I am sure," murmured Ballochean with that armed, somewhat remote air which any mention of his wife never failed to bring.

Nobody knew what depth of remorse and unavailing regret was in that tough old heart over the gentle, sweet creature whose love he had so tried and whose heart he had so wrung. Very few would have believed that Gavin Hamilton kept, or could keep, in his heart a shrine before which, at rare intervals, now, alas! growing rarer, his wild soul could bow in secret.

"I have a bit of family news to impart to you," she said with great deliberation after a brief pause. "It is very new in the family as yet, but there is no one to whom I would more quickly tell it."

"Ay—what is that?" he asked interestedly. "Perhaps you are thinking of marrying again," he suggested, with a faint twinkle in his eye. "None could blame you, and he would be a lucky man."

"Hold your tongue, Ballochean. That's not the way to speak to a possible and probable grandmother. My son is going to get him a wife."

She watched him narrowly and was rewarded by observing a sudden stiffening of his figure and a curious narrowing of his brows until they actually frowned.

"Indeed! Well, it is what they will do—these young ones, putting us old fogies in the shade. And who is the fortunate lady whom he is to marry?"

"Surgeon Dove's daughter," said Lady Kessock with the same deliberate air, and her tone was a little merciless. "It was settled last night."

There was a moment's complete silence; and, when Ballochean spoke again, his voice had a new quality in it—a vibrant quality which indicated some disquiet within.

"Surgeon Dove's daughter!" he repeated. "But surely, Lady Kessock, that is no great match for the Laird of Sangster, and your son——"

She shrugged her shoulders.

"It might be worse. She is a gentle, sweet thing, and her father is one of the best. She has a silly mother, but she can be kept in her place. It might very well be worse, Gavin, for I am not minded to go away from Sangster, if I can help it; and I think that Ellison is one that will be glad of my counsel and chaperonage—at least, until her wings be grown."

Ballochean had his doubts. But at the moment his only concern was Meg and how this would affect her. At the back of his mind through all the dread and despair of these last days, which had culminated in an extraordinary proposal, there had lurked the hope that things would come to a happy settlement between Kessock and his daughter, and that, through their marriage, he might climb to some semblance of freedom and respectability.

He was so astonished and so dumbfounded by what Lady Kessock had told him that he could not take the trouble to hide it altogether.

"I confess you have surprised me, Lady Kessock. Surely it is rather sudden and unexpected. I have never heard any rumours to prepare me for such intelligence as this."

"There have not been any rumours. In this they have been wise. When Hew came to tell me last night, I was pleased and I told him so."

"Then it all happened yesterday, I suppose?"

"Yesterday afternoon, I believe; and the engagement will be short. It is better so in a place where gossip has neither beginning, middle, nor end. And they have nothing to wait for."

"I suppose not. It's a leg up for the Doves—folk I could never bide, though Meg goes about with them."

"So I understand," said Lady Kessock, wincing slightly. "Mrs. Dove has been kind to your motherless girl, Gavin. I've always been sorry for her."

"Have you indeed? But your sorrow never got you the length of being even as kind to her as Surgeon Dove's wife has shown herself, Anne," he said with a cynical uplift of his brows.

She coloured a little; and then, sitting forward, she looked him straight between the eyes.

"It was not that I would not have been so, Gavin, but I was afraid of your daughter. She is not like other creatures. She would have made dispeace in Sangster. She will make dispeace wherever she goes. Perhaps it is not altogether your fault, but you have done very ill by your girl, and I am surprised that you, with all the knowledge of women you have—or used to have—have not had your eyes opened long ago."

"There is none to hold a candle to her in all the county, Anne," cried Ballochean in high rage and scorn. "For looks—who can touch her? For spirit—none can break it! It is because you know how superior she is to them all that you have kept her at arm's length and have never had her to visit you at Sangster. But, thank God, both Meg Hamilton and her father can live without the goodwill or favour of Sangster or of the set it represents!"

He was now in a towering passion, and the interview which had begun so well was like to culminate in complete rupture.

Lady Anne had a bitter retort on her lips when, just at the moment, the train stopped at Paisley Station and the door of the carriage opened to admit another passenger, and their intimate talk was at an end.

At Ayr station they parted with a formal, curt nod, and Gavin Hamilton set out to walk to Ballochean with a good hour in front of him in which to cool his ire.

He had sustained a frightful disappointment, and he began to fear that he had perhaps counted too much on Meg's help for the future.

If Anne Kessock's was a fair sample of the opinion in which she was held by the county—then where were her chances?

Altogether this had been a disastrous day for Ballochean—one of the worst he had ever experienced.

The walk, however, did him good, and he was in more equable mood by the time he reached his home, which had never seemed dearer or more desirable in his eyes than now when he was threatened with its loss.

"Miss Meg—where is she?" he enquired of Jean, who was laying the table for dinner.

"She's only just come in, sir. Gone up to dress, I think, answered the girl who had seen Meg, evidently in a state of great perturbation, fly across the park, and dash into the house through the conservatory door.

"And Mr. Guy, where is he?" the Laird next asked.

"In the library, sir, waiting for you to come home."

Gavin Hamilton passed on to the library, where he found Guy smoking hard and apparently trying to read a sporting paper.

"So you've got back?" he said laconically.

His father had not taken him into his confidence regarding the business at Glasgow, and Guy was feeling himself an ill-used and unfairly treated person, who could get no satisfaction out of anybody.

Ballochean closed the door and sat down rather wearily. He had taken the four-mile walk from the station rather fast, and, besides, the strain of the day had been great and was now telling on him.

"I've had an infernal run of bad luck in the last year or two, Guy, and it isn't going to mend. The place will have to go."

"Ballochean, you mean?" asked Guy rather stupidly.

The old man nodded.

"What else could I mean? It's all we've got. That's what Van Leyden and his nephew came for yesterday."

"These insufferable bounders!" cried Guy. "You don't mean to say they've got the whole thing in their clutches!"

"That's just what I do mean to say. You needn't glower at me like that, Guy. After all, it's none of your business. If anybody has a grievance it's Ludo, and he never said a word. He has taken the only sensible course, and gone out on his own. You'd better follow his example."

Guy was speechless for a moment, wondering what would come next.

It was the first time that he had ever heard his father allude civilly to Ludo, and the idea of praising him for having taken prompt action had its comical side. But Guy was not, just then, in the mood to see comedy in anything.

"And when the place goes, what becomes of us all—but principally of Meg?"

Ballochean shrugged his shoulders, assuming an indifference he was far from feeling. He was by no means comfortable in his mind about his daughter, and he was privately incensed because, as he might have expressed it, she had played her cards so badly.

"She might have landed Kessock," he answered with a shrug of his shoulder. "She had him in her hand, but she has lost him. He's going to marry Surgeon Dove's daughter. Lady Kessock told me so to-day, as we travelled down from Glasgow together."

Guy turned aside, and his face assumed an even deeper gloom.

He had entertained some hopes in that direction himself, and had Ellison had any money he would not have allowed the grass to grow under his feet so long without making a serious effort to win her.

"Infernal bad luck all round," he muttered. "But do you actually mean to say that these harpies who were here yesterday are going to have Ballochean?"

"I don't see what is going to prevent them. They are coming down to-morrow for the week-end. They seemed uncommonly well pleased with their last visit, and they want to repeat it. I shall have to souther up Meg. She didn't like them; but it's essential that they should be kept in good humour."

He walked to the cupboard, mixed himself a stiff brandy and soda, and began to fill his pipe.

"After all, what good is the place to us under present conditions? We can't do anything with it. We've no money to pay anybody. It's a poisonous existence. When our feet are cleared we'll know where we are."

"A little house in Ayr, I suppose, and not a bit of horseflesh or a trap to drive in," said Guy in deep disgust. "Final extinction of the Hamiltons, in fact. As well put a bullet through oneself and be done with it!"

"You needn't talk like that, Guy. You're young, and you've the world in front of you. You can go out to one of the colonies and seek your fortune. I'd go myself, in fact, if I were ten years younger, and had the liver I used to have."

What wonder that at the dinner table that night the acme of gloom was reached!

The two men dined alone, Meg having sent down a message that she had a headache, and didn't want anything. This in itself was unusual enough to cause some comment, even a little consternation, on the part of her father and her brother. But neither of them ventured to go upstairs to make personal inquiry.

It may be that a certain shame kept them back, for, undoubtedly, between them they had destroyed Ballochean and made of it a poor home for the only woman of their race.

Next morning Meg appeared at the breakfast table as if nothing had happened in the interval. Never had she looked more cool and careless, more defiant, or more strong. But, had there been any interested enough to take particular note, they would not have failed to observe the hard brilliance of her eyes, the deepened lines about her mouth, the sedate and somewhat gloomy air.

She had slept but little. In the night watches she had fought her battle, tried to tear the image of Hew Kessock from her heart and to trample on every memory of him. And, though Meg's nature had a volatile side, things took a grip of her, and this had not been easy. But no one would ever know what it cost her—Kessock, least of all!

She had mapped out her procedure for the day. Quite early in it she would walk or ride into Ayr and pay her personal visit of congratulation to Ellison, just to show that her engagement to Hew Kessock was a matter of supreme indifference to her.

Talk did not flourish at breakfast. Her father was unusually silent, but, towards the end of the meal, he looked across the table and addressed her.

"Those men who were here the other day are coming this afternoon to spend the week-end, Meg. Make the same arrangements for them as before."

"You mean the Dutchman and his wax figure of a nephew?" she asked with a slight curl of the lip.

"Yes. See that there is plenty of food in the house and find out, if you can, what Van Leyden likes for breakfast. If he's a strict Jew, he won't, of course, eat bacon. Order up plenty of fish."

These directions brought to Meg's mind the matter of Macmichael's account.

"Say, father, did you know that we owed so much money to Macmichael?" she said quietly.

His brow darkened.

"Has the rascal been bothering you about his little bit of a bill?"

"I asked him how long it was since he had sent in an account."

"The deuce you did! Well, that was about as stupid a thing as you have ever done, my dear—and that's saying a good deal!"

"The account amounts to a hundred and seventy-three pounds," went on Meg mercilessly; "and then there's the baker, and the fishmonger, and the grocer. What are you going to do about it all?"

"Settle them soon—sooner than you think—probably next week," he said, and he signed to Guy not to intervene. "Things will depend on Van Leyden's visit. He's coming to have a good talk over everything."

Meg rose, heavy-hearted, even appalled, at the prospect of having to endure the presence once more of such visitors—more especially of the one who paid the compliments. He was really a very estimable and clever young man, with a sort of genius for finance, which would have been better employed in more dignified directions. But in Meg's estimation he was a perfect bounder and completely and absolutely outside the pale.

"Father, couldn't I invite myself down to the Sandersons to stay over the week-end? Bobbie and his wife would be quite pleased to have me, I'm sure," she suggested. "You would be far better without me while these men are here. I'll arrange everything before I go—order in the food, and put old Greig on her mettle. Only I don't feel as if I could be civil to them for three whole days if I were here."

"Nothing of the kind! You needn't see much of them—only at meals. And we can cut these short as decently as possible. Van Leyden made a special point of seeing you. Somehow, you seem to have impressed him favourably, though I can't say I noticed any indications of civility on your part."

Meg uplifted her brows and curled her proud, sensitive mouth.

"Spare me any more about Van Leyden, if you please. I've had quite enough. I must dree my weird, I suppose. But, just at present, life doesn't seem worth living. If I were you, Guy Hamilton, I'd take the wings of a dove and fly away."

Somehow, the casual mention of the word "dove" seemed to bring home to her the perfidy of her friend, and she rose abruptly and left the room.

She had a sickening feeling as if she were being hemmed in on every side, as if soon there would be no escape.

From what she was trying to escape she did not know. All that she knew was that all things were horrible and out of joint.

She saw to her household affairs, and had one strenuous hour with the aggressive Mrs. Grieg, who threatened to strike on account of so many additions being made to the meals. As usual, however, her young mistress came off victorious.

About eleven she got out a ramshackle old bicycle, gave it a polish with a stable rubber, drew on her gloves, and set out to congratulate Ellison Dove.

CHAPTER X

THE NET

WHEN Meg arrived at Prospect House she was shown with unusual ceremony into the dining-room, which was the living room of the Doves, except on days when callers were expected. She looked surprised, not being aware that Mrs. Dove from her bedroom window had seen her ride along by the side of the links, and had issued her instructions to the maid accordingly.

Presently Mrs. Dove herself came to greet the early guest. The little woman, in spite of the song of triumph swelling in her heart, was obviously nervous.

Meg, however, instantly put her at her ease.

" Why am I treated in this ceremonious fashion, Mrs. Dove ? " she cried merrily. " I've come to see Ellie, and to congratulate her. Father came down from Glasgow with the Dowager last night, and heard the news from her."

Her tone was gay, her smile pleasant, her whole appearance that of one who rejoices in the good fortune that has come to a friend.

Mrs. Dove, in much relief, positively overflowed with friendliness.

" My dear, how sweet of you—how positively sweet ! " she said, and, clutching Meg, she kissed her on both her unwilling cheeks. " Ellie is, of course, a little upset. As a matter of fact, she is getting dressed to go up to Sangster to spend the day there. Sir Hew is driving down presently to fetch her."

" Oh ! " said Meg, with an uplift of the brows. " Can't I just run up and see her ? "

Mrs. Dove looked dubious for a moment. Ellison had declared emphatically that nothing on earth would induce her to see Meg, and she had almost hysterically begged her mother to get rid of her as quickly as possible.

But, observing Meg so bright and gay, and apparently only ready to rejoice, and regarding the complexion of affairs as much altered for the better thereby, Mrs. Dove assented, though rather apologetically.

" I am sure I don't mind. But Ellie is feeling very shy, and strange, of course. It all came about so suddenly."

" Oh ! did it ? " asked Meg briefly. " I was wondering how it happened. I'll just pop up and ask her."

She was gone before Mrs Dove could prevent her, and that good lady, who pursued the policy of avoiding unpleasant things as much as possible, remained where she was.

Meg, who for the last five years had been almost like another daughter in the house, opened the door of Ellison's room without ceremony, and found that young lady completely dressed in a very becoming frock of a delicate mauve colour, drawing on her gloves.

" Whatever do you mean by sending your mother down to me, Ellie ? Is this a sample of the treatment I am to expect from the future Lady Kessock ? "

Ellison flushed almost guiltily, laughed nervously, and sat down on the nearest chair.

" I hardly know where I am to-day, Meg. And it all happened so suddenly —oh, so very suddenly—that I felt as if I wanted a few days—don't you know ?— to realise things."

" I don't wonder at that. Still, you can't blame me for wanting to be the first to offer my congrats. It was awfully good of you to write. I don't believe that, in similar circumstances, I could have been capable of doing it myself."

" I promised, you see, and I felt that you ought to know at once," said Ellison, much interested in the fastening of her glove.

" Well, I wish you good luck, Ellie, and I hope you'll get on with the Dowager. Take my advice, and begin with her as you mean to end. She's a Tarter ! "

"Oh, not at all! You are quite mistaken. She has been most sweet and kind to me," said Ellison demurely. "She is going to show me everything to-day, and I'm sure I shall be very happy with her. Everything depends on how one treats people. You know, Meg, I have never shared your bad opinion of Lady Kessock."

"Oh! haven't you? I thought I had heard you more than once call her a cat, but I may be wrong, of course. Anyway, it's the right spirit you're exhibiting now, and, no doubt, you'll get on a treat at Sangster. I have a lot of shopping to do in the town, so I hope you'll excuse me for cutting my visit short. But I felt I simply must come round this way to be the first to congratulate you."

"Awfully sweet and good of you, Meg, I am sure. But aren't you going to kiss me before you go?"

Meg made a little wry face.

"You know I loathe pecks, Ellie. I can be sincere enough without them. Ta-ta! I hope you'll still be having a nod for me when you're driving in style behind the Sangster horses. I must say that I envy you them. They're perfect darlings."

So Meg got pretty well out of the difficult situation of her own making, and, on the whole, she felt satisfied as she rode away.

But she had not yet put herself through all her facings. Instead of riding into the town she turned round by the links, and deliberately and very slowly proceeded to ride up the road by which she knew Hew Kessock would have to come, unless indeed he had already gone into the town.

She would ride a mile or so along the Sangster Road, and would perhaps inquire at the nearest lodge-gate whether he had passed Poor Meg wanted and intended to get the whole thing over in one day! Her heart beat feverishly, her eyes had a kind of hard glitter in them, and she was in a state of ferment, both body and soul. But no thought of shirking the unpleasant task imposed on her by her proud spirit or of hiding for a moment a diminished head occurred to her. On the contrary, she must hold her head higher than the best of them!

She was rewarded at a sudden sweep of the road by the vision of Hew Kessock's fine drag with the splendid pair of roans between the shafts bowling along in fine style.

With a little reckless smile on her lips she swerved to the left, as the law of the road decreed, and, riding very slowly, she met him directly in the face. She saw him redden, and, though he saluted her, he would have driven on without speaking, had it not been that she held up her right hand and dismounted, holding her bicycle between her and the drag.

Fortunately for both there was no groom with him, his absence being due to Kessock's intention to take his new sweetheart for a considerable drive before finally they arrived at Sangster for luncheon.

"Would you cut an old friend because she happens to be riding on a dilapidated bike?" she asked mockingly. "I have ridden this way on purpose—to be first with my congrats."

She extended one slim, gloved hand towards him, and he perforce had to stoop to take it.

"Thanks, awfully," he said awkwardly. "But how, in heaven's name, have you got to know so soon?"

"Oh, Ellie wrote to me last night, and your mother told my father yesterday. So it has been a twice-told tale. You're going to be very happy, of course. But it would have only been fair, wouldn't it, if I had known a day or two ago of your intention?"

He reddened again.

"Meg, 'pon honour, when we met the other night on the shore, I hadn't the remotest intention of asking Miss Dove to marry me. It was only after you had treated me so beastly shabbily that I went there, and—and was caught in the rebound, don't you know?"

Meg's clear laugh rang out a little shrilly on the morning air, and Kessock did not like the sound of it.

Most men are acutely sensitive to ridicule, and he was particularly so. He felt that Meg had him in the hollow of her hand, and somehow, now that, through his own action, she was altogether out of his reach, she had never seemed so adorable or so desirable. She was a woman of whom no man could tire, for her moods were as innumerable and as changeful as the wandering winds that swept up from the sea.

"Hope you'll have a long and happy life." she said gaily, as she mounted her machine and rode away.

She turned off at a little side road which would take her by a circuitous way back to Ayr, and she was not sure as she dashed something from her eyes whether she had made a fool of herself or of Hew Kessock.

As luck would have it, at some farm cottages she beheld Bobbie Sanderson's gig, and at the moment she was riding by he came out of one of them.

At sight of his good-natured, placid face smiling at her from under the brim of his bowler hat, a sudden, unreasoning jealousy of him, his wife, and his comfortable, well-ordered life and home seized her. How was it that she, of all men and women, should be singled out for disaster, humiliation, and defeat?

"East wind this morning?" he said significantly, for Meg, as was natural, dismounted to speak to him, and her face, he observed, as she approached was one big cloud.

"Yes, and the snellest at that," she answered. "I'm wishing this morning that I'd never been born, Bobbie, or at least that you had made me say 'Yes,' instead of 'No,' that day at the Maidens when we fell out over matrimony."

Sanderson merely laughed, not taking her seriously.

"Things worse up at Ballochean?" he asked sympathetically.

"Yes, just as bad as they can possibly be. And I have to go home presently to make myself as agreeable as I know how to two strange men who, I believe, have got us all in their power. It isn't fair, Bobbie, it isn't fair!"

It was the battle-cry for that freedom to which each human soul is in some measure entitled, though some mistake license for that finer liberty of soul which alone makes men free.

She was greatly tempted, having now not a single woman friend in the whole wide world, to make one of her old lover; but she was happily prevented by some inner and finer sense from so much as mentioning Kessock's name to him. In affairs of the heart the narrower the border of discussion the better, for there is no area of life which can so quickly become a vulgar place.

Bobbie, whose calling as a healer was not restricted merely to the practice of his profession, regarded her with deepening interest and kindliness.

"Look here, my dear. Come down to the Broad House and stay there for a few days. Come this afternoon. I'm going home to one o'clock lunch, and I'll tell Edie to expect you. She and the baby will do you good."

"It is what I would like to do, Bobbie; but when I mentioned it to father that I would like to come to you, he simply put his foot down and said I must remain at home. By Monday, Bobbie, if there is any remnant of me surviving, don't be surprised at anything!"

Meg was much given to extravagance of speech, but Sanderson, making due allowance for that habit, nevertheless easily divined that to-day there was some actual reason for her acute depression.

He walked about five hundred yards with her trying to comfort and reassure her, and his last words often recurred to Meg's mind when she had taken the great plunge and the clouds were thick and impenetrable about her life.

"You may take it from me, Meg, that what I am going to say is true, for I've observed it again and again—why, even this morning in that bit cot-house I have just come out of I've seen the quick swing of the pendulum before the limit of endurance has been reached. It may be that this very thing which you are dreading, that the transactions in connection with Ballochean which are undoubtedly going on, may turn out the very best happening that you have yet encountered. Try to take that view, and possess your soul in patience, my dear, and, above all, remember that things done in a hurry are meat for repentance!"

"Preaching's no good, Bobbie, for I've got the devil in me this morning. So good-day to you."

A little later in the day, when, in another house of call, Sanderson heard both rumour and confirmation of the Kessock-Dove engagement, he cursed himself for a blind ass and imagined he had found the key to Meg's reckless mood.

Once in the streets Meg pulled herself together, and placed her orders at the shops. To Mr. Macmichael, the butcher, she addressed herself with a kind of pathetic dignity, the memory of which lingered long in the man's kindly soul.

"I've spoken to my father about your account, Mr. Macmichael, and he is going to give it his immediate attention. Some time next week you may expect a cheque and full settlement."

But she smiled drearily to herself as she rode away, for though inwardly conscious that there were great happenings with regard to Ballochean impending in the immediate future, she was certain that, if the money for the settlement of Mr. Macmichael's just claim was to come out of the barter of Ballochean, nobody but he would be the gainer.

She arrived home in time for luncheon, and she was again struck by the evident uneasiness and restlessness of her father.

"Tell me what orders you gave in Ayr, Meg." he said peremptorily—a procedure so unusual on his part that to Meg it was full of the most ominous significance.

With a strange meekness she gave him an account of her stewardship, her narrative being interrupted occasionally with this suggestion or that from him until at last she flared up.

"If you want all these things you will need to go down to the kitchen and tackle Mrs. Greig yourself. She won't do them, I tell you, even if she could! If these people who are coming know we are poor, as I dare say they do, they won't expect too much. It will be the more fitting that they should be fed in a simple way."

He was struck by the evidence of subtle wisdom and foresight displayed in this remark.

"Well, see at least that there is plenty of good, wholesome food. I'll chuck the other things—all except the savoury. No man likes his dinner without the savoury. Go and see Mrs. Greig about that."

Meg's hands were full that day in very truth, for none of the household were in sympathy with the coming guests. For one thing, they had gone away at the end of their former visit without leaving any *pour boire*, and Jean tossed her head when she spoke of the eternal ringing of bells, to which neither she nor any of her colleagues were accustomed, all their own folk being singularly independent of personal service.

The day wore on. Meg made no inquiry as to the possible moment of their arrival, but as she had received her instructions to have dinner ready at eight she expected they would reach Ballochean shortly before that hour at latest.

About half-past seven, as she was dressing in the old schoolroom, she heard the sound of wheels, and understood from that that the guests had come by the seven o'clock train. But she did not move to the window to look out, nor did she make any attempt to discover whether they had actually arrived.

At her father's suggestion the fire in the drawing-room had been lit, the shabby old chintzes hauled off the faded velvet and woolwork of the furniture to make the room seem more homely.

It was a great barn of a place, with no touch of beauty or originality about it. Long mirrors set on gilt console tables added fictitious space to its already vast area, and the walls, denuded of the picture treasures which they once had carried, and the cabinets, rifled of anything that was worth looking at, seemed to proclaim with no uncertain voice the fallen fortunes of the house.

But the cheerfully burning fire did wonders, and when the long curtains of the richest crimson silk damask, which somehow had escaped the appraiser's eye, had been drawn across the long windows, the room presented some slight semblance of comfort.

Meg, in the old blue gown, into which she had hurriedly run a chemisette of fine lace in order to hide the snow of her bosom from these alien eyes, moved with a certain dignity across the floor, put another log on the fire, and was pulling out the bunch of tawny chrysanthemums at her belt when Mr. Morris Bien entered to pay his respects.

He was clad in evening dress and had a vast expanse of white shirt front, with an immense diamond stud glittering in the midst thereof, which, catching the light, looked like the flashlight of a motor car. His figure did not lack distinction, and his clothes fitted it to perfection; his tie was a marvel of art, while the scent of the gardenia in his buttonhole mingled with that of the brilliantine on his sleek hair.

"Ah! Miss Hamilton, I am in luck," he said joyously, and with very little trace of a foreign accent. "I hope I see you very well?"

Meg was determined not to shake hands with him. In amends she bowed graciously, and even mustered a somewhat weak smile.

"I am quite well, thank you, Mr. Bien. I hope your uncle also is?"

"Oh! yes, he is jolly—is Uncle Solly. His name is Auguste Solomon, and we boys, whom he has brought up, call him Solly for short."

"Oh, then, there are more of you," said Meg with a curious note in her voice.

She was standing by the hearth with the point of her old dancing-slipper of blue satin resting on the faded border of the fender stool—the work of some bygone dame of Ballochean. Her head was held regally, and a gleam from the candelabra, all alight on the mantelpiece, just caught her hair and transformed it into gold.

"Two of us altogether—myself and my brother Karl. He is in Frankfurt in the big banking house of our family," he answered with a certain pride.

"And why are you here in Scotland?" she asked. "One would think that there is not much of a field in our poor country for—for gentlemen of your financial abilities," she added lamely, for a less complimentary word had very nearly slipped out.

Morris Bien took the words as a compliment, and he showed his dazzling white teeth in an appreciative smile.

"Ah! there you are wrong, Miss Hamilton. There are great opportunities for every kind of genius in Scotland. It is a great country! Is it not the home of genius? Witness this very county, where your national poet was born!"

"Poor old Robbie!" murmured Meg, feeling an irresistible desire to laugh.

As she contemplated this resplendent being there arose before her mental vision, in acute contrast, a picture of the ploughman poet in his working garb, patiently turning up the furrows on Lochlea or Mossgiel, with the lilt of immortality in his heart!

"Poets know very little about money, I have heard. They are not good at keeping it, and, in fact, they don't need it. Their riches are within," she said, and she wondered why it was that she, of all the persons in the world, should speak thus, as if reading out of a book.

It was certainly the oddest experience of her life, and she was enjoying it with that strange perverseness which is ever a part of a complex personality such as hers.

She loathed the adorned and scented dandy before her, but she had neither the desire nor the right to deny that he possessed some qualities which commanded respect. He was certainly no weakling. The breadth of his brow and the swift penetration of his glance bore testimony to that fact. She even felt that she would like to pit her fighting forces against his, and to watch with breathless interest to which side victory would lean.

Their conversation was interrupted by the entrance of the others, Ballochean himself carefully guiding the steps of his elderly guest, who looked even more distinguished than his nephew, as he had certain orders pinned across his breast, and his fierce white hair brushed straight on end, the effect being that his massive features were in no way softened, but, on the contrary, stood out with a strange compelling kind of strength.

Meg turned to him with relief, and, taking some steps across the room, met him with a smile. The old financier with the manner of a courtier almost bowed himself to the ground, and in voluble and picturesque, if very guttural, language, expressed his pleasure at meeting her again.

Dinner passed off pleasantly, and Meg, sitting like a stately young goddess at the head of the table, directed the most of her remarks to Mr. Van Leyden. In spite of herself she was interested by what he had to say about the life of his own country, and by the knowledge of men which he displayed, while his close acquaintance with the histories of those in high places on two continents seemed to her both sinister and uncanny.

But, with it all, there was a kindly gleam in his eye, and always, when its glance would rest on the fair face of the daughter of the house, it would soften into a strange tenderness.

Just once or twice, encountering on her left the more ardent gaze of the younger man, Meg felt a sort of terror creeping over her heart, and her tongue for the moment would be paralysed.

She felt like a bird in the snare of the fowler.

She would not have been reassured had she overheard a scrap of conversation between uncle and nephew, which took place late that night in the Red Room —the chamber reserved for special guests—which had been prepared for Van Leyden.

"Yees, my boy, she is a peerless creature! Ach, she is fit for any throne! It is a prince that she ought to be vedding. She vould vear a crown royally, and vould command homage. But she is not for ze hearth, Morris, Now that you haf seen her, tink vell. There is no peace in ze home of a man vith such a voman. She is for a stimulant, adoration, homage outside, but for ze hearth, for ze mothering of his children, and for ze gifing of him peace and comfort—nein! Tink vell, my boy, before ve speak."

"She is the only woman I've ever seen for whom I would give up my freedom, Uncle Auguste. And it is a fair bargain! I hear that she has not a chance in her own country among her equals in rank and position. But as my wife she would be able to snap her fingers at them."

"Zen, you will not gif her up?"

"I will not."

"Ach, zen you vill haf to go slow, for it is ze lightning zat is in her heart. She is of ze thoroughbred zat cannot stand ze goad or ze spur. She vill haf to be von royally, Morris, and royally held. And even zen there vill be no peace. Therefore, I say—tink vell!"

CHAPTER XI

THE INTERLOPER

MEG got through that Saturday better than she expected. She took care to be busy about the house all the morning, and after luncheon cleverly eluded Morris Bien, who asked her to walk with him in the park.

She got out the old bicycle and rode desperately into Ayr, where, however, she had no luck. She did not call at Prospect House, and she found that the Sandersons had gone to Glasgow for the day.

Then came dinner at Ballochean, with Meg at the head of the table, a guest on either side.

" And vat has mademoiselle been about all day dat she has not permitted ze light of her countenance to shine upon us ? " asked Van Leyden, as he spread his napkin over his knees and tucked one corner in beside the red silk handkerchief showing at his shirt front.

Meg crumbled the bread at her plate. The old man's questioning she did not mind. It was the eyes of the young one that struck rage and terror into her soul.

" I've been doing the usual things a woman has to do," she answered flippantly—" ordering food. And then I rode down into Ayr to find out why some of it hadn't come."

" You rode into Ayr on what ? " asked Morris Bien.

" An old bicycle worth just eighteen shillings," she answered. " And I had a burst tyre on the way which it took the man an hour to repair."

" I should have enjoyed the walk with you," said Morris Bien reproachfully ; " and you know you promised to walk with me some time to-day."

" That was before I knew the food hadn't come," she answered in the same flippant tone. " Say, Mr. Van Leyden, tell me more about the burst dykes in Holland. While they were patching my tyre, I tried to find a book in the Free Library on the subject, but they haven't anything."

" Ach, you are interested in Holland, mademoiselle ? " said Van Leyden joyously. " Perhaps you and your vorthy father vill pay a visit to our people there. Ve could show you mooch to interest you—could ve not, Morris ? "

" Miss Hamilton would like Frankfurt better, Uncle Auguste," said Morris Bien. " Holland is a dead country in the winter. I hope we shall show you Frankfurt one day."

" It doesn't interest me," said Meg carelessly. " Father, I heard to-day there's going to be a general election in the spring, and they are looking for a new member."

Van Leyden looked interestedly down the table at his host.

" Politics vould call you, Mr. Hamilton. You vould stand, perhaps ? "

Gavin Hamilton laughed bitterly.

" I'm afraid I haven't sufficient reputation in the county for that, Van Leyden. Politics are not much in my line."

" People take them seriously in Scotland," said Van Leyden. " But you are a serious nation."

" It is because none of us have enough money, Mr. Van Leyden," put in Guy, who since the arrival of these inexplicable guests had found himself a person of no importance. " As a nation we've been hampered through lack of funds."

" Ach, but there are qualities vich flourish in poverty, my young sir," said Van Leyden, fixing him with a penetrating eye. He had already taken the measure of this worthless and idle youth, and decided that he required no consideration.

Guy gave a shrug of the shoulders.

" I'd uncommonly like to have a chance of seeing what qualities would flourish in an atmosphere of affluence. It would be a happy change."

"Do you care for money for its own sake, Miss Hamilton?" inquired Morris Bien interestedly.

Meg replied without a moment's hesitation.

"At the present moment it is the only thing that matters in my life. It is certain one can do very little without it."

"First sensible remark I've heard you make of late, my dear!" said her father grimly. "I'm with you there. Our friends, of course, can't expect to understand just how we feel about it, can they?"

"Are you so very rich, then, Mr. Van Leyden?" inquired Meg, fixing her big, childlike eyes on the old man's rugged face.

Van Leyden gave his characteristic shrug.

"We haf enough. But vile money is good, mademoiselle, belief me it cannot purchase von hour of happiness or peace."

"I'd be willing to risk it," she answered quickly, and then coloured, imagining that she saw uncle and nephew exchange glances.

"Ach, mademoiselle, vat is money but to roll at ze feet of such as you? It griefs me to hear vords so bitter on lips so beautiful. You haf but to say ze word and ze flood vill roll to your feet."

Meg laughed ruefully.

"I say the word, then!" she answered recklessly. "Now, let it roll!"

"Ach, but vat is ze word, mademoiselle? Ve shall talk again of dis matter—to-morrow, perhaps. Vill you honour ze old man by showing him vat you call 'My Lady's Garden?' Like Morris, I pine and die because you keep not your promises to me."

"Oh! Mr. Van Leyden, you are a foolish old man, and it is like reading a translated novel to hear you speak," cried Meg, now laughing in spite of herself.

Gavin Hamilton listened, well pleased, to these passages between Meg and his guests, delighting in her ready responses and in Van Leyden's evident joy in her. If only she would prove amenable when the matter of serious business came to be discussed—hey, presto!—all their troubles would vanish into thin air.

She sat longer with them that evening at the table, though her face was more often turned towards the uncle than towards the nephew. There was a great deal of by-play, and Guy, looking on, listening to Meg's casual and perfectly unpremeditated remarks, marvelled at her high spirit, her courage, and her beauty.

Never had all these qualities been more brilliantly shown, and, had he been less vitally interested in the little drama being played out in the first stages, he could have taken the keenest enjoyment in it.

After dinner they came quickly to the drawing-room, the piano was opened, and Morris Bien discoursed such music from it as had never been heard in that room since it was built. He was a splendid musician, and he forgot himself the moment his fingers touched the keys.

Meg's soul vibrated under the spell of it; yet, in the midst of it, moved in some strange, subtle way, she rose up and crept out of the room without so much as bidding the others good-night.

And once more she went to sleep with the strange, fluttering consciousness that some net, impalpable but strong, was being woven around her destiny.

Next day being Sunday there was no escape from the guests possible to Meg. Church-going had for years had no place in the calendar at Ballochean, Meg's every-day garments not being suitable for comparison with those of the well-dressed crowds who flocked to the parish church every Sunday.

Immediately after breakfast Van Leyden claimed the fulfilment of her promise to show him "My Lady's Garden." His nephew went off to the stables with Guy; and, had not Meg been singularly guileless, she might have suspected a little arrangement between uncle and nephew.

She was quite pleased to spend an hour with the old man. Anything was better than a *tête-à-tête* with Morris Bien, which she had been dreading all the morning.

After lunch, she reflected, she must find out means of escaping for the whole of the afternoon. She felt sorry that in the meantime Prospect House was barred as a place of call. She dared not venture thither lest she should encounter Hew Kessock. What more likely than that he should spend the better part of the Sunday with his lady-love?

"Everything has gone to rack and ruin about poor Ballochean," said Meg sadly to Van Leyden, as she pushed open the trellis gate between the high beech hedges which shut off "My Lady's Garden" from the shrubberies. "I believe this garden was made by my great-great-grand-mother, who, by the way, had some connection with Holland. I believe her husband was an exile there for some years—but I'm rocky in history."

"You are vat, mademoiselle?" he asked, puzzled by the unusual word.

"I mean I am not a well-read person. Indeed, I am hopelessly ignorant," she said, smiling into his kind face. "I ought to know the whole story of my great-great-grandmother—only I don't. All I can tell you is that she made this garden, and that it was called the Dutch Garden in her time. I suppose you've many like it in Holland, Mr. Van Leyden?"

The old man stood still, leaning heavily on his notched stick, and his eye seemed to twinkle comically.

"It is a sweet spot and a true garden, mademoiselle, for it offers retreat. But, belief me, I haf nefer seen anything in ze least resembling it in Holland."

"Of course it's all run to seed now. Just look at these box hedges and at the queer trees which used to be quite trig beasts and birds when they were properly clipped and kept! Now they are like ragged spectres. Come here in the bright moonlight, Mr. Van Leyden, and you would be quite frightened!"

"You shall bring me, mademoiselle, and I shall enjoy a new sensation."

"Have you never been frightened in your life, then?"

"I cannot remember. My heart has melted within me, but not with fear. It vould take mooch to frighten you, mademoiselle!"

"Oh, I don't know. Just lately I seem to have got very downhearted."

"Ach, yees—and no vonder! It is lifting up you need, mademoiselle—some von to care for you and spend himself for you. All this trouble about ze place is not for you, mademoiselle. Ve, I hope, haf come to end it."

Meg stood still on the moss-grown path between the box hedges, and looked at him searchingly. She really liked the old man. He had won her confidence, and she wanted desperately to know just what lay in front.

"Mr. Van Leyden, may I ask you a few questions, if you please?"

"You may, mademoiselle, for certain; and it vill be my extreme pleasure to answer them."

"Well, why have you come here?"

"Ve haf come, mademoiselle, to see you, of course."

"Oh, yes, I understand that. But that's not quite what I mean. I know so much—but not enough. I suppose that my father has borrowed large sums of money from you—that you hold what is called a mortgage on Ballochean."

"Yees, mademoiselle, dat is so."

"And what does that mean quite? I do want to know, Mr. Van Leyden—in fact, I must know, for I am miserable in the dark!"

"It means, mademoiselle—since it is ze truth you vill haf, dat Ballochean is no longer your father's. It belongs to me."

"Oh!" said Meg with a little gasp. "Is it so bad as that?"

"It has been going on for long, mademoiselle—let me see?—for quite seven years. And your father has been—shall ve say—foolish right through. And now he cannot redeem himself."

"You have come to turn us out," cried Meg, with all the passion of her soul in her vibrant young voice, which had lost its caressing sweetness, its singular charm.

"You put it harshly, mademoiselle," said the old man suavely. "Haf ve, zen, made so poor an impression on your mind?"

"No, no. But what you say can have only that meaning. If Ballochean belongs to you—then it cannot belong any more to us, and we shall have to go. It is terrible!"

The man looked with compassion into the girl's wrung face. It was long since a woman-creature had interested him so deeply, and he had said repeatedly to his nephew that she was the only bit of gold in the house of Ballochean.

"You are right so far, my dear mademoiselle; but there are other ways. It is possible for us to share, for instance—to make some compromise—to vat you English call gif and take," he observed shrewdly.

"I don't understand," said Meg hotly, "for if we have nothing left what have we to give?"

"Listen, my dear, and I vill explain," said the old man, with a great and quiet patience, which was not without its effect on the girl's troubled soul. "It is not so cold. Shall ve sit on dat old bench at ze end of ze box-walk? Zen perhaps some spirit of ze old-time quiet will descend upon us."

His picturesque language—so different from and so much more interesting than that she was accustomed to hear—acted like a charm. Somehow she had the feeling that this strange old man, who doubtless had come into her life for some purpose, was more than disposed to be friendly towards her.

He was rich, he was powerful, he had all in his hands. She must listen to what he had to say.

So she sat with him there on the gnarled old wooden bench in the mellow glow of the autumn sunshine, and waited.

"Listen, dear mademoiselle. It is of myself I vould talk, and for that I must go a little back."

"Vonce in ze long-ago time, ven I vas a young man and ze blood vas hot, I lofed von voman who had for me ze kind vords. For a little time all vas vell. Zen my brother, whom I had lofed and vorked for, stepped in and stole her from me."

"How wicked of him! But that happens every day in this horrible world, Mr. Van Leyden," cried Meg, with the sting of her own hurt in her soul.

"Ach, yees, it is so. But, in my case, mademoiselle, there vas ze most lying treachery. I vas made vat you call black in ze eyes of ze voman I lofed; and in ze end she became my brother's vife. It vas as I expected and knew—for that type of man can be true to none. He broke her heart, and she died in a few short years, leafing her sons to my care. For some years before she died she had gone back to her old profession of music—my Minna—and she sang under her own name. That is vy he is called Morris Bien, and not Van Leyden, vich vas his father's name."

An indefinable change crossed Meg's vivid face. It was as if her warm interest had been suddenly dashed.

"Oh! is he her son?" she asked.

"He is ze boy. I haf had him vith me since he vas eleven. And he is a good lad. I can vouch for him vith my soul!"

"And you never married?" said Meg quickly, anxious only to escape the tale of Morris Bien's good qualities.

"Ach, no; for ven ze heart is seared—as mine vas—there is no more spring. But I do not complain. Somevere my Minna and I vill meet vonce more and be in ze happy fields together."

Had some of the clients of Auguste Van Leyden heard these extraordinary utterances they would undoubtedly have been struck dumb with amazement.

The incongruity between these and his profession struck even Meg Hamilton, and she gazed fascinatedly at his rugged face, which bore traces of the emotion called up by the memories that he was evoking for her benefit.

"I came to London ven ze misfortune of ze heart overtook me, and I vas for many years in business in ze great city. I prospered as men prosper who haf nothings at stake. Afterwards I followed to Glasgow a great friend of your nationality, who helped to restore my faith in my kind. And dat is my story, mademoiselle, to vich you haf had ze goodness to listen."

"It is all very sad," murmured Meg in a voice of astonishing softness, "and nobody would ever dream that you had it all shut up inside of you."

He chuckled at her expression, and then patted her arm reassuredly.

"I tell it you, mademoiselle, because it vill help you perhaps to understand. I vell know how it is in ze world—how ze men in my business are credited with no bowels. If all were laid bare, mademoiselle, ve very often vould be found to be ze victims of ze folly and dishonesty of people who haf no use for ze honour. Unfortunately it cannot be helped dat for ze great mass of human veakness it is ze few who haf to pay."

As this bit of philosophy fell from the old money-lender's lips, the momentary softness disappeared from Meg's face, and it became set in a kind of dull resentment. It brought her back sharply to the point at issue.

She had had no hand in the scattering of Ballochean, yet something told her it was she who would have to pay.

"Now ve come back to ze question of gif and take," he began after a moment's pause. "Tell me, mademoiselle, do you remember coming a long time ago—it vas, I think, in ze summer of last year—to my offices in Bath Street, Glasgow?"

"I remember going to an office with my father one day, but I am certain I did not see you, Mr. Van Leyden. If I had I should have recognised you directly you came last time to Ballochean."

"Dat is so. Ve had a stormy interview dat day, and your father showed himself vithout reason. I am obliged to say so to you, mademoiselle, for, now ve are embarked on dis discussion—von of such high importance—ve must shirk noting."

"Well—and what happened?"

"You do not remember seeing my nephew coming through ze room vere you sat to wait?"

Meg shook her head.

"He might have passed through, but I have no recollection of having seen him," she replied truthfully.

Her answer seemed to disappoint the old man.

"Ach, dat is how it is ven a man puts his heart in ze hollow of von voman's leetle hand! She sees him not, but leafes him to despair."

It was impossible to mistake the significance of his words, and Meg flushed uneasily. But she could think of nothing to say.

"Listen, mademoiselle. Since ze time ze boy first saw you he has not been ze same. For vy?—you haunt him day and night. At first he fight against it, and I know notings. But because he is so good and von apple of mine eye, I vatch him and see dat he has sometings on his mind. I put it to him—oh, yees, scores of times—for he has been such a son to me dat I vould get him ze moon, if I had it in my power. I could nefer in a long day of weeks and years tell you of all ze goodness of dat boy. He is kind, he is true, he is straight, he vould not hurt von leetle fly!"

Meg remained silent yet rooted to the spot, waiting with a kind of sickening apprehension for what was coming.

"For your sake only, mademoiselle—none other—ve keep on doing vat you call obliging Mynheer Hamilton, who has strange ideas of right and wrong, and no soul above money. How he came to father a pearl like you none knows!"

There was something merciless in this diagnosis of her father's character, and though Meg felt that she ought in loyalty to protest she was still held dumb.

"Ve go on obliging till everything is svallowed up. Zen the crisis must come. It came last week ven ve come down here to see ze place and to talk tings ofer. Before ve come dat time Morris speaks out and tells me vat he vishes most in ze vide vorld."

Meg rose and placed her hand to her faintly beating heart.

"All this cannot interest me, Mr. Van Leyden. I think we had better be getting back to the house."

"Von minute more, mademoiselle. Ze time has come to speak. I varn him dat vat he seeks is impossible—dat von born as you are vill not mate with a foreigner, dat there is all of tradition and family pride to conquer. But ze boy he heeds not. Zen I tell him dat in such a marriage there could be leetle chance of happiness."

"What marriage?" cried Meg, and her high, clear young voice seemed to beat upon the air.

Her eyes were flashing, but they never for a moment left the old man's kindly, earnest face.

"Ze marriage I tell you of—between you and Morris Bien. It is ze way out! Marry him. Make two men—ze old von and ze young—happy, and all ve possess ve lay at your feet. Ve make all right for your father, and ve tie all up tight for you and your children. All dat, mademoiselle, you haf in your power. Ze destinies of so many lie in ze palms of your leetle hands."

"You must be mad, Mr. Van Leyden," she said quietly, but her voice cut like a whip. "Marry your nephew, Morris Bien! Why, I would much rather marry you. I must go. If I stay I shall say what I might be sorry for."

She turned and fled, the old man looking after her with a strange expression on his rugged face. Leaning his hands on the knob of his stick, he uplifted his eyes to the clear vault of the sky, and spoke softly—

"Minna, forgif me, I haf fail."

CHAPTER XII

THE HAVEN

Robina Dunlop, housekeeper to David Sillars at Langdyke, took the opportunity when her master was dining out to spend the evening with a friend who was cook in one of the fine mansions built on the high ground above the Esplanade. She left in charge her niece, Ellen, a strapping damsel of nineteen, with rosy-red cheeks, a tremendous appetite, and a good capacity for work.

About half-past eight o'clock, and not more than an hour after her aunt and her master had left the house, the girl was disturbed by a tremendous peal at the front door bell.

Ellen was without fear, for no marauders could actually get to the house door without first passing the porter at the gate as well as the watch-dog on the chain in the yard. She therefore approached the front door without the smallest hesitation, only devoured with curiosity regarding the intruder who was seeking admission at such an untimely hour.

Her master had a few bachelor friends who dropped in of an evening for a talk or a quiet hand at whist, but the majority of these would that evening be at the dinner, which was of a public character, taking place in the Tontine Hotel.

Ellen took the precaution to turn the gas in the hall full on before she undid the door, in order that she might be better able to see who stood without.

"Scotty," the little Aberdeen terrier, accompanied her along the passage, all the bristles of his brindled back standing straight up on end and his ears being fully cocked.

To Ellen's surprise, she beheld standing just within the porch the figure of a woman carrying a bag in her hand.

"I want to see Mr. Sillars, if you please. Is he in the house?"

"No, an' that he is no'. He's dinin' oot," answered Ellen; and then, to her no little amazement, she recognised both face and figure as belonging to Miss Hamilton of Ballochean, with whose appearance, of course, she was perfectly familiar.

"Mercy me, Miss Hamilton, is it you?" she inquired, with that friendly interest which, though resented by some, when exhibited by a maid is seldom intended for presumption.

"Yes. May I come in for a moment? Is Mrs. Dunlop in?"

"No. Auntie has gone up the Lyle Road to see a neighbour," answered the girl. "Come in, of course. Have ye just come from Ayr?"

"Yes. I'm very much disappointed not to find Mr. Sillars. I made sure I would catch him at his dinner."

"So ye would on an ordinary nicht, Miss; but he's at the Tontine at a big denner, an' he has to make a speech. He telt auntie when she gaed up to lay oot his things that, if it hadna been for that, he wouldna have gane. An' he said he wouldna be late."

Meg drew off her gloves, looked restlessly round, and appeared wholly at a loss. Ellen regarded her with sympathetic interest, which, however, offered no solution of a knotty problem.

"I don't know what to do. I simply must see Mr. Sillars. He said he would not be late? What does he mean by that?"

"He means ten o'clock. He hates thae lang denners wi' speeches—I've often heard him say it. There's a nice fire in the library. The dinin'-room ane was let oot efter lunch as the maister wouldna be usin' the room the nicht again."

Meg set down her bag, looked at the leather watch-strap on her wrist, and gave an impatient shake of her head.

"It's only twenty minutes to nine. I shall have to wait an hour and a half."

" Oh, but ye'll be stoppin' the nicht—will ye no', Miss ?—seein' ye have brocht a bag ? "

Meg looked at the bag, and then at the girl, and felt sundry qualms which had not visited her since she started out in a moment of desperation to seek her only deliverer.

" Well, I must wait. Nobody but Mr. Sillars can tell me what to do."

Meg set down her bag, which Ellen promptly lifted to a far corner of the hall. She then opened the library door.

A warm, comfortable air met them, which was grateful to Meg, for an early frost had set a chill in the atmosphere, of which she had been conscious as she rode in the open cab from the station.

She was none too warmly clad, having come off in her homespun coat and skirt and her old hat of suede leather, which, though becoming enough, could not be said to be smart wear.

She looked round interestedly on the snug apartment where Sillars spent most of his leisure after working hours were over.

" Are ye no' hungary, Miss Meg ? You've missed your denner. There's plenty in the pantry. Let me set oot something for ye in the dining-room. I'm sure the maister and Auntie Beenie, too, would like me to do that."

" I shouldn't mind a cup of tea," said Meg gratefully. " I forget when I had food before. I believe it was yesterday. Yes, thank you, I'll take anything you like to set before me."

The girl ran off, delighted to do her service. She was too simple a creature to ponder on the strangeness of this visit ; she was only too glad of it as it served to break the monotony of a long evening alone.

She foraged well in the pantry, and made tea, too, and set out a very appetising meal.

While the girl was thus engaged, Meg was taking an inventory of David's room. It interested her immensely, as everything concerning him must needs do, since he was going to be of such tremendous importance in her life.

It was a good-sized room. In order to obtain the space he wanted Sillars had knocked down a partition wall and thrown the drawing-room and the back bedroom into one. The effect, if long and narrow, was quaint. Books were everywhere, and a few fine etchings in ebony frames on the sea-green walls, a warm red Turkey carpet on the floor, an immense leather-covered sofa, and big easy-chairs that simply yawned invitations to rest combined to produce a general air of luxurious comfort.

An old-fashioned fender-stool with bead roses on it was the only feminine touch in a man's room. Meg guessed that it had come from Kildoon.

She remembered having heard that David's mother had been very fond of the little house at the works, and had paid more visits to it than her circle in Ayrshire approved. Oddly enough, the girl's thoughts continued to dwell on her, assisted, perhaps, by the sight of a very lovely miniature which stood on the mantelpiece, flanked by two old-fashioned cut-glass candlesticks with hanging drops.

By the time Ellen, visibly inflated with a sense of her own importance at having to do the honours of the house to such an unusual guest, came to summon her to the dining-room, Meg was beginning to feel physically comfortable and mentally at home. She was so safe there under the roof of David Sillars, so remote from menace or hurt, that she had no room for anything but thankfulness.

What he had said in the Howff Wood when she had thrown herself on his mercy from a purely mean and selfish motive she had already forgotten or forgiven. He would never, she was sure, cast her off now that she was in the depths of such unutterable woe !

" The pheasant was made for the maister's lunch, but he only ate a bit o' bread an' cheese," Ellen explained with pride in the good show her table presented. " An' here's cauld ham, an' I've boiled twa eggs, Do ye think that'll be enough ? "

" Hardly," said Meg, with a little twinkle in her eye. " I believe I require a joint of beef and a few pies, or something even more substantial ! Why, it's lovely, Ellen, and I don't know how to thank you ! "

Much gratified, Ellen withdrew, thinking gloriously of the surprise that awaited her aunt, and congratulating herself on her good luck in coming in for this fine adventure.

Then Meg addressed herself with a will to what she imagined the best meal she had ever tasted in her life. She had had no tea, and lunch at Ballochean had been a mere farce owing to the strange conditions prevailing in the house; and in her anxiety to reach the haven where she would be she had not paused to seek even a light refreshment on the way.

When she had eaten enough, though not enough to satisfy Ellen's jealous expectations, she rang the bell, profusely thanked the girl again, and went back to the library to wait for Mr. Sillars.

"Would you not like to wash your hands, Miss Meg, and put off your hat? I've ta'en your bag up to the spare bedroom an' lighted the fire."

Meg thought she would. It was now nearly ten o'clock, and it was hardly likely that David Sillars would deny her shelter for the night. She followed Ellen upstairs into the somewhat small bachelor chamber which was all that Sillars had to offer in the way of sleeping accommodation to his friends.

The fire made it cheerful, however, and after Meg had washed and brushed her hair she felt better. She hesitated about removing her boots, to which the good Ayrshire clay still clung, and she finally decided to keep them on.

When she sat down before the library fire once more, and when the heat crept about her, she felt drowsiness creeping over her, and, in spite of sundry efforts to keep awake, she fell sound asleep in David's big chair with her feet resting on his mother's beaded stool and her head lying against the cushion that his mother's hands had embroidered. Her sleep was that of sheer healthy fatigue, and she heard nothing until Sillars stood before her in the flesh. He returned about twenty minutes past ten to find his housekeeper waiting for him in the hall with a certain mysterious air.

"Somebody has come, sir. She's in the library—Miss Hamilton frae Ballochean."

In the act of unfastening his fur-trimmed overcoat, Sillars paused, staring incredulously.

"Miss Hamilton from Ballochean here?—in this house, Robina! You must be dreaming!"

"No, sir, she's there richt enough. I gaed up to High View to see my auld neibour, Betsey Templeton, and Ellen let her in aboot half-past aicht. She was baith tired and hungry, and the girl got her her supper and made the spare bedroom ready, which showed mair gumption than I thocht she had. Ha'e ye ony orders, sir?"

"I don't know. Don't go to bed yet, Robina. I must see Miss Hamilton. It's the most extraordinary thing I've ever heard! Something must have happened at Ballochean."

He spoke quietly, but he was seriously disturbed.

Robina disappeared through the baize door to discuss with Ellen the portent of this unusual visit. Being a woman of greater experience than her niece, Robina was perfectly well aware that Miss Hamilton's action was not only out of the usual, but that it was open to very severe criticism and question on the part of the busybodies of Ayr and its neighbourhood.

"Something'll come ooten this, Ellen," she said solemnly. "Maybe a mistress for Kildoon."

Ellen simply bristled with excitement, being then in the throes of a threepenny novelette in which the hero and heroine made a runaway match which was wholly uncalled for and most injudicious, but in which they had her entire sympathy.

Sillars walked into the dining-room, looked rather longingly at the syphon of soda and whisky decanter put ready for him on the sideboard. He felt the need of it to brace him for what was in front of him, but it was characteristic of the man that he should turn resolutely away from it. He had dined well, and the one glass of champagne he had permitted himself had already lost its evanescent effect.

He was looking absolutely his very best. Evening dress became him, and he was able to wear it with a certain distinction which many of his compeers envied. His tall, slim figure seemed to gain both height and grace, and the expanse of white in no way shamed the colour of his face.

He pushed his fingers through his hair, thrust one hand into his trousers pocket, muttered something under his breath, and finally pulling himself together made for the library door.

But there he hesitated, as a man might hesitate before taking some irrevocable plunge. He did not minimise the significance of the foolish thing that Meg Hamilton had done in seeking the protection of his bachelor abode. It would take a good deal of explaining away; in some parts of the county of Ayr no amount of explanation would ever condone or wipe it out.

Ellen had lit the centre lamp on the table, but the fire had burned low. The fragrant smell of the half-burned log that had fallen on the hearth greeted him as he opened the door, but for the moment he did not see Meg.

He closed the door softly and walked forward, and there she was sleeping like a child, partly curled up in the big chair, with her dimpled chin resting on her hand, and her feet, with the brown, clay-stained brogues, on the fender-stool!

Her face was softly flushed, and all the childlike charm which so often had been the undoing of Sillars stood out. Her ruffled hair had the gleam of gold on it, and it seriously disturbed him to see a tear, not yet dried, on her cheek.

"Meg!" he called rather loudly—"Meg, wake up! Why have you come here?"

It was a very bald greeting, but it served to arouse the sleeping girl, and she opened her eyes. Then, seeing him, she pulled herself together with a start and sprang up. As she did so the unbidden tear that had lain on her cheek fell on her hand and was indignantly shaken off.

"Oh, David, please don't look at me like that!" she cried. "Be glad to see me! I had just to come."

"Why?" he asked in a grave, judicial voice. "It was a foolish thing to do. Where have you come from?"

"From Ayr, of course, and I got all wrong with the trains and things. I had no idea Greenock was so far away and so difficult to get at. I seemed to be hours and hours in getting here."

"I'm sorry. But why have you come? Has anything happened at Ballochean?"

"Oh! yes—everything has happened; and I'm never going back there as long as I live! Don't keep on looking at me like that, David, as if you wanted to put me in a black box and send me right away again. I've only come to ask you to give me Ludo's address and to lend me enough money to let me go out after him. And could you let me go to-morrow, please, for I don't ever want to see father or Guy again. I must get clean away before they know where I am."

Sillars perceived that something fresh and terrible must have happened at Ballochean to account for the girl's overwrought state of mind.

He did not want to hear what it was. He would have given five years of his life cheerfully to escape ever hearing it. But what could he do?

She stood there in front of him with fingers hotly interlacing, with the note of rebellion and determination sounding in her clear young voice, and he was the scapegoat for the moment!

His voice softened in spite of himself, for surely under high heaven there could not at the moment be a more forlorn and desolate creature than Meg Hamilton, who had burned her boats behind her!

"What you ask can't be done, my dear. There is no place for a woman where Ludo has gone. He will be living in the bungalow with three white men, and all the others on the plantation are black."

"Oh, never mind. I'm not afraid of men—at least, not of some men," she added, hastily correcting herself. "If there's a bungalow—that's a house, isn't it?—there must be something in it that a woman can do. I could learn to cook and to wash clothes, and I should want very little for myself. You must help me, David, for in all the world there is only you."

Sillars glanced at the clock, and took swift counsel within himself.

It was now twenty minutes to eleven o'clock, and it was impossible that Meg could leave the house that night.

How he wished he had obeyed the secret injunction of the soul that had warned him against going to the dinner at the Tontine! Had he been in the house when she arrived it would have been possible to have made some arrangement to dispose of her. But now nothing could be done. To take her to the hotel would but widen the area of discussion and comment.

" Sit down, Madge, until I speak to Mrs. Dunlop. You'll have to stay here till the morning, of course."

He did not like his task, for he had a natural pride which forbade his discussing private and intimate affairs with a servant. But Robina Dunlop was the soul of prudence and reliability, and he felt that he had no alternative but to trust her unreservedly.

He walked along the narrow passage and pushed open the swing-door.

" Are you there, Mrs. Dunlop ? "

" Yes, sir, comin'," she answered with alacrity, and presently she appeared, ready to hear what he had to say.

He motioned her into the dining-room.

" This is rather an awkward thing that has happened, Robina, and we must make the best of it," he said quietly. " Miss Hamilton has run away from Ballochean. She has not yet told me very much, but I gather that there has been some sort of a quarrel between her and her father, and that she considers it irremediable. Of course, that is a mistake. I will take her right back in the morning."

" Yes, sir. I'm sorry for her, and hae aye been. Ballochean has never been a place for a lass-bairn since the mistress died."

" You never spoke a truer word, Robina," said Sillars, inwardly blessing the woman for her quick understanding. " She came here to-night to ask me—what do you think ? "

" I'm sure I couldna say, sir."

" To send her out to Jamaica to her brother Ludo ! Of course, that is altogether out of the question. There are no women on the plantation to which he is going, and even if there were, it would be impossible for her to go there."

" I should imagine so, sir. Among blecks !—the very thocht gi'es ye the cauld shudders."

" I have told her that. Presently I shall go and explain to her how imperative it is that she should go back to Ballochean in the morning. I came to tell you what I have done and to ask you whether her room is ready."

" Yes, sir, I telt ye it was."

" Ah, that is good. Well—one other thing. Miss Hamilton has done a foolish thing, Robina, which, if it became known, might easily be misconstrued. She is not like other young ladies of her age and position—she acts on impulse simply because she has never had a mother since her childhood to teach or guide her."

" I understand, sir; and it will be necessary for us to keep quate about it, you mean ? "

" Precisely. In the meantime, at least. I am very much obliged to you, Robina. I suppose Ellen can be relied on ? "

" She can," said Robina grimly. " She's a besom in some things, but her tongue's not that bad. I'll see that it's clipped aboot this. I'm very sorry for Miss Meg, sir, and I hope you'll be able to help her. Onybody that has to live wi' the Laird o' Ballochean noo needs baith pity and help."

Once more Sillars devoutly thanked her.

" You can go to bed now, for I must hear the story of what actually happened from Miss Hamilton's lips. I could dispense with the hearing of it, but probably when I suggest that she should go back to-morrow she'll have something to advance against doing it. But it is the only thing to do."

" I can sit up, sir, if you would like me to show her to her room after you've dune speakin'. I'll send Ellen to her bed and tak' my stockin' by the kitchen fire. I'm not a bit sleepy. I had tea at Betsey's at half-past nine, and that aye waukens me up."

Sillars nodded in acquiescence, and, as he walked back to the library, he wondered that he had not realised even in the ten years of Robina's faithful service all the sterling qualities she possessed.

When he re-entered the library Meg was sitting with her elbows on her knees and her chin on her hands, glowering into the still glowing heart of the fire.

" Wouldn't you like to go to bed, Madge ? " he asked kindly, feeling that he would give much if he could postpone further explanation until the morning.

She gave a start of defiance.

" I can't go to bed, David, until I've told you what happened. Don't you want to hear? You must hear, or you'll never understand what has made me run away. You couldn't think of anything half so awful as has happened, if you tried for a year of days!"

"What's that? Has your father married some impossible person, and thrust you out?" he inquired, hoping that that might actually prove to be the case.

"No, no; nothing to do with him. It's only poor me, the everlasting scapegoat, that is in the toils. Hear what happened."

She began to talk with all her might, sitting bolt upright, with her firm young right hand gripping the arm of the chair like a vice, and with her eyes glowing like twin stars in her head.

CHAPTER XIII

THE DELIVERER

"DAVID, you remember my telling you about those men who came to Ballochean—old Van Leyden and Morris Bien?" she asked, with her stormy eyes fixed on Sillars' face.

"Yes, of course," he said shortly; and he might have added with perfect truth that he forgot little or nothing she ever told him.

"Well, they came again last week. It was on Friday. But what day is this?"

"This is Tuesday."

"Oh, yes; I could not remember. You see it is a million years since yesterday!"

"These strange visitors have been at Ballochean again," he repeated, trying to lead her back, as if she had been a child, into some definite path from which she had strayed.

"Yes. They came on Friday. Papa was careful and troubled about them, just as he had been before, and I am sure there never has been so much talk about food in Ballochean since I can remember! Why, I had to spend an entire morning in Ayr, going from one shop to another with a piece of paper and pencil in hand to get all the things that he thought necessary for their entertainment. They arrived on Friday in time for dinner, and we had the same sort of entertainment as before: I sitting at the head of the table with one on each side of me, and papa at the bottom glowering up at me, so that I might keep myself civil. It was quite easy to do that with the old man, for, if he were not a Jew and obsessed with all sorts of strange and perfectly impossible ideas about things which he could never understand, he would be quite a dear. But, somewhere behind it all, he is a gentleman."

"For which much thanks," murmured Sillars furiously, wondering what he was going to hear, and already, figuratively speaking, on the warpath.

"But his nephew—I can't tell you what he is like, and I am not going to try. He is over-dressed, oppressively polite, and most—most damnably clever!"

"Madge! Madge!"

"David! David! this is a night on which I beg leave to use strong language. Give me leave. Don't pull me up or harrow me till I've done! Then do what you like. I didn't like it when they were there before, David. But this time, from the moment I knew they were in the house, I was afraid. Can you imagine it, David? I, Meg Hamilton, was afraid! I don't know why or of what, but the fear was there, like a horrid little snake wriggling all over me and showing a nasty head and hideous eyes and a forked tongue! I just had the feeling that, I am sure, the poor wee bunnies have when they are in the snare. How often I've taken them out and bandaged up their poor legs! But nobody is going to take the trouble to open the gin to let me out."

"I'm waiting to hear what happened; and, if you please, may I smoke while you are telling me?" asked Sillars, moving uneasily against the mantelpiece, where he stood with his hands thrust deep in his pockets, an odd, deep wrinkle between his level brows.

"Smoke? Oh, yes—I shall love it. I've come from an atmosphere of oppressive politeness, where everybody bowed himself before me to the earth, as the sheaves of his brethren did before Joseph's sheaf."

Sillars gave a queer smile as he opened his cigarette-case.

He felt himself being slowly worked up into a state of excitement, and the extraordinary vividness and picturesqueness of the girl's language, combined with something electric which seemed to emanate from her, produced a dramatic atmosphere which was at once stimulating and exhausting.

"The Wax Figure, in particular, was prodigiously polite, but I kept him at a distance. To escape conversation with him I devoted myself to the uncle, and we had tremendous talks about everything under heaven. That went on till Sunday, when it began. We were walking in 'My Lady's Garden,' and he began to tell me the story of his life. It was like something from a story-book, David—all about his Minna who was not true to him but married his brother. If I could set it all down just as he spoke it it would read like a penny novelette. It was all told with a purpose. The Wax Figure, David, is the son of the woman who played him false and of the brother who deceived him. Yet he forgave everything and took the boy to live with him and brought him up. I forget the tragedy that went in front. There was something, anyway, that the old man had explained. He bore no malice, however, just the same as they do in story-books, but never in real life. On the contrary, he brought up this imp of darkness in the lap of luxury and made him a money-lender—only they don't call it that among themselves. They are financiers! And Van Leyden says that Morris Bien's proper place is in Frankfurt, where financiers are made, and where he ought to be at the head of his house. Then I asked him why his nephew didn't go to Frankfurt and stop there, but he did not know what to answer.

"After a small while, however, he began to explain at great length why they preferred to stay in Scotland, and to tell why they want to have a permanent home in it. The home they want—and have got—is Ballochean!"

"No!" cried Sillars. "Surely it hasn't gone so far as that."

"Much further, David—oh, much, much further—and I'm coming to that, if I can find the words that will tell it. All this picturesque story was told for my benefit—don't you see?—and presently he came to the crux of the matter. They've got Ballochean. They can take it from us now and turn us out at a moment's notice without a stick of furniture or a red cent to our name! He did not use these words, David, for princes of finance clothe their ultimatums in flowery language fit for the ears of a woman—when they happen to be dealing with one. It would have been all splendid from the point of view of a listener or a looker-on—a fascinating game to watch, but not for the insect in the toils! He said they were homeless men, and that they longed for a home; and then he began to say—how can I tell it to you, David? My tongue is paralysed with the shame of it!—he began to explain how, once last year when I had been with papa at their offices in Bath Street, Morris Bien had seen me and how he had never since forgotten me. When they came the first time to Ballochean he saw me again, and then, I suppose, he—or the two of them together—conceived the monstrous scheme which Van Leyden put before me. Are you following me, David?"

"I am, and I think I can dispense with the rest," said Sillars, and his voice sounded a little thick as it came from between his clenched teeth.

"Oh, but you must hear it! I've been through it, David, and I don't let you off so easily. He told me that his nephew aspired to marry me—I think that was the word he used—and that, if I would accept his hand and heart, Ballochean would be left in the family, the only difference being that Morris Bien would hang up his hat. There would be plenty of money forthcoming, and everybody would be nice and comfortable—including, I suppose, Mrs. Morris Bien!"

Sillars muttered something under his breath, and his cheeks went a little paler.

"But, of course, there was but one answer to that, Madge?"

"I had only one answer, and I gave it to him. I can't remember how or in what words. They rushed out anyway, and I didn't leave him in any doubt as to my meaning. Later in the day I had to go through it again, but in a worse and more sickening form with the Image himself, and it seemed to put madness in my blood. Everything went against me on Sunday, David," she added, and her eyes, burning with strange fires, travelled wistfully to his face. "I had nobody to speak to. I rode desperately to Ayr. But all the Sandersons were out, and, of course, I can't go any more to Prospect House. So I had just to wend my way back again and shut myself up. I did not go down to dinner on Sunday night, nor did I see them on Monday morning. They left about eleven o'clock. I watched them from behind the schoolroom curtains, and when they were gone I began to cry, David, as if I had been a kid. I could not stop for a whole hour."

"But it's all over, my dear," said Sillars, and from his voice, though it had lost its pleasant cadence, nothing of his inward feeling could be discerned.

"Over!" She laughed shrilly. "That's only the first chapter! It's going to be continued in our next!—and so on for ever and ever. That is why I am here."

"But surely they took their answer like men. You did not leave them in any doubt?"

"No, and that I did not! But after papa came back from driving them to the station there was the most awful scene. Heavens, how I lived through it I don't know! There was papa on his knees crying to me one minute, and the next storming and raging like a fiend!"

"But, in the name of Heaven, why?"

"Because I refused to save him and Ballochean!"

"He would be willing for you to marry that outsider, Meg?"

"Willing! It's what he wants more than anything in the world. And more, he said that he had told them not to accept any answer of mine as final, declaring that I would do as he wanted, if they would only give me time, that they had rushed the thing too much, and that they must come again."

"Oh, my dear, it is unthinkable!"

"It happened, David—every dreadful moment of it. I hated my own father so much that I don't know how I was prevented from taking down a rifle and killing him!"

"But Guy? Surely he had more spirit and a true sense of the enormity of the bargain!"

Meg shrugged her shoulders.

"It made Guy very sick. And, though he did his best, he is without backbone, and he is afraid of his own skin. There are no men in the house of Ballochean."

"Well, and what happened?"

"Oh, the storm rose and raged. Papa accused me of having no natural affection, and urged that it was a very small thing that he was asking—only that I should marry a perfectly irreproachable young man of good family and enormous wealth. He pointed out that there is nothing in the world but money that is worth thinking about, and he asked me how I would like to go out as a housemaid or a nurse, which was what must happen soon if I persisted in my refusal to marry Morris Bien. They will foreclose now, I suppose. So, you see, I had just to come away. I would not have come here, David, for I know how deadly sick you are of me, if there had been anybody else in the wide world I could think of. But there is none. And it is not very much I ask—only enough money to take me to Ludo, or somewhere else, where nobody can find me. And I'll pay it back, David, every penny of it, if you'll only trust your old pal so far."

Sillars threw his half-burnt cigarette into the fire. There ensued a strange silence, during which Meg sat glowering beyond him into the red embers, her face white, save where the fierce red streak of indignation and womanly shame burned in either cheek.

"David," she said at last in a low, thrilling voice, "do you think there is any power under heaven that can make me marry Morris Bien?"

"No, my dear, there is none," he answered clearly and firmly. "Now that you have told me the story you will go upstairs to your bed and try to sleep. You are looking thin and worn, and you'll have a breakdown if you're not careful."

"A breakdown—then perhaps I should die! That, perhaps, would be the easiest way out. But I don't want to die yet, David; I am not old, and I love to live."

Sillars never forgot the pathos of these words. She was nothing but a child in heart, and the unconventionality of the thing she had done in throwing herself on his mercy here, in his lonely house, troubled her not at all. It had not once occurred to her even to imagine that anybody might wonder or cavil at her action.

He was her only friend—proved through all the years. Therefore she was in his house.

She rose obediently, and, now that the excitement had died down and that the strain had relaxed, the pallor of her face was very marked.

"I don't think that I've ever been tired in all my life until to-day. I could ride to hounds for nine hours at a stretch without feeling it. I suppose, however, that after twenty one begins to feel old."

Sillars smiled queerly, but his face seemed wrung.

" Twenty is a great age, I believe. But it is so long since I passed it that I've quite forgotten how I felt."

" You will never grow old, David ! " she said impulsively. " And you look lovely in these clothes, which make most men look like waiters."

The queer smile lingered on Sillars' face, for he was remembering how not long ago she had hurled his years at him in the Howff Wood ! But this was no time for such reminders or recriminations.

" You will do something to-morrow, David ? " she said swiftly, touching his arm as he began to move towards the door.

" Yes," he said curtly ; " you may rely on it that I'll do something to-morrow—but I can't say exactly what. I'll have a pipe now and thrash it out."

" Thank you so much. Good-night, David. I don't need to ask questions or to bother any more, for when you look like that and say you will do it, it is as good as done."

" We must find Mrs. Dunlop, my dear," he said, opening the door quickly. " She hasn't gone to bed. She'll get what you want and look after you generally."

" I don't need anything in the world but just to sleep, David, and to wake up knowing I am here," she answered as they passed out of the room.

Mrs. Dunlop, on the alert, came through the swing-door and was ready to offer such services as was in her power.

" Take Miss Hamilton to her room, Mrs. Dunlop, and get her everything she wants. I'll see you when you come down. I'm going to have a pipe," her master said.

" Yes, sir. I've been up seeing to her fire and the room is very comfortable. Come, Miss Meg," she said, smiling in friendly fashion into the girl's white face.

In a quarter of an hour's time Meg was in bed, and the moment her head touched the pillow she was asleep.

" She's clean dune, sir," said Robina when she appeared in the library in answer to her master's request. " Whatever has happened to her ? "

" There has been trouble at Ballochean, Mrs. Dunlop. But you don't need me to tell you what the Laird is. Let Miss Hamilton sleep on till twelve o'clock to-morrow, if she likes ; and we'll take the two-ten back to Ayr. I shall have to see Mr. Hamilton. I am not at liberty to tell you more."

" No, sir, I quite understand. But it is time that somebody spoke up to Ballochean, for—ech me !—thon's a puir hoose for ony lass-bairn. An' so sweet an' gentle she is ! She was jist like a bairn wi' me up there. They lee aboot her at Ayr, Maister Sillars. Wicked lees ! I'll choke some o' them first time I get back ! "

These words were grateful to David Sillars, who had just tried to pull himself together and get the better of the astounding softness of his own heart.

" Ay, it's a pitiful case, Robina, and I'm not seeing the way out. But anyway, back to Ballochean she must go to-morrow, and the remembrance of this night must be wiped out as if it had never been."

" Yes, sir. Guid-nicht, an' dinna sit late, for ye are tired yersel'," she said with all the freedom of the faithful and privileged servant.

She closed the door softly and mounted to her own room on the stroke of midnight, thinking her own thoughts about what had happened at Ballochean.

Sillars paced the floor.

He could not sit still, for all his mind was in a tumult, and his pulses were bounding at fever pace. But, after a time, the strong pipe began to calm him, and he sat down quietly to think.

The story to which he had just listened would have been incredible had he heard it from any other lips.

To marry her to such a man—one of an alien race, a money-lender who had her price in his hand—it was appalling !

" But, by God ! " he cried, with clenched fists, " it shall not happen ! "

He and he alone would prevent it.

He sought diversion in trying to make a rough estimate of the value of Ballochean. It was an impoverished estate from which every saleable piece had long since passed into the hands of others. In the early days of Gavin Hamilton's succession it had been twice as large as it now was, for he did not suppose that its present acreage exceeded two thousand. But all these particulars should be in his hands before the close of another day, after he had had his interview with Gavin Hamilton.

There was something to be done before then, however—some words to be spoken to Meg which would decide the issue of the day. A strange upheaval of emotion was at his heart at the prospect.

But he set his square jaw firmly and laid his plans.

Had he spoken the words in the charged tenseness of the hour which she had spent with him in that very room, doubtless she would have agreed at once. But that was not Sillars' way. Though in some respects quixotic, he had abundance of worldly wisdom.

In the clear light of day Meg should have the situation put before her, and be told the only remedy.

Then he would act. Before the day closed her future would be assured.

He unlocked the front of the bookcase, and when the flap fell back it revealed an inner nest of drawers, all answering to a master-key. Here were stored all the private papers relating to his business in Greenock, which he kept quite separate from the accounts of the Kildoon estate.

He had the neat, rather precise, habits of the bachelor of orderly mind, and he could, at a moment's notice and without a moment's hesitation, lay his hands upon any document that might be required.

He found without difficulty the pass-book which set forth in simple terms his financial state. It was even more satisfactory than he had expected to find it. He had the wherewithal to lift the burden from Ballochean without so much as being hampered by the expenditure of the money required for the purpose. It only meant realising some more lucrative investments, but that he could afford to do.

He spent a considerable part of an hour over facts and figures, and by one o'clock he had arrived at a complete and definite intention.

He locked the desk, smoked another pipe, and finally turned off the lights and went upstairs on his way to bed.

He stepped lightly past the door of the room where the girl who had trusted him slept dreamlessly, conscious of nothing except that she had come to David with a heavy burden which, as so often aforetime, he had taken on his own shoulders and rolled clean away from her heart.

What he was going to do, or how he was going to do it she knew not—no, nor cared—as she had lain down to sleep.

The one deliverer was there and he would not fail!

CHAPTER XIV

THE WAY OUT

SILLARS kept a riding horse in the Greenock stable, and before seven o'clock next morning, though he had sat till after one, he was in the saddle. For a good hour he rode over the uplands, from the highest point of which, the sunshine being particularly clear, the loveliest panorama in the world unrolled itself before his eyes.

But its enchantment had lost its power to charm. In deep absorption he rode, now fast, now slowly, always brooding, uncertain what the issue of the day might be. Yet, though unconscious of it, undoubtedly in some way the subtle hush and spell of the pure morning, undefiled by man, enveloped and uplifted him, and by the time he reached his home he had ceased to fret. There was only one way out, and Meg must take it—nay, Meg and he together.

Mrs. Dunlop, busy about the breakfast table, came out to greet him.

"Miss Hamilton's up, sir. We heard her singing, an' I ran up wi' her hot water. She askit for a bath, an' she had it cauld. So I'm hurryin' up the breakfast."

Sillars nodded and proceeded upstairs to change his clothes.

Having a journey in front of him, he put on a suit of blue serge which he usually wore for travel purposes, though at Kildoon a shooting suit was his favourite garb. Sillars had all a rich bachelor's fastidiousness about his clothes, and he was never seen untidy or unsuitably dressed.

Singing with the dawn, he thought, as he mounted the stairs, her brief despair of the night swallowed up! How characteristic of that volatile heart—a heart which yet perhaps might be easily broken!

He was concerned with the mettle of it, since presently he hoped to have it in his care.

They met on the stroke of nine in the cheerful dining-room, and there was no shyness in the girl's eyes—only frank and grateful comradeship—as she bade him good-morning.

"I've had a glorious night, David—eight hours' solid sleep, and now I'm fit for anything! You have been riding, Mrs. Dunlop tells me. What energy! I am sure you set an example to all your folk here, just as you do at home. How nice it must be to do the right thing always and to find it easy!"

"That is the lot of few," he answered, as he set a chair for her and asked whether she would take coffee or tea.

"Oh! tea, always. Perhaps it is because we can't make coffee at our house. Papa is always going on about it. What will I eat? Well, anything I can get, David, thank you; but don't you wait on me! I am not used to it. It embarrasses me."

"You are a guest in my house," he reminded her, "an honoured guest."

Somehow, the tone in which he spoke made her grave, and she began to eat in silence with her eyes fixed on the plate.

"What a pity new days can't stay as they are born!" she said presently. "When they come to us they are for happiness. But quite soon we begin to fill them with all the strife of living, and then they become long and grey and sometimes intolerable. When I awoke this morning I felt like a child, but already age is creeping on."

Her mouth was smiling, but her eyes swam in tears.

Sillars could find no words by way of answer; but he tried to change the subject by referring to some item of intelligence staring at him from the front page of the morning paper.

"When you are here by yourself you have the paper propped up against the loaf," said Meg suddenly. "Put it there now, David, and I shall feel better. Do you go into business immediately after breakfast?"

"No—not till ten usually. The breakfast hour in Greenock is from nine to ten."

"And does everything stop—all the engines and chimneys and machines when all these fiendish whistles blow at one fell swoop at nine o'clock, deaving the folk?"

"Practically, yes."

"So you live by steam whistle, David? Aren't you glad to get back at week-ends to bonnie Doon?"

"Uncommonly glad."

"I'll always be glad I have been here, David. Now I shall be able to picture you as you are every day of the week. Up till now you were only a Friday-to-Monday David, with a dark past, a yawning gulf, hidden in between."

"But you will come again, I hope," he said quickly.

"It's not likely."

Then suddenly her eyes swooped on him, and her lips put the crucial question: "Well, what are you going to do to-day about me?"

"Take you back to Ayr first thing—as soon as we can conveniently get away. But we've got to have a little talk before that. If you have had enough breakfast to carry you through, we might go to the library now. We have half an hour before the whistle blows again."

"Very well."

She rose without haste or apprehension, stopped for a moment to speak caressingly to a beautiful canary in a gilt cage that had been trilling its heart out since daybreak; then she followed him to the other room.

Sillars closed the door. His face had lost the flush of the morning ride, and his hand had a tremor in it as it touched the handle of the door.

"You are going back to Ayr with me. And what after that?" she asked as she stood before the fireplace with her hands clasped behind her back, her clear eyes without a hint of misgiving in them enquiringly fixed on his face.

"I sat up late thinking over it all, Meg," he answered, steadying himself in response to her appeal. "There's only one way out."

"Yes? I am glad to hear that there is a way," she answered tranquilly. "I knew that, if anybody on earth would find one, it would be you."

"You couldn't imagine or guess what it is, I suppose?"

"No, I could not, I am sure."

"It isn't easy for me to talk about it—especially in the morning, my dear," he said with a slight grim laugh. "But there doesn't seem to be any alternative. You must give me the right to intervene on your behalf."

"Well, I have given it. Didn't I come for the purpose? Didn't I say to myself, when the big tide came rolling in, 'There's David—nobody else can help?' And here I am!"

"But there is only one kind of right. You must give me authority to go to your father and put an ultimatum in front of him."

"Oh, yes! It is the thing he requires above everything else—somebody to stand up to him. I don't know what you are going on about, David. If you think that is the thing to do—and obviously it is the only thing—well, do it."

"Then you'll have to marry me, Madge, and that just as soon as it can be arranged," he went on rapidly. "I must go to your father to-day and say, 'Look here, I'm going to be one of the family, and I propose to stop what's been going on. I will take over the mortgages—buy out the Hebrew crew.' But all the same, it is you, my dear, who will have to pay."

She stared at him steadily with lips parted a little and with wide open eyes.

"I shan't mind that," she answered steadily. "I shan't at all mind paying to you. I will marry you, David, any day you like—and there's my hand on it!"

But he did not touch it.

"I haven't forgotten that day in the Howff Wood, Madge, and I'm expecting nothing," he said in a quiet, low, but very clear, compelling voice. "I do this because it is absolutely the only way out that I can see. These Jews have got Ballochean fast, and nothing but hard cash will buy them out. I have got the hard cash, and I shall spend it in buying them out. But it is only by making you my wife that I shall give myself the right to do so and justify you in the eyes of the world."

He had to pick and choose his words with the utmost care, for the ground he was treading on was delicate exceedingly.

But Meg listened in unperturbed tranquillity.

"Then you propose to go to father to-day and to tell him that we are going to be married and that you are going to pay up?"

"I do. I haven't thought out the details yet."

"And will father stop at Ballochean?"

"Yes, of course."

"And Guy?"

Sillars made his mouth into a long, thin line.

"No. Guy must fend for himself—he must be thrust out ruthlessly into the world to find his feet, or he will go to the devil in a year or two. I shall have one straight talk with Guy when you give me the right, Madge. Do you give it?"

"Yes, of course I do. And I will live at Kildoon, I suppose, at the week-ends and come here in the middle—how quaint!"

"Your home will be at Kildoon, of course," he said evasively. "This is only a workshop and no place for ladies."

Meg's eyes danced.

"Oh, but, David, I shall be all over the place. You won't be able to keep me out of it! And when—and when—shall we get married?"

She spoke of it as if it were an expedition to the nearest shop.

Something swept over Sillars—a mighty pity and fear for the thing he was going to do was fraught with risk the most appalling, and no man knew or could know what the issue would be.

She did not appear to realise the magnitude of it all, or even what it was costing him to propose it.

"It will be time enough to settle these details after I have seen your father. I propose that we go up on the eleven-fifty to Glasgow, lunch in town, and run down to Ayr at two, if that meets with your approval. I'll wire them to send to meet us, and we shall go straight out to Ballochean."

"Right-o, David!" said Meg easily. "What a fright we shall give them!"

"You've probably given them that already. Did it never occur to you that they might grow anxious about you—might even drag the Doon for you?"

Meg laughed.

"Oh, no! that is the last thing that would occur to them. I've often stopped a night with Ellie Dove, if it happened to be too wet to walk home; and long ago dear Miss Anne Sanderson sometimes gave me a bed at the doctor's. They never trouble their heads about me at Ballochean."

"I can hardly believe that. Well, now, I must go into the works. The trap will be ready at half-past eleven to take us to the station.

"Can't I come into the works, David? I should simply love to see them."

"Not to-day. Next time you come back I shall take you through them myself. I have a great many orders to give to-day, and I would have no time to show you anything."

Meg did not suspect that he did not wish her to be seen unnecessarily by anyone. So she went off to get together the few things she had brought with her, her outlook considerably brighter.

Not in the least in love with Sillars, she yet now felt supreme content at the idea of becoming his wife. Marriage with David would immediately lift her from a position of uncertainty and misery into one of shelter, ease, and freedom from every sordid care.

If Meg had been asked to put her sentiments into words she might with perfect truth have declared that she expected by her marriage to get even with a great many people! To the solemnity of the step she was about to take, both for herself and the man, she did not give one passing thought.

Poor child, she was as ready now to play with life as she had ever been! Marriage was only a fresh phase, and it was one which she thought would please her.

Of the great deeps unstirred in her heart, of the unawakened womanhood soon to be thrust back upon itself in a loneliness more utter than anything she had yet experienced, she had not an idea.

But Sillars was fully aware of all that, and the shadow of what was coming lay rather heavily upon his heart, imparting an unusual gravity to his looks and making his words fewer even than usual.

But Meg's volubility made up for his silence. During the brief fifty minutes' run to Glasgow she was gay and happy, chattering about many things, though she did not allude at all to the subject of their conversation that morning.

It was Sillars who recurred to it in the first-class compartment where he and Meg were alone together as they went down to Ayr.

"Have I your permission, then, to speak out with complete frankness to your father?" he asked with a curious note in his voice. "It will be rather a difficult interview. I'll need all the bolstering I can get, Madge."

"But I shall be there," said Meg confidently.

Sillars shook his head.

"I don't think so."

"Oh, but yes! I must simply see my father's face when I come back with you! I believe you are the only man in the world whom he really respects and whose good opinion he wants to keep. Besides, I want to hear what you have to say to him."

"It's impossible that you should be present, my dear. In an interview of this kind there will be things said on both sides that a woman need not hear. Anyhow, I shall take care that you don't hear them," he said with that authoritative air of finality which somehow cowed her.

The words were spoken very, very quietly, and yet she knew it was not a bit of good trying to argue with him or to get him to change his mind.

"David, I'm not sure whether you are not going to be rather terrible," she said impulsively.

"Terrible as an army with banners," he laughed back. "Well, I've got a mighty unpleasant job in front of me, my dear."

"To ask for me?" she said with a twinkle in her eye. "Is the idea so very unpleasant then?"

"There have to be certain conditions laid down first——"

At this point he broke off and leaned forward, looking at her with great intentness.

But she did not shirk it.

"Well, what next?"

"It's a big thing, Madge, for us both—matrimony with very little to start it on! Are you afraid?"

"No—when it's you, David, for I know how good you are," she said simply. "And I take back all those horrid things I said in the Howff Wood, and I'll be the very best kind of wife I know how to be to you, if only you won't be too hard on me at the first."

"Hard on you, my dear? I won't be that! I haven't forgotten altogether what took place in the Howff Wood, and I know that it is for your family you are making this sacrifice—that it is to save the good name of the Hamiltons from being dragged for ever in the dust."

"And what are you doing it for, David?" she said suddenly, and at the question the flush mounted to his cheek.

"I've told you. It is because I don't see any other way out of this unholy mess, and because there isn't any reason why we shouldn't jog along comfortably and show a decent face to the world. Anyhow, I shan't expect what I won't get, and when that's once realised it's not a bad start."

Meg did not altogether grasp his meaning, but she was as yet without fear.

"Will it be soon, David—before Hew Kessock and Ellie get married?"

"I don't know their plans. But I think we can easily be in front of them," he said quietly. "And would you like to go abroad for a few weeks? You have never seen Paris."

"No, I won't go anywhere except to Kildoon. And when I get tired of that I can come to Greenock. Then, there will be Ballochean. You're going to save it, aren't you, David?"

"If I can," he answered, and with these words they ran into the station at Ayr, where they transferred themselves to the high dogcart which had been sent for them, and which Sillars, sending the groom off to walk home, resolved to drive himself.

Then of a set purpose he drove through the town, in order that all who were abroad might see them together. As luck would have it, they met the Sangster carriage, with Ellison Dove sitting demurely in it by the side of her future mother-in-law.

Meg experienced an unholy joy to be seen sitting behind the beautiful piece of horseflesh belonging to David Sillars, and she flashed a sort of triumphant glance at Ellie, over which that damsel secretly pondered.

"Odd, isn't it, Ellie, that these two should be together; and what is Mr. Sillars doing in Ayr in the middle of the week, I wonder?" said Lady Kessock.

Ellie propounded her theory, which, however, was not anywhere near the truth.

It was a lovely clear afternoon, and never had Ballochean looked more entrancing than it did now, with the autumn sun adding a ruddier tinge to the yellowing leaf and with the delicious crisp autumn feeling in the air.

The Laird, who had been taking an afternoon nap, had just rung for a cup of tea to be brought to him when Jean announced that Miss Meg had just come home with Mr. Sillars and that he wanted to see Mr. Hamilton at once.

"Sillars? Sillars? But I thought he was in Greenock in the middle of the week, lass!" cried the Laird, leaping from the old leather sofa and shaking himself as a dog might have done. "He wants to see me? Well, show him in."

Sillars came into the library alone, and never had Gavin Hamilton seen such an expression on his face.

He closed the door, ignored the Laird's offered hand, and came striding forward.

"I've brought Madge back, Mr. Hamilton," he said briefly.

"Back from where?" asked the Laird, trying to assume a blustering air.

"From Greenock. I was dining out last night at the Tontine Hotel, and when I got back between ten and eleven o'clock I found her in my house."

"In your house?—are you meaning Kildoon?"

"The Tontine Hotel at Greenock, I ought to have said, though there isn't one that I am aware of in Ayr," said Sillars with exasperating coolness. "It's my house at Greenock I'm speaking about."

"In your house in Greenock, the deuce take her! Why did she go there? I fancied that she was with the Doves at Prospect House."

"You never troubled to inquire where she had gone, Mr. Hamilton, though I gathered from what she told me that she had left you in a kind of frenzy. What have you to say for yourself? Many a girl has been lost through less."

"Tut, tut—not a girl like Meg! Never was one born better able to take care of herself. And the jade was downright rude to me, merely because I tried to point out how she might do a good stroke of business for herself and at the same time get me out of the biggest hole I've ever been in. I suppose she has told you all that?"

"Yes, she has," answered Sillars, and the measured tone of his voice, so vibrant with contempt, succeeded in lashing Gavin Hamilton's well-nigh dead manhood into something of the old flame.

"You know what Meg's tongue is. She was not herself when she left here. You are a sensible man, David. You discounted at least half of what she said?"

"The facts she imparted to me admitted of no discounting, Mr. Hamilton. How dared you suggest that she should give herself to a money-lending Jew just to save your precious skin and your hungry acres?"

Sillars let himself go, for the tone and the attitude of the old man and his utter callousness to what might in the interval after she had left him have happened to his girl, outraged him beyond endurance.

"Ca' canny! I know the yarn she would spin. But you should have come here to get the truth. It was a magnificent offer that Van Leyden made, and Bien himself is a man whom any woman could live happily with and be proud of. Maybe he wouldn't count in Ayr, that is full of stinking pride and hunger; but I tell you they're aristocrats in their own country."

"Let them stop in it, then," said Sillars dourly.

"Well, I'm waiting to hear what Meg wanted from you? To be so high and mighty, she took a foolish step, I think. It's a thing that a father might have very properly had something to say about."

At this the passion which Sillars had been sternly checking burst the bounds, and he strode forward and simply clenched his fist in the astonished face of the old reprobate.

"Hold your tongue, you old sinner, or I'll forget your age and fell you!" he said. "Your daughter came to me because she could trust me, and because, thanks to you and your misbehaviour, I'm the only friend she has in the world. And I'm here because of that to deal with you and to take her clean out of your clutches."

"Come, come! Who are you, David Sillars, that you should speak to me like that? I knew your father and your grandfather before you. I'll stand that kind of talk from no man, much less from you!"

Sillars stepped towards the door, turned the key in the lock, and sat down on the edge of the round table, on which poor Ludo had been wont to study the maps of the world, which he had longed so ardently, but had never expected, to see.

"Look here, Mr. Hamilton. It's quite evident that you are dead to every feeling of decency and that somebody has got to rub that fact in. This monstrous thing can't be done! Why, man, the whole county would rise up against you and drown you in the Doon or lynch you at the nearest pole! I would be the first to lead them on. You may thank your stars that Madge had the good sense to come to me and not to go to the Doves, or even to the Sandersons. For this thing need go no further. She and I are going to get married, and it will be my unsavoury business to sort out the affairs of Ballochean."

CHAPTER XV

THE ULTIMATUM

BALLOCHEAN stared in the utmost amazement, and for a second or so found no words in which to express it.

"You and Meg to get married!" he stuttered at length. "Ho, ho, so this is the upshot, is it?"

"It's the only thing to be done to save the situation, Mr. Hamilton; and Meg is willing, not because she particularly wants to marry me, but because it will save her from something worse."

Gavin Hamilton shifted from the one foot to the other, eyeing Sillars narrowly with the air of a man not yet sure of his ground.

In spite of all his bluff, he was secretly afraid of Sillars, for, as a general rule, the man who has left the straight path shrinks from the one who remains steadfast in it.

"And you've come here to ask my consent, I suppose?"

"I have not. It can be dispensed with—the thing is arranged," he said quietly.

"Then what do you want?" asked old Hamilton insolently. "Perhaps you're married already?"

"No. But we shall be in a few days' time—in fact, just as soon as it can be arranged."

"And what, may I ask, becomes of me?" asked Hamilton blusteringly. "She leaves her old father in the lurch, I suppose—ungrateful creature that she is!—for I've never crossed her since she was born, David; and no woman is fit to stand such indulgent treatment! She doesn't know what it is to be thwarted."

Sillars scarcely smiled at this atrocious statement, though there flashed across his innermost mind a fleeting wonder at the aberrations and absurdities of which a poisoned nature can be capable.

"That's what I've come about, Mr. Hamilton, for Meg has told me of the desperate pass to which you have come. She is right, I take it, in saying that the Jews have got you in the hollow of their hand."

The old man glared, for the remnant of self-esteem still left in his proud nature writhed at the tone of the words as well as at their dire significance. But realising that, now that Meg had completely failed him, Sillars was practically his only hope, he capitulated there and then.

"They've got me like the devil, David," he acknowledged; "and the trouble is that they've fallen in love with the place. They want it almost as much as they want her. I believe," he added with a queer, quiet chuckle, "that they have some idea of founding a new family down here."

"We needn't go into that," said Sillars, stopping him short. "Let me tell you what I am prepared to do."

Still sitting on the edge of the table, he made a statement which fairly took away the old man's breath.

"You're prepared to pay up to the last farthing to—to free the place? My God, it'll be the first time it has been free in my time. But what about me?"

"You stop here, of course, and look after it. There are conditions, however, which can be entered into later."

"And Guy, does he stop here, too?" asked the old man eagerly, his pulses bounding at the thought of being freed from the millstone that had so long hung about his neck.

"No. Guy must fend for himself. I will require you to pay a rent for Ballochean, Mr. Hamilton, and I hope that when we go into things you will see the reasonableness of it and profit by the chance that has come in your way."

"I'm seeing it now, by Gad! to be quit of them all, David! They've been like harpies gnawing at my vitals. Times out of number I've been on the point of making a bullet end of the whole business."

"Small good that would have done, for the mess would have been left," said Sillars, who had no sympathy with such talk, even if he had taken it seriously. But, in spite of his words, the idea of suicide and Gavin Hamilton were miles apart, and would remain so, the old reprobate being too heartily in love with life to seek to escape from it.

"Ah! but you have never known the lack of a pound or two," he said appealingly; "you don't know to what straits an honourable man may be brought."

Sillars slid off the table, determined to have done with the distasteful interview.

"You'll give me the address of these men, Mr. Hamilton, and I'll see them to-morrow."

"I'll go with you. I'd like more than I can tell to be present at that interview! It would do me uncommon good to see old Van Leyden's face when he hears what you have to say."

But Sillars shook his head.

"I'm afraid I can't agree to that, Mr. Hamilton. It will be better for you not to be present. If you reflect a moment, you'll see reasons enough for that."

"Van Leyden himself is not a bad sort, David. He's the decentest money-lender I've ever come across. That's where Meg and I came to loggerheads. You see, she made no distinction. They were simply money-lenders and nothing more."

"So far as she was concerned that fact was all that mattered," observed Sillars drily.

"But Van Leyden's a gentleman," persisted Ballochean; "and she had got at the soft spot in his heart. When I think what she might have done with that millionaire's money, David, the thought turns me sick!"

"I'm sick at the bare mention of it," said Sillars curtly. "Well, the address? I must get back to Kildoon at once, and I'll be off by the early train to-morrow morning."

"Won't you stop and dine, David?" urged the Laird.

"Not to-night, thank you."

"Well, don't you think this deserves a dram?" asked the old man with his longing eye fixed on the cupboard door.

Sillars laid a warning hand on Ballochean's sleeve.

"If there had been fewer drams, Mr. Hamilton, you would not be in such a pass to-day as you have brought yourself to. The dram will have to come into consideration among other things when the deeds are signed."

"You would make a mealy-mouthed teetotaller of me, David. By Gad! I'd rather go under the clean water at once and be done with it! Water in a glass is an abomination—no fit drink for a gentleman."

Sillars faintly smiled, but something in the depths of his glance kept Ballochean away from the cupboard door.

"Are you going to put me to school again, lad, when you're my son-in-law? Mrs. David Sillars of Kildoon!—by Gad! it'll make them sit up. It's a proud woman she ought to be, for it's the oldest name in the county—even Kessock can't match it."

"It will be honoured by its new bearer," said Sillars absently. "But, Mr. Hamilton, the less said about this the better meanwhile. May I ask you to hold your tongue? Your daughter and I desire above everything that we should not be made the subject of gossip at the present moment. And you know what the town and the countryside are."

"I do. You can no more stop jaw about a marriage than you can stop the cawing of the rooks in the trees. I tell you, David, there's something in the air that proclaims it—the very laverock in the lift sings it out at the top of its voice! Mrs. Sillars of Kildoon!—I would give a tenpound note to see Anne Kessock's face when she hears it! She gave me a warm five minutes the other day about the lassie, David. To hear her speak one might have thought she was not fit to marry a hind—let alone the best match in the county!"

A faint shadow showed momentarily on the grave brow of Sillars. He knew only too well what was said in the county about Meg Hamilton. He had seen the pitying shrugs, the uplifted brows when her name was mentioned, and, though he knew the purity of her heart and all the individual charm and honesty of her, still it hurt.

"Guy is deep in the dumps somewhere, David," said Hamilton presently, as Sillars made a movement towards the door. "This will make a mighty difference to him."

"It will, for there won't be any place for him in the new order of things at Ballochean," said Sillars grimly. "None at least, unless he is prepared to turn over a new leaf and play the part of a man in the world. Will you ask him to come over to me to-night at Kildoon? I can't wait any longer now, and you haven't given me the address yet."

"David, I'm going with you to-morrow to hear what you've got to say to these rascals. But, I say, have you any idea of the sum total that you will have to pay? Why, man, I've had thousands from them and from others! They've shouldered the lot now, of course. They hold everything, and you'll have a job getting the title-deeds out of their hands."

"I don't think so. After all, it's a mere question of money—the passing of a big enough cheque. Well, since you make such a point of it, will you meet me at Ayr station to-morrow morning in time for the eight-fifty? I suppose we can find them at their office at ten o'clock."

"I can wire them to-night, David. I'll send one of the stable lads into town with a telegram now."

"Very well. Eight-fifty to-morrow morning. And don't forget to send Guy to me."

Sillars spoke quietly, but with an air of great authority. After considerable counsel with himself, he had decided to take a high hand at Ballochean, for only by doing so would he get a wholesome grip of the situation.

Negotiating with the Laird and with the money-lenders was not a job he liked, but at the back of all his sensitiveness and refinement there was a harder, shrewder strain—the strain that goes to the building up of a great fortune. Sillars, whom so few understood—Meg, least of all—was a man of far more complex character than anyone dreamed.

"You're going now? You don't want to see Meg before you go?" said Gavin Hamilton fussily. "I haven't seen the lass yet myself."

"Don't say much to her, Mr. Hamilton. She's not in the mood to endure much more. She has been hurt. Give her time to heal."

Gavin Hamilton blinked at the strange choice of words made by Sillars. He followed him, however, with much respect to the door, where a stable lad was holding his horse.

Meg was nowhere to be seen.

Sillars drew on his driving-gloves, and, before he mounted, he looked Gavin Hamilton straight in the eyes.

"Eight-fifty to-morrow morning, then, and nothing said in the interval, Mr. Hamilton, if you please. This is nobody's business but ours, and it is Meg's express desire that there should be no talk about it. I'll see what can be done with regard to hastening the marriage."

"Where will it take place?" asked Hamilton easily. "Are we to make no show over it?"

"None. That's the last thing either of us would desire. What you have got to understand, Mr. Hamilton—only you seem denser than usual—is that this is a desperate step. Your daughter has consented to take it because it is the only honourable way out. Try to remember that, and bring your best feelings to bear on it."

Gavin Hamilton stared stupidly.

"If that's the set of it, David—then I'm hanged if I see what you're going to get out of it," he said bluntly, hitting on the truth blunderingly, as the fool sometime does when wise men fail.

Sillars laughed drily.

"That is hid in the womb of the future, Mr. Hamilton. Meanwhile keep it dark, and don't forget to ask Guy to come over to me to-night."

He sprang up, took the reins, gave a nod, but offered no hand; and the next moment the wheels grated and the thud of receding hoofs beat on the air.

Meg, from behind the curtain in the old schoolroom with a strange beat of the heart watched her lover ride away.

In the space of a few hours how greatly all had changed!—even her opinion of David Sillars! He had now become the pivot of her existence—the arbiter not only of her destiny, but of that of all Ballochean!

The interview with Sillars had sobered Gavin Hamilton, and he sat down to think mightily—a task to which he was altogether unaccustomed. But some strange odd feeling—a mingling of delicacy and shame—prevented him from seeking his daughter. Nay, he even dreaded the moment when he must meet her face to face.

He had been sitting alone for about half an hour in the library when Meg opened the door quite quietly and came in. He rose fussily, and, pipe in hand, eyed her somewhat askance.

"Good-evening, father," she said, in an even, passionless voice, very different from the ringing note of anger and scorn that she had hurled at him little more than forty-eight hours ago. "You have seen David?"

"Yes, I've seen David," he answered in a queer uncertain voice, yet inwardly relieved that it had not fallen to him to make the first advances; "and I haven't got the better of it yet."

She leaned wearily against the edge of the round table, and looked at him with a singular mingling of wistfulness and dignity.

"This is a wonderful thing he is going to do for us all, father, and we shall never be able to repay him."

"I want to know why he is doing it, Meg. I asked him, but he did not seem to be very clear about it," said Ballochean bluntly.

"It is because he has a great heart, father—the same heart that felt for Ludo and sent him away to begin such a fine career."

Something remote, unfathomed, but wholly moving about his girl touched a deep chord in the old reprobate's heart.

"But it is you who will have to pay the reckoning, Meg—you and nobody else."

"I know, and I'm not afraid, father. David, you see, is different from all other men. He makes everything easy."

She spoke with the uttermost confidence. But there was none in the heart of Ballochean, for he knew women well, and, in the days of his youth, he had had much skill in the lore of the heart.

The greater Meg's confidence the keener his doubt. Strange that, though he would have wed her to Morris Bien without a pang, the contemplation of her mating with David Sillars could so disquiet him! It was one of those inexplicable gleams of vision that are almost prophetic and that sometimes flash out in quarters where they are least expected.

"I hope it'll turn out well, Meg. I hope to God it will! I am sorry for my part in bringing it about. If I could go back on my life, Meg, I'd be a different man."

Meg smiled a little wintrily, for all of a sudden the romance had fled from the high adventure and it was reduced to the level of common things.

"I hope it will improve things here, father, and that both you and Guy will consider David, for it is a very wonderful thing that he has undertaken to do."

"He gets you, Meg," he said harshly, "and there are men who would say that he fares well."

Meg laughed a little at that.

"I am worth nothing," she said lightly. "But I will be better than I have been—I must be better, for David's sake."

Meanwhile, heart and brain afire, the new arbiter of destiny for Ballochean drove rapidly along the high road towards his home. And on the way he met Guy, riding the one sorry nag that the stable of Ballochean could now boast.

Sillars at once drew rein and beckoned him.

"Unless you have something important waiting for you elsewhere, Guy, I want you to ride to Kildoon with me. I won't keep you more than an hour."

Guy looked surprised and tugged the untidy end of his moustache.

"Why are you here in the middle of the week?"

"Come on, and I'll tell you. I've just come from Ballochean. I left a message for you to come over to Kildoon. As you are half way there this will save time."

"All right," said Guy, nothing loth to accompany him, for there was little cheer at home, and almost anything that would delay his return was welcome.

There was no speech on the way, Guy riding ahead mostly, and in about fifteen minutes' time they were inside the house.

Leaving his horse in charge of the groom, Guy followed Sillars to his den, where he waited with considerable interest and some apprehension for what was coming. That Sillars had something of dire importance to say he gathered from the gravity of his mien.

"I'm here because I had to bring your sister back. When I got in late last night from a public dinner I found her at my house."

"Here, do you mean!" asked Guy, making the same mistake as his father.

"No—at Langdyke. It was nearly eleven o'clock at night when I got home, and it was impossible for me to bring her back earlier."

"Um!" said Guy, and his face assumed the oddest expression; but he evidently thought that silence was at the moment his wisest cue.

"She came to me because she believed I was the only friend she had in the world. I suppose you know what had happened. By God, Guy! I don't know how you could stand by and see it done!"

"You are meaning the Bien affair, I suppose. Well, I couldn't prevent it, and, after all, she had the option of refusing," he said sullenly.

"She ought not to have been subjected to such a vile thing at all," said Sillars in the same measured, stinging tones. "I said as much as I thought wise to your father; but he is an old man. You ought to have had some manliness still left in you. Your sister came to me to ask me to help, and I have come here for that purpose. Sit down, Guy, and let me make a proposition to you. Your father is past redemption in the sense that we need not look for honest work from him now. He has lost the capacity for that. What he wants is to be relieved from every atom of responsibility—to be allowed a certain sum for his own spending, and to be given house-room—no more."

"He hasn't had as much of late years. It has been hell at Ballochean, David —nothing more or less!"

"I know; and what I lose patience with is the fact that you boys should have stood it so long. But to come back to the proposition—supposing Ballochean were pulled together, the mortgage paid up, and you had a chance to look after the place—to farm the home-farm, say, and put in honest work with some hope of earning an honest living, is it in you to do it, Guy?"

"I wish somebody would give me the chance."

"It would be work, Guy—genuine, honest work. There are three hundred and fifty acres in the home-farm, and I hear that Rintoul would be glad to quit at Martinmas. He's an old man, and he wants to retire—he himself told me so only last week. He has made enough off these acres to retire on, Guy, and if you took them in hand and gave your mind to working them, you and your father could live comfortably and independently at Ballochean, and you, at least, would be a happier man."

"I don't doubt it, but who is going to give me any such chance, David? These cursed Jews have got us tooth and nail, and now that—now that Meg has disappointed them they'll put on the screw, I have not the least doubt."

"But the Jews can be disposed of. As a matter of fact, I mean to dispose of them to-morrow."

"You do?" said the lad, looking with eyes of wonder into the grave, determined face of Sillars. "But what in the world are you doing it for? You've always been decent to us, David—the only chap in the county who has. But why this?"

"Well, we can't stand by and see Ballochean parted among the Israelites," he answered, trying to speak lightly. "But it is as a business proposition I'm attacking this, Guy. I don't intend to lose a fortune over it. My money will pay off the mortgages. But they will be in my hands, and I don't know that there will be so very much difference."

"It'll make some difference to us poor dev——"

Then he stopped, for Sillars raised a warning finger.

"Look here, you're over twenty, aren't you? It's about time you were making yourself a man of some account. Why, man, there is no reason why, if you lay your mind to it—and your body as well—that you should not clear the place in a few years' time. I'll help you all I can. Let's co-operate and get rid of the scandal that Ballochean has for so long been. I'm interested in it; I want it done; but it can't be done unless you step into the breach."

Guy did not speak for a moment, and Sillars misunderstood his silence.

"The alternative to my proposition is that you take a hundred pounds and go to Canada to make a kirk or a mill of it," he said, his tone perceptibly hardening. "Understand clearly that in the new order of things there will be no room for a loafer at Ballochean."

"I understand. I'll do my best, David."

"Go home and think it over, and talk it over with your father," said Sillars more kindly. "But don't be under any delusions. I'll be a hard taskmaster, and, for everybody's sake, I must take my pound of flesh."

"But why are you doing all this—what are you going to get out of it?" cried Guy impulsively. "Seems to me that everybody scores in this deal but you."

Sillars gave him no satisfaction on that head, however. And it was only when he burst with the same question into the presence of his father and his sister that his eyes were opened.

They were half way through dinner when he got back to Ballochean, and, with a nod to Meg, he flung his eager questioning at his father.

"Say governor, what's happened? Meg, how did you get round old Sillars to that extent? I want to know what he's going to get out of it?" went on Guy. "It's the queerest thing I've ever heard tell of in my life."

The old man pointed an unsteady finger at Meg's conscious face.

"Don't you worry about Sillars, lad. He gets that"—an announcement which so overwhelmed Guy Hamilton that he was unable to eat any dinner!

CHAPTER XVI

MARRIAGE AND GIVING IN MARRIAGE

Surgeon Dove's wife had become a woman of affairs.

Such scheming and planning, such interminable days spent in the shopping areas of Glasgow, such consultations with dressmakers and milliners and purveyors of trousseaux—she simply revelled in them all.

Even the Surgeon-General—most good-natured and enduring of men—began to get a little weary of it.

" Glasgow again ! Bless me, my dear ! " he said one morning over his shaving, " neither you nor Ellie will live to see the wedding day if you go on at this rate. One would think that nobody had ever been married before ! "

Mrs. Dove, buttoning her neat gown over her skimpy bosom, surveyed him with active disapproval.

" No quarter-deck for me, Tom, if you please," she said, though his tone had been one of the mildest. " It is you who have no proper sense of gratitude, or of propriety, or of anything ! "

" An abandoned wretch, Clara—and have ever been ! " he retorted grimly. " And everybody knows it ! "

" Aren't you even decently glad that your child is to become a great lady ? "

" Um, yam, fiddlesticks ! I might be glad if I knew what a great lady is, Clara. Perhaps you might enlighten me amidst the mysteries of the toilet. It would be good for us both."

" Idiot ! " said Mrs. Dove sharply, for she was familiar with these vagaries of her husband's wayward mood, and she was fully aware that, so long as he was under their dominion, nothing could be done with him. " I shan't speak another word to you, Tom Dove, if you go on ever so ! You don't deserve it ! Anyhow, it is a certain fact that you never did, and never would do, anything to help your own child to her proper place in the county."

Tom Dove irreverently smiled, and he very nearly cut himself in the process. The county was so old a bugbear, and to him it mattered so little. He had no quarrel with Fate—no fault to find with his own place in the county. A good friend or two, willing to listen to his yarns of the sea, a clear-blowing pipe, a corner in the Club on a wet day, and a good round of golf on a fine one—these were the Surgeon's requirements, and they were so modest that they were seldom or never denied him.

" I haven't got over wondering yet how you engineered it, Clara," he said.

" Engineered it, Tom ! You're worse than undeserving—you are vulgar ! " said his wife in cold scorn.

" I suppose it is vulgar in the county to call a spade a spade. Things have changed since my young days. I've no objection to Kessock in the abstract, and Ellie seems happy enough."

" They are both as happy as there is any occasion for, Tom," snapped his wife. " Personally, I have never considered matrimony any occasion for rejoicing."

" No. It is an occasion for humiliation and prayer—but not unadorned," replied the Surgeon, with a little humorous smile playing about his mouth. " Well, and what are you going to do in Glasgow to-day ? "

" Choose the wedding gown."

" Oh, ho ! so important as that. Is Lady Kessock to be at the choosing ? "

" No. I am the proper person to choose my daughter's wedding gown," she answered, with lips primly set. " And you are the proper person to pay for it. There is to be no haggling over the price this time, Tom Dove. Ellie must go to Sangster properly dressed, for oh, that old woman makes me deadly sick ! "

The words were out before she could keep them back, and instantly the laughter and scorn died out of Tom Dove's honest eyes.

"My dear, out with it. Confession is good for the soul."

"I'm glad that Ellie's future is settled; but I shall never feel perfectly safe until she is Lady Kessock. When it's all over I'll get even with that woman for her insulting, patronising ways if I die for it!" his wife continued hotly.

"Do you think Ellie will be happy with her?" inquired the Surgeon-General earnestly, for peace being the one desire of his kindly soul, he set much store by it for others.

"No, and that I don't," she snapped back. "But she'll have the whip hand, and directly they come back from their honeymoon I begin moving heaven and earth to get the old woman another establishment. I believe Hew himself would like that—only his mother's got him tied to her apron-string. But when he has us to help him he will see to it, never fear."

"Be careful, my dear. You don't want to have 'meddling mother-in-law' thrown in your teeth at Sangster."

"I mean to get even with Anne Kessock, Tom, if I die for it!" she repeated imperturbably. "She's lending her veil and her lace flounce for the wedding frock. And it will be printed in the newspapers. Oh, Tom! why haven't we ancestors with lace veils and flounces to trim our wedding gowns——"

Her voice was querulous to the verge of tears, and the Surgeon-General began to have dim realisation of the pangs of ambitious discontent through which his wife was passing.

"Never mind, Clara. Who cares about ancestors in these days?" he said soothingly.

"Oh! but they care here yet—care about them above everything else on earth. Haven't I had it rubbed into me since I came here? Southsea was nothing to it. But Ellie will make them sit up. You don't know what's in that child, Tom. She amazes me afresh every day."

"I hope she's going to get some happiness out of the thing, Clara, for, after all, that's what matters chiefly," said the old man, voicing his own simple creed of life.

"Fudge! People find happiness in the amount of things they can get—chiefly in the amount of money. Fortunately, there will be plenty of that at Sangster, and I mean to have a share of it. I haven't endured purgatory meekly here for nothing."

"We don't sponge off Kessock, Clara—not if I know it!" said the Surgeon sharply.

"Now you are vulgar again. Who wants to 'sponge'?—though, looking at the clothes you wear, anybody would be within his rights in suspecting you to be capable of it."

"As it's the wedding gown to-day, the wedding itself must be getting near. Is the day fixed?" he asked interestedly.

"Idiot!" said Mrs. Dove again.

But the epithet thus used had little significance. In private life Mrs. Dove had always indulged in considerable latitude of language, though she was so prim outside.

"It's going to take place on the eighteenth day of December," continued Mrs. Dove. "That's next month—four weeks to-morrow exactly."

"Here, in this house?"

"No. In the parish church, of course. And a very few will come on here afterwards. Lady Kessock and I agreed for once that there should not be much fuss. She talked of a hotel reception in Glasgow, but I said you had put your foot down!"

"Heavens, Clara, I hear it now for the first time!" said her astounded husband.

"Of course you do. If you had heard it before you would have put your foot in it," she said tranquilly; "you always do. Was I going to carry the thing to Glasgow, and be swallowed up?—not likely. It will take place in the parish church, which will be crammed to the door for I have already told Mr. Murchison that nobody is to be refused admittance. Everybody who is interested shall see her. Then a few select carriages here, and just the right guests arriving and departing, and Ellie going away from her father's house, as she ought—and no hotel about it! Don't you approve, Tom?"

" I approve of her going from here, of course. A hotel wedding is an abomination."

" There is somebody coming next week to make an arch between the drawing-room and the spare bedroom. When that's done we shall have quite a decent reception room."

" Knock down the partition, do you mean ? " asked the Surgeon aghast.

" I mean just that."

" But it will have to be built up again, or old Kemp will kick up a dust."

" Old Kemp !—don't name him. He doesn't enter," she said in swift contempt of a landlord who had occasioned them a good deal of worry during their tenancy of the house. " And I've ordered a new carpet to cover both the rooms—a lovely Gobelin blue—Ellie's colour."

" Goblin blue ? Anything to do with fairies ? "

" G-o-b-e-l-i-n," she spelled out provokingly. " It's a lovely shade—just like Ellie's eyes. And we'll have a bell of white flowers at the arch and Hew and Ellie will stand under it."

" What for ? "

" To receive congratulations, of course. And a first-class Glasgow firm will send down to do the decorations and the buffet. I'll show them what can be done even in a small house by people who have seen something of society outside a Scotch provincial town."

" You're a great woman, Clara ! And what about bridesmaids ? "

" There is to be only one—the Hon. Miss Cochrane, Hew's cousin—and there will be two little pages in kilts. It's not an indecent show we want to make. Besides, a crowd of bridesmaids is a mistake, for they sometimes throw the bride into the shade. Ellie is the chief figure on the eighteenth of December, and I intend that nobody shall forget it."

" You'd have made a wonderful general, Clara," said her husband absently, as he wiped his razor and carefully returned it to its case. " Only one bridesmaid ! I should have thought now that Ellie would at least have had Meg Hamilton, who was her best friend for so long."

Mrs. Dove pursed her lips into a slightly knowing smile. Of her husband's intelligence in the ordinary affairs of life she had no great opinion, though she could boast on occasion of his professional skill and of the high place he had won for himself in the Service.

" Tom, if you had any perception at all you wouldn't need to be told why Ellie would have too much good feeling to ask Meg Hamilton to be a bridesmaid or even to invite her to the wedding."

The Surgeon-General presented the usual blank front.

" I've no perception at all, Clara. Supposing you tell me the reason."

" Well, the poor thing wanted to be Lady Kessock herself, and, I believe, she expected to be so. But—as I pointed out to Ellie, at the same time telling her how grateful she ought to be for a proper upbringing—men may laugh and joke with girls like Meg Hamilton, but they don't marry them ! "

" Oh ! " said the Surgeon-General. " You seem to know a good deal about men, Clara. I wonder where you got your information. Now, if I were a young man, I should not be afraid to marry Meg Hamilton. She's as straight as a die and as true as steel."

" No doubt," said Mrs. Dove, with a suspicion of iciness in her voice. " Well, if you are nearly ready, we'd better go down. That was the gong a minute ago, and our train goes at nine-forty."

After he had seen his wife and daughter into the station fly the Surgeon-General played nine holes on the old links of Ayr, though he had meant to have a proper morning's golf at Troon. Then he came in to an early lunch.

All the morning he was pursued by what his wife had said about Meg Hamilton. It had made him so thoroughly uncomfortable that, after a good pipe and forty winks in his easy-chair, he set out to walk in the direction of Ballochean in the hope of seeing or hearing something about her.

It was a mild, grey November day. The walking was a little heavy, and very soon the Surgeon-General, who was a great walker and who knew every field and bypath and short-cut in the neighbourhood of his native town, turned off the high road and struck into the Howff Wood on the Kildoon side.

He looked as his watch when he emerged from the wood on the confines of the park at Ballochean, and he found that it was twenty minutes to three o'clock.

As he walked in a slanting direction through the great spaces of the park, he beheld two vehicles follow each other in quick succession up the avenue. The one was a closed brougham, the other was a high dogcart, and it was being driven with great rapidity. He was too far off, however, to recognise the occupants of the latter.

Both had disappeared apparently in the direction of the stables by the time he reached the house door. When he rang the bell, Jean, the tall parlour-maid, answered it, and she looked at once excited and puzzled.

"Good-day," said the Surgeon-General pleasantly. "I want to see Miss Hamilton, if she is in the house."

"She is in, sir, but——"

As she hesitated, quite at a loss what to say, some one came across the hall from behind. It was Meg herself, in a grey gown of some soft, clinging material and with a bunch of red chrysanthemums in her belt.

She had no hat on, and her beautiful hair seemed to have been arranged with some care, and altogether she had made a much more elaborate toilette than the Surgeon had ever seen before. She looked beautiful with a kind of stately coldness about her which was most striking.

"Who is it, Jean?" she said quite clearly as she came forward. "Oh, it is you, Dr. Dove! I am very glad to see you. Please come right in."

Jean immediately withdrew, and Meg, with her colour rising a little and with rather an odd smile on her face watched him draw off his gloves.

"I ventured up, my dear, because it seemed such a long time since I had seen you. I really couldn't stop away," he said simply. "Why have you deserted us so completely?"

"Oh! I've been busy—very busy," she answered. "It is odd that you should have come to-day—just in time. Will you come right in with me to the library? You may as well see it through."

"See what through? If there is any sort of function going on," he said, drawing back—"and from your dress I gather there is—I shall just slip away. I'm not dressed for that sort of thing, and, besides, it would be an intrusion."

"Oh, no! dear Dr. Dove, for this is my occasion, after all, and we shall all be very glad to see you. Please, come with me."

Her face and voice seemed to compel him, and without further demur he followed her down the long corridor to the library door.

She stopped there, smiling a little unsteadily, and put her finger on her lips. The next moment, followed by him, she had passed into the room, and from that moment he felt and acted like a man in a dream.

In the room stood Gavin Hamilton and his son Guy, and David Sillars in a tweed travelling suit, and the Reverend Mr. Murchison, the parish minister, and his wife, and on the table lay a Bible and certain papers that looked like documents.

"Father," said Meg clearly, "here is Surgeon Dove. I happened to come down just as Jean was going to turn him away. I invited him in. I am sure you are pleased to see him."

Ballochean looked the surprise he felt, and contented himself with nodding across the room to the Surgeon. Sillars, however, came forward and shook hands warmly, for he had a great respect for Surgeon Dove. The minister and his wife made greetings likewise. Then there was an awkward pause.

"We are not waiting for anybody, are we, Miss Hamilton?" said the minister after a few seconds in his pleasantly inquiring voice.

"No, Mr. Murchison. And I'm quite ready. Please be as quick as you can."

"Stand here, then, my dear," he said, in a voice of fatherly kindness.

And Surgeon Dove, dumbfounded beyond all telling, stood back, and, watching stupidly, saw two tears rise in Mrs. Murchison's kind eyes and roll unheeded down her cheeks.

Sillars stepped forward and took his place beside Meg in the open space in the great bow-fronted window, and then the minister opened the Book.

Dove listened for what was coming, and then he realised all of a sudden that he was witnessing a marriage between David Sillars and Marjorie Hamilton. It filled him with amazement so intense that he did not hear a single word until the minister uttered the sentence "I pronounce you man and wife."

Then the Laird, nudged by his son, stepped forward and made his awkward congratulations, bestowing a swift perfunctory kiss on his daughter's cheek. Guy followed suit, as did the minister and his wife.

"Haven't you anything to say to me, Dr. Dove?" said Meg's voice, a little clear and metallic in its tone.

"I'm bowled over, my dear! But I say 'God bless you and Sillars.' It's the best thing I have witnessed for many a day, for there are few like him. But, oh, my dear! this is not the kind of wedding you and he should have had! The whole of Ayr should have danced at it."

"Oh! but that wouldn't have suited either him or me," said Meg demurely, and she cast a queer, half-appealing glance at her new-made husband, the remembrance of which lingered in the old man's mind long after her words had been forgotten.

"You've cheated us, Mr. Sillars," he said as he shook hands with the bridegroom. "But—but you're worthy of her. She is a bit of bright gold, my man. See to it that you cherish her."

It was the one and only injunction laid on David Sillars that day, and Surgeon Dove marvelled that he had so little to say in response.

There was champagne presently for those who cared for it, and the Laird's tongue was loosened thereby, and the queer look of strain was lifted from his anxious face. Dove noticed with satisfaction that Guy did not touch it, and that there seemed to be some change in the lad, a look of new resolve, a strange humility begotten of some mysterious prompting from within.

The Surgeon-General, being a man of discernment, easily divined that much water had flowed under the bridge since he had last seen Meg beneath his own roof. He hoped all was well, and yet he feared and that greatly. For there was none of the usual joyance visible on the faces of the bride and bridegroom, and they seemed rather to avoid than to seek each other.

In a short time Meg made her escape in charge of Mrs. Murchison, and the men were left to themselves.

But the talk in the library was only of impersonal matters, and there was a little uneasiness in the air.

In about half an hour's time Meg came down, dressed for her wedding journey in a dark blue frock and a long travelling coat with a sable collar, a gift of the bridegroom, in which she looked regal as a queen.

And the brougham being at the door, there was no delay, very little leave-taking, and not a tear except in the susceptible eyes of the good Mrs. Murchison, who felt that there was something not quite right about it all.

And almost immediately the married couple were off, and Meg's face, as she turned it at the last to say good-bye to her father's house, had a strange whiteness and a wrung look upon it, as if she realised for the first time how great and irretraceable was the step she had taken.

When the carriage disappeared round the curve in the avenue the minister spoke gently to his wife.

"Get your cloak, Lucy, and let us go. Mr. Hamilton will wish to be alone, I am sure, after all this."

Then he turned to the Surgeon-General.

"We can take you, Dr. Dove. There is a vacant seat in the old family chariot, and it will give us uncommon pleasure if you will occupy it."

The Surgeon-General thanked him, and they all left with a feeling of relief. Not a word was spoken until they had swept through the gates of Ballochean.

"Surely this is the queerest wedding I have ever been at," said the Surgeon-General at last, unable to contain himself.

"They wanted it to be very quiet. It was in accordance with the wishes of the bride that it should be so," answered the minister quietly.

"But it was a shame all the same," said his wife indignantly, "for she ought to have had a proper wedding, and my heart is sore for her, and I hope—I hope she is going to be happy."

"Did anybody know it was coming off?" asked Dove bluntly.

"Apparently not. But then Miss Hamilton, as you know, is a little unconventional in her ways, so that need surprise nobody," said Mr. Murchison. "I don't know what you are crying for, Lucy, for she has got one of the best men as well as the most eligible *parti* in the county," added the minister, looking with disapproval at his wife's still burning eyes.

"That may be. All I can say is that if I had a girl I shouldn't like her to be married like that, and I'm glad that you, Dr. Dove, hold the same opinion."

They allowed the Surgeon-General to get down at the nearest point to his home, and it was only then that he began to realise the astounding nature of the news which he had to impart to his wife and daughter.

They had spoke of getting home by the four-ten train, and it was now nearly five o'clock. He went into the house, asked for his tea, and was about half-way through with it when they came in, laden, as usual, with parcels, and both apparently radiantly pleased with themselves.

Fresh tea was brought, and for ten minutes or so he was deaved with the details of their day's shopping.

"Did you get your game at Troon, Tom?" his wife asked at last, struck by the unusual silence that was being maintained by her husband.

It was his custom to poke fun at them over their shopping, but to-day he scarcely opened his lips.

"No. I had nine holes on the old course, came home to my lunch, and then went to a wedding," he said stolidly.

"Went to a wedding!" they both repeated in amazement. "You mean you popped into the church in passing, I suppose. But nobody that we know was getting married to-day, eh, Ellie?" said her mother.

"Oh, yes. Somebody that you know very well was married to-day. The marriage, however, was in no church—it was in the library of Ballochean at three o'clock this afternoon. I just wandered up, thinking I might see Meg about somewhere and ask her why she has been so little to see us of late. I arrived in the very nick of time, and I saw her married to David Sillars. So she has stolen a march on you, Ellie, and they'll all be so busy talking about the new mistress of Kildoon that they'll hardly have time to be interested in the new Lady Kessock."

CHAPTER XVII

THE WEDDING JOURNEY

MEG had changed her mind about going home to Kildoon from Ballochean, and they drove direct to Troon Station and journeyed to Kilmarnock to join the south-going train *en route* for Paris.

She was perfectly composed and cheerful, even taking a certain childish delight in the details of the wedding journey, the first stage of which was to end at Carlisle.

At Kilmarnock they were recognised by two Ayr people, who, not knowing that they were married, treasured up the occurrence for discussion and dissemination on their arrival home.

Sillars, who left nothing to chance, had reserved a compartment in the Carlisle train, and the stationmaster, suspecting what had happened, was most solicitous and attentive.

The heavy baggage was put in the van, and Sillars swung his wife's dressing-case to the rack.

" Perhaps you would find a maid in Paris, Madge," he said. " It will be a fag for you looking after your own things."

Meg laughed lightly.

" Oh, no ! I should not know what to do with a maid. She would get in my way. I daresay there is a housemaid at Kildoon who would be able to do all I want. I should like that Ellen creature I saw at Greenock, David. She has understanding."

" I daresay you could get her, my dear," he answered. " Won't you take off your hat and make yourself comfortable for the rest of the journey ? We shan't get to Carlisle till half-past eight."

" My hat isn't heavy. Besides, some one may come in."

" Nobody will. I've reserved the carriage. You are tired, and you don't want people to be staring at you," he answered, with his usual kindly consideration.

" You think of everything, David," she said, as she took out the pins, and laid the hat on the seat beside her, at the same time leaning back with a sudden gesture of weariness. " I'm really dead-tired. I can't think what has come to me lately. I feel such an old crock ! I didn't sleep last night. It's a dreadful thing not to sleep, David—it makes the night hideous."

" I know it—but you are going to rest now. You are clean away from everything that will worry you. I've wired to Carlisle, and they'll make us comfortable at the hotel there, too. To-morrow we'll go to London, and we will have a few days at the Metropole or the Langham. Or would you like something gayer—the Carlton or Prince's ? We don't get married every day, Madge."

" No, but I don't want you to spend too much money on me, David. I keep thinking of what you have to do for Ballochean and my folk. It is that that keeps me awake at nights."

" I'm sorry to hear it. Why should it keep you awake at nights ? "

" Well, because it hurts—you can't imagine how it hurts—and I haven't done wondering yet why you should take the whole burden on your shoulders, as you have done."

" Oh ! it'll pay me in the long run," he assured her. " I'll get my money back —that is, if Guy sticks in and goes on as he has begun," he said hopefully. "Anyway, it's not a thing you have any occasion to worry about."

" It's easy for you to speak. You are the benefactor, David, and you have never had to owe anything to anybody. To be under obligation is the sort of thing that weighs me down to the very dust. And I must tell you here," she added, leaning her elbows on her knees and looking across at him with that deep, searching disconcerting glance that had at once something of the woman and something of the child in its depths, " that I shall not spend an unnecessary penny at Kildoon, or cost you anything more than I can help."

" But that would displease me very much, my dear ; and the first thing we shall do when we get to Paris is to spend a hundred or two on clothes for you."

" A hundred or two of pounds, do you mean ? " she asked aghast.

" It is what I do mean," he answered, smiling back into her eyes.

In spite of all his former misgivings, in spite of the strange rôle he was playing, and intended to play, he was subtly conscious of a sense of joy at being there in the compartment alone with her. She did not love him, but at least no other man would make love to her now. She would be loyal enough to prevent that. And perhaps some day her heart might awaken, and she would turn to him of her own accord.

" But I won't let you, David," she remonstrated. " A hundred pounds' worth of clothes ! Why, my wedding frock cost only five, and it will last me ever so long!"

" Ah ! stop till you see the shops in the Rue-de-la-Paix and the Place Vendome. Then you'll change your tune, my lady," he said.

" Won't you smoke a pipe, David ? Then I should feel more at home."

He obeyed with alacrity, and she leaned back, while he placed his own suit-case for her feet, and arranged the rug about her knees.

" Don't wait on me like that. I'm not used to it. I won't be mollycoddled, David. And I can't believe that we have really got clean away from them all ! Oh ! wasn't it glorious that Dr. Dove just came in in the very nick of time ? He's told them at home by now ! What would I not give to see their faces ? "

She was a girl again, full of girlish inconsequence, laughing over the march that she had stolen on her sometime friend.

Presently she put another question.

" David, how rich are you ? If I am your wife, mayn't I know ? "

" I can't exactly tell you at this moment. But there will be enough for this jaunt anyway, and a little something left over to go on with when we get back to Kildoon."

" And when we do get back we go on just as you were doing before—the week-ends at home and the middles at Greenock ? I'm going to like that, I think. The dear little house at the works ! I'll never forget it, David."

Sillars got up suddenly and busied himself about the fastening of the window. And Meg did not get an answer then to her question about the arrangement of their lives after they should have returned to Kildoon.

Sillars was an accomplished traveller, and he had been practically all over the world. In his father's lifetime he had even spent two years on the plantation in Jamaica, for old Robert Sillars had believed in training those under him in the way that they should go, and he had not spared his son.

Work, however, had never been a hardship to David ; and though he could now afford to take considerable leisure, he had of late been much of a stay-at-home.

In other circumstances what a joy it would have been to him to have introduced his wife to scenes and treasures which he had himself enjoyed. She was wholly unawakened, uninterested even, simply because she had seen so little and had no idea of what the world beyond the confines of their own sea-board was like.

He tried to interest her with talk about the great capitals which she would shortly see for the first time ; but, though she listened politely, he could see that her thoughts were otherwise engaged.

It was something of a relief to him when they came at last to Carlisle, where they found the hotel porter waiting to convey their luggage.

" I suppose you won't unpack your trunk," said Sillars inquiringly. " Have you all that you want in the dressing-bag ? "

" I think so. Do we go off quite early in the morning ? "

" Just as early as you feel inclined. There is no need for haste about anything. We are going to stop away a month."

" A whole month ! " she exclaimed blankly. " But shan't we get very tired of it ? "

" I don't see why we should. We need not stop long in any one place. There is the whole Continent of Europe in front of us."

Meg stepped out of the train, appearing to ponder deeply ; and while her husband was talking to the hotel porter she looked vaguely about the big station, thinking queerly of the strange change that had come over her life. Yesterday—nay, that very morning—she was a free agent, little more than a bit of driftwood on the shore ; and now she was under jurisdiction, her comings and goings subject to the will and the power of the tall man who everywhere seemed to command respect and attention.

True he was the kindest of custodians, consulting her desires at every turn, but always with him rested the final word. And, since he had decreed that they should be wanderers for a whole month, then wanderers they must be, and she must resign herself!

It was an odd experience for Meg Hamilton, and in that strange pregnant moment on the platform at Carlisle Station she came face to face with the reality of things. But not with the full reality. For as yet she was perfectly quiescent, mortally tired of everything, glad to be with one who would undertake for her. The day of suffering was to come!

Inside the hotel the instructions of Sillars, received by letter, had been scrupulously attended to. A small suite of rooms had been reserved for his wife and a room for himself on a different floor. He had offered no explanation of this to the management, nor did he explain to Meg. She accepted the situation as she found it, and, if she was surprised, or hurt, or mystified, she made not the smallest sign.

Declining the offer of the chambermaid's attentions, she shut the door, looked round the rooms, which were well furnished and perfectly comfortable, a cheerful fire burning in both sitting-room and bedroom grates, and everything arranged as for a guest to whom money was apparently no object.

She took off her hat and coat, touching with lingering and appreciative fingers the lovely sable of the great roll-collar, and, approaching the long pier-glass, she took a long survey of herself. She was struck by her slimness, which the straight lines of her plain, well-fitting blue gown seemed to accentuate. But the face, somehow, did not look like her own. The strain of the last week and the ravages of overwrought feelings had left their traces on it.

" I'm getting old," she said viciously. " I've got crows' feet near my eyes and horrid lines round my mouth! And I had the sauce to tell him only a few weeks ago that he might be my father!"

Her colour rose a little, and with some haste she began to undo her frock. Then, finding some of the fastenings baffle her, she was obliged to summon the chambermaid.

" I'm sorry to bring you back, but I thought I could manage for myself," she said apologetically. " I hope you had not to come far ? "

" Oh ! no, miss—I mean ma'am," she said, catching sight of the plain ring on the lady's beautiful hand. " I sits on the landing till half-past eleven."

" What a queer place to sit on ! But why do you do that ? " she asked interestedly, being quite new to the ways of hotels.

" Oh ! to be handy, ma'am, for the bells. There's two of us on each landing. We does a bit of needlework after the rooms are done, and we attend to the bells. Can I take out your things ? "

" There is only a little silk frock in the bag. Yes, you may lay it out, thank you, while I wash."

She felt suddenly glad to have the companionship of the girl, for it seemed a very large place, and David had disappeared. There was no self-consciousness about her. She had given very little thought to the new estate on which she had entered, and nothing that was happening now had the power to disturb her seriously.

But the girl who attended was in a state of lively curiosity.

" Can't make it out," she said, when, after having fastened the lady into a pretty gown of blue silk, she had gone back to her companion on the landing—and she spoke in an excited whisper. " Looks like new-married—but they can't be ! Somethink up—him nowhere to be seen ! As good as a play, Liza. Hope they'll stop a bit and let's watch it out."

Now fully dressed, and not knowing what to do next, Meg sat down before the fire to wait, and presently back came the maid with a little apologetic tap at the door.

"Please'm, the gentleman has sent up to ask if you are ready. He's waitin' for you down below."

"I am quite ready," answered Meg, and off she went, leaving her dressing-bag open, without giving a thought to possible marauders.

Half-way down the stairs she found Sillars, who had changed into a dinner-jacket and a black tie.

"I ought to have come up to fetch you," he said, and when the maid overheard these words she felt reassured. "They are still busy in the dining-room, but they have cooked something special for us."

Meg, rather interested, for this was her first experience of hotel life, followed him across the big hall—where some of the early diners were already at coffee—and into the large, brilliantly-lighted restaurant.

"What a lot of people!" she cried excitedly as they entered. "Are all hotels crammed like this?"

"Not always. There is a conference of some kind going on in the town this week, and that accounts for the crowd. I've stopped here when it was deadly dull. I hope you like your rooms, and have found there everything you want."

"Oh, yes, they're all right," she answered casually. "I do believe I am hungry, David. I don't remember having had any lunch to-day, and, before leaving Ballochean, I drank only one cup of tea, which Jean brought to me upstairs when I was dressing. Chronic hunger seems to be my state when I am with you! Do you remember that meal at Langdyke? But you can't, for you were not there to see it. It was a Gargantuan feast, and I became torpid immediately after."

Sillars smiled at the reminiscence, relieved to find his wife so perfectly natural, apparently so little disturbed by the new conditions in which she found herself. If only she would remain so, and be the pleasant comrade and cheerful travelling companion, they might rub along. It was all he hoped for, perhaps desired—just that they should rub along!

She seemed deeply interested in all the people about her, though they were a highly conventional and rather dingy crowd, as the practised attenders of conferences often are, being given to bestowing more attention on their minds than on their physical adornment.

She speculated on them all in turn, and highly amused Sillars by some of her comments, being quite unaware that they, in turn, were objects of much interested curiosity to their fellow-guests.

By the time they had finished dinner, to which Meg did ample justice, it was ten o'clock.

"We had better take coffee in the lounge, as I daresay they want to clear up—and you must get to bed soon," he said when they rose. "Well, what about to-morrow? Would you like to stay in Carlisle till lunch-time, and have a look round some of the places of historical interest?"

"Yes, if you like. I don't mind. As you have said, there is no hurry, and perhaps we may never be back in Carlisle again."

They stepped out into the hall, took their places at a little table, coffee was brought to them, and Sillars lit a cigar.

A handsome, well-matched pair they looked, and many regarded them with both interest and approval, all quite unconscious of the strange web of chance in which they had become enmeshed, and so had been placed in circumstances fitted to try their finest mettle.

Though Meg was fortified by the dinner, Sillars, watching her closely, saw that unutterable weariness was stealing over the girl, and he understood that, now the final plunge had been taken, the strain of the past weeks must inevitably have begun to tell on her.

"I think you should go to bed," he said gently, not looking at her as he rose. "I'll take a turn outside, I think, and have a pipe. I hope you'll have a good sleep and be ready for sight-seeing to-morrow. Be sure and ring if you want anything. The more trouble you give in a hotel," he added with a touch of cynicism, "the more attention you are likely to get."

"I have all I want, David, thank you. Shall I go up now. Then, good-night. In the morning shall I come down here for breakfast?"

"Yes, about nine o'clock, if that will suit you."

He walked with her to the foot of the stairs, did not offer to shake hands, however, and with a kindly nod walked rapidly away.

Meg ascended the stairs alone, passed into her rooms, and shut the door, immediately slipping the bolts.

Her bedroom was the picture of warmth and comfort, but a sudden sense of the most appalling desolation swept over her, and she stood quite still in the middle of the floor and wrung her hands.

She was David Sillars' wife in name, and that was all. Without doubt he intended her to remain so; and for the rest of their lives they would be like casual travellers lodging at an inn together, with some slight threads of mutual interest to bind them together—but nothing more!

She tossed her head proudly, walked once more to the long mirror, and looked at herself. A kind of startling beauty was reflected back upon her, and, for the first time, she realised that she was very fair. In all her life she had never given a thought to her personal charms; but now she took inventory of them, one by one, with a kind of merciless exactitude.

Critical to the last degree, Meg beheld nothing there to make her gnash her teeth, for the vision was more than fair. The exquisite blue of her gown became her, the colour was high in her cheek, and a kind of wild, rebellious fire was in her eyes.

"Very well," she said to herself, as she began with nervous, even angry, fingers to tear off her gown, "if that is what he wants—why, then, he shall have it! But perhaps the day will come——"

The strain did not lift, however, and she went sobbing to her pillow, because of all women she felt herself the most accursed.

But she was very young, and was physically tired, and sleep quickly wooed her. She slept dreamlessly, and was only awakened by the chambermaid's small, insistent knock at the door when she brought the hot water.

When she sprang up a gleam of wintry sunshine lay across her bed, and eight o'clock was pealing from a church tower in the immediate vicinity.

The shrill scream of steam whistles and the noise of shunting trains, which had been going on all night without awakening her, now seemed to fill the air, warning her to rise to begin the duties of the new day.

Duties? What were they? She wondered, as she dressed, how she would be able to live through the whole month of complete idleness, of this strange, detached life, and how she would feel towards David Sillars at the end of it.

By nine o'clock she was quite ready to go down, and, looking very trim and fresh and attractive, she left the room and descended to the hall, where she found Sillars standing by the great fire-place with a newspaper in front of him, in the contents of which he was evidently entirely absorbed.

She was quite close to him before he became aware of her approach.

"Good morning, David. Am I not very punctual?" she asked in her clear, cool voice, in which there was not a hint of embarrassment. "I hope you've slept well?"

He dashed the paper down and looked at her keenly, well pleased to see that she appeared rested, and that there was no shadow on her face.

"I hadn't a very good night. My room, unfortunately, was on the station side, and the noise was fiendish. I hope you are rested."

"I never woke once until somebody fetched hot water. How is the congress this morning? Has it breakfasted, individually and collectively?"

"It's at breakfast now, I believe. Let us go in," he answered, his relief deepening now that he was assured that she was in quite a tranquil and happy mood.

Her spirits did not flag that day, nor did they on any of the days they spent in England.

They remained over the week-end in London, which, being altogether new to Meg, was a great revelation. They went about like brother and sister, or like comrades, both to outward seeming finding the arrangement perfectly satisfactory.

On Monday morning they took the boat-train to Paris, which they reached in time for dinner.

Sillars had booked rooms at the Continental, and when they reached and entered it Meg was a little awed by its magnificence. But the brightness and gaiety pleased her, for she was young, and was susceptible to all outward impressions.

" How I should like to know all about the people in this room, David," she said as they settled to their places in the dining-room for dinner. " I am sure their stories would be more enchanting than anything one reads in books."

" I dare say," admitted Sillars; and rather absently and privately he wondered whether the story of any in the room would be more interesting then their own.

Meg was looking radiant. The week of perfect rest and immunity from care had restored the roundness to her cheek, and her eyes sparkled and shone. Looking at her, one could have imagined her the happiest creature, without a care.

A good many regarded them with interest, and Sillars was proud of her and she of him in an odd, secret way, which neither of them would have cared to acknowledge. Again and again Meg had felt a little thrill of pride at the distinction of the manner and bearing which, though quiet and unobtrusive, invariably obtained him prompt attention, and people obeyed him naturally, and never withheld from him the regard to which he was entitled.

Even here, in the great Paris hotel, where distinguished guests were the order of the day, he could hold his own.

" Say, David, look at that perfectly sweet old lady, with her hair dressed just as if she had stepped out of an old French picture—there, over in the corner. Do you think the man beside her will be her son ? "

Sillars looked in the direction she indicated, and beheld a small but very stately old lady, wearing a gown of old-fashioned brocade, much trimmed with lace, and a beautiful cap of lace, which made an exquisite frame for her fine, high-bred face. With her at the table was a handsome man of about thirty-five, who looked like a soldier, and who apparently was waiting on her with the greatest tenderness and assiduity.

" Probably he will. They're a handsome pair," he said; and at the moment he saw the man's eyes fall on Meg's face and linger there with interest.

" I suppose one never gets to know people in hotels," said Meg regretfully. " This is the third that we've been in, and I have never spoken to anybody except servants."

" It's unusual; and hotel acquaintances, as a rule, are not very desirable. But, if we go on to Nice or Monte Carlo, and make a stay, I dare say we might make an acquaintance or two. But one has to be careful."

" But I should love to speak to that old lady ! She must be French, of course. But he looks like an Englishman. Let us romance a little about them ! She isn't his mother at all, but just his aunt, or his godmother, and he has brought her to Paris for a little trip, and is going to show her everything. She is very fond of him. Perhaps even she has brought him up, and he has no other mother. Don't you think that that might fit the case ? "

" It might," said Sillars, much amused.

" And she simply adores him, and thinks there is nobody in the world like him," went on Meg. " And, if he ever wants to marry, the position for the girl whom he marries will be very difficult, for she will never be able to pass the bar of the old lady's judgment. I'm not sure, now I get a better look at his face, whether I quite like it. What do you think of him, David ? "

" Looks a trifle heavy and dour, doesn't he ? An army man, I could bet my bottom dollar. I think they feel that we are talking about them, Meg. We'd better get on with our dinner."

Meg dropped her eyes on her plate at once.

" I believe they're interested in us. There's one thing certain, anyway, and that is that nobody could possibly take us for a newly-married couple," she said quietly.

" Oh, couldn't they ? But that's what we are ! How do you make that out ? "

" We don't look like it. I told that funny little maid at Carlisle that we had been married a million years ! You should have seen her look at me."

" What made you say that ? " he asked with a puzzled air.

" Well, because she was so frightfully curious that I thought I should give her something to think about. Now, they're sitting up. She has a jewelled stick. See how lovely he is to her ! She does look as if she had stepped out of a picture ! I should just love to know her."

" It's unlikely we can attain to that," said Sillars, " unless we find some mutual acquaintance to introduce us."

But, to please Meg, he determined to make some inquiry as soon as he had an opportunity.

As it happened, however, when Meg went into one of the drawing-rooms a little later in the evening, while Sillars was occupied in answering some of the letters which had been sent on from Scotland to Paris, she found its solitary occupant to be the old lady who had so deeply interested her at the dinner table.

She was reading one of the French evening papers, and Meg began to wonder what would occur if she should happen to speak to her in French. Should she ever be able to answer her? Once she had known French fairly well, for her father spoke it fluently. But of late years it had seldom been heard in the house of Ballochean, and Meg's had grown rusty.

She took up one of the illustrated journals, and sat down in a corner of a settee at a respectful distance from the old lady, who presently peered over the top of her newspaper at her, and, after that brief observation, addressed her in good English, with, however, a strong foreign accent.

"Will you not come nearer the fire, madame? It is cold out of doors in November."

Meg rose at once, for the voice was so winning and kind that it somehow compelled her.

"Thank you. I do not feel cold. I come from Scotland, where the weather is never very hot, and, besides, this hotel is delightfully warm."

"You think so? I find it draughty; and I always prefer something smaller. But every other here is quite full. I am only here for a few days. I came up from Touraine to meet my nephew. He is on leave, and we go by the end of the week further south."

"To Nice, perhaps?" said Meg, eagerly, thinking how delightful and fortunate it was to hear in one sentence all she wished to know.

"No—to Cannes at first. We have some relatives who have a villa there. You also, perhaps, go south?"

"We may. I think my—husband wants to go; but I am not sure."

She hesitated on the word, and her face flushed when she at last got her tongue round it.

The old lady smiled delightedly, pleased with the simplicity and modesty of the girl whom her nephew had so much admired in the restaurant.

"Ah! and so you are married, madame? We wondered—Hubert and I. When one is idle one is interested in the passing show. We meant no rudeness, madame."

"Oh, no, of course not!—how could you? I, too, was making up a story about you," said Meg, with a laugh.

"Ah, so! You speak French, perhaps? Indeed I think so. You ought to, and I am much more at home in my own tongue."

"I could speak it once," answered Meg, in French, rather hesitatingly. "But in Scotland one has little opportunity of practicing it."

"Ah, so! You come from Scotland, where I have many good friends. Your name, if you please, madame?"

"Mrs. Sillars," answered Meg, and once more the red flooded her cheek. "Before I married it was Hamilton."

"Ah—Hamilton! That is one of the best of your country's names. I knew some Hamiltons in Paris. But that is an old story. Yes, Hubert, I am here, and being vastly entertained."

The young man came forward, and the old lady briefly introduced him.

"This is Major Kettering, my nephew, Mrs. Sillars. I am the Marquise de Balincourt. You have been stationed in this lady's country, have you not, Hubert? She is from Scotland."

"Yes—at Edinburgh—and at Glasgow, for my sins," he answered lightly. "But I ask your pardon. I ought not to speak disparagingly of what you love."

"I don't love Glasgow," said Meg with a smile; "and I know very little about Edinburgh. My home is at Ayr."

"At Ayr! I have been there twice, Mrs. Sillars—once on a visit to Sir Claude Oliphant at Garsdale, and once to spend a day at the races."

The Marquise rose and said they had better be going since the carriage was waiting.

" We go to see an old friend who is an invalid, madame. Good-night and good-bye. But it is my hope that we may meet again."

" And mine," echoed Kettering, as he bowed low at parting.

And Meg had the feeling which she could not have put into words that it was a hope likely to be realised, and that some day, somewhere, she would meet Hubert Kettering again.

CHAPTER XVIII

BIRDS OF PASSAGE

At Nice, to which they travelled fully a week later, to Meg's delight, they came upon the Marquise and Kettering once more. Walking on the promenade, they beheld the young officer strolling dutifully beside the old lady's chair, and his eyes brightened at sight of Meg's face under the brim of her shady hat.

The glorious flood of sunshine in which the whole Mediterranean seaboard was bathed came as a revelation to the girl, accustomed, as she had been, to long grey winters by the northern sea. Her joy in it was that of a child, while the delight of Sillars consisted in watching her and the effect which her various experiences were having on her.

Sometimes he found himself a trifle startled, and he could not help wondering what the years in front, spreading out in an illimitable vista, would bring to him and her. When such thoughts swept over him like a resistless flood, he found untold comfort in the reflection that he would still have the middle of each week at Greenock immune from all the dangerous lure of her presence.

For often he found it difficult to maintain the mask of indifference, even though she apparently was perfectly satisfied with his treatment of her. A kinder friend, a more solicitous, considerate travelling companion than Sillars it would not have been possible to find, and Meg found the days speeding with much haste.

The slight feeling of home-sickness which, at the beginning, had undoubtedly often visited her heart, quickly disappeared, and, like a flower, she seemed to open in the sun, becoming a radiant creature.

She had begun to take an interest in the beautiful things to be bought out of shops, and she no longer protested when David asked to be allowed to buy them for her. Poor Meg, who had never had one superfluous penny in Scotland, on discovering that Sillars apparently regarded money as an article made to roll, became, for her, most frightfully extravagant.

It was things pertaining to the toilet that she chiefly desired—pretty blouses, dainty laces, trifles for her neckwear, sunshades, becoming hats. The windows of jewellers' shops did not tempt her, for she wore no jewels, and she often said that to hang chains of gold or of precious stones about one's neck was to proclaim oneself a barbaric creature.

When they met Kettering and his aunt it was Meg who involuntarily stopped. She was so natural in all her movements and in all the impulses of her heart, and she had seen so little of the conventions of society, that she did not know that she ought to have waited for recognition from the older woman, especially from one of such high rank.

But the Marquise showed no displeasure—nay, her keen eye brightened at the vision of the girl in her white embroidered frock and shady hat and parasol of daring red.

"Ah! good morning. And is this the husband, my dear?" said the old lady, leaning from the side of her bathchair and extending a perfectly gloved hand.

"Yes," answered Meg, a trifle shyly; and Sillars, whose manners never left an impression of awkwardness, immediately stepped into the breach.

He was quite well aware that both the Marquise and her English nephew were regarding him with critical eyes, and with some curiosity also, as the husband of the girl whom they had already met.

He looked well and irreproachably dressed, but the years had told. His appearance, however, pleased the Marquise, accustomed, as she was, to marriages arranged by parents with due regard to position and family interest and with none at all to individual taste.

" I am pleased to make your acquaintance, monsieur, and, if you will walk on with Major Kettering, I shall like very much to have a little talk to your most charming wife."

Sillars smiled, and that smile, so rare and winning, left its impression on the Marquise's womanly heart. Kettering, however, did not look so well pleased as his aunt. He would have infinitely preferred to have been allowed to continue the walk by the side of Meg and to have had further opportunity of watching the play of light and shade of expression on her lovely face. Nevertheless, the Marquise had her will, as was invariably the case, for, in her way, she was a little queen, and might have held court there in Nice had she chosen, among all the aristocrats—herself one of the most distinguished of them all.

Meg had no idea what a signal mark of approval the old French lady had bestowed upon her by thus permitting her to walk beside her chair in intimate converse—a privilege permitted to a very few indeed, for the Marquise belonged to the old regime, and was well known as one of the most exclusive visitors to the Riviera in the season.

" I am pleased to make the acquaintance of your husband, my dear," she said graciously, as she watched the two men walking on in front. " Tell me, is this the wedding journey ? "

" Yes," answered Meg without a tremor, for already her wedding day seemed like ancient history. " It is."

" How long since the happy event ? "

" Three weeks only. I was married on the twentieth day of November, madame."

" Ah, well ! this is the halcyon time of joy in your life ! "

" Is it ? " asked Meg simply. " Well, certainly it is lovely here."

The Marquise laughed and tapped with her lorgnette on the side of her chair.

" Do not put on that woman-of-the-world air. It does not at all suit you," she said kindly. " If one is full of joy, why should not one show it ? The world needs it, my dear. Never seek to hide the happy heart. For, look you, there are hundreds with hearts at the breaking point, rushing hither and thither, trying to find distraction from secret care."

" I suppose so," said Meg in a lowered voice, for these words had surprised and startled her, with such a passion were they spoken. " But mostly it is people's own fault, don't you think ? They do the wrong thing."

" Ah, my dear, you have said it ! But I like not such worldly wisdom from your lips. Surely you at least cannot have had care as yet ? "

" I ? Oh, I was cradled in it, madame ! I've never known anything else. But sometimes one can forget, and then nothing matters."

She spoke in French because she knew that the Marquise preferred that language, and that gave a kind of halting certainty to her speech, which somehow accentuated it.

" Ah ! but now the care is past, my dear, I am sure. That husband of yours with the grave, kind face and the perfect manner will not ever permit any care to approach you."

" He is very good," said Meg quietly, but there was an entire absence of warmth in her voice.

" And it is well that a woman, when young, should have one a little older than herself to guide her. Believe me, my dear, these are the happiest marriages. Here one sees so very often mere children on their wedding journey ! They come from England, of course. Such things are not permissible in France."

" They arrange people there, don't they, madame ? I have heard so."

" They do. And nowhere are there happier homes than in France. I tell my nephew that, if only he will permit me to be a French mother to him and arrange his marriage, I can promise him all the happiness that would be good for him and which he will never find for himself, for in the affairs of the heart men are like children, my dear, ever crying for the moon ! "

" Are they, madame ? " asked Meg, much interested.

" I want to hear more about your home in Scotland," said the old lady presently. " Have you brothers and sisters ? "

" Two brothers, a father, and no mother. I have not been well brought up, madame—at least, that is what they say."

The Marquise smiled.

"The finished product, at any rate, is very good," she said indulgently. "But now you will go back to fill the position your husband has given you with honour and dignity. It is what men prize. But so many of our sex hold their vows lightly in these days, thinking of nothing but selfish enjoyment and pleasure-seeking. This place is full of them."

"Oh! but I think men need to be reminded of that, too," said Meg spiritedly. "The selfishness and the pleasure-seeking are not all on our side. I've not seen very much of life, but I have observed that."

"That may be so; but it does not lessen the sum of our responsibility. Always remember this, my dear, that it is to us, the women of all nations, that God has entrusted the high task of keeping the standard of life pure. Forgive my little homily. A little faster, Alphonse, and we shall come up with the gentlemen. It is time for me to go in now."

Presently they came up with Kettering and Sillars, and for a brief moment they and Meg made a little group about the Marquise's bath-chair.

"You will bring your most charming wife to dine with me one night at the Villa Beau Site, monsieur?" said the Marquise, smiling graciously. "Shall we fix it now—to-morrow evening, perhaps?"

"Thank you," muttered Sillars, not very cordially, having no valid reason for refusing.

Perhaps he had not liked his brief conversation with Kettering, or perhaps he did not like the admiration he saw in the eyes which dwelt on Meg's face. But the fact that Meg seemed utterly unconscious of the admiration reassured him, and the little arrangement was satisfactorily made, and they parted with many bows and smiles.

"She's a lovely old dear!" said Meg enthusiastically. "But you're looking most awfully glum, David. Didn't the Major come up to expectations?"

"He fancies himself—as the British officer is apt to do—and he talked very tall. He was very anxious to find out all about us, but I kept him on short commons. We'll go to-morrow night, of course, since you seem to have fallen in love with the old lady and she with you. But after that we'll just drop them gradually. You remember what I said to you about chance acquaintances?"

"I do. But then, they are rather amusing, David; and, after all, we can't live all our lives without talking to outside people. Think how soon we shall be back at Kildoon, where we shall never see anybody! Have I got anything to wear to-morrow night suitable for one who has to dine with a real Marquise?"

"Supposing we go back to the hotel and see," suggested Sillars, with a smile at her childish enjoyment of the passing show. "If you haven't it might be possible to find something suitable in the course of twenty-four hours. It is all a question of payment, I believe."

"Oh! but, David, haven't I been extravagant since we have been here? You gave me ten pounds the day before yesterday, and it is nearly all gone."

Sillars smiled.

"I laid aside as much as I thought we should spend on this trip, my dear, and there's a margin yet, so don't pucker your brows."

"That's all right, then. Of course, as you're so much older and wiser than I am, David, it would be your own fault if I spend too much. All you have got to do is to stop giving me money. Then, you see, I won't be able to buy the things."

Sillars did not smile this time. He was super-sensitive with regard to the adjectives she had applied to him.

"And, after all," Meg continued, "I'm your pupil. I started out meekly, and I was full of good resolutions. If you had encouraged them you would be at least a hundred pounds richer than you are to-day."

A brief inspection of her limited wardrobe convinced Meg that she had nothing suitable to wear at the dinner at the Villa Beau Site. This rendered necessary the spending of an afternoon at the shops. She found what she wanted in one of them—a little gown of white satin veiled in green chiffon which set off the amazing fairness of her beautiful skin. The price staggered her, but when Sillars said she might have it she was filled with all the joy of a novice in possessing such dainty attire.

And when she came to array herself, certainly the vision reflected back from the long pier-glass was a little overwhelming in its magnificence.

Even Sillars was startled by it when she came down with her cloak over her arm.

"You look stunning, Madge, and I'm a bit afraid of being seen with such a vision splendid. I think I had better get you back to bonnie Doon as quickly as possible."

"Do you? But the gown is quite simple, David, and not at all low-cut; for, see, I made the dressmaker put another tucker in the bodice, and we had quite a fight over it before she would agree to do it. She said it was not half smart worn so high, and nobody wore them like that. But I will be decent, and I had my way."

She spoke to him precisely as if he had been another woman or a brother whose taste she had to consult; and Sillars smiled a little grimly to himself as he fastened her cloak and helped her to the waiting carriage.

They were the only guests at the Villa Beau Site, where a small dinner, most perfectly cooked and served, was got through in about an hour's time.

Then the Marquise suggested that they should take coffee on the terrace, which commanded a magnificent view of the bay, where the lights twinkling on the yachts made a lovely panorama.

Oddly interested in the pair, the old lady sent Kettering and Meg to walk down to the lower terrace, in order that she might have the opportunity of having a little talk with the husband of the girl who had awakened such warmth of feeling in her heart.

Kettering, hugely pleased with this arrangement, offered Meg his arm as they turned to the terrace steps. But she lightly shook her head and said she could walk alone.

Drawing her fur-trimmed wrap about her, she stepped down the broad path, her eyes glowing and shining like twin stars in her head.

She was intoxicated by the beauty and the novelty of her surroundings.

"You have never been here before?" he said interestedly.

"Never. It is the first time I have ever been out of Scotland," she answered, "and I had no idea the world could be so beautiful."

"It would always be beautiful for such as you," he said involuntarily.

"Do you think so? Oh, but you are quite wrong!" she answered quickly enough. "And though I am pleased to see all this once, of course, I can't imagine why people should want to come out here year after year, and just loaf about as I see them doing. It is such a horrible waste of time."

"But that is what most of them are here for, Mrs. Sillars—just to kill time."

"How strange! I am glad I don't feel like that. I could always find things to do with my time."

"Tell me about your life in Ayr? You can't think how much I am interested in it; and, you see, I know something about Scotland."

"There is very little to tell. I just lived in my father's house until I married," answered Meg in the most matter-of-fact tone. "When I go back I shall live in another house—and that will be all the difference."

"It does not sound very interesting. Is your husband a very busy man with large estates to manage?" he continued, in pursuit of his enquiries.

"Oh, no. His estate is quite small, but his business is large, and it is not in Ayr, but in Greenock. He has never had a holiday for two years, and I hope this one will do him good."

"It ought to—travelling in such company!" said Kettering, who was never at a loss to find a pretty speech to address a pretty woman.

Meg took no notice of it. If she heard it—which was doubtful, for her attention was absorbed in the scenery—it made not the smallest impression.

"I shall hope to re-visit Ayr some day. I have a standing invitation from the Oliphants. I suppose you know them?"

"I know who they are, and they know me. But we are not friends, Major Kettering," answered Meg truthfully.

"But their place is not very far from yours, is it?"

"About four miles. It is not a question of distance. Only my family do not happen to be sociable. How perfectly charming your aunt is," said Meg, bent on changing the subject. "I have never before met anyone quite like her."

"She is rather charming. She has been most awfully good to me. I lost my own mother when I was quite young, and she has brought me up, in a sense. I have spent most of my leave with her. She alternately spoils and scolds me; but I could not imagine life without her."

He spoke with a good deal of genuine feeling, which raised him somewhat in the estimation of Meg. She had not been drawn to him until now. Somehow, he seemed to strike a note of insincerity. He was too much a man of the world to find favour in her eyes. She had no experience of such as he, and she did not care for the subtle flattery of his speeches. She even resented them as impertinent, though the fact was that, coming from Kettering, they were a quite genuine tribute of admiration.

The couple interested Kettering, and he wondered whether a story lay behind their marriage. For already he had decided that the big, slow-going, taciturn Scotsman was no fit mate for this radiant creature, in whose eyes lay unrecked of and unkindled fires. He had great experience with women and had many love affairs. Nothing would have pleased him more than to have been allowed an opportunity of making some small impression on the heart of this girl-wife, who was obviously, so he thought, not appreciated as she ought to be by her middle-aged husband. But he had no opportunity, for Sillars, who had not enjoyed his evening at the Villa Beau Site, announced as they drove to their hotel that he thought they would move on next day.

Meg had no objection—none, at least, that seemed worth mentioning.

"How many places are there to see, and how long shall we be staying abroad yet?"

"Are you tired of it?"

"It seems purposeless to me; and, somehow, this sunshine right in the middle of winter doesn't seem appropriate. It doesn't come up to a good canter on the Ayr sands with a good west wind in front. Shall I have a horse at Kildoon, David? I should like to have one. Father always promised me one when his ship came in!"

"A horse? You shall have half a dozen of them if you like," said Sillars, with an abandon which rather surprised Meg.

"I think one will do. I shall have to restrain this spendthrift habit of yours, David, now that I've had my fling!" she said demurely. "May I ask you something else?"

"Surely! whatever you choose."

"Then tell me what old Van Leyden said when you paid him the money to redeem Ballochean? Did he know you were going to marry me?"

"Your father told him."

"And did he say nothing?—for he was an old dear, David. I think I told you that, even when he was most impossible, he was an old dear; and I am sure he would not be so very angry with me."

"He wasn't angry. He gave me several pieces of advice."

"Did he? Tell me what they were. I am sure they would be worth remembering. He is really most frightfully clever—like a sort of prophet or philosopher."

But Sillars did not satisfy her curiosity at that time, nor did he do so until long after, when there was no barrier between them.

A few more days' wandering, in the course of which Meg got more and more restless, and then they journeyed back to London, arriving early in the evening at the Carlton Hotel.

Meg put on one of her Riviera frocks and went down to dinner prepared to enjoy herself to the full. A singular elation of spirit was hers because she found herself in England again, and already the call of home was in her blood, and she felt that she would be genuinely glad to see the long, grey line of the Firth of Clyde, with Arran in the distance, and the rolling Carrick hills losing themselves in the rim of the low, grey sky.

"David, I shall never be able to settle in Kildoon after all this," she said, nodding across the table at him.

It was now rather more than a month since they left Scotland, and never once in all these days had she lost her temper or been a stupid or a difficult companion. She had amazed Sillars at every turn, and he experienced a strange stir in his blood when he thought that soon they would be together under the roof of his old home, and that their actual everyday life together would have to be faced. This moving from place to place, and this constant sight-seeing was mere play, and so far Meg had appeared to enter into it with her accustomed verve and joy of life.

But the long, quiet days at Kildoon when he would be in Greenock would try the mettle of her pasture, and sometimes in his solitary hours and moments he was afraid.

There was no cloud on her brow now, however, as she sat at table, and there was not in all that gay throng a finer embodiment of radiant youth then she.

The pride which Sillars had in her was as high as the heavens, and he had no idea, because his eyes were holden, how much of pride went to sustain the gallant bearing, or how many secret tears had contributed to the flashing clearness of those starry eyes! Nor did he know—how could he?—of the vow that she had taken to punish him for his slight of her, and to make him rue the day on which he had elected to keep her outside of his heart.

"David, David Sillars!" she said presently, in a breathless whisper. "Don't look round for a second. Let the man put down the fish before you do. You will never, never guess who have just come into this room!"

Sillars very naturally turned his head at once, but a tall palm hid the table, which, however, Meg could see perfectly.

"Now you may look."

"I can't see anything. In what direction do you want me to look?"

"There—just beyond the woman in the red frock and the man with the medals on! Can't you see? Oh, how tiresome you are! Why, it's Hew Kessock and Ellie! This is the twentieth of December, and they were married the day before yesterday. How could I forget?"

"Oh!" said Sillars, and his look was a little blank.

But though he eyed his wife keenly he could detect no sign of perturbation on her face—nothing but the liveliest excitement and a sort of merriment such as a child might have displayed at some unexpected entertainment provided for her delectation.

"They look horribly glum, and Ellie's frock is ugly—a horrid champagny colour which makes her all of one hue! Do I look nice, David? Tell me quick, do I look most awfully nice? My very best? Because I want to. I must—just to get even with them!"

"There isn't a woman in the room fit to hold a candle to you," he answered proudly, and for once all a lover's fire leapt into his eyes.

"Not even the red woman with the ropes of pearls?" eagerly inquired Meg. "Oh, how perfectly ripping! Now I shall patronise Ellie, because I've been married so much longer than she has. We'll just finish dinner quietly, David, and then we shall stroll round that way and appear most frightfully surprised when we come upon them."

Sillars laughed. He could not help himself; she was so much a child. Perhaps he laughed, too, because of the feeling of relief that was in his soul. For surely the wound that Kessock had inflicted on her heart could not have been very deep, else she could not speak thus.

Meg's dinner ceased to interest her, and her eyes kept wandering in the direction of the table where the newly wed pair were sitting together, Ellie obviously feeling a little awed and out of place amid surroundings so gorgeous.

She had none of the natural charm and grace of Meg Hamilton; her distressing consciousness of herself being always uppermost. And the narrow limits of Prospect House had hardly prepared her for this.

"Now, David, if you think you've eaten enough, let us go round," said Meg presently.

"I shall have to pay two guineas at least for this little lot, my dear, so please sit down and finish your dessert," said Sillars whimsically.

"Oh, David! You've no soul! Just think of the fun I'm going to have presently. Do let us go!"

Sillars rose and laid down his napkin, and, turning round, caught Kessock's eye. The recognition, of course, was natural and instantaneous, but before he could draw Ellie's attention Meg was half-way towards them.

"How do you do?" she said, her voice high and sweet, and even a little triumphant. "I've been watching you for the last twenty minutes. But this tiresome man would not hurry. How odd that we should meet here."

Lady Kessock blankly stared. It was the voice of Meg Hamilton that she heard, but this radiant creature in a gown which, though simplicity itself, somehow eclipsed all the glories of Ellie's Glasgow-made trousseau was not, could not be, the Meg Hamilton of the leather-bound skirt and the brogues heavy with good Carrick clay.

"Goodness gracious, Meg!" she gasped at length, and Meg, reading surprise, envy, disgust in Ellison's eyes, felt a little ease at her twice-wounded heart.

CHAPTER XIX

THE END OF THE PLOY

THERE could be no awkwardness in the movement which Meg carried off so superbly.

" How do you do, Sir Hew ? " she said, extending a frank hand with a smile. " A hundred thousand congratulations ! We forgot until we saw you that your wedding-day had come and gone."

The inference intended to be drawn by the Kessocks was that Meg and her husband had been so much occupied with themselves that they had no thought to spare for others.

Kessock was more than amazed—he was dumfounded.

Nothing increases a man's respect for a woman more than the assurance that she has become wholly uninterested in him, or his charms, and has put him entirely outside of her life. Being treated in this way also piques his vanity.

" Why, how did you come here, and where have you been hiding all this time ? " he said stupidly.

" Have we been hiding, David ? " asked Meg merrily. " We've just made the usual honeymoon journey. We came from Paris to-day. Are you going there ? "

" Yes, to-morrow, answered Ellie eagerly, anxious to be upsides with her quondam friend, yet somehow feeling that Meg had stolen a complete march on her.

" We're keeping Sir Hew and Lady Kessock from their dinner, Madge," said Sillars, feeling, for some obscure reason, a little sorry for them. " Perhaps you'll join us at coffee out in the Palm Court ? We'll wait for you."

" There's no ' perhaps ' about it," answered Kessock eagerly. " We're nearly through."

Meg nodded, smiled kindly, if a little patronisingly, at the new Lady Kessock, and then turned away.

A good many eyes—Hew Kessock's among the number—followed her as she moved with stately grace across the room.

" By Jove ! she rather fancies herself—eh, Ellie ? " said he in a somewhat savage undertone, as he dropped into his chair again. " It's a new rôle she's playing, and no mistake. I'd uncommonly like to get at the bottom of it. But there's no doubt she has Sillars on a lead. I'm sorry for him, poor beggar ! "

" I didn't want to see Meg Hamilton here, Hew," said the new bride, with a little distressed pout. " She's always getting in my way."

" Well, as we're going on to-morrow we needn't see much of her, my dear," he said as he poured for himself another glass of champagne. " And, anyway, I didn't know she was here."

Ellie subsided into contemplation of her plate.

" I suppose she really is married ? " she said viciously.

" We read it in the newspapers, didn't we ? " replied her husband. " Besides, old Murchison tied them up as firmly as he tied us up. Told my mother so. And I'm not sure that they had not the best of it—they got out of all the beastly fuss, anyway."

Kessock had not enjoyed the carefully-ordered pomp and circumstance of his wedding day. Few men do ; but, in his case, there were incidents connected with it which had specially irritated him.

He had begun to doubt, even already, whether the " Dove " he had caged was as gentle as her name ; and now, as she sat there puckering her brows, doubts again assailed him.

" Don't screw your face in that fashion, Ellie ! It doesn't become you, and it certainly doesn't improve you. And, if you don't want to see Meg Hamilton here, it won't be very good policy to let her see that, will it ? "

"Don't be horrid, Hew!" she answered with a considerable snap in her voice and a toss of her head. "What can I possibly care whether she is here or not? I think you're quite right to pity poor Mr. Sillars. She'll lead him an awful dance and spend his money like water. People like her always do."

She had contrived to preen and smooth her ruffled plumage again by the time they had joined the other pair at the little table at the bottom of the stairs in the beautiful Palm Court—a table which was cunningly set among the green, and from which a complete view of that fascinating rendezvous of the fashionable world could be obtained.

Meg, with a provoking smile on her lips, watched them approach—Kessock looking well in his evening dress, though his heavy face was a little glum, and Ellie, attired in her much-trimmed "champagny" gown, trying to walk with dignity, which, being a matter of original endowment rather than of acquired habit, had never been one of her strong points.

Sillars rose, set a chair ready for her beside his wife, and they all sat down apparently on the best of terms.

Perhaps the one of the party most at ease was Sillars, who, being a student of men and of things, rather enjoyed this little study in psychology. The conclusion he came to was that either Meg was a consummate actress or the impression Kessock had made on her heart had been completely obliterated.

"Why did you run away, Meg?" inquired Ellie, saying the wrong thing at the wrong moment with surprising exactitude.

Meg's smile suffered the smallest possible quenching; but, instead of answering, she looked straight across the table at her husband.

"David, why did we run away?"

Sillars laughed.

"Faith, and I don't know, unless it was because we both hate fuss."

"It made a most frightful lot of talk, didn't it, Hew?" said Ellie cheerfully. "And there didn't seem a bit of sense in it!"

"But your wedding came along and gave them something else to talk about, didn't it?" said Meg teasingly. "And no doubt they have forgotten all about it by this time."

The man brought the coffee at the moment, and Sillars adroitly changed the subject by inquiring what sort of itinerary Kessock had in his mind's eye after they should have left London.

He had all a woman's keenness of perception, and he did not want that sort of personal questioning to be pursued to the extent of making Meg uncomfortable, though he knew that she was perfectly capable of parrying all Lady Kessock's little thrusts.

They spent a pleasant enough half hour together, at the end of which Kessock suggested that Sillars and he might take a stroll outside, leaving the women to their talk.

"Have you anything to show me, Ellie?" Meg asked when they were alone. "I suppose you got a perfectly gorgeous trousseau?"

"I did get a good many things. Whatever did you marry like that for, Meg? What fun was there in it?"

"No fun at all. But, then, I don't think people get married for fun. And I had very few clothes—only one new frock, Ellie—and I set out on my honeymoon journey in that old serge coat and skirt you've so often jeered at. We stopped in London, however, for a few days, and David bought me some clothes, and I got some more in Paris, and some more again at Nice. I crossed the Channel with one small box, and I've come back with three big ones! It was great fun. I never knew that buying things could be so fascinating."

"Where did you buy that?" asked Ellie, touching the pretty restaurant frock with envious fingers.

"In a little shop at Nice, recommended to me by the Marquise de Balincourt. In fact, she was with me when I bought it. Very French, isn't it?"

"Did it cost a lot?"

"Twenty-five pounds."

"Oh, Meg, Meg, how awful! Why, I haven't anything that cost more than ten! Wasn't Mr. Sillars angry?"

" Oh, no. I could have had a lot more, if I had wished. I'm afraid Mr. Sillars is most disgustingly rich, Ellie, for he simply never thinks about money," said Meg with a serene and unconscious air, hating herself all the while for the poor, mean revenge she was taking, for the smallness and selfishness of her outlook, for her positive delight in the situation.

When a woman asks another woman for her dressmaker's address, as Lady Kessock had done, it is an admission of failure.

" I suppose that's real lace on it," said Ellie with a sigh. " I really wish I knew why you and Mr. Sillars got married in the way you did. It made a most frightful lot of talk."

" Why should it have done so ? It was all very properly managed, with Mr. and Mrs. Murchison and your father as witnesses. By the way, how is dear Dr. Dove, Ellie ? What ages and ages it seems since David and I left Ayr ! "

" Oh ! father's all right. When are you going back ? "

" At the end of the week."

" To live at Kildoon ? "

" Yes, I suppose so."

" And will Mr. Sillars give up business in Greenock ? "

" Gracious, no ! He will have to be at it harder than ever now that he has to keep me."

" But won't it be dull for you all by yourself ? " asked Ellie, continuing her catechism. " Surely he will never go to Greenock five days out of seven, as he used to ! If he were my husband, I would never permit it."

" If Mr. Sillars were your husband, Ellie, you would have to do as you were bid," said Meg quietly. " There isn't anything soft about him ! "

" Oh ! but a wife has certain rights," retorted Ellie. " I'm going to make Hew give up a good many things when I get back to Sangster," she added with great assumption. " I'm studying him at present. His mother has simply ruined him by her mode of bringing him up ! "

" You have something in front of you, Ellie. And I see that marrying a man without relations has compensations," said Meg demurely.

" There aren't any of these that matter except his mother, and she shall go," said the new Lady Kessock calmly. " Mother and I have talked everything over. Of course, we shan't do anything in a hurry. But I really don't see why that pretty old house at Girvan should be let, or lent to other people, when it would make such a nice home for the Dowager."

" Oh, Ellie ! she'll never go there—never in this world," declared Meg.

" Won't she ? Then I will ! " said Ellie, snapping her small mouth together ominously. " But don't let us talk about her now. I mean to have my honeymoon, at any rate, in peace. Now, let's go upstairs. I want to see your things and to show you mine. What floor are you on ? "

" The first," answered Meg.

" The first ! Why, I believe we are six or seven, or something even higher ! I'm afraid you are wickedly extravagant, Meg, and I'm astonished at you."

" It is not I who do the spending. It is David who insists on spending the money."

They ascended the lift together to Ellie's room, where her frocks and some of the jewellery that she had received as wedding presents were duly inspected and admired.

" The presents made a lovely show, Meg," said Ellie impressively. " You missed that, anyway. Fancy not having a single present ! And not even a bit of jewellery ! How dull ! Hew gave me this pearl chain and pendant. Didn't Mr. Sillars give you anything ? "

Meg's bosom suddenly heaved.

" I don't care for jewellery. I shouldn't wear them if I had ropes of pearls. He has given me everything I wanted—and a great deal more than I deserve," she added, and that was the truest word she had spoken the whole evening.

" Let us go down now and see your things," suggested Ellie, after all the silks and furs and other things had been disposed of in the capacious wardrobe.

But Meg seemed suddenly to have become remote and inaccessible.

" There isn't anything much to see," she said evasively ; " only a few frocks and blouses and some furs which David bought me at Revillon Frères in Paris."

"I simply must see them," insisted Ellie, "in order that I may tell Hew. Come on, Meg. Don't be mean and horrid! After all, isn't it great that we should have met here? There is so much that we can both be interested in now, having been married about the same time. I never thought it would happen!"

Meg had no valid excuse for refusing, and presently they entered the lovely suite of rooms which Sillars had provided for his wife.

Ellie looked around discontentedly and enviously.

"You must either be millionaires or be having a frightful burst, for which, of course, you'll have to pay afterwards! And what tidiness! Wherever does Mr. Sillars keep his things? I'm always at Hew for leaving his lying about. Don't you think men are untidy, Meg?"

"I haven't noticed it."

"But I don't see a thing of Mr. Sillars'!"

"He keeps them in his drawers and wardrobes, same as I do."

"It's distressing to have a man so tidy. I suppose it is because he was such an old bachelor that he has learned to put everything away. He's making you turn over a new leaf, I see."

"Come and see this, Ellie," said Meg, with a queer, strange note in her voice; and the next moment the wardrobe and the drawer were opened, and Ellie was deep in the mysteries of Parisian clothes.

"I can't believe that it's really you who are showing me all these things," said Ellie as they descended in the lift to see whether their men folk had returned. "I suppose you are going to cut a tremendous dash in the county when you get back?"

"I don't suppose I shall. I'll get into the old leather-bound skirt and the flannel blouse with lightning speed. This is merely an episode," said Meg, and something crept into her eyes.

The new Lady Kessock, being without discernment, saw nothing. But she did mention to her husband that it seemed very queer not to find the least trace of the presence of David Sillars in his wife's rooms.

"Not so much as a tie was hanging on the dressing-table glass. So please take note, Hew. And, by the way, I want some furs like Meg's from the Revillon Frères, and a frock from the same place in Nice where she got that one she had on to-night."

Meg said good-night to her husband on the landing outside her door.

"Thank you so much, David. I have enjoyed myself. I'm nothing but a poor, mean, spiteful worm, after all, and I am ashamed of myself; but I have enjoyed myself, and thank you very much."

"There is nothing to thank me for. This play—or ploy—or whatever you call it, is over, Madge," he said, drawing back with a strange roughness, as if he feared she would touch him. "To-morrow, or the day after, we must get back to real things. Good-night."

"Good-night," she said, and both voice and face hardened as she closed the door.

CHAPTER XX

HOME AGAIN

Two days later David Sillars and his wife arrived at Ayr, where they were met by the brougham from Kildoon.

" I wired to your father asking him to come over with Guy to dinner this evening," said Sillars a trifle nervously when the luggage was on the tray and the restive horses had started forward. " I thought that would be better than feeling ourselves quite alone in the house at first. That would have been a bit trying for you, wouldn't it?"

" I don't know," said Meg, and her voice had a spiritless sound. " I suppose all the servants will be expecting us, David," she said presently, " do you think they will mind ? "

" Mind what ? " he asked, quite at a loss.

" Having me there ? "

" Why should they ? They have been informed that their new mistress will arrive to-night, and that is sufficient for them."

" I shan't upset them, David. You've had them a long time, haven't you ? "

" Some of them have been there since my mother's time," he answered evasively.

" What did they say when you told them that you were going to get married ? " she asked.

This was the first occasion on which she had expressed the smallest interest in the household of Kildoon, and now there was something pathetic in her questioning. Sillars could see that she was a little afraid.

" They were surprised, of course, to hear it ; and Mrs. Maxwell, the housekeeper, said that she would wait until you came home, and that then she would see," he answered with a smile.

" Which means that I'm to be on my trial," said Meg swiftly. " I don't bear any malice against them. I quite understand how they feel. In their place I should hate such a change myself. But I think they will find that I won't worry or upset them. I never yet had any trouble with servants, except old Greig—and she's impossible ! All the younger ones at Ballochean were pleased to serve me. I'm not going to upset arrangements at Kildoon, David."

" I have never for a moment thought that you would," he answered.

" I won't make myself a nuisance at all," she assured him. " And, of course, if we go to Greenock in the middle of the week we shall just be week-enders at Kildoon, so that it won't really make much difference to the staff."

Sillars pondered a moment, let down the window another inch, remarking that the air seemed warmer there than it had been at any place which they had struck since they left Scotland.

Then he spoke up.

" It won't be possible for you to go to Greenock, Madge. It would be preposterous to think of it."

" But you will go, I suppose—or perhaps you are going to give it up ? "

" I can't give it up," he said. " It's my daily bread. Besides, I like my work there. Up till now it has filled my life."

" I see. And you won't mind going away for all these days every week. I quite understand," she said, and though the wounded note in her voice was quite obvious, he hardened himself against it.

" I dare say you will find plenty to do and ways and means of amusing yourself. You will have to pay frequent visits to Ballochean and keep your father and Guy up to the mark. Perhaps you might take to hunting again, if you care for it. It will be quite an easy matter getting you a good mount."

" I don't know that I should want to hunt without you, David, and I'm surprised that you should suggest it. But I daresay I shall find means of filling up my time all right. I'm not one who is ever at a loss for an occupation. Is this the lodge already? How the horses do go the pace! I'm looking forward to making acquaintance with the stables to-morrow."

Sillars was quite conscious of an odd thrill, partly of anticipation, partly of discomfort, as the lights of Kildoon, lying low at the water's edge, began to twinkle through the trees. He could imagine what his home-coming might have been had he been sure of his wife's heart, had their marriage been one of affection and not of arrangement.

He had had a good many difficult hours during the weeks they had been away together, but this one at hand was the one which would try their mettle beyond them all! For the house was hallowed by memories of his mother, who, in the last years of her life, had often spoken to him about the wife whom he would some day bring to take her place. When he had assured her that he was not a marrying man she had only laughed at him, and told him that his day would come. And, lo! it had come in a very different guise from that which either of them had anticipated.

A little nervousness began to creep over Meg, too; and when the carriage stopped and he took her hand to help her out, he felt it tremble.

"All right, my dear. It'll be all over in a minute," said he kindly. "There's your father in the hall. Why, here he is at the door—and Guy just behind! See how smart your brother is; dressed for the occasion, and no mistake!"

Meg sped forward, and her father took both her hands, and, after looking at her with an odd mixture of inquiry and tenderness, kissed her cheek.

"Welcome to your new house and home, Meg! Where's David? I wish to see him that I may thank him for asking us over to dinner. It's a pretty dull, rotten time we've had during the weeks you've been away."

The Laird of Ballochean had done his best to honour the occasion. Meg, eyeing him keenly, could quite well see from his appearance that he had been imbibing less freely than usual in their absence. His eyes were quite clear, his face had lost its purplish hue, and he carried himself with increased dignity.

Guy, too, looked somewhat different; but his greeting was rather casual, and in a minute or two he was out after Sillars, who, in his eyes, was the person of supreme importance at Kildoon. Meg was a mere accessory, and Guy was eager to tell his brother-in-law what he had done in his absence during the few short weeks in which he had had the home-farm under his care.

At the farther end of the hall there was assembled a small group of servants headed by the somewhat austere and awe-inspiring Mrs. Maxwell, who had been housekeeper at Kildoon for over thirty years.

Meg, eyeing her doubtfully for half a second, marched up to her and, pulling off her glove, frankly held out her hand.

"How do you do, Mrs. Maxwell, and everybody? I'm glad to see you all, and it is very kind of you to welcome me as you are doing, for I'm sure that, deep down in your hearts, none of you wants me in the least!"

"Oh, ma'am, don't say that!" said Mrs. Maxwell, completely taken aback by this greeting. "We are all glad to see you, and we wish you many years' happiness in this house. May I come up with you, ma'am, and help you, for dinner is almost ready, and the gentlemen from Ballochean have been waiting a long while?"

Meg nodded, and went up the narrow, winding stairs in the wake of Mrs. Maxwell.

"It's the rooms of the auld mistress we had orders to get ready, ma'am," she said, in a puzzled voice. "I hope you'll like them. Some new things have been sent from Glasgow, but we did not ken where to put them. And I couldna help thinkin' that maybe you would like to keep them just as the auld mistress had them."

"I am sure that is what I shall like," answered Meg, as she flung back her veil with a nervous hand. "I just want to say one thing, Mrs. Maxwell, and perhaps I had better say it now. I don't come to Kildoon to upset or change anything. Life is to go on here in every respect just in the way that Mr. Sillars has been accustomed to. I hope every one of you will stop on and help me to make it go on smoothly. I need you to be kind to me, Mrs. Maxwell, for I don't know very much, and to-night I am a little afraid."

At these broken words the old servant's heart melted like snow off a dyke before the sun.

"Oh, my dear! what for should you speak like that? There's naething here to be feared for. Ye ha'e gotten the best o' men. I say it that have been here 'maist since he was born! I was only thinkin', before you came, that I am auld and a wee bit auld-fashioned, and that maybe a young mistress would like things different—have her ain weys, like. But we'll a' stop since you ask us, and only be prood o' the chance to serve ye."

"Thank you very much," said Meg more composedly. "The rooms are most beautiful, and I will not have any of the new furniture put in them. It can go back to the place it came from."

"Let me tak' off your boots," cried Mrs. Maxwell, her heart completely won, and now as eager to serve as an hour ago she had been inclined to stand on her dignity. "I am glad that you like the rooms. They are the best in the hoose, as it is fittin' they should be. The Laird was very parteecular that you should ha'e the best."

Meg began in haste to throw off her cloak. Above the mantelpiece there was a picture of the woman who once had lived in these rooms, tasting all life's joy and sorrow. Her eyes seemed to dwell upon the forlorn young creature who had come to such a strange and rough bit on the road of life.

Mary Maxwell could not sleep that night. She lay wide-eyed till the dawn, marvelling that the two in whom all the hopes of Kildoon were centred should be like strangers under its roof.

CHAPTER XXI

THE NEW HOME

NEXT morning in the low, wainscotted breakfast room at Kildoon appeared a new Meg—or rather the one with whom Sillars had been familiar so long in the days before their marriage.

On her wedding journey she had been a thing of smiles and softness and charm, of womanly graces and alternate fire and pathos, a wonder and a puzzle to herself, and a perpetual lure and menace to Sillars.

But now the old Meg had come back. She wore the leather-bound skirt of Harris tweed, the white flannel shirt with the loosely knotted green tie, and the brogues which had so often offended the fine sensibilities of Ellison Dove. Her hair, with the sun on it, was demurely brushed and loosely coiled behind, though in the pleasant land of France she had each day tried some new method of enhancing its beauty.

Sillars, springing up from his letters, regarded her somewhat askance.

" Don't stare, David," she cried in a gay, defiant voice. " I'm only clothed and in my right mind. As you said in London, the ploy is over."

" I thought you would have left the old garb at Ballochean," he said shortly. " Not that I have any fault to find with it ; but surely you could find something to put on that is more up-to-date."

" No, David. This is the garb for everyday wear. Only when I have it on shall I be like myself—or, rather, shall I feel like myself, which is more to the purpose. How ever did you put up with me while we were away ? And, in heaven's name, how much of your money have I spent ? "

" That is neither here nor there, my dear," he answered more shortly still. " Come to your breakfast, and tell me what you are going to do to-day."

" I've been up since half-past six, and I have paid a visit to the stables. There are seventeen dogs of sorts, David, nine of which have arrived since you went away. They'll keep me busy enough. I should like to have them all in the house together."

" I'm afraid Mary Maxwell would have several different kinds of fits if you brought them there," said Sillars somewhat anxiously.

" Oh, no, she wouldn't. We've had it out. We're going to be chums. She'll let me do everything I want."

" Will she ? " he said drily.

There was, however, deepening interest in his eyes as he looked up the table to where she sat behind the tray, busy about the cups.

" Oh, yes. But as I have assured her that my way will consist in leaving everything as I found it she's going to like me very much. We are agreed that you must never be put out, David, whatever happens."

" Since when have I become a sort of Bluebeard ? " he asked a trifle harshly.

On her lips rippled a tiny smile.

" It isn't that, David, and well you know it ! Only, you must be master in your own house. Well, then, after I had seen and feasted my soul on all the live stock and had had a cup of tea in Mary Maxwell's very own room and the most delicious bit of toast I have ever eaten, I went up and unpacked my clothes and put them all away in that most astonishing place called the wardrobe room." When Sillars made no remark she continued, " When it is too wet to go out I can amuse myself there, for it is full of stuff. Do you know how full it is ? "

He shook his head.

" The things there were my mother's," he said shortly. " But you, of course, are at liberty to turn them all out."

" Why should I turn them all out ? And why do you speak like that, as if I were a Vandal or a hooligan ? I've come to build up, not to destroy," she added with one of her oddly apt, if somewhat freely rendered, Scriptural quotations. "Any fool can destroy. I've put away all the outward signs of extravagance and folly, and I have returned to the simple life."

"Are you talking about your clothes?" he asked in a somewhat puzzled tone.

"I am," was her laconic answer.

"But why lock them away? Won't you wear them every day as you have been doing?"

"No, no; they belong to the ploy, and you've said it is over," she said quietly. Then quite suddenly she leaned her elbows on the tray and looked over the top of the embroidered tea-cosy gravely into his face. "David, will you do one more thing for me?" she asked.

"Of course—it's done before you ask it!"

"Allow me to take down that picture of your mother which hangs above the mantelpiece in my sitting-room?" she said somewhat timidly.

"Of course you can take it down. The rooms are yours to alter as you please," he answered, but his tone was a little cold. "Some new things ought to have come. I ordered them thinking you might not care for the old sticks. Did Mary say nothing to you about them?"

"Oh, yes! They have come and I have seen them, but I won't have them at any price. What was good enough for your mother is good enough for me, David; so you can send them back to where they came from."

A moment's silence fell, and Sillars kept his eyes fixed on his plate.

"What is your objection to the picture?" he asked at length. "My mother was a very harmless and inoffensive, not to say good-looking, old lady."

"Her eyes follow me about," answered Meg calmly. "Some day I shall find them full of tears. Then I shall run away. Please don't say any more about it. I'll take it down to-day."

She dismissed the subject immediately; but Sillars was destined to ponder on these cryptic words for many a day without arriving one whit nearer to their meaning.

"What are we going to do to-day? Can I go to Ballochean, David?" she asked presently.

"Of course," he at once assented. "I'm going there myself, in fact. Shall we drive?"

"No, I want to walk; and, please, can I take as many dogs as I like with me?"

Sillars showed irritation at this question.

"I wish you would try to be a little less childish and not come asking my permission or consent for every trifle, as if I were some sort of a schoolmaster. Understand that you are mistress of this house absolutely, and that nobody has the right to deny you anything or to hinder you from doing whatever you wish."

"Oh!" said Meg with an odd little snap and a contraction of her brows. "I'm sorry I've made you angry. I'll try not to offend again."

Then Sillars, conscious that he had shown unnecessary heat, felt that he ought to, and even wished to, apologise; but he did not.

"How soon?" she began as she rose; and then, remembering that she had just been told not to ask foolish questions, she abruptly broke off and turned her intended query into a statement. "I have to see Mrs. Maxwell about the housekeeping. How much nicer she will be than cantankerous old Greig! I'll be ready to start for Ballochean in about an hour's time."

Then she walked out of the room.

Sillars wiped his mouth with his napkin, rolled it absently, and stuck it in the curious old ring with the Sillars crest on it.

"The sooner I'm off to Greenock the better. This is Saturday morning. Forty-eight more hours will see it through."

Strange words these for a newly married man! But already Sillars, though he had not been in the house for much more than half a day, was finding the strain of life at Kildoon under altered conditions much more trying even than the wedding journey.

With the best intentions in the world, David Sillars at this crisis in his life began to make the mistake which came within an ace of wrecking his life and that of the woman whom he had vowed to shelter.

From her own lips, on that foolish but unforgettable day in the Howff Wood, he had learned, as he believed, her true opinion of him, not only that she did not and never could care for him, but that, from her standpoint, he was old, impossible, the last man on earth she could marry. She had even likened him to her father in respect of age, he remembered.

In the long silences of the last weeks of his bachelor solitude he had thrashed the thing out and had decided on his course of action.

The dignity of his name, the shelter of his house, he would give to Meg Hamilton —and no more. He would never ask for her affection, her wifely duty, nor would he ever by a single betraying sign allow her to guess that he desired it.

A strong man in all the ordinary affairs of life, he was unaware till now that the task which he had set himself was beyond the power of him or of any man to accomplish, and, further, that it is not possible for husband and wife to live together under such conditions without disaster ensuing.

Much wisdom was stored in the head of David Sillars, but at this crisis in his life he made one vast and over-weening mistake.

As they walked together through the fields with a couple of setters, an Aberdeen terrier, brother to the one at Langdyke, and a weird mongrel, named Mike, who attached himself with special affection to his new mistress, Sillars thought with an odd pang what a child she was. She flew with the dogs a breadth or two and then came back to his side, apologising for her pranks.

" It's in the air, David, it's sheer, unadulterated gladness at getting back to Scotland ! It's no use for real Scotch folk to gad about—they are never really happy except under their own dear, frowning skies. Now, I wonder where Sir Hew and Lady Kessock are and whether they are very well this morning."

" In Paris likely," answered Sillars absently. " Kessock said he expected to be a week there."

" Ellie will drag him to shops, but she can't buy clothes. I really think, David, that if I were to try very hard, I might become a connoisseur in dress."

" I am sure you could—you always buy the right thing and wear it like a queen," he answered without a moment's hesitation.

She threw a rather startled glance at him.

" That's a queer speech to come from you to me, David. It's one which Major Kettering might have made. Did I tell you he was hoping to come to Garslade for the races this year and for a little shooting afterwards ? "

" No, you did not," he answered rather curtly, not seeming altogether pleased with the prospect of the visit suggested by her words.

" Do you think, if he did come, that I might invite his aunt to Kildoon, David ? "

Sillars looked the surprise he felt.

" You might. But it is doubtful whether she would come—and she is a very great lady, Madge. She might consider it presumption on your part to ask her. She has entertained royalty at her château in Touraine."

" Oh ! but she is so sweetly simple that I should not be in the least afraid of her if she were in a position to accept my invitation and come here. Really great folk are simple, I think. It is only people like Lady Kessock who put on airs. How simple you are, David ! " said Meg with her slight, adorable smile.

" Now you are laughing at me," said Sillars a trifle dourly, becoming with the passing of each hour ever more sensitive to the cadences of her voice.

" Am I ? When I dare to laugh at you, David, I shall not be fit to live, and you have my leave to make an end of me," she cried ; and she darted off in front with the dogs, which presently were yelping and chasing the rabbits in the Howff Wood and having the time of their lives.

In such fashion they came at length to the Park at Ballochean, and when half way across it Sillars made an abrupt pause.

" I think I'll take the short cut to the home-farm, Madge," he said. " Guy will probably be there, and I wish to see him. Will you go on to the house ? "

She nodded and left him at once without so much as a good-bye.

But when her face was clean turned from him it assumed an expression of strange bitterness.

" Oh, my man !—but the day is coming when I shall punish you ! I can wait for the coming of that day—I can wait, but, oh ! I hope it is going to come soon before I do something desperate."

By the time, however, that she arrived at the door of her father's house she looked demure enough, and she even smoothed her hair and set her cap straight before she presented herself to the inquisitive eyes of Jean Drysdale.

"Oh, Miss Meg!—I mean, Mrs. Sillars," cried the girl, blushing all over her face, "how nice it is to see you again!"

"Thank you, Jean. It's very nice, I assure you, to get back. Where is father? In the house?" asked Meg eagerly.

"No, miss—he's at the farm. Both your father and your brother are at the farm every day now, and Mr. Guy gets up at six o'clock every morning."

"Good! And how are you all in the kitchen—particularly Mrs. Greig? Is she attending to my father's meals?"

"Not so bad, miss. But, oh! we do miss you. It's not the same house as it was when you were here. I do wish you would come back," said the girl with an expression of so much genuine feeling in her voice that Meg was touched.

"It's very kind of you to say that, for I thought you would all be glad to see the last of me. I'm afraid, however, that I am not likely to come back now, and I hope that you will all stop on and make father and Guy as comfortable as possible."

"We're not thinking of leaving—in the meantime, at least. We were waiting until you came back. Are they a' stoppin' on at Kildoon?"

"Oh, yes!"

"Even Mrs. Maxwell? We heard that she was to leave on the day that you arrived."

"I think she has changed her mind. I was drinking tea with her at seven o'clock this morning in her room, and she seemed quite pleased with me and all my works. I've had a splendid holiday, Jean, and I bought something for each one of you in Paris. But I have forgotten to bring it with me. You must come to Kildoon and get it. And we met Sir Hew and Lady Kessock in London. They were staying in the same hotel."

"They had a grand marriage, and three columns in the paper," said Jean jealously. "We were a' chawed when we read it, Miss Meg."

Meg laughed merrily.

"I am glad we escaped such a vain show. Well, I think I'll walk over to the farm as they are all there. But, before I go, I'll run upstairs. I've never been so long out of Ballochean in my life. It all looks quite different now, somehow."

"Kildoon's very nice, isn't it, Miss Meg? We heard that a lot of new furniture had come frae Glesca," said Jean inquiringly.

"I believe Mr. Sillars ordered some for me, but I prefer the old. It is a very beautiful house, Jean, and you must come over to tea next Sunday and see it."

So saying, Meg ran lightly up the stair, painfully conscious, as she had never before been, of the shabbiness of everything. The Brussels carpet was almost threadbare, and everywhere there were signs of poverty. But it was all dear—oh, very dear! A stinging moisture was in her eyes as she sped to the old schoolroom where all her girlhood had been spent—the girlhood that, though removed but by a few months of time, already seemed so very far behind her.

"Do I want to come back, I wonder?" she asked herself as she closed the door and stood in the middle of the room, looking round.

It was all dismantled. A huge dust-sheet covered the bed and the dressing-table, and everything seemed forlorn and quite unlike what it used to be.

Perhaps the greatest change of all was in herself, however. She was not happy in her new home; and, had she dared to analyse her inmost feelings, she would have been obliged to admit that. But, as yet, Meg carefully avoided any such analysis. Perhaps she knew it would be a dangerous pastime to indulge in.

"Everything's different and can never be the same again," she muttered to herself, and she was glad to leave the room, shut the door behind her, and turn her back on the house.

There was a short-cut to the home-farm by way of the kitchen gardens, and half-way through them Meg met her father hastening back to receive her.

"I am sorry nobody was in the house when you arrived, my dear," he said, with the strange new deference in his air and manner which Meg found most embarrassing to herself, and regarded as unbecoming, if not humiliating, on her father's part. "I've left David and Guy discussing things. It's very queer and unbelievable,

Meg, the way in which Sillars has awakened up the lads and made them not only think of working but actually take to work ! I never could."

" He showed them something worth working for, I suppose," answered Meg soberly. " Jean tells me that Guy gets up at six every morning now."

" He's throwing himself tooth and nail into the farming business, and he swears that he will make it pay. David and he are discussing the breeding of horses at this minute. There are grand stables down there, Meg ; and, of course, there's room for a lot of horses at Ballochean too. If they go in for that, I could be of use to them and maybe make a bit on my own as well, for there's nothing about a horse I don't know, Meg, and I've never been cheated with a bit of horseflesh yet."

Meg was instantly and deeply interested, and was likewise amazed afresh at the resourcefulness of Sillars. Not only had he redeemed the place, but he was laying himself out to discover the very best use to which he could put Guy, and he had put his finger unerringly on the spot.

" I was telling David as we came over this morning that he is a great man. Don't you think he is, dad ? "

" He's a clever one, anyway, and he has a remarkably good business head. He's keen, too. He'll keep Guy up to the mark, I'll be bound. I tell you there's money in horses," he added excitedly, " and horse-breeding on a big scale by folk that understand it would pay better than anything—especially in this country."

When Meg made no answer to this he looked at her anxiously.

" Are you like to be comfortable at Kildoon, lass ? " he asked, rather awkwardly.

" Comfortable ?—oh, yes ! Why not ? It's a very fine house, and nothing is grudged in it."

" Servants coming in to heel, Meg ? But I need hardly ask that, for you know how to manage work-folk."

" There will be no trouble on that score," she answered quietly.

" I suppose David will not stop during the week in Greenock now—go perhaps one day a week ? " he ventured to ask.

" He will make no change in the order of his life," she answered steadily.

" And will he leave you at Kildoon from Monday to Saturday ? "

" So he says," she replied with apparent unconcern.

" Humph ! " said Ballochean. " But that way of going on will never last. He'll find it won't work. It will be terribly dull for you. But we'll be right glad to have you back here, if he has to stick to business so close as all that in the meantime."

Meg sighed a little as she turned away. Something within whispered that never more would Ballochean be home to her, that she had burned her boats, and that henceforth she must sink or swim with David Sillars. That he should leave her to sink was unthinkable after the magnitude of the thing he had already done.

There was a shadow on her face. Her father wondered what had brought it there, and deep down in his seared heart stirred once more the strange father-feeling, the vague anxiety, that had tugged at its strings that day when he had beheld her stand up before God and man to take the vows of wifehood upon her.

" He is kind to you, lass ? " he said roughly. " David Sillars could never be other than kind to any woman, surely ? "

" Kind ? Oh, yes ! His kindness is prodigious." she made answer swift enough. " Tell me, do you ever hear of old Van Leyden now ? "

" Never. I was too glad to be done with the whole affair to have any more to do with him. But I hear that his nephew has gone back to Frankfurt."

" Oh ! " said Meg wonderingly, with an odd softness of heart that had certainly never before mingled with any thought she had had of Morris Bien. Perhaps he too suffered, and all the world was full of pain !

The day was put in not so badly, and on Sunday morning Sillars and his wife walked to Alloway Kirk and sat in the Kildoon pew amid a great congregation that had come out from Ayr to behold them.

But they saw naught save a sober-faced man and a young and most quietly dressed bride, both apparently absorbed in the service and flaunting nothing of the happiness of their new estate for the delectation of curious eyes.

The last ordeal over, Sillars prepared himself with uncommon alacrity to return to Greenock and to take up once more the order of his life.

Monday breakfast was always early at Kildoon, and it was always served in the small breakfast parlour soon after seven o'clock. As Sillars descended the stairs that morning dressed for his journey, he hoped most fervently that his wife would not come down. Indeed, he had suggested as much to her as they had walked home from Ballochean together after supper the night before. She had answered him not a word then, but when he entered the parlour he found her seated at the head of the table ready to make his tea.

"It's a shame for you to get up at this hour to see me off, and it's unnecessary as well," he said in a low voice. Probably you will find the day long enough without rising so early."

"Oh, no!" she answered airily. "I am full of affairs."

"What kind of affairs?" he asked rather anxiously.

"I don't know just yet," she answered. "But if I am at a loss to put in the time, it will be the first occasion in my life, David. So long as I am able to get out of doors you needn't trouble about me."

He ate his breakfast in silence and with little relish, and before he had finished the cart was at the door with his bag, already packed, placed below the seat.

Meg walked out to the door with him, gave the mare a bit of sugar from her own hand, and laid her cheek for a moment against the velvet of her neck. The creature, responsive to her touch, whinnied with delight and nestled her nose to the kind hand.

"I must go, my dear. It'll take me all my time to catch my train. Good-bye. I'm sorry I have to go, but there is no help for it. Business must be attended to. I hope you won't weary while I am away."

"Oh, no! Good-bye. Will it be Friday before you come back?"

"I may write. If possible, I'll try to come on Thursday; but I've been over four weeks away and things accumulate. Besides, there will be a good deal to do in view of the New Year holidays next week. Good-bye. Right, William."

William, who had discreetly looked the other way, was sure, talking afterwards about this first parting of husband and wife, that no kiss had passed between them. He had a sweetheart himself—a housemaid at Garslade—and it astonished him to think that love's ardour could cool so soon after marriage!

Meg stood still and waved to the departing trap; but Sillars, with his lips sternly set, never once looked back, nor did he speak even a casual word to the groom all the way to the station.

William came to the conclusion that the two had had their first quarrel, and his sympathy was entirely with the mistress!

She went back to the unfinished plate, laid her head down on the tablecloth for a moment, and let the firelight play upon her hair.

But there were no tears in her eyes when she raised them—only a dull, defiant glare.

He had chosen, and the way was open for her to walk alone.

Well, she would walk in it. It was his look-out whether the walk proved to be one of which he could approve!

She had done her best, and she had failed.

He had done his best—as he had imagined it—and he had succeeded only too well!

The rest lay on the knees of the gods.

CHAPTER XXII

THE AWAKENING

David Sillar's wife was sitting on the library window-seat at Kildoon a few weeks later, reading the pages of a local paper. It was more than usually interesting, seeing that it contained a full and circumstantial account of the home-coming of the Laird of Sangster and his bride.

Apparently nothing had been lacking to render it impressive and memorable, and not one time-honoured custom attendant upon such occasions had been forgotten or suffered to lapse. The paper stated that " the preparations for giving Sir Hew Kessock and his bride a hearty and rousing welcome to their historic home were most complete."

The narrative went on to tell how that, as Sir Hew and Lady Kessock drove in the family carriage from Ayr Station, a band of willing devotees were waiting at the bottom of Kessock Hill to give them a joyous and enthusiastic reception, and how the horses were quickly unyoked, and the Laird and his lady were drawn up to the doors of their ancestral home by the sturdy arms of these.

The floral and other decorations, seen by torchlight, had been most effective, and the entry to the park specially fine, the village boys having been lined up on either side of the drive, holding aloft flaming torches, which lent a weird charm to the scene.

Sir Hew had evidently been both pleased and touched by this tribute of affection, and was observed to turn often to her ladyship, making some pleasant comment.

On the terrace steps the house party, consisting of the Dowager Lady Kessock and Surgeon-General and Mrs. Dove and the head servants, waited for the arrival of the carriage.

In the course of a short, but singularly happy speech, Sir Hew had returned thanks for the warmth and heartiness of their welcome, and had emphasised in neat, well chosen phrases the happy relations which had always existed between Sangster and the people on the estate, both tenants and employees. It would be his aim, he had said, and the aim of the gracious lady by his side, to foster and continue these relations, and he had expressed the hope that they were entering on a new and happy and prosperous year for all concerned.

Surgeon-General Dove had also made a few humorous remarks, which were evidently much appreciated.

The account concluded with the following :—

" We are requested to state that there is no truth in the rumour that the Dowager Lady Kessock is to retire to the Dower House at Girvan, the lease of which is likely to be renewed to its present occupiers.

" General satisfaction will be expressed at this decision, as the removal of Lady Kessock from the district would be a great loss to Sangster and the neighbourhood."

Meg smiled a little as she read the latter paragraph, and, dropping the paper on her seat, stared through the rain-blurred panes with a rather bitter expression in her eyes.

Perhaps it was the contrast suggested by what she had been reading that pained her. She saw the gay scene, the animated faces, the assumption, at least, of joy and welcome, and the conscious, self-satisfied smirk on the face of Ellie Dove.

How different had been the home-coming of another bride and bridgroom not so many weeks before ! Almost like thieves in the night they had crept back, and none had bidden them welcome, save those within the house who were in duty bound ! And she was alone now in the great house, where she would be alone for ever more !

It was Friday afternoon, and her husband had been gone since Monday for the second week in succession since the resumption of work after the New Year holidays. And not a line or sign of any kind had come from Greenock in the interval ! Nor had she written. They were as much detached as if the breadth of the seas divided them. Her woman's heart had quailed long since at the prospect of the unrolling years and of a possible half-century of these to go on like this!

She had no interest in life. In that well-ordered, comfortable house there was nothing to arrange, to cavil about, to fight for—nothing, in short, admitting of improvement. All went on as if by clockwork—smoothly, silently, without a hitch. Well-trained, and certainly most kind, servants were there to do her bidding, and she had the sickening consciousness that she was an object of speculation and pity in the kitchen quarters, and that any kitchen wench escaping from Mrs. Maxwell's vigilance to meet her lover at e'en had a better part in life to play than that of her mistress.

The new hunter was in the stable; but, while she would creep to his side and lay her cheek on his velvet neck, and make love to him, as she did to all animals, who were docile as kittens in her presence, she had no desire to mount him or ride him before the wind, to feel the fever of the chase coursing in her veins.

The salt of life had lost its savour, and she longed with a strange, wild longing for the old sordid, fighting days at Ballochean, when each new dawn brought some problem to be faced.

At least that was life, while this was mere existence, and Kildoon nothing but a gilded prison, where neither heart nor soul was free.

She turned round on her slender finger the plain gold badge of her bondage, and she longed with a passionate longing to go down to the tumbling Doon, which a wild night of rain had converted into a raging flood, and drop it in deep, deep, where it would never more be found or be seen by her eyes or the eyes of any other.

The ring was without meaning, it encircled nothing; it was a hollow mockery to deceive the world!

And her strong, true nature scorned deception. She did not care at that moment though the whole world should know upon what terms she and David Sillars were living together—no, not together, but apart in the house of Kildoon!

Presently, across the rain-blurred landscape, up through the dripping trees which lined the long avenue, came a carriage swiftly, and drew up at the door.

The library being remote from the front avenue, Meg did not hear the sound of the approaching wheels, and she was startled out of her reverie by the sudden opening of a door and the announcement of an arriving visitor.

"Lady Kessock!"

Meg sprang up, flushing almost painfully, for it was as if a sudden and ruthless witness to her discontent had intruded on her.

Presently enters Ellison Dove, ostentatiously wrapped in the sables which she had persuaded Kessock to buy for her in Paris, her small head held erect with pride and with all the conscious dignity of her new estate.

"Oh, Meg, Meg, darling! how are you? I simply had to come! Such a day, isn't it? But I was dying to see you!"

"I am pleased to see you, too, Ellie," said Meg, and, in a sense, she honestly was. "I've just been overwhelming myself with the account of your dramatic arrival at Sangster. It reads like a fairy story."

"It was one," said Ellison enthusiastically; and, having kissed Meg, she threw back her sables to reveal her Paris-made frock, being at the same time astonished to behold Meg in the abbreviated leather-bound skirt which so often scandalised her, and even in the brogues, the plain flannel shirt, and the knotted tie!

Not one item changed—and she the mistress of a great house awaiting callers at three of the afternoon!

"Why, Meg, have you got into that old thing again? Why do you? It doesn't seem to be the thing," she stammered, as her perfectly gloved hand arranged the lace at her throat which the clinging fur had ruffled.

"This is the kind of clothes I like, Ellie. Never mind, you are smart enough for two," murmured Meg, as she threw another log on the fire, and stirred it to a brighter blaze.

It was nearing the end of January now, but the wind was easterly, and, somehow, Meg felt suddenly cold.

"It's all right, if your husband doesn't mind. I find husbands so particular," cooed Ellison, with a conscious laugh. "I shouldn't dare to appear before Hew so plainly dressed as you are. He loves to see me in lace and silks, and blue is his favourite colour. I did get the furs from Revillon's, you see, and I brought them over so that we might compare prices and qualities. It's delicious to think that we have so much in common, isn't it ? "

" I suppose it is," said Meg in a perfunctory tone. " Mine are all locked away. I don't suppose I shall wear them here. Somehow, they don't fit the landscape. I can't think how I could behave so like a baby on my honeymoon journey, and make Mr. Sillars spend so much money. I'm ashamed of myself now."

" Oh ! but, Meg," cried Ellison, puzzled by this new Meg, so different from the radiant creature whom she had last beheld in the Palm Court at the Carlton Hotel, " you'll have to wear them when you begin to pay your wedding calls. I don't suppose you'll go to Garslade or Rubers Castle, or even to Sangster, in that old rag."

" I don't think I'll trouble about the calls, Ellie. You see I'm not a new person in these parts, or among these people," she answered, with a little touch of maliciousness, for which she afterwards took herself rather severely to task.

The new Lady Kessock looked blank at this.

" Oh ! but, Meg, you will have to pay calls—or, at least, to return the wedding ones. My mother-in-law lays great stress on all these things, and, of course, she knows the usages of the county better than most people. Hasn't anybody called ? "

" Oh ! a few," answered Meg, in a tone expressive of complete indifference.

" Tell me who ? " said Ellie excitedly. " Lady Kessock will be sure to ask me whenever I get back what callers you have had. She rather wanted to come with me to-day, but I circumvented her cleverly by saying that I wanted to go to mother's to tea, as I hadn't seen her a minute alone since we came back. Of course, after that she could hardly insist on coming, could she ? "

" I suppose not," assented Meg absently. " A good many people have called," she added in answer to Ellie's first question. " But, somehow, I always happened to be out until yesterday, when the Countess of Rathillis came."

Ellie stared in open-mouthed awe.

" Did the Countess of Rathillis come ? " she asked, after a pause. " She doesn't call at Sangster, I think—at least I have never heard the Dowager speak about her."

" I think she doesn't call," said Meg quietly.

" But perhaps she'll come now. Oh, Meg ! you must positively get her to come. It would be such a score off ma-in-law ! Won't you ? " entreated Ellie.

Meg shook her head.

" I couldn't suggest anything of the kind to her, Ellie, I'm afraid. She is very old and very dignified—but very, very nice."

" Why did she come here ? "

Meg hesitated for a moment, thinking of the strange half hour she had spent yesterday in the company of the most exclusive of all the women of the county.

" Well, I think she came entirely because she was so fond of David's mother. She talked about very little else indeed except David and his mother."

" It doesn't matter what brought her so long as she came. Was she nice to you ? "

" Oh ! very," answered Meg, and a little indefinable shade of emotion just trembled for a moment on her lips.

" And, of course, you'll pay a return visit to the castle ? "

" Some day—yes. She is to arrange that. She wants me to spend a whole day with her."

" Then that would be your chance to mention poor little me, Meg," said Ellison imploringly. " You could work it in so sweetly, saying I was your best friend, don't you know ? You could say that without telling any lie, Meg. And just think what a triumph I would have over the Dowager ! "

Meg made no promise.

" Did you see that hateful and quite uncalled-for paragraph in the paper to-day about the Dower House ? " continued Ellie. " She made them put that in. Hew didn't know a thing about it. But, I'm going to work for that, Meg. You can't think how horrid she can be, and what a struggle I shall have to assert myself against her. She thinks—I can see quite plainly—that I'm a nobody, and that she will go on just as she has been doing, bossing everybody. But I'm just taking my time, Meg. I'll get her out yet."

Looking at the small, shrewish face, set just at that moment in its least attractive expression, Meg had not the smallest doubt of her final success.

" And she is so spiteful, too," went on Lady Kessock. " She is just as fond of gossip as any kitchen girl could be. She has got hold of a story about you, Meg. I had to stand up for you this morning, I can tell you. She didn't want me to come here this afternoon—why, do you think ? "

" I'm sure I couldn't say," answered Meg, reaching for another log, and getting down on her knees to lay it on the fire.

In that attitude her face was hidden, and the firelight playing on it covered its natural blush.

" As I have said, she has got hold of some silly story about you and David before you were married. It seems that her maid had it from somebody that Mr. Sillars employs at Greenock. The story is that you went there late one night to see him and had to stay in the house all night, and that that is the reason why you got married in such a hurry, with nobody knowing anything about it."

Ellison paused a moment, waiting for an answer, or, at least, for some light comment from Meg, but none came.

" Of course, I flared up when she told it, and stood up for you—in front of Hew, too. And he was pleased with me for doing it. I just told her quite plainly that you were not that kind of girl, and that such a thing could not possibly have ever happened."

" But it did happen," was the startling answer that came very quietly and deliberately from Meg, seated on the fender-stool. " Every single item of it happened. So, you see, your mother-in-law was correctly informed after all."

Ellie threw down her muff and sat forward, her small face eager and strained.

" Oh ! but, Meg, you never did. You couldn't ! It's unthinkable ! "

" Yes, I did. I went to Greenock at nine o'clock that night and waited till David came in from dining out, and stayed all night at his house, and he brought me back next day—and I don't care if all the world knows it ! "

" Oh, but Meg, dear ! you mustn't be so reckless as that. Young women in our position can't be too careful what they do or say. Since I've been married to Hew I have come to know how men think and speak about such things. You should have heard Hew this morning when his mother told us that story at breakfast. He was simply furious, and that showed how much he felt it. I mustn't tell him what you have just said, and I'll try to forget it, dear. I think you have spoken recklessly, just as you used to do in the old days about things. But you will have to be more careful now."

Meg stood up and leaned her slim hand on the dark oak of the mantel, and turned her beautiful, quiet face towards the excited one of Hew Kessock's wife.

" Every word of what I have said is true, Ellie, and there was nothing wrong in what I did. I was in trouble. David Sillars knew something about it, and he was the only one that could help me, so I went to him."

" But—but in the light of what happened after—your hurried marriage, and all the secrecy—you would never expect people to believe that ? "

" I don't care what people believe, Ellie—not one atom. The less they believe that is good of me the better I shall be pleased."

" But if ma-in-law spreads this story and if I can't contradict it—why, even the Countess of Rathillis might get to know of it, and perhaps believe it ! In that case I don't suppose she would ever come back to see you."

" Possibly not ; though perhaps when I go to spend the day at the castle I may tell her myself," said Meg, and a strange little thrill came into her voice.

At this unexpected announcement Hew Kessock's wife became speechless. She had the odd feeling that there was something behind it all which she need not hope to be able to understand.

CHAPTER XXIII

A CHANGE OF FRONT

MEG pulled the bell-rope, and presently the man entered with the tea-tray.

Then Ellie sat back, critically comparing the whole of the arrangements with those at Sangster, the result being that she was privately and grudgingly compelled to admit that, of the two homes, certainly Meg had the more beautifully appointed. Such silver, so immaculately kept, such wonderful old decorated cups she had never before seen. If there were any such treasures at Sangster, they were not fetched out for daily use.

Meg took it all in the casual, indifferent manner of yore.

"Do you go much to Ballochean?" Ellison asked, while the man was still in the room.

"Every day," answered Meg; and, turning to the man, she thanked him with that sudden, sweet smile of hers which played such havoc everywhere with hearts.

Already she had grappled all the household to her with hooks of steel which nothing could break.

"And is it true what mother tells me—that things are different there, too: that Guy has taken over the home-farm, and is working on it just like a common ploughman?"

"Yes. I saw him driving a team to-day. But he does the work because he likes it," answered Meg, whimsically wondering how much more of the family history up-to-date Ellison had garnered during the incredibly few days that she had been at Sangster.

"Well, I'm sure you must be glad that he has turned so industrious, though Mr. Sillars may not like his doing such common work. And Lady Rathillis would be horrified! Such nice tea, Meg. And how lovely you have everything here!"

"It was like that when I came; it has always been like that, and it will go on being like that for ever and ever," answered Meg, as she lifted the beautiful old Derby cup of green and gold to her lips.

"I can't make you out, Meg," said Lady Kessock discontentedly, and with the air of one who has been baffled. "But I hope you and Mr. Sillars will come and dine with us one evening so that we can go over our continental experiences together. The night, I suppose, will have to be a Friday or a Saturday, if Mr. Sillars is going to keep on being away all the week at Greenock," she added inquisitively. "Couldn't you fix on a night now?"

"I can't fix anything when David is not here, Ellie. And I don't think we are dining out yet. Why, even you must get a few days to settle down before you begin entertaining."

"I want ever so many new things at Sangster," said Ellie with a sigh, as she pulled on her long, mouse-coloured suede gloves. "A lot of things there are really very shabby. It's my belief that ma-in-law has been feathering her own nest all these years."

"No, no," said Meg, repelled by the vulgarity of this speech. "She would have her own jointure. Women like Lady Kessock don't do that kind of thing, Ellie."

"Don't they, though? I've found out that she buys cheap butter in Ireland and has frozen meat sent out twice a week from Glasgow," said Ellison with a shrewish, ill-natured laugh. "I'm not going to practise that kind of economics! As I told mother, I married to get away from them."

Meg's expression was a little detached, and as Ellison meandered on she became aware that she was getting only a divided and somewhat listless attention.

"I can't think what has come over you, Meg. You don't look a bit like what you did that night at the Carlton in London. I was quite jealous of you. Hew kept raving over your style and your frock—but if he could see you now! I never heard of anything so atrocious as your locking up your Paris clothes! Why, I bought mine to wake up the county with—not to shut them away."

Meg smilled.

"I hope you'll get a lot of fun over it, then, Ellie."

"I must go and call at mother's before I go home," said Ellison as she rose to leave. "Lady Kessock will be sure to be asking me questions about the visit I said I was to make there. When are you coming to see me at Sangster? I suppose you have horses?"

"Five of them eating their heads off. David has bought me a new hunter; but I haven't been farther than the paddock yet on him."

"Well, ride over to lunch one day soon. I must show ma-in-law that I mean to keep my own friends. I suppose you won't mind coming in spite of what I told you she said about you to-day."

"Oh, no! I don't mind at all. I have nothing on my conscience, and I care very little what people say about me."

"My! Lady Kessock will be wild when I tell her that the Countess of Rathillis has been to call on you. I'm simply dying to tell her."

So saying, the empty-headed little bride fluttered away out to her waiting carriage, being eager to drive along the race-course road before the swift darkness fell, in order that she might have the chance of being observed by any who might happen to be abroad.

Meg dropped down on the fender-stool when she was left alone and glowered long into the glowing heart of the fire.

So that was what the world was saying, she reflected, and that was the reason, doubtless, why David Sillars had thought it his bounden duty to offer her the shelter of his name and of his roof! He, too, had known what would be said, and his pity got the better of his judgment.

Her face grew harder and harder the longer she sat; and, in a sudden fit of anger, she took the wedding-ring from her finger and laid it deliberately on the table on David's own writing-book, where already some letters that had come that day lay ready for his inspection.

When she heard the roll of the dogcart wheels about an hour later she stood still and waited for him to come there to the library to seek her.

His expression was eager as he came into the room, but she had no welcoming word or smile for him. He closed the door and stepped forward, holding out his hand.

"How are you, my dear? Aren't you well, Madge?—or what has happened?"

"Nothing much. I've just had two hours of Lady Kessock—Ellie Dove that was, I mean."

"Oh! Is she the only caller you have had this week?"

"No, there have been others. Lady Rathillis came yesterday."

He looked much pleased.

"Did she? You would like her, Madge, I'm sure? She has not been here since my mother died."

"I liked her very much," answered Meg steadily.

Presently she watched him as he approached the table where the wedding-ring gleamed on the white expanse of the clean blotting-pad.

"Why, what's this?" he asked stupidly, when his eye was caught by it.

"It's my wedding-ring," she answered in a low voice. "I can't wear it any longer, David. Please put it away."

"But what has happened?" asked David, his brow darkening—"something that little wild-cat has been saying, I don't doubt. But you ought to know her well enough by this time to pay no heed to a single word that falls out of her mouth."

"I don't want to discuss, or even to tell you, what has happened, David," said Meg, with an air of great weariness, and in a tone of finality that there was no mistake. "Take up the ring and put it away."

He lifted the shining thing, from which the glitter of newness had not yet gone, and laid it flat on his palm. It was very tiny, it had cost him only forty shillings, but it was a symbol of bondage for him and Meg more utter than anything he could have conceived. By means of it he had bound himself and this wayward woman-creature in a union which possibly naught but death could dissolve.

" But, my dear, it is unusual for a married woman not to wear a ring. People will talk. Hadn't you better——"

She flashed her glorious eyes upon him in sombre fire.

" If they talk about that, they will find that it fits in with the rest. I ask you to forgive me for what I have done, David. Why is it that God—if there be a God !—withholds judgment from women and from so many men ? "

There was a hint of reproach in the words—or so he conceived. It seemed to him almost as if she had asked him what years were for if not to be filled with discretion. Sillars perceived that at the moment nothing could be gained by discussion.

He slipped the ring into his pocket.

" It can stop there until you ask for it," he said, with the kind of patience which had marked his earlier attitude towards her.

" Lady Kessock has lost no time in paying her respects. I thought it would have been your social duty to go to Sangster first," he continued, trying to divert her thoughts into a lighter channel.

" I should not have been in a hurry to do that—and now I shall never go," she answered, and the flush was hot on her cheek.

Once more Sillars wondered greatly what the little wildcat, for whom he had but the scantiest respect, could possible have said so to wound to the quick that proud spirit.

" A gnat like that is not worth minding, Madge," he said, trying to speak naturally. " Now tell me about the visit of Lady Rathillis. She has not been in this house since the day after my mother died."

" So I gathered from what she told me. She thinks that there have been only two people born in Ayrshire with a rightful claim to a halo," she said rather hardly. " Your mother was one, and you are the other. I'm to do my duty to you, David, and all my other duties, social and religious, in season and out of season ; but, as I said to her, I have none to show me how."

Sillars observed that the experience of the afternoon had tried her mettle, and he wished that he could have spared her.

He was quite well aware of the high ideal of personal conduct in a woman and also of the poor opinion of Meg Hamilton entertained by Lady Rathillis, who had never met her until the day of her visit. After his engagement to Meg she had openly remonstrated with Sillars, stopping her carriage on the road for the purpose, regarding his marriage, though she had in the same breath promised, if possible, to befriend his wife.

She had called on Meg with that object in view, but apparently she had not achieved it ; for, out of very devilment, it seemed, Meg withheld from her husband the slightest inkling of the sweet intimacy of that half-hour's conversation and the extraordinary sympathy which had been immediately established between her of the riven heart and the fighting spirit and the woman whom life had so purified and refined in the crucible of human pain as to leave her only meet for the Kingdom.

Things instead of mending seemed likely to get worse in the house of Kildoon, and Sillars groaned in spirit, and wondered whither the thorny path on which his feet and Meg's were set would ultimately lead.

Suddenly, as Meg, who had had enough of being indoors, was about to leave the room, he bethought him of something pleasanter than the theme of his meditations.

" I had a letter from Ludo yesterday evening. I thought of sending it to you. Then I reflected that if I brought it with me you would have it just as soon. It is good reading, Madge. Take it with you."

He drew from his pocket-book a fat envelope containing many sheets of thin foreign notepaper, closely written, and she took it ungraciously.

Coming at this crisis in her married life, when she was cherishing such hard thoughts of her husband, it seemed but to emphasise the fact of the amazing debt which she and her people owed to David Sillars—the debt she had begun to pay, but of which so much still remained to be paid.

At the moment she had no desire to read it ; courtesy, however, forbade her to refuse it when held out for her acceptance. She took it from his hand, but her eyes did not meet his as she did so, and, immediately leaving the room, she closed the door.

"By God!" said Sillars to himself, as he passed his hand distractedly across his brow, "a few more scenes like that and the situation becomes impossible! What am I to do?"

He threw his pocket-book on the table, walked to the window, and, looking absently through the rain-blurred panes, he beheld his wife running through the blast without hat or wrap, like a wild thing seeking kinship with the storm!

David did not know what such an action portended, for there are moments in the life of the best of men when they can be amazingly blind, and when they have no understanding worth mentioning of a woman's heart.

They pride themselves on being able to understand the weaker vessel and to tabulate all her qualities, both good and bad, while all the time they are but beating against the secret door that yields to one key only, and that has to be polished till it shines like fine gold in order to open it.

Sillars, imagining he had loved Meg Hamilton all her life, never understood her less than he did now.

But certainly he almost cursed the day and the hour when he had been tempted to offer her a way out of the sea of trouble in which she was like to be engulfed.

When they met at the dinner table that evening the storm had apparently passed. She came demurely, with a white frock on, guiltless of ornament. She looked very young and girlish, though the light that shone in her eyes was rather pitiful.

She did her best to make conversation so long as the man who waited on them was in the room, and Sillars, albeit his heart was heavy, responded as best he could with a grave courtesy.

"I've read all Ludo's letter," she said, when they were left alone. "I will bring it to you presently. He seems to have no quarrel with anything. Is what he says about Jamaica all true?"

"Yes, of course, every word. When you go there first it is like an enchanted isle. I can never forget my first impression of it."

Sillars was wondering what she had thought of Ludo's remark about their marriage, of which he had just heard. In the circumstances it was perhaps natural that he should continue to glorify and exalt the man who had so greatly benefited him, and that he should belittle the value of his sister's part of the bargain.

Nobody had as yet told Ludo the complete truth of the transaction, and the whole burden of his letter was the good luck of Meg in securing such a prize. Sillars had indeed pondered on the expediency of keeping back the two sheets of it that were mainly filled with praises of him; but reflecting that if he did so Meg would certainly attribute it to some sinister motive, he had finally decided to give her the letter entire.

But Meg had not read all that these sheets contained. Quickly grasping their tenor, she had, of a set purpose, skipped them.

"How far is it, and how much does it cost to go out to Jamaica?" she asked presently.

"It costs anything up to fifty pounds, and you may spend either a long time or a short time on the journey. There are different routes by which you may go. The busy man takes the shortest, which is likewise the most expensive way."

"Don't hedge with me, David," she said impatiently. "I was only wondering whether I should ever be able to go out and see Ludo."

"If your heart is set on it, I'll take you some time in the autumn, when we can afford leisure for another holiday."

"The autumn!" she exclaimed, and she seemed to repeat the words wonderingly. "This is only the end of January, David. It's a year—a lifetime—an eternity till the autumn! The end of the world might come before then."

"True, but so also might it come to-morrow, for the matter of that. The autumn would be the best time for you to go, and it would not be possible for you to go alone."

Again he spoke with the finality of the man who orders and ordains for his women-folk what, in his estimation, is for their good, and, in doing so, pays but small regard to their own wishes in the matter.

"David," she said quite suddenly, "father is failing. I can see a great change in him lately. It does not suit him to be good."

The words had in them a most moving pathos, and they affected Sillars so profoundly that he could not for a moment or two command his feelings.

"I don't quite understand," he said formally, as he very neatly and precisely pared and cored an apple and passed it on a plate to his wife.

"Oh, you must understand! Father is like me—he likes the broad road. We can't be hampered, or tied, or—or dragged up to impossible heights. I am understanding him better every day than I used to."

Sillars winced; the inference was obvious.

"Who hampers and ties you here, Meg?" he asked a trifle harshly. "Can mortal man do more than I have done, or leave you more entirely to your own inclinations and resources? It is because I recognise the fact that my presence is irksome to you that I have done all I could to give you as little of it as possible."

"I'm not complaining of you. You have certainly done your best, and your best is astonishing. It fills me with a daily amazement," she said with a faintly mocking air. "I am quite willing to take all the blame. I do take it; but, if I have to go on living here, David, I shall most certainly die."

"Never did woman look less like it," he answered, with the haste of a rising passion. "And this is a poor sort of welcome to come home to! Not that I do expect, or ever have expected, much, but even that little I do not get."

"You expect so much that it is not in my power to give it all," she retorted, the sombre fire leaping in her eyes once more. "But, seeing that I disappoint you so frightfully, couldn't I go to Ballochean on Friday and stay there till Monday during the time that you are at home? In that way I should not disturb the order of your life, which was so happy before I came into it. Oh! if I had known, David—if I had only known."

The anguish in her cry was poignant; but Sillars, interpreting it as being due only to an increased dislike and distaste of himself, hardened his heart against it. His face, a little white, was set like the granite rock, and his eyes had gloomy and answering fires in them, as they were bent on her face.

"Look here, Madge. By an unfortunate chain of circumstances we have taken an irrevocable step, and what we have both got to realise is that it is irrevocable, and that we have to abide by the consequences. Do you understand that?"

She shivered, for certain words spoken by the Rev. Mr. Murchison anent the vows he was laying on them that marriage day at Ballochean swept back to her remembrance.

"It is irrevocable only if we make it so, if we choose to have it so," she said recklessly.

"Then I do choose," he answered deliberately. "And this I will have you understand—there is not going to be any scandal in my house, nor are we to make ourselves a world's wonder. I shall require you to disguise as best you can your hatred and your indifference towards me, and to make as good a show in the world's eyes as you can. And, while you are at liberty to spend as much time at Ballochean in my absence as you like, I shall require you to be here when I come home, and remain here while I am at home, and further, to conduct my house as I wish it to be conducted. You can fill it with folk, if you like. I shall myself begin by inviting some for next week-end. And we shall take our place in the life of the county—dine out and dine folk in return—and everything, in short, shall go on just as if there were no skeleton in the cupboard. Do you understand?"

"I understand."

Her tone was low, and she beat a tattoo on the table with her forceful fingers.

"I require that every call be returned," he continued, "and that a proper hospitality be shown in Kildoon by its mistress. In return, I promise not to molest you in any way or to inquire how or where you pass your time, and I promise also to give you everything that the heart of a reasonable woman could desire. Now, do you understand?"

"And if it should be the heart of an unreasonable woman?" she asked him demurely, with her eyes still fixed on the pattern of rich gold on her plate of old Sèvres blue.

"Don't quibble with words," he rebuked her sternly. "Do you know what

I mean and what I will have? And the first thing is that you put this on your finger again"—taking out and handing her the marriage ring—"now—this very moment—before we leave the room."

In handing to her the offending circlet it fell from his fingers and rolled across the table so that it hit with a quick and vivid tinkle against the wonderful old Waterford glass standing by her plate.

She made no move to touch it, and the same provoking smile was on her lips.

He rose and pushed in his chair, and stood behind it, leaning his hand on the back of it.

"I have no wish to be rough with you, nor do I intend to be so, Madge. But there are certain things to which I am entitled, and these I mean to have. You have understood what I have been saying?"

"I'm not sure. Say it all over again, just to make certain," she answered, with what he regarded as mocking insolence.

He bit his lip, and the colour rose in the face that the strain had paled, but he repeated in substance what he had already said.

"I require that there shall be no scandal or occasion for talk in the house of Kildoon, and that—outwardly at least—you pay me the respect that every decent woman is willing to pay the man whom she has married, whether she cares for him or not. I also require that the house's tradition for hospitality be upheld, that you take your proper place in the county, and—and, as I have said, that you give no occasion for talk. And the beginning—the sign and seal of your purpose to defer to my wishes and obey my injunctions—is, that you put that ring on your finger again."

"And if I refuse?"

His arms went limp by his side.

"You can't refuse," he said doggedly. "You have no choice."

"And what, may I ask, do I get in return for bearing this—this tremendous burden you seek to lay upon me?"

"You made a bargain," he said hardly. "You—you thought that you had got good value, I remember, that night at Greenock."

The very name of the place seemed to sting her into an unreasoning fury.

"I was trapped, David Sillars!—trapped!—and I did not know it! How could I have any knowledge of the wicked tongues, the unclean minds, of the world, or of the things that it would be base enough to say? I came to you in my trouble with the confidence and simplicity of a child—and you were kind. But your kindness stopped there. You don't know what you have done—probably you will never know. But something has been killed in me and will never live again. I—I will do all that you say. There is not an item of the many things you have mentioned which I will not carry out to the uttermost, if that is your idea of what constitutes the payment of the debt—the great debt—which I owe to you. It is a millstone about my neck. It will always be that until some day it will drag me down—if not to hell, at least to death. And when that day comes it will be the happiest in all the life that has had so little peace in it. I put on your ring again. It is the symbol of the thing I will do and the obedience I will render. But—but God forgive you, David Sillars!—I never can!"

She thrust the shining thing on the white flesh of her finger and walked from him and from the room like a veritable tragedy queen, nothing in the manner of her exit being in the slightest degree melodramatic.

So the last storm for many a day died down in the house of Kildoon, and a great peace descended on it.

But it was like the peace of the grave.

Sillars, actually wretched, his brain reeling with the baffling mystery of her whole procedure, had no idea that the incidents of that night had closed the door of hope, and that the real tragedy of his life was about to begin.

Next morning Mrs. Sillars came down to breakfast in her riding-habit.

It was a new one, designed and made by a Glasgow expert, and in it she looked adorable. The white stock seemed to accentuate the slimness of her throat, and the heavy green cloth of the robe seemed moulded to every line of her perfect figure.

Sillars looked the supreme surprise that he felt. The hunter had been bought, the habit fitted and sent home; but, though there were still three days' hunting in the week available for lovers of the sport, his wife had not, so far as he was aware, been even once in the field.

"Why, is this a hunting morning?" he asked, and he was unable to veil the admiration which showed in his eyes.

But that she did not see, or seeing, took no heed of.

"Yes—the meet's at Garslade at half-past ten," she answered. "Will you come?"

Sillars seemed to hesitate. Once he had been keen enough on hunting, but of late he had almost given up the sport.

"I should like, but I'm not sure about my things being in order."

"They are all ready. I gave orders about them last night, and 'Diamond is ready, too, and in the pink of condition. I think that after what occurred last night it will be better if we put in an appearance together at Garslade. After we are in the field we needn't ride in company, unless it is necessary."

She spoke with great calmness and with a dignity there was no mistaking.

"Very well. When you put it like that I can't refuse; but I'm afraid I've forgotten my hunting-seat. I haven't been in the field for seven or eight years."

"The man who has once had a hunting-seat never forgets it, David," she assured him. "And you know you were the best jumper in the county. So don't vamp up excuses."

So natural and pleasant was her manner of speaking that the nightmare of the ghastly hour over the dinner table last night faded as a mist before the rising sun.

Great was the surprise and unspeakable the joy of the more intimate of the servants at the spectacle of their master and their mistress going forth together in hunting-kit, Mrs. Sillars radiant as a dream and according with her beautiful mount as if they perfectly understood each other, and Sillars himself looking gallant in his red coat.

"Now that is as it should be," observed Mary Maxwell to her trusted subordinate. "And there won't be anybody to hold a candle to them the day at Garslade!"

To Garslade they rode through the soft grey morning easily, and with evident relish.

It was only a distance of four miles to the meet by known short-cuts, and when they rode on to the lawn in front of the big house, where the hounds were already clustering about the Master, and a good many followers were riding in, their arrival created something of a sensation.

The M.F.H.—old General Oliphant—rode forward, held his hat down by his side, and made a low salute to the mistress of Kildoon.

"Now, this is a sight for sair een, my dear!" he said to Meg. "And I'm sensible of the honour you have done me. Thank you, Sillars. It's a proud man you should be this day! I see you for the first time for many a long day where you should be, and I'm glad your charming wife is bringing you so finely to heel."

Sillars turned off this speech with a joke. Then young Oliphant—captain of a regiment which had had an almost unprecedentedly long term of service in India—also advanced and asked to be introduced.

"I suppose I must have known you as a child, Mrs. Sillars," he said, baring his handsome head, so like his father's. "But fifteen years is a big slice out of a man's life. By Jove! to see you like this and married to Sillars makes a chap realise what he has lost!"

All this flattery was as wine to Meg Sillars, and she repaid it with her most radiant looks. It was good, very good, for David to hear what other men thought of her; and she promised herself that he should hear it until it deaved him!

"Say, Mrs. Sillars," he continued—and Sillars, hard by, could not help hearing—"I've been thinking of calling to give you a message from a pal of mine who is recruiting in the south of France. I think he had the felicity of meeting you at the house of a relative."

"Major Kettering?" said Madge at once with a quick, bright smile.

Oliphant assented by a nod.

"That's the chap. He was my superior officer in India, and we've seen a lot of each other. He came here to visit my folk on one occasion, but I was absent. He wants to come again. I suppose he'll wait for the races now, as the hunting will soon be over, and we haven't much to offer a chap till the shooting commences again."

"I shall be charmed to see him when he comes," said Meg, with an air of sincerity, "Is it likely, do you think, that his aunt—the Marquise de Balincourt—will accompany him?"

"Oh! I don't think so. You see, my people don't know her. I know of her. She's a very great lady and is devoted to Kettering. He expects to be her heir. She has historic palaces or castles in Touraine, I believe."

"She is a lovely dear," said Meg. Then her eyes danced with pleasure. "There's Bobbie Sanderson," she said to the captain by way of discharging him from her service, "I must go and make love to him! Oh, I am going to enjoy myself to-day! Everybody I want to see is here."

She pranced off down the avenue to meet Bobbie Sanderson, whose one recreation was a day with the hounds, as it had been his father's before him.

At the moment, up the other side of the drive came a smart dogcart, in which Hew Kessock was driving his wife to the meet.

When they both saw Sillars and Meg looking so handsome, and apparently so well satisfied with each other, both looked surprised.

Ellie was conscious of a feeling of chagrin, and she could not avoid showing it. She was ambitious, she was clever, she was in some respects unscrupulous, but she knew in her inmost soul that she could never sit on a horse like Meg Hamilton, or acquire her regal air, or bring men to her feet as the mistress of Kildoon could do with a glance.

"If you had seen her yesterday, Hew," she said bitterly, "you would have said she was a little shop-girl or a gamekeeper's daughter—and you wouldn't have given twopence for all she had on!"

"She's got 'em all on to-day, anyhow, my dear," replied her husband; "and there isn't a thing in the field to touch her," and Kessock's eye was roving as he spoke.

The Master at the moment said pointedly to David Sillars that he hoped he was duly sensible of his amazing luck in having won the Pride of Ballochean—the toast of a county—the sweetest thing ever seen in a hunting field!

If Meg meant to punish a laggard husband, she had chosen the best weapons and the very proper place for doing so.

CHAPTER XXIV

THE NARROWING CIRCLE

" BOBBIE," said Mrs. David Sillars, marching into Dr. Sanderson's consulting-room at the Broad House, in Ayr, on a summer's day, " I want you to tell me what is the matter with my father."

Bobbie, taken unaware, hardly knew what to say in response to this very direct and peremptory demand of Meg's.

Old Ballochean was breaking up, Nature revenging herself for all the insults to which she had been subjected through all the wastrel years—and they had been many. But no doctor with a heart or any feeling of delicacy would have cared to say these things of a father to his daughter, and Bobbie, who had such a high regard for Meg, simply loathed the idea of telling her.

" He is an old man, Mrs. Sillars," he at length began, but he got no further, for Meg broke in.

" Enough of that, Bobbie. It won't do, you know," she said, and never had her tongue had a sharper edge. " My father isn't an old man yet, and don't you ' Mrs. Sillars ' me ! How dare you call him an old man when you have in front of you our M.F.H.—General Oliphant—to say nothing of your own lovely father ? Why should he break up at sixty-five, while they and others I could name, years older, are still pictures of health ? "

Bobbie eyed her doubtfully, saw resolution stamped on every feature of her face, and then realised that the truth would have to be told.

" He's getting so thin that he looks like a scarecrow," continued Meg, " and he takes so little interest in anything. I know you go to see him because he has told me so ; but, haunt Ballochean as I may, I never seem to be able to get a hold of you. So I am here to get the truth. Please tell me what is wrong and if there is nothing you can do to mend him ? "

Her eyes were troubled, the radiance of them dimmed.

Never had the Pride of Ballochean so well deserved her name as during those early months of her married life when she was before the county in all her beauty and spirit.

And the county gloried in her. Her name was on every lip, and David Sillars was the most envied of men. So far as outward appearances went there was nothing in the relations of these two to cause comment. Sillars, to be sure, still pursued his solitary mid-week course of bachelor freedom in Greenock, and some much-married husbands declared that that was what kept the freshness and the charm in the ménage at Kildoon so vivid.

The conditions under which he and Meg lived there had not been talked about beyond the gates. Complete and most rare loyalty on the part of the household, drilled to that end by Mary Maxwell, and, in addition, perhaps, a certain delicacy and pride that forbade them to speak of the subject, had kept the secret safe.

Even Bobbie, who at the beginning had undoubtedly had sundry misgivings as to the likelihood of their marriage proving a success, had concluded, as the result of such observations as he had been in a position to make, that few were better able to manage their own affairs than David Sillars and his wife.

Sometimes, indeed, he had fancied that he detected a covert sadness in her eye, but surely it was no business of his to call attention to it or to demand the cause of it.

Possibly Sillars as husband lacked something, for he was large and deliberate and slow, being besides unaccustomed to the vagaries of womankind. In knowledge of the sex and its whimsies Bobbie Sanderson was an authority, and he seldom made a mistake in his management of them, so expert and skilful had he become.

But Meg had eluded the inquisition of all her critics, however searching and persevering—of all save her own hot and restless heart.

"I'm waiting, Bobbie, for you to speak. If you know what is the matter, please tell me right now so that I may know what to do," said Meg.

"Your father, Mrs. Sillars, has been a hard-living man, and has treated his body with scant respect."

On this she made no comment of any kind, waiting with such patience as she could command for what he had still to say.

"Also," he went on, "he has been a fairly hard drinker, and he has often made drink take the place of meat. It is because he has lived so long and so habitually in the open that he has hitherto escaped punishment. But now it has got him hard and fast."

"What has?"

"A malignant disease of the kidneys, for which, I fear, nothing can be done."

"A malignant disease of the kidneys for which nothing can be done!" repeated Meg stonily. "Then what is the good of you?"

Bobbie Sanderson showed no resentment towards her for putting such a query, because, as a matter of fact, he felt none. He knew that swift, incisive tongue of yore.

"Faith, and you've pinned me, Meg," he answered in a perfectly natural voice. "It's often I'm asking myself the same question, for it's little we doctors can do, after all—even the best of us—except help lame dogs over stiles."

She seemed to ponder with her chin upon her hand. When she spoke again her voice was low and singularly sweet.

"Bobbie, I thought they did wonderful things in surgery now—that there was nothing that could happen to a person's body that they couldn't do something to mend. Can't anything be done for my father?"

"There is an operation that would prolong his life, if he would submit to it," Bobbie replied uneasily. "But that is the utmost we could promise."

"Have you mentioned it to him? Does he know that he is—he is marching on to the grave?"

Her voice broke, and her great eyes were piteous as she raised them to his square, kind face. That glance of hers stirred old memories in Bobbie Sanderson's heart, and his face wore its softest look.

"He knows everything. He demanded the naked truth, Meg—and he has had it."

"And he never said a word to me, or to anybody," she said, struggling with something in her throat that threatened to strangle her.

"No. All that he said to me when I told him was that the old fox would die game."

She started up, dashing something stinging from her darkling eyes.

"When you—when you told him the horrible truth did you also mention to him that by undergoing an operation he might prolong his life?"

"I did," was the laconic answer.

"And what did he say then?"

"He said that no butchers should hack at his poor old carcase," said Bobbie, with a faint, compassionate smile, "and that for the sake of a few more months of life it would not be worth while submitting to the pains of getting himself patched up."

"And what did you say to that?"

"I forbore to urge it. It was merely my duty to mention it."

"And how long——?" she asked, with a choke in her voice that prevented her from proceeding further with the question.

Bobbie Sanderson, however, completing it for himself hesitated for a moment.

"This is mid-June. October, my dear, will see him through."

"And if—and if—supposing he could be made to consent to an operation—how long——?" and again she could not finish the question.

"Oh! as to that it is impossible to speak with certainty," answered Bobbie, knowing what she meant to ask. "You see, until the knife is actually used, we can't say precisely what there is for it to do," he said, trying to pick his words so that, while they were fully significant, they should not needlessly hurt. "And the results vary. I have seen the same kind of operation give one man a lease of ten years' life, while with others there was a quick recurrence, and all was over in a few weeks or months. It depends greatly on what reserves of strength or what recuperative power the patient has."

" And he would not die under the operation ? " asked Meg dubiously.

" That is unlikely."

" Bobbie, tell me, if it were your father, would you advise the operation ? "

" No, I would not—because of his age. But if he were only sixty-five, I should certainly advise it. Only, the final choice would have to be left with your father. A man can't be operated on against his will, my dear, even if he is dying, and even if his doctor is absolutely sure that his life would be prolonged if he submitted. Consent has to be gained somehow."

" But if his submitting to it would give me father for, say, ten more years, it would be worth it, Bobbie. You see, I can't imagine how I am to live without him ! "

Bobbie merely nodded understandingly. He had his own thoughts of Ballochean, but his girl-child's deep affection for him wiped out many sins. He wondered whether the blue-eyed mite in his own nursery, who already brightened at his approach, would feel as much and say as much for him at sixty-five !

" I'll go up to Ballochean and have a talk with him," resumed Meg, after a moment's pause. " Thank you very much, Bobbie, for telling me the truth. If—if I can persuade him to the operation, it can be performed at Ballochean, I suppose ? "

" It could. But I would myself advise a nursing-home."

" Oh ! I am sure he never would consent to that. Have you had another opinion, Bobbie ? Wouldn't it be a wise thing to have a big surgeon down from Glasgow to see him ? "

" We've had him—the biggest—Carruthers, and the diagnosis was confirmed," he answered briefly.

A slight resentment gathered in her eyes.

" All this happening at Ballochean and I not told ! " she cried rebelliously.

" As a matter of fact, the interview with the surgeon took place at Glasgow, and it was Mr. Hamilton's express desire that not a word should be said to you about it."

" I'll ask him what he means," she said as she rose to go.

Her face had lost its radiance, and her lips looked a little drawn.

" Good-bye, Bobbie, and, again, thank you. You may see me to-day yet. How is Edith, and how is dear Miss Ann ? "

" They are at Pirn Mill, and so is my father, with the bairn, who has had whooping-cough—worse luck ! These are the sorrows of parenthood, Meg, and when a man becomes a father he is a person of no account."

" So much the better for him," she answered ruthlessly as she went out by the door.

In the street beside her dogcart—Mrs. Sillars was never seen in a carriage or a closed trap, if she could procure an open one—the new two-horse brougham from Sangster was drawing up at the kerb.

The footman had just stepped forward to ring the doctor's bell, and the face of his mistress, a little sharper and more peaked than usual, looked out, and when she saw Meg was suddenly wreathed in smiles.

" Come here, Meg, and give an account of yourself," she called out imperiously. " Why have you never been to see me since the deluge ? I have been expecting you for months."

" I have been busy," answered Meg evasively. " I have to be so much at Ballochean on account of my father's illness."

" Well, when are you coming ? "

" I don't know, Ellie —some day," she answered, in the same evasive tone.

Ellie's restless eyes travelled up and down the trim, slender figure in its linen coat and skirt and dainty blouse of white lingerie of a cut and style not found in Scotland.

" Have you been to see the doctor ? Is he at home ? "

" Dr. Robert is—the old doctor is at Pirn Mill with Mrs. Bobbie and the baby."

" I see," said Ellie, and she seemed to hesitate for a moment before going on with her questions. " You like Dr. Robert, don't you, Meg ? You'd feel yourself safe with him, would you ? " she asked presently and meaningly.

" Safe ?—why, of course ! I've known him all my life ! " answered Meg promptly.

" Do you think he is a good doctor ? " asked Lady Kessock, following up the subject in the persistent and interrogatory manner that characterised her mode of carrying on what she called conversation.

" The very best," was Meg's answer, given with decision.

" Then you would have him supposing——"

It was impossible to mistake the significance expressed in the small, shrewish voice. Meg coloured crimson, and looked a little wildly away.

" Oh ! I don't know. I've known him all my life. I haven't thought about it. Why do you look at me so stupidly, Ellie ? I must be going. My father is expecting me at Ballochean."

" How grudging you are, Meg, of your time and of your confidences ! You've quite gone back on me—and that, too, when I have such oceans to talk about, and so many things to tell you. I'm having a lovely time just now, making—what do you think ? "

She lowered her voice and whispered delightedly in Meg's unwilling ear. " Ma-in-law has turned up quite trumps ! She sent to Jane Mason's in London for a complete set of heavenly things trimmed with real lace. She's making them from the pattern. I never thought the old dame had it in her. So, meanwhile, I am lying low and keeping dark about the Dower House at Girvan."

Meg's smile was cold. She did not even ask to be enlightened as to when the happy event might be expected. But presently she was in possession of that tit-bit likewise.

" October, my dear—about the fifteenth ! Mother is so pleased. Of course, it makes everything secure when one presents one's husband with an heir to his estates. Besides, it is one's duty ! " she said with the proud and happy air of a prospective mother.

Meg smiled with amazing brilliance, and said she quite agreed. Then, with a hurried handshake she leapt to her seat in the dogcart and sent the mare flying off.

Never had she covered the miles between Ayr and Ballochean in such a short time. The groom on the back of the cart held tight to his perch, and could not manage to keep his arms folded in orthodox fashion across his breast. He could not see the face of his mistress. It was set darkly, however, and in her eyes blazed the sombre and beautiful fires that Sillars had learned to dread.

But these died down, and were succeeded by an expression of amazing softness when presently she beheld the strange and moving spectacle of her father, looking bent and feeble, walking with the aid of a stick on the terrace before the house.

" Take ' Beauty ' to the stable, George, and rub her down," she said to the groom. " You may go to the kitchen for tea, if you like, for I shall be here for an hour at least."

Then she sprang forward, and stood in front of the old man. And he gathered from the look on her face that she knew.

" I've seen Bobbie," was all that she said, and she put her hand through his arm and leaned her head on it, and her shoulders heaved.

" Wheesht, lass—it's not worth greetin' for. What's the smashing of an old crock like me ? Why, just nothing at all," he said blithely. " But how dared Bobbie tell you ? He had my commands not to."

" He had also my commands," said Meg, straightening herself with an effort. " And now I'm going to give you yours, dad. I can't let you go out of my life ! You are the only thing that matters in it."

" No, no, Meg ; don't say that ! " he cried, seeming to wince at her words.

" But it is true," she insisted. " I have been talking to Bobbie Sanderson, and he says that he has known cases as bad as yours cured by operation and ten good years added to the sufferer's life. If that can be done for other men, it can be done for you, dad, and it is your duty to us all—but most of all to me, who will not let you go —to allow it to be done," she added, and again her emotion was like to choke her.

The old man's face worked for a few moments, and such a wistfulness crept into his eyes that all traces of the evil of the past seemed to die away, and leave something of the semblance of a child, which is never wholly eradicated even from the hearts and minds of even the worst of men.

" It's not that I am feared for their knives, Meg," he said, after a pause ; " but what's the use ? It would cost a hundred pounds or more, and what I said to Bobbie when he proposed it was that I wasn't worth it—and neither I am," he added.

Meg bit her lips, and her eyes had rebellious depths. For the performance of the operation and the expenses of the nursing home meant piling up the debt to David Sillars—the debt which had so irked her all these months, and of which she could not even bear to think without a feverish surging of her blood.

" But Guy's going to do well with the harvest this year, he says, and certainly his crops are looking splendid. Surely the money for that could come out of the farm ; and if not, why, then, I can find it. David gives me so much, and I spend as little as I can upon myself. The money I have saved is accumulating in the bank, and there might easily be a hundred pounds."

Ballochean hesitated, seeming to hold intimate communion with himself.

" What I wonder, Meg, is whether it would be easier for the lads if I were away. What am I now but a cumberer of the ground ? "

" Hold your peace, old man ! " said Meg, and her tone was shrill with pain ; for, listening to these words coming from her father's lips, she had no doubt that death was lying in wait for him, and might even then be at the gate.

She seemed to cast a fearful glance across her shoulder, and horror was in her eyes.

" Father," she said, and her tone was pitiful, " it was better for us before all this happened ! We were poor, we were rough, we didn't know where to turn for an honest penny ; but at least we were happy and no man was our master."

" We had a good many masters, lass—at least I had before David despatched the lot," her father reminded her.

" I am not so sure," she said in clear-cut tones, " whether Van Leyden would have made a bad master. He had a big, kind heart. If it had not been for that worm he wanted me to marry—why, then, I think we might have done worse than have stopped in the clutches of Van Leyden."

" No, no, Meg ; you don't think what you are saying. Could there be any finer consideration shown to anybody than David Sillars has shown to me and mine ? Look at his way with Ludo and with Guy "—" and with you " he was about to add, but something in the expression of her face forbade him. Something bleak and unapproachable, it was capable of conveying a thousand hidden and sinister meanings.

" Well, I came here not to listen to pæans in praise of David," she said shortly, " but to arrange about the operation. For my sake, father, do submit to it," she pleaded, laying her hand gently on his arm. " I've had it out with Bobbie. He suggested that you should go to a nursing home in Glasgow, but I said you would never face that."

" But I would," he assured her blithely. " What would it matter where the thing was done ? And going there would hardly be more expensive than bringing nurses down here. I've heard that they make nothing but devilment in most of the houses they enter. If it is to be done, the where and how of it had best be left in Bobbie's hands, for I trust him as if he were my own son—and far more, indeed, you will be saying, than I ever trusted either Ludo or Guy. I shall never to my dying day forget what Bobbie was to me that day he took me to Glasgow to see the surgeon."

" And I shut out, father !—oh, fie ! " she cried, and her bosom heaved.

" I forbade Bobbie, and Bobbie forbade me, to tell you ; so you were between the devil and the deep sea, lass ! But our one motive for keeping silence was to save you trouble and vexation of spirit."

" I see ; but both you and Bobbie ought to have known me better, and I am not sure that I shall ever forgive him. Well, then, have I your leave to see Bobbie again, and arrange it with him, if he thinks it wise ? "

" Yes, my dear, certainly. I have not much pleasure in life as it is, Meg. I can't walk the length of the farm now, and I have no stomach for my meat."

Meg remained at Ballochean for tea, and when she left, instead of going straight home, she drove once more into Ayr and drew up at the Broad House.

It was six o'clock, and Dr. Robert had to be summoned from his evening surgery to interview Mrs. Sillars once more.

" I've been to Ballochean and had it out with the old man," she said. " He has consented to the operation, Bobbie, and he says he will put himself entirely in your hands. How soon can you arrange it ? I suppose it is a case of the sooner the better ? "

" Undoubtedly. I would say this week, if it is to be done at all. Every day increases the risk. Beyond doubt the thing is growing rapidly ; and I may tell you now that there would be a period of suffering in front of your father, if it were long put off, which would try us all. So it is better in every way that he should go to the nursing home."

" What will you do then ? " asked Meg, with her quick incisiveness. " Will you telephone, or wire, or write ? "

" I can do all three. But I'll come and see you at Kildoon in the morning after my arrangements are made."

She nodded, and, saying she would not keep him, drove away back to her empty house.

Her heart wooed her to Ballochean, but there was really no urgent need for her presence there, and, besides, she had to see Bobbie in the morning.

After she had dined she sat down to write a letter to her husband, informing him of what she had learned that day, intending to leave it unposted till she should hear from Bobbie in the morning what had been decided.

Sillars was not yet forty-eight hours gone—for that was but Tuesday evening, and he had expressly said that he would not return till late on Friday evening. Sometimes, now, he did not even come till Saturday, and Meg was quite indifferent to the time of his coming and going—or pretended to be so, which, in the circumstances, was quite as well.

Before ten o'clock next morning the doctor's gig was before the door of Kildoon. Meg, on the look-out, received him in the hall, her face eager with expectancy.

" It's all arranged, my dear," said Bobbie gravely. " To-morrow morning, at Carruther's Nursing Home in Bath Street—the place, I mean, where he sends most of his cases. Your father will have to go in to-night."

" It's a very rapid way of doing things, isn't it ? " asked Meg, and her cheeks paled.

" Not more so than usual," was the reply. " These things are always arranged at a few hours' notice. What I want to know is whether you can go with him this afternoon, and see him comfortably established—or shall I ? I can make the time, if you would prefer that I should go ? "

" Oh, I can go. But you will be there to-morrow morning, Bobbie ? Promise me that nobody shall touch him unless you are there ? "

An odd softness deepened the kindliness visible in Bobbie's eyes.

" That's right, my dear. I'll be on the spot. Carruthers will expect me to be, and he will probably ask me to assist. But you won't stay the night in town ? "

" Yes, I will—and in the Home, of course."

" I hardly think they'll allow you to do that, but we'll see. You have a way of getting things. Well, you'll go to Ballochean and get Mr. Hamilton's things together, and I'll go back and tell Miss Macdonald to expect you about tea-time, or a little later. Will that do ? "

" That will do," she answered.

Then they went into details as to what things would be required for a sojourn in a place which had never been other than a faint name to Meg Hamilton. She was learning day by day fresh lore regarding the pain of the world and the sacrament men call life.

She said good-bye reluctantly to Bobbie, who had a tremendous day's work in front of him, his father being on holiday.

Then she sat down to finish her letter to her husband. In the middle of it she broke down and sobbed like to break her heart. But though Sillars saw the blur upon the page it never occurred to him that it was the impress of his wife's tears !

CHAPTER XXV

THE HOUSE IN ORDER

DAVID SILLARS received his wife's letter with the last post on Wednesday evening and, as a result of what he had read therein, he took an early train on Thursday morning for Glasgow.

Meg had told him certain things, but she had omitted to mention the address of the Nursing Home to which they were taking old Ballochean. She had given the surgeon's name, however, and a telephone message to his house in Kelvinside did the rest.

Sillars arrived at the door of the demure, rather grim-looking house in Bath Street about half-past nine, just at the moment when the issues of life and death were being decided for poor Gavin Hamilton in one of the upper rooms.

Shown into the superintendent's sitting-room, he found Meg there, walking to and fro, with her hands clenched, and with a somewhat desperate look on her young face. She feared little under heaven, but on this day she had come into conflict with forces of which she had no knowledge and which therefore baffled her.

All the deep tenderness embedded in the nature of Sillars sprang to the surface as he saw her distraught face, and almost he could have taken her in his arms.

She, it seemed, turned to him with a blind desire for help. Then she drew back, even as he had done, restraining his impulse, and spoke formally.

" It is good of you to come like this, David. But there is nothing you, or I, or anyone can do! It is the waiting that kills."

" It will not be long, let us hope," he answered gently. " I got your letter by the late post last night. I need not say I am sorry, my dear. I can see you feel it desperately. Is Dr. Robert here ? "

" Oh, yes ! Without him I should not have allowed them to touch Dad. And he has promised to come to me the moment he can. Oh, I wonder how much longer they are going to be ! "

" It could hardly be done under an hour, I think," he answered, " and it is only a quarter to ten. The time will soon pass."

She looked at him vaguely, wringing her hands.

" David, had you any idea of this ? " she asked presently, as if some fresh thought had struck her.

" I saw that he was going down the hill, of course ; but I had no idea what was the matter. Somehow, I never see Sanderson now, though, of course, I might, and perhaps should, have made it my business to see him."

" It wouldn't have done any good. If dad dies, David, I'm done. I shan't care for anything any more."

Sillars had nothing to say. It was not the first time he heard such a cry from the lips of the bereft. Nay, he had himself felt like uttering it on the day when they had come and told him that his mother had left him alone in the old house of Kildoon.

But it was futile and, at the moment, it would have been unkind to remind her that the tide of human affairs flows on in spite of all the heart-break in the world, and that a little more or less matters not at all !

The minutes dragged ; but punctually on the stroke of ten the door opened, and Bobbie came in. He recognised Sillars merely by a nod, surprised perhaps to see him there, though undoubtedly that was his proper place.

Meg flew to the young doctor, clasping imploring hands on his black coat-sleeve.

" All right, my dear—all right ! He has stood it A1. And—yes—there is every hope. He has not come out of the chloroform yet."

" Can I just pop up and look at him ? " asked Meg eagerly.

Bobbie shook his head.

" No, no, you can't see him before the afternoon—if then. He will most probably sleep for the most of the day. Sad business, Sillars; but I think we'll pull him through."

Meg walked to the window and, through the swaying curtains, looked out upon the dingy street. Her relief was great, for she had worked herself to expectation of the fullest tragedy. She felt weak now—weak and spent, and very near to tears.

" I think you should take your wife out, Mr. Sillars," suggested Bobbie. " There is nothing she can do here, and they are not keen on having too many visitors in the house. There isn't room for them. It would be much better, really, if Mrs. Sillars would go home to Kildoon."

At this Meg looked rebellious.

" He might ask for me," she said quickly.

" He won't to-day," Bobbie assured her.

" Where are you staying, Madge ? " asked Sillars. " Did you sleep here last night ? "

" Yes. I stayed with dad till after ten o'clock. Miss Macdonald was very kind; but she told me that I couldn't have the room after to-day."

" Then we'd better go to St. Enoch's, my dear," suggested Sillars. " Go and see about your things, and we'll take a cab over and get a room."

She went with astonishing obedience.

When the two men were left Bobbie looked straight into the eyes of Sillars.

" The poor old chap's done," was all he said.

" Why, I thought you said the operation had been successful ? " said Sillars, surprised and rather displeased.

" So it was up to a point. What Carruthers did was all right. But he can't do enough. Something had to be left. If Mr. Hamilton ever gets up it will mean a recurrence. The best thing that can happen will be that he should peg out now."

Sillars looked inexpressibly shocked.

" It was a pity, perhaps, not to have told my wife the truth," he said rather stiffly.

" She is not in a fit state to hear it," answered Bobbie rather curtly. " And don't you tell her it. It'll come to her gradually. He'll rally a bit; then there'll be a gradual sinking. The way will be smoothed for her, I don't doubt, as it is for others."

It fell out just as Bobbie had predicted.

Gavin Hamilton recovered from the immediate effects of the operation, and Meg and he had some delightful days in the upper room of the Nursing Home—days on which all the years seemed to have rolled back and made her a little child again, toddling after her father to the stables to be set in turn on every bit of horseflesh in them. All the old time—the good time before the blight had fallen on Ballochean—was lived over again, and it would have been hard to tell which of the twain was the greater or the more lovable child !

All the household frankly worshipped them both, and Gavin Hamilton sometimes said jestingly to his kind nurses that he was having the time of his life.

Then quite suddenly and perceptibly he began to decline. At the end of the third week there was no betterment; on the contrary, there were certain signs and symptoms that there was no mistaking.

One day when Bobbie Sanderson arrived early to see the dying Laird, at an hour when he knew that he would not be likely to encounter Meg, he said to him suddenly —" Bobbie, I want to go home."

" Time enough, Mr. Hamilton. Next week, I think, we may safely let you undertake the journey."

" I shan't be able for it next week, Bobbie. I'm going down the hill fast. I want to go home to-day."

" I'll telephone to Carruthers to come out. I'll wait for him here."

" It's no good. He says the same as you, and bids me wait till next week. I want to die in the old house, Bobbie—in my own bed, d'ye hear ? "

" I hear," answered Bobbie Sanderson; and he looked like one stricken, for he knew that the call from afar had come to the soul of Gavin Hamilton, and that nothing could stay its flight.

" I'll wait till to-morrow—not a day longer. I'll tell Meg when she comes up this afternoon. So you can arrange it as best you like, my man."

" There will be no trouble about the arranging—just an ambulance to the station and a proper invalid compartment. Very well, Mr. Hamilton, it shall be as you say."

Bobbie's immediate capitulation was significant; but his heart was heavy, not so much for the old man, who was done with the things of time, as for her who clung to him so desperately, and who would be so forlorn when he should leave her.

"What day is this, Bobbie?" inquired Ballochean, moving his restless old white head on the pillow.

"This?—oh, Wednesday. One loses count sometimes."

"Well, I want you, when you go down or out of the house, to telephone to David Sillars and tell him I want to see him."

"To-day, do you mean, or after you get back to Ballochean?"

"To-day—this evening after Meg is safely back at Ayr. She mustn't know. It's private business I have with my son-in-law, Bobbie, understand, and I might find it difficult to get the privacy at Ballochean, where, I suppose, Meg will establish herself when she understands."

Bobbie said he would see that Sillars had the message.

"And there'll be no telling her, Bobbie," continued the Laird. "Just let it drift in on her as it drifted in on me. She'll get used to the idea before the poor old candle blows out. Ay, ay, a queer—a mortal queer—thing is life!"

"But death unravels it all, Mr. Hamilton," said Bobbie out of the fulness of his heart. "The more I see of all the mysteries the more reconciled I am to death. It is not the end, as most folk think—it is the beginning for most."

"Ay, ay, who knows? The old reprobate might get a clean slate up there," he mused with his tired eyes half-closing. "He will, if she can do anything! She's not so far away, Bobbie—Meg's mother I mean. It would not surprise me to know that she is in this very room."

Bobbie hastened to take his departure, not so much from disbelief—for he had seen many strange things in the supreme moments 'twixt life and death, and he had not the scoffer's mind—but because he observed that great weariness was stealing over the worn-out frame and that the Laird would immediately sleep.

He went downstairs and, from Miss Macdonald's sitting-room, rang up Sillars at Langdyke. A very few words served to put Sillars in full possession of the facts; and, though shocked and grieved, he was by no means overwhelmed with surprise.

"Tell him I'll be up there about six. I suppose Mrs. Sillars will have gone by then?"

"I'll make sure," Bobbie answered, as he rang off.

Then with a heavy heart he returned to Ayr, and his first road was to Kildoon.

CHAPTER XXVI

THE PASSING OF BALLOCHEAN

It was now glorious summer weather, with just a touch of the crisp harvest fulness in the air, and Kildoon was looking it's very loveliest. The Doon, which the dry summer had somewhat reduced in volume, sang between its pebbly banks, lined with the willow and the birk and the rowan, on the last of which the flame was already creeping over the luscious fruit.

It was only noon, and as he turned his horse's head round the last bend in the avenue he saw Meg's trap before the door.

" By Jove ! just in time," he muttered, and hastened forward to the door.

He found her in the hall, giving some instructions to Mary Maxwell. At sight of Bobbie she visibly paled.

These days of sharp anxiety had told on Meg, and she had undoubtedly lost some of her radiant bloom. But there was an inexpressible sweetness in her sharpened features and a quietude in her whole demeanour which struck Bobbie Sanderson rather poignantly.

" She is aging, poor lass," he said to himself. " Life is working its will with her."

" Good morning, Bobbie. You haven't brought me bad news, I hope," she said with difficulty.

" No, no. I ran up by the eight-thirty to see him, and I find him fretting to get home. Nothing is to be gained by keeping him in the Home any longer. So, if you'll make the necessary arrangements at Ballochean we'll get him down to-morrow."

She looked at him searchingly.

" I want to know exactly what this means, Bobbie."

" Faith, then, and I can't tell you," he said, trying to speak lightly. " There is no more for Carruthers to do. The wound has healed, and he can be moved with perfect safety. He's hankering to get home, and the nurse whom he likes best can come with him, and you will be nearer him. It's his own wish, Mrs. Sillars, and you'd better grant it—indeed, there is nothing to gain by thwarting him now."

Comforted by the assurance that the wound had healed so completely, Meg immediately became a woman of affairs.

" Does he expect me to-day ? " she asked.

" He did not say. But I think you had better run up by the twelve-thirty, if that is the train you were going to catch. There will be plenty of time after you come back to arrange things, and, if you like, I can drive round by Ballochean and prepare them for your father's return. They could be airing the room, anyhow, and getting ready. I might see Guy, too."

" Thank you, Bobbie, if you will. Well, if I am to catch that train, I'll have to go now and drive ' Beauty ' like the wind. Good-bye."

She was off with a nod and a wave of the hand, but with no accompanying smile.

" I believe," mused Bobbie, " that she understood without further parley or words that the end is drawing near." For the things of the spirit are unfathomable, and knowledge comes from afar, borne on the wings of invisible messengers who never fail to accomplish the behest entrusted to them.

Sanderson drove round by Ballochean, found Guy at his luncheon—which he proceeded to share with him—and prepared him for what was coming. There being no particular need to spare Guy's feelings, he told him that his father's ultimate recovery was doubtful, even unlikely.

Although happenings of this kind were part of Bobbie Sanderson's daily experience, he was conscious of a singular sadness and depression of spirit for the rest of the day. Associated as he had been with Ballochean from his earliest years, he felt that in the gradual breaking up of the family life there was a tragedy of no ordinary kind. Soon Guy would be left sole representative of the old name in Ballochean. But it was of Meg that he thought most.

Shrewd and observant above the common, Bobbie had now come to see that things were not as they should be between David Sillars and his wife. Their upkeep of appearances in public in no way deceived that astute student of human nature and of life, and his personal interest in Meg rendered his intuition in all matters concerning her unerring.

She was unhappy, she was eating her heart out at Kildoon, and David Sillars was either wilfully or ignorantly and deplorably blind. Bobbie did not actually know what was the matter, but something told him that the relations between the two must march to inevitable tragedy, unless something intervened to lift them to a level of more perfect understanding of each other.

He had no doubt that Ballochean's death, when it came, would hasten this crisis.

A little sick of things as he drove that morning, he determined to write to Pirn Mill telling his father that he must come home now and bear the brunt, for he was needing a spell of quiet and of the society of the bairn to do him good.

At the close of his working day Sillars journeyed to Glasgow, reaching the Nursing Home about six o'clock.

He was evidently expected, and was shown up to Mr. Hamilton's room without a moment's delay. He found him sitting up in bed—a gaunt figure, with all the grossness and the high colour purged from his face, which, however, was perfectly serene; and his smile of welcome had no shadow as he reached out to take his son-in-law's hand.

" Sit down, David. You're a man of your word. I'm glad to see you. Did Bobbie tell you they were getting me home to-morrow ? "

" He said something about it."

" Ay. I've been here long enough. It was a lot of expense for no particular end, David. But I don't know that I'm grudging it, for they've taken my pain clean away and given me peace to think."

To that Sillars could make no answer. A man of few words at all times, he never found it possible to coin them to suit occasion.

" Has Meg told you," pursued the old man, " that I'm going home to get ready for the kirkyard ? "

" It's what we're all doing," said Sillars rather desperately, for the speech moved him.

Ballochean gave a little chuckle, and the ghost of a smile flickered a moment across his wasted face.

" And that's true, too—only some of us get there quicker than others, and by harder riding. But when I was your age, David, I had small truck with a kirkyard, or, for the matter of that, with the kirk itself. Yet, lad, it's the queerest thing, but, since I have been lying here wi' naebody aboot me but kind women and just seeing Bobbie and you occasionally, it's all wiped out—all the devil's marking, I mean—and I feel as if I were a bit bairn washed in the clean water of the Doon ! "

Sillars rose up from the chair by the bed and took a turn across the floor, not trusting himself to speak.

" Has Meg been here to-day ? " he asked at length.

" Yes. She came up about lunch-time and stopped rather shorter than usual, being in a hurry to get home and make ready at Ballochean. Bobbie himsel' is coming to take me down the morn, and you'll come over at night and see me, I don't doubt."

" I will that," answered Sillars fervently.

" Guy is the one I've seen the least of, David, and the last time he was here he grat like a bairn ! The queer thing is that nane o' them should hate me, lad, for the kind of father I've been to them, and the ill turn I've served them ! There should be a letter from Ludo soon, for Meg wrote to him the day of the operation.

" Ludo is doing well, Mr. Hamilton. The manager has nothing but praise of him."

"And all due to you, David. You've saved the lot," said the old man with a thrill in his voice.

"Hold your tongue, Mr. Hamilton! If that is all you have to say to me I'll be going," said Sillars hastily.

"It's the truth, my man. Come and sit down, and I'll try to keep off that subject. I suppose you will not object to tell me what will become of Ballochean after I'm safely in the mools?"

"The lads will have it. Ludo is the heir, Mr. Hamilton. He will have to come home."

"And Guy? He is putting his heart into the place as he has never done to anything else; and the horse-breeding business will pay, David, if it's given time, and if a bit of money is spent on it."

"Then, why not divide the place, Mr. Hamilton? Give Guy the home-farm and The Knowes, and let Ludo have the rest," suggested Sillars, leaning on the bottom of the rail of the bed and speaking with a deliberation which showed that the idea was no new one to him. "Ludo is very happy meantime out in Jamaica, and, if he liked, he could leave Guy to look after the place till he is minded to come home. They were fairly good friends before Ludo went away, were they not?"

"They did not quarrel—if you mean that, David. But Ludo was aye at his books, and they had but little truck with each other. Each, I think, despised and misunderstood the other. It was Meg that saw good in both."

"Well, if you think the suggestion worth anything, Mr. Hamilton, it will be as well to have Kirkbride up as soon as you are able to see him."

"Anyway, you will come too, David, for, after all, yours is the biggest stake."

"I will come, of course. But I am only anxious that the interests of your sons should be safeguarded, Mr. Hamilton. I will rid them of obligation to me as soon as I legally and wisely can. I have no axe to grind for myself."

Old Ballochean, eyeing him keenly, with vision sharpened by detachment from the things of time, saw the cloud deepening on his brow. He sat forward suddenly and pointed his finger, and his sunken eyes were full of strange fire.

"David, what is the matter between you and Meg? You are both miserable. It is written no less legibly on your face than on hers."

Sillars flushed and would have turned away, but something in the old man's penetrating gaze held him to the spot.

"Since you have put it like that, the marriage was a mistake, Mr. Hamilton. I was too old for her, and, besides, I was not the kind of man to make her happy."

"Have you tried?" came mercilessly from the old man.

The question staggered Sillars, and for the moment he looked as if he would take offence.

"I have done my best," he said stiffly. "If she has said anything else, she has not given me my due. I have given her everything in my power, and have taken care not to force myself upon her, understanding from the beginning that it was a mere marriage of convenience in which her heart could never be. Neither of us, I fancy, imagined how difficult it would be for us; but we are not actually unhappy. I am certain that nobody thinks there is aught amiss between us."

But Ballochean was not satisfied.

"It's an ill thing meddling with married folk, David, and among all my faults and my escapades I've steered clear of that. But in my younger days I knew something about women, and I have seen into the hearts of not a few. And this I can pass on without hurt to my daughter or to any other woman. It's love they need, and, even when it is given in full measure, pressed down and running over, they never have enough. It's the very marrow of their bones, and they will forgive anything in a man who does not stint them of that wine of life. Take that home with you, David, and ponder it in your bachelor days and nights at Greenock, which are an insult to the bonniest woman in the county. Her heart is starved, my man, or I am sair mistaken. Now we'll change the subject. Will you make an appointment with Kirkbride to come to Ballochean, and will you come with him yourself the day after the morn, unless you hear to the contrary?"

Sillars promised, and the interview was not prolonged.

Gavin Hamilton bore the journey well, and seemed glad to be at home.

Meg was waiting at Ballochean for him, and she intimated that she intended to take up her abode there meanwhile. Nobody demurred or said her nay.

But she was not needed long. Having set his house in order, Ballochean fell asleep on Saturday night with a smile on his lips, and the dawn of the fair Sabbath morning found his spirit freed from the bonds of the flesh and away—whither, who can tell?

If the expression on his face meant anything—then he had sensed some happier region, where all the sins and sorrows and struggles of earth are forgotten or wiped out for ever more!

CHAPTER XXVII

BOBBIE INTERVENES

BOBBIE SANDERSON had a long round and a busy day. Four of the afternoon found him within half a mile of the village of Maidens, where he had a call to pay on some Glasgow folk who had a house there for the summer, and who, owing to the illness of one of the children, still remained.

It was October now—grey, stormy weather, with occasional blinks of sun, and with high winds which lashed the sea to foam and sent wonderful shoals of clouds scudding across the sky ; weather for lovers of the open who did not mind the tang of the salt wind on their faces, or its wildness in their blood.

Bobbie had been hard at it since eight o'clock in the morning, and his day was not near done ; yet he came with a joy which never failed to the picturesque old-world village in the cleft of the hills, with its golden fringe of sands, where he had paddled and picnicked many a long day in his boyhood.

He drove in a high gig, lightly hung and seated for two, into which a fresh horse had been put at two o'clock in order that no time might be lost upon the road. He himself was driving, and he had not spoken a word to his young groom for a good hour. But such long silences, necessary to the man who had much on his mind, in no way disturbed the happy relations existing between master and man. Jake Nisbet had been about the Broad House stables since he was fourteen, and no mood of the master had ever had power to trouble his placid soul.

" There's a big swell on, Jake, and I wouldn't wonder to see rain before nightfall," said the doctor, at length breaking the silence, as his eyes roamed the vast expanse of the tumbling sea, which was so misty to westward that Arran was lost to view.

" Ay, I wadna wonder. It's gey coorse-like," answered Jake stolidly.

Then his gaze was rivetted by the sight of two persons riding on the sands. Bobbie also saw them, but his eyes were not so gleg as Jake's, and he was unable to identify them.

" Mrs. Sillars and the major frae Garslade," observed Jake laconically. " I see them yesterday, too. But you didna notice, so I said næthing."

The doctor appeared not to notice now—at least, he made no answer, though a frown darkened the pleasant expression on his face.

To discuss the wife of David Sillars with a stable-boy was obviously impossible, though he gathered from Jake's tone that he might have told a great deal more. The lad's father was gardener at Garslade, and he spent his Sundays at home.

Bobbie watched the figures cantering along the sands contentedly together, and when the gig had to turn away from the sea he still kept silence.

He paid his visit, informed the folk that it would now be perfectly safe to remove the child to Glasgow, and then returned by the road he had come. And there, at the head of a lane, he met the riders full in the face.

Meg was looking radiant. A splendid and quite fearless horsewoman, she looked her best in the saddle ; and Bobbie Sanderson, well as he knew her, was startled by her beauty, which was almost uncanny.

Her companion fitted well into the picture ; in all the shire there could not have been found a pair more perfectly matched. Both looked pleased with themselves, and at the unexpected rencontre Meg showed not the smallest embarrassment. She gaily waved her switch, and shot Bobbie a defiant, laughing glance as the two of them sped swiftly by.

Bobbie's hands tightened on the reins and he glowered straight in front of him and flecked the mare with the whip sufficiently to send her madly flying—an action by which Jake Nesbit was immediately made aware that his master was angry.

When the doctor had gone about a quarter of a mile he drew the mare up so sharply that she nearly came on her haunches ; then he turned her about.

"I have to go to Rathillis," he said shortly, "and I think the farm-road will take us there sooner. It'll cut off half a mile anyway."

Jake assented with his particular brand of nod, and sprang down to open the gate into a turnip-field, up the side of which there was a rough track.

There was not a by-road or a short-cut in that side of the county unfamiliar to Dr. Robert, and he could engineer them on the darkest night with complete confidence and skill. This particular road entailed the opening and shutting of no fewer than five gates, but finally they emerged on to the magnificently wide and smooth avenue leading up to the castle, which they reached in a few minutes' time.

It was one of the show places in Ayrshire, if not, indeed, in Scotland. Cradle of an old race and custodian of romance, it had Scotland's song and story inseparably associated with its grey stone battlements, to which the ivy clung.

As they swept up to the door a fierce red gleam from the half-defeated sun shone forth and wrapped the place in an indescribable glory.

It was very still and quiet all around; even the thinning trees seemed to be hushed. The Doon did not trepass here, and so some subtle charm was lost to Rathillis.

But the family had their own traditions of Burns, the inspired singer of the stream, as well as those of earlier and more warlike heroes. Bobbie never approached the place without a thrill.

He came there to-day entirely on his own account, acting on a sudden impulse that was almost an intuition. There was no sickness in Rathillis, and in his professional capacity Bobbie had never been inside the house in his life.

A sort of panic seized him once he had asked for Lady Rathillis and been invited to enter. But, gripping his courage in both hands, he followed the man up a winding stair and was, without further ado, shown into the presence of the countess.

She belonged to the old school, and never made excuses or pretences, or parried with what she considered her duty. In spite of her age and the many claims upon her she received personally all who called, and no servant was ever put to the trouble of coming to inquire whether she would or would not receive. If she was in the house she received all.

Her tea table had been laid in the window of the round tower, which was her favourite sitting-room, and when the man announced Dr. Sanderson she turned to greet him with the liveliest expression of pleasure.

"Now, I take this as truly kind, Robert, though I am perfectly well and not needing your ministrations. I hear you have put your father's eye completely out in the county. But you may tell him from me when you go home that, if a message should come from Rathillis, and he should dare to send any whipper-snapper to me, he will never hear the end of it!"

Her eyes twinkled, and the smile on her small, cameo-like face was a mingling of sweetness and archness, and her whole endeavour was to put the young man completely at his ease. Her handshake was very warm, and she motioned him to a chair, instructed the man to bring another teacup, and sat forward, prepared to enjoy herself.

She was very small, but never was a completer dignity embodied in so little compass. She had been one of the beauties of the older time, and she still retained much of her charm, her grace and lightness of figure, her wonderfully clear colouring, and her engaging smile.

Yet in certain quarters she was feared, and with reason. For she was a very great lady indeed, who had small sympathy and patience with the trend of modern life, clinging with pride and steadfastness to the traditions of other days. True as steel, straight and honourable, keen and proud, she was a friend worth having; but because the gift of her friendship was so great it had been vouchsafed to very few.

She was a childless woman and dwelt alone in her house of memories, which, after her death, a very distant kinsman in Australia would come home to inherit. And that was a grief of no ordinary kind, for Rathillis was a home and a heritage which ought to be worshipped and revered.

"I hear that you are often at the Maidens in these days, Robert. I cannot call you 'doctor,' for it is no time since you used to come with your father, sitting between him and the groom in the gig, and many a cake and bit of barley-sugar I have fed you with just to hear you say you were going to be a doctor, like 'Daddy.' Has it come up to expectation?"

" My business, do you mean ? Oh, yes, Lady Rathillis, I have no cause to grumble, though sometimes when night comes I may be too tired to sleep."

" And now you are a married man with a bairn of your own. Tell me, how does that queer composite arrangement at the Broad House suit ? Your father and Miss Anne are there still, I understand."

" Yes. It works all right. The house is big, and my wife is sweet-tempered, and there are no ructions, or even the sign of them," laughed Bobbie, with all the assurance of the man whose house is built on a sure foundation.

" Ah, then you should thank God for her ! She must be a pearl of price in these days of unsexed women. How many lumps of sugar does she permit you in your tea ? "

" As many as I ask for. I like it sweet, Lady Rathillis."

" There you are, then—four lumps, and the basin to your hand ! And what is the news of the county ? You who are never done flying to and fro in it should be able to gather the cream. Tell me, has the heir arrived at Sangster yet ? "

" Not yet, but may any day now. I was there yesterday. Lady Kessock is very well, and there is no anxiety."

" And is it true that Anne Kessock is going to Girvan after the happy event is over ? "

" The house is being got ready, I believe. But I have known a bairn's hands to work wonders before now, Lady Rathillis, and perhaps it will end in her finding another tenant for the Dower House."

Lady Rathillis nodded.

Then, quite suddenly, Bobbie plunged, afraid lest he should be tempted to leave without coming to the point.

" I did not come this afternoon to pay an idle call, Lady Rathillis. That I had no manner of right to do," he began a little nervously. " And even now I am not sure whether I may presume to mention what is in my mind."

" You have my leave ; and if it is anything in reason that you want, it is granted, Robert."

" As I came along the road about half an hour ago I saw on the sand on horseback Mrs. Sillars and a man who is stopping at Garslade," he began hurriedly. " He came there to shoot by Billy Oliphant's invitation a good month ago. It is very few birds, I am thinking, that have fallen to his gun. His time is spent chiefly at Kildoon."

Lady Rathillis listened intently, her face betraying nothing but interest.

" I don't know whether you have heard anything," Bobbie went on, conscious that he was blundering horribly, and wishing himself well out of it, yet determined to go through with his self-imposed task. " They talk of nothing else at our end of the county ; and unless something is done—well, there may happen that which all of us would be sorry for."

" You mean that the soldier is making love to the wife of David Sillars in his absence, and that she is encouraging him ? "

" I don't know what has actually happened between them. All I know is that I meet them together in all sorts of odd places, and that I am getting desperate. I like her. I should hate horribly that anything should happen to her. And I like Sillars, too—though there's something about all this that I don't profess to understand. How anybody who calls Meg Hamilton wife can be away from her more than half the time, when there's no need, is beyond me. I've thought of speaking to Sillars," continued Bobbie, " and again I have thought of writing to him at Greenock. But, hang it all ! a man hesitates when it is a question of dropping poison about ; and it surely is his business to look after his own wife. But to-day there is a mortal fear on me, and I have the feeling that something has got to be done, and that at once. The doing of it, however, is not a man's work—least of all is it mine. But will you do something, Lady Rathillis ? I know that you have approved Mrs. Sillars, and that you go sometimes to Kildoon. Will you go now and try to save her ? "

" You think it as bad as that ? "

" I do. And she is wayward and very much alone. And this Kettering is an attractive beggar—just one to take a woman's fancy—and he is skilled in all the arts. And that fool Sillars, with his eyes shut, is grubbing among his sugar-bags, or his money-bags at Greenock, and, pouff !—the next thing will be that she'll be off ! It mustn't happen, Lady Rathillis, for, in spite of all they say, she's one of the best.

She's pure gold, but—but she has never had the right folk about her, or anybody to give her what she needs."

"She has got a good husband, Robert—one of the best, too. But I'll see what I can do. I thank you for coming to me to-day. It was good of you. It shows you have a heart, and it's not a thing that many men would have done."

"It was not an easy job, Lady Rathillis," admitted Bobbie, with an oddly nervous laugh as he ruffled his sandy hair with his long, virile, characteristic hand—the hand of the healer. "But I'll sleep the sounder now I've told you. Please forgive me; and—and you will not lose any time?"

A tear was in the old lady's eye as she held his hand; and then, suddenly moved, she offered him her cheek.

That was one of the proudest moments in Bobbie Sanderson's life, and he never forgot it to his dying day!

Next morning, soon after ten o'clock, a carriage, with a groom bearing a note marked urgent, drove from Rathillis to Kildoon; and Meg, alone in the house, read the message:—

"My dear, I am sending for you to lunch with me to-day, for I am not very well, and it is borne in upon me that I need to see you. Please send me no excuse, but just return in the carriage. I will let you go immediately after lunch. I am waiting for you now."

The signature was that of the Countess of Rathillis, and Meg felt that she had no choice but to go.

She had an engagement. It was for the afternoon, however, and it would not take her far away from home—only down the winding Doon a mile or more, to an unfrequented bend in the willow-lined banks beside a pool, beloved of every angler in the shire, but permissible only to very few, for it was the richest as well as the most beautiful part of the Kildoon stretch of the Doon water. And Meg had become very skilled with the rod, plying it from her vantage point by the side of the old mossy brig.

Pondering on the summons, a trifle startled by it, perhaps—for she had not seen Lady Rathillis since immediately after her father's death—Meg yet discovered that the idea of going pleased her.

"Tell Lady Rathillis' coachman that I shall be ready in five minutes' time," she commanded her own man.

Then she ran upstairs, not to change her gown, for the neat, tailor-made skirt and white blouse, with the black tie and pearl pin, became her rarely, and were perfectly suitable for a lunch *à deux* at Rathillis.

She reached the castle about half-past eleven o'clock, and was at once conducted to the presence of her old friend.

The storm had quieted now, and a fine, thin rain was beginning to fall from skies uniformly grey. But the round tower was the picture of comfort. It was fragrant with flowers, and Meg's welcome was of the warmest.

"You've not treated me well, my dear," her hostess reminded her. "What did you promise me that day when I saw you after your poor father's burying? Was it not that you would come whenever you had a lonely, unoccupied hour, and did I not assure you that you would find this door ever open? It is six weeks—six good weeks and more—since you have crossed my threshold, and now I only get you by main force, as it were."

Meg smiled, but her colour rose high. She was conscious of something deeper than usual in the kind scrutiny of these keen old eyes.

"I don't know how the time goes, but it does seem to slip away, Lady Rathillis," she said a trifle confusedly. "I am sorry for my remissness, however, and I promise to behave better in future."

"Come and sit down here beside me on this couch. I have sent for you to-day for two reasons, my dear. Firstly, I wanted to see you because I love you and you don't come to Rathillis half as often as I should like; and secondly——" she paused.

"Yes?" said Meg inquiringly, quite unembarrassed, however, for the idea that Lady Rathillis, who lived remote from the world and disdained to associate herself in any way with its evil or foolish gossip, would stoop to speak to her about such a trifle as her fooling with Major Kettering, never once presented itself to her mind.

"I want to hear such a lot of things about you, especially as to how you pass the time at Kildoon all those days of the week when you are left alone. It has often troubled me. It is a lonely life for a young woman."

"Yes," answered Meg hardly, "it is. But, then, I knew that it would be like that. Most lives are lonely. I know that your share is, because you have told me so."

"Ah! but I am only dreeing the remnant of it. Once my life was as full as there was any need for—fuller, indeed, than I desired sometimes. And it is best when one's faculties are in their prime that they should be completely exercised. Do you housekeep, or read, or garden—or how do you fill up your time?"

"I do a little of most things. My housekeeping doesn't amount to much, to be sure, because Mrs. Maxwell is so competent. And I love to exercise my horses and my dogs."

Lady Rathillis dropped her fine chin on her hand and eyed the beautiful, vivid young face in front of her with deepening kindliness, touched with anxiety.

"I had hoped that by now you would have something to tell me—that one day we should be welcoming an heir at Kildoon."

Meg flushed, and then paled desperately.

"There is nothing of that kind in prospect—there never will be," she answered hardly.

"Oh! but you must not talk like that, my dear. I am a childless woman myself, and look what it means when one is old and has lost the one being on whom all one's hopes and affections were fixed! It is only half-living. And I did not expect to hear your mother's daughter talk like that, my dear. It is wrong and wicked an unwomanly. After all, if one marries, one takes certain vows which no woman, even the most advanced, has the right to break."

Meg laughed suddenly, and the sound had something hollow and rather repellant in it.

"You are quite right, Lady Rathillis. In marriage one does take tremendous vows without in the least understanding or realising what they mean or involve. I think it would be no bad thing if there was a class for matrimony as there is a class for confirmation in the English Church. It might help a good many girls afterwards."

Lady Rathillis was displeased at this apparently flippant answer, which she conceived to be in the worst of taste. She was very clever, but she had missed the way with Meg Hamilton, to whom all along she had done injustice the most profound.

"I don't like to hear you, my dear, and it makes me sad to think how you have deteriorated in the last six months. Do you think this is quite fair to your kind husband?"

"Oh, yes," said Meg quietly, "quite fair."

"Then I do not. But what you say gives me courage to mention a matter which has kept me awake all night. I have been hearing a good deal about you which I would rather not have heard, Meg. Is it true that you have been so far disloyal to the husband who trusts you as to go about with Major Kettering and—and to suffer your name to be linked with his in a manner that no self-respecting woman or wife should do?"

"Yes," answered Meg steadily, "it is quite true. Major Kettering is my kind friend. He has made life brighter for me since he came to Garslade. The days on which I see him are the happiest in my life."

"Meg, Meg, do you realise whither you are drifting?" cried the old lady rather desperately.

"Yes," answered Meg, in the same steady, strange voice, "I realise it quite well."

Lady Rathillis sat back in horror.

"Has it gone so far as that, you poor, misguided child? Have you even contemplated taking that frightful, that irrevocable, step which a woman regrets only once after it has been taken—and that is for the rest of her natural life?"

"Yes," answered Meg evenly. "I have even contemplated that—I am contemplating it now."

There was a moment's rather dreadful silence. Then, quite suddenly, Meg burst into a passion of weeping, and, falling upon the floor, hid her face on the trembling knees of her old friend.

CHAPTER XXVIII

THE CRISIS

LADY RATHILLIS, much shaken, suffered the storm to have its way, and for a few minutes there was nothing but the sound of sobbing in the room. Then, with equal suddenness, Meg sprang up, and a fire came into her eyes which dried her tears at their source.

"I know what you are thinking—how much you are blaming me, Lady Rathillis. And, because you are the only person in the world for whose opinion I care anything I will open your eyes. It is not I who am to blame for what has happened, and for what may happen. It is he, the husband whose interests you are so anxious to protect. Listen, and I will tell you if I can for very shame! I want you not to interrupt me once, dear Lady Rathillis, but just let me tell the whole story from start to finish. It is my story. Afterwards, if you like, you may go to David Sillars and hear his version. But what I am going to tell you is true, and it will perhaps explain what is happening now."

Meg commenced her narrative. She went back to the beginning of things—to the visit of Van Leyden and Morris Bien to Ballochean, and to the desperate remedy that she had sought at the hands of David Sillars.

Her recital was brief, vivid, graphic, and through it all the heart of the woman scorned seemed to beat loudly upon the tense atmosphere, and to be heard in every thrill of her vibrant voice.

The old lady, in whom the intense love of life was not yet dead, listened in the utmost amazement.

"So you see," concluded Meg, "I owe no duty to David Sillars. I have lived for almost a year in his house as his housekeeper, but he does not really need me. The house was, if anything, better kept before I came, for Mary Maxwell, out of her love for me, has slackened off, and keeps thinking only of how I may have my due. Do you blame me, if I take the joy of life as it is offered to me? I know what I shall do on the night when I wrap my old Ballochean cloak about me and go out of the house of David Sillars for ever! I shall take nothing of his away—not even his regret. My presence is irksome to him. I've destroyed the bachelor symmetry of his life and upset all his arrangements, and he will be glad when I go. And I am going!—oh, yes!—it is but a question of time, and I am rather sorry that you should have been troubled with my unhappy story; though afterwards, when everybody is blaming me, you will be able perhaps just to put in a word and to say that, had things been different with poor Meg Hamilton—had she ever had a chance—she, too, might have been different.

Up rose Lady Rathillis, and it seemed that a new majesty of mien dignified her slight figure. In her eyes there was a mingling of indignation, determination, and yearning affection.

"Come here to me, Meg—right over here!"

Meg came to her slowly and was folded to her heart.

"My bairn, my dear, own, suffering, ill-treated bairn! I'm your mother from this time henceforth. Had God given me such a daughter as you, not David Sillars or any other should have made such shipwreck of your life! But, please God, we will find the way out, my dear—we will save you yet, and the honour and the love of Kildoon."

* * * * * * *

Sitting over his solitary breakfast in his house at Langdyke on a grey-red October morning, David Sillars read these words:—

"At Sangster, Ayrshire, on the 16th inst., the wife of Sir Hew Montgomery Kessock, Bart., of a son."

He dropped the paper as if he had been stung, and there came to his face a sudden hardening that had something evil in it. The fiercest jealousy that can consume a man tore at his heart-strings, and, pushing back his chair, he left his meal unfinished and went out into the open.

A son and heir to Hew Kessock of Sangster, while his name, as old, as honourable, as well worth passing on, would go down to the grave uninherited, like those of the beasts that perish—unwept, unhonoured, and unsung!

The newspaper notice gave Sillars a shock of surprise, for, though the event recorded had been daily expected in the county and had been matter of intimate gossip and speculation for weeks, no hint of it had ever come to his ears.

It was the last—the very last—subject, of course, on which Meg would speak to him. Now, indeed, there were few—very few—matters that he and she discussed together, and the week-ends spent at Kildoon had become such nightmares to Sillars that he was even then casting about in his mind for some means of escape from them.

The morning's mail from abroad had furnished him with one. A letter from his Jamaica manager informed him that he had the opportunity of acquiring at a quite moderate figure a neighbouring plantation on which the firm had long cast a covetous eye.

Sillars took swift resolve. He would make the journey to Jamaica, come to a decision about the purchase of the plantation, and take counsel with Ludavic Hamilton regarding his future.

Affairs at Ballochean were in abeyance, as it were, until the new Laird should declare his intentions. In the meantime he seemed very loth to leave the lovely tropical island where he had become a man, had achieved a certain amount of independence, and had won a happiness to which he had been a stranger in the house of his fathers.

The Scotsman at the head of affairs, fully trusted by Sillars, had made a study of the lad and had helped him as only a big, strong-hearted man can help a weaker brother.

For a few weeks after Ballochean's death things had gone a little better at Kildoon. Broken with grief, Meg had been grateful for the unfailing tenderness and consideration shown her by her husband. He had tried everything he could think of, save the one thing, to console her, and had even offered to take her to Jamaica, but she had declined all his kindly, well-meant proposals.

Though old Gavin Hamilton's words spoken that night in the Nursing Home seldom left his mind, he had been unable to act upon them. He had tried, but Meg's stony stare and half-armed neutrality had caused him quickly to forbear. The brief spell of tenderness past, they again hardened themselves towards each other, as was inevitable, and as the end of their perilous year hove within sight they were almost completely estranged.

Supervening on the surprise and chagrin caused to Sillars by the sight of the Sangster announcement, there came another feeling, strong, and sharp, and disagreeable—a sort of sensing of trouble at his own house of Kildoon.

Of late tongues had been busy with the name of Mrs. Sillars, and people were watching with breathless interest the unfolding of a very pretty comedy which might any day be swiftly converted into tragedy.

On coming to Garslade for the shooting in the late September, Major Kettering had lost no time in finding his way to Kildoon. Perhaps only Mary Maxwell knew how often he was there, and how little shooting he did even on the well-preserved coverts at Garslade.

The Oliphants, however, knew; but though the M.F.H. had spoken once to Kettering a word of warning as to how easily the poisonous tongues of the county could tarnish a reputation, his words had made no difference. The old man had thereupon privately informed his son that he must contrive somehow to bring Kettering's visit to a close—an admittedly difficult matter, when their splendid traditions for hospitality were considered.

Sillars knew that Kettering was at Garslade, and he had surprised him once walking by the Doon with Meg. But there was nothing in that to arouse his suspicions, and, moreover, there was no hint of consciousness or guilt in their demeanour, and he had tried to dismiss his vague fears.

But to-day, following upon the unpalatable news of the birth of Sangster's heir, recollections of what he had seen and heard rushed upon him in a resistless flood.

He spent half an hour in the counting-house after breakfast and before noon was in the train.

Arriving at Kildoon in time for a late luncheon he found that his wife was absent from home. Not caring to ask the footman where she was, he made his way to Mary Maxwell's room, where she was taking her after-dinner forty winks in her easy-chair.

She jumped up, confused and apologetic, to greet her master.

"It's all right, Mary—sorry to have disturbed you. But I've had an urgent letter from abroad this morning. It may be that I shall have to go to Jamaica."

"Oh, sir!" said Mary—and there was consternation on her face—"you'll take the mistress?"

"No. I can't very well do that, for the journey will be hurried. Besides, she would not care about going. She refused in August, you will remember, when I thought the voyage might do her good."

The words were, in a sense, defensive, as if he sought by them to justify some shortcoming of his own.

Mary Maxwell regarded him stolidly.

"And you'd leave her here for three—or maybe six—months, sir," she said quietly. "Then God forgi'e ye—that's a' I say."

She had exceeded her duty, and the reddening of her master's face indicated his resentment.

"You forget yourself, surely, Mrs. Maxwell. Can you tell me where Mrs. Sillars is to-day?—at Ballochean, probably."

"I don't ken where she is, sir," answered Mary in a low voice. "But I do ken who she is wi'—and it's that man who's stopping at Garslade. And if something's no' dune sune, there'll maybe be something that'll keep ye frae Jamaiky. I canna help it if ye are angry and send me aboot my business. But my hert's wae for my dear mistress. There's mair nor her gangs greetin' to their beds in this hoose ilka nicht."

Sillars stared hard at her, but his pride—his colossal, insensate, ungovernable pride—forbade him to discuss such a subject with a servant.

He flung himself from the room, and there was raging in his heart a fire which was like to consume him.

He went downstairs, wandered idly through the rooms, declined the food that had been hastily prepared for his consumption, and, clapping his cap on his head, wandered out into the still sunshine of the afternoon.

The place was fair, its sylvan loveliness being unsurpassed in all that land of enchanting beauty. But at the moment Sillars hated it with the hate of hell. A curse was upon it, a blight lay on the yellowing trees and the gay flower-parterres, and even the gurgling waters of the Doon, which had so often soothed a poet's frenzy, were all discord.

The fiercest passions which can ravage the soul of a man had Sillars in thrall, and all his vaunted dignity and self-control were torn to ribbons and cast at his feet. He was nothing but a primeval man, eager to wield a club and to assert his right. How dared she—how dared she, after all he had done, make such a vile return! How dared she bring even the hint of scandal or dishonour on the name she bore!

He grew frenzied on the river path, and presently he was striding back again, thinking of a horse, the fleetest in the stable, on which he might pursue and overtake the woman against whom his rage was burning so fiercely.

And all the while, had he but known it, a few more steps by the water-side and he would have come upon Meg and the major in scenes hallowed by many a love-idyll and even then witnessing a fresh battle betwixt love and duty being waged!

As Sillars left the river path and stepped upon the clear gravel of the avenue there fell on his ear the swift roll of approaching wheels.

Pulling out his watch, he saw that it was now ten minutes to three o'clock, and quite possibly an early caller might be coming to Kildoon. Half-tempted to escape and yet half-hoping that the conveyance might be bringing home his wife, he stood still until the equipage came swiftly round the bend.

It was an old-fashioned barouche, hung very high and drawn by a pair of coal-black Belgian horses that spurned the ground in their speed. In the carriage sat the Countess of Rathillis alone.

Her surprise at sight of Sillars was very great; for, knowing the habit of life at

Kildoon far more intimately than he imagined, she had come prepared to find his wife at home and alone.

A certain satisfaction, however, dawned on the fine old face, and as the coachman slowed down and Sillars advanced, cap in hand, she even faintly smiled. Her face, nevertheless, wore its gravest look, and the smile faded as quickly as it had come.

" I am fortunate in meeting you, Mr. Sillars ; but I did not expect it. My visit is to your wife."

" I arrived about an hour ago unexpectedly, Lady Rathillis. I am afraid my wife is not in the house. But will you come in and wait a few moments ? It is possible she may be here before long."

" I will come in—not to wait for her but to talk to you," was the unexpected answer, and the carriage slowly made its way to the door, Sillars walking by the side of it while they talked the convenient trifles which always serve to take the edge off our most poignant moments.

At the door Sillars assisted her with great care and tenderness to alight, for he revered her as the only intimate friend of his mother now surviving, and as one whose very name was worthy of reverence.

" I am not sure of the drawing-room, Lady Rathillis. My wife seldom sits there. But the library fire will be all right. It is our principal living room."

She nodded understandingly, and, leaning somewhat heavily on his arm, came to the library.

When Sillars opened the door the smell of cigar-smoke greeted him and caused him to start unpleasantly, for he had not been in the room since his arrival, and, unless Meg herself smoked—which was unthinkable—she must have had a man visitor.

Lady Rathillis, of course, thought the very perceptible odour due to the presence of the master of the house.

Two easy-chairs drawn up to the hearth and a half-finished cigar lying on a small table suggested quite recent occupation. Sillars swept the offending reminder into the fire, asked whether he might set open one half of one of the French windows, and drew forward a comfortable chair for his visitor.

She took it, and, leaning somewhat heavily on the crystal-topped stick, looked round the room interestedly.

It was full of flowers, and, but for the books and the tobacco odour, might easily have been taken for a woman's boudoir. It was in this room that Meg chiefly lived, when alone, though at the week-ends she seldom entered it.

" You have come from Greenock only to-day, Mr. Sillars ?—but there ! I think I must call you David. Your dear wife has given me leave to call her by her Christian name—then why not you, whom I have often dangled in my arms, though of late years we have met so seldom and you have shown Rathillis Castle the cold shoulder.

Sillars did not know where to look.

" I am sorry if I have given offence, Lady Rathillis. But you know what bad habits an old bachelor gets into ! "

" You are not an old bachelor now," she said, fixing him with her coal-black eyes, " and your wife has been my constant visitor at least up till the last few weeks. I saw her yesterday, however."

" I am grateful to you for your kindness to her, Lady Rathillis," he murmured, and he had the odd feeling of being a schoolboy up for swift condemnation and condign punishment.

" Humph ! Somebody had need to be kind to the poor, forlorn creature since you, whose first duty it was to be so, have so miserably failed."

Sillars whitened about the gills and drew himself up. Lady Rathillis was pleased to observe these signs of manliness, for in the last twenty-four hours she had been entertaining little but feelings of contempt for the son of her old friend.

There was a moment's strained silence, which Sillars could not break, since to defend himself by word of mouth offended all his pride. He must wait for further developments, and as he stood there, the picture of discomfort, he realised that there was more in it all than met the eye.

" David, it's a long time since your mother and I were like sisters, and when she went away, she begged me to continue my interest in you, and more especially to be kind to the wife you would some day bring to Kildoon. I promised, and I have tried to redeem that promise, though you have needed little of me until this day."

Sillars fixed on her high-bred old face a strange kind of uncomprehending stare, which might have disconcerted anyone but her.

" We all thought you a confirmed bachelor, David, and when you married Gavin Hamilton's daughter in a hurry I was as much surprised as the rest of them. I had given up visiting for many years, as you know, but I went out of my way to pay a call on her—Mrs. David Sillars—when she came to Kildoon."

" She appreciated it, Lady Rathillis," said Sillars quickly ; " we both did."

" That is a matter of no consequence. But my heart went out to her, and, as I drove home that day, I had nothing but reproach for myself for not having seen and known her earlier. She is that rare creature, David—a woman perfectly pure, fearless, and frank. And when I thought of the lies that had been told about her my old heart was hot in my breast—hottest of all in its wrath against myself."

Those fine words warmed David's heart, for it is pleasant to a man to hear praise of the woman he loves.

" I think that she liked me too," continued the countess, " and she came sometimes—though never so often as I would have liked—to the castle ; and every time I saw her I loved her more. How is it, David, that you, having won a prize so rare, have somehow failed to value and to keep it ? "

Her eyes were merciless as her tongue But Sillars merely stood dumb and red before her, wishing that the terrible old woman would either go or hold her peace.

She had no intention however, of doing either until her task was accomplished.

" When she came to me first, David," she went on, " there was nothing in her heart but gratitude and tenderness towards you—too much gratitude, indeed—and more than once I reproved her for it, pointing out what she had given in exchange in giving herself. But, though she has a high proud spirit, and a big, dear heart, she has none of that sickening vanity or conceit which spoils so many women who have less to be vain or conceited about. She had too poor an opinion of herself and was for ever crying that she would not be able to repay you. I naturally wondered what lay behind all this ; but it was not till yesterday that the whole fell story was poured into my ears."

Sillars started visibly, but he had no power to stem the torrent.

" I have said that at first she was full of gratitude and tenderness towards you ; but these began to wane, and now they are as dead—as dead as the bough that the wind breaks off and casts into the Doon when in flood. And you have killed them ! " She paused.

" I have done my best for her," repeated Sillars stiffly ; " and if she says aught else it is not the truth she speaks. Have I ever interfered with her or laid commands on her or—or forbidden her anything under heaven ? "

Then a strange fury seemed to lay hold upon Rose Rathillis, and she was tempted to shake her stick at him.

" Listen to the man—the poor, foolish, misguided creature ! That is just where you failed. You expected nothing, you asked for nothing, you demanded nothing, but you just left her like a bit of drift upon the shore ! Yet you would wonder if she seeks another haven ! Good Heavens ! the blindness and foolishness of man ! "

Sillars, now thoroughly roused, met her flashing eyes with kindred fire in his own.

" Lady Rathillis, you mean well, I am sure, but you do not understand."

" You are mistaken," she put in quietly. " I understand all."

" There are wheels within wheels," continued Sillars, ignoring—or pretending to ignore—her interruption. " Meg Hamilton and I married not for our own sakes."

" The more fools you, then, since you and no others have to bear the burden ! " she again broke in.

" Not for our own sakes ! " he repeated hotly, " but for the sake of smoothing out the affairs of Ballochean. I knew that she did not care for me, for she had with her own mouth laughed at me, telling me that I might have been her father ! "

" A lassie says many foolish things, and, if they are to be harboured against the day of judgment, then woe is me ! "

" I promised her shelter, immunity from care, relief from her anxiety about her father," went on Sillars, " and I have given her all these. I have failed in nothing of what I set myself out to do."

Lady Rathillis looked at him steadily for almost a full minute. The fire died out of her eyes, and an ineffable sadness took its place.

" Listen, David. I saw your wife yesterday, for a friend, to whom you and yours will, I hope, owe a debt of gratitude that nothing will ever wipe out, showed me where my duty lay. Having left your wife's heart empty even when it was turning to you, you have lived to see it filled with the image of another You took that young, forlorn, motherless creature into your keeping, and you have left her entirely to her own resources, flouting her at the very beginning of her married days and showing her that you could and would live without her. Can any woman stand that ?—very few, and Meg Hamilton least of all. Now, what are you going to do to save her ? "

He stared at her open-mouthed, and she perceived that he had no idea of her meaning. The sight of him caused her almost to stamp her foot.

" Heavens, man ! do you mean to say you've been grubbing away among your sugar-pokes at Greenock without so much as knowing that a handsomer, if not a better, man has been busy about Kildoon ? Have you not heard of the gallant who rides from Garslade to Kildoon every day of his life to see its sweet mistress ? "

" I have heard," he answered dourly, " but I thought I might trust my wife."

Then anger shook her again, and she was hard put to it to speak with any semblance of calmness.

" You are past speaking to, David Sillars. Before we say another word, tell me if you love your wife, or if your heart is cold and hard as the nether millstone to her?"

Then there was wrung from him a swift confession.

" I love her so that I have no peace from her either night or day, and I wish to God that I had never seen her ! " was his passionate cry.

" That's better," said the old lady, with a touch of supreme satisfaction. " Now we have something to work upon. Listen, David. You've got to remain at home and make love to your wife and take her from the very maw of that man, were he twice the gallant that he is ! It can be done—I've seen it done, and, please God, I shall see it done once again before I die ! So, now I will go, and good luck to you ! Find her to-day—now—at once, and show her what you are."

" She has no use for me," he cried, his dour pride rising again.

" Then you are a poor creature who had such a chance given you and have refused to take it ! " she cried spiritedly, " and my patience is at an end."

She gripped her stick, drew her ample skirts about her, and began to make for the door.

There she paused and turned to him sorrowfully.

" Life is a bitter thing, David Sillars, and for the heart of a woman impossible, unless she has love to help her to bear it. Your wife, poor lass, has had little ! She never knew a mother's, and, though it does not become us to speak ill of the dead, you know, none better, what Ballochean was. You have failed in your duty to her whom you swore to protect and to cherish. You have permitted your wicked pride to come between her and you, and you have hardened your heart against her when it ought to have been at her feet ! Worth it—she is ten times worth it. She would bring sons to Kildoon—sons that would restore the ancient glory of the race. She has a big heart ; and—and, bend your head, David, and I'll tell you something for your comfort, though never did man deserve it less—that heart of hers is yours, and no other's !—she sobbed it out upon this breast ! "

Then, blinking the tears away, she strode out with much dignity to her waiting carriage, and so left him without another word or without even a brief good-bye.

And when she was swept beyond sight of the old house she bent her head and closed the eyes to which the mist still clung, and prayed that the God of his fathers would not forget David Sillars, but would bring him and his to lasting peace.

Sillars, like a man dazed, could not stop in the house. His being was shaken to its very foundations, but the only words he remembered were the last ones that his faithful friend had spoken—" That heart of hers is yours and no other's."

God, if it should be true ! Then, where was Eden on earth, if not here, at his own door ?

Walls could not hold him. He strode into the open and plunged once more into the path by the Doon, whose gurgling voice had sung the accompaniment to many a love song. All his pulses were bounding, his heart beating and calling for his mate. Illimitable vistas of glory seemed to open before him, but not yet——

Suddenly the heart of him seemed to stop beating, the blood receded from his face, and his eyes fell with horror upon a scene which seemed for the moment to freeze his blood.

On a mossy stone sat two—his wife and Hubert Kettering—and their attitude was that of lovers. Kettering's look was impassioned and imploring; Meg was pale, and she seemed to hesitate.

Sillars saw red, for never in his darkest hour had the thought of such treachery shaped itself in his mind. He had trusted his wife, and, beyond doubt, that trust was betrayed!

Meg turned her head and saw him. Then, springing up, she stood still.

"My husband!" he heard her say in tones which fluttered from her trembling lips.

CHAPTER XXIX

ALL'S WELL

KETTERING did not look ashamed. He stood as a man might stand to a gun on the last ridge swept by the enemy's fire, the expression on his face being that of one who is not afraid to lead the forlorn hope.

"Well," said Meg, with her head high in the air, addressing her husband, "what have you to say?"

David Sillars, drawn up to his full height, looked magnificent. It was a desperate moment; he faced it, a desperate man!

"I have to say two things," he said, and his voice rang clear upon the crystal air. "And you, Kettering, will stand by and hear them."

"Yes," answered Kettering steadily. "I am glad you give me leave, for stay I should, in any case."

To his wife then did Sillars turn, his eyes cleaving to her face.

"The first thing I have to say is that I have here and now to ask your pardon. To-day my eyes have been opened, and I have come to my senses. I ask your pardon," he repeated, "and if it will prove me more sincere, I will ask it on my knees."

She looked bewildered and her courage wavered. Both men observed the tremor of her lip.

"My pardon for what?" she asked, expecting to have heard words widely different.

"You do not need me to tell you. I ask your pardon for my blindness and my folly. I ask you to wipe out from your remembrance the year that has nearly gone. Do you follow me?"

"I follow you, of course, but—but I don't yet understand," she said, and her breast began to heave.

"Never mind, provided you grasp my words. Their meaning will dawn more fully on you later. When you have forgiven, or, if you like it better or it seems easier, when you have blotted out that year—then we know where we are. The second thing I have to say is that we two, standing before you, both love you. For myself, I can answer, for you are the only woman that has ever been in my life or ever will be. It is because I have loved you so well that my eyes have been holden. This man, we may suppose, also loves you, else he would not be here. Am I right?"

He suffered his eyes to dwell for a moment on Kettering's changing face, and his tone, though cuttingly cold, was perfectly courteous.

Kettering, finding no words, merely bowed his head.

"Then," said Sillars, turning again to his wife and folding his arms across his breast, "it is for you to choose. Forget the year that is almost gone, and choose between us the better man, or—or," and here his voice faltered, "the one you care for."

Meg's eyes, full of a strange light, seemed riveted to his face. It was as if some new man, some man whom she had never before met, had come into her life, filling it to the exclusion of all else!

There was a moment of intense, almost hideous, strain, broken only by their breathing, and by the low croon of the Doon water rolling to the sea.

"You won't keep us waiting too long, Meg, for these are unendurable moments, nor is this a scene to be prolonged. I would not speak a word to bias your choice. I have forfeited that right—only, I beg you to be merciful and quickly choose."

She looked from the one to the other, and when Kettering would have spoken, she silenced him with uplifted hand.

"My choice is made. I will go home with my husband, Major Kettering—so good-bye."

Then she turned upon her heel and fled away, leaving the men behind. What passed between them she never heard, nor would it further this history to relate it.

In like case murder has often been done, but these two, threshing it out, parted, if not friends, at least not deadly enemies.

Kettering left Ayr by the night mail for London.

Sillars made no haste to go to his house. Indeed, he almost feared to enter it. The soft twilight fell and found him still within sight and sound of the Doon, trying to calm his wildly-beating heart.

She had chosen, but, after all, how much or how little did her choice mean? He had a long way to travel yet, he imagined, before he found the key to Meg's heart. But at least the open tragedy had been averted, though he shuddered to think how nearly he had been too late.

When at last he came within the house its silence was profound. Presently, however, through the open dining-room door he could hear the clink of silver and glass where the man-servant was laying the table for dinner.

It was twenty minutes past six, and the usual dinner hour when the master was at home was at seven o'clock. He passed into the library, where the curtains had been drawn and a fresh log placed upon the fire, but where the lights were not yet turned up. Approaching the fireplace he was amazed to find his wife huddled up against the chair with her face hidden on the cushions.

"My dear," he said with a great gentleness, though his pulses began to throb wildly once more, "don't be like that! I can't bear it. Please get up and let me see your face."

She lifted her head, and he saw that her face was drawn and sharpened as if the plough of sorrow had been at work upon it.

"My dear," he repeated, "get up. Go to your room and let Mary Maxwell come to you and put you to bed. You look ghastly."

"That is how I feel," she said wearily as she rose to her feet. "No—no light, please. I have some things to say to you, David, and I will say them now."

"I want to hear nothing. You have made your choice, my dear. Let us abide by it."

"No, no," she cried, a little wildly. "After to-night we can wipe things out. But I must tell you—I must! I had very nearly promised to go away with Hubert Kettering. He had asked me for the third time, and I think that to-night, if you had not come, I should have gone."

"But you are not sorry you didn't, my dear? You made a free choice?" he asked anxiously.

"Oh, yes! At the back of my heart I did not in the least want to go. Something kept crying out in me, and when I saw you come—then I knew that I had been praying without knowing it."

He had no answer to these moving words, but stood watching the firelight playing on her tragic face.

"Was Lady Rathillis here this afternoon, David?"

"She was, but before she came there was something within warning me that things were coming to a crisis. That is how and why I am here. I have had no peace at Greenock this week. God forgive me that I should have had even as much peace as I have had at that accursed place!"

Meg might have smiled, only her lips seemed to have forgotten the upward curve.

They stood apart, and Sillars had no power to speak the words that surged within his heart. "That heart of hers is yours," Lady Rathillis had said. But there was no sign that it was so. How were barriers swept away? In what words does a man tell a year-old wife that he loves only her and begs her love in return? Something was between them yet—something intangible, yet strong—which neither could grasp nor yet demolish.

"It must be nearly dinner-time," she said nervously. "I think I had better go up and dress. I am not sure if you will get anything to eat, unless Mary Maxwell has stepped into the breach. But you won't be hard to please to-night, perhaps."

She began to move towards the door, and, hastening to open it for her, he inadvertently brushed close to her. Then something came to him, and, lifting her face in his hand, he stooped to kiss it. Then he folded her to his heart.

* * * * * *

Mary Maxwell, conscious of strange happenings with the deep consciousness of an anxious, brooding love, waited in vain for her mistress to come upstairs. Mary had added another to her numerous, though often self-imposed, duties. She had constituted herself sole waiting-maid to her mistress, and she suffered no hand but her own to touch her.

The fire was burning brightly, three frocks were laid out on the bed, and she was all impatience when Meg suddenly burst into the room. Mary had heard the flying feet through the open door, but she was not prepared for the vision of loveliness which broke upon her startled gaze.

"Oh, my dear mistress, what a colour!" she cried. "My—my dear, whatever is it?"

Then, quite suddenly, Meg threw herself upon that ample bosom, hugged her faithful waiting-woman close, laid her hot cheek against hers, and hid her happy eyes.

"Oh, Mary Maxwell! it's heaven come down to earth—that's all. Take away all these black clothes, and let me whisper something in your ear. Do you know where my wedding frock is—that little grey thing which Miss Carrick made and which I wore at Ballochean last year?"

"Yes, my dear. I put it away with my own hands, as you bade me, for you said you never wanted to see it any more."

"Go and bring it, and when you have got that, get me some roses. Roses are love's colour. Oh, Mary Maxwell!—I know now how the banks and braes o' bonnie Doon can bloom sae fresh and fair!"

Mary Maxwell's old legs made swift pilgrimage to the wardrobe room. The wedding gown was fetched and donned, and, though a little loose in fit, was found becoming But when the roses—no match for the twin roses in Meg's cheeks—were tucked in her belt, she was a picture fair to see.

Mary was still in the dark, but she dared not ask a single question. She only hoped that all was well.

Down in the big hall a strange shyness came over the mistress of Kildoon, and she got no farther than the fireplace, where she stood with the tip of her dainty grey suede shoe on the fender, waiting for her husband. When he saw the frock his colour rose.

"It is my wedding frock, David," she said shyly. "Do you remember it?"

Remember it! Had he not counted the pin-tucks from the wrists to the elbow upon that never-to-be-forgotten afternoon in the library at Ballochean, when they had stood before the Rev. Mr. Murchison to take upon them irrevocable vows?

He dared to touch that sleeve now with a lover's touch.

"Fifteen of these queer little ruffles to the elbow," he said whimsically. "I counted them every one."

"Tucks, you foolish boy—tucks," she said and hid her happy eyes, lest the man, walking decorously by them with the old silver soup-tureen should observe anything unusual. As a matter of fact, he did, for though the breadth of the table was between him and them, and though they talked soberly of things that did not matter, the air seemed charged with electric forces and twice they laughed together. From Meg's lips the laughter was like the music of the spheres.

"Don't let us stop here, Madge," David whispered the moment they were alone. "We don't want any more to eat—though, when I come to think of it, I have seen you eat very little.

"Have I eaten little? I have no idea what was set before me or where it went!" she said sweetly, flashing him an adorable glance.

They went together to the library, and Meg, with her swift, commanding air, made him be seated, filled his pipe, and drew to his feet a footstool of which she made herself a throne.

And there the discreet Malcolm found them when he brought the coffee-tray, and thence he went, red and spluttering, back to the kitchen to report!

There was very little talk through that happy silence. Meg laid her head on David's knee and drew his hand under her cheek, the firelight playing on her sweet face, from which every line was smoothed away, leaving it soft and gracious as a little child's.

As for Sillars, none would have known him—Meg least of all. It was as if the veil of the years—the years of whose disqualifying effect his imagination had so exaggerated—had been lowered with merciful fingers, hiding for evermore all the bitterness, even the passage of the days that had been so wearily long.

And now they were simply boy and girl together, with love in their hearts and all life before them!—an intoxicating thought, which yet had power to awe them into long and frequent silences!

"Megsie," he said after one of these pauses, with his lips on her hair, "I am going to Jamaica next week to see Ludo."

"All by your little self?" she asked.

"If that is your will," he answered. "I wait on that now for the rest of my natural life!"

"Oh, but David, it must not be that way! I will not have it! Did I not promise to obey?"

"Then I order you to get ready for Jamaica, and we'll start to-morrow."

She laughed, and the sound made pure music in the glowing spaces of the old room.

"I go to get ready, my lord," she answered meekly; but she made no movement save to nestle closer to him.

Then they began to talk lovers' talk of the first moment, now the heart of each had awakened to the other. But even that was difficult because of the searching pain of the year of peril.

"Don't let us talk, David. Let us do as you say—blot it all out. We were fools and blind—now we see!" she said quaintly, harking back, as ever, to her Scripture quotations. "Oh? I am so tired, David—so worn out and battered, just as if I had been to Arran and back in a salmon coble. I think I will go to bed. May I ask you something first?"

Instantly his head was close to hers, his eager ear waiting her behest. Her white arm touched his neck, and her cheek was against his as she made her request.

"To-morrow, David, I shall be ready for—for the wedding journey," she said falteringly. "And will you take me to the little house at Langdyke and let us begin our honeymoon there?"

"It is as you will—but why not here?" he whispered with his lips on her hair.

"Because—because—there you were my David, though you left off being that immediately after, and never were that again until your stupid eyes were opened. Take me there, David, where we shall be quite alone, with only Mrs. Dunlop to mother us."

So Meg had her way. But before she slept she wrote just one line to her who had saved them and whom, manlike, David in the selfishness of supreme happiness, had forgotten.

"God bless you for ever and ever for what you have done. You have given us Heaven, my dearest dear, and to-morrow we are going away. I will not, must not see you yet, but when I come back—oh, God bless you, and good-bye!"

* * * * * *

The mother of Sangster's heir, convalescent and looking uncommonly sweet in her blue peignoir, wrinkled her brows over a letter which had reached her, bearing a foreign postmark which she could not decipher.

The handwriting, however, she recognised, and the letter she tore open with eager fingers. Her interest in mundane things had revived, and she had asked again and again about Meg Sillars, professing herself hurt and surprised that not a hint that she was aware of the birth of the heir or a word of congratulation on the event had reached her.

To Ellie's astonishment, she found the letter dated from on board ship. Thus did Meg write to her old friend who already seemed remote from her and all the life she had known :—

" Steam Yacht ' Ailsa,' off—I don't know where !

" DEAREST ELLIE,

" I am sure you are thinking of me and, no doubt, calling me a proper pig for not having written to congratulate you before this. But, my dear, I am so full of affairs with a masterful husband, who gives me small chance to assert myself, that I seem to have just let slip everything in Scotland.

" We are somewhere on the high seas—though where I haven't the least idea. Jamaica, however, is our ultimate haven. Mr. Sillars found that he had to go to Jamaica, and I thought that I should like to see Ludo—at least, it is decent to put it like that, though I don't suppose any notice would have been taken of my scruples, if I had had any about going. I had no choice.

" We left Kildoon rather hurriedly, for David's business was pressing and he had intended to catch a certain boat at the Tail of the Bank. After we got to our little house at Langdyke, however, he changed his mind. He said the boat was not good enough for me, and so he extravagantly chartered this yacht. I dare say Sir Hew will remember it on the Clyde last year. It belongs to Lord Dunoon.

" And here we are—nobody but him and me and a little maid from Langdyke to look after my clothes. Oh, Ellie ! the Riviera and Paris and Monte may do very well as honeymoon places for ordinary folk, but none of them has a chance beside this ! Life on these sunny seas is just like being in heaven, and I'm learning everything there is to learn about the yacht, and David is even wondering whether he might not buy it and make me commodore !

" So you see how we are playing ourselves !

" As for coming back—well, we are not there yet, and I don't suppose either of us will mind though we lose our compass or chart—or whatever it is that keeps boats in their rig t and proper course.

" Now, after all that, let me say God bless the little heir of Sangster, and send that he may grow up fine and beautiful to bring joy to the hearts of his father and mother. Give him a kiss for his Auntie Meg, and whisper in his ear that she will try to find him something wonderful in the shape of a birth-gift in the new lands she hopes to see.

" I hope you have recovered. I need not ask whether you are happy. You ought to be, having got all a woman's heart could desire, and all at the fit and proper time. But you were always one to do your duty, while poor I have ever been a reed shaken with the wind ! But now I am in my anchorage, and perhaps when I've stopped in its blessed calm for a little while I too may begin to grasp the meaning of duty.

" Remember me to Sir Hew and Lady Anne and to Mrs. Dove and the dear Surgeon-General, whom you may tell, if you like, that he was a privileged person that day in the drawing-room of Ballochean when he stood there and saw graceless Meg Hamilton married to the best and the dearest man on earth.

" So no more now from your affectionate and thrice-happy.

" MEG SILLARS."

Ellie read and re-read this missive, and her starched and frilled nurse observed the pucker in her brows as she did so.

" You've no bad news, Lady Kessock, I trust ? " said the woman's smooth voice soothingly. " We don't want any set-backs now."

" Oh, no nurse ! Only a letter from an old friend, a rather surprising letter. Is that you, Hew ? Come here and read this extraordinary outburst from Meg Hamilton."

Sir Hew, come to pay his morning respects—a very presentable and fine figure of a father in his shooting suit of Harris tweed and brown leggings—stooped to kiss his wife's fair face, then reached for the letter.

The predominant expression on his face, as leaning against the table, he read it through, was one of bewilderment, for, like the rest of the world, Kessock had expected to hear something very different concerning the ménage at Kildoon.

"It can't have been true, Hew—at least, not a tithe of it—about Major Kettering, I mean," said Ellie as she watched the varying expressions chase one another across her husband's face.

"Looks as if some of it had been lies, dear. But of course there was something, because in October, just when you were first laid up, he and Meg were never apart. Depend on it, something's happened."

"Perhaps Sillars went mad and carried her off. I've heard that he can be rather terrible in a passion, and of course the mere suggestion of a scandal in connection with Kildoon would send him into fits."

"If she's captive, never was woman a more willing captive and never did woman bear captivity so joyfully," said Kessock as he folded the thin sheet a trifle lingeringly.

"Oh, but you don't know Meg Hamilton, Hew!" said Lady Kessock maliciously. "She's got the very devil in her when her back's up! If Sillars was really bullying her, she'd pretend that she adored both him and the bullying."

"There's no pretence about this," said Kessock as he laid the letter down. "She's in Paradise—they both are. Whatever has happened before, they've found the key to that gate!"

"Don't put on that hang-dog look, Hew," said his wife pettishly. "One would think, to hear you speak, that you hadn't a chance of Paradise. I'm sure you ought to be a happy man—everybody says so."

"Well, and have I said anything different?" he asked banteringly.

"No. But sometimes you don't look so happy as you might. Your mother hasn't been in this morning yet to see me or baby."

"Hasn't she?" asked Kessock, though he was perfectly aware that she had not.

"No. Has anything been settled about Girvan, Hew? Have you spoken to her yet?"

"No, I haven't," he answered, and he lowered his brows.

"Well, you have got to speak to her," she said quietly. "I have told you that I will neither come downstairs nor arrange about baby's christening nor do anything until it is settled when she is going to Girvan."

"My mother doesn't want to go to the Dower House, Ellie, and why should she? This one is big enough for us all," he said dourly.

"Not for both her and me," his wife made answer, and she laid herself back languidly among her pillows with the exasperating expression of a woman who means to have her way and who knows she will get it.

Kessock turned on his heel, and, without so much as glancing in the direction of the blue, lace-trimmed nest in which the heir of Sangster was taking his morning nap, strode out of the room.

He was face to face with a stiff problem—that, namely, of how to keep the peace between his mother and his wife, and how to get the internal affairs of Sangster put upon a more harmonious footing.

Something stirred in his heart—something that was more than a vain regret; for if he had been more of a man, if he had been true and loving and kind, then he might have been on the happy seas with Meg Hamilton by his side!

* * * * * *

One more letter, a little later, found its way from the happy isle to an old house frowning on its rocky steep beyond the Heads of Ayr.

Thus did Meg pour forth her heart to the woman who had saved her:—

"Santa Lucia, Jamaica,
November 20th.

"My Dearest Dear,

"This is the anniversary of my wedding day, and I celebrate it by writing to you who have given me the happiness that I did not deserve, but which I will bless you for till my dying day.

"All my other letters you will doubtless have had, and though I am hungry for one from you, I know I shall have to wait. But the days are winging; soon perhaps I shall be on my way to Rathillis Castle to sob my heart out again on the kind breast that has mothered me so dearly.

"Is this Meg Hamilton who is writing—who finds poetry for her pen in every beam of the sun and every quiver of the leaf in God's good world? Oh, my dear! happiness is wonderful. You wouldn't know me. I have grown and bloomed till I hardly know myself. When Ludo saw me he simply stared, and then he laughed at David and said, 'Who painted Meg's face like that, David—why, she's beautiful!'

"Why do I tell all this to my dearest dear? Why, just because I know it is what she wants to hear, and because I know it will make her glad!

"But, in spite of all my happiness, I am very humble and often broken-hearted because I so ill deserve it, and because I am so afraid that it won't last, so wonderful is it!

"Of my husband I can't write, only I should like to let you know that all you said of him was true, and the half has never been told! Oh! when I get back to Kildoon I will try—and you will help me—to be a good wife, to be all his mother would have wished me to be to him.

"How is it, I wonder, that when great happiness comes to us we think so constantly of those who have gone away? I feel as if I knew my mother, as I never did in life, and father too not far away. I feel that they are together somewhere, where we can't follow them, and that they are glad in my happiness. It cannot be wrong to harbour such thoughts, for surely they are sent to us from afar.

"All is well in this beautiful tropical island. Ludo has grown and altered. He is thin, but he looks taller and his shoulders have broadened. And he is so keen about everything here. At first he showed no desire to go back to Ballochean; but David has been talking to him—David, who talks so wonderfully to everybody, saying the right word and striking the right note always. And we can now see that his heart is beginning to turn homewards, and that some day Ballochean will be restored to its place of honour in the county.

"And David will have done it all—David alone! Surely you must see how entitled he is to the blind worship of his wife's heart!

"We all come back together on the 'Ailsa,' and should reach home somewhere about the beginning of the New Year. I am in no hurry. My dearest dear, I care no longer for places or things but only for people and, above all, about deserving the happiness that is mine.

"I can't write any more. I long for you. I need you even more now in my happiness than I did in all my pain. Thank you, thank you, and God reward you for what you have done for

"Meg Sillars."

Low was bowed the proud old white head of Lady Rathillis on the fine white hands, and a prayer of thanksgiving fluttered from her lips. Put into words, it might have tallied with the petition of Simeon of old, who, granted the desire of his heart was ready to depart in peace.

But the tiem, was not yet ripe for her going.

The Countess of Rathillis must wait until she beheld her whom they had named the Pride of Ballochean become in truer, richer sense, the Pride of Kildoon.

THE END

THE STEPMOTHER

BY

ANNIE S. SWAN

SUNDAY MAIL EDITION
1933

CONTENTS

CHAPTER I

WHO IS THE WOMAN?

THERE were visible signs of displeasure on James Cardine's face when he descended to the dining-room of his house in Huntley Gardens and found nobody at the breakfast-table. It was then twenty minutes to nine—the breakfast hour was half-past eight—and there was no sign of the appearance of the meal.

Now, though a good-tempered man, Cardine was a very punctual one, and, reflecting that out of a household of five, he alone made any pretence of being in time, he proceeded towards the bell-pull and tugged at it mightily. There was a scurry on the back stairs, the swift creaking of the service-lift, and presently a heated table-maid came into the room and moved towards the door of the service-lift in the corner.

"Late again, Barbara! I'd like to know how many times it has happened this week?"

"Sorry, sir, but it's cook: she's—she's very thrawn this morning. She wouldn't put a thing on the lift!"

"And what, may I inquire, makes cook so 'thrawn'?"

"I don't know, sir," answered Barbara. "She's very ill to live wi', and I'm thinking of giving Miss Cardine notice this very day."

"I'd wait, if I were you, unless you have some other fault to find with the place."

"Oh, I've no particular fault, sir; but—but——"

"But what?" inquired Mr. Cardine. "Please speak out. We have not been so comfortable lately as we might have been, and I should uncommonly like to know the cause?"

"Well, sir, there's too little management. It's orders here, and orders there, Miss Cardine says one thing, and Miss Nancy another—but the worst of all is Miss Bella."

"Ay, and what's wrong with Miss Bella, my girl?" inquired the master of the house, with rather a dry note in his deep, pleasant voice.

The girl looked scared, and pushed back her cap streamers with a fling.

"Oh, I don't know that I ought to be saying anything about the young ladies, especially as I'm not stopping. Everything's on the table now, sir. May I sound the gong?"

"In a second or two. I don't suppose they are ready yet. And I particularly want to know what is the matter with Miss Bella?"

"Well, she's the mistress, sir—the real mistress—and she's always finding fault. If it was Miss Cardine none of us would mind. She's too 'ordery' for one thing. Service is not what it was, Mr. Cardine, and girls won't be ordered about nowadays as if they were dirt under your feet!"

Barbara Watson delivered herself of this statement with considerable relish, fully aware that, unless she had been leaving, she never would have dared. She had the greatest respect for her master, but it is the women of the house who create the domestic atmosphere, and things were all at sixes and sevens in the big Glasgow mansion, where there were six servants, much waste, and, comparatively speaking, but little comfort.

Mrs. Cardine had now been dead four years, and it was no exaggeration to say that no day passed when she had not been thought of and mourned by her widowed husband. She had been a woman of no brilliant parts, rather shrinking and homely; but she had made a home. And that, after all, is the woman's first business, and until she has mastered the elements of that science, she may consider herself more or less of a failure.

"So Miss Bella makes you feel as if you were dirt under her feet—eh?"

"Yes, sir, she does: and——"

But Barbara stopped there, for she had been about to utter a word of warning regarding a matter wholly out of her province. "I'd better sound the gong, sir," she said, and darted through the door, relieved to make her escape.

She fled down the kitchen stairs, and proceeded to enliven the kitchen breakfast-table by a highly embroidered account of what had passed in the dining-room. The others regarded her with amazement, and inquired, in a body, how she could have had the cheek! For once, Barbara got even with Mrs. Leggatt, the cross-eyed cook, and felt correspondingly uplifted.

Mr. Cardine began to eat his solitary breakfast, with the quality of which he was quite ready to quarrel had he thought it worth while.

His housekeeping, both at Huntley Gardens and at Ardgoil, in Bute, cost him considerably more than it had ever done in his wife's lifetime, and he had much less comfort.

As he consumed his mouthfuls of flabby fish, cooked so unappetizingly, he recalled, in a swift pang of memory, old, old days at the beginning of his married life, when there had been only one servant in the flat in Great Western Road, but where meals fit for a king had been served. For his wife—his Isabel, as he still fondly called her in his lonely heart—had been a clever housewife, and, even when riches came, had never slackened her hold on domestic affairs. Her three girls, in spite of all her efforts to bring them up to be useful and efficient in the housewifely arts, had hardly attained them. The eldest, Jean, was interested in "Causes," and her name was on more committees than she could conveniently attend.

The youngest daughter, Nancy, the prettiest of the trio, and much run after by young men, needed a stronger hand than had been ever stretched out to her. She was wilful, impulsive, foolish to a degree, and it was regarding her latest indiscretion that Barbara Watson had intended to speak when she drew herself up in time.

Bella, the middle daughter and the plainest, was discontented, ill-natured, and ambitious for herself—an odd combination, which required very careful handling at the outset. Such handling it did not get.

Two sons completed the household. The elder, Alexander, was married, and lived in a house of his own at Dowanhill; while Harry, the fourth of the family, had only lately left the University and entered the Bridgeton Works.

Such, then, were the members of the household who will play out this little drama; to outward seeming, an ordinary, prosperous family, whose days might be supposed to glide along evenly, without much excitement, and certainly without tragedy. Yet both excitement and tragedy were lying in wait for them at the moment when we meet them first.

Mr. Cardine was wrestling with a very hard-boiled egg, when the door opened and Harry came in. An extraordinarily handsome youth, with a winning way, he "took the first word" of the scolding.

"Sorry to be late, Dad, but I'm not the only one. We didn't get in till half-past two in the morning. Did you hear us?"

"Yes, I did. It was too late for Nancy. I don't suppose she's up yet?"

"Not she! I daresay she'll sleep till lunch-time. She danced enough if you like! And Dad——?"

The lad's face was slightly clouded as he turned from the side-dishes, from which he was about to help himself. "I don't think she ought to go to those regimental balls without somebody to properly chaperon her."

"Why, where were Jean and Bella?"

"Jean wasn't there at all, Dad; and Bella was too much taken up with her own concerns."

"What about Evey? Usually she is very kind about Nancy."

"She wasn't there. Alexander only looked in for about an hour, and he said Evey wasn't well, and he wouldn't stop."

"What was the matter with Nancy? Didn't she have the right kind of partners?"

"Plenty of partners. But I wish she would pick and choose. She danced far too often with Gilder. He's an outsider. I've told her so, but she won't listen. I wanted to bring her home between twelve and one, and then his name was five times on the programme."

The father's eye darkened, and his face seemed to become heavier and more forbidding. Usually it was a pleasant enough face, though it had a good deal of the strength characteristic of the man who had fought his way up.

"Seems to me—seems to me, Hal, that things want pulling together a bit in this house—eh?"

"They do," said the lad, and his eyes shadowed a bit.

He had never forgotten his mother. Of all the family he was the most like her in nature, and none of them guessed how terrible a blow her death had been to him. They were reticent concerning emotions and feelings, as most Scottish households are, and were even remote from one another in a greater degree than many families. Now that the bond, the connecting-link, of the mother-love was away, they had drifted even farther apart, each one going his or her own way pretty much, and seeking very little community of interest. The loneliest of them all, undoubtedly, was James Cardine himself, though when people spoke about him they invariably said how well off he was with his family, and what a comfort his daughters must be. He was one of the men—they sometimes added—who would not have a ghost of an excuse for marrying again.

Just as Mr. Cardine rose from the table his eldest daughter, and housekeeper, entered the room.

"Sorry, Father; but we were late last night. I sat up for the girls, and we talked afterwards, of course. Have you finished your breakfast already?"

She made a little jerky motion with her eyeglasses which had the effect of making them fall off her nose. She did not really need them very much, but imagined that they improved her looks, and gave her a more intellectual air.

She was a tall, rather angular person, who affected a severe style of dress. Her one beauty was her hair, which was shining and abundant, and, in spite of all her endeavours to treat it decorously, it seemed to riot about her face. She was now twenty-six, and had been keeping her father's house, after a fashion, since her mother died. But she had no method. She did not really care for it, and far too much was left to servants. The old ones, who felt keenly the change from their mistress's well-ordered regime, had gradually left, one after the other, and the only one now remaining was Maggie Ferguson, the sewing-maid, who "did" for all three. And she only stayed on because she had been the nurse originally, and had no other home to go to.

"I've had something to eat, but it couldn't, by courtesy, be called a breakfast." her father answered drily, but Jean, who happily—or, perhaps, unhappily—was not sensitive, merely laughed.

"They are careless," was all she said, as she passed to the head of the table.

"The governor's wool's off, Jean," said Harry, his blue eyes looking out from under the brown curls warningly.

"Oh, no, dear; he's all right," she answered absently, her eyes already glued on the pile of letters by her plate.

She did not go out of the room to see that her father had his gloves, or that his hat was properly brushed, nor did Barbara Watson, though supposed to do a certain amount of valeting, trouble herself to come up the back stairs. Barbara had arrived at the stage when she only came when rung for, and then unwillingly.

Presently Harry and Jean were disturbed by the banging of the outside door.

"Oh, I say!" exclaimed Harry. "That's Father off. He's angry, Jean, and no mistake!"

The lad looked genuinely troubled, but Jean was not much perturbed.

"Probably he has somewhere to go before Bridgeton," was all she said.

In this conclusion she was perfectly right—though she could not have located his mission.

He walked down the hill, out into the Great Western Road, and then made a little detour into a cul-de-sac of small, old-fashioned houses which had escaped the laying out of newer Glasgow.

Caddam Square was much sought after by those who liked a quiet dwelling for which they did not have to pay too high a rent; and they were mostly solid, old-fashioned folk who dwelt there, many of them elderly, who owned their own houses and had no desire for change.

A pretty and well-kept garden in the middle, further added to the amenity, and there was seldom a house to let within its precincts.

James Cardine walked up the slope of Caddam Square with no uncertain step, and at the house at the far end, made pause and rang the bell. He was answered by a middle-aged servant, who, as she gave him good-morning, appeared to be surprised by his early call.

"Is Miss Bruar down yet, Kirsteen?"

"Oh, yes, sir. She's had her breakfast, and is busy with the paper. Come in."

But Miss Bruar had heard her brother-in-law's voice, and now appeared in the little hall behind Kirsteen.

"Mercy me, James! What brings you here at nine of the morning? Nothing wrong at Huntley Gardens, I hope?"

"Nothing. And, to be quite correct, it is half-past nine, Mary Bruar!" answered Cardine, feeling his spirits rise at sight of that blithe, contented face.

She was one of those small, bird-like women of extremely precise appearance, not a hair out of its place, capable, kind and cheery. Miss Bruar, known as Aunt Mary Bruar to a very large coterie outside her own family, was quite a well-known figure in the west-end of Glasgow. She was very old-fashioned, but it gave her an odd charm. Who but Aunt Mary Bruar could have worn Early Victorian clothes, frilled skirts, and elbow sleeves with full wristlets of white lawn, with such a becoming grace? Even the apron, without which she was never seen in the house, and it was fringed all round, too, seemed part of a personality at once engaging and unique.

"Well—half-past nine, my man; and surely time ye were at business."

Aunt Mary Bruar, while not speaking exactly broad Scotch, had preserved a flavour of the old-time in her language also, though it was always precise, because she and her sister had kept a small dame's school near Charing Cross, just about the time the School Board system of education came into operation. But it had not hurt their school nor their reputation as teachers and it had only been given up when the younger sister married James Cardine.

It had been a good thing for Mary Bruar, too, for her sister's husband had proved indeed a brother to her in every sense, and she had the greatest respect and admiration for him, though she mourned in secret over the foibles of his family, of whom Harry was her favourite.

"I'm on my way. But I want to speak to you, Mary Bruar," he answered, as he hung up his hat and followed her into the cosy little, red dining-room, where, on more occasions than could be counted on his hands, a confessional had been set up.

"You're very small in Caddam Square, Mary Bruar, but you've got the knack of comfort," observed Mr. Cardine, as he dropped into a chair. "There's none at Huntley Gardens."

"What's upset you this morning, Jamie?" asked his sister-in-law kindly; but her hands moved just a trifle nervously, for she was whole-heartedly interested in her sister's children, though she had no jurisdiction over them.

"Everything! You did me an ill turn when you would not give up your house and come to us when Isabel died. It was your duty, Mary Bruar."

She began to tremble a little at that, for the matter had been one of extreme tension at the time, and she had only held out by sheer force of will, as it were.

"I don't see it, James. I didn't see it then and I don't now," she said manfully. "Your lassies ought to have been capable of managing the house they had lived in so long. If they were not, why not?"

He shook a dismal head.

"I don't know. But that there's something the matter with the women of our day is a sure thing. They seem to lack something—a sense of responsibility and an understanding of duty."

A faint, a very faint, smile flitted across Mary Bruar's face.

How often had she seen her sister's wise handling of this big, strong, dour man, who was at heart but a little bairn! With him, his children, all but Harry, had missed the way just as he had missed the way with them.

"I grudge them nothing, but they do nothing for me," he went on, permitting his long-pent bitterness expression. "There's never one of them there when I happen to need them. I had to breakfast this morning by myself, off stuff that would have disgraced the Sautmarket! Any wife at the close mouth could have fried her haddie better! I'm not going to stand it, Mary Bruar, and if you won't come to Huntley Gardens and take Isa's place, I must hit on some other plan."

"A housekeeper, maybe—a thorough, capable woman. I might try and find that for you, James, and I think I could," she said cheerfully. "Then the lassies would have time for their ploys, and the house would be looked after better."

Mr. Cardine gave a kind of grunt.

"I've thought, once or twice in the last year, Mary Bruar, that the man who marries again soon after he is left a widower does the most sensible thing in the world. And the folk that judge him most, probably know nothing at all about the circumstances that have forced him to it."

Mary Bruar gave a little start, and looked attentively into her brother-in-law's gloomy face. She had known the perfect union, the by-ordinary love that had existed between her sister and her husband, and that had been the only thing that had reconciled Mary to separation from Isabel, and to her own loneliness. Therefore, she could not, and did not take him seriously.

"You would never do that, of course, James. There are a hundred reasons why you would never think of it—reasons, apart from her that's away," she said quietly. "But the first and foremost is that your last state would be worse than your first. Put a stepmother in among your lively crew and—and even your worst enemy needn't envy you."

James Cardine gave his shoulders a slight shrug.

"At least, I might have somebody to speak to, and might reasonably expect value for money expended in the house," he answered heavily. "Well, I'll be going. Good-bye, Mary Bruar. You have never a great deal to say, but you somehow put heart into a man, and the best solution of the difficulty would be if you would marry me yourself, and come and look after my unruly crew."

She laughed at that, but the tear was not far distant from her eye. She loved James Cardine as a sister might, and not one flaw or jar had ever marred their relationship, through all these perfect years. It was, in its way, a unique relationship, for, so highly did James Cardine value his sister-in-law's opinion and judgment, that he had confided to her a good many of his more speculative business undertakings even in his wife's lifetime. And, though she did not take him seriously at the moment, there was both truth and passion in his voice; and, certainly, had she been available as a wife, he would have sought no other. But as the law stood, and as all the conventions stood, they were as much apart as if the breadth of the seas had rolled between them.

"You'll feel better the morn, my man," she said, as she saw him kindly to the door. "By the way I'll take a walk up to Huntley and give them a word."

About twelve, she left the house, and took the car to the nearest point to Huntley Gardens, arriving on the doorstep just as Jean was coming out.

"Oh, good morning, Aunt Mary Bruar," said that self-possessed young woman cordially. "I'm late with my morning shopping, but there isn't anything I can't order over the telephone. Come in, and hear the news."

"Your mother never ordered meat or drink over the telephone, Jean; and I'd rather walk out to the shops with you now."

"Oh, no; there isn't any need. It's only the fish, and some fresh flowers, anyway. Come in. They're not down yet—Nancy or Bella—but they're both out of bed. You'll see them at lunch-time."

Miss Bruar, because she really wanted a word with her niece, permitted her to fit her key in the latch, and accompanied her into the pleasant morning-room or parlour—as it was usually called—the favourite rendezvous of the family.

"Your father came to see me this morning, Jean," said Miss Bruar as she sat down by the table.

"Oh, that is where he was off to in a hurry! Queer time to pay a call—wasn't it?—on the way to business, too!" said Jean, but her tone was not actively interested.

She had a most irritating, indifferent air of detachment, always, both in speech and expression, which conveyed, perhaps unintentionally, the impression that she was completely indifferent to whatever theme happened to be under discussion, and that she had far more important schemes of her own to interest her.

"He wasn't in a good mood, my lassie. He isn't satisfied with the way things are going on in the house, and I thought I'd just pop up and give you a bit warning."

"Oh, that was because the fish wasn't properly done this morning. Poor Father! He is always so finicky about his food. Mother spoiled him. There are so many other things in the world of bigger moment than what we eat."

"A man's food, when he is middle-aged, and works as hard as your father, is a very important matter indeed, my dear," protested Aunt Mary Bruar. "And you make a mistake in not paying more attention to it."

"Was father complaining, then, all round?" asked Jean rather more interestedly.

"He was. And he said a thing which stuck in my throat, Jean. He said, nobody could blame the man who marries again, and that circumstances would need to be taken into consideration in his case before he was blamed. He——"

"Hulloa! Who's thinking of getting married, and how are you, Auntie?" inquired Bella's rather thin, penetrating voice in the doorway.

She came up and gave her aunt a little peck on the cheek, and then sat down on the edge of the table to hear the news. There was nothing distinguished about Bella Cardine's appearance. Her figure was inclined to stoutness, and her face was round and commonplace; her eyes hard and keen, and her mouth rather fond of assuming a mournful curve. She was very trim and neat in her dress, and prided herself on her dainty foot-gear. She was, perhaps, the cleverest of the three sisters in a worldly sense, and far sharper than Jean in grasping a situation.

"Who were you talking about, Auntie?" she persisted, when nobody proceeded to enlighten her.

"Well, it was your father, my dear," her aunt answered. "He's been to me this morning and he had a good deal to say in the way of grumbling. But the thing I liked least was, when he remarked that nobody could blame a man for marrying again."

"Did father say that?" asked Bella shrilly.

"He did, my dear; and it's for you and your sister to tak' tent in time."

"Oh, I say!" cried Bella, in her most penetrating tones, "I wonder who is the woman?"

CHAPTER II

THE KIND FAMILIAR FACE

A WORD, a look, a mere suggestion will sometimes fix an idea in a man's mind.

Although James Cardine had alluded to a second marriage merely in jest to his sister-in-law, he began, as he made his way to the factory at Bridgeton, to ponder on the possibilities.

He was at that acute stage of personal loneliness which makes a man peculiarly susceptible to sympathy—especially to feminine sympathy. He was not thinking of any particular woman, but rather of woman spelled with a big W—the wonderful, subtle influence that had, without his knowledge, so ably and finely controlled his life. He was like a ship without a rudder now; or a compass without a needle; and the unwise virgins in the house with him had not had sufficient discernment to try to make up to him for the want of their mother.

With all the splendid selfishness of youth, and something of its cruelty, they had looked upon him rather as a figure-head and universal provider, than as a living human being whose heart and impulses and outlook were all youthful for his years. These years were but fifty-one, but to the twenties, such an age seems remote and ancient, if not actually hovering on the brink of the grave!

The Bridgeton factory of Messrs. Speed, Cardine & Co., gave employment to a large number of women and girls, in whose welfare the late Mrs. Cardine had taken a motherly interest. To her they owed the improved conditions of working, the new dining-room and recreation room, and the scale of wages which compared very favourably with that adopted by similar firms in the West of Scotland. She had never been a fusser, and, though she came sometimes to the factory, and was known to just a few—and these, the ones who had been in trouble of one kind or another—it was rather as a sweet gracious influence than a presence that she was remembered.

There were no Speeds now in the Bridgeton factory, Cardine and his elder son being the sole partners. It was a very lucrative concern, and one to whose operations there was practically no limit.

Outside of his business, James Cardine had fewer interests than most men of his age and ability in the most forward city of the Empire. He had been so much of a home-lover and home-keeper that he had never taken any part in civic life, nor had he cultivated any outside hobby. An occasional dinner at the house of a friend, a lecture, a concert, or a theatre, summed up the list of his outside interests, and now that there was none to share them, and the children were all scattered immediately after dinner, if not before it, on their own concerns, he had found his evenings often dull.

When James Cardine reached the factory that morning, about ten, he found his elder son already there.

Alexander was a preternaturally solemn young man, a complete slave to business, out of which he was determined to make the most he could. This was quite necessary, as he had married an extravagant and ambitious wife, who desired to shine in society and give dinners that would be talked about.

James Cardine was not difficult to get on with up to a point; that once reached, however, he could become stubborn and immovable as Dumbarton Rock. Once or twice, Alexander had come up against that impenetrable wall in his father's character, and had to retire discomfited. For "the old man," as he was sometimes irreverently called (it is amazing how quickly we become "old" to our children, possibly because we always represent and embody ancient history to them) was still absolute master and head.

A brief "good morning" passed between the two men, and as Mr. Cardine went to the cloakroom to dispose of his hat and overcoat, he inquired whether Harry had come

"Yes, about ten minutes ago. He seemed surprised that you weren't in front of him."

"I walked as far as your Aunt Mary Bruar's," his father answered him. "Anything fresh this morning?"

"Some. We'll need to make a push with that big order from Sampsons, father. There'll have to be overtime, or it will never get in up to contract."

"What do Sampsons say?"

His brows narrowed a bit, as he drew in a chair to the immense writing-table in the centre of the room, on which the morning mail was spread. His face seemed to change, and he became once more the acute, alert man of business, giving his whole mind to one thing at a time.

"Um. I'll write them myself this morning. There was no word of all this last March when the contract was laid. Seen Gemmill?"

"No. I've only just come."

"I see. Evey all right this morning?"

"Quite. She had her own reasons for not going to the ball last night. Trust a woman like Evey for knowing what's what!"

"I suppose so," observed Mr. Cardine rather drily. "But it wasn't fair on the girls. Nancy ought to have had a chaperon. Perhaps you'll kindly let me know next time she can't go? Aunt Mary Bruar hates dances, but she'll go if we want her. Why didn't you look after Nance better?"

"Well, you see, I didn't stop long enough," answered Alexander, surprised into self-defence. "What was she doing, anyway? And couldn't Bella keep her in order?"

"I don't want her to be too thick with that crowd, Alec. They're birds of passage, and one never knows the truth about them."

"Rather rough on the Army!" observed Alexander, with his odd, cackling, little laugh, that had no gleam of mirth in it.

"She's had no mother's care," his father went on, with great deliberation. "And, I confess, I'm rather anxious about her."

"Oh, Nance will come out all right, Father," observed Alexander, more and more surprised. "Jean and Bella are solid enough surely to keep her in ballast."

"Doubtful. Jean's taken up in public work, and nobody ever gets to the bottom of Bella's intentions. Well, we'd better get to work."

But all through what was undoubtedly the most pregnant hour of the day, when father and son were accustomed to discuss business policy and prospects, Alexander was conscious of an odd detachment and slackness of interest about his father. Once or twice, even, he looked at him with a furtive anxiety, wondering whether he was in his usual good health. There was, however, nothing in his looks to cause the slightest concern. Never had he looked more fit or younger, his colour was ruddy and healthy, his eye clear, his whole appearance pleasant to behold.

When they got through the subject matter of the mail, they separated, and James Cardine made his way into various departments of the great building where three hundred women and girls were happily employed, and about a hundred men and boys.

He came at last to what was called the finishing shops, where goods were packed, ready for export, and for delivery to home firms. If was one of the largest and finest departments in the whole establishment, and had been part of the latest addition to it. In this large, light place, the girls worked under the pleasantest conditions, and, though nearly a hundred were engaged in one room, there was no sign of crowding, but, instead, a feeling of space, and leisure, and comfort. Berths in Cardine's packing-room were much coveted in the Glasgow labour market, and certainly the present occupants looked a very healthy, happy crowd.

They were in charge of the head of that department, Margaret Oswald, considered one of the most trusted and valued employees of the firm.

She sat at a long table at the head of the room, a neat and attractive figure of a woman, about thirty-five, becomingly dressed in a frock of dark blue cashmere, relieved by a touch of white at the neck. She had white linen sleeves up to the elbows to protect her gown, and a white apron, which was very becoming.

If not exactly a lady, she had an air of refinement and common sense, which made her a pleasant picture to contemplate.

There were no signs of excitement or of embarrassment, either on her part, or on the part of any of those under her, at the entrance of the master.

Where there is nothing to hide, there can be perfect ease of manner, and Miss Oswald's department was admittedly a pattern to the whole house. She had been much liked by her employer's late wife, who had discussed every matter relating to the welfare of the women and girls with her, and she had the complete confidence of both Cardine and his sons.

She looked up, with her pleasant smile, as he approached the long table, and rose up, as it was fitting that she should, to greet him.

" Good morning, Miss Oswald. Everything up to the mark, as usual ? " looking with approval at the trim figure, the pleasant, kindly face, and the little flush of colouring on the cheeks, the clear, grey eyes, and the pretty hair which, though slightly tinged with grey, was very luxurious and abundant.

She was slightly above the average height, and carried herself with a good deal of dignity. She looked what she was—a woman who knew her position, and was sufficiently proud of it to adorn it.

" We shan't be quite so tidy for the next few weeks if it's true what Mr. Alexander was telling me this morning, that we have to get that big order out before Easter."

" I'll see Sampsons next week. I daresay we can get them to modify their demands. Come in here a minute."

" Here " signified a small room which had been partitioned off from the bigger one, and which was Miss Oswald's own, where she put her hat and coat, and could eat her lunch if not disposed to go out. It had been a great boon to her, for which she had never ceased to be grateful to Mrs. Cardine, whose thought it had been.

She had the greatest respect, and even a kind of mild affection for her master, and, just of late, she had noticed various signs of worry about him which she knew had nothing to do with business. She knew a good deal about the conduct and progress of the business, for both father and son, finding her a wise, sensible, and kindly, as well as a deeply-interested person, had got into the habit of discussing with her business details, quite outside her department.

She was the very best type of the industrial woman, sane, and evenly balanced, thoroughly capable, and with a heart as well as a head for her work.

As James Cardine closed the communicating door and put his back against it, he became suddenly conscious of a change in his attitude towards this woman. With the exception of Mary Bruar, she was the only one that really counted in his life, and he suddenly asked himself what he should do if a day should dawn when Margaret Oswald would not be there when he wanted her.

" I hope you are all well at home, Miss Oswald ? " he said with the faintest touch of awkwardness.

" Quite well, thank you. You've no idea what a pleasure my father takes out of his garden, and he will always be grateful to you for letting him have that extra corner ! He is getting in vegetable seeds just now for all he is worth ! "

Margaret's father was a retired ship captain of the merchant service, who, with her mother, lived in one of a row of small villa houses which Mr. Cardine had lately built at Bearsden. She had only one brother—also a captain in the merchant service—and her home was quite a happy one. She earned a handsome salary at Cardine's, and, on the whole, had no fault to find with life.

" I must come out one of these afternoons and have a look at the place. Should I find him at home on Saturday afternoon ? "

" Yes—or any afternoon. How pleased he would be ! I'm so glad he has got this hobby, Mr. Cardine. He was a miserable man in the Shawlands flat."

" Ah, I dare say ; a man wants some occupation. Say, Miss Oswald, don't you get a bit sick of the routine here ? "

She shook her head, smiling brightly.

" I should be a wicked, ungrateful woman if I did ! I like my work, and there are few women-workers who have such favourable conditions to work in. I'm always rubbing that into the girls, but indeed I think they realize it. We have a very nice lot just now, don't you think, Mr. Cardine ? "

She put the question rather anxiously, because she imagined a cloud on her employer's brow. It was quite usual for them to have a little private talk in her room, and nobody in the big room beyond ever took notice, or wondered about it.

But, somehow, Margaret felt there was a difference that morning, and that Mr. Cardine had something on his mind.

"I am sure the working woman is the happiest, Miss Oswald," he said suddenly. "If my daughters had some definite occupation, they would be both happier and better women."

"But Miss Cardine is very busy about the Suffrage, isn't she ?" asked Margaret, with a slight smile. "I heard her speak one night in Bearsden, and really she was very good."

Mr. Cardine looked the disgust he felt.

"I don't know that I'm against Votes for Women, exactly, but before they ask for votes they should do the job lying nearest to them. Jean is to take her mother's place, and I can't honestly say she's doing that."

"But nobody could ever fill that place," said Margaret softly, and her eyes became suffused with tenderness. "Don't expect too much of them, Mr. Cardine. They are young, and life will teach them."

"And, meanwhile, I have nowhere to lay my head," he said, with a kind of strange abruptness.

Margaret looked at him with a quickened interest that was almost anxiety. They had discussed many things in that little room, but Cardine had never brought any member of his family under review before the forewoman. His natural pride forbade it.

"I think you can't be very well, Mr. Cardine," she said gently. "It is about this time you take a little change usually. I suppose you will be going to Ardgoil soon."

"They don't like Ardgoil except in the yachting season, when they can spend their time on the sea," he answered gruffly. "If I happened to want a quiet week-end down there in the off season, I should have to take it by myself. No—if there's to be any change, it will have to be a big one," and with that he went out by the door, as if afraid of further speech.

Margaret lingered for a few moments in the quiet of her own room, strangely disturbed. But not half so disturbed as her master, who knew within himsel what was going to happen. For, looking on the kind face of Margaret Oswald, meeting the straight full glance of her sympathetic womanly eye, he suddenly realized that he wanted to marry her, if she would consent. But that was neither the time nor the place for the question.

How does such swift resolve come to a man in the moment he least expects it ? It was within the mark to say, that when James Cardine entered his own factory that March morning, he had not the smallest intention of asking Margaret Oswald to marry him, had not, indeed, any concrete intention of marrying at all. But there, in that quiet room, with the hum of the busy working hive wafted to them through the partitioning walls, listening to her kind voice, the idea had suddenly crystallized !

But he was shaken, for, looked at from any standpoint but more especially from his own social and family standpoint, it was not a marriage to be desired.

Probably, if ever it did take place, there would not be one voice raised in his behalf, amid the united chorus of dissent. Even Mary Bruar would probably be alienated. Margaret and he would have to stand alone.

"Margaret and he !" He smiled grimly to himself, as he felt his middle-aged pulses thrill at the combination.

When does interest in woman die in the heart and life of a man ? Why, never, if he is an ordinary human man, with a full grip of life.

That was a poor business day for James Cardine, the poorest he had put in since the time of anxiety and stress when he was waiting for the issue of life or death in his wife's last illness.

Margaret was hardly less disturbed, though her thoughts had no definite object or cohesion. To one so absolutely sensible, and free from the stupid coquetry and self-consciousness, which sometimes militates against a woman's business life, and complicates existence for others, it did not occur what could be the meaning of this strange half-confidence her employer had bestowed upon her. Soon after he had left the vicinity of the packing-room, and while she was still trying to collect her thoughts, someone else sought her—a middle-aged man, of sturdy well-set figure, with a somewhat full, florid face, bold, bright, black eyes, and a dark moustache—Bruce Gemmill—the manager of another department, though not closely associated with hers. He managed that they should meet often in the course of a day, and, just lately, Margaret had begun to weary of his attentions. He had only been in the employment of the Cardines for about eighteen months, and, though a capable servant, had managed already to make himself heartily disliked throughout the entire place.

He belonged to the bullying order, and could never give the smallest item of instruction or command without a suggestion of threatening in his voice and manner. That was not and never had been the policy of the Cardines. They were more broad-minded and sensible, and believed that the best service is got by consideration and kindness, combined with the necessary firmness. They aimed at raising the standard of the relations between employer and employee, and industrial discontent was very rare at the Bridgeton factory.

There had been one or two rather sharp passages between Gemmill and his employers on this very head, as well as several very warm discussions between him and Miss Oswald. She had, in the end, absolutely forbidden him to meddle with her department, of which she claimed to be the undisputed head.

It was so unusual for a woman to stand up so stoutly for her rights—in his former place Gemmill had found them rather downtrodden and quiescent, even under obvious justice—that his attention was arrested, and pretty soon he began to take a personal interest in Margaret Oswald, which was far more offensive to her than his criticism or arguments concerning business affairs. She, indeed, heartily disliked the man, and since his coming to Bridgeton, a few personal jealousies in the place seemed to have become accentuated. He had the faculty of bringing to the surface the least desirable attributes in those among whom he worked.

He met the master as he came out of the packing-room that morning, but only a nod passed between them. Gemmill strode down the long room. The girls, for some reason of their own, had nick-named him " the night hawk."

Finding Margaret apparently doing nothing, and looking a trifle unlike herself when he entered her room, Gemmill immediately assumed an air of proprietary concern.

" What's upset the aipple cairt—eh ? " he asked in his full, guttural tones. " I've just met the boss. Has he been on the warpath ? "

" Oh, no," answered Miss Oswald, pulling herself together, and at the same time opening a drawer in the corner cupboard as if looking for something. " Do you want anything, Mr. Gemmill ? For I've plenty to do next door. Heard of the time limit for Sampsons', I suppose ? "

" Oh, there's time enough—don't be in a hurry. I say, Tree's coming to the Royal next week. If I get two stalls, will you come ? "

" No," she answered steadily. " But thank you all the same."

" Why not ? You have gone with me before now," he said ingratiatingly. " What's happened just lately to make you give me the cold shoulder ? "

" Nothing particular. But it's not convenient to go to the theatre at night, living at Bearsden, and having to get to work by eight in the morning."

" Oh, that's fudge ! If you wanted to come, that wouldn't hold. Well, look here. When can I come out to see you ? Saturday afternoon—eh ? I want to smoke a pipe wi' the old man. Him and me's thick." he added, with a pleasantly facetious touch.

In spite of herself, and for no known reason, the flame leaped in Margaret's face.

" Not Saturday," she said quickly. " And, really, I must go and see what they're after."

But Gemmill, now really angry, for she had managed to convey to him, in some subtle way, her full lack of appreciation, and he understood that he and his advances were not welcome to her—flushed darkly.

" I tell you what. Something's happened, Miss O. Higher game, eh ? "

CHAPTER III

ANCHORAGE

CAPTAIN ROBERT OSWALD of the merchant service was converting into a show place his Anchorage at Bearsden.

The appropriate name was printed in large gilt letters on the glass above the door. A fine model of the *Clydesdale Mary*, in full sail, stood on a small table between the muslin curtains of the parlour window, and was an object of never-failing interest to small boys out with their nurses or mothers for walks. The garden paths were outlined with a neat pattern of shells and white " chuckie stanes," and, altogether, the little domain presented a very bright, cheery aspect, such as an old salt likes to create when he gets a fair chance.

About four o'clock on Saturday afternoon, when Captain Oswald, in his shirt-sleeves and with a short pipe in his mouth, was very busy measuring and laying out his little extra piece of ground into seed beds (the digging happily finished), there came down the Station Road, among other passengers by the late afternoon train, the tall, fine figure of Mr. James Cardine.

Margaret was already home, and had done her best to get her father to leave off working and tidy himself for tea. But she had not given him any valid reason why he should lose a grand working afternoon, so he had not heeded her request.

Margaret had not insisted, because she was by no means sure. She might have said, indeed, that Mr. Cardine would think no more about his suggestion to come out to Bearsden and see how the new garden was getting on. She might have said so, but, in reality, she was quite sure that he would come, and when, she heard men's voices in the garden she did not so much as look out of the window because she knew what had happened.

Even her mother—a small, gentle, white-haired old lady of much activity of body and very little of speech, there being no room for anyone else's voice, in her opinion, in the vicinity of Captain Robert Oswald—had noticed a queer restlessness about her. One thing, however, Margaret had resolutely refrained from, and that was making any personal preparations for the visit of Mr. Cardine.

She still wore her working blouse. True, it was a clean, white silk one, very dainty and fresh-looking, and of a better quality than she usually wore in the workroom, and she had donned it that morning with the strange feeling that this was going to be an epoch-making day in her life. What she expected she had not an idea! She was only conscious of some disturbance of the heart and spirit, which was at once painful and pleasant.

She had not seen Mr. Cardine that day, nor even heard whether he was in the factory.

A low wall, surmounted by a painted railing, enclosed the triangle, and directly Mr. Cardine came up to it he made pause and called out a cheery " Good afternoon, Captain ! " across the intervening space.

The captain made abrupt pause, then, recognizing his interrupter, took his pipe from his mouth, shoved his hand through his stubbly grey hair, and came forward, smiling capaciously.

" Mr. Cardine ! I'm proud to see ye, sir. Will ye come in ? Micht it be that ye have come specially to veesit the Anchorage ? If so, it is a good day for the Anchorage."

" I believe I did come to see how you are getting on. You've done wonders Captain ! " said Mr. Cardine admiringly.

By this time the captain had made a bee-line for the Anchorage gate, which was always kept rigorously shut to keep out marauding dogs. And, when the gate was duly opened, a hearty handshake passed between the two, the captain's working hand being first vigorously rubbed on the spacious sides of what he facetiously called "ma gairden breeks."

For several minutes they stood contemplating the little domain, while its owner pointed out all the improvements he had made, as well as several he had still in contemplation.

"Margit's hame," continued the captain, as they began to move towards the house. "You'll come in, I hope, and see the mistress, and drink a cup o' tea? Naething stronger permitted noo"—he added, with a delightful wink of his scarred eye, which gave a peculiar zest to it. "We're a' T.T. at the Anchorage."

Cardine laughed, his spirits infected quite sensibly by the captain's cheery optimism, and, presently, they were clearing the gravel from their feet on the wire mat; then, rubbing them on the fibre one, according to the unwritten laws.

Mrs. Oswald, with her kind smile of welcome, not at all embarrassed, came out from the parlour to greet the guest, and Margaret, sheltering in the rear, welcomed him too. Then they all moved into the parlour, where Mr. Cardine immediately became absorbed in contemplation of "*Clydesdale Mary's*" fine lines and noble show of canvas.

"Tea is laid in the kitchen, Father," said Margaret. "I hope you will wait, Mr. Cardine, until it has been brought in here."

She said it quite deliberately, because she could pretend nothing, and even had she been quite sure of his coming, some inner pride would have forbidden her to make an elaborate preparation. He turned swiftly to smile in her face.

"I hope you will give me that treat, Miss Oswald! A kitchen tea! I haven't had one since my mother used to give us them in the Carluke farmhouse where we were born."

"I'm sure Father doesn't approve," she said, seeing that he was about to burst forth into protest.

But, with a laugh, she escaped at the moment, to see that all was well in the family living-room.

Now, Mr. Cardine, possibly out of gratitude for the Carluke memories, had made the kitchen a great feature of his houses at Bearsden. It was larger than the parlour, and had a deep bay-window to the garden, and the apartment was cunningly arranged with the cupboards in the wall for shutting off all unnecessary reminders of kitchen work.

The range, too, was something special, with a white tiled back, and hearth of the same; and, when the floor was covered with linoleum, and had a pretty rug before the fireplace, it was as snug and spacious a family living-room as any ordinarily fastidious person could desire.

The Oswalds kept no servant, though a woman came in every day to do the rough work; they thus preserved the complete privacy and amenity of their home. Margaret liked housework, and was always busy with her needle. She had made the chintz covers for the old settee and the two easy-chairs, and curtains of the same hung at the sides of the bay window, besides the short muslin one with the crochet trimming, also her work.

The fire was bright, and the smell of buttered toast most appetizing. The cheery warmth and homeliness of it that blustering March afternoon laid hold of Cardine's heart as he was invited to enter.

"What a beautiful, homely, cosy place!" he exclaimed involuntarily, and Margaret's eyes brightened, for she was proud of her home and loved it, too.

She hadn't an atom of false pride about her. A working woman, she was immensely proud of the fact that she had made an undoubted success of her life.

The captain, having washed his hands and donned an old smoking jacket, was ready to do the honours of the table, and it is a question whether a happier little party was to be found in the whole of Bearsden that Saturday afternoon.

The slight embarrassment Margaret had been conscious of when contemplating a possible visit from her employer, had altogether disappeared now it had become a reality. It suddenly appeared the most natural thing in the world that he should be sitting there, drinking her mother's tea, and praising her scones, and the particular brand of spiced beef for which the Anchorage was famous.

The fact that her father and mother apparently saw nothing more than a landlord's kindly visit in Mr. Cardine's presence was distinctly reassuring. So Margaret poured out innumerable cups of tea, and even made a fresh pot, her face softly flushed and her eyes shining with the simple pleasure of it. It was all so much happier and easier than she had expected.

Cardine was happy, too, for he had come of homely folks, and, though his position had necessitated a social rise in the world, he had never taken kindly to formal dinners or drawing-room teas—more especially in the form they had taken since his wife's death. What he needed, and missed, was a home.

The captain was in his best form, and, after tea, he carried Mr. Cardine off to his den in the attics, to show him curios and smoke innumerable pipes, and talk of his old sea-faring days. So it was six o'clock when they came downstairs and Margaret was nowhere to be seen.

" She was sorry, but she had to go out and ask after a sick friend," Mrs. Oswald explained. " She said she would not be any more than half an hour. Will you wait, Mr. Cardine ? "

" You forget, my woman, Mr. Cardine sees Margit every day ! " put in the captain facetiously.

" I won't wait, thank you. Perhaps I shall meet her," said Mr. Cardine. " I have to thank you for one of the pleasantest afternoon teas I've had for a long while, and I hope you will let me come again, Mrs. Oswald."

" Surely, sir. As often as you like," she assured him ; but there crept into her eyes an odd, puzzled look, as her hand lingered a little in his kind clasp.

James Cardine walked on to the station, and beyond it, and, led by some impulse for which he could not account, quickly found himself in a pretty country lane, such as is still to be discovered not far beyond the precincts of the great city, by those who care to look. And, not much farther on, he met Margaret, as he knew he would meet her, returning from her walk.

" You have missed your way, surely, Mr. Cardine ! You have passed the station," she said, and this time she was quite evidently embarrassed, and her somewhat quickened speech and step betrayed it.

" I know. I passed it on purpose. I came to meet you. Will you turn back and walk a bit with me. I want to speak to you."

She seemed to hesitate, yet had no excuse for refusal.

" I should be getting home " she murmured confusedly. " This road doesn't lead to anywhere in particular. I've been at the last house in it, and there are only the fields beyond."

" Let us go to the fields, then. It won't be dark for another hour."

He had a kind of compelling force about him, and Margaret turned obediently, and began to retrace her steps.

" Your father is a very jolly, happy man, Miss Oswald. I quite enjoyed my talk with him. He is full of interesting stories and information about the places he has seen, but I think he is quite pleased with his Anchorage."

" Of course he is ! He is as proud as he can be of it, and I am happy about it, because he was really fretting when we lived in the town. He felt so shut in, and had nothing whatever to occupy himself with."

" Your mother, too, looks well and happy, and active for her age. They don't really need you there, Miss Oswald."

" Oh, but I think they do ! You have no idea what a busy, housewifely person I am ! I get up at six every morning, and do quite a lot of things before I leave the house at twenty minutes to eight."

" You lead a strenuous life," he said with a glance at the fair, sweet outline of her face. " Don't you ever get tired of going up to Bridgeton ? "

" Oh, never ! I've always been in business, you see, since I was sixteen ; and I'm fond of the girls. I take a lot of interest in them. You would be surprised what things they tell me, and what a little world full of tragedy and comedy my workroom is ! "

" I could believe that. It is sympathy you give them—the most precious thing in the world, and the rarest."

" It doesn't cost anything," answered Margaret blithely. " And I was born interested in folk."

" It's rather strange then—seeing the kind of woman you are—that you have never married," he said daringly.

Her face flushed naturally at the remark, though she did not resent it.

" There isn't anything strange about that, Mr. Cardine. It is not every woman, you know, who wants to get married. I've known quite a lot who never thought about it."

" But you could have been, I don't doubt."

" I'm thirty-five years of age," she answered unexpectedly, " and there are very few women of that age but have had an offer of some kind."

She smiled as she said that, because the absurdity of the turn the conversation had taken suddenly overpowered her. She could hardly believe that it was she—Margaret Oswald—that was walking in the Bearsden fields beside her master, discussing the reasons why she had remained single!

" But you haven't any deep-rooted objection to getting married—have you ? "

" Oh, no. Only I think it is a fairly hard way of getting a living—worse than the packing-room, in some instances."

" Ah, but if one is happy, that wouldn't matter."

" Perhaps not."

" You haven't taken any vow not to marry, then ? "

" Oh, no," answered Margaret, and her foot stumbled a little as she laid hold of the upper rail of the stile to which they had come. " Don't you think we should be getting back ? " she asked nervously. " Where are we, anyway ? This path goes on for miles and miles. I've never explored it really. I've never been farther than this——"

They both stood still at the stile, and there was no sound about them but the sighing of the March wind in a line of poplars near by, and the distant trill of a lark lost in the upper air.

" I came down this afternoon for a definite purpose, Miss Oswald," said James Cardine quietly, though there was something which thrilled in his voice and gripped the heart of the woman listening to him. " To ask you to marry me. Will you ? "

Margaret cast upon him a startled glance, almost a distressed one : yet in her heart of hearts she was neither startled nor distressed. She knew, now, that she had expected it, and that she had known the day would not close without bringing this strange crisis into her life.

" Oh, Mr. Cardine," she said quietly, " I am very much obliged. I'm even proud. But—but, it's quite impossible—quite ! "

" And why is it impossible ? " he asked, and, leaning his elbow on the rail, he looked intently into her face. " Is it I, myself, that is impossible ? Could you never bring your mind to entertain the idea of me as a husband, instead of a master ? "

" It is not that," she said, trying to speak naturally, and without the slightest trace of coquetry. " But you see, it wouldn't do—it would never do at all ! We wouldn't have a chance of happiness."

" Why not ? "

" Well, you see we are not the same. You are a rich man, moving in grand circles."

" In grand circles ! " he interrupted, and gave a little, mirthless laugh. " I don't know where they are. I'm a lonely man, without a home—that's what I am."

" And I'm a working woman," persisted Margaret steadily. " I would be quite unfitted for the position."

" I may be permitted to be the judge of that, surely. Any more objections ? "

" Yes—there is your family. She would be a brave woman who would go to the house in Huntley Gardens and upset them there ! I'm not brave enough for that, Mr. Cardine."

" I can understand that objection, but I think it can be swept away. I believe that my family would be very glad. Not one of the girls cares about the house or the responsibility it entails. They are everlastingly grumbling about it, and there is no real mistress. The servants are always either going or coming, and I never know when I may see a fresh face at the door. That sort of thing doesn't suit me, and I'm going to put an end to it."

Margaret continued to shake her head.

" I'm much obliged to you, Mr. Cardine ; but I couldn't do it."

A look of deep disappointment overspread his face.

" Miss Oswald, you know what my wife was ; you know, too, how happy we were—don't you ? "

" Yes, sir ; I know all that," she answered in a low voice, and turned away her head as if she would hide something from him.

" And I loved her to the day of her death. I love and revere her memory at this very moment. And I believe that she knows what is happening between us at this moment, and approves of it, because she knows the intolerable loneliness of my life."

Margaret gave a little start, but did not turn her head.

" I'm not pretending to that sort of love, because I believe it only comes once in the life of man or woman. But you were her friend, and you've been mine for ten years and more, and I know what a heart you have, and that a man could rely on you, and rest his life on yours, and be neither disappointed nor ashamed. That is the kind of woman a man wants in his home, and, if you will come to me, I will promise to do what I can to make you happy, and to care for you to the end of your life—so help me, God ! "

Margaret walked away a few steps, and he did not follow her. Perhaps he understood.

When she came back, he saw that she had been weeping.

" Mr. Cardine," she said—and a very sweet note had crept into her always kind voice—" I won't deny that it is a temptation. I won't hide from you that I've had my dreams of a home of my own. I would like—I would like to help, and—and comfort you, but honestly, I'm afraid of your children. I'm a strong, capable woman in some respects, but there are things—there are things—that would take the heart clean out of me, and that would be one—to have your sons and daughters say I came in and broke up their home would break my heart. I can't do it. I'm afraid ! "

" But if—if I could smooth the way—make it easy, assure you of a welcome—you would come ? " he said eagerly, and leaned towards her.

" I might think of it then. But I don't see that there is the faintest chance of that. I hear now and again about your daughters, Mr. Cardine, and I know what an ordeal it would be for any woman to go in there among them. Neither she nor you would have a chance of happiness. It would only be complicating your life, and tapping fresh sources of misery."

" But, at least, there would not be the personal loneliness, there would be somebody that understood," he put in quickly.

" There might be that. But I question whether it would be worth while. Wouldn't it be better to have a good talk with your daughters and try to point out to them that you are disappointed ? "

" When a man has to do that it's practically all up, Miss Oswald. Happiness that has to be explained and bartered for, as it were, has no real existence."

" And that's true, too," she admitted. " What about Miss Bruar ? Wouldn't she give up her house and go to Huntley Gardens ? I've often thought it would be a splendid arrangement."

" I asked her this morning, and she refused."

" So you really don't want to marry ? " she said, with a little humorous upturn of the lips, which seemed suddenly to bring her girlhood back. " It's just somebody to manage for you, you want ? "

He answered with a perfect candour.

" That was what I thought till I went into your room on Thursday morning. Then, when I saw you, something else was born—I don't know what—the desire for personal happiness, for somebody who cared. And it is that that brought me here to-day. It is hard to go away disappointed."

"There are plenty of ladies in your own class who would not be frightened," she suggested. But the words came more slowly.

"I won't ask any of them. It is you I want, Margaret Oswald, because I know what you are. You are the only woman I would ask to fill my wife's place, and, if you refuse me, I will go on, as well as I can, in the old way."

For the first time she suffered her eyes to meet his. Then, quite suddenly and simply, she laid her hand on his, where it rested on the bar of the stile.

"If you can get them to receive me kindly, I'll come. I care enough for that."

CHAPTER IV

BELLA ON THE SCENT

NEXT day was Sunday—a day on which James Cardine usually saw more of the family than on week-days. They breakfasted at nine, and in the mother's lifetime had been in the habit of attending together at the nearest parish church.

They dropped in, one by one, as usual, to the breakfast-room, and by half-past nine, when the head of the house had all he wanted, the table was complete. But he did not leave them to finish by themselves, because, quite suddenly, individually and collectively, they presented an entirely new aspect to the father—they were possible enemies !

He had but to open his mouth, tell them that he was going to bring a new mistress to Huntley Gardens, and what might not ensue ? Even he quailed a little at the thought presented to his mind.

" Anybody for church this morning ? " he asked, when Bella dropped in last to her chair. " An Edinburgh man preaching to-day—Doctor Weddell. I think I'll go."

" I'm going," said Harry, when nobody answered. " It's about time you were turning in, for your sins, B. How long since you darkened a kirk door—eh ? "

" That sort of thing hardly counts in life, now," observed Bella tartly. " The Churches are losing their hold, and they don't even try to find out why ! I could tell them——"

" Tell me, instead," suggested Jean, looking narrowly across her eyeglass, with a good deal of quiet scorn, at her sister's rather nippy face.

" They don't strike the note of modernity," asserted Bella calmly. " They go on in the old way, preaching to babes and sucklings, and the new generation has grown up—that's all—and wants something more and better than spoonmeat."

Cardine had heard much of the same empty chatter before, and had sometimes smiled at it ; but, for some reason or other, it nettled and vexed him that morning.

" They preach the old Gospel which has served to keep men and women in the right way for generations before you were born, my lass," he said quite gravely, and, at this new note, four pairs of astonished eyes instantly turned on his face. In Bella's there was a furtive watching gleam of which her father's new self-consciousness was fully aware.

" Going to have an illness, Father ? Sure thing ! You'd better ring up Dr. Lumgair."

" I'll have an illness of the mind, if I hear much more of this sort of thing, lass," her father answered, a note of sternness accentuating the gravity of his tone. " Maybe you think it smart, but it's all of a piece with the rest of things. There isn't a bit of sincerity, or depth, or feeling for others, in what you call your modernity, and the sooner it's swept off the face of the earth the better ! "

Bella gave a cackle, Jean bent her eyes on her plate, slightly disconcerted, for their father's anger was rare, and she did not like it. Nancy, unafraid, moved her chair a little, and snuggled her hand under the tablecloth to his knee. His fingers closed over it with a small convulsive touch, of which the child was quite conscious.

" Dear Daddy," she said in a low voice. " Don't mind them. It doesn't matter anything, not a single thing—it's nothing but words."

It was not often Nancy joined in the critical, censorious remarks so frequently indulged in, regarding most things under heaven, and even, on occasion, of heaven itself, which they affected to regard as a wholly mythical place. She was a sweet, wholesome little thing, with all a pretty girl's love of life, and a desire for adventure in the fields of love, which sometimes disquieted her Aunt Mary Bruar, and made the mystery of her sister's untimely death more insoluble than ever. For if ever girl-child needed a mother it was Nancy Cardine, and her sisters had neither the understanding nor the wisdom to guide her. They were blind guides, and had wandered, themselves, far enough from the path wherein the heart of woman finds happiness and peace.

Over Cardine's troubled face stole a ray of light, and he smiled into the big, innocent, trustful eyes.

"I'm glad to hear you say that, Nancy. But we've had more than enough, of late, of this kind of talk."

"Votes for Weemin!" drawled Harry, as he spread on the marmalade with lavish hand. There was a merry twinkle in the glance he shot at Jean, who preserved a dignified silence for a brief space. When she did speak her tone was acrid.

"A concrete example of the density and prejudice of men," she said then. "Everything that just doesn't agree with all their antediluvian ideas—which, incidentally, mean complete exaltation of themselves—is marked down under that head."

Then the fun waxed fast and furious, but Cardine took no part in it. The expression of his face indicated that he was remembering past Sunday mornings in his life, when the atmosphere had been different!

Bella, easily the sharpest and most observant of the four, was seriously exercised regarding this sudden change in front on her father's part, and connecting it with Aunt Mary Bruar's remarks a day or two back, began to wonder what was happening.

Cardine, increasingly and uncomfortably conscious of that watchful scrutiny, presently rose from the table, pushed back his chair, and left the room.

A little later, Mr. Cardine and Harry sallied forth to attend morning service.

Conscious of something different about his father, but not connecting it in any way with the random words uttered by Bella, the lad tried to be cheerful and attentive. He really had an immense affection and admiration for his father, born partly of the opportunities he had of seeing him in the world of men. And he hated to see him look dull and vexed, as he had looked during the last weeks.

"It would do Jean and Bella a lot of good if they could get married, Father," he suggested. "All that is on the surface."

"I doubt it, lad. Women have changed—are changing every day; and unless you are very careful, you won't have much chance of happiness—the kind of happiness I had with your mother," he added, with rather a painful note in his voice. "My advice to you is to look out for one of the old-fashioned sort."

"I'm going to," said the lad, and had his father not been so completely absorbed by his own thoughts, he might have seen how the sensitive colour rose in Harry's face.

Just at that time the Cardine family were more or less in the melting-pot, and the next few weeks were to prove to the uttermost the stuff of which they were made.

James Cardine gave but a detached attention to the preacher that morning, and the sight of his sister-in-law, Mary Bruar, in the pew, sent his thoughts in another direction. What would Mary Bruar be likely to say? Whose side would she be on? She had a strong and vivid personality and exercised a good deal of quiet influence over her nieces. It was important, he knew, to get Mary on his side. He decided that, perhaps that very evening, he would take a walk round to Caddam Square and talk it over with her. But first he must pay another visit to Bearsden in order to make sure that it had all happened and that Margaret Oswald was prepared to stand to her word.

He did not know whether he felt any happier in the knowledge that she was willing to marry him. Certainly he had a stupendous ordeal in front, from which many a stronger man has shrunk.

In the old days it was certainly less of an ordeal. Then a man was absolute head of his house, and, as husband and father, his word was law, which nobody ever dreamt of disputing, however unjust and unfair it might be. But the old order had changed, and youth, with all its splendid selfishness and cruelty, was now leading the van.

A heavier meal than usual was partaken of by the Cardine household on Sundays, and, following the immemorial custom in middle-class families, there was an abundant evening supper of cold viands to which anybody the young folks liked to ask was welcome.

The heavy midday meal made them all disinclined for exercise, and usually Cardine retired to the library and had a good sleep on the deep leather settee, while the girls yawned and read and drowsed in the drawing-room.

On that Sunday, however, both Jean and Nancy went out of the house before three, and Bella was left to her own meditations.

She was sitting at the window, idly watching the dull street, when she heard the front door close, and, to her astonishment, saw her father emerge. He was smartly dressed in a new spring overcoat, and a tall hat, and walked away briskly from the door, as if he had quite a definite object in view.

This was so unusual that she was filled with astonishment, and went off in search of Harry. But, apparently, she was in sole possession of the house, and her curiosity and ennui made her so restless that she began to wonder what she could do to pass the interval till tea-time, which was not until five o'clock on Sunday afternoons. Finally, she decided that she would go out to Bearsden and see a friend who had been at the Hanover *pension* with her, and who had lately married and gone to live in a splendid new mansion, in the planning and building of which Bella had helped to advise.

There was no particular reason why she should go to Bearsden on that Sunday afternoon. Things happen like that in life, leading one almost to conclude that they are all part and parcel of some concerted plan or game in which human beings are mere puppets.

Bella, a very trim figure in her neat spring suit and fox furs, arrived at Bearsden soon after four, but, to her chagrin, found her friends not at home.

"They've only gone for a walk, Miss Cardine," the maid assured her. "And they're coming back to tea."

"Oh, well; I'll wait," said Bella, much relieved, and entered the pretty hall, whose design and equipment were of the very latest Glasgow school of decoration.

Punctually at half-past four Mr. and Mrs. Gavin Halliday returned, together with a couple of fox-terriers at their heels, looking very fit and healthy, and well pleased with themselves.

A very good-looking and well-matched pair they were, and Bella, in spite of all her cynicism and worldly wisdom secretly envied Nora Halliday her happy lot and her handsome, devoted husband.

They welcomed her warmly.

"Now this is most awfully good of you—isn't it, Guy?" said the bride, as she kissed her old friend, and said how glad she was to see her. "Whatever put it into your head?"

"I don't know. I took it all of a sudden. You, see, for some unexplained reason, the family seemed all to have important engagements this afternoon. Jean and Nance went out before three, and Father soon after, and nobody ever knows where Harry goes of a Sunday."

"Well, that's funny, Bella, because we've just met your father—haven't we, Guy?"

"My father!" cried Bella with a small squeak in her voice. "In the name of goodness where?"

"In the fields—walking with a lady, too!" said Mrs. Halliday.

Halliday himself went out of the room at the moment. Struck by Bella's odd silence, the bride approached her side.

"What is it, Bella? Why do you look like that?"

"You're sure, then? You didn't make any mistake? It was Father, Nora?"

"Why, of course! We said how-do-you-do. He seemed very fit and jolly. He was enjoying himself, Bella."

"But who was the woman?"

"I don't know. Haven't you any friends out here besides us?"

Bella shook her head.

"None that I know of. Tell me what she looked like—every single thing about her that you can remember?"

"There was nothing striking. She wore a blue serge coat and skirt—quite well cut, for I noticed it, as they passed. She wasn't quite young—over thirty, I should say. A very pleasant face, not exactly pretty, but nice, you know the sort of face you trust without knowing why."

" I wonder now—I wonder who it could be ! " cried Bella, and her brows narrowed, her chin became just a trifle peaky, her lips hard and thin.

Her tone and look were so significant, that Mrs. Halliday hesistatingly put a question.

" You're not—you're not thinking it could be a love affair with your father, Bella, surely ? "

Bella nodded vigorously.

" That's just what I'm not sure about, Nora. I've my suspicions. Bearsden ? —Bearsden, now who lives at Bearsden ? "

She kept on knitting her brows. Then a light seemed suddenly to dawn on her.

" I know ! Margaret Oswald ! Describe her again, Nora. Was she of decent height—not very slender, and had she most awfully pretty brown hair ? "

" I did notice her hair. Certainly, it shone like gold, under her hat. I mentioned it to Guy after we had passed them."

" It must be the same woman ! She's a forewoman at Bridgeton. Good heavens, Nora ! Don't you see what's going to happen to us ? We're to have a stepmother ! A common woman from the factory ! A forewoman in the packing-room ! It can't have any other meaning."

Mrs. Halliday looked appropriately interested and excited.

" Oh, but, Bella—Mr. Cardine never would ! Why everybody says he's a very proud, exclusive man ! He is the last man to do that sort of thing. It simply couldn't happen."

" But I tell you it's going to happen ! I feel it in my bones ! I've been feeling it for very nearly a week back. He's been grumbling most frightfully of late, and leading poor Jean an awful dance. That's the preliminary canter—don't you know ? —when an old man is going to make a fool of himself he starts on the grumbling line so as to furnish the necessary excuse."

" Your father isn't that sort, I'm sure. And he doesn't look old at all. Guy just remarked on his splendid looks after they had passed."

" How did he look when he saw you ? Had he a sort of caught expression ? For, of course, he must have known that you would tell me you had seen him."

" He looked very happy. They were both smiling before they saw us. But I hope it isn't true, all the same, really, Bella. It would be horrid for you all ! Especially a woman like that, though I must say she looked very nice, and not at all common. I hope you've made a mistake."

" No mistake, you may take it from me. Don't say anything to Guy. I can't discuss it just yet ! " said Bella hastily as the maid opened the door to bring in tea. " I haven't got over the shock. Talk about other things, and give me a little time to recover—there's a good girl."

Mrs. Halliday, sympathetic and fully understanding, did her best, and there was plenty of chatter over the teacups ; and Bella recovered herself sufficiently to take an interest in all her friend's new household arrangements.

She stayed, perhaps another hour, with her friends, and, when she left the house, if she had known in what direction her father's property in Bearsden lay, she would have taken a walk that way. But she did not know, and when she arrived at the station she found she had about twenty minutes to wait for the train.

Walking up and down the platform, chewing the cud of angry reflection, living, in anticipation, the scene with her father, if it should all be true, the moments sped quickly enough.

As the last signal dropped, two figures came through the doorway from the booking office—her father and Margaret Oswald. She shrank back as far as she could, and from behind a tall shrub watched them where they stood talking animatedly. Her soul was filled with an unholy rage, as she stood, a silent witness to the evident understanding between them, the tender, protecting air with which her father regarded Margaret Oswald, and the sweetness of the face upturned to his.

Nothing appealed to her womanly instincts. The idea that a man could ever feel the need of a close personal sympathy, the need of love, at her father's time of life, would only have filled her with immeasurable scorn. A sort of bitter glee mingled with her other emotions, at the reflection that she had caught them so neatly ! She held back of a set purpose until the train was in, and her father had taken his seat in a first-class compartment. Then she pushed forward, passed by Margaret, and opened the door.

There were two other passengers in the compartment besides her father. It was, therefore, impossible for them to speak a private word. Their eyes met as Bella moved swiftly to her seat.

Under the veiled mockery in those of his daughter's, Cardine's fell, and his face uneasily flushed as he lifted his hat gravely to the woman standing on the platform who had not seen Bella's face, or recognized her. The doors banged, and, the next moment, they were off.

CHAPTER V

BREAKING IT

THERE are several different kinds of silence. Most of them speak louder than words, and are more baffling.

Somehow, though he had no positive grounds for his supposition, James Cardine was aware, as he sat opposite his second daughter in the train, making the short journey from Bearsden to the city, that she actively disapproved of him.

The other passengers journeyed all the way with them, and when they alighted at the Central Station still Bella did not speak. A remark made by her father about the weather, and the number of people travelling on Sunday, was met by the same stony silence.

Slowly, but quite perceptibly, Cardine's choler began to rise.

"Wait till I get a cab," he said briefly and sternly, at the station gates, but Bella merely shook her head swiftly, and sped from his side into the throng of the street.

He entered the cab alone, and reached home in front of her to find no one there. It was only half-past seven, and supper was not until an hour later. Glancing into the dining-room he beheld the table already spread with the customary abundance of cold viands, which could be eaten at any time, and for which the attendance of no servant was required.

As he came out of the dining-room another cab rattled up to the door, and presently Bella rang the bell. Her father opened the door to her, said briefly "Come in here," and led the way to the library.

"Now then," he said shortly and sternly, "I'd like to know what's the matter with you, Isabel, and for what reason you imagine you have the right to behave so rudely?"

"You hardly need to ask," she said then, and her tone left nothing to the imagination. "It isn't a pleasant thing to be told that one's father was out roaming in the fields with—with a woman of that kind, on a Sunday afternoon, for anybody to see."

"I require you to speak with a little more respect of the lady I am going to marry," said Cardine, finding it difficult with that small hard, scowling face in front of him, to speak with the dignity and authority he could have desired. He would have liked to shake her on the spot, to tell her, in no uncertain voice, to go to her own room until she was ready to beg his pardon. But, in the twentieth century, with a grown-up daughter, these things are not done. Instead, men and fathers and brothers have to listen to their strictures, and digest them, too, as seems good in their sight!

"The lady you are going to marry!" she flung back the words in scorn to him. "God forgive you for an old fool!"

It was unpardonable—it was revolting—no nice-minded girl would have hurled such words at her father. But they summed up the entire situation as it appeared in the eyes of Bella Cardine. Never had she spoken with greater force or courage. And her hard eyes did not quail before the anger in his. Whatever she said, she was willing and brave enough to stand by, though her knowledge of the world was too limited to enable her to judge the possible consequences at the moment.

"If that is all you have to say to me," said Cardine, and though his tone was quiet and dignified, he was made subtly conscious of its utter futility, "we needn't go on talking here. In fact, it is a matter I won't discuss with you. Later, when your brother and sisters come in, I will lay the matter before them. You have already put yourself outside the pale."

He turned from her, and walked out, took his hat and coat from the cloakroom, and left the house.

The scene for which Bella had primed herself had been brief enough, and all she had learned was the indisputable fact. But in the meantime it sufficed, and Bella, lashing herself into fresh fury, waited with an impatience she could hardly curb, for the moment when they should all return, and she could floor them with her information, throw the precious bomb at their feet.

It would be a bomb and no mistake! For two more unsuspicious persons than Jean and Nancy did not exist in the world. Bella told herself that she was the only person with open eyes, and, further, the only one really capable of dealing with the situation. She enrolled herself on the spot as the general of the campaign about to be waged, which, she hoped, would have the effect of turning her father from his disastrous purpose.

Bella was not heart-sick, nor sorry. No sentimental regrets, or genuine sorrow over a mother supplanted, surged in her soul. It was all purely material, selfish, an appeal and response to the side of her nature which loved strife and dissension. Like a war-horse, scenting battle, she made ready for the fray. Of its disastrous and far-reaching consequences she did not dream.

She summed up the whole situation thus: Their father was about to make a fool of himself. It was their bounden duty, as a family, to prevent him, in their own interests, and also in his.

Cardine, breathing a trifle heavily, for the short scene with Bella had been rather poignant, and such as a man of his temperament could not but feel acutely, made a bee-line for the house of Aunt Mary Bruar.

He was in the mood, if need be, to proclaim his decision and intention to the entire world, and he would himself tell the sister of his late wife, so that no second-hand or prejudiced version should reach her. It was not less his duty than his pleasure, and, at the back of his mind, was the dim hope that she might stand by him. But he could not be sure. There seemed to be no surety in women now.

When he had buried the dear companion of his life, four years ago, she had carried something with her which would never be regained—that heart's grace, that big motherliness which makes for the healing of the nations.

Was there any of that left among women? Was the new age to be hard, merciless, and cold? Where were the mothers of the sons to be? He could not picture Bella with a baby at her breast, her small, narrow face, her cold, clear eyes, her sharp tongue, all melted to tenderness before the love which transforms the world.

His thoughts of the woman who had promised to share the remnant of his life with him had altered in a hour's space. He could not ask her to face his house as it was, or subject her to the daily torment of Bella's hostility.

Torn this way and that, he arrived at his sister-in-law's door.

The order of the Sunday evening life there never altered. Kirsteen went out—her mistress stayed in, guarded by faithful Fidra, the little Scotch terrier. Together they took care of the house. Mary Bruar was never dull. She had her books, her letters to write, all the little satisfying occupations with which the woman of quiet leisure and quiet tastes could fill up her time. She, at least, had no desire for clamour, or the clash of words. Peace was dear to her soul. She had discernment, however, and some inner consciousness assured her that a crisis was approaching in the household at Huntley Gardens, where so much of her dearest interest lay.

She was glad, therefore, when she heard Cardine's step and ring, and she had the warmest welcome for him. She gathered, from his looks, that he was disturbed in mind, and she drew him into the warm cosiness of her little dining-room, and pulled forward the most comfortable chair, and told him to get out his pipe.

"By and by, Mary Bruar," he said, with a slight melancholy smile. "Maybe, when you hear what I'm going to tell you, you'll not ask me to smoke again by your fireside, or even bid me come across your doorstep."

"It'll have to be something very bad, then, James," she answered readily, though her heart-beat quickened.

"Oh, I daresay you can guess. I'm thinking of marrying again."

He brought out the words with a kind of jerk, but his eyes did not quail. Hers did, as she braced herself for what might come.

"Sit down, my man," she said a trifle unsteadily. "And tell me all about it."

He shook his head, leaned against the edge of the table, and looked keenly and a little wistfully at her, as she seated herself with a little tremor, in her chair by the fire.

" I hardly know how it came about, Mary. It seemed to happen all of a sudden-like. You remember I was in here, Thursday morning, on my way to Bridgeton ? "

" Fine I mind it. I went out to Huntley soon after, not easy in my mind, and had a word with the girls."

" Well, that morning though the idea of marrying had occurred to me, and I even spoke to you about it, I had nobody in my mind, nor any serious intention of doing it. About half-past ten I went into the packing-room to speak to Margaret Oswald. And, when I saw her, I knew she was the woman I wanted to marry, and yesterday I went out to Bearsden and asked her."

" Margaret Oswald ! " repeated Mary Bruar in a low voice. She's a very decent, fine woman, James, but you cannot expect your daughters to like it."

" They don't—at least, the only one that knows as yet, and that's Bella. But let me get on with my story."

" Yes, your story ? You went out to Bearsden, and asked Miss Oswald. And what did she say ? "

" Refused me, point blank, at the first. And after I had talked to her for a while, she said she would only come if my bairns would welcome her. I don't think they will. That is, if I'm to take Bella as a specimen. And I've come to see what you are going to do about it, Mary Bruar, for you count for a lot in all our lives."

Mary Bruar did not answer for several minutes. Her kind, tired eyes were on the fire, her heart was bowed down with innumerable thoughts. She was not angry, but an ineffable sadness seemed to surround and encompass her. And once more she felt inclined to question the dealing of the Almighty, who had seen fit to take away a woman whose price was above rubies, and without whom a home was going to pieces !

" Of course there is trouble ahead," she said at last. " What I would like to know is whether it is worth it ? "

Her tone was so reasonable and kindly that it gave him an amazing courage. Here was somebody he could talk to, and explain the situation, even touch upon his innermost feelings without fear of being misunderstood.

" I think it will be worth it," he answered quietly, as he seated himself on the edge of the table. " You don't need me to tell you that I won't forget Isabel, nor ever will forget her. We were happier than most, and I believe—I believe that I made her a good husband."

" The very best ! " Mary Bruar hastened to say, and dashed away a tear. " She told me, the day before she died, that she had been a very happy woman, and her whole concern was for you, James, and her cry about your loneliness. She seemed to know that you were dependent on her, and that you would miss her more than any of them."

" That is exactly what has happened. It is the want of someone to speak to when my day's work is done, the certainty that I'll find nobody ready to listen to what I have to say—it's—it's just everything, Mary Bruar ! You're the most understanding woman, next to Isabel, I've ever come across, and, though you've never been married, a man can speak out plainly to you, without fear of being misunderstood. I'm only fifty-one. I may live another twenty or even thirty, years—the Cardines are a long-lived race—and frankly, I can't face it alone."

" There is no reason why you should. But—but I'm not sure but that you might have found somebody more suitable than Margaret Oswald. She'll stick in their gizzards, James, for you've brought them up to have plenty of pride."

" They did not get it from me, nor from their mother," he protested. " It's just born of the circumstances of their lives. I know what Margaret Oswald is. She is the right kind of woman to make a man happy—she's another Isabel."

If Mary Bruar secretly winced at this she made no sign.

" She is sensible, she is kind, and she has plenty of brains. She will never make a fool of me," Cardine went on.

" But the west-end of Glasgow is getting stiffer every day, James, and, just lately, the girls have got in with a new lot of folk."

" It may stiffen into stone before it affects me, my dear ! Well, now that we have thrashed it out, are you going to turn your back on me, on the head of this ? "

She lifted her head, smiled at him, and held out her hand.

" That would very ill become me, for you've been more than a brother to me, James Cardine. I must say frankly, that I wish it had not happened, but if you are willing to face the consequences, well—surely the least I can do is to stand by you. And I will."

Cardine was conscious of a swift strong wave of emotion, which made words impossible for a moment. He grasped the proffered hand, and bent his head to it till his lips touched it.

" Thank you, Mary Bruar! From Isabel's sister, that means a lot. It is almost as if she had bidden me God-speed herself."

Mary Bruar drew her hand away in rather a quick shamefaced manner, for they were not emotional folk, and the moment was an awkward one.

" Now, having got through that, what's the next move? Are you going to tell the assembled multitude to-night?"

" I am, and I'll go back now and do it."

" You wait here, till I put my bonnet on."

" You would come, Mary Bruar! My patience, but you are a brick!"

" If I'm to stand by, now's the time," she flashed back brightly as she pushed away her hair. " I'll tell you what—it's Alec's wife I'm afraid of. I suppose he did well for himself, in a sense, when he married a Whitehorn, but she carries a very high head! The lassies have not been the better of Evelyn Whitehorn, James."

" She needn't count; she's not in the house."

" Every little counts, and she can egg them on. But we'll see. I'm trusting a lot to Jean's common sense, and, of course, a kind word will win Nancy. If it was only Nancy, there would be nothing to fear."

Mary Bruar donned her long sealskin coat, and they set out. The sky was star-gemmed above them as they walked, and, though the air had an undoubted nip, it was ideal for walking.

" Are you thinking of an early marriage?" asked Mary, as they moved out of the seclusion of Caddam Square.

" We haven't made any plans. It was only yesterday the question was put, Mary. Neither of us has got accustomed to the idea yet. But there is no reason for putting off, that I can see."

" She will have a difficult place to fill," went on Mary. " But, as you say, she is a fine, sensible woman, and won't expect too much. I'll go and see her to-morrow, if I don't write to her to-night. But, first, you've got to get this ploy over. There was none of them in the house but Bella, you said, when you left it?"

" Nobody. But they'll all be in for supper now, I don't doubt."

They were, and the meal had begun, when the excited, talking quartette heard the latchkey being fitted in the door.

Bella was holding forth in her shrill, piping treble when the dining-room door opened, and their father, accompanied by Aunt Mary Bruar, who had left her coat on one of the hall chairs, quietly entered.

" Evening, all of you!" said she. " You seem to be making a bit of a noise. Get me a chair, Harry. I'm ready for a snack, and I'm sure your father is."

" We didn't wait, Father," said Jean, with an odd, furtive glance in Cardine's direction, " because we hadn't an idea when you would come back."

" When I mean to be out for meals I generally say so, I think," observed Cardine drily. " But it's a matter of no consequence. What can I offer you, Aunt Mary?"

In these guarded courtesies the meal progressed to an awkward close, and the only remarks that had any semblance of naturalness were those made by Aunt Mary Bruar.

Bella therefore concluded that she knew nothing about what was impending. Of the four, Harry looked the most miserable. Mostly he kept his eyes on his plate, and took no part whatever in the slight conversation there was. All were relieved when the meal came to an end, and Cardine, who had eaten very sparingly, pushed back his chair.

" I'll be much obliged if you will all come to the library for a minute or two," he said formally. " I've got something to say to you."

It might have been comic, if it had not been a little pathetic, to observe the small procession cross the hall and step down the passage towards the library. Jean and Bella held their heads high, but Nancy was plainly weeping. The things Bella had already said had seared her soul.

When they all were in Cardine closed the door.

" I have only to tell you bairns that I have made up my mind to marry again. I don't propose to go into the reasons that have brought about this. The lady I am going to marry is Miss Margaret Oswald. You all know her. I only ask you to give her—and, incidentally, me—a fair chance. If it is possible to live at peace, we shall do it. I will do my duty. I look to you to do yours."

It was an odd, jerky appeal, and, in the background, Mary Bruar almost smiled at it. But it was no easy job, with those four hostile young faces in front, with the knowledge of what they held in their hands.

There was a moment's tense silence. It was broken by Bella, who turned to her Aunt:

" May I ask what you think of this—this arrangement, Aunt Mary ? " she asked shrilly. " Has it your sanction and approval ? "

" That is neither here nor there, Bella," answered Aunt Mary. " All I have to say is—and I've come here for the purpose of saying it—you have had a good father, who has worked hard for you, and lavished everything on you, and it is open to you now to show that you are grateful. He has a perfect right to please himself. His reasons for taking another wife are sufficient."

" What are they ? " inquired Bella, and high scorn was in her face.

Nancy opened her blue eyes wide, Jean gripped the back of the chair, Harry looked down on the floor.

" I will answer that question as well as it's possible to answer it," put in Cardine sternly. " I don't admit that I am obliged to endure a court martial here. I want a little comfort in the house. I need a home. I haven't had one since your mother died. We need somebody to keep us together, as a family."

" And we are to have a factory hand ! " quoth Bella rudely. " Nice, happy prospect ! Well—I, for one, won't stand it."

" Then you can do the other thing," her father answered. " Understand, that neither Miss Oswald nor I wish any change. We don't want any of you to leave the house. I will arrange my affairs so that you will each have an increased allowance, and will have to ask for nothing. Everything that is just and right I will do, and nobody will be interfered with."

" That's what you say, Father, but what about her ? " put in Jean, speaking for the first time.

Though she had said nothing she was not less acutely affected, and her pride was hurt. Likewise, she realized, though she would not have admitted it, that the failure to make a home was partly hers. Bit by bit she had been drawn into the vortex of Movements and Causes, Meetings and Committees, till the care of her father's house—left in her hands by her mother—had been mainly relegated to servants and to the vagaries of tradespeople.

" She will wish to live at peace, I know. At this moment you have it in your power to make or mar the happiness of a good many lives. Think well how you are going to act. For certain things done can never be undone. Hard words are easy to speak, but they leave their mark. That, I think, is all I have to say, except that the marriage will take place in the month of May."

He waited, and, when nobody spoke, he turned about quietly and left the room. So far, the hostility had been felt, rather than expressed.

But, at the closing of the door, the storm broke in earnest, and it was Aunt Mary Bruar who had to bear the brunt of it.

" Aunt Mary ! " cried Bella shrilly, " you spoke a minute ago as if you were on his side—as if you even approved of this monstrous thing ! Do you think it decent that a woman of that class should be foisted on us in our mother's place ? "

" Don't speak like that, Bella ! " said the little, old lady sharply. " It can do no earthly good, and it hurts everybody."

" The truth generally hurts," said Bella tartly. " But we're out for truth—aren't we, Jean ? We aren't children. We are quite capable of facing the facts of existence. We're up against them anyway, seeing that in little more than a month we shall be homeless."

The stupid remark filled Mary Bruar with righteous wrath.

"Well, then, if you are out for the truth I'll give you a little. If you had taken the smallest trouble—any one of you—to follow in your mother's steps, and keep your father's house together, and look after him, and be at hand when he was lonely and sad, this might not have happened. If there is any blame, tack it on to the right folk. But there is no blame. The root-causes of this thing are beyond your handling, and the sooner you recognize it the better. Your father is not an old man, he has a long life in front of him, and is it likely that he is going to hang it on to your whims and fancies? There isn't one of you to be depended on an inch farther than you can be seen! That's the 'truth' then! Your father has a perfect right to please himself, and, though your mother was all my own I had on the earth, I'll be kind to the woman he is going to put in her place out of gratitude for what he was to my sister, and because—because I'm heart-sick and sorry for him, so there!"

This amazing and unexpected outburst quelled them for a minute.

"Good old Aunt Mary Bruar!" murmured Harry, with a queer, quivering smile, and crept out of the room.

CHAPTER VI

BELLA ON THE SCENT

ANOTHER pair of hostile and surprised eyes had watched James Cardine and Margaret Oswald parting at Bearsden Station, and when Margaret stepped out to the quiet road again she found Bruce Gemmill waiting for her.

She looked annoyed, for she had never liked the man, nor had she forgiven him for the gibe he had flung at her a few days before, when she declined his invitation to accompany him to the theatre.

He seemed humble enough, however, as he raised his hat and stood in the way so that she could not pass him without some sort of recognition.

" Good evening, Miss O.," he said, and somehow the abbreviation of her name, which Margaret had never liked, struck with a particularly jarring note on the ear attuned to something more courteous and appealing. " I've come to make my peace. I own I had a good cheek to speak as I did the other day—even if it was true. I had no business to say it."

" Then, as it's past," she said a trifle stiffly, " why go back on it ? "

" Well, because I don't want to cast out with you, or, more properly, you to cast out with me," he said eagerly. " In fact, it's a thing that just can't be ! Can I walk back a bit with you and come in and see your folk ? "

It was not the first time that Bruce Gemmill had dropped in at the Anchorage on a Sunday evening, where he had been made quite welcome by the captain, and had often shared their evening meal. Margaret had no valid reason for refusing, though she had never liked the man's visits, and had resented, with all the force of her quiet nature, his very obvious, and often clumsy attempts to win her favour.

" You can come back, I suppose, if you want to. Father and Mother will be pleased to see you," she said unwillingly.

" But you won't—eh, Miss O. ? "

" I wish you wouldn't call me that ridiculous, horrid name ! Why can't you say it properly ? I won't answer if you say it again."

The petulant note, so unlike Margaret's usual reserve, seemed to tickle Bruce Gemmill's fancy, and he laughed.

" Beg pardon ! Won't offend again, Miss Oswald. A fine night, isn't it ? It's clearer out here than in Glasgow. Well, then, may I come to the Anchorage ? "

" I can't prevent you if you want to come," again she answered unwillingly, beginning to move along the road.

It was only a short distance between the Anchorage and the station, but Gemmill intended to make the most of it. He had come out to Bearsden with a set purpose, and though the sight of James Cardine being seen into the train by Margaret was sufficiently disquieting, he did not attach any serious meaning to it. He meant to clear it up, however, and proceeded to attempt it in the clumsiest possible way known to him.

As he glanced with an open admiration and longing at the clear profile of her face, he wanted desperately just to ask her point blank whether there was any personal element in their employer's visit to Bearsden, but something warned him he had better not.

Gemmill was a Glasgow man, and he had the history of Glasgow folks pretty well at his finger-ends. He knew all about the Cardine family—including some figments of imagination which would have surprised nobody more than the Cardines themselves; trading on the assumption that knowledge is power, Gemmill was one of those unpleasant persons who may always be trusted to call up disagreeable truths, or untruths, about people, on the shortest notice. He was a male gossip-monger, of whom there are more in the world than is usually imagined, and before whose embroideries of facts the feebler traffic of the feminine tea-table is as water unto wine.

"It's a very fine night," he repeated experimentally. "It's a positive shame to go in yet. Won't you take a turn with me up the road till supper-time, as you are kind enough to invite me to supper?"

Margaret did not remember that she had done so, but did not cavil at the words. She merely said that she would not walk any farther, but must take a straight cut home.

"You've got terrible grudging, all of a sudden, Miss O.—I beg pardon, Miss Oswald. Do you mind that lovely walk we had over the braes, last October? I've never forgotten it."

"Oh, that's ancient history," she said with a faint smile. Then, suddenly she changed the subject. "We'll be kept very busy in the next six weeks with Sampsons' order. I hope we'll be able to get it through in the time. My lassies are all quite keen. They really work splendidly!"

"It's folk like you and me that build up fortunes for the Cardines and others like them to spend," said Gemmill, "Capital and labour all over again! Things are moving, though, and there's going to be a grand adjustment soon."

"And where will you be when it is over?" asked Margaret.

"Oh, somewhere near the top, you may be sure! I would not be feared to try my mettle against any Cardine that ever lived. The boss is not so bad, but take Alexander. What does he know about the industry that supplies Mrs. A.'s Paris frocks? And he's not even ornamental. It is well for him that he had a father! Harry's not that bad for a youngster. He is shaping well enough, though he has a bad habit of prying in where he isn't wanted. But if the like of us had our chance, where would they be? Just nowhere! I'm looking for a decent partnership. I've saved a tidy bit, but I've never been a spender. I'm hoping that somebody is interested. You must know, Margaret—may I call you Maggie?—that it's all being saved up for you. Just name the day and we'll be as happy as twa doos in a doocot—to use a very auld simile that's hard to beat."

He laid a hand on her arm, but Margaret drew back, almost in horror.

"No, no! I've told you before, Mr. Gemmill. I can't think why you won't take a telling. I can't marry you! I never would, if there was nobody else in the world! I'm obliged to speak like that, for, apparently, no other kind of speaking has any effect on you."

"I believe that faint heart never won fair lady," he answered gallantly. "And a man who takes a woman's 'no' at the first time of asking is a poor fool! They aye say no when they mean yes. I want to tell you all about my little investments, Maggie, and to show you that you would be upsides with any Cardine among them."

"I don't want to hear about your investments nor anything else," said Margaret desperately. "Why won't you take your answer like a man? I don't care for you, and I can't marry you, and unless you leave off talking about it I won't walk another step with you."

By this time she had worked herself into a kind of mild passion. For over six months the man had pestered her with his attentions, assuming, and hinting to others, that all was well between them; and it was pretty generally believed that a match would come off between them sooner or later.

Nothing Margaret could say or do had repulsed him, and even yet, he seemed incredulous, until his eyes met something in her eyes, a look of personal antipathy which no man, not even the densest, could mistake.

"It's just as I said," he observed sullenly. "You're hoping to hook the governor. But you won't. He'll never marry again. There are private reasons why he can't. Trust the quiet psalm-singing, church-going kind! A bird in the hand, my dear, is worth two in the bush. You had better tak' tent in time, or you'll be left permanently on the shelf!"

He had not the slightest ground for these atrocious innuendoes, but the manufacture of scandal, the blackening of private character, was his trade, at which he was much more efficient than at his legitimate business for which he was paid.

Margaret's blood ran a little cold as she listened, and, though her loyalty was not shaken, she realized what power for evil this man could be in a censorious world.

"I'm not going to talk another single word with you, Mr. Gemmill. You don't deserve it. And I wonder you are not afraid to say such vile things about innocent people! You'll be had up for libel one of these days, that's what will happen to you, and you'll have nobody to blame but yourself. I've often warned you."

He laughed disagreeably.

"I'm taking the risks! You may take it from me, Miss O., there are pages in most lives that are the better of being glued down. Our boss is no exception to the rule. But I don't want to make trouble. You may take it from me, however, that if he ever contemplates a second marriage, which, indeed, he would be a fool to do with such a crew in Huntley Gardens, there would be—well, to put it quite plainly—the devil to pay. Well, after all that, and begging your pardon if I've offended you, can I come and see your father? I'd uncommonly like to."

He laughed at the blank stare on her face.

"I'm not thin-skinned, thank the Lord! It doesn't pay in this world to which we are condemned for our sins, and I won't offend again—till the next time! But, oh, woman, I want you badly! I'm not going to pretend, at my age, that I've not had other affairs. A man who doesn't know something about women at forty, is a poor fool! But this is the real thing, and I would work hard for you, my dear, and try to give you just everything you could want in this world. I would even build a house for you, out here, near the Anchorage. I have my eyes on the very site!"

He spoke now with considerable passion, expressing feeling more sincere and deep than Margaret had credited him with. But she merely shook her head and quickened her steps.

So they came to the gate of the Anchorage, and as Gemmill set it wide, he looked at Margaret Oswald with a sudden access of respect, such as comes to men who have thought that all women want to get married, and who, one fine day, are confronted with the fact that their assumption has been too sweeping. He fancied himself hugely, and had no doubt, even yet, but that he would be able to persuade her to listen to his suit.

Both the captain and his wife looked surprised when Margaret brought another man into the house.

"That sounds like Gemmill's voice, Susan," he observed facetiously to his wife. "Oor Margit's going it!"

Margaret did not follow Gemmill into the sitting-room, but permitted him to make his own announcement. When she came downstairs, she went into the kitchen where her mother was getting some extra dainty out of the larder to put on the supper-table.

"Mother, I'm sorry I had to bring that man back. I can't abide him. I met him outside the station and he simply glued himself on to me. But I don't want him here. Do you?"

"Well, my dear, I canna say I'm that terrible keen on him, but he amuses your father," said Mrs. Oswald, smiling a little as she arranged the parsley round the meat on the dish.

"I wish he had never come here. I was trying to remember how it happened he came at the beginning, but, of course, he just called without invitation, and has gone on calling on Sundays ever since."

"Of course, it is you he comes for, Maggie, suggested the mother, as she crossed her hands above her black silk apron, and lifted her quiet kind eyes to her daughter's disturbed face.

"It is, and that is why I hate it so much, for I've told him I won't have anything to do with him, ever! I told him, long before I ever thought there would be anything with Mr. Cardine——"

Mrs. Oswald's face delicately flushed.

"Then there is something wi' him? I was afraid of it, but I never said a haet to your faither, for, you know, men can't hold their tongues."

At another time, Margaret would have relished this quaint controversion of usually accepted facts, but she merely answered quietly:—

"Oh, yes! I'm going to marry him, Mother, in less than six weeks' time."

"Oh, my dear! My lassie!" said Mrs. Oswald, and laid a somewhat unsteady hand on Margaret's now trembling arm. " Ye are not feared ! He has a lot of bairns—hasn't he ?—all grown up. Are ye not feared ? "

" No—I'll do my best," she answered steadily. And then added : " And God will help me, I'm sure."

It was so unusual for such words to fall from Margaret's reticent lips that the discerning mother knew that the thing must have gone very deep.

" That is how you feel about the man, Maggie ? You would go through fire and water for him ? "

" Yes, Mother, that is just how I feel."

" Then you'll do it, my dear ; and, as ye say, the Lord will help ye," said Mrs. Oswald, and the tears were raining down her cheeks.

" Say you are pleased, Mother, and that you like him ? " pleaded Margaret humbly, eagerly as a child.

" Why, of course. Who could help liking a fine man like that? It's not him I'm feared for, I've heard how happy he made his first wife. But the stepmother's road is a hard road to travel, Maggie. I ken, for I was brocht up by a stepmother."

" I'll do my duty and try to win them," faltered Margaret.

" I am sure ye will. Are we to tell Faither yet ? "

" Not for a day or two."

" But, if the marriage is to be so soon, ye will not be bidin' on at the Bridgeton ? "

" He wanted me to stop off at once, but I will go back, at least for this week. He is telling his family to-night—and his sister-in-law, Miss Bruar. He seems as anxious about her as about any of them, because she has a lot of influence with them at Huntley Gardens."

" Ah, well ! Ah, well ! " said Mrs. Oswald, shaking her head and drying her eyes. " You deserve happiness in this world, Maggie, if ever woman did. For there are not mony like ye. Now we had better go ben."

" Go and bathe your eyes, Mother. Anybody could see you have been greetin' ! I'll set on the rest of the supper for that man—though I could see him far enough ! "

Nevertheless, her face was perfectly serene as she bore the cold chicken into the dining-room, and set it on the table.

Gemmill and her father were already deep in talk, and the pipes were lit. Gemmill had a way with him—a kind of hail-fellow-well-met style, which specially appealed to a man of the captain's temperament, and he was a prime favourite with the head of the Anchorage.

The meal passed off quite comfortably, though the conversation was almost entirely sustained by the two men. Quite well satisfied with themselves, however, they did not notice any of the unusual silence of the women-folk, and when they had risen from an excellent supper the pipes were lit again, and Margaret went off to the kitchen to help her mother wash up, as the little servant always went home on Sundays, and was never missed.

CHAPTER VII

THE "IN-LAWS"

MARY BRUAR did nothing by halves. Finding that it was more difficult to write a letter to Margaret Oswald than she had anticipated, though she spent a good hour in the attempt after she got back to her own house on that eventful Sunday evening, she made the journey out to the factory at Bridgeton the following afternoon.

Making her way into the inner precincts of the business offices, she found Alexander in his father's room alone.

Bella and he resembled each other in looks ; he had not the father's fine figure nor open, frank face. A smallish man, with a thin, rather shrewd face, he possessed the business faculty without that charm of manner and appearance which does so much to forward business projects successfully.

Cardine had already found his younger son a more valuable asset in that direction, and looked forward to the day when Harry should take his place as a junior partner.

Alexander's astonishment at sight of his aunt was evidently keen.

"Hulloa, Aunt Mary Bruar! What brings you here—eh? The general stramash at home? I suppose you've heard?"

"Oh, yes; I've heard, Alexander. That is why I am here. How are Evey and the children to-day?"

"The kids are all right, but Evey's on the warpath with the rest. She's gone over to Huntley Gardens this morning."

"When did you hear? Did your father tell you?"

"No; he left us to hear it over the telephone from the girls. Evey's pretty wild about that, I can tell you!"

"Evey would be upset, no doubt—a good deal less upsets her," observed Mary Bruar a trifle drily. "But I hope you'll keep her from going to too great lengths. At a time like this it is very easy to say things that can never be forgotten, and which bear bitter fruit in days to come."

Alexander looked at his aunt uneasily. He had a great respect for her, but his wife's antipathy to Mary Bruar made it difficult for him even to seem to agree with anything she might say. He had not sufficient courage to have opinions of his own, except in business, where he was keen to the verge of unscrupulousness.

"Of course, we are surprised, as a family, that you should be taking Father's side," he began in a conciliatory voice.

Mary quickly held up a deprecating finger.

"All the sides we take won't prevent what is going to happen. And I've lived long enough in the world to have proved that the line of least resistance, except in matters of principle or conscience, is the best for most folks."

"One would think you had forgotten your only sister—that's what Evey says——"

"I'm not needing to hear what Evey says, my man! She hasn't the right to say anything, because it doesn't affect her. And what you should do is to go home and tell her to hold her tongue. But I don't suppose you'll do that."

"No," answered Alexander with a somewhat slow grin; "I'm not likely to do that."

"Then I will tell her, not that it will do any good, but outsiders should abstain from adding fuel to the flame in family matters. I'm all for peace, and that is why I'm here this morning. I'm going up the lift presently to see Miss Oswald."

"And fall on her neck, I suppose!" said Alexander with a slight sneer. "I must say it seems to me a bit superfluous. And you don't seem to understand what a state the girls are in. They never slept a wink all night, and Nancy has had hysterics."

"Which she wouldn't have had if she had been let alone. I saw that last night. I could have shaken that Bella, and the very best thing she can do is to leave the house and earn her own living! It would teach her what she has never yet known—the value of her father's home."

"I believe she'll do it. Both Jean and she are talking that way."

"It's mere froth! Neither of them would have the courage," said Aunt Mary Bruar stoutly.

"I believe Evey will try to put them off that tack. Naturally she wouldn't like it, and all the Whitehorns would be up in arms."

Aunt Mary Bruar smiled a slight inscrutable smile as she rose to her feet.

"You take it from me, Alexander—you're all on the wrong tack. Your father has the right to please himself. Your mother made him happy while she lived, and it is the same kind of happiness he is craving now. I believe Margaret Oswald is the woman to give it to him. And I'm going up the stairs now to tell her that, so now you know just where your Aunt Mary Bruar is!"

With that she tripped out of the room, for, indeed, to argue with or try to convince Alexander Cardine was a perfectly futile task. He was but the pale reflection of his wife's opinions, and although Mary had intended to discuss the matter with Evey she had not the smallest hope of doing any good.

She was quite familiar with the interior of the factory, and most of the older officials knew her. She found the packing-room without difficulty.

When Margaret saw Miss Bruar, she coloured violently. Seeing this, Mary did her utmost to set her at her ease.

"I must apologise for intruding in business hours, Miss Oswald," she said, with her gay little smile. "What a lot of girls! Surely the packing-room has grown bigger since I was in it before?"

"The work in it has almost doubled," said Margaret, as she returned the kind hand-clasp. "And two years ago this end bit was taken in. There are seventy in this room, and twenty-eight in the side room."

"Dear me; then your hands are full enough! Can you leave the girls for a few minutes?"

"Oh, yes. They don't need such close watching as all that," answered Margaret, as she led the way to her own little sanctum.

When they were both inside and the door shut, Mary Bruar looked at the changing face of the woman in front of her, and said quite simply:

"My dear, my brother has told me, and I've lost no time in coming to say that, so far as I am concerned, you will be made welcome, and whatever a first wife's sister can do to smooth the path for you will be done, and that right cheerfully."

Margaret's eyes filled with tears, and Mary Bruar, laying her little hand on her shoulder, gave her a kiss, and continued:

"He might easily have made a choice that would have been more difficult to welcome, for I don't forget that my sister knew and loved you."

Margaret flushed again, and her lips moved as if to speak. But it was not until long after, when they had both been through many deeps together, that Mary Bruar learned what had been on her lips that day.

"Now, let us sit down and talk it over. You won't have an easy time nor a soft bed, my dear, for they're all on the warpath!"

"Are they?" asked Margaret faintly.

"Every one of them," answered Mary cheerfully. "But you'll not be discouraged. A little time and patience and you'll win them yet."

"Ah, but I'm afraid, Miss Bruar! Who am I to bring such dispeace into a family? It would not be right. And I told Mr. Cardine that unless they are prepared to welcome me I would not marry him."

"Then, my dear, you might just as well have said 'No' at once, for I question whether you would find in the whole of Glasgow, or in the world, a family who would perform such a magnanimous feat! Don't you expect it! Just make the best of what it is, and go in and try to win them."

The sweet assurance that a person so beloved and so important as Miss Mary

Bruar had entered into combination with her, was an immense comfort and strength to Margaret Oswald, and gilded the rest of the day for her.

But though Mary had done her duty, she was not less heavy-hearted than she had been as she wended her way from Bridgeton back to her own haunts. She could not help asking herself what effect the hostile and difficult atmosphere might have on Margaret Oswald, who, though naturally sweet-tempered and wholesome-natured, might have the other side of her character brought into being by opposition and prejudice and active resentment.

Mary foresaw dark days for her brother-in-law and his family, and asked herself, with a little wistful sigh, whether the small amount of personal happiness James Cardine might reasonably expect to get out of a second marriage was likely to be worth the price which would inevitably have to be paid. It was little she or anybody could do to smooth the thorny path. For youth is high-handed, relentless, oft-times cruel.

CHAPTER VIII

MAN AND WIFE

CONSTERNATION and speculation were rife at the Bridgeton factory when, one morning two weeks later, a new superintendent appeared in the packing-room, to be initiated by Miss Oswald into the duties of the place.

Bruce Gemmill, who had heard of it in the course of the morning, made it his business, at the dinner-hour, to seek out Margaret to ask whether she was actually leaving. He found her alone, eating her modest luncheon of sandwiches and coffee in her room, the successor having gone out to a substantial meal at a restaurant. Margaret did not look by any means pleased to see him, and he was quick to remark upon it.

"I suppose the new woman has but one meaning," he remarked gloomily. "You're leaving?"

"Yes," she answered quietly, "I'm leaving."

"What's the reason? Are you going to get married—or what?"

She hesitated a moment, coloured angrily, and then, reflecting that the secret could not be kept much longer, she answered in the same steady voice:

"Yes, I'm going to be married."

"To the boss?"

She nodded and turned her head away, while she bent over the fireplace to see whether her coffee had warmed sufficiently.

"Imphm!" observed Gemmill with his sourest look. "Well, I suppose you expect our congratulations?"

"I neither expect nor desire yours," she answered spiritedly.

"But it's more likely commiseration you'll need before you're through with it, Miss O.! No doubt you think you're doing a mighty fine thing for yourself, but——"

"I don't want to discuss it with you, if you please, Mr. Gemmill," she said rather proudly.

He shrugged his shoulders.

"Getting on your high horse already! Well, since you're so mighty civil, I'll not inflict myself on you any longer, but you'll not have your sorrows to seek—in Huntley Gardens—more, and different kinds of sorrow than you've ever imagined! You would have done better for yourself to have been content with the villa on the hill at Bearsden, a humbler, but, maybe, a better man, was willing to build for you."

Margaret's expression became so strongly forbidding that he began to move towards the door.

"I wonder that a good woman like you, who poses for all that's saintly-like, would be the means of breaking up a whole house. It's all over the west end already, and, they say, the second daughter is negotiating for a milliner's shop near Charing Cross. But I've no doubt it is easy to reconcile yourself to such things when one's own nest is to be feathered! Don't think I blame you. It's the way of the world; only, you see, you had led us to believe that you were a cut above it. Nevertheless, I wish you well, and all the happiness you think you are likely to get out of such an arrangement."

With that he took himself off.

Now, though Margaret both heartily disliked and despised the man, his words had power both to wound and to rankle. She had, on Mary Bruar's advice, written to all the Cardines, and had not, so far, received an answer from one of them. Harry had spoken a few awkward words to her the first time they met face to face after his father had broken the news, and since then they had been quite good friends, and it had been commented on how often Master Harry slipped through the packing-room to Miss Oswald's sanctum in the last week.

She was sitting before her rapidly cooling coffee, when she saw another figure through the glass screen coming up the long room—a figure she recognized at once. It was Cardine, who had met Gemmill at the door.

"That was Gemmill, wasn't it?" he asked the moment he stepped inside the glass door. "What was he doing here?"

Margaret did not immediately answer.

"He came to speak to me. I suppose he got into a habit of dropping in here at the dinner-hour, for which reason I've sometimes gone out."

"What did he say to-day? Something that has vexed you, I could take my affidavit!"

"Well, he did. But, please, don't ask," pleaded Margaret, trying her hardest to smile, and failing rather miserably.

"But, I just will ask, Margaret! I've the right to know. I don't like the man, and never have, in spite of his ability. He's a low down sort of chap. What did he say to you?"

"Of course, he was surprised and curious about Miss Richardson, and asked me, point blank, whether I was going to be married."

"And what did you say?"

"I said yes."

"And what after that?"

"He asked whether it was to you, and I answered yes, too; for I think it is well enough known, somehow, in the place. I can tell it on their faces."

"Well, and what did he say after that?" said Cardine, persistently.

"Oh, the usual things folk do say in such a case! Warnings, chiefly, about the stepmother's lot. Don't let us think about Bruce Gemmill. One of the things that makes me glad to leave the factory is that I needn't ever see him again."

"He's been making love to you, then?"

"After a fashion, I suppose, he has. But don't let us speak about him."

James Cardine looked daggers, but Margaret's kind warning smile restored him.

"If people would only mind their own business!" he fumed.

"He told me that your second daughter is actually negotiating for business premises at Charing Cross. Is it true?" she asked then.

Cardine shook his head.

"I don't know, I'm sure. And, at the present moment, I am not minding much. Let them have their fling. I suppose none of them has answered your letters?"

She shook her head.

"Never mind, my woman! You'll win them yet, I believe. Well, now we've settled the date, where shall we go afterwards? Would you like a trip to London, or to Paris?"

"I don't mind, I'm sure," she answered, as she turned away. "What would you like to do?"

"Personally, I should like to go to Ardgoil."

"Oh, yes, let us go there!" she cried eagerly. "I have never forgotten the one week-end I spent there. Do let us go there!"

He was surprised at the warmth and eagerness with which she spoke.

"Very well, my dear. It shall be Ardgoil. We can go south later, if we find that a little change would benefit us, or would be advisable."

"And we needn't stop long out of Glasgow, need we?" she asked wistfully. "Now that it is coming so near, I seem to want it to be all over, and to know just exactly where I stand."

"You wouldn't come out to Huntley Gardens one day, and see them?"

She shook her head, and appeared to shrink from the thought.

The family life in the Cardine household was now pretty intolerable—meals a species of nightmare, during which either there was no conversation at all, or a kind of wordy warfare, which gave the girls an opportunity of displaying their skill in snapping at one another.

Cardine, a man of peace, hated it all, and was intensely miserable.

That day he made one more attempt to arrive at a more amicable understanding with his family. For this purpose he went home earlier than usual, and was fortunate in finding all his daughters at home in the drawing-room. Two carriages at the door indicated that they had callers. He put down his coat and hat, and, without a moment's hesitation, ascended the stairs to the large fine room which had been the scene of a good many happy social gatherings, but which, of late, he had not entered very often.

They were all there—his son's wife, also; and the way in which she suddenly came to a standstill in her rapid talk, indicated that he had been the subject of it.

As he strode across the space from the door, Cardine was intensely conscious of the quick and actively disapproving hostility of at least five pairs of eyes. The sixth pair belonged to an oldish woman—Mrs. Dinwoodie, a friend of his late wife—and they were distinctly more kindly.

She rose up as Mr. Cardine entered, and they met at the narrow end of the long room where, if voices were lowered, it was quite possible to carry on a conversation inaudible to the people at the other end.

"Don't go, just because I happen to come in, Mrs. Dinwoodie," he said. "We haven't met for a long time."

"No, we haven't," she answered, and something in her face made him walk with her to the door, and out to the landing.

Cardine closed the door, and Mrs. Dinwoodie, from the flap of her little handbag, took out a small visiting card, and offered it for his inspection. On it was printed:

"THE MISSES CARDINE—AT HOME."

and down in the corner, the letters "P.P.C." which, Cardine knew, were used on cards indicating farewell.

"I think it would have been better if you had prevented this afternoon, Mr. Cardine," she said, with a kind, straight glance. "The whole of Hillhead, and a large part of Kelvinside and Dowanhill, have been here this afternoon, and the cackle has been tremendous!"

"You may take it from me, I didn't know anything about it," said Cardine tensely. "Surely it was in the worst of taste!"

"It was. The whole thing is a pity, I'm sure; and it would have been better—both Robert and I think—if you had tholed the widower's life. After all, there are worse sorrows than death."

She passed out with that, without speaking a word of heartening to a man who was craving for it. She was one of the late wife's intimate friends, and he could see that while not actively hostile, like his daughters, she was coldly disapproving. He saw her into her carriage without another word, and once more ascended the stairs. He met the last caller as he ascended, and she passed him with the briefest nod.

His face set rather sternly. He proceeded to the drawing room and opened the door, taking care to close it behind him. At the far end of the room, grouped about the tea-table, were his three daughters and his son's wife, who, however, had risen, and was beginning to adjust her sables.

Holding the piece of cardboard he had retained from Mrs. Dinwoodie in his hand, Cardine approached them, and, without other greeting, asked curtly:—

"Who is responsible for this?"

For a second or so nobody spoke. At last, Mrs. Alexander, with a slight uplift of her head, made an answer:

"Well, since you ask, Mr. Cardine, it was my suggestion. It is better to get disagreeable things over all at once, so to speak!"

"And you thought it necessary, and apparently decent, to proclaim the state of this household to the entire west end of Glasgow?" asked Cardine in his voice of ominous quiet.

"No proclamation was necessary," she answered coldly. "Unfortunately, these unpleasant facts are always better known and with fuller details to outsiders than to the family circle they immediately and disastrously affect. We heard a good deal this afternoon—didn't we, girls?"

"Yes," answered Jean dully, while Bella's lips curved in a small, inscrutable, mocking smile.

Cardine preferred not to ask what they had heard. The cackle of west-end Glasgow did not so much concern him at the moment as the attitude of the women before him. He looked again at the card.

"The letters indicate a good-bye, I understand. Does it mean, then, that you are all going to leave your father's house, and that you, Evelyn, aid and abet them in this disobedience and folly?"

Evelyn shrugged her shoulders.

"You will find that the sympathy of most people is with them, Mr. Cardine, and that, if they do leave the house, nobody will blame them."

"And what, may I ask, do they intend to do when they have left it?"

They looked from one to the other, and again nobody spoke. Nancy's face had paled a little, and her small hands were working nervously on the folds of her pretty afternoon frock. She was such a childish, pretty creature, with curls of gold set closely about her head, defying all attempts to keep them in order, yet infinitely becoming to her features. Nancy was just eighteen, but looked young for her years.

"I was told to-day that you, Bella, had taken, or were about to take, some business premises. Is that true?"

"It is quite true."

"And may I inquire who has become surety for the rent, and who is going to lay down the money to start you?"

No answer.

"And where do you propose to go, Jean?"

"Oh, I expect to get a secretarial post; I'm negotiating for it now!"

"And Nancy?"

"Nancy will find a home at Greenbank in the meantime," put in Mrs. Alexander's cool, clear voice.

She looked as if she was immensely enjoying the scene, which had become far the most poignant that had yet taken place.

Mr. Cardine drew himself up, partly turned his back on his daughter-in-law as if he did not recognize her interference or right to hear anything discussed, and addressed himself to his daughters.

"I am going to be married on the 28th at Bearsden. Your brother Harry has promised to be there. I suppose I need not expect any of you?"

"Certainly not!" Bella made haste to answer.

"Think better of it. It would not cost you so very much. I give you another chance. I have used every argument of kindness and consideration I can think of, and Miss Oswald has far exceeded anything that could possibly be expected of her. Are you all finally decided that your present attitude is to continue?"

"You leave us no choice!" Bella hastened to say.

"Then listen to me. This house is your home to which you are all welcome so long as you offer me and my wife the ordinary courtesies of life. Further, you will have a hundred pounds a year each, for your own use and spending, and nobody will ask you what you have done with it. Further, I and the woman who has been good enough to promise to undertake this difficult business, will do our utmost to make the home happy and comfortable. But we can't without your co-operation. Will you co-operate? If you persist in leaving the house, you will be allowed to leave it, unhindered by me. But think well what you are doing, for I will give no allowance, nor help you to make homes elsewhere. And that is my last word."

He looked at them wistfully, yearningly, for a moment, and, when no one spoke, and the stony silence once more descended like a pall between them, he turned on his heel and left the room.

A week from that day the marriage took place at the Anchorage, at Bearsden, the only members of the family present being Cardine's younger son and Miss Mary Bruar.

. . . .

It was a lovely evening when the boat, bearing the newly married couple among the passengers, entered Rothesay Bay.

Mr. Cardine was well-known on the island, of course, having possessed one of the most desirable properties there for the last fifteen years. There were several smiles and salutations as they stepped off the boat and walked along Craigmore Pier.

The two horses and the carriage had been sent down for the week, which had occasioned further talk and chagrin at Huntley Gardens.

The new wife, in her long, well-fitting sealskin coat, her bridegroom's gift, had an expression of mingled happiness and anxiety on her face.

The final step had been taken, and, though the presence of Harry and Aunt Mary Bruar had helped considerably, her thought of the trio at Huntley Gardens lay, like a pall, over everything. That morning they had astonished their father by appearing at the breakfast-table in black frocks, unrelieved by so much as a white collar. That was Bella's idea; Bella, who prided herself on her originality! Cardine, however, had not taken any notice; having made the final appeal, he had closed the doors of his heart meantime, and of his purse.

He had not taken very seriously their threat to leave the house. He could not believe their folly would go so far. Because, unless they had some extraordinary, and quite unusual, stroke of good luck, their little flutter in the labour world was not likely to be permanent. As for Nancy becoming an inmate of the house at Greenbank, Cardine merely smiled at the thought. Evelyn was not the woman to make a third person very happy, or to be put out of her ordinary way unless something was to be gained by it.

As the carriage swept in through the open gateway of Ardgoil, Margaret could not repress a little exclamation of admiration. The high rhododendron banks were in full and exquisite bloom, every imaginable variety of spring flower brightened the borders, and vied with one another to bid her welcome. In that sheltered nook, where no adverse wind could blow, Nature had a chance to flaunt her gayest colours early, and a perfect pageant was spread before the delighted eyes of the new mistress of Ardgoil.

The house was usually left in charge of the gardener and his wife, who lived in the kitchen premises. Christina Rogers had been a kitchen-maid in Huntley Gardens before her marriage, and knew all about the Cardines. She was an excellent cook, and a very trig, tidy woman, generally smiling, and ready to welcome any of the family from Glasgow. But, as she came out to the front door, at the sound of the carriage wheels her face wore an odd, rather nervous expression. She had heard, from some of the servants at Huntley Gardens, regarding the upheaval about to take place in the family, and her master's letter, briefly instructing her to prepare for him and his wife on a certain date, had put her into a tremendous flutter.

"How do you do, Christina?" he said in his most friendly voice. "This is Mrs. Cardine. I hope you have made the house comfortable for her. It is cool in the evening here, even when the days are fine and warm."

"Yes, sir; everything's ready, I think," answered Christina, and, when her eyes met Margaret's, she smiled in spite of herself, for there was kindness and truth in these eyes, and even something which appealed.

"Thank you," said Margaret gratefully, as she held out her hand. "I am glad to make your acquaintance, Mrs. Rogers, and I am sure that I shall be comfortable in this beautiful place."

Cardine turned away, relieved, and said he would go round to the stables and have a look at the greenhouses.

"I did not open up the drawing-room, ma'am, as I got no orders, and I knew the maister likes the wee parlour best. It has such a lovely view. You see, he got the trees cuttit doon, just in front, so that he could see the sea. There's a fire in the dining-room, and one upstairs as well. I hope everything will be right."

"Thank you. I'm sure it will. I can go up now, I suppose? I believe you are quite alone here, but we shall not give much trouble, and, of course, I'm accustomed to help myself."

"Oh, that's a' richt!" answered Christina, with a prodigiously cheerful sigh of relief. "We'll get on fine. And, I must say, I like my kitchen to mysel'. When they come doon frae Huntley Gardens I canna ca' a thing ma ain! Of course, Wullie and me goes to the ludge when they come doon for the simmer."

Thus, garrulously talking, Christina made haste to show her new mistress to her rooms. She was agreeably surprised and pleased with her, and all day had been, in a sense, nervously on the defensive. But she knew now that they had told her a pack of lies in the Glasgow letters, and she was far too just and sensible a woman to permit her mind to remain prejudiced a moment longer than need be.

A little later she confided to the stolid-faced William that the new mistress "wad dae."

A very appetizing little meal had been prepared, and, when it was partaken of the newly made husband and wife entered the little smoking-room, and sat down to enjoy their first evening together.

"Let me do that," said Margaret, when she saw him get out his pipe. "I'm used to doing it for father, and I'm wondering whether I could pass muster with you."

She was smiling now, and looked so sweet and womanly in her pretty frock of grey silk, that Cardine drew her to him fondly.

"At least we'll have these few days' peace, my woman, and they'll make us strong for whatever may come."

She left her hand on his shoulder, and with a very sweet, serious look on her face, said in a low voice:

"I think I'd like to tell you something here, Jamie."

"Yes, my dear?"

"It is about her——" she said, as she bent her head lower, so that her chin rested on his hair. "Do you mind when I went to see her that last week when she was in the Nursing Home, and you found us together, and we were crying?"

Cardine said he remembered.

"She told me she knew she would not get better, and her thought was all for you, and of how lonely you would be. She seemed more afraid about you than any of them—except, perhaps, Nancy."

"Yes, my dear; and what then?"

"She said to me that if she had a wish it was that I might one day take her place. She told me that she loved me, and that she knew—she knew I had the gift of making happiness and caring for folk, and she asked me, if it ever came to pass—and, somehow, it was very queer, but she seemed to think it would—I was to remember that she wished it, and that she would know about it over There, and bless us both, and be glad about it."

Cardine was too deeply moved for speech.

"And I am so glad to come here," Margaret continued, "for this house belonged to her, and she often told me how much she loved it—that it was her real home. And I—I think she is here, to-night, in this very room, and, because of that, I'm taking a fresh vow to serve you and your bairns to the very end of my life."

CHAPTER IX

BEARDING THE LIONS

Before the week was out business letters began to filter through from Glasgow.

" I'm very sorry, my dear, but I'm afraid I'll need to go up to-day, and not only to Glasgow, but to Edinburgh," said Cardine, as he passed over a communication that had arrived by the morning post. " That's from Harry. Alexander and his wife have gone to London, and this man will have to be seen. Now, I wonder whether I can do it in a day ? " He took out the little time-table from his pocket, and, after studying it for a few brief moments, said, disappointedly —" I doubt I can't manage it. The very last boat sails from Gourock at six thirty-five, and, as it is, I can't possibly get to Edinburgh now before two o'clock. Even then, I may have to wait for the Australian. He's a big man, and, as I say, he must be seen."

" Why, of course," said Margaret, smiling across the table. " When does your boat leave this morning ? "

" Just missed one. Next, eleven o'clock."

" I'll walk in with you to the pier."

" But I don't like leaving you. And supposing I don't get back to-night ? Will you not come with me ? " he asked, as if a happy thought struck him.

" Oh, no. A business man doesn't want a woman tied to his coat-tails. I'll be all right—just fine, in fact. I can write some more letters and potter about the garden, and go out in the boat."

" You don't go in the boat without William—remember that," he warned her.

" All right, my man—though I'm not a bairn, and I was born at sea ! " she reminded him.

It was when she stood on Craigmore Pier, waving to the boat, becoming a rapidly decreasing speck on the shining water, that a sudden idea came to Margaret Cardine. Seven days they had been on the island, and, so far, not a line or a sign had come from Huntley Gardens.

Cardine himself had been able not only to throw off his depression, but most of his anxiety and responsibility concerning his daughters. Not so Margaret. She had brooded, more or less, on the coming ordeal and problem all the week. Why not get it over alone ? she asked herself, as she turned away from the receding smoke of the Gourock boat. It was as if the opportunity had been created for the occasion.

" When is the next boat ? " she asked the piermaster, with her friendly smile.

" Naething now worth your while till twelve thirty-five," he assured her.

" And after that ? "

" One forty-five."

" I'll try and get back for the twelve thirty-five if I can," she answered, as she thanked him and turned away.

What a triumph, supposing she should pay a visit to Huntley Gardens, see them all, and, in a sense, have it out. Then some sort of working basis for their lives could be established ! Even if she should fail, nothing would be lost. They would, at least, not be worse off than they were now.

She was fairly cheerful when she got out at Glasgow, and, after making pause to get a little lunch, took the Kelvinside car. It was a quarter to three, by the University clock, when she got out at Huntley Gardens, and walked up the hill to the house at the top.

Her heart beat quickly as she ascended the steps, and she paused half a moment before she pulled the bell.

Barbara Watson, whom pure curiosity had kept in the house after she had given Miss Cardine her notice, opened the door, after an interval which even a basement kitchen could hardly excuse. Her cap-streamers hung at a particularly aggressive angle when she faced the visitor.

"I wish to see Miss Cardine," said Margaret quietly. "Is she at home?"

"She's in the house," answered Barbara, rather favourably impressed by the looks of the caller, of whose identity she had not the smallest idea. "But my instructions was 'not at home.' She's packing up. I might just take your name. I can do that, though I'm not very sure if she will see you. Unless—" she added, a bright thought striking her, "unless you've anything to do with the Suffrage?"

Margaret smiled.

"I have nothing to do with the Suffrage, and I would rather not give my name. Just ask Miss Cardine, will you, whether she will be so kind as to give me a few moments of her time."

"I suppose I can say it's important business?" suggested Barbara, as she held the door wider, with an encouraging smile.

She had decided that she liked the lady, who was very well dressed, and she wondered who she was. Margaret nodded, stepped across the threshold of her new home, alone, for the first time, and, as the door closed, an indescribable quiet descended on her spirit.

She was put into the morning-room, or parlour, above the mantelpiece of which hung a large framed portrait of the first Mrs. Cardine. She stepped forward, to look more nearly at the sweet face, and it almost seemed to her that the kind eyes smiled steadily upon her. "Oh, my dear," she said, with a little sob, "I wonder whether you know, and whether you'll come and help me to-day?"

She was kept waiting about ten minutes, and, when the door opened at last, she was standing by the table, on which her hand was laid rather firmly, as if craving its support.

"Good afternoon," said Jean, with the casual indifference of the busy woman who meets a stranger for the first time.

She did not, at the moment, recognise Margaret, who had her back to the light. It was several years since she had seen her, and Jean's sight was a little treacherous at the best of times. She still wore her morning skirt and blouse, and her hair was a little awry. All these things Margaret did not fail to notice, though her principal concern was with the personality within.

"You don't know me, I think?" she said, in her steady, quiet voice. "I'm your father's wife."

Jean gave a great start, her face coloured violently, and she stepped back.

"Oh," she said confusedly. "But how does it come that you have arrived to-day? We did not expect you home till next week. Has anybody had a wire? You can see for yourself, there is nothing ready for you."

"I have not come to stay to-day," answered Margaret. "Your father had to go up on business, and has gone on to Edinburgh. The idea was mine. He does not even know I am here. I—I—came to see whether we might not—might not—arrive at some kind of understanding, so that he might be spared pain or discomfort later on."

The voice was very appealing, the eyes especially so; and Jean was momentarily shaken. After all, it might easily have been worse! She really looked very well—so quietly and nicely dressed, such good style, and, above all, so obviously unassuming.

"Perhaps I had better bring my sister. We—we do everything together," said Jean, stretching a point in her discomfort and anxiety to get away. She did not feel herself competent, single-handed, to deal with the situation. "Of course, you know we are leaving. Nancy has gone to London with our sister-in-law, and she will go straight to Greenbank with them when they come back."

"But why?" asked Margaret steadily.

"Oh—you know—of course, we simply can't stand it! But I'll fetch Bella. She can always express herself. I'm not good at it."

She made her escape, closed the door hastily, and got up the stairs two steps at a time.

"Bella!" she called out excitedly. "Come—come quick. Where are you? Who do you think has come?"

Bella, in her own room, with all her possessions scattered on the floor, and numerous trunks yawning about her, turned a bored and irritated face towards the door.

"Whoever it is, tell Barbara to chuck them out!" she said crossly. "And don't come bothering me."

"But we can't Bella! It's—it's Her!"

Bella, staring incredulously, climbed to her feet.

"You mean?—you mean the new Mrs. Cardine—in other words, our dear, delightful stepmother?"

"Yes."

"What does she want? I call it confounded cheek," said Bella springing to her feet. "Why didn't you just tell Barbara Watson to say we were not at home?"

"She didn't send in her name, and Barbara didn't know who she was. Besides, Bella, don't you see, she has a perfect right to come in? In fact, it's her home, now."

Bella's eyes ominously glared.

"I don't call it fair of father to let her steal a march on us like this. There isn't any dignity in it, to begin with," she said, moving to the mirror, to arrange the hair her packing exertions had slightly disturbed.

"She looks dignified enough," answered Jean, as she nervously wiped her eyeglasses. "But, the question is, what are we going to do?"

"I'll go down," said Bella determinedly, "and tell her, quite politely, but without any unnecessary embroidery, that if she'll only give us another night—or even a few more hours—she'll have the house to herself."

Margaret had not moved during the five minutes she had been left, and when she saw the sisters enter together she gripped the table a trifle more firmly, and sent up an inward prayer for strength to cope with this critical situation.

"Good afternoon, Mrs. Cardine," said Bella coolly. "I've just come down to say that as father did not choose to give us any intimation of your arrival nothing is ready for you. As a matter of fact, you were not expected until next week."

"He does not know I am here," answered Margaret quietly. "Please shut the door. I came of my own accord to-day, moved by an impulse which, I hoped, might be a happy one. Of course, I know that you have all threatened to leave the house, and I want to ask why. And to try whether things can't be arranged differently."

"We are leaving," said Bella coolly. "And there is no other arrangement possible. If you will give us a few more hours we shall be gone, stock, lock, and barrel."

"Where to?"

"That, surely, is our affair."

"Pardon me—it is also mine," said Margaret, still quietly, but without the slightest trace of hesitation or nervousness. "Although you gave me no answer to the letters I wrote to you about a month ago, I am ready to repeat what those letters contained. I am not coming here to make dispeace or to meddle with any of you."

"The dispeace is made already," retorted Bella tartly. "It was made when you got my father to ask you to marry him."

The insult, which was not even veiled, caused a flutter of the eyelids—that was all—on Margaret's face. But she passed it over in silence.

"We need not discuss that. Every word I said in those letters was true, and I am prepared to hold to it. I wish only to make your father happy, and I can't do it without your co-operation. He will be very unhappy, I am sure, if you all leave the house."

"He should have thought of that before the mischief was done," said Bella with the utmost coolness. "When a man of his age is guilty of such folly, he has to pay for it—that's all."

Margaret, inwardly indignant at the tone and the words, realized that, probably, they were mere aggravations, arising out of the crisis, and tried to smile at them.

"After all, your father is not an old man," she said suddenly. "And he has been a very good father to you. Even if you don't approve of his conduct"—here she smiled more broadly—"I think he deserves a little more consideration at your hands."

Bella shrugged her shoulders.

"The situation is quite plain. We are grown-up women, Mrs. Cardine, and we can't face the changed conditions in the house. We have not had anybody to interfere with us since we lost our dear mother. To begin with—we resent most awfully the idea of anybody being put in her place."

Margaret winced a little, and, to their surprise, turned her eyes for a second to the picture above the mantelpiece.

"We resent, naturally, the disrespect to her memory."

"Whose disrespect?" asked Margaret, a sharp note sounding through her voice for the first time.

"Why, his, of course, and yours," retorted Bella boldly. "I don't think, really, that we need prolong this disagreeable interview. Would you like to go over the house, or to see cook, or to interview Barbara Watson? Most of them have given notice, but their time isn't up till the first of June."

"I don't want to do any of these things until I come to stay," answered Margaret steadily. "Your father has gone to Edinburgh, and it was only after he had left that the idea occurred to me to come here alone, and see whether I couldn't do anything to mend matters."

There was a moment's silence then, and the three regarded one another with evident distrust, and a furtive anxiety. The two younger faces were forbidding enough in their expression—Bella's, especially, being hard and defiant.

Even before she made it, Margaret felt sure that her final appeal would fall to the ground.

"Won't you—won't you think better of it?" she said, with her most winning look. "I quite understand, in part at least, what you feel; but, I do assure you, I am not the kind of woman you imagine. I'm a builder—not a destroyer. And, if we only bear a little with one another, I'm sure we should get on quite well. Won't you wait, at least until we come home, and give me a trial?"

It cost something to make such an appeal, to speak humbly when a kind of natural anger was burning in the background. For these two young women, who had hardly ever done a serious hour's work in their lives, who dallied with the issues of life, and talked as if they were arbiters of fate—their own and others—who were at once her censors and her judges, had not the right to take up this attitude. Her husband had told her many things about his home-life which had filled her with a holy indignation, and she longed, woman-like, just for a moment to speak up to them, even as Aunt Mary Bruar sometimes spoke up, and tell them plainly what she thought. But, happily, she was better advised by her inner consciousness, and so kept to her quiet, womanly appeal.

"It wouldn't do any good," said Jean dully. "Besides, our minds are made up. I begin my work at the Institute next Monday."

She spoke the words quite proudly, and with an air of finality which, apparently, admitted of no dispute.

"It isn't the work I would mind, for, I'm sure, everybody who works is happier and better for it; but, why leave your father's house? You have every right to it."

"Or had," put in Bella significantly. But once more Margaret passed by the deliberate offence.

"It will make him very unhappy if you leave, and me also. Do think better of it, and give the new order of things a trial."

"I begin my work week after next," said Bella stonily. "My place of business will be out of the painter's hands next week. I am going to live at it, and my sister will live with me. As for Nancy she will divide her time between us and Greenbank—our brother's house."

Having thus proudly flung the whole programme in the stepmother's face, as it were, Bella glanced significantly at Jean, and added that they had better go.

"I've started to make an inventory of things in the house," said Jean then, "but, of course, I'm a busy woman, and if you'll let me know exactly what day you are coming, I'll try to have everything ready, and we shall have departed with our belongings."

They went out together, and left Margaret standing, either to go or stay as seemed good in her sight.

She departed. Her face wore an expression of acute disappointment and sadness as she rapidly descended the hill. She had made a stupendous effort, had put herself voluntarily and alone into a position from which a braver woman than she would have shrunk. And she had failed.

CHAPTER X

THE NEW RULE

MR. CARDINE did not get back to Rothesay until the last boat. The carriage was waiting at Craigmore Pier, but, somewhat to his disappointment, his wife was not on the pierhead.

She was waiting at the door for him, and at sight of the expression on her face all his qualms vanished. There was real welcome there, wifely and womanly joy, at the return of one who had been missed.

"What a thing it is to be met with a smile at the door!" he said, as he kissed her. "I do believe the want of that is the widower's lure."

She smiled back at him and hoped he had had a successful day.

"Very. And it was a good thing I went to Edinburgh, unwilling though I was! I've done a good bit of business through it. And what have you been about, my woman?"

"I've been to Glasgow. But I'll tell you about it later, Jamie—after you have had your dinner."

"All right, I'm in no hurry. I was thinking as we came across from Wemyss Bay, whether, if you didn't happen to care for Huntley Gardens, we couldn't stay all summer here?"

"But you would have to travel every day?" she said anxiously.

"Five days a week. But I could make them short days. If I slacken off a bit, it would give Harry a chance. By the by, I saw him to-day, and he's coming down to-morrow, for a week-end. Do you mind?"

"Mind? No! I'll be more than glad to see him," she answered with a confident smile.

"Now run and change your coat and shoes, for dinner is quite ready, and you must be needing it."

They enjoyed their homely meal together, and immediately it was over retired to the snuggery, where the air was so warm it was possible to leave the verandah window open, and see the moonlight on the Clyde.

"Now, I'm ready to hear an account of your day, my woman," he said with a sigh of infinite content, as he dropped into his favourite chair and took out his cigar case. He had had a long, tiring, exacting day, and the rest of home was sweet, the light on Margaret's face good to see.

She drew a low chair a little away, but just opposite, so that he could see her face.

"Well, after you went away this morning, I thought, all of a sudden, I would go to Glasgow, and go out to Huntley Gardens to see your daughters."

Cardine paused in his work of trimming his cigar and sat forward tensely.

"Well, and I'm not sure whether that was wise. Did you do it?"

"I did. I went up by the twelve thirty-five boat, and between two and three got to the house. I was shown into a little morning-room and, after a few minutes, Jean came."

"Ay," said Cardine drily. "And what did Jean say?"

"Nothing at all. She seemed frightened. She ran away, and brought in her sister."

"Well?"

"I can't remember every single word that passed, Jamie, but the visit was a failure as far as I was concerned, and it is quite true that they are packing up to go away."

"So Harry tells me. Well, then, lass, they must just go, that's all."

Margaret wrung her hands a little on her lap.

" You keep a calm sough, my dear, and don't bother your head too much. We have Harry on our side, and we'll get Nancy, or I'll know the reason why ! "

" Hadn't we better have Miss Bruar down to-morrow, too, if Harry is coming ? " suggested Margaret, after a minute or two. " It might be more comfortable for us all if she came."

It was a happy thought, and on the Sunday, when they had a delightful walk along the shore road, Margaret had an opportunity of getting to know Cardine's younger son better.

Harry was then in his twenty-second year, a fine, well-set-up youth, good-looking and very attractive, especially to women, with whom, however, he was shy. Margaret drew him out, and was greatly pleased with the lad, with his views on life generally, his clean, wholesome outlook, his manliness, and candour, and frankness.

" I think it's pretty rotten—the way they're going on at Huntley Gardens," he said a trifle shamefacedly. " When I told them I was coming down here, yesterday, you should have heard the jaw ! I don't believe you'll find anybody, when you go up. When are you going ? " he asked, with a somewhat shy glance at her kind face.

" To-morrow. Miss Bruar suggests that she and I should go up together in the afternoon. You and your father will go by the early boat."

" Oh, but—don't you and the pater want to go out together in style ? " he asked with a slight smile.

" No, it's the very thing we want to avoid ! " she said with an answering smile. " There's no occasion to make a fuss. I suppose your sisters told you of my visit on Friday ? "

Harry nodded.

" I heard all about it the moment I got home on Friday night, and probably a good deal more than actually happened ! But I say, you'll try and get back Nancy, won't you ? It doesn't matter about the others now."

" I'll get back Nancy," she answered. " It is what I'm going to start out to do, whenever I get home."

" I can't think why they should keep on being in such a wax. I said to them they might give you half a chance. I begged them, only yesterday at breakfast, to wait a few days at least. I told them you are a good sort—the sort a chap could take to—don't you know ?—without fear of being misunderstood."

Margaret's face was very sweet as she heard these kind words.

" And if a chap were in trouble, I'm nearly sure he could go to you, too—couldn't he ? "

" I've had a good many come to me with their troubles, both young men and women," she answered softly.

" That's what I thought. Well, don't be surprised if I come some day. I'll remember what you've said."

" I don't think you are the sort to get into trouble," she said, smiling into his face, but at the moment something flitted across it—an indefinable expression which caused her a moment's uneasiness.

" Oh, you're wrong, though ! It's the most unlikely folks that get themselves into tight corners. But a chap could tell you, I'm sure."

His face had flushed a little, and it almost seemed as if he were on the brink of some confession ; but, at the moment, as they turned a bend in the road, Cardine and Miss Bruar were waiting for them, to direct their attention to a very fine yacht bearing down on the bay from the Port Bannatyne direction.

Margaret told her husband a part of that little talk that night, but kept to herself the slight qualm which had flitted across her mind at the moment when she caught that particular expression on Harry's face.

" He's a good lad," said the father warmly. " He has never cost me a moment's anxiety. His mother's son, he is , and a general favourite with everybody ! I have no hesitation in calling him the pick of the bunch ! He won't marry in a hurry, you'll find. And Harry's wife will be somebody worth looking at, I don't doubt ! "

" She'll be a very happy woman that gets him," said Margaret.

But that night she dreamed of the boy—that together they were standing on a narrow plank amid seething waters, from which there seemed to be no escape.

That Sunday evening closed the brief respite from business and family worries which Mr. Cardine had permitted himself, and next morning, in accordance with the settled plan, he left Rothesay by an early boat with Harry, leaving the ladies to come together later. A telegram had been sent to Huntley Gardens, warning them to expect them to lunch, and Mary Bruar drove all the way with her new friend to the house in Huntley Gardens, and was on the doorstep with her when Barbara Watson, who had evidently dressed in a hurry, opened the door.

"Has Mr. Cardine come home yet, Barbara?" asked Mary Bruar in quite her ordinary voice.

"No, Miss Mary; not yet."

"Then I must introduce your new mistress," said Mary, who always said the right thing in the right place. "I hope you'll serve her well, and not be in a hurry to leave a good place. Are the young ladies in?"

Barbara, who had heard very good accounts of the new mistress from Christina Rogers, murmured something which nobody could catch. She had had her own fling on the subject of the new mistress, and had only stayed in the house out of sheer curiosity to be a witness to the final act of the domestic drama.

"I'm sorry, but the young ladies were all away by ten o'clock."

"Away? Where to?"

"To Miss Bella's new place at Charing Cross," said Barbara with quite a broad grin. "They really flitted on Saturday. There was a man from the upholsterer's came and took everything away—eleven boxes, besides bags and dressing-cases, and a hamper with silver in it."

She glanced furtively at the new mistress as she delivered this item of information, as if fully expecting her to betray signs of annoyance or indignation. But Margaret, though pale, made no comment.

"We had better go upstairs. I suppose lunch is ready for the master, Barbara?"

"There's nothing but the cold meat from yesterday's dinner, miss. I asked Miss Jean if I could not telephone for some fish, or cutlets, or something, but she said it was not necessary."

At that moment the telephone bell rang, and Barbara, whose duty it was to answer it, flew into the parlour. Presently she came back, looking flushed and important.

"The master, ma'am; wantin' to speak to you from Bridgeton."

Margaret went to the receiver and, after a brief colloquy, turned to inform Miss Bruar that Mr. Cardine could not get out to lunch as he had expected, and that he had asked how they found things.

Miss Bruar smiled grimly.

"You and I had better set to, and attack the cold mutton, my dear. I'm sorry for you, but perhaps the end will be better than the beginning."

Long afterwards, Margaret reminded her of these words.

But both their faces were a cloud as they sat down together to the unappetizing lunch. Neither of them cared a fig what they ate, but Mary Bruar was angry because so little respect had been shown to the new mistress, and even blamed Cardine for not setting everything aside to come out to be present at his wife's home-coming.

"It's like a badly-managed stage play, and if you were not a very sensible woman, you would be in a towering rage!" she said, as she waved her muslin elbow sleeves restlessly about the table. "Well, what am I to do? Would you like me to stop and see you through? Show you the house, and introduce you to the rest of the servants?"

"No," said Margaret calmly; "I've got to live here, and I'm not afraid of them. I'll put my things away and go through the house myself."

Margaret saw that Mary Bruar would be glad to get away, and realized that, after all, though she could rely on a certain amount of sympathy, the battle and the victory, if it ever came, would have to be fought and attained singlehanded.

Mary bade her good-bye; urged her to try and keep her heart up, and departed in hot haste, to have it out with her nieces at Charing Cross. She had never believed that they would actually take the plunge, and she was filled with a strange mixture of indignation and curiosity to see for herself what they were actually going to do.

Margaret walked back to the dining-room and stood for a few moments quite still in the big, spacious family room, in which she found herself alone.

It was a finely proportioned place, handsomely furnished, and with some fine pictures of the Glasgow school of art on the panelled walls. A sober richness was its chief characteristic, but it was rather dull and sombre, and had nothing about it calculated to raise the spirits of the woman who stood there by the table, a solitary unit, an interloper in the eyes of some. She did not even know whether she had a friend under its roof. Her face hardened slightly, and, just for a moment, she felt that she was completely at a disadvantage, and that the home-coming, if without fuss or show, was likewise without dignity.

Some other method would have served the occasion better.

But her common sense and resource did not fail her. They immediately suggested an independent course of action. She moved to the fireplace and rang the bell. In due course, and rather more expeditiously than usual, Barbara Watson appeared on the scene.

" As it is not possible for Mr. Cardine to get home to luncheon, Barbara, I had better see the cook about dinner," said her mistress quietly.

" Yes, ma'am. Will I tell her to come up now ? " inquired Barbara with evident relish, for she had just left Mrs. Leggatt discoursing at length over a special pudding that had been reserved for kitchen use, on what she intended to do to assert her position with the lady upstairs.

" In a moment," said Margaret quietly. " How many of you are downstairs ? "

" Me and Mrs. Leggatt and Agnes Spears, the housemaid, and Tweeny—or, at least, she's supposed to be Tweeny ; but, as she's Leggatt's niece, she takes care to keep her pottering about the kitchen an' the scullery a' day. There was a proper kitchenmaid in the first mistress's time, but naebody can stand Leggatt's temper. She wad like to get her relations a' wormed in here, an' I for wan am no' carin', efter I'm away."

" Are you going, then ? " inquired Margaret calmly.

Barbara slightly reddened.

" Well, you see, I had gi'en notice. It has not been a comfortable place for a long time. Too much has been left to Mrs. Leggatt, an' she's—she's——"

" I'd rather not hear tales," said Margaret quietly, but firmly. " I daresay I can find out for myself about Mrs. Leggatt. The question is about you. Did you give notice or get it ? "

" Sort o' betwixt and between. But I'm willin' to stop a month, at least, to see how we get on, if—if you want me to ? "

" Go down now and tell them all to come up to me here."

" Leggatt too ? I don't know if she'll come ! She has a very queer temper."

" She will come, I think," said Margaret quietly. " In ten minutes' time I shall expect you all in this room."

Barbara Watson flew, in much excitement, to the lower regions to communicate with a great flourish of trumpets the first command of the new mistress. It was received by the redoubtable Mrs. Leggatt with loud scorn and defiance.

" Me, in the middle o' my lunches and wi' a denner to get, to wait on her at two o'clock in the day—no me ! If she ken't onything she would ken that ten o'clock in the mornin's a mistress's time. I'm no' gaun wan fit."

" I think ye'd better. She means it," said Barbara gleefully. " Here, you Tweeny, away an' wash the smudges aff your nose, an' I'll len' ye a clean apron."

The ten minutes passed. When they were exceeded the bell rang again. By this time Mrs. Leggatt had donned a clean apron, smoothed her black hair, and, with a very red face and defiant air, stood irresolute, still declaring her intention not to " budge a fit."

But when Barbara proceeded to lead the way to the back stairs, she brought up the rear with muttered thunder.

She was one of those unsatisfactory persons who, on entering a house as temporary help at a high wage, had stopped on simply because those in authority were too slack to take the necessary trouble to find the right person. For fifteen shillings a week Mrs. Leggatt did as seemed good in her own eyes, ordered and dispensed stores, and incidentally handed out a considerable part of the same to a married daughter at Govan. In return she cooked meals as the spirit moved her, though she had been at one time under a hotel chef, and knew the elements of her business, at least, had there been anybody to compel her to apply her knowledge.

It was doubtless a secret sense of her own shortcomings which made her resent the too speedy interference of the new mistress, and before her heavy breathing had reached the front hall she had decided to leave on the spot.

But when they filed into the dining-room and saw the new mistress standing, alert, capable, wholly unafraid, and with a conspicuous dignity, waiting for them, the spirit of Mrs. Leggatt inwardly quailed. For she knew that she had met her match. She merely scowled in response to Mrs. Cardine's pleasant greeting, and, folding her red hands, waited for what was to come.

"Good day, all of you," said Margaret in her quiet, steady, pleasant voice. "As the young ladies in the meantime have left the house, it is necessary that I should see you all at once. I have just one or two things to say. I have no intention of making any very great changes here; my only concern is the comfort and well-being of the master. As you know, I have been a working woman, and I intend to continue one, in the sense that my new duties will take my whole attention. At Bridgeton it was my business to see that a hundred and twenty girls and women did the work for which they were paid. It will be equally my business here to see that you four do it. You'll find me just, generous, and kind; but I intend to be the mistress, and to see that the work is done. Now, do you understand? Are you willing to remain on these conditions?"

"I'm no'," said Leggatt sullenly. "I'll leave this very nicht."

"Without wages, then," said Margaret calmly. "I would advise you, Mrs. Leggatt, to go down and think it over. I'll give you till three o'clock, when I will come down and see what is in the larder for dinner. You, Agnes, and you, Tweeny —I suppose you have some other name?"

"Oh, I'll stop!" said Tweeny, a smile brightening her anæmic face.

"De'il a fear!" said her aunt in a loud, aggressive voice. "Ye leave the hoose wi' me!"

"And you, Agnes?" said Margaret kindly, and her eyes travelled with relief to the open, rosy face of the housemaid, who, so far, had not spoken a word.

"Oh, yes, ma'am!" she answered immediately. "I'll stop, and be glad to stop."

"You can go. And I'll see you, Mrs. Leggatt, at three o'clock, downstairs," said Margaret, and they departed as they had come, the large cook, however, visibly disconcerted, though still breathing forth threats.

Margaret had taken the wind completely out of all their sails by declaring herself a working woman and laying down her policy. Evidently she was not ashamed of the fact, but proud and confident, because experience had taught her how to use her power.

At three o'clock she descended to the kitchen, found it tidy, and Mrs. Leggatt in a better temper. A little more talk ensued, and they arrived at a possible working understanding.

That night James Cardine ate the best dinner in his own house that he had tasted for many a day!

CHAPTER XI

NANCY IN THE TOILS

MR. AND MRS. ALEXANDER CARDINE, in a third-floor bedroom of a first-class hotel in Russell Square, London, were having a small matrimonial discussion.

" Don't you see, Alec," she said, as she brushed out her fine luxuriant hair, without looking directly at him, as she could see his face in the mirror, and study its expression, " that it would be far better if Nancy didn't go home just yet ? Give them another week to get settled in Glasgow. Now, why shouldn't you go home alone to-morrow and let Nancy and me stop another week ? "

" I've no particular objection, but it's jolly expensive here, Evey. The bill last week was over fifteen pounds."

" Oh, but that was pension and extras for three ! After you're gone, of course, we could do differently. We could move up another floor, and one decent room would serve us. Or we could even go into rooms. I know of some nice ones in Seymour Street, recommended by Lady Belmuir."

" They're not likely to be economical if recommended by Lady Belmuir," said Alexander rather grimly. " And, anyhow, if it's only to be for another week, it doesn't seem worth while to change."

" There's no doubt Nancy's enjoying herself," said Evey, looking gratified at the partial success of her suggestion. " Poor child, she has simply seen nothing ! And, you know, I could take her to Aunt Eliza's dance next week in Grosvenor Place—a chance of a lifetime ! We oughtn't to miss it, Alec. It's our positive duty to try and marry Nancy well—she's so pretty, and everybody likes her ! "

" By the by, where is she this afternoon ? " asked Alexander. " I'm not sure that she ought to be let out careering about London alone. The old man wouldn't like it."

" Much he cares ! " said Mrs. Alexander with curling lip.

" You haven't told me yet where Nancy went this afternoon. I'd like to know, Evey, for, after all, we fetched her away, and we ought to look after her."

" Well, if you really must know, she's gone on the river with Captain Gilder."

Alexander did not appear to be reassured.

" I don't like Gilder, Evey. There's something underhand—not quite O.K.—about him. I'm nearly sure the governor wouldn't approve of him as a suitor for Nancy."

Mrs. Alexander laughed, and, as she deftly coiled the last strand of her hair about her shapely head, turned round to see the effect in the side-glass on the dressing-table.

" You think that ? Well, I think Nancy would have to be congratulated if she was so successful as to rope in Clement Gilder ! He's one of the most fastidious men where women are concerned."

" He isn't good enough for Nancy, however—besides being much too old," maintained Alexander doggedly. " And if it's only to give her more opportunities to go round with that Gilder chap, I don't think I will give in, after all, to your staying here another week. She'd much better go and face the music at home."

Evey laughed.

" Poor old Alec ! What a kill-joy it is ! Do hurry up, and I'll go and find out whether Nancy has come back. It's the opera at seven-thirty, in Aunt Eliza's box."

" How did Gilder get off just now ? " he asked, as his wife drew on her silk dressing gown, preparatory to going across the corridor to Nancy's room. "I thought they were all in the thick of getting ready for camp at Barry."

"Oh, he can always get the week-end. He's in favour!" answered Evey carelessly; and though her face distinctly reddened, as she slipped out at the moment, he did not notice it.

She was gone only about five minutes.

"Nancy's home, safe and sound. She's had a lovely time, she says, and her eyes positively danced at the idea of stopping on another week. How badly you have tied your tie, old man! Come here, and let me make you presentable."

Her deft white fingers soon remedied the defaulting white tie, and she gave him a little pat on the cheek when she had finished, and smiled into his eyes.

"Thank you so much for giving us such a good time! And I promise to settle down and be ever so good, and not ask another change! I shouldn't even mind if we didn't go to the coast this summer. I daresay Grandpapa won't grudge the poor kiddies a few days at Ardgoil."

Half an hour later a hired brougham, irreproachably turned out, for which Alexander would have to pay at least a guinea, bore them to Covent Garden, where for over four hours they listened to an opera which only genuine music-lovers and enthusiasts could really appreciate. For this reason Lady Farquhar had lent her box, while she herself was enjoying the latest musical comedy at the Lyric.

At the end of the first act two men from the stalls promptly made their way to the box. They were Gilder and a friend whom Alexander Cardine recognized as an officer he had seen at the last regimental ball they had attended in Glasgow. With this man Evelyn had danced sufficiently on that occasion to make herself conspicuous, but when her husband remonstrated with her she only laughed.

Although he watched her closely, Cardine could not observe any particular signs of embarrassment or self-consciousness about her; and the episode seemed all quite natural and even pleasant, for they had fine manners, plenty of small talk, and Gilder especially seemed to have either a personal or a casual acquaintance with everybody of consequence in the house.

Gilder sat next to Nancy, into whose small, delicious ear he poured outrageous flattery, which caused her heart to flutter and her cheek to redden like the rose. He was a man of about thirty-five, well set-up, soldierly, good to look at; but the lines of his face were harshly set, his mouth was not kind, his eyes had a shifting, furtive look, and could glitter very hard at times.

Next morning Nancy did not get down in time to say good-bye, but Evelyn went to the station to see her husband off, and was very wifely and affectionate at parting.

"I really wish I'd been going, too, now I'm here, Alec," she said, as they stood on the platform together after his traps had been deposited in the corner seat. "I hope you'll find the kiddies all right. Mind you wire the minute you get home. It's really for Nancy I'm so anxious to stop. It's such a pleasure to see her enjoying herself like that!"

"But, after all, she ought to be at home, Evey, and I think they've all made a frightful mistake burning their boats like that!"

"Oh, it won't last," she said flippantly. "Inside of a month you'll see they'll all be settled in Huntley Gardens again. And then, though I think the second Mrs. Cardine the absolute limit, I shan't envy her! Don't you see, I'm rendering a genuine public service trying to do my best for the girls? Of course, Jean's impossible! No man would put up with that sort of thing in a wife, and the best she could hope for would be some long-haired reformer who spouts on the Green, and wants a bath badly. Indeed, Nancy is the mainstay, and the bright particular star! You may be sure, if Aunt Eliza invites a man to her house, even as a dancing partner, he's all he ought to be! She's had the reputation of being the most exclusive hostess in her set, and she doesn't even allow one of the new step dances in her ballroom. So there! You can go back, old croaker, with your mind at rest."

Alexander Cardine smiled as he kissed his wife good-bye. She had still the power to lure and hold him, all the more marked because she gave so little of herself. She was one of those intensely modern wives who regard matrimony merely as a means of self-advancement. Sick of the poverty and grinding limitations of her life in her father's house, Evelyn Whitehorn had accepted

Alexander Cardine mainly because he was, or she imagined him to be, the son of a very rich man.

A good deal of the bickering which had marked their married life, especially of late years, arose from the fact that in her estimation her father-in-law had not come up to expectations in the matter of income, for Alexander, at thirty-one, was not even yet a full partner.

Her ambitions had no bounds, and just lately a sort of recklessness both of appearances and of consequences had marked her actions and caused her husband anxious days, and sometimes restless nights. To his two children he was passionately devoted, and, fully aware that there would be no more, for his wife had left him in no doubt as to that, he watched them with a solicitude that was wholly absent from their mother's casual interest.

Alexander Cardine indeed was by nature cut out for the rôle of quiet, domestic, family man, and would have been happy in a suburban garden, pottering away his leisure hours among his flowers. He had married the wrong woman. He still loved her, however, after the way of the faithful, dogged person, and gave in, often against his better judgment, to her whims and often impossible desires.

For instance, now, he was by no means sure about the wisdom of leaving her in London, although her aunt's ball was, of course, a fairly good reason for her desiring to stop another week.

The London season was in full swing, and as her aunt, Lady Farquhar, was a woman of fashion, and quite willing to show a little kindness to the niece she saw so seldom, there were plenty of interesting events.

That afternoon they drove with the Farquhars to Ranelagh to see a polo match, and before tea-time Gilder and his superior officer turned up on the ground. Lady Farquhar was rather interested to see the quick flush and the bright gleam of Evelyn's eye when they appeared, and in a quiet way watched her for the rest of the afternoon.

She soon discovered which of the two was attracted by Nancy. She had no daughters of her own, and only one son at Cambridge, who was going to the Bar, and hoped afterwards to follow his father into Parliament. She felt sorry to see Nancy evidently attracted by a man of Gilder's type, and she took an early opportunity of putting a question to Evelyn about it.

"I say, Evey, it looks as if it were going to be serious for that little girl with Captain Gilder. I can't say I particularly like the man. Who is he, anyway?"

"I thought you would have known his name, Aunt Eliza," said Mrs. Alexander with well-feigned surprise. "He is very well connected, though not too well off, but the Cardines are rich, and that wouldn't matter. Surely her father would make a good settlement, or would have done before this woman came on the scene. Every day seems to make it worse. Aunt Eliza, I'm surprised you don't look at it as I do!"

"Well, you see, I haven't seen the woman," said Lady Farquhar. "But, about Nancy—I can't say I'd like to see her marry that man. She's the sweetest thing I've seen for many a day! If only Heaven had given me a child like that! Now, she would be a sweetheart for my Colin! Next week is May week at Cambridge. Let us go down for a couple of days and let them meet."

"How very kind of you, Aunt Eliza! And, I'm sure, Nancy would simply love it. I'm afraid I've tied myself up pretty tightly for next week."

"I don't know how you managed to do that, as yesterday you said you weren' at all sure whether Alexander would let you stop on!"

Evelyn reddened slightly at the home thrust.

"Well, I gave conditional promises—don't you know?—to people like the Arbuthnots. I don't think I could possibly fit Cambridge in, for we must go home not later than next Thursday or Friday. But do take Nancy—she would love it!" After a second or so she added quickly: "Do you mean to say, Aunt Eliza, that you meant what you said a minute ago about Colin? Why, I should have thought nothing but the Peerage would have satisfied you now!"

A somewhat tired little smile flitted across Lady Farquhar's still beautiful face.

"Ah, my dear, I'm afraid I'm a little old-fashioned. What I should like for my boy is that he should marry young, for love, and for happiness. It is a man's best safeguard. His father thinks so, too, and he has quite fallen in love with

Nancy himself! Here's your Major coming to claim you again. Be careful, Evelyn! It is easier to play with fire than to escape from it unscathed."

It was the only word of warning Lady Farquhar felt it incumbent upon her to utter to her niece, whom she supposed capable of looking after herself. But with Nancy it was different. As she watched her engrossed with her mature admirer, where they sat on two chairs remote from the general company, she had more than one qualm. She would have had several could she have heard the gist of the conversation that was dyeing the child's cheeks crimson and setting her pulse beating wildly.

Gilder had decided that he would not lose any more time. For the first time in a life which had not been guiltless of intrigue and of love affairs too numerous to mention, he was honestly attracted by simplicity, purity, and all the exquisite charm of girlhood in its first blush.

"Darling, you look perfectly enchanting to-day!" he murmured, bending his handsome head as near to hers as he dared. "I simply can't look at you and keep my head. You know I love you, don't you, Nancy? The moment you left it, Glasgow became a howling wilderness. I wonder whether I have the ghost of a chance?"

"Of what?" asked Nancy, turning her innocent blue eyes to his.

Her white frock, with the broad ribbon of blue at the slim waist, and the hat-strings tied in a big bow under her bewitching chin, made a picture which refreshed the jaded eyes of the man of the world, and made him wish himself worthier for her sake.

"Of—of—you know—of winning you for my own darling little wife, of course. I know I'm not worthy to kiss the hem of your frock, but I'd have a jolly good try to deserve you, and I would be good to you, Nancy. I've never loved anybody like you."

"Never anybody?" she asked wistfully, and just for the moment there was all the yearning of a woman's heart both in her look and tone.

"Never anybody!" he repeated emphatically. "Of course, I've admired pretty faces, as other men have done, but this is the real thing, Nancy! I've never felt like this in my life before!"

"But you are so clever! And then, your people are very grand—aren't they? Would they be pleased with me?"

"Pleased with you!" he laughed with a slight hardness as he repeated the words.

She did not know of the sordid vision the word "people" called up, of a squalid Southsea Villa, where an ill-assorted pair, his father and mother, were living out an unlovely old age on half-pay, and cursing the day they had met one another!

"The question is whether I shall pass muster with your father!"

"Oh, father won't take much interest in us now," said Nancy with a faint, pitiful droop of her lips. "He has turned us all out of his house practically. You know, I'm living with Alec and Evey now, and the other two have gone away, too. I shall be very glad to have a home of my own. It isn't nice not to have a home—is it?"

Gilder's face slightly fell.

"No, darling, that it isn't. But, of course, your father won't keep it up. I've heard from Mrs. Cardine—your sister-in-law, I mean—that he didn't actually turn you out, and that you can go back when you like. Of course, it would be much better to be friendly all round. We must be friendly, if it can be managed at all."

He did not say why, and Nancy shook her head. Her nature had been poisoned through the influence of the others, and she was for the time being incapable of taking normal sensible views of life. It had all been a whirl of excitement and adventure which had borne her along, and culminating thus in this delightful London visit and a handsome soldier lover at her feet, Nancy was no longer herself.

"I have your permission to speak to your father, then, have I, darling?" asked Gilder rapturously.

"Oh, if you like. But I think you'll find that father won't take the slightest interest. How could he, when he has just been married himself? It is so ridiculous—isn't it? Why, he is quite, quite an old man. He must be quite fifty!"

"I am thirty-five," said Gilder ruefully.

"Oh, but you don't look it," said Nancy, looking straight into her lover's handsome, flushed face. Her own eyes fell before the ardour in his.

"You haven't said that you love me, yet?" he said, lowering his voice to a passionate whisper.

"I can't say it. But—but I think I do," she answered, and slipped her little hand into his.

Lady Farquhar saw this little action, and immediately bore down upon them. "Come, come, Captain Gilder! You have monopolized the flower of my party quite long enough. Come, dear child! Tea is ready, and Evey has been looking for you."

"Lady Farquhar," said Gilder gravely, as he took off his hat, "I have the honour to inform you that Miss Cardine is my promised wife!"

CHAPTER XII

THE NIGHT HAWK

MARGARET CARDINE, most inoffensive and peace-loving of women, who might, with perfect truth, have boasted that she had not an enemy in the world, had by one act thrown herself into a hostile atmosphere, and converted indifferent people into antagonists where she was concerned.

Foremost among these—though, certainly, she gave him the least thought—was Bruce Gemmill. The man had received a blow, not only to his affections, which had been involved to a degree which surprised nobody more than himself, but to his vanity, which was colossal. He imagined himself a ladies' man, before whom—to use one of his own choice phrases—" the lassies would go down like ninepins!"

During the months he had been paying assiduous attention, the only kind known to him, to Margaret Oswald, he had never had the slightest doubt up till the last that these attentions were welcome. Proceeding on the assumption that he and Margaret would ultimately make a match of it, he had behaved accordingly, without the smallest ground for such assumption or assertion.

He was not a man to appeal to a woman of Margaret Oswald's clear perceptions and decidedly fastidious tastes. She had done her best to give him the cold shoulder, and had sometimes been at her wits' end to escape him when it was borne in upon her that nothing she could say or do had power to repulse him.

Although he was not immediately concerned with her department at the factory, the same roof covered them in working hours, and there was nothing easier than for Gemmill to create opportunities for seeing her and getting a passing word with her.

Himself the head of a department, and very capable at his job, especially where keeping the nose of subordination at the grindstone was concerned, he had, of course, a certain amount of personal liberty in the place, and was under nobody's jurisdiction except that of the masters.

Outside, he was suave and cheerful as usual, but when Cardine and he met for the first time since the return to Huntley Gardens the former was conscious of a strange, subtle, but almost overpowering sense of personal antipathy.

The mere fact that he had presumed to enter the list of suitors for Margaret's hand wounded Mr. Cardine's self-esteem. In spite of his simplicity of life and manners, Cardine was an austere, proud man, and, on some sides of his nature unapproachable. Even while discussing with Bruce Gemmill the merest technical details connected with the work, he was mentally resolving that he would take the earliest opportunity of getting rid of him. As he had not any actual fault to find—for, within limits, Gemmill was an excellent servant—he must find him a better job with some other firm at some distance from Glasgow. He decided to endeavour to accomplish this in the immediate future.

" I hope that Mrs. Cardine is quite well, sir," said Gemmill smoothly, after business had been discussed.

" She's quite well," answered Cardine brusquely, then immediately added a belated " thank you."

" She's much missed here, sir; and I hear things are not going so well in the packing-room."

" It would naturally take some time for a new person to get into the routine. We must not expect too much. I hear from Mr. Alexander that he will be home to-morrow, so it will have to be all hands to the pumps next week."

"Yes, sir," said Gemmill; and as he went out by the door Cardine was conscious of nothing but a smile, which he considered offensive, and his own overwhelming desire to kick the man for the same!

Up till now he had scarcely given Gemmill a thought. But, somehow, Margaret had made a difference, and the thought that, in a past which was quite recent, Gemmill had had the right, with all other men, to approach her with his attentions, left a sting. Already another small serpent had entered James Cardine's Eden, and its poison was destined to spread.

A few days later an offensive postcard was discovered among the letters waiting for Mr. Cardine's attention at the factory. He saw its coloured edge peeping out from under the pile, and out of curiosity drew it forth. He beheld the vulgar picture of two lovers on the seashore and read the words, written in the familiar backward hand of the manufacturer of anonymous stuff. He coloured violently and his eyes flashed fire.

On the back these words were written:—"The elderly Lothario thinks he has won a treasure, but he is reminded by a friend that there is such a thing as a Woman with a Past."

The post-mark was Paisley, and, of a set purpose no doubt, two words were spelled wrong, undoubtedly with the object of putting the recipient off the scent. The writer of the anonymous letter or postcard is seldom an illiterate person. It requires a certain amount of cleverness and mother wit to do such devil's work. Happily for humanity he cannot press babes and sucklings into the service. Their ministry has been retained by the angels!

On the spur of the moment Mr. Cardine turned to throw the vile thing into the fire, but, thinking better of it, he pushed it into a drawer and went on with his letters.

A little later in the morning, going his usual round of the factory, he encountered Bruce Gemmill. He did not know what prompted him, but, keeping his eyes keenly on the man's face, he asked casually:

"Do you happen to know anybody at Paisley, Gemmill?"

Gemmill's heavy face presented an admirable picture of blank amazement.

"Paisley? Let me see. No, I don't think I do. Queer, isn't it? For almost everybody kens somebody in Seestu——"

Cardine, with the jerk of the hand, drew forth the post card. "That is my reason for asking. I suppose you don't know anybody in the place who would be guilty of such a crime as that?"

Gemmill gazed upon the offensive rag with an appropriate expression of disgust and surprise.

"Well, I never! I'd pay no attention to it, Mr. Cardine. Some waster who is jealous or disappointed over your good fortune; maybe some lassie Mrs. Cardine had to get rid of when she was Miss Oswald—that's the most likely explanation."

At this suggestion Cardine certainly looked relieved.

"Ah, no doubt that is the explanation. Thank you, Gemmill; it did not occur to me."

"You'll not mention it to Mrs. Cardine, sir? It micht vex her," said Gemmill, with another appropriate expression.

Cardine slightly smiled.

"What do you take me for, Gemmill? I'm not quite a baby in arms! Thank you, all the same. If there are any more of them I'll hand them over to the police. This sort of thing, even coming from a quarter beneath contempt, ought to be nipped in the bud in the public interest."

So saying he passed on. Bruce Gemmill waited until he had left the shop before he permitted himself the luxury of a smile. He was setting a train of explosives for the Cardine household, and it pleased him that the first had not missed its mark.

On the following Sunday he went down to Paisley on the tram for the purpose of fathering another of his poisonous postcards on that unoffending town. It was a beautiful afternoon—an ideal summer one—and every car was packed to its utmost capacity.

As he was wending his way across the Square to the General Post Office he suddenly caught sight of what seemed to him to be a familiar back—that of a young man in a tweed suit, a straw hat, and a cane swinging in his hand. Naturally secretive, and possessing some of the attributes of the successful detective, Gemmill instinctively stepped back into a convenient doorway and watched. Presently he was rewarded by seeing Harry Cardine's face. When he disappeared round a corner Gemmill followed. For a little over a quarter of an hour this little pantomime went on. The zest of the pursuit was undoubtedly enhanced by the fact that the neighbourhood towards which Harry Cardine was evidently hastening was not the residential one in which he might naturally have been expected to have his associates.

He came into a working-class area where there were rows and rows of small houses with little gardens, all as like as peas in a pod.

All unconscious that he was being watched and tracked down, Harry Cardine swung onwards with the air of a man who has a goal in view. Suddenly, before one of the little garden gates at the far end of the street, where the road opened upon green fields spreading away in the Johnstone direction, he paused, and then made his way to the house door, which he entered without knocking, also without looking round, which gave Gemmill opportunity to watch him more intently.

But when the door was closed nothing further could be done. He made careful note of the name of the street—Woodbine Gardens—and also of the number of the house, in his little pocket-book for handy reference, and walked away, musing deeply.

Now, if Harry Cardine was sufficiently intimate in a house of that description to enter it without knocking, some explanation seemed necessary. Who lived there? What was concealed behind its prettily-curtained windows alluring enough to bring a gentleman of his position there on his principal afternoon of leisure?

A born plotter and schemer, Gemmill decided to leave no stone unturned to find out what it meant. If quite harmless—why, it would, at least, satisfy his insatiable curiosity and do nobody any harm. If, however, it hid something else which would add to the exciting chapter of the Cardine family history, then it was equally important that he should know it.

Since Margaret Oswald had become a Cardine there was nothing concerning the family too mean or trivial to interest him.

Mr. Cardine and his two sons were in close attendance at the factory all that week, and great strides were made towards the fulfilment of Sampsons' contract.

Gemmill noticed, or imagined, that they were less friendly than of yore, but, try as he would, he could not discover anything about affairs at Huntley Gardens. He was badly in want of an informant in the house itself, and set himself to try and find out how he could get one.

On the Wednesday he had a sharp and altogether unexpected encounter with his employer, who met him on the packing-room floor, in the corridor, in fact, not far from Miss Richardson's door. The sight of him there brought back to Mr. Cardine the memory of what Margaret had told him about Gemmill's frequent visits to the packing-room, and, acting on the impulse of the moment, he decided to put a stop to it once for all.

"Have you any particular business on this floor, Gemmill?" he inquired curtly.

"I wanted to speak to Miss Richardson, sir," answered Gemmill, distinctly taken aback.

"What about?"

That nonplussed him, for he could not actually say he had anything to say to her referring to her work or his own.

"It was a matter of private business, sir," he said, his heavy face flushing slightly.

"Then I must trouble you to discuss it outside. I will tell Miss Richardson the same thing, Gemmill," said the master quietly, yet in his most decisive voice. "There is no occasion whatever for you to be on this side of the building; and I must trouble you to keep to your own department. Any message for Miss Richardson from your department must go through George Kelly. Do you understand?"

"Oh, very well, sir—through Mr. George Kelly. Perhaps you would prefer to see him in my place?"

"That is as it suits you. What I do require is that you confine yourself to your own side of the building. You know the rules about the women's departments. I require them more strictly adhered to than you have been in the habit of doing."

"I'll leave this day week, Mr. Cardine. A man like me doesn't need to stop in Bridgeton factory to be insulted!" said Gemmill stormily.

"Very well, Gemmill. I have not dismissed you, remember. But a week to-day, unless you take time to reconsider."

James Cardine passed on, conscious of an extraordinary and profound relief that the thing had so ended.

CHAPTER XIII

UNDERCURRENTS

JAMES CARDINE had avoided the vicinity of Charing Cross since the day when a man he knew had asked him in the car whether he had seen the little, white-fronted shop with his name above the door. He had answered surlily in the negative, and had, both by manner and word, convinced his casual and tactless acquaintance that probably the Miss Cardines deserved all the pity they had got, as their father deserved all the censure.

On the afternoon of the day on which he had dealt with Gemmill, Mr. Cardine purposely went round by way of Charing Cross, and, without difficulty, found the place he sought. He was somewhat relieved to discover that it was not a shop on the ground floor, but apparently a flat, or two flats, above a florist's. Across the window, in slanting gold letters, ran the legend:

" CARDINE—ROBES AND MODES."

A solitary hat of tremendous dimensions, was on a stand in one of the windows, and the froth of white, lace-trimmed lingerie was displayed in the other.

Now James Cardine, who had worked in his father's factory from the lowest rung upward, could estimate honest work at its full value. He had regretted permitting Alexander just to drift into the business by way of the office stool, with the result that technically he was at the mercy of those who knew better. He had, therefore, reversed the order of things with Harry, foreseeing the day, which would inevitably come, when the business would require another head.

Harry had not grumbled, and had turned out cheerfully at half-past five on dark winter mornings and fallen in line with his father's plan of life for him, both because his sunny disposition made it easy, and because he had a shrewd head on young shoulders, and had grasped his father's meaning at once, when he had informed him that there could not be room for fine gentlemen at Bridgeton.

But there is a difference between honest work and masquerading, and the masquerade of robes and modes exasperated James Cardine and made the expression of his face sardonic, as he opened the little white door next the green-grocer's and deliberately walked upstairs. He was fortified by a sheaf of unpaid bills in his pocket, which, acting on Miss Cardine's instructions, the decorators had rendered to Huntley Gardens.

On the first landing, which was rather dark, he thought he had better knock at the door. It was answered by a small girl with a frizzled head and a pert, eager face.

" I want to see Miss Cardine," he said brusquely.

" She's engaged, but you can wait," she said condescendingly, for, as he could not be a customer, it was not necessary to be polite or even specially attentive.

" Right! Take me where I can wait, and be sharp about it."

The child, unaccustomed to such accents, stared, and did as she was bid. He was shown into the smallest waiting-room in the world surely—where one chair stood amid a wilderness of pasteboard boxes all bearing the same legend in green letters on a delicate fawn ground—" Cardine—Robes and Modes."

Now, though Bella Cardine undoubtedly had clever fingers, and had been able to work strange and sometimes effective transformations in her own wardrobe and that of her sisters at Huntley Gardens, there is a wide difference between a natural aptitude dependent on whim or chance and skilled knowledge of the intricacies of a fashionable woman's toilet.

The west end of Glasgow pays handsomely for its clothes, but it likes good value for its money; and Bella Cardine was soon to discover that, while a good many would give her a chance or a single order for good luck, or out of curiosity, the transfer of a single customer completely was another matter.

For a few days everything had gone merrily, but this was now the third week, and not a fresh order had come in.

When the door swung open, and Bella, in the tightest-fitting and skimpiest black satin frock imaginable, appeared, it was her turn to be surprised. Then she laughed, just a trifle embarrassedly.

"Sorry to have kept you waiting. I had an important customer. Will you come into the next room?"

He rose heavily, and, in his haste, knocked over a pile of boxes, which he viewed with sour disgust. Following her across the passage, he entered the saloon itself, a large, light, and really beautiful room, furnished and decorated in fawn and a delicate shade of apple-green which had been much admired. A mere suggestion of almond blossom on the frieze gave the finishing touch.

Bella was undoubtedly a little nervous, for she guessed her father's errand. He stood by the ridiculous white table with the finely-turned legs and took out his pocket-book, from which he extracted two business envelopes.

"There has been a mistake," he said coolly. "These bills have been sent to the wrong name and address. They are not for me."

She knit her brows, and took them up gingerly. Finally she decided to brave it out.

"There hasn't been any mistake, Father," she said coolly. "Of course, I told the people to send you the bills. What else could I do?"

"I won't pay," he said quietly. "I thought I had better fetch them myself and inform you of the fact. I daresay, if you adhere to the prices current in places of this kind," he added, stimulated by the recollection of the many sheaves of bills he had paid in his time, "you will soon clear off two accounts of seventy-five pounds and thirty-nine respectively."

"I can't pay them," she said, giving them a push towards him. "We are doing quite well, but it will be some time before there is a margin of that kind. We expect that you will clear us and give us a fair chance. Jean was just speaking about it last night."

"You had no ground for any such assumption," he answered grimly. "I told you quite clearly what I would do, and that it was only if you stayed at home and behaved yourselves that I would pay the allowance I mentioned."

Bella looked nonplussed. She had not expected this, and, in their calculations, the sisters had invariably counted on the fact that the promised allowance—amounting to two hundred and forty pounds—would enable them to live comfortably and not get into debt.

"I'm afraid you'll have to pay, Father," she said, quite quietly.

"I won't, I tell you. A man only pays cheerfully for what he thinks good value. This sort of thing is below the belt, and I could take my affidavit you won't make salt to your kale off it!"

"We took orders for thirty pounds the first week," she said defiantly.

"And how many the second?"

"About the half."

"And the third?"

"This is only Wednesday—" she began, but her father interrupted her with a short laugh.

"It's fizzled out, like a glass of stale champagne, lass! And the fourth week—you'll have to face the music! What's Jean doing?"

"She didn't get that secretaryship at the Institute, after all," said Bella, betrayed into a sort of forced confidence. "It was a case of horrid jealousy and spite. Another girl got it—some pet of the Committee's."

"And is Jean also among the unemployed?"

"No. She's doing some secretarial work for Tom Burgess."

Bella spoke rather defiantly, uttering the name of a well-known Socialist, one of the moving spirits on Glasgow Green, a man whom most employers of labour had reason to dislike and distrust.

James Cardine's strong, mobile face expressed the depth of his disgust.

"A nice pair of daughters! Calculated to fill the heart of a father with pride!" he said sarcastically. "And where is Nancy? I suppose she came home with Evelyn the other day?"

"No, she didn't. She's gone to Southsea, to make the acquaintance of her future 'in-laws,'" said Bella, enjoying immensely the item of intelligence she had received that very day from Alexander's wife. "She's engaged to be married to Captain Gilder," she went on, nodding delightedly. "Evey brought it off in London, I believe. So you'll be quit of the lot!"

Cardine was now a little white. Of all his daughters, Nancy most closely resembled her mother, and she had worked herself into the very recesses of his being.

"Nancy cannot marry anyone without my consent. She is under age," he said harshly. "Well, if that is all you have to say to me, I'll be going," he said, rising heavily to his feet. "You have cut the ropes pretty short, and burned your boats. I'll leave you your precious bills. I'm not responsible for them, happily, and I don't intend to pay."

"You won't mind, then, if you should see your name in the papers?" said Bella, a little shaken by the determination in her father's tone.

"Why should I mind? Better men have had their names in the papers, and for less. I haven't done anything. You had a fair offer—a generous offer—made to you, and you refused it. It's closed—that's all. And, unless you exhibit a proper spirit, and apologize for your outrageous and uncalled for behaviour, both of you, you must just sink or swim together!"

So saying, he went out, leaving Bella distinctly chagrined and chilled by the interview.

It was not possible for Cardine to obtain the full flavour from the personal happiness which Margaret had undoubtedly given him, for his corroding care regarding the other members of his household. But of one thing he was now sure—an ever-ready and sympathizing ear into which he could pour his anxieties, without the smallest chance of being misunderstood or misjudged, and that, to a man of Cardine's temperament, meant a great deal.

Margaret, indeed, felt these anxieties with a poignancy far exceeding his, because she was not altogether free from the knowledge that she had unwittingly added to them. For that reason she was full of projects for healing the family differences. But she was so constituted that she could not act on impulse nor in a hurry. Everything she did must have well-considered reason to back it.

"Where's Harry?" he asked, looking round irritably when Barbara Watson closed the door, and prepared to dispense the soup from the sideboard.

"He telephoned about an hour ago to say he would not be home to dinner," his wife observed, noting the deepening cloud on his brow.

"He has only been in to dinner twice this week. I'd uncommonly like to know what he does with his evenings. You needn't wait, Barbara, we can ring when we are ready."

Barbara went out discreetly and closed the door. Domestic matters were now arranged in the house, and none of the servants had left, but had apparently settled down to the new rule, which, if a trifle strict, was certainly both kind and just.

"I'm certainly not easy in my mind about Nancy, and I'll go to Southsea to-morrow, I think, and bring her back. We could be home Saturday morning or Saturday night, at latest."

Margaret sighed faintly, but perceiving that some sort of action had become necessary to allay his more acute anxiety, she encouraged him in his plan; and, next morning, saw him off to London by the ordinary day express.

She was not altogether averse to the prospect of having three days to herself. She would go out and see her father and mother, and one or two friends, and, perhaps, if the spirit moved her, make another attempt to see the girls at Charing Cross.

But, before she could employ her hands and heart with all these benevolent schemes, something else, wholly unexpected and serious, turned up to fill them.

CHAPTER XIV

THE NETWORK

In the course of the next twenty-four hours Margaret received two telegrams—one from London and one from Southsea. The first merely intimated her husband's safe arrival; the second was very reassuring—"Arrived, Southsea. Found all satisfactory. May stop over Sunday and bring Nancy home Monday." The second message lifted an undoubted load off Margaret's mind, and yet it so surprised her that she could not take all the satisfaction possible out of it.

Margaret told Harry the good news and he ran his eyes over the telegram, but his face did not conspicuously brighten.

"I don't understand it. They've thrown dust in Dad's eyes somehow," was all his comment. "I don't care what they say—Gilder's not the man for Nancy. He's nearly twice her age. He's an outsider, and his moral character won't bear investigation. I shall have to speak very plainly when Dad comes home. Why, Nancy's a mere child. The whole thing is rotten, I tell you!"

Margaret's face expressed her utmost concern. "I've heard things about him, and he has said to a man who told someone who told me," said Harry, with a rueful smile at the intricacies of gossip, "that he'd only go through with the match if proper settlements were made! It's Evelyn who has done this. She's far too thick with the military crowd. Some of them are just splendid chaps, but it's the rotters she goes in for. I'm sorry for poor old Alec, but he should have put his foot down long ago."

Never had Harry spoken with so much candour, and Margaret felt that, while it seemed to increase the sum of perplexity for the future, it was evident that she had won the full confidence of at least one member of the family.

"If he stops till Monday that means you and I have the house to ourselves on Sunday. Let's go down to Ardgoil," he added eagerly. "That was a most awfully jolly Sunday we had when Aunt Mary came! Do let us go to Ardgoil."

"We shall have to make sure first that your father won't come home unexpectedly. It would be a very sorry welcome to find an empty house! And I am counting great things on having Nancy back."

"Oh! Nancy will be all right when she's away from the others," said Harry confidently. "And when she finds out what it is like at home she'll settle down all right, I'm sure."

Margaret's face flushed softly.

"Then you don't think it's so very bad after all?" she asked shyly.

"Bad? I think it's just splendid!" he said eagerly and warmly. "I met Jean yesterday in Sauchiehall Street. She was talking to an awful-looking bounder in a red tie, but I just waited about till I got speaking to her. Then I told her straight how kind you were, and that the best thing they could do would be to come home without further delay."

"What did she say to that?" asked Margaret, intensely interested.

But Harry looked the other way.

"Apparently they haven't had enough of it yet, though I gathered from what she said that business is rather slack at Charing Cross, and that customers haven't come up to the scratch. Jean hasn't anything to do—at least, nothing at which she earns money, so more than probably it'll end in Father paying their debts and clearing things up generally."

Margaret's face grew wistful again, for the thing worried her now in the new aspect of an economic problem. Waste of any kind was hateful to her, and she had found certain leakages in the house at Huntley Gardens, which had filled her with righteous wrath. But she had said nothing about them, not even to her husband, realizing that he had enough to worry him already, and fully conscious that her position needed no strengthening.

Every day she cared more for him. He was a very lovable, human man, by no means perfect, but like the best of his sex, even those who achieve the greatest things in the world, he needed mothering at home, and was grateful for it.

After that little talk with Harry, Margaret went out to Bearsden to see her father and mother, with whom she spent the day.

On her return, she had intended to go to bed early, but eleven o'clock, when she heard Harry's latchkey in the door, found her still at the desk in the morning-room, writing a letter to an old school-friend, who had married a traveller in silk, and lived in Lyons. It was a somewhat tardy reply to wedding congratulations, which had come from a great many unexpected quarters. Margaret had, indeed, been more than amazed at the interest the world seemed to take in her in her new rôle of stepmother!

She had just written these words—" You ask me how I am getting on as stepmother to four, but when I tell you that since my marriage I have never seen any of them except the youngest son, you will understand that, so far, I haven't had a chance of playing the part with any likelihood of success."

At that moment the door opened, and Harry entered, looking so little like his usual self, so tired and harassed, that, involuntarily, she sat round with a look of inquiry on her face.

He still wore the tweed suit common to his working hours, and looked very little like a man who had been out for an evening's enjoyment.

" My dear, how tired you look! Would you like a cup of tea or coffee?"

" No—I don't know—perhaps, later on. It was good of you to sit up for me."

" Oh! I didn't do that," she answered brightly. " I'm not watch-dogging! I've been out to Bearsden spending the evening with my father and mother, and after I got in I started on letters. It's wonderful how they gather up—isn't it? —even with a person of no importance!"

Harry hardly smiled, but dropped into an easy-chair with the air of a man who had all the care of the world on his shoulders.

" You look as if a quiet dinner at home would have suited you better," she said, turning round on her chair to get a better look at him.

" Say, Mrs. Cardine—" he sat forward suddenly, and a quick flush overspread his boyish face, which yet for a moment looked curiously old and anxious, " I've got myself into a beastly hole, and—and—well, hang it all!—you're so kind I thought maybe you'd help me out of it."

" So I will if I can, of course," answered Margaret, and into her eyes there leaped the soft light which is the sign and seal of motherhood all the world over. " It's what I'm here for."

Harry rose up instead of saying anything more, and began to pace the floor.

" I'm rather glad it happened like this—I mean that father had to go away— as it gives me this chance," he went on, rather dismally. " We know a lot of people, but isn't it a queer thing how few people there are a chap can say anything to, when he is up against it?"

" And that is very true, Harry. Most folks' friends can be counted on the fingers of one's hands," answered Margaret readily. " But what are you up against?"

" Rather a big thing," he said, stopping short in the middle of the room, and looking at her with a rueful smile.

" You see, it's this—I've gone and—I've gone and—in fact, I'm a married man!"

CHAPTER XV

MAKING A CLEAN BREAST OF IT

MARGARET looked at the pale, strained face of Harry Cardine, full of deep consternation. He seemed such a boy, that for the moment she wondered whether it was not some nightmare of an imagination distraught.

"May I tell you all about it from the beginning? God, what a relief that will be!"

"Yes, yes; of course. Everything—from the beginning," repeated Margaret feverishly. "Sit down, won't you? And try to look more like yourself."

"Like myself!" he laughed with an odd catch in his voice. "I haven't been that for many a day. I feel about ninety or a hundred, and I've known in the last month or two what makes men commit suicide or flee the country!"

These words naturally made Margaret anticipate some frightful tragedy, yet the tale was simple enough.

"It began ever so long ago—soon after my mother died. Everything seemed to go wrong from that very minute. She—she was a servant in this house.—Oh, I know—but when a chap's lonely and can't bear himself, and there is somebody kind and—and sweet as well, what is a chap to do?"

It was the whole matter in a nutshell, and what could Margaret do but sigh in acquiescence?

"Her name was Katie Lang. They called her little Kate here. She was very wee, and not very strong, and it made me blaze the way she was put on in the house from Jean downwards. Often I've met her on the stairs carrying scuttles of coal nearly as big as herself? Of course, I helped her, and the thing began."

Margaret was just a woman, but also a shrewd one, and her long experience of Club girls had given her an insight somewhat uncanny into their minds and habits of thought and life. But she refrained from suggesting that perhaps the pose on the stairs might have been less pointed had the looker-on been anybody else than the handsome young son of the house!

"I spoke to the girls about it, but they either didn't listen or just laughed. That horrible Mrs. Leggatt never rested till she got her out, and her own relation put in her place, and the way she put on Katie was something awful!"

"So you made yourself a champion?" said Margaret, with a faint, melancholy smile. "It was a dangerous thing to do."

"It was what any man with a spark of decency in him would have done. And she was an orphan, too. She came from one or other of the homes my mother used to be interested in and subscribe to. She liked her, I know, and nobody mourned when she died more than Katie."

"Well, and what happened? Tell me all the story," said Margaret, with a note of pity and tender sympathy in her voice.

"Oh! it just went on in the usual way," said Harry, with a kind of a shame-faced candour. "We got to like one another. I found out that she was quite a nice girl. She hated kitchen gossip, and she was fond of reading, too, and had spent all she could on nice books. Well, to make a long story short, I began to see her outside on her nights out and her Sunday afternoons off. Neither of us thought of anything wrong—and—and she's the dearest and best little woman in the world, Mrs. Cardine, and I'm ready to stand up for her to the whole world."

"But instead you took the thorny, difficult way of secrecy and concealment."

"Well, we didn't seem able to help ourselves. Everything was at sixes and sevens at our place. You know how it was when you came? Jean always out,

Bella squabbling with the lot at home, and Mrs. Leggatt getting drunk, and generally kicking up hell downstairs! You see, I know more than most, for Katie told me all that went on down there, and if people knew what went on in their kitchens when they haven't got the right sort of woman there their hair would stand on end!"

Margaret smiled in spite of herself at these side-lights on life below stairs. The Cardine history was certainly a varied one, and, as it happened, she was permitted to know it from every side.

"Finally, Katie was sent off at a moment's notice. I needn't go into the sordid, horrid story; but Jean wouldn't give her a reference, and was as hard as the nether millstone about it all. She said it was quite time that that class had a proper lesson taught it, and that unless you held the reins pretty tightly, you got nothing for your money. And all the time the cook was drinking and wasting downstairs, and Jean was afraid to dismiss her in case she wouldn't get another, or it was too much trouble to seek one. The fact is, they're all incapable. They don't know the elements of their business. Hardly any of the girls in our class do, and that's why men get off the line sometimes after they are married. They haven't got either decent comfort or value for the money they pay out.

"Well the long and short of it was, I married her, and took a little house for her down at Paisley, and of course I've been spending as much of my time as I could with her. That was eleven months ago, and now—and now——" Here his face flushed, and he turned an odd look of appeal on Margaret's face. "Now I'll have to acknowledge her, and tell my father, and all that, for, in two months' time there'll be another to consider; and, though Katie has never made a complaint, and is as happy as possible, it isn't right; and I'm not going to live like that any longer."

Margaret's eyes filled with tears. In her long experience among working girls, she had encountered many strange life stories and some tragedies; but nothing so simple, moving and straightforward as this! It showed the real grit of which Harry Cardine was made. While quite unconscious of what was passing in Margaret's mind, and though perhaps a little disappointed that she had so little to say, he went on:

"I'm not a bit ashamed of Katie, understand, but I hate telling the pater. Of course, he's very proud in some directions; then, he has had such a beastly lot of worry lately. I hate adding to it. I thought that, perhaps, you'd help me—not to tell it—I'll do that myself—" he added, drawing himself up with an involuntary and very manly gesture—"but perhaps, you'd put in a good word for me, if he happens to cut up rough about it?"

His eyes became wistful again, and, when he turned them on Margaret's face, and saw the tears in hers, his face both softened and brightened.

"Of course I'll help you, dear boy. I don't think it will be very difficult, for if I know anything about your father, he'll be proud of the way you have behaved. You see, you had the chance to behave like a scoundrel, and, instead, you behaved like an honest man and a gentleman to the girl who trusted you."

"Oh, that was easy enough. You see, Katie isn't—well—the kind you're thinking of. It wouldn't have been possible for a chap, even had he been a bounder, to say the wrong thing to her."

"If that is so, she will make a home for you, Harry, and you will be happy together."

"That's what I want, and must have!" he cried eagerly. "In the meantime, she's in a small furnished house that belongs to a seafaring man. They're gone on a six months' voyage, and as his wife hasn't been very strong, the doctor said the sea would do her good. But they're coming back inside of a month, and want the house. Besides, I must get a home of her own for Katie on account of what is coming."

"What name is she living under?"

"Her own—just Mrs. Lang. But, of course, I'm going to change all that."

"Then you haven't regretted it?"

"Oh, no!" His eyes kindled a little. "We'd be quite happy—more than happy!—if our minds were relieved. She's—she's the right sort, Mrs. Cardine. The only fear she has is that she may have hurt me, or hindered me by marrying me—when I didn't leave her much chance of refusing!"

"I'll go and see her to-morrow," said Margaret, on the spur of the moment.

His face brightened.

"Oh, will you? That would be kind. I could take you, as it's Saturday afternoon. I'll come and fetch you—or we could meet, somewhere in town?"

"We can arrange that in the morning," said Margaret. "Meanwhile, we'd better go to bed, I think, as it's past midnight."

As Harry stood up to open the door for her, holding out his hand, she lifted her face and kissed him.

"You poor, foolish laddie! Taking a man's responsibilities on you at your age! But we'll see you through——"

"God bless you," said the lad, and his bosom heaved. "If you knew how differently I feel, now you know! I'll sleep to-night. Just lately, I've had bad nights and anxious days. I'm—I'm glad you're here, and if they'd only see it, you've come to make everything better for us all. You're that sort."

Margaret's eyes overflowed with foolish tears as she climbed the stairs to her own spacious room. The harvest was beginning already, and as she knelt for a few moments by her bed, to ask for a blessing on the house to which she had come, she had a special word for the lad who had borne such a burden of secrecy, though not of shame.

Next afternoon, about four o'clock, they journeyed out together on the top of the tram to Paisley, and Margaret was conducted to the little house in Woodbine Gardens. As they approached the door a somewhat pale, wistful-looking face was seen between the curtains at the near window, but it was quickly withdrawn.

Harry opened the door, and they passed into the sitting-room where the young wife waited, nervously clasping and unclasping her hands, though she had been made aware, by a few lines from Harry, that she might expect them that afternoon.

"Mrs. Cardine has come to see you, Katie," said Harry, a little awkwardly; then, observing something odd and strained in the expression of the two women's faces, he made himself scarce, retreating to the kitchen, where he shut the door and started a cigarette.

After one look, poor Katie Lang, trembling a little, stepped forward, and Margaret took her in her arms.

"You poor, foolish bairn!" said Margaret, feeling her heart stirred to an extraordinary tenderness. "What is this you both have done? A pair of bairns, to be playing at housekeeping, and getting yourself into this scrape!"

"Oh, oh, I'm sorry! I didn't mean it, but—but I love Hal, Mrs. Cardine; and I'd go through fire and water for him."

Margaret patted her shoulder, then held her back a little, and looked into her pretty face from which the rounded contour had gone, and the lines of approaching motherhood taken its place. There was nothing greatly striking in the face to have attracted a man like Harry Cardine, but Katie was sweet, and clinging, and very, very humble, as well as eager to try and atone for what was an imagined wrong.

"I wanted to wait, Mrs. Cardine," she whispered. "I could have got something to do, but Harry wouldn't wait. Do—do you think his father will be very angry? Is there anything I could do to help, for oh, I hate to see him look so worried and anxious? Sometimes when I'm alone, and thinking about it—there is nothing else to think of, down here—I could very nearly kill myself for what I've done!"

"Oh, don't speak like that, my dear," said Margaret, seeing that the girl needed mothering above all else. "It'll come all right if only you have a little patience. It was a foolish step, maybe, for you are both ridiculously young, but it might have been worse."

Margaret had the true womanly instinct which prompted her to try and ease the awkwardness of the situation. She had also a considerable quiet charm of manner, and, by her behaviour that afternoon, knit the heart of Harry Cardine to her in indissoluble bonds. She stayed to tea, and left Harry with his wife, suggesting that he should remain at Paisley till Monday.

"How awfully good and thoughtful you are!" he said gratefully, when they left the house together on the way to the station, Margaret saying that she would go back by train, as a thin, fine rain was now beginning to fall.

"There isn't so very much kindness about that, Harry. The poor lassie needs someone to be beside her, just now, and there is nothing to hinder your stopping till Monday, as your father won't be home till Monday night. What I would like to do, is to send her down to Ardgoil to Mrs. Rogers to be taken care of till after the event. I'll speak to your father about it. But nothing can be done until he is told."

Harry's face positively glowed.

"And, between while,"s said Margaret, "if your father consents to the Ardgoil plan—it's a shame for that beautiful place to be standing empty, and so many folks needing rest and change—we'll get a house ready for her against the time you and she will set up housekeeping in earnest. What would you say to Bearsden—near my father and mother, perhaps? My mother is a perfect dear, Harry, and she would just enjoy mothering your Katie."

"I say!" said Harry, and his voice shook. "It's just as if my own mother had come back? That is the way she used to speak and think for everybody. But, of course, if she had been living I never would have got into this hole, because Katie wouldn't have been put upon in the house."

"You are quite right about your mother, Harry, and it was she who taught me to think about folks—as you express it. But for her I never should have got to know all about my lassies at Bridgeton as I did. I do miss having them come to me with their bit stories! But it has given me the understanding heart. Well, good-bye, my boy. I'm glad you've trusted me, and, I repeat, I'll do my best for you. But just wait a day or two in case your father has had enough of worry in town."

Harry nodded.

"Right you are!" said he, and wrung her hand at parting, and looked as if he wanted to pour forth more gratitude. But she stopped him short, and bade him go home and take his wife out for a drive, and make their plans for the future.

She spent a very quiet Sunday in Huntley Gardens. Miss Bruar came round to tea. They had a good deal of family business to discuss, but Margaret said nothing about Harry and his affairs, except that he had gone away for the week-end.

On that Sunday evening as Harry went out, rather late, for a stroll, he was surprised to encounter Bruce Gemmill at the end of Woodbine Gardens. His face flushed guiltily, as Gemmill thought, and, involuntarily, both paused.

"Hulloa, Gemmill! What are you doing in these parts?" he asked carelessly "Are you working in Paisley now?"

"No, I'm no'," answered Gemmill, with his disagreeable and slightly knowing smile. "I haven't taken a job yet, though I've had the offer of one in Yorkshire."

"You'd better take it, then," said Harry, on the spur of the moment, his old antipathy to the man asserting itself.

"Ay, I daresay you think that. You'd like to get me out of Glasgow! I know too much, maybe, about Bridgeton, and Huntley Gardens—eh?"

"I don't know what you mean, Gemmill," said Harry, drawing back with a certain hauteur. "Whether you go or stay can't possibly affect us. You were a fool to speak as you did to my father, and get the chuck. Berths like Bridgeton aren't picked up every day!"

"Perhaps not. But I've got several crows to pick with the Cardines yet!" he said with a kind of studied insolence. "I might ask, for instance, what you are doing on the prowl down here? Woodbine Gardens, Paisley, is a bit of a come-down from Huntley Gardens—isn't it?—and a bit suggestive, shall we say, of the double life?"

For a minute Harry Cardine saw red. Never in his life had such a passion of rage overwhelmed him. His fist involuntarily clenched, but reflecting, that he would not soil his fingers by touching such a cur, he stepped back.

"I'll say good evening, Gemmill. Either you've been drinking or you've forgotten yourself. In either case, I'll bid you good-night."

"Oh, not so fast, young sir! I see by your face that I've nabbed you! How long has this little game been going on? And what do you suppose your father will say? He took a wife out of the gutter himself, but the sins of the fathers don't excuse the sins of the children—eh? To the third and fourth generation, what does the Bible say? He's an elder in the kirk—isn't he? And you were supposed to be going to follow in his steps! But the little doocot in Woodbine Gardens will take some explaining away, and I'd like to be the one to do the explaining!"

"If you don't get out of my way, you insolent blackguard, I'll fell you!" said Harry thickly. "Or hand you over to the nearest policeman. I suppose it's blackmail you're after—eh?"

"Well, it might pay you, if you want it kept quiet."

Harry Cardine swallowed something in his throat, and turned deliberately, so that the light from the gas-lamp shone full on his face. When he spoke it was in a voice of studied quiet.

"You're an outsider, Gemmill, and it's a good hiding, or kicking, you need. But I'll let you off this time. I'm living with my wife. We're going down to Ardgoil presently for the rest of the summer; so you can put that in your pipe, and smoke it, and the next time you want to push your dirty fingers into other folk's business, you'd better make sure of the kind you have to deal with. And I'd advise you to clear out to your Yorkshire job with as much speed as you can; for Glasgow, apparently, has no use for you—and I have less than none!"

Harry turned contemptuously on his heel and walked off. Had he been a little older he would probably have been more dignified, and have kept his own counsel.

Bruce Gemmill's expression was malignant, even devilish, as he was left to pursue his solitary way. He was not done with the Cardines yet.

CHAPTER XVI

THE NEW COMRADESHIP

JEAN and Bella Cardine were sitting rather gloomily over their Sunday afternoon tea in the flat at Charing Cross.

The one inexperienced maid, whose modest wage had become part of the acute problem of their existence, had gone out for the afternoon, and they had the house to themselves.

Bella had got the tea ready. To do her full justice, she did not shirk any of her self-imposed duties. These weeks had taught both the young women certain facts concerning themselves and other people which they could not have learned in their father's house. They had discovered that willingness to work does not constitute ability or success, and that certain conditions govern the labour market which are at once inexplicable and just.

The last week had been positively disastrous from a business point of view, not a single order having been booked with "Cardine—Robes and Modes."

"Evey ought to do something," said Bella gloomily, as she cut herself a "doorstep" off the loaf and inwardly sighed for the dainty bread and buttered wafers that used to be sent up to the drawing-room at Huntley Gardens. "Let us go out to Greenbank and see."

Jean did not seem elated at the suggestion.

"Anyway, if she doesn't," continued Bella, "I must get some money from Alec. After all, we are entitled to a living wage, and Father promised it. Of course, it's that woman's fault that not a penny has been paid."

"I don't think that, Bella. From the little I saw of her I think she would probably behave more generously than Father."

Bella, imagining too much relenting in the tone, flashed on her sister a look of contempt.

"Jean, I don't believe you'll ever fight it out! I will, if it's over a hunger strike —and I suppose it will come to that if Greenbank won't do something. We can't go on running up bills for ever. I do wish I knew the law exactly about fathers and daughters. Couldn't we raise six-and-eightpence to go and ask somebody?"

Jean neither demurred nor assented. She had a detached air; indeed her thoughts were far enough from the problem under discussion.

"Can't you get anything to do?" questioned Bella irritably. "Will not one of your pals lend a hand or put a thing in your way? What's the good of all their boasted devotion and enthusiasm for one another if they can't do something for one in an emergency?"

"Well, you see, I'm not suffering these disabilities for the Cause," said Jean shrewdly. "And some of them think it was a mistake to leave Huntley Gardens. I'm beginning to think that myself."

"The next thing, I suppose, you'll be going back to let our sweet stepmother wipe her feet on you!" cried Bella, springing to her feet. "Not I! I'll leave you to clear up, and go out to Greenbank and see what they say. Failing Alec and Evey, I must get some money from somewhere to go on with. What about Aunt Mary Bruar?"

"You know her sentiments well enough," said Jean, as she, too, rose. "She's never hidden them, and she has never looked near us since the first week we were here."

Bella walked all the way to Greenbank, partly because she enjoyed it, and partly because pence for car fares were now luxuries. This in itself was an excellent experience for those who had been accustomed to toss coppers about as coins of no importance. The sisters now treated a penny with respect.

Jean washed up the tea-cups, put everything straight, and sat down with the latest pamphlet on social questions, but found her attention wander. At half-past six the street bell rang. Then the colour leaped, warm and soft, to her cheeks, and her heart began to beat quickly.

At twenty-five Jean Cardine had never had a lover, nor had even met any man who had evinced the slightest desire to become one. She was not of the type which attracts men, and her pronounced modern tendencies, though they were merely on the surface, frightened them away.

By the time she had got to the outside landing to pull up the lever of the street door, she had recovered herself, and when Tom Burgess came up the stairs, two steps at a time, whistling softly, she was able to meet him without any outward or visible sign of perturbation.

"Good evening," he said, and there was no doubt about the warmth of his greeting, as he clasped her hand and looked straight into her eyes.

He was attracted by the very qualities which had repelled others—the intense earnestness, the desire to do something with her life, though she had missed the first demand of usefulness, that it shall apply itself to the nearest duty, however irksome and unwelcome. Then she was not of his class. Her refinement and daintiness, her fastidiousness, both physical and mental, had appealed to one who, born in a rather low-class home, amid sordid surroundings, had had his youth cursed by aspirations above it all.

The history of Tom Burgess's early years need not here be told, though it would make interesting reading. Undoubtedly the sorrows and wrongs of his boyhood had helped to make him what he was.

"I hope you are quite well? It's glorious outside. Won't you come out for a stroll? We could get on to the car to the country, and walk in the fields."

But Jean shook her head. She was not ashamed of her interest in Tom Burgess, but she was ultra-sensitive regarding the outside world's opinion and verdict on it, Bella having left her in no doubt as to its possible nature.

"I'm all alone in the house. My sister has gone to Greenbank. I don't think I want to go out particularly, and, anyway, I must stop in, for if she doesn't find them at home she'll come right back, and she hasn't a key."

"Right-o!" he said, as he followed her, nothing loath, into the charming little house which, after his poor lodgings, seemed a very luxurious and beautiful place.

Burgess was a tall, slim figure of a man, wearing the orthodox blue serge suit, loose, soft collar, and red tie, which, in his case, were immensely becoming. One might easily have imagined a studied grace in the careless knot of the tie, and an eye for effect in the arrangement of the plentiful black hair which, having a natural wave, was much admired in certain quarters.

He was quite at home in the room, alone with Jean Cardine. It was the other sister who made him uncomfortable, and put him on his mettle. A good deal of sparring had taken place between them, and he found Bella much less pliable and more difficult to impress with his specious arguments, every one of which she was ready to challenge. His hearty approval of the step they had taken, and which he viewed from quite another standpoint than theirs, did not blind Bella in the least to its economic drawbacks, Bella, indeed, had decided that a great deal of the Socialist party's contention was nothing more than froth!

"So you're all alone?" he said, sitting down opposite Jean, and not seeking to hide his satisfaction. It did not occur to him that in receiving him there alone she was outraging one of the most cherished conventions of her class. He would have laughed at the idea. Burgess was nothing if not an apostle of complete personal freedom. Indeed, in this respect he had left most of his associates far behind. "I've got some news. It's all settled about the trip to the colonies. The money's been found, and the sailing date fixed."

"Soon?" asked Jean, rather faintly, for she knew by the sinking of her heart that the prospect of parting from him troubled her.

"Not before September. As long as we get back before the general election, which is bound to come next February, the time doesn't much matter. But one has to study times and seasons, hot weather, and such-like. The conditions are different from what we have them here."

"Anyone going with you?" asked Jean interestedly.

"Not that I know of yet. But I'm hoping that somebody will."

The tone was significant enough to make the girl's colour rise. She rose nervously and moved towards the window, remarking that it was hot and she would like a little more air.

He sprang to her side, and, standing closely by her, against the window panes, looked into her eyes.

"This is the comrade I'm hoping will be brave enough to take the long voyage—the voyage of life—with me!"

Jean laughed a little nervously. The next moment his arms were round her and she was a prisoner against his breast.

"You care—don't you, lassie?" he asked, and his voice had a ring of genuine passion in it.

She tried to speak, but her breath came quickly.

"Oh, yes; I think I care. But, please let me go! it's all so new and strange, I can't believe it yet!"

"But it's the oldest thing in the world!" he said triumphantly. "It began in Eden."

He did not let her go altogether, but, with one arm thrown round her waist, guided her to the sofa, where they sat down together.

"The very first time I saw you—do you remember that night in the ante-room at the Athenæum?—I said to myself, 'This is the woman who is going to count in my life!' What a difference it makes! What did you think, that night?"

"I had sympathy with you, and your eloquence was wonderful. But I really don't know very much," said Jean humbly. "I'm a mere baby about all these big questions, and I never can understand how people can be so sure of their ground about them. To me there seems to be so many cords all pulling different ways."

"Ah, but you have the open eye and ear, and the understanding heart!" said Burgess confidently. "And you're getting just a little further emancipated every day you live. Now, when you and your sister came here, it was a big step towards that personal freedom to which every human being is entitled."

"Oh, but," said Jean doubtfully, "we can't make a living. It is all very well to have ideas about personal freedom, and living one's own life, and all that; but, unfortunately, one's body needs food and drink and clothing! And soon, I don't know where we are going to get it, unless Capital comes to the rescue."

"Life is burdened with the weight of things we can do perfectly well without," asserted Burgess with full assurance. "The simple life is the best."

"Granted. But even the simple life has to be paid for, at so much per day!" maintained Jean wistfully.

"I've reduced it to a fine art!" said Burgess whimsically. "If I can't actually live on a straw a day, at least I can support existence upon bread and water. And one's reward for that crucifixion of the flesh, is a clearness of vision, a loftiness of aim, which can never be attained among the fleshpots."

"But the fleshpots are very nice," protested Jean with a small sigh, and involuntarily she drew herself a little apart. "For instance—thin bread-and-butter is much nicer than 'doorsteps,' only it takes more butter, and that has to be reckoned with when one is positively poor."

"But where love is, these things don't matter!" asserted Burgess boldly. "Would you be afraid to set out on the self-denying road with me?"

"Oh, no!" she answered, and the glow was on her cheek again, and the moment was a lover's one, of which he took full advantage. "Things are really rather desperate with us," she said, by-and-by, and her face was transformed by the new sweetness which had come into her life. "We owe money. You see, my father refused even to clear the bills for getting us in here. He wants to compel us to go back to Huntley Gardens."

"But you are determined not to?"

"Bella is determined. Personally, I shouldn't care much. Does it matter, after all, where one lives or in what environment? The inner life, the things of the spirit, are one's own."

"Then you are thinking of going back?"

"I am afraid we shall be compelled to; but Bella won't, until that moment arrives. She's gone over to Greenbank now, to see whether my brother Alexander can suggest any way out of the difficulty, or advance some money for our immediate needs."

"I hear quite good accounts of your stepmother. She is a favourite among working girls. I happen to know the woman who ran the Bridgeton Working Girls' Club with her. Perhaps it wouldn't be so bad to be under the same roof with her—she would approve of our comradeship——"

The choice of the word was an odd one, but Jean, accustomed to hearing extreme views expressed in extreme language by Tom Burgess, took no special notice of it. The idea of comradeship in conjunction with love was passing sweet, nay, more, in her estimation it was positively ideal! It seemed to equalize everything, to lift a woman up, to give her the position and the privileges which has been denied her by convention and by man-made laws for centuries.

It was all in harmony with Jean's own crude, only half-digested opinions regarding the relations between the sexes.

"I don't suppose your father will pay those bills. Shall you ask his approval before we set out on the long voyage together?"

"Why, of course! He's my father, and although we've drifted apart a bit just now, I shouldn't like to marry without his consent and approval. I don't even believe I should be happy without it."

Burgess rose suddenly, as if something had been said to startle him. He took a turn across the floor, and Jean, watching him somewhat apprehensively, saw that his brows were knit in an unmistakable frown, and that his mouth had taken a line with which his platform appearance when he was on the most debatable ground had made her familiar.

It was a hard mouth, even relentless in its moulding, and, somehow, she felt a little chilled. For Jean was quite a human and womanly creature, and half of her extreme opinions constituted a pose much in vogue among a certain section of advanced womanhood in Glasgow, and, indeed, all over the kingdom.

"Marriage!" he repeated. "It's a relic of barbarism, and men and women will never be really happy till they bind themselves to one another by the simple oath of fealty. It ought to be enough, between two who love one another. Don't you think so, Jean?"

He paused before her, and his eyes, full of passion and entreaty, were on her face.

Hers faltered then, and her colour rose again more vividly—even a little shamed.

"Oh, I don't think that. There must be surety—something to bind people together!" she cried, a little wildly. "We are not near enough perfection for anything else."

He seemed disappointed.

"Comradeship should be enough," he said, rather gloomily. "It is enough between two who really love and understand one another. Compulsory union, sanctioned by Church and law, has conspicuously failed. The marriage laws are in the melting pot at the moment, and have been proved a complete and ghastly failure."

"Oh no; hardly so bad as that! There are a good many happy couples," asserted Jean faintly.

"They present a conventional face to their world; but get behind the scenes, and down to bed-rock, what do you find? Weariness, ennui, heart-sickness, chafing against the bond!"

"But that has nothing to do with the bond, and would be there just the same if there was no bond! Probably, it would come even more quickly and surely if there was no bond."

"No. You are begging the question, dear woman. Haven't we agreed, times without number, that liberty is the first and the most insistent need of the human soul?"

"Yes, but that can't be pursued to its extremest point," contended Jean gallantly. "It is the very foundations of life and society you are laying the axe to, and what are you going to put in its place. There must be something to keep people together!"

"Now I see that you really haven't advanced far from the primeval state!" said Burgess rather disappointedly. "I thought you had got clear into the light—that faith and freedom stood, hand-in-hand, in your heart."

"I haven't parted with my common-sense," was Jean's unexpected answer. "And the thing you are advocating is only free love under a different name. It's end would be disaster, and not happiness. How would the family, or the home, be safeguarded under such conditions?"

"Oh, ye of little faith! Then I needn't count upon my comrade?" he said, coming quite near to her again.

She had grown strangely pale now, and her eyes were shining, like lamps, in her head.

"I would like you to put in plain language exactly what you mean," she said steadily. "You want me to go to Australia with you—as what?"

"My wife and comrade."

"Your wife—but without any marriage ceremony?"

"You know I don't believe in that old fetish, on which so many hearts and lives have been broken. The new era is not going to have any room for it. It is going to be re-built, on a finer, more glorious foundation."

Jean shook her head.

"I could not go with you on these conditions."

"Then you don't love me as I love you."

"That may very well be. No—you are quite right! I don't understand that kind of love. Mine would make sacrifice, but not foolish sacrifice; and it would demand some guarantee for the future."

"Love gives itself, and is not bought," he quoted glibly.

Jean's lips curled, ever so faintly, and her eyes shadowed darkly. For she had gotten a cruel stab. She knew now that she had been building on this man's love, but every fibre of her shrank from his point of view.

And Burgess, strong and unreasonable in the shibboleths of his creed, was quite merciless, and had no idea either of the depths of the wound he had inflicted or of the priceless treasure just slipping from his grasp!

Imagining that she wavered, he threw an arm about her again, and would have drawn her to his breast.

"Darling!" he cried, "if we love one another does anything else matter? Surely, love and faith walk hand-in-hand in the best natures. And we can be independent of the shibboleth of the marriage service. I would make my vow to you on my bended knees, and, certainly, before whatever Power there is, that is higher and dominates men's minds, my vow of fealty and life-long devotion would be registered. Can't you trust me? Do you think I would fail you? Aren't we both strong enough to show to the whole world, if need be, the power and the beauty of the love and comradeship which ought to be between men and women, but which, by reason of these very conventions, has never had a chance?"

Jean listened, and, even for a moment, permitted his embrace, because she had given her heart, and, when such a woman gives, it cannot be lightly or in a moment recalled. But, almost immediately, with a little shiver, she drew herself apart.

"I am afraid. No! No! If you cared, you would not suggest this thing. If the marriage service is such a trifle as you say, why should it be a stumbling-block? But to me, it is not a trifle at all. I am thinking of—my mother. Have you forgotten yours?"

A strange, slow smile curved the man's mouth, but before he could speak the street-bell rang with no uncertain sound.

"Bella come back!" cried Jean, and flew, with relief, to the door. But, when she drew up the door-lift, and stepped upon the landing, thankful for the timely interruption, great was her amazement to behold, on the dimly lighted stair, the figure and face of her stepmother.

CHAPTER XVII

WORKING TO WIN

MARGARET stood on the landing with a little anxious smile on her uplifted face.

"I hope you are going to ask me in?" her pleasant voice said, "because I have come purposely to see you."

Jean made no immediate answer. She seemed, for the moment, a little dazed. But when, somewhere in the background, a man coughed, the colour flooded her face.

"Bella's out; and I have a friend in the house whom, perhaps, you would not care to meet. It is a man friend," she added, with a slight touch of defiance. "His name is Tom Burgess."

"I have heard of him, and I would like to meet him very much," said Margaret with perfect good humour and cordiality. "And I don't mind about Bella, at the moment—it is you I have come to see."

If Jean wondered at the words, she gave no sign, but stood back, so that her stepmother might cross the threshold she had momentarily barred.

Margaret followed her into the sitting-room, where Tom Burgess stood.

"Mrs. Cardine, Tom," said Jean simply and baldly; and if Margaret felt inwardly a trifle startled by her familiar use of the Christian name, she betrayed no sign.

"How do you do, Tom Burgess? I know you don't like to be called 'Mister.' I heard you say that, one night on the Green," she said, as she extended her hand, with her kind, friendly smile. "You are the man who wants to abolish everything. I could pick a few crows with you!"

Jean turned away abruptly and walked to the window. Not only had Margaret appeared opportunely, but, with unerring precision, she had hit the nail on the head! It was almost uncanny. Incidentally, never had she shown to greater advantage. She was looking very handsome in a well-made and most becoming frock, and she had an assured air of happiness and confidence which, somehow, immediately made itself felt.

She represented the type of womanhood against which the Tom Burgesses of our civilization may pit themselves in vain. They haven't a chance, because women like Margaret Cardine, the potential mothers of the nation, are in unity with nature, and the combination of forces is irresistible.

"I only wish I could stop and have it out, ma'am," he said, obviously impressed. "But I'm due at a conference in Sauchiehall Street, at 8.30, and it'll take me all my time to get there. But, perhaps, you'll give me another chance?"

"As many as you like!" she smiled gaily back. "And I'll get my armour polished up in the interval."

During this brief interchange, Jean had not spoken, but had actually turned her back on them. Margaret decided that her arrival had been opportune, and that, for some reason, Jean welcomed it. She shook hands with Burgess again, and Jean accompanied him to the door. She was not long gone, and, if it were a lovers' "good night," certainly it had not been unduly prolonged.

When Jean re-entered the room, all her colour receded, and she was now wan, while her eyes had a look of strain in them which went to Margaret's heart.

Margaret had seated herself, and was about to rise and put an anxious question, when, without warning or word, Jean suddenly threw herself on her knees beside the chair, and, hiding her face, burst into a storm of passionate weeping.

Margaret, greatly perturbed, tried every known method of pacifying her, and realizing that such a nerve-storm could only clear the air and bring relief in its train, she desisted presently, and simply contented herself with stroking the bent head, and murmuring kind, loving, motherly words.

"There, there, my lassie! It's all right. Yes—it'll help; I know it will. Many's the good greet I've had myself. Nobody, but only the God who gives us tears, knows how to deal with a woman's heart."

Presently the passion was stilled a little, and Jean, wiping her eyes, drew herself a little away.

"I don't know what you must think of me. I couldn't help myself," she said, a trifle shamefacedly. "It came over me all of a sudden-like. But I'm glad, I'm glad it was you; for Bella never would have understood."

"Sit still, my dear, and let your poor heart get quite quiet, while I tell you how I came here to-night. I was sitting all by myself, in the drawing-room at Huntley Gardens, with a book. I had had your Aunt Mary Bruar to tea, and she was very keen on taking me to the kirk with her, to hear some grand American preacher from a Fifth Avenue kirk in New York. But I just didn't go. I was reading quite quietly, and there wasn't a person near me in the house, all the servants being out but two, when somebody spoke my name. I got up, and so real and quick was it all that I answered 'Yes' before I knew where I was! Then, quite distinctly, I saw your face, and knew that you needed and wanted me, so I just came."

"How very strange! I believe my heart called to my mother," said Jean simply.

"And, as she is not here in the flesh, she sent me," said Margaret. "That is how it is, for, on her death-bed, my dear, she bade me take care of you all, and give you mothering, if I could."

"Did she?" asked Jean with wide-open eyes. "And see how we have behaved!"

"Oh, that will soon be all forgotten. Now, if you feel you can tell what has happened to upset you, do. If not, I'll never ask a question save one—Was that your lover who went out a minute ago?"

"My lover!"

Once more the blood crept up to the girl's neck and cheek, and brow.

"Yes. I suppose he is—or was. Now I don't know whether he is anything to me. I am going to tell you, though it won't be easy; but I must know what somebody wiser than myself thinks, though I have decided for myself."

When Jean hesitated there, Margaret said kindly:

"I believe the man sincere. I have never heard anything but that of him, and he has certainly been through the hards, Jean. But his outlook on the world is perverted, and he can't see round a question, or even look into it whole."

"Oh, that is so true! I have often been repelled by it, and he has such power and force! His personality is dominating. It has been dominating me, ever since I have known him."

Then Jean told Margaret of Tom's suggestion—all that had passed between them. When she had finished, she sobbed again, and Margaret's kind hand fell on her head and rested there.

"It has hurt, of course. It must do so when we find the idol has feet of clay. But you have left him in no doubt?"

"None," answered Jean firmly. "But he thinks I don't care for him, and that I never could have cared. But now I know, when he is gone, that he filled all the spaces of my life, which was empty in spite of all I was for ever trying to put into it."

It was the natural, the womanly, the self-revealing cry. Margaret's own eyes filled as it smote upon her ears.

"It would be wrong, wouldn't it?" the girl asked, lifting her face as trustful as a child's to the one bent above her in love. "Of course, people brought up as we have been would be shocked infinitely at the idea. But do you think it possible that that sort of freedom could ever come? That men and women could reach and keep such heights of fealty and devotion?"

"Never, while we are clothed with the body of this flesh!" said Margaret quite solemnly. "And, as I said before, the man would lose nothing, while the woman loses all. We must get him out of your life, Jean, and out of your heart."

"I wonder how? For, though I have sent him away to-night, I'm not prepared to let him out of my life altogether. He meant so much in it—you have no idea!"

"I think I have. But someone else will come and fill it. Someone worthier, and about whom your mother's heart would be glad."

Just for a brief moment the wonder of the thing that had happened banished the more poignant thing from Jean Cardine's mind. She and her stepmother were talking as intimately and naturally as if they had been friends of a lifetime!

Jean's sins, however, where her father's second marriage had been concerned, were chiefly sins of omission rather than of commission; her errors, those of judgment rather than of intention. At heart she was a reasonable creature if handled the right way. She had suffered herself to be dominated by Bella's more overmastering temperament.

"How true and right Aunt Mary Bruar was about you!" she said suddenly. "And how silly we have been! I don't feel safe here any more!"

"Then you'll come back, my dear, to the place you ought never to have left!" cried Margaret, as she took her two hands fast in a warm, compelling grasp. "Come back with me to-night, and let your father, when he brings Nancy home to-morrow, have the joy of seeing you there!"

"Do you think I might? I want to, most awfully—not to-night, exactly, but soon. Perhaps some time to-morrow. Of course I'll have to consult Bella, and try to persuade her. She's most frightfully worried, for she didn't take a single order last week, and, of course, we are already in debt. We don't get the food even that we've been accustomed to, for though people are quite willing to give a Cardine credit up to a certain point, Father said, quite definitely, to Bella that he wouldn't be liable for any debts she or I might incur, and we don't know just what that might mean."

Margaret did not enlighten her, though well aware that Mr. Cardine would never permit extreme measures to be taken towards his daughters.

"I think you had better come home without further delay. Do you think you could persuade Bella, or shall I wait here and try?"

"I don't know. She wasn't in a good mood when she went out. She has gone to Greenbank to see Alec and Evey, and, I believe, to try to get some money from them to carry on with. But Alec has hardly ever a spare penny. Evey spends it all."

"I think I'll go back home then, my dear, and perhaps after you and your sister have talked it over you'll let me know what you decide. To-morrow I'll get your rooms ready, and order a bigger dinner, and live in hope."

They parted affectionately, and though Jean expressed no further gratitude they understood one another.

About half-past nine Bella came home. Her expression was not any brighter than it had been when she went away, and she tossed her gloves and hat down on the table as she cried pettishly:

"If there's a selfish wretch on earth it's that Evey Whitehorn, Jean! I'm properly fed up with her, and no mistake! You should have heard her to-night! She wasn't any too pleased to see me. I don't know where Alec happened to be, but she was entertaining Major Howden to supper, and I just stayed on to spite her. I pretended I had important business with Alec, but at last I left, and I met him at the bottom of the Gardens; and, of course, he hasn't a red cent to bless himself with! No man who had married Evelyn Whitehorn ever would have! So I don't know what's to be done next."

"Well, I'll tell you what I'm going to do," said Jean unexpectedly and with a certain quiet deliberation. "I'm going back to Huntley Gardens to-morrow!"

"You're what? To be chucked out by that woman, or at least made to feel small and mean? You'll never do it, Jean! Why, anything—even this would be better!"

"But this can't go on. Unless we get money from somewhere we're bound to shut up shop."

"I tried to get Evey to give me an order and to promise to bring Lady Farquhar. She's expected at Milbreck's next month. But Evey wouldn't do a single thing! She's ashamed of us, Jean. And I know that somehow she isn't playing the game."

"I told you she wouldn't do anything for us," said Jean coolly. "I say, Bella, she's been here."

"Who has?" asked Bella as she took up her hat and began to even out the rose-leaves with careful fingers. " Aunt Mary Bruar, do you mean? It's just about time she did look us up! I wonder if she'd be any good for a hundred or so? I've a very good mind to pop round even yet and ask her."

" It wasn't Aunt Mary. It was Mrs. Cardine."

" Mrs. Cardine! Heavens, what brought her?"

" She came to see us," said Jean, and the colour flickered unsteadily in her cheek. " And she was most awfully kind and nice, and agrees with me that we'd better go home. Let's go to-morrow!"

Bella regarded her sister steadily, and with a certain mingling of surprise and suspicion.

" I thought you expected Tom Burgess to-night?"

" I did."

" Well, and didn't he come?"

" Yes. He was here when Mrs. Cardine came."

" How interesting! Did they get on together?"

" Not very well. He didn't stop long after she arrived," said Jean, steadying her voice by an effort, and determined not to tell Bella what had actually happened.

" Oh, but she ought to understand him," said Bella rather slightingly. " She belongs to his class. How long did she stop? I rather wish I had seen her."

" Do you want anything to eat, or a cup of cocoa?" asked Jean.

" I had a very genteel supper at Greenbank, but I couldn't enjoy it, knowing perfectly well that Evey was wishing me at Timbuctoo. I could be doing with a cup of cocoa and an egg, I believe. I should like a good square meal again! Wonder when I'll get it?"

" To-morrow night—in Huntley Gardens," suggested Jean as she went to put the kettle on the gas-ring. " She's going to order a bigger dinner on purpose."

Bella, however, did not take that at all seriously, but she had less to say in demur than usual.

Next day Margaret had her hands full. She surprised the housemaid by giving instructions that all the young ladies' rooms were to be put in readiness for them, and herself went up later in the day to make sure that all was right.

A little smile of satisfaction was on her kind lips as she did so, for if she could once get them under the roof she would not despair of the rest.

She was as happy as a girl all that day, and towards evening so restless, and even agitated, at the prospect of the welcome home! How much she had missed her husband she could not have put into words. A few months back she could quite truthfully have asserted that it was not in her nature to care so much for any man!

It had been arranged that Harry would be at the Central to meet the travellers. Margaret herself had not the slightest desire to go. She bestowed great care on her toilet, putting on a beautiful gown of a lovely, soft amethyst shade, which suited her to perfection. A great bunch of violets she tucked in the corsage, and had just gone into the dining-room to see that the table was all she desired it to be, when she heard the rumble of the cab wheels.

" Two more places, Barbara! I'm nearly certain Miss Cardine and Miss Bella will be round to dinner, even if they don't stop all night," she said hurriedly, the colour coming and going pink in her cheeks like any girl's, as she heard Cardine's voice in the outer hall.

He came striding in first, looking everywhere for her, and, careless of the on-lookers, kissed her fondly.

" My own dear woman, but I am glad to get back to you! Here's the truant. Come and show yourself, Nancy."

The girl came forward shyly, her eyes shining like twin stars under the brim of her coquettish travelling hat.

Margaret had no flowery phrases, but honest gladness was in both face and voice as she held out both hands to Nancy.

" I'm so glad you've come home, my dear," she said simply, and Nancy, touched and made repentant, on the spur of the moment, lifted her face to be kissed.

" Gilder came down with us, Margaret, and I asked him to come and dine. He'll be here by half-past seven. I hope you don't mind?"

" Oh, no. I ordered dinner for seven, but I daresay it can be kept back all right," she answered. "I've told them to make your old room ready, my dear. And your Aunt Mary will be here, I hope; so we shall be very happy."

She did not mention the names of the other two girls, because she was not sure whether they would come. The day had passed without bringing any message from them.

After Margaret had taken Nancy to her room she went back to her own to see about her husband's things. Cardine closed the door, and drew her to him fondly.

"Eh, but I'm glad to get home, my dear! Look me in the face and tell me you're as glad to see me as I am to see you?"

"Why, of course I am! I haven't been able to settle to anything to-day," she said, giving his cheek a wifely pat. "I'm sure you're tired with all that travelling, Jamie?"

"I am. But it was worth it. I think Gilder's all right, Maggie. I've put him pretty well through his paces, and seen his folk, and, though they are queer, according to our standards, and he has nothing but his pay, it might have been worse. I'm relying on your opinion, however. You'll see him to advantage to-night. And now, tell me what you've been about, my lady, since I've been away?"

Margaret coloured a little as she stepped back and began to busy herself about his suitcase.

"Oh, I haven't eaten the bread of idleness. I'll tell you bit by bit, as it comes up," she said, thinking of all that had happened in his absence. Harry's affair was naturally uppermost in her mind. "I'm very glad anyway that Nancy is here. What a bonnie little dear she is! She ought never to have gone away."

"You're right there. Have you heard anything of the other two?"

Before she could reply a low knock came to the door, and the housemaid opened it.

"Please'm, that's Miss Cardine and Miss Bella come. And I've put them in the blue room. Was that right?"

"Quite right!" cried Margaret, and she flew to the door. "Have they brought their boxes?"

"Oh! no, ma'am. They're in their evening frocks and cloaks."

"Very well. I'll come to them immediately."

She closed the door and turned a radiant face to her husband.

"That's what I've been busy about, my man, while you've been away. Just nothing but you and your bairns and your affairs! I'd better go and see them. I'll tell you all about everything later on. My! what a lot there is to tell!"

She was more than pleased that the girls had come, because their father's happiness over that would no doubt help him to get more quickly over the disappointment and shock of Harry's marriage. That the news would both shock and disappoint him there could be no manner of doubt.

She was pleasurably nervous as she sped along the corridor to the blue guest-chamber, where Jean and Bella, with an odd feeling of strangeness, were feeling themselves for the first time merely guests in their father's house.

All day long, Bella had protested that nothing on earth would induce her to go near Huntley Gardens; but, when she saw Jean fully dressed, she had flown to get into a black evening frock, and had said, with a touch of sullen defiance, that she wasn't going to be out of it, and must go, to see that they didn't sit in judgment on her in her absence.

Some trace of that unlovely attitude of mind was visible in her expression when their stepmother entered the room, smiling slightly, but very sweetly, in welcome.

"I'm so glad you've come, my dears. Thank you very much," she said, and, having kissed Jean, turned to Bella. But that prickly person stood back.

"I'm not going to be a hypocrite! I'm only here because I'm fed up with things generally, and Charing Cross in particular; and because I wasn't going to be judged and condemned when I wasn't there."

"I don't mind what brought you, now you've come," answered Margaret, without a trace of resentment. "Nancy's in her own room, and yours is all ready —sheets and everything. So if you change your minds, you can stop all night, and go and fetch your boxes to-morrow. We'll see later. Anyhow I've told your father you're both coming back to-morrow. Now I must go and help him to dress, for your Aunt Mary Bruar will be here immediately, and Captain Gilder is coming at half-past seven. I'll leave you to your own cracks, but I'll just say again that you've made me very happy to-night, and I thank you very much."

"She's a good sort," said Bella, somewhat grudgingly, as they were left alone. "But I confess I couldn't climb to such heights! If any woman had said the things to me I said to her, and about her, I'd cut her for the rest of my natural life! Let's go and see Nance."

Twenty minutes later, Margaret descended alone to the drawing-room to wait the coming guest. Aunt Mary Bruar had arrived, but was upstairs with the girls, rejoicing over the miracle that had been wrought. She did not know how it had been wrought, but the evidences of victory were there; and, in the meantime, nothing could alter the happy fact that the Cardines, to outward appearance, were once more a united family, from whom the eyes of a censorious world might now be withdrawn.

Margaret flitted about the drawing-room, changing a cushion here, pulling forward a flower-vase there, and, generally speaking, in that state of happy restlessness which arises out of a quick succession of events, most of them pleasant.

Before anyone came to join her, Barbara Watson, in an obvious state of elation and excitement, announced Captain Gilder.

Margaret turned swiftly, but the welcoming smile froze on her face when she beheld the man advancing up the long room to greet her with the polished veneer of social usage.

"You! You!—it is you!" she said.

He, obviously startled and dumbfounded, could not for the moment find an answer. Just then Cardine followed him, rubbing his hands together, with the satisfied air of a man from whose mind and heart a load has been lifted.

"You've surely done it in record time, Gilder!" he said. "I suppose my wife has introduced herself."

Fortunately Aunt Mary Bruar and the others entered at the moment, and the instant of undoubted strain passed.

But Cardine saw that his wife's face had lost its natural serenity, and, once or twice during dinner, his eyes wandered anxiously down the long table, wondering what had happened to upset her.

CHAPTER XVIII

ANOTHER POINT OF VIEW

CONSIDERING the fact that those seated round the table represented so many different kinds of drama, and that almost every individual present had an under current of some kind in their lives, there was a surprising amount of quite natural interchange of conversation during dinner.

The two most natural and unconcerned were undoubtedly Cardine himself and Mary Bruar. She, kind soul, rejoiced unfeignedly to see her sister's children once more gathered about their father's table, and inwardly blessed the woman whose tact and sweetness of disposition had triumphantly overborne and demolished every difficulty.

Margaret herself probably spoke least of all. Courtesy had demanded that Captain Gilder should have the place of honour by her side, but Nancy, on her lover's other side, naturally monopolized a good deal of his attention.

On the whole the dinner passed off better than might have been expected. Bella was very quiet, but fully appreciated the excellence of the food placed before her. A course of scrap-meals and cocoa suppers had given her appetite a good edge. She was obliged to admit, somewhat grudgingly, that even her own mother had not more beautifully filled the part of house-mother and house-mistress.

Margaret put on no airs ; she was perfectly natural, pretending nothing ; while, at the same time, she had sufficient dignity to bear herself with a certain distinction. Indeed Gilder, who had seen her in far other circumstances, marvelled at what he now saw. But he was very uneasy in his mind, and, when not talking, his expression was furtive.

After a very good, well-cooked dinner, Margaret rose, and the others followed her to the drawing-room. It was a wet night, and she had ordered a log fire in the drawing-room, which added greatly to its comfort.

Bella was basking in the extraordinary sense of physical well-being, which had enveloped her since she had crossed her father's threshold once more. After all, independence and living one's own life involve a good deal of discomfort for young women of Bella Cardine's type ; and only a few of them stand fast, without sighing for the fleshpots of Egypt !

As Bella curled herself in the corner of the big, old Chesterfield, she was wondering what would be the most diplomatic ground for surrender. After all, the stepmother was not so bad at all. She was not even common, but had a gracious naturalness of manner, as well as a kindness of heart, which set her apart.

Jean was quiet, and rather distrait. Nancy, in the glamour of her first love affair, was radiant and restless too. When she had swallowed her coffee, she went to the piano, and began to play waltz tunes.

Jean drew up to her Aunt Mary, on the fender stool, and, after a moment's cogitation, Margaret came over, quite deliberately, and sat down beside Bella. While dinner was in progress, she had conceived a scheme for getting hold of Bella, and obtaining some assistance for herself.

Bella made as if to rise, but Margaret smiled, and said she only wanted the other corner.

" I hope this means you are coming back to-morrow ? " she said quickly. " You must have seen how happy your father is. I haven't seen him look like that since I came to the house."

" I'm surprised," said Bella, and, try as she would, she could not keep the nip out of her voice. " I thought he had everything he wanted, now."

" He is a man who likes all he cares for about him, Bella, and is there any reason now, why he shouldn't have it ? "

" Not so very much, perhaps. I will go as far as say that if I'd known as much about you as I do now, I wouldn't have left."

It was a concession, and Margaret accepted it.

" That is something, anyway ! But as it happens, you simply must come back. The sooner the better—to-morrow, if possible. I've a job in hand I can't put through myself, and I was wondering, at dinner, whether I might ask you to help me ? "

Bella looked both piqued and interested.

" I'm not much good. But, of course, if it's anything I can do, well, I will—and so I ought, after to-night."

" It happens to be a rather urgent matter. Could I see you, do you think, to-morrow morning—either here, or at Charing Cross ? It is something I want to talk over with you ; something of the first importance, arising out of to-night."

Involuntarily Bella's eyes travelled towards her little sister at the piano.

" Has it to do with Nancy ? "

Margaret nodded.

" It isn't possible to say any more here, or to-night. What about to-morrow ? "

" Perhaps I'd better come to you. Jean can look after the place. I daresay you know there won't be any customers," she added, with a faint, bitter smile.

Margaret passed that over.

" May I wait till a little later, and just tell you, before you go, where we had better meet ? "

" But, I say ! My advice won't be much use to anybody. And I can't think why you want to be so civil to me."

The last words rushed out rather quickly, and the first gleam of softness Margaret had yet seen was visible in Bella's eyes. It was not possible to pursue the subject farther, however, because, at the moment, the men came up from the dining-room.

Gilder had hardly the look of a happy lover, as, following close upon the heels of his future father-in-law, he came within view. Relieved to see Nancy at the piano, playing softly, he at once made his way to her side.

" Darling," he whispered passionately, " I wish I could get you away from this crowd. Couldn't we have a few minutes alone, somewhere ? "

Nancy looked round in rather a startled way, the shimmer of the blue frock she was wearing scarcely bluer than her eyes. Her smile was shy, the colour pink in her cheeks. She was maddeningly fair !

" Oh, I don't know. They would wonder. I don't think we'd better—to-night. And I'll see you to-morrow—won't I ? "

" Not even to say good night ? " he persisted. " For I'll have to go soon. I ought hardly to have seen you here, even, but you make a man forget everything, Nancy ! "

Nancy smiled, well pleased, but continued to shake her head.

" Isn't there any place—a little sitting-room, a conservatory ? Surely, in a house of this size, there must be a corner for two not very big lovers ! "

But Nancy, new to lovers' ways, and shy yet, made no move.

" I can't, you see. There's my stepmother—she's been most awfully kind, but she mightn't like it. We've got to consider her."

" I'll tell you what, darling—I'll go and plead with her. There isn't anybody talking to her just now, and, as you say, she's got to be considered. I shan't be gone long."

He walked deliberately up the long room, to the sofa on which Margaret sat looking over the columns of the evening paper. Bella had moved off. Cardine was talking to Mary Bruar, and there was nobody exactly within ear-shot. Margaret stood up when she saw him come.

" Where can I speak to you ? " he said, in a low voice. " I must know whether you are going to put a spoke in my wheel. Is there a chance, to-night ? "

"No," she answered coolly. "But if you will call here to-morrow, between eleven and one o'clock, I will see you."

"I would rather not come to the house," he answered briefly. "Couldn't you meet me at the gates of the Botanic Gardens at eleven o'clock? That might easily appear accidental—a meeting here might occasion comment."

Cardine, wondering, perhaps, why they talked so earnestly together, after glancing once or twice in their direction, took a step towards them.

"Very well," said Margaret hurriedly. "Inside the Botanic Gardens gates, at eleven."

Then she turned, with an immediate and visible relief, from the somewhat sinister face of the man of the world, to her husband, to whose fine face the serenity and much of the old happiness had been restored.

It was the thought of the hidden fires of human conflict in that room, the forces which make for dissension and peace, which troubled her, because she saw from his expression that he imagined all was well with him and his, and that a new era in his family life had been happily inaugurated.

For Nancy's engagement Evelyn Whitehorn alone was responsible. Very well did Gilder know it; and, when he left the house in Huntley Gardens, he looked at his watch first, and then asked a policeman to direct him to the nearest telephone office.

Arrived there, he rang up Greenbank, and, much to his relief, was answered by Mrs. Alexander Cardine's clear, high treble.

"Who?—Oh, Captain Gilder! Yes—but where are you speaking from?"

"From Hillhead telephone office. May I come out for half an hour? I have something very important to talk about."

"Why, yes—delighted! I'm all alone. My husband is at a textile dinner at the Windsor, and won't be home before eleven. It's only half-past nine now."

"Right-o! Thank you, I'll come now," said Gilder, and, ringing off, he went out to the street to hail the first passing cab. Inside ten minutes he was shown into Mrs. Alexander Cardine's presence.

"I quite thought you were dining *en famille* at Huntley Gardens, and I can't imagine how you got away so soon," she said as they shook hands. "Wasn't it a success?"

"No, it wasn't," he answered, as he sat down uncomfortably on the edge of a chair, with the air of a man somewhat at a loss.

"Why, whatever happened?" asked Evey, with the liveliest interest. "Do tell me every single thing! Wasn't the new woman nice?"

"It's about her I've come to talk, and before I can explain the situation I'll have to go back a good while—more than a year and a half——"

"Oh, why? Did you know her in the old days, when she was a working woman at the factory?"

"For my sins, I came in contact with her, and I saw, from her face to-night, that she means to have her knife in me. I simply couldn't stop in the same room with her, because I did not know what might happen any moment. If I'd known who the second Mrs. Cardine was, I'd have given the house a wide berth—at least until I'd got my bearings, and had had a chance of explaining."

"Well, what is there to explain? Have you something to tell me?" asked Evelyn, settling herself comfortably in the corner of the big silk-damask couch, and reaching for her cigarette case. "This is most exciting!"

"I must tell somebody who understands. A woman of the world—like you—because it is necessary, for I may want somebody to take my part at Huntley Gardens."

"Oh, but I'm a broken reed, in that direction! For I'm not a *persona grata* at Huntley. Surely you know that? I'm even out of Aunt Mary Bruar's good graces. She's the one to play up to, if you need a champion. If she takes to you, she'll go any length to befriend you. I don't happen to suit her tastes, but there's a lot more in that Early Victorian dear than you would imagine. I'm quite sorry to be on her black list, at present. I miss her, rather, and she always has had a good deal of influence over my father-in-law. In fact, I've often said to my husband that if the law had allowed it they would have got married soon after granny died."

" All this doesn't help me much," said Gilder ruefully. " May I smoke, as you are so encouraging as to light up ? One of the very best cigars I've sampled in a blue moon was spoiled for me by that woman to-night—confound her ! "

" Light up, of course. They are Egyptians in the silver box. My brand is a mild Virginian," said Evelyn. " Well, what are you going to tell me about your former acquaintance with my stepmother ? Fancy you with a past, and she in it ! "

" Well, as it happens, I have had a bit of a past, and she was in it, though not quite as you think," said Gilder, making a wry face. " I'm going to make a clean breast of it, Mrs. Cardine, for I know what a sensible woman and a good pal you are. And you don't belong at all to the middle-class set you have married into."

" Of course not," said Evelyn, with an air of satisfaction. " But when one is the eldest of a family of eight—six of them girls—one has to do many things. In my case it was accepting the first man who came along offering me a good time."

At another time Gilder, who was never uninterested in any personal talk with his women friends, might have pursued the subject, but at the moment he was wholly engrossed with his own affairs.

" I understand," he said rather absently. " It is three years since I came to Glasgow, and when I came first, I found it dull enough. It was a while before I found my set, you know, and, in the interval, I had to amuse myself somehow."

Evelyn nodded, and watched the rings of smoke curling above her head.

" It's a beastly dull hole this when a chap has no friends ; and, until Howden came, I somehow didn't get to know the right people. We had a pretty average slow crowd at Maryhill my first year. Well, among other things, there was a little girl I got to know. She was a seamstress, or milliner, I believe it was ; awfully pretty. She lived with her mother, who was a widow. We got rather chummy, don't you know, and I spent a good deal of time with her. Then, of course—well, I must be honest, as it happens, because I'm in a pretty tight hole now, and, if you are to help me, you must know exactly where I stand. There was trouble. She—she got ill, and—and died."

" Through you ? " said Evelyn, sitting forward with a look of tense interest on her face.

" It isn't any use denying it. It was through me, in the first instance ; but she needn't have died if she had had any stamina. I did everything I could for her, and even went the length of offering to provide for the mother, but she wouldn't have anything to do with me."

" Then what had Mrs. Cardine to do with it ? "

" I'm coming to that. She made herself unnecessarily and objectionably busy about it. This girl happened to be in some club, or association, or something which Mrs. Cardine ran. I never heard her name, though I saw her once or twice, and I never, for a moment, associated her with the woman Mr. Cardine had married. She came to see poor Mollie several times while she was ill ; and, once or twice, I had the misfortune to meet her there, so now you see where I am."

" It isn't a pretty story," said Evelyn, who had no difficulty in filling in the gaps. " And it is most unfortunate that Mrs. Cardine should have known anything about it. Of course, she'll tell. Probably by now she has told. That kind of woman takes a positive delight in waving the moral flag very high ! And, if she works on Mr. Cardine's feelings sufficiently—well, you have said, or will have to say, good-bye to Nancy—that's the whole matter in a nut-shell."

" I'm most awfully fond of Nancy. She's the sweetest thing and the dearest I've ever seen ; and she could make anything of me ! I want to settle down. And I'll make her a good husband—that, I suppose, is what the holy Mrs. Cardine could never be able to understand—that a man might repent of the sins of his youth, and be sincere in his resolutions for the future ! "

Evelyn Cardine looked for a moment in attentive silence at the selfish face, the cold, clear eye, the hard, heavy jaw, and had a most unusual qualm. After all, Nancy was such a child !

" I'm bound to tell you, knowing the Cardines as I do, Hugh, that I don't think you've the ghost of a chance," she said decidedly. " Unless you can shut her mouth for ever, I'm sure that my father-in-law will show you to the door. He's a stickler for religion and morality, and it is not a story he would accept and pass by. I do believe that perhaps it might be better if you just backed out of the engagement somehow."

"I won't," said Gilder, jumping up, his face set in its hardest lines. "By heavens, and that's just what I won't do! I'll fight them to a finish, and, if I can take Nancy away from under their very noses, I'll do it!"

"If you care as much as that I ought to wish you well," said Evelyn with a faint smile.

CHAPTER XIX

THE DARK FLOWER

"I'LL just take one pipe and come up, Maggie, for it seems as if there was a lot to talk about. It's been a successful evening on the whole, better than I expected," said Cardine to his wife, when the family party had broken up.

"It has, and, Jamie, I want you to be grateful for your mercies, for they are many," she said rather solemnly.

"Why, my dear, so I hope I am: but, more especially, for you! This house is a home to-night, for the first time since Isabel left it, and they are all learning to know and to feel it."

"Then, if that is how you feel, promise not to be hard on the bairns. They are all young, and it is just guiding they need more than anything."

He looked at her, more and more surprised, and also deeply moved.

"You're a wonder, Maggie!" he said rather thickly. "I'll be up inside of five minutes."

But Margaret knew better. As she went upstairs there was prayer in her heart, and once in the big, spacious room, she busied herself taking off her frock and getting into her dressing gown. Then she began to take down her hair and brush it out, also very slowly, feeling her nervousness increase.

It was right that Harry should himself speak to his father, and he had promised his stepmother he would do so that night. She wished she could have had a chance to prepare the way a little. Already she had proved that Cardine, though he had the sense and equity of justice highly developed, could be hard and even relentless; and this marriage of his younger son, on whom so much of his hope was built, would undoubtedly disappoint him keenly, and in his dearest part.

When her hair had been put into two long thick plaits, which gave her a very Madonna-like look, she walked through the dressing-room and out to the landing to listen. But not a sound came up from the room below. The lights were all lowered, and the house was already silent as the grave.

She busied herself for a few moments putting away her husband's things that had tumbled out of the bag, the housemaid having had no time for the usual valeting owing to the increase of work in the dining-room and in the kitchen, made by four extra for dinner.

Eleven rang, and Margaret was becoming the prey of acute nervousness, when she heard someone coming up. She flew to the door. It was Harry, and his face was utterly woe-begone, even distraught.

"You have told him, Harry?" she said from the threshold of the door.

"Yes. He's taken it badly. He simply won't see reason. He says the best thing I can do is to go abroad. He spoke to me precisely as if I had been a scoundrel! Evidently it pays to be like Gilder—a polished villain! Next time I'll try the rôle."

Margaret did not seek to detain him, because she saw that nothing could be gained by further talk between them. She had suffered him to go off without a "good night," and herself ran down the stairs.

She had no hesitation. She simply opened the smoking-room door, walked in, and carefully closed it behind her. Cardine was in an easy-chair, sitting slightly forward, with his fingers lightly interlaced, his face wearing the most forbidding aspect Margaret had ever seen. Even at the factory, when things went wrong and business worries pressed, she had never seen him look so gloomy.

Although he turned his head, he did not smile at her entrance. She glided to his side and dropped her hand on his shoulder.

"Don't take it like that, Jamie. It might so easily have been worse."

He flung up his head.

"Oh, so you know, do you? How long have you known?"

"Didn't Harry tell you?" she asked in surprise, gathering much from his question regarding the bitter nature of the interview.

Cardine shook his head.

"He told me last Friday, and I went out on the Saturday to see the poor lassie. She's all right, Jamie, and I do assure you it might have been worse."

"I can hardly see how it could have been," he said hardly. "A bit servant lass! It's galling to a man's pride; and, as I said to him, he might have had his pick! I thought him the best of the lot, Maggie. He has brains, looks, a way with him."

"I grant all that. But he has something worth all these put together—he's an honest man. Don't you see that he might have behaved very differently? Left the poor thing to her fate, as—as others have done?" Here she faltered involuntarily. "And what you have got to do now is to make the best of it, and remember his mother would have been pleased, because, though he may have been foolish, he has not been bad or heartless."

Cardine listened attentively, though outwardly there was no sign of softening.

"What I can't make out is how a woman of that class could appeal to him at all, or what he saw in her. I remember her well enough, of course—a small, jimpy thing, with no looks to make a man throw everything else to the winds for her. And as for brains! How could a bit kitchenmaid have brains to match with Harry Cardine's? As I told him to-night, it's a lifelong business he's laid up for himself as well as for us."

"Oh, it isn't so bad as that," said Margaret cheerfully. "She certainly is a cut above the usual run. She's interested in books, and she's been doing her best to improve her mind."

"Tchut!" said Cardine contemptuously, as he rose to his feet. "We may leave that out of the count. We know just how much it means. The best thing we can do is to ship them off to Canada and let them dree their weird. I told him I would give him in moderation to stock a small farm, and he can make a kirk or a mill o' it."

Margaret's own face hardened a little.

"I think it would be cruel and hard as well as unnecessary to send them away to Canada or anywhere else, as if they had committed some crime," she said bravely. "After all, whose business is it except yours? Give them enough to start on and to live on, and you'll never regret it. Meanwhile let her go down to Ardgoil and Christina Robb will look after her."

Cardine stared. The feeling heart, the organizing brain, had never been more clearly demonstrated. He felt himself wavering, grateful even for this strong and sane intervention, suggesting the most common-sense way out of the difficulty.

"You have often said you couldn't do without Harry at Bridgeton," she went on, emboldened by the impression she felt she had made. "Why should you rob yourself of all he is and is going to be in the business? It isn't common-sense! Give them a chance to be happy, and to make the best of everything! I'm sure you won't regret it, Jamie! To begin with, you'll get all his gratitude and love—instead of the face I met just now on the stairs."

"You're not feared, my woman! Nobody has ever before spoken to me like that. There might be something in it, after all; but it'll ruin him socially. Folk like the Whitehorns don't forgive that sort of lapse, and then, there is Gilder and Nancy to be considered now. His folk are mighty poor, but they're mighty proud with it."

Margaret's lip curled up, but she turned swiftly away to hide it.

"Captain Gilder isn't a member of the family—yet. And, if he is going to swerve in his allegiance and affection for Nancy because of this, why then, we are better without him!"

"You didn't take to Gilder, Maggie. Anybody could see that."

"No, I didn't take to him," she answered. "But don't let us talk about him just now. It's Harry we're on. Aren't you going to change your mind, and be a little kinder to him? He feels things more acutely than any of them; and this may, very easily, be a crisis in his life."

Cardine made no answer, and she ventured to lay a wifely hand on his arm again.

"Jamie—I can't think it would have pleased you better had Harry betrayed that poor lassie?"

"Good heavens, no! I would have been done with him, then. But the whole thing is so beastly underhand and low-down. It takes a lot of swallowing. Maggie. Give me time."

"All the time there is, my man," she answered and lifted her face for his kiss.

"Well, what now? You've got something else up your sleeve, I can see," he said, with a glimmer of a smile.

"I only wondered whether you wouldn't go up and say another word to Harry? There's no sleep in yon eyes, Jamie, and he has suffered a lot already."

"Humph! You've a hard job wi' me and my bairns, lass. Off to your bed, and I'll be up presently."

He did not promise, but she went upstairs hopeful.

She had hardly got inside her own room, and the door shut, when she heard her husband's foot coming up. Listening, with her hand on the fastening of her wrap, she heard the heavy, measured tread come up the stairs and go by her door. He was on his way to Harry's, and it was fully five minutes before he joined her.

"I have done what you bade me, Maggie," he said, as he shut the door. "So now, maybe, you'll be good enough to let me get a wink of sleep. I've had precious little since I was in London! They put me in a room facing the Euston Road—as well have perched me on the roof at once!"

He spoke lightly, to disguise the feeling under which he was evidently labouring.

"You spoke a word of comfort to him—thank you, Jamie!"

"I don't know for what you should thank me. All the thanks ought to come your way. And they are coming—I see them! That lad fair worships you already!"

"And you'll furnish a house for them, out at Bearsden, and let me take her down to Ardgoil, and—and be generally a very good, kind father, who will be rewarded in this world and the next!"

Cardine laughed as he threw off his coat.

"I'll leave you to tell everybody all about it, for, if you can bewitch them as you have bewitched me, I daresay it'll end in general rejoicing."

He fell asleep quickly, tired out with the journey and the excitement of the day; but Margaret was long wakeful, thinking of the ordeal of the morrow, and what she should say to Hugh Gilder. She had not an idea; she could only pray that she might be guided; that wisdom and the fitting word might come to her from afar.

Nancy did not come down to breakfast next morning, and Margaret was glad of it. She went up to see her, and recommended her to rest till lunch-time; then having seen her husband and Harry off to business, and seen to the ways of her household, she dressed and sallied forth to keep her appointment at the Botanic Gardens.

She was there a few minutes before the time, but Gilder, looking very spruce and well-groomed, though his expression was not very amiable, was waiting for her. A brief salutation passed between them, and they turned, and began to walk towards a secluded part of the grounds.

It was a most lovely morning, but too early for the gardens to be crowded, only a few nursemaids, who had taken time by the forelock, being visible with their charges. It was perfectly easy to find a place where they could not be overheard, or even seen.

"Well," said Gilder, making pause by a seat under a tall acacia tree. "What are you going to do?"

"I have not made up my mind," answered Margaret calmly. "I would only ask you whether you consider yourself a fit husband for a girl so pure and sweet and young as Nancy Cardine, who deserves, and could very easily get, the best."

"That is for her to judge, surely."

"Is it?" said Margaret significantly. "Then has she been, or is she to be, told of what happened in the past in your life?"

CHAPTER XX

TO SAVE NANCY

WHEN Margaret asked him if Nancy had been told the story of Mollie Semple, Gilder muttered something under his breath, but he tried to keep control of himself. He had to be both respectful and conciliatory in the presence of this woman, who had the power if not to break his engagement, at least to put difficulties of no ordinary kind in the path. It was important that no hitch should occur, more particularly where Mr. Cardine was concerned, he having intimated his intention of making a very handsome marriage settlement on his youngest daughter.

But Gilder had no knowledge of the type of womanhood Margaret Cardine represented. Her outlook, her prejudices, and her impregnable moral code were alike a sealed book to him. He was therefore handicapped throughout their interview.

Now, with Evelyn Cardine, he was quite at home, and had discussed the whole story with her from the standpoint of the man and woman of the world, to whom such incidents, though regrettable, were not insurmountable.

But Mollie Semple's death had made a profound impression on Margaret, and she had never felt that the girl's forgiveness of Gilder at the end was justifiable.

" Of course, I realize quite well, that you can put a nasty and probably an efficient spoke in my wheel, Mrs. Cardine," he began, in a conciliatory voice. " But what I would ask you to consider is, what's the use ? What good would it do ? I care for the girl, she cares for me. I'll make her a good husband. I'm not the only man who has had a lapse of that kind before matrimony, and it's a certainty I shan't be the last."

Margaret had no answer as yet. If she had hoped for some genuine penitence, some bitter regret and shame over that unhappy story, she was keenly and promptly disappointed. Gilder regretted it, of course, as most men do regret the irretrievable errors of their youth. But he had neither Margaret's appreciation of the situation, nor could he brook the blame she was ready to bestow.

" It was a bit of cursed luck that this should have happened," he went on, watching her face narrowly. " I say again, what's the good of throwing this fat in the fire ? Nancy won't go back on me, I hope, and am nearly certain. Why trouble her little head with that old story ? I know you pride yourself on your Christianity. Well, there doesn't seem to be much Christian charity about your attitude towards me, Mrs. Cardine ! "

Margaret swallowed something in her throat. Conscious of a rising anger, she began to wish with all her heart she had not come.

" I think it will be better if we do not discuss it any further," she said coldly. " It is a matter for Mr. Cardine."

" Then you intend to tell him ? "

" I do not see that I have any alternative. You have been able to satisfy him, so far, but I am as certain as I stand here that if he knew the story of Molly Semple he would not give you his daughter. He would make any sacrifice first."

" I don't see how you could be positively certain. I think I ought to get the benefit of the doubt."

" You make very little of what you did, but the whole affair was tragic. Not the least part of it was that you introduced yourself to Mollie Semple under a false name, and that I did not know that you and the man who ruined her life were the same, until we met last night."

" A man in my position has to take certain precautions," he began.

Then Margaret's anger blazed forth.

"I refuse to have any further talk with you, sir. You are less fit even than I thought you to be the husband of any decent girl! I shall tell my husband the whole story and leave him to decide what is to be done."

So saying she walked away.

So far as any settlement or solution of the matter was concerned, the interview might just as well not have taken place.

But Margaret did not know the infinite resource of an unprincipled man of the world.

Margaret did not remember that she had arranged to go to Bella at twelve at Charing Cross until she was nearly half-way home. Then she regretted it, for she perceived that this was a matter with which only Mr. Cardine had the power and the right to deal. But no thought of slipping out of the engagement occurred to her, though her feet were certainly reluctant as she turned them in the direction of Charing Cross.

When she reached the flat, Bella admitted her, her face wearing an expression of pleasure.

"Good morning! I was beginning to think you weren't coming."

She led the way into the showroom, and through that, to the little sitting-room in which, on Sunday evening, Margaret had spent another and very fruitful hour. As she sat down at the table, and began to draw off her gloves, she suddenly realized how full life was, and what demands it was making on her resources of head and heart.

Even all her experience among the joys and sorrows of the young lives she had sought to guide in other walks of life, had hardly prepared her for these poignant experiences.

The last hour had tried her mettle, and had proved her, as she imagined, wholly incapable of dealing with such big moral questions. She felt the need of independent opinion, more especially that of some other woman. And she had chosen Bella for two reasons—she had already proved her active grip on affairs, her fearlessness where any big issue was concerned; and, secondly, she thought that by making this appeal, she might pave the way to some common meeting-ground, some community of interests, which would make the family life, presently to be restored, more permanent and lasting.

"I wanted your opinion on a question of conduct, last night," she said, as she laid down her gloves. "Conduct—no, I don't think it is that; but something rather deeper."

Bella, feeling rather flattered, leaned against the table, looking with interest on Margaret's kind face, seeing there qualities and attractions she would not have conceded a month ago.

"Why do you want to ask me? I'm not a very capable person. Look what a mull I've made of this!"

"Oh, that isn't conduct!" answered Margaret with a slight smile. "That comes under the heading of economics, and you haven't had a chance of studying these. But this experience won't be lost—nothing ever is. I just want to ask you one or two general questions, but they are based on one essential, I believe. There's a tremendous lot of talk, in these days, about the equality of sexes, but it seems to me that the only equality worth struggling for is that in the region of morals."

"What is it apropos of?" asked Bella shrewdly.

"I'm thinking of marriage at the moment. Don't you think that a woman has the right to expect and to demand the same standard of morality in life and conduct from the man she is going to marry as she has to offer for herself?"

Bella looked a trifle startled—the question was so entirely removed from anything she had expected.

"She may expect and demand it, but how often does she get it? The standard isn't the same, unfortunately."

"That's my point—it ought to be!" cried Margaret passionately. "And if all your reformers, men and women, would make that the principal objective of their efforts, why then the world would stand a reasonable chance of improvement."

CHAPTER XXI

CARDINE'S INDIGNATION

BELLA was surprised at the passion with which her stepmother spoke, and felt an inward sense of apprehension. Could she, by any chance, be thinking of her own personal experience? But that was impossible! She dismissed the idea with haste, as base and unworthy.

"Let me put it a little differently. Supposing a man of the world, with a particularly shady past, full of cruelty and baseness to at least one other woman, should wish to marry a pure, sweet, young girl, just like a flower—Do you think that would be a fair exchange?"

"I don't," said Bella shortly. "It would be an unfair exchange, and it shouldn't be allowed."

"Well, that is the position, where your sister and Captain Gilder are concerned," answered Margaret quietly; then, quite deliberately, she sketched the story of Mollie Semple.

Bella alternately paled and reddened; and at last angry tears stood in her eyes.

"It must be stopped, Mrs. Cardine! Say you'll stop it! We can't let it go on. If it were Jean, or me, it wouldn't matter. Our eyes are open a bit—and we know what goes on in the world. But Nancy! You just described her a moment ago! She's like a flower. Do you know, as I saw them sitting at table together, last night, I couldn't help thinking that Captain Gilder was not suited to Nancy. She looked almost like his daughter! And she ought to have some splendid boy to match herself. That would be the natural and fitting marriage for her! Oh, it has got to be stopped!"

"That is what I feel. But what are we to do? I've just come from him, and, I assure you, he is full of fight!"

"But he can't deny it, if the facts are all as you have stated."

"He doesn't deny it. His contention merely is, that most men have a past, and that it should be wiped off the slate, and they given a chance to make good later on. But I say he isn't fit for Nancy, and I can't bear the idea of it. Besides, apart from the morality question, he's a hard, unfeeling man. He would wound her heart every day; and I don't believe that she really cares for him! She's flattered, pleased, carried along on a certain wave of excitement. And I do blame your sister-in-law, Mrs. Alexander Cardine, for hurrying this affair on, as she undoubtedly has done, for what reason, who can tell?"

Bella's lips shut together with an undoubted snap.

"Oh, Evey's the limit, Mrs. Cardine! The absolute limit! I daresay she knows enough about Captain Gilder's past to sink a ship; but what does she care for Nancy or any of us? Look here, Mrs. Cardine. What's your idea? What were you thinking of doing, before you told me?"

"Well, only of telling your father. I think this is really a matter for him."

"But he won't tell Nancy! You don't know father as well as I do, Mrs. Cardine! He'll fly into a rage, of course, and forbid Captain Gilder the house, and simply say to Nancy, 'You can't see this man any more. I don't approve of him,' and, though Nancy is only eighteen, she's wilful. Don't you see, that will just be playing into Captain Gilder's hands?"

"Then what would you propose?"

"I would propose that you should tell Nancy yourself."

But Margaret visibly shrank. The Cardines had made considerable demands on her since she entered the family, and this was an ordeal from which her soul shrank.

" I don't want continually to be a prophet of evil, a bird of ill omen," she said forlornly. " Else you will all hate me, and with good cause."

" I don't think we shall," said Bella, with an odd softening in her face. " And I may as well be honest Injun, now, and say I'm awfully ashamed about the way I went on. How silly we must have all seemed to you, now I know what you are ! "

" Oh, don't let us go back on all that," said Margaret, momentarily comforted. " But you see, don't you, that you had better come home without delay. We shall have to stand shoulder to shoulder through this."

" Oh, we're coming right enough, and Jean has begun to pack up already ! But father never said a word about it last night. Do you think he expects us, and will be glad to see us ? "

" Why, of course. I'll see to that," said Margaret. " I'm most awfully sorry this has happened, for he hasn't got over Harry's affair yet."

" Goodness gracious ! Don't say that kid has been getting into trouble too ! " cried Bella in tones of consternation.

Margaret had no choice but to put Bella into possession of the facts concerning the complications in Harry's life.

" Oh, I say ! What are we coming to as a family ? A nice kettle of fish you find yourself mixed up with ! A little kitchen-maid or 'tweeny' ! Of course, I remember the girl perfectly. Though there was nothing to make anyone remember her by ! She was so colourless, so absolutely just nothing, that whether she was in the house or out of it, was a matter of no consequence. And now she is Mrs. Harry Cardine ! "

Margaret gravely inclined her head.

" Can you tell me what has happened to us, as a family, all of a sudden ? " asked Bella, rather tragically. " For years and years we go on in the same groove, with positively nothing happening, and then all this ! I can't understand it ; and if you will throw any light on it, I shall be much obliged."

Margaret slightly smiled.

" The explanation is quite simple. You have all grown up. Your personalities and characters have developed, and, most of all, you have missed your mother——"

Bella looked at her stepmother attentively.

" Do you really think it matters so much as that ? Our mother was so quiet and gentle. She certainly had less to say than any woman I've ever known, and not one of us is in the least like her in that respect. I don't just see that her power could have been so tremendous."

" Ah, but that is just where you are wrong ! That was her power. She guided and directed without any of you being conscious of it, and when she went, the elements just scattered, like so many loose threads."

" And now you've come to pull us together again ! I begin to see that there might be more in a second marriage than meets the eye."

" I can never fill her place, but I knew and loved her ; and she—and she——" Margaret hesitated, just a moment. " She asked me to take care of you all."

" She what ? Do you mean to say mother spoke as if this might happen ? "

" She did not specify in what way I might help ; but I saw her, in the Nursing Home, two days before she died, and she asked me to do what I could for you."

" I wonder, now, if she said anything of that sort to father ? "

" She did not," said Margaret. " But it has been a help to me—it even made it easier for me to decide—knowing that she would not mind."

" Heavens, what pigs we've all been ! but you're not going to keep up any grudge—that's what's so sporting about you ! " said Bellar frankly. " Now, it only remains for Jean to marry her Socialist, and for me to run away with the milkman, to finish the charming history of the Cardines ! "

" Neither of you is going to do anything so foolish. In the meantime, you are coming back, to help us to restore the balance at home."

With that Margaret went away, her heart at rest concerning the two who had been the stormiest elements in her new life.

But she grew more and more uneasy about Nancy, and, as she sat with her alone, at luncheon, and heard her gay prattle of her London doings, her heart sank over the thought of the trouble ahead.

" Really, Mrs. Cardine, the bit I enjoyed most of all while I was away, was the two days I had in May week at Cambridge. Lady Farquhar took me down. It was simply ripping."

"Who is Lady Farquhar?" asked Margaret, her interest not very vivid.

"She's Evelyn's aunt—such a dear! She has only one son; he's at Trinity, and he wanted to give me the loveliest time! We would have stopped another day, only Hugh wouldn't let me. He kept writing and telegraphing—between ourselves, he was quite jealous!"

"Of whom? Lady Farhuhar's son?"

"Yes—Colin. Such a dear boy, and so handsome; and—and I don't mind telling you, that if I'd never met Hugh, I might have fallen in love with Colin Farquhar. You couldn't help admiring him in his boating things! He's a great rower, you know, and doesn't go in the boat crew because his father is more keen on his working than sporting at Cambridge."

Margaret, listening to this delightful prattle, took heart of grace.

"Perhaps it would have been better, had you waited for someone nearer your own age to turn up, dear," she said, smiling into the girl's sweet, piquant face. "Captain Gilder is rather old for you—he must be quite thirty-five."

"Oh, but I don't mind that. He is so kind and thoughtful. And though I had such a ripping time at Cambridge, I was sorry he was so vexed about it. Lady Farquhar seemed only amused, and she said she would try and get father to let me go back with her for the very end of the London season. You know, she's coming to see Evey quite early in July. She promised me the Cowes week. Of course, that would be lovely! Only, I'm nearly sure Hugh wouldn't let me go."

"After all, he can't prevent you, my dear. You're not married to him yet." said Margaret, at the same time inwardly resolving that Nancy would have the Cowes week with the Farquhars if she could compass it.

But this little talk, and its revealing light on Nancy's mind, certainly relieved her, and rendered easier the task of laying the whole story before her father.

When Margaret saw him so happy with them in the evening at dinner, both Jean and Bella having come round again, she felt inclined to postpone the trying moment. But her fear was that Captain Gilder would take some step before her which might make it impossible for her to tell the story with any effect.

She, no less than Nancy, was surprised that Gilder had not come near the house that day, nor sent any message. Margaret did not like that silence. In her estimation it boded no good.

She had to wait till late before she had a chance of speaking privately to her husband. The girls had gone, and Nancy, still feeling the effects of the journey, and all the excitement of the home-coming, and, perhaps, secretly disappointed at her lover's non-appearance, went early to bed.

Harry had gone down to Paisley immediately after dinner to acquaint his wife of the happy change in the situation and affairs.

"I'm surprised that Gilder didn't turn up to-night, Maggie. Do you think Nancy was disappointed?"

"She didn't show it, and I rather hope she wasn't, Jamie," said Margaret, a trifle nervously, and even paling slightly with the strain of the moment.

"You didn't care for the chap, then, Margaret; but I hope and believe he'll improve on acquaintance."

"Not with me, Jamie. For, you see, as it happens, I knew him before."

Something in her tone arrested him, and he laid down his pipe.

"What is it, Maggie? Some fresh trouble, if your face means anything."

Quite simply, in as few words as possible, Margaret told the story. It needed no embroidering or emphasizing; nay, the simple narration had a certain power.

Cardine alternately flushed and paled, as she proceeded, and when she had finished, he stood up and brought his fist down upon the table with a bang which shook the coffee cups and the glasses on the tray.

"And that damned scoundrel, with all that at the back of him, had the damned impertinence to ask me for Nancy! What an escape the bairn has had! Rather than give her to a man like that I would see her in her grave!"

"I was afraid you would take it like that. I felt wretched last night. Do you wonder I did not look like myself? I have seen him this morning by appointment, and I told him I should tell you."

" Ay, and what did he say to that ? "

" He took up the rôle of an injured penitent, and said it was the duty of Christian charity to cover up sin, and not to hound it to publicity and punishment. Oh, he is full of specious excuses ! And if he gets Nancy's ear——"

" But he won't ! " cried Cardine, and down came the fist again. " She'll go to Ardgoil, safely out of his way. I'll see him the morn, and make short work of him, I can tell you ! The scoundrel ! And Nancy the pick of the bunch ! Her mother's ewe lamb ! Oh, my woman, what I owe to you ! "

Margaret struggled with her tears. She did not cry easily, but Cardine's depth of feeling moved her profoundly. In a way, she was proud of it, because it assured her that he took straight, clean, strong views of life, and was not afraid to face the facts.

" We'll have to decide what Nancy is to be told," she said when she found her voice.

" Told ? She shall be told nothing ! I forbid you to mention the thing to her. I'll speak to her myself. I'll simply tell her that Captain Gilder is an unsuitable husband for her, and that she must trust her father and those who know better to judge for her. She's such a bairn, she won't fight. Gad ! What an escape she has had—and the man had the audacity to plead for an early marriage, even suggesting July or August, at Ardgoil ! "

" My dear, we shall have to walk warily. Captain Gilder is a dangerous man, and very clever. He will find ways and means of working on Nancy's feelings ; and even of getting at her. It might even be worth while to send her abroad for a time, with Jean or Bella. Bella for choice. I hope you don't mind, but I told Bella this morning. I had to. After I had seen him I felt I must talk to somebody."

" But why Bella ? " asked Cardine, rather struck. " Why not Jean or Mary Bruar ? "

" I don't know. But I just thought Bella was the one. She is very clever, Jamie, and not afraid to look things straight in the face, and there's a kind of strength about her."

" Well, and what did Bella say ? "

" Practically what you say. But she agrees with me, that we shall have to behave very carefully ; and, remember, that if Gilder has set his heart on winning Nancy, he won't stick at anything."

Cardine set his stern jaw, and looked capable of any fight !

CHAPTER XXII

THE SERPENT IN EDEN

"I'LL see Gilder to-day, Maggie," observed Cardine, next morning at breakfast. "Say nothing to Nancy. It'll give him a chance to explain, if he can."

"He may try, but he can't explain away the facts," she said sadly.

"I didn't mean that. But I'd like to hear how he would explain his presumption. As soon as I get down to Bridgeton I'll telephone through, and ask him to meet me in my office. I would ask him to lunch, but it isn't likely to be a friendly occasion. Gad, how I hate it all!"

"You look as if you did," said Margaret sympathetically. Then suddenly a wistful look crossed her face. "You don't think I should have held my peace, Jamie?"

"Good heavens, no, my woman! That would have been worse than all! The air must be cleared. See here, Maggie—if most men knew what their families were going to cost them, first and last, they would hesitate a good deal longer than they do about marrying! That young fool, Harry, now! But there, I'd better get out, and see whether an honest day's work will restore the equilibrium I've lost."

It was not until he had got his hat and gloves and umbrella, as rain was threatening, that he appeared to have time to consider her.

"A fine hornet's nest you find yourself in, Maggie! And it doesn't look as if you and I were going to get much peace out of our little quest for happiness. I daresay you're regretting it already."

"Oh, no," she said brightly. "I've always said the strenuous life is the best."

"There are different kinds of strenuousness, and few of us like the rack for most of the time. Are the other two coming here to-day, then?"

"Yes, some time, I hope. I may pop round this morning, after Nancy gets up, and see what's going on."

"I suppose I'll have to clear up after them at Charing Cross. It may cost me a couple of hundred pounds. Well, they'll pay it back—every penny, Maggie! They can do with what clothes they've got, or run up cheap stuff with their own fingers, till we get square again. They must be taught, somehow, that neither life nor money is made to be played fast and loose with."

With that, he kissed her, and left the house.

She did not take his moods at all seriously, though she began to understand more completely the history of the past four years, which had covered the period of his widowhood. He was, in a sense, a big child, that had been petted and cared for by a wife who had thought very little about her own personal claims. The natural result was evidenced in a great impatience of trifle and detail, a quickness of temper, an exacting disposition which his family, engrossed with their own concerns, and regarding their father chiefly in the light of universal provider, and occasionally a nuisance, had paid no heed to.

This attitude on the part of the family is by no means uncommon. It provides a good deal of the bitterness which sometimes saddens middle life.

Margaret did not love Cardine less because she knew him better, but she was made of slightly different stuff from Isabel Bruar, and had the rare gift of being able to look round all sides of a question. Her chief concern was, in the meantime, for Nancy. The father's irritation over this horrid disturbance of what he had accepted as a satisfactory arrangement was of no account beside Margaret's deep anxiety regarding that sweet young life, and her determination to guard and protect it.

This feeling had nothing to do with the fact that Nancy was Mr. Cardine's daughter, but had its root in the springs of Margaret's own being. She was a builder-up—not a destroyer.

She thought of Mary Bruar with some yearning, and about ten o'clock, having found that Nancy was still asleep, she left the house.

She had taken the precaution to look over the letters, as they lay on the hall table, but there was not even one for Nancy. She was not aware, however, that the express messenger whom she passed at the bottom of the gardens bore a missive for Miss Nancy Cardine in his wallet; indeed, she did not even observe him.

The letter was delivered, and as it was marked "express," and seemed to be of some importance, Barbara Watson took it upon herself to take it up to Miss Nancy's room. She was just waking up, and smiled at the girl as she stepped inside the door, not even noticing that it was the table-maid and not the girl who usually attended on the top floors.

"Oh, is it time to get up, already?" she said sleepily. "Has the first bell rung?"

"Oh, Miss Nancy, it's twenty minutes past ten o'clock! Everybody had had their breakfast, and gone away out. The mistress was the last. She went on the stroke of ten. Here's a letter for you, come by express messenger."

"Oh!" said Nancy, stretching out her hand for it with a faint blush. "I've never had one before. I suppose it's some sort of telegram—isn't it?"

"Well, it's in a hurry, anyway. Will Jessie bring up your breakfast now, miss?"

"Yes, if she likes," answered Nancy, already deep in the sheet she had extracted from its official cover.

Surprise and other feelings struggled for the mastery, as she read the impassioned lines.

"DARLING," it ran, "I must see you at once. I am sending this, hoping it may have the good luck to fall into your hands before any meddler gets hold of it. If it does, please come out and meet me at the Botanic Gardens gate, just inside. I'm going there now, and will wait as long as I can. I have an appointment in the city later, but must see you first.

"My angel, understand this is urgent, and don't let anything stand in your way of coming out to meet me. Don't say a word to anybody, nor let out where you are going. Just come to your anxious and devoted lover, H.G."

Nancy was on her feet in the middle of the floor next minute, and when the maid arrived with her breakfast, she was brushing her hair.

Under half an hour she was out of the house, and she made her way as quickly as possible to the Botanic Gardens gate.

Gilder was just inside, pacing a side-path, out of sight of the main entrance, even while keeping an eye on it, so to speak. With lively satisfaction he sprang to meet the pretty figure in light grey coat and skirt, carrying a ridiculous parasol, in case of a shower.

He was intensely relieved to see that her sweet face was quite unclouded, her colour rising softly under his ardent gaze. He drew her hand through his arm, and together they sought a secluded path, where they could talk unobserved.

"It is so good of you to come, darling! I was almost afraid to expect it!"

"Why shouldn't I come? I've had an awful rush, though. Fancy! I wasn't up when they brought me your letter. Everybody had gone out, so nobody asked a question about where I was going. Not that I need have told them, of course. But what's it all about?"

Gilder tried to draw consolation from the fact that so far, evidently, not a word had been said derogatory to him in Nancy's hearing. But, with the peremptory telephone message from Bridgeton ringing in his ears, he felt that some explanation was necessary.

"Nobody has said anything to you then, darling, about me?"

"Nobody has said horrid things, if you mean that," the girl answered, with a little wrinkle in her brows.

"Well, I don't doubt they are going to. Your father rang me up on the telephone about an hour ago, just before I wrote that letter, and asked—no, commanded me to come over to Bridgeton at once, as he had something important to say to me."

"Didn't he tell you what?" asked Nancy.

"No; and I didn't like his tone. It wasn't friendly. Now, darling, listen to me——" he said impressively. "I don't want to make dispeace, or to pick quarrels with anybody, but I'm nearly certain your stepmother is at the bottom of this."

"Oh, but, Hugh, how do you make that out? I'm sure nobody could have been nicer than she was; and look how she got Jean and Bella back! You have no idea how abominable Bella was about her, at the beginning. She said simply awful things, both about her and to her face"

"You didn't observe, then, how very little she had to say to me at dinner?"

Nancy shook her pretty head. Being, as she imagined, the chief centre and object of interest in the house, she had not observed anything that was not pleasant and delightful!

"She had precious little to say, and that wasn't what it ought to have been. I may as well tell you that I had met her before."

"You had met my stepmother before! But where?" asked Nancy, now genuinely surprised. "She used to work in the factory, you know, though I must say that nobody would have guessed it! Of course, clothes make a lot of difference. And that was a lovely frock she had on!" prattled Nancy. "But where did you meet her?"

"Well, as it happens, I'm not at liberty to tell you the full particulars, because she has not said anything. You see, a man has always to hold his tongue where a woman is concerned. It's the unwritten law."

"Is it?" asked Nancy, not in the least grasping his meaning. "But I don't see why you shouldn't have said, quite straight out, that you had known one another before. It would only have made last night more interesting."

"Ah, but you see the circumstances in which we met before were not exactly or altogether pleasant; and, of course, Mrs. Cardine had her own reasons for holding her tongue about it."

At this atrocious and deliberate lie, for, although it contained no direct charge, the words were significant enough to arrest even Nancy's rather wandering attention, she looked round inquiringly into Gilder's face, which was now set keen like a hatchet.

He had not known or decided, when he met Nancy, just how he was going to explain the situation or justify himself. But the method accompanied the occasion, so to speak—the method which a rather desperate man is seldom too scrupulous to hesitate about using.

"Oh, do you mean that you knew something about her which, perhaps, my father or the rest of us wouldn't like to hear?"

But Gilder was far too wary to commit himself.

"Well, you see, darling, as I said a minute ago, a man has to hold his tongue where a woman is concerned. And, if Mrs. Cardine had left me alone, I would have been the very last man to say a word!" he said, with perfect truth. "Don't let us study that aspect of the question or discuss her. The world has set the mark of its disapproval on stepmothers, and, in real life, most of them earn the criticism they get. I'm sorry that yours seems likely to follow in the usual train. Of course, a man who marries out of his class, as your father has done, has to take all the risks. Quite evidently she has said something to your father—probably because he noticed how she treated me, and questioned her about it. And now your father has sent for me. Do you follow, and can you understand, darling, my anxiety to see you first?"

"Of course I understand," said Nancy slowly. "And it is all rather horrid. I don't want that kind of thing to happen, and, somehow, I can't believe it; for she doesn't seem like that at all! She's really most awfully kind!"

"Darling, have I said a word against her? I'm sure she's kindness itself, when things go her way. Most of us are. All I want is an assurance of your trust in me, and your promise not to bowl me over whatever they may say?"

"Oh, but Hugh—it will never go so far as that! Of course, you'll have to tell father something, if he asks you questions. Can't you give me any idea of what it is ? "

" No, darling. Your white soul ought not to be clouded with the evil of the world," he said, and his words were spoken with a passionate sincerity, for he regretted the turn events had taken whole-heartedly.

Nancy shivered a little as she drew away. The serpent had entered her Eden, and a sudden, quick apprehension of trouble seemed to fill the air.

Gilder, quick to see the change in her, brought all his lovers' art to her comforting.

" Darling, it's only a little, little cloud, which will blow over. Only, we've got to deal wisely and firmly with it. I'm hoping that, after my interview with your father this morning, there won't be another word about it. If I hadn't been afraid they had said something to you last night, I wouldn't have written that letter, nor asked you to come out. But I can't afford to lose you, Nancy. I can't—and, by heaven, I won't ! "

He spoke with such passion that Nancy was thrilled. She was at the romantic age, and he behaved like the lovers in novels, who are prepared to go any lengths for the women they love !

" Of course, it won't make any difference—nothing will, Hugh ! " she assured him.

" And you'll stick to me in face of them all, and refuse to believe any lies they may tell you about me ? You see, darling, it's like this—people are not too scrupulous what they say when they desire to achieve some end of their own. I could see, last night, that your stepmother had made up her mind she would part us. But you won't let her—will you ? "

" Oh, no ; most certainly not. But I'm sure it won't come to that. It will be so easy to convince father that there isn't anything to trouble about. Don't look so glum, Hugh ! I don't think I like you, like that. I should be afraid of you. I'm sure your men must be if you scowl on them like that ! "

" Oh, the Tommies—poor beggars ! They're hardened to that sort of thing. It's all in the day's work. I beg your pardon, dear. It's my fearful gnawing anxiety, lest they should steal you from me. Promise again, you won't let them, or believe anything they say, and that you'll always believe and trust in me ? I promise I won't fail you, Nancy. By God, I won't ! "

Nancy, carried along on the whirlwind of his protestations, gave the required promise, which, as they were alone in a secluded spot, could be ratified in the lovers' usual way.

" Now, darling, I want you to do something else for me. Go round to your sister at Greenbank, and wait there till I come back from Bridgeton—will you ? "

Nancy brightened at the prospect of seeing Evey ; and telling her all about that night rather appealed to the girl.

" Oh, I should like that ! Yes, I'll go. You'll get back by lunch-time, surely. I'll stop there to lunch. I can easily 'phone to Huntley Gardens and tell them not to expect me to lunch."

" Don't 'phone or do anything till you see me or hear from me," said Gilder feverishly, and looking at his watch, said he would have to go now and keep his appointment.

He, however, walked so far on the way with Nancy to make sure that she actually would go to Greenbank. On the way he explained that Evelyn knew all there was to know about the affair, and that, as she was the friend of both, they could talk to her freely. He did not say, however, that this little programme had been all arranged over the telephone with Mrs. Alexander Cardine before he came to the Botanic Gardens to see Nancy.

They parted at a convenient corner, and Gilder, setting his teeth, proceeded citywards, to keep his unpleasant and momentous appointment with his future father-in-law.

He had been very successful in his appeal to Nancy, and decided to try the same line with her father. But a straight talk between two experienced men of the world is a very different matter from a man's treatment of the same subject when talking to a mere girl like Nancy.

He was about seven minutes late in arriving at Bridgeton, but was shown at once into Mr. Cardine's presence.

Gilder could not have shrunk from the interview more heartily than Cardine did, and the traces of his mental state were visible on his face. He gave Gilder a curt "good morning," without offering his hand, and indicated a chair which, however, Gilder declined.

"I am glad you were at liberty to come at once," said Cardine with all the stiff reluctance of a man handling a hated task. "I daresay you are not so much surprised, after meeting my wife yesterday."

Gilder replied as stiffly.

"I don't understand. You will have to be quite explicit in your language, Mr. Cardine, as I gather that a charge of some kind has been made against me, and that your attitude towards me this morning has altered from that of the night before last."

"There isn't any use playing with the matter," said Cardine, with a kind of stern kind of weariness. "My wife acquainted me, last night, with certain facts regarding your life, which, if true—and, I may say, I don't doubt them for a moment—render you an unfit husband for my daughter. The engagement is, therefore, at an end. That is all."

Gilder swallowed something in his throat. He was not young; he was an officer in command, unaccustomed to such treatment, and he had a hard job to keep his temper. But, fully aware that nothing was to be gained, but everything lost by not keeping his head in this crisis, he tried to maintain a quiet and decorous demeanour under this staggering blow.

"Of course, this is a very serious affair, Mr. Cardine, and I won't take it lying down. May I be permitted to ask exactly what Mrs. Cardine told you last night?"

Mr. Cardine's face slightly reddened.

"She told me the story—unfortunately a too common one in this city and elsewhere—of a girl's wrong, and fall. In the case of this girl, whose death my wife lays at your door, the circumstances are peculiarly sad and revolting. I take it, you are unable to refute the facts."

Gilder looked Mr. Cardine steadily in the face.

"I could modify them," he said quietly. "But that would entail a certain stricture on the dead, and—and—well, an indictment of the living. I prefer not to do so, for, though you are not treating me well, Mr. Cardine, I have no desire to introduce strife into a household not altogether free from it. I hope I make myself clear?"

"You do not. Your remarks are open to two interpretations. You would impute some blame to the poor girl who is dead; and also motives, the reverse of honourable to my wife. I don't know what prevents me kicking you out of this office, Captain Gilder!"

"You are allowing your imagination and your wrath to run away with you, sir," observed Gilder coolly. "Pray let us look at this as sensible men. You seek a husband for your daughter who shall be as immaculate as she is. I ask where you are to find him? In my life there have been episodes—as, doubtless, there have been in yours—which I regret. That was one of them. But I was neither wholly to blame for the tragedy, nor was I the only person involved. More I am not at liberty to say without—without, as I say, suggesting dispeace in your household. Look at this, as a man of the world, Mr. Cardine. Would it not be better to bury the past, with its mistakes, and to give me, and others, the chance to atone for our mistakes? I offer your daughter a sincere devotion. I will spend the rest of my life trying to make her happy. We love one another, and remember that you cannot punish me without punishing her."

Cardine did not waver. An acute distaste of the man, both physical and mental, rose up, like a barrier, between them. He realized that he belonged to a different world, that Gilder's code was not the code whereby he believed happiness and peace could be achieved; and he smarted under the personal indignation of having aspersions cast on Margaret.

"I have made up my mind, Captain Gilder. There would be no possible chance of happiness or peace with this in the background. Pray let us close this interview."

"On what terms? Am I to understand that my engagement to your daughter is at an end?"

"Yes."

"And that you will not give me an opportunity of explaining the position to her?"

"If necessary, she shall be told the full truth. It is what my wife desires, I know, but I will avoid that, if possible. You may write to her at once, but I shall require to see the letter. I will, myself, tell her to-day when I go home that she must not see you again."

Gilder's face became livid. He saw that Mr. Cardine's mind was fully made up, and that nothing he could say at the moment would avail in the slightest degree.

"You impose a hard and impossible task on me, Mr. Cardine, and it is infamous that the word of a jealous and apprehensive woman should be taken, absolutely, against mine! No—I don't take back my words! We fight with weapons suitable to the occasion, and I will not give Nancy up!"

He strode out of the room and the place, leaving Cardine in a towering rage, though, upon reflection, he tried to dismiss the grave discomfort Gilder had caused, and to assure himself that his conduct was natural in the circumstances.

CHAPTER XXIII

GEMMILL—THE MISCHIEF-MAKER

THERE is a kind of slow, revengeful person, who is never happier than when nursing a secret resentment against a person or persons who, he imagines, have done him an injury.

Bruce Gemmill was such an one. Although the circumstances of his dismissal from the Bridgeton factory were by no means out of the common, he brooded so persistently on what he inwardly called his wrongs that he had gradually become assured that he had been the victim of persecution and injustice. Mrs. Cardine was, of course, the principal instigator and perpetrator of these wrongs.

He had honestly cared for her, as far as one so selfish and self-centred could care for anyone ; and as, in his own mind, there never had been a doubt but that when he spoke she would be willing to marry him, it was only a step further for his imagination to decide that she had promised to do so, and had basely broken that promise, simply because she had a chance of doing better for herself.

Then, in spite of his braggart speech, he had been really sorry to leave Bridgeton, which had a good reputation for its treatment of employees. And all his gorgeous tales of the fine berths, with high salaries and participation in profits, were also largely figments of his imagination.

The month of June saw him still unemployed in Glasgow, leading the idler's life, which is peculiarly favourable to the growth of revengeful feelings. When a man is actively engaged, all his faculties fully occupied, he has seldom either time or inclination for brooding over personal wrongs.

Bruce Gemmill, then, was in this parlous state during that summer in Glasgow, and though by no means hard up, for he was a careful man, who had saved and invested money, he was quite ready to be led off the straight line in any direction which promised him the sweets of revenge.

One day, drifting about Bridgeton, and almost determined—after fortifying himself with a glass at the corner public-house—to inquire whether Mr. Cardine couldn't do something for him, he saw Captain Gilder leave the big gates which shut in the factory, with hasty step, and a countenance which left Gemmill in no doubt as to his state of mind. It was an opportunity he could not afford to miss. His mind, quick as lightning in certain directions, decided that there had been a stormy interview between Mr. Cardine and the man once, if not still, his prospective son-in-law. Risking the possibility of being kicked out of the way, he crossed the lane, and, touching his hat as he faced Captain Gilder at the corner, said, inquiringly:

" Captain Gilder, sir ? "

" Yes," answered Gilder, rather threateningly. " But I don't know you. What do you want with me ? "

" Only a word, sir. My name is Gemmill. I used to be employed at Cardines, and I want your advice about the way I have been treated."

At an ordinary time, undoubtedly, Gilder would have had more sense and pride than to bandy words with a discharged man, on the edge of a public pavement ; but, at the moment, he was hardly normal ; in fact, he was in a blazing passion and eager to pitch into somebody. He appeared to hesitate, while he eyed the not too well-favoured specimen in front of him suspiciously.

" I don't know why you should pester me. I've a very good mind to call a policeman. What do you suppose I could do for you ? "

"I don't know, sir. I only thought that you would like fair play, and, maybe, be interested in some of the so-called philanthropy of the family; more especially, the new mistress."

It was quite a bold card to play, and it succeeded.

"Come in here a minute," Gilder said, on the spur of the moment; and, next minute, they had passed through the swing-doors of the tavern at the corner, which, at that hour, was so quiet that they had no difficulty in finding a corner where they could talk undisturbed.

CHAPTER XXIV

GILDER'S PLOT

CARDINE loathed that public-house, which had occasioned the downfall of more than one good workman, and he had made every effort to get it removed. But the vested interests had been too strong for him to fight successfully, and there the place remained—a yawning pit for the trapping of the weak and of the unwary.

"And what have you to say to me, my man?" asked Gilder in his curtest, most offensive voice.

"I know, of course, that you are going to be married to the youngest Miss Cardine, said Gemmill smoothly. "All Glasgow has been talking about it, and I thought that, maybe, you would speak a word to Mr. Cardine for me."

The suggestion was purely experimental, in order that, before proceeding farther, he might discover, if possible, the exact terms on which Gilder now stood with the Cardines.

"I'm afraid there is little I can do for you, my man. Mr. Cardine is one who would not brook much interference in his business affairs, but you may tell me your story, if you like."

He ordered two whiskies, but did not touch his own. It was, of course, not possible for him to drink with a man of Gemmill's class. Gemmill, however, who never refused a free drink, and who had of late taken much more than was good for him, drank off his at a gulp.

Then he proceeded to tell his own version of the private affairs of the Cardine family, which had now assumed extraordinary and vivid proportions, yet was so naturally told, that Gilder swallowed it whole. The bit relating to Mrs. Cardine was of special interest, since she alone was responsible for the sudden downfall of Gilder's hopes.

Though by no means a stranger to intrigue himself, or the subtle workings of a revengeful temper, he realized that it was necessary for him to be on his guard with a man of Gemmill's class and description, and that he must, on no account, place himself in the smallest degree in his power. Although Gemmill's story, if true, undoubtedly placed in his hands a most powerful weapon to be used against Margaret Cardine, the utmost care and discretion would have to be observed.

Gilder knew far more about the law as relating to libel than Gemmill, and he had no mind to put himself anywhere near the reach of its operations. Also, he had proved, not half an hour ago, something of the stern temper of James Cardine, who, if any attack were made, or any aspersion cast on his wife, would use his power and influence to the uttermost.

So, while inwardly intensely interested, and even, in a sense, elated by the story which was capable of an interpretation which put Mrs. Cardine's moral scruples in a very different light, make them indeed wholly ridiculous and untenable, he preserved outwardly a show of admirable indifference.

"I'm very sorry for you, my man," he said quietly. "It isn't a savoury story and shows, once more, the fallacy of the attitude of the people who live in glass-houses—you know the rest. But I don't quite see your object in telling me."

"Well, you see, sir," said Gemmill, slightly disconcerted, "my idea was, that if you are going to be a member of the family, you might be able to speak a word for me to Mr. Cardine."

Gilder neither denied nor affirmed, and waited for Gemmill to proceed.

"And, of course, you know what awful trouble the stepmother has made in the house? They generally do; and she seems to have been specially successful in that direction. And it isn't fair on the young ladies, sir. That's the opinion of Glasgow folks. It's the old story of what happens when beggars ride!"

"Quite so," said the Captain, rising. "Well, Gemmill, I'll think over this story. It can be substantiated, I suppose?"

"There's nobody knows the inwardness of it, sir, but her and me," said Gemmill stolidly, though his eyes gleamed with an unholy fire. "And, of course, as it's her word against mine, I'll go to the wall. She's got the master's ear, and there are no fools like an old man in love."

Gilder smiled faintly.

"All I thought was, that maybe, when you get a chance of her, you would put in a good word for me," continued Gemmill eagerly. "When she knows that you are acquainted with the facts, maybe she'll see the wisdom of it."

"I can't make any promises, Gemmill," said the Captain with all the well-assumed reluctance of the man who does not wish to be mixed up with unsavoury family matters. "But I won't forget you, when the opportunity arises, I'll do my best. You had better give me an address which will find you, in case I should happen to want you."

Gemmill scribbled the address in St. George's Street on a leaf torn from his pocket-book, and they left the place together, parting, however, immediately, at the door.

Gemmill was no match for Hugh Gilder. He had given everything away—a great deal, in fact, which did not belong to him, or had any real existence—and all he had obtained in return was a vague promise that he would be borne in mind, if occasion arose!

He had not even got the smallest inkling as to the nature of the interview which had undoubtedly taken place inside the factory gates.

Small wonder that Bruce Gemmill cursed his luck, and the fates which seemed to pursue him so relentlessly.

Gilder, however, departed in triumph up west, with the splendid card of Gemmill's providing up his sleeve.

CHAPTER XXV

THE CORRUPTING OF NANCY

WHEN Gilder was shown into Evelyn's drawing-room, she gathered from his face that he had bad news to impart.

Nancy rose up, her lips parted, the colour fluttering in her cheek.

"Darling!" he cried quickly. "I've got my *congé*. Your father has forbidden me ever to speak to you again."

Nancy took hold of the back of a chair, and burst into tears.

"Oh, Hugh!" cried Evelyn, "surely it can't be so bad as that! It's so unreasonable! But it can't be irrevocable. There must be some sort of explanation."

"He would not listen to reason," said Gilder gloomily. "They've got their knife in me properly, and no mistake! It's only my word against your stepmother's, and, naturally, he has taken hers."

"Oh, but, Hugh!" cried Nancy, suddenly dashing her tears away, "never mind. It won't make any difference. I shall believe in you, and stick to you."

"Bless you, darling! But, unless I run away with you from under their noses, its all up with us. Any attempt at explanation would be simply hopeless. They can't see reason, any of them, and somebody's not too particular about the truth."

"I won't give you up!" cried the girl determinedly. "Don't you think I'm right, Evey? You would stick to him—wouldn't you?"

"Oh, I should, of course—but then, I'm not a Cardine," said Evey significantly. "And I don't want to be too conspicuously mixed up in it, either, for the door is firmly shut against me at present, and likely to remain shut."

Gilder begged Nancy to sit down, for he saw that she was trembling violently. Standing in front of her, with his hand on the table, he began his impassioned appeal.

"Listen, darling—if you really will persist in your determination to stick to me there are going to be hard times in front. When you go home—or, at least, when your father comes home—you'll have an awful time with him. He's in a towering rage, and he says he will never let you marry me. Do you think you are strong enough to stand up against them all?"

"Oh, yes, of course; for I shall see you sometimes—shan't I?" asked the girl piteously.

"Yes, of course, here," put in Evelyn quickly. "Didn't I promise to stand by you. We shall have to enter into a little innocent plot to circumvent them."

"But can't I know what it is all about?" asked Nancy wistfully. "Whatever they say, I can tell them it isn't true—can't I? I don't see why there should be so much mystery."

Evelyn and Gilder exchanged glances. Then he spoke.

"Fact is, Nancy, all the trouble is being caused by your stepmother. If you will excuse me saying it, she isn't in our class, and she doesn't understand certain things which we think and say and do. Then, of course, she's immensely proud of being Mrs. Cardine, and won't lose a chance of asserting herself. As I happen to know something about her, she knows she can't pose in front of me; so she wants to get rid of me. That's the whole matter in a nutshell, and it is quite easy and simple to understand—isn't it?"

"Yes, quite easy. But she will find that I can be determined, too. Will you come round this evening, Hugh, and hear how I shall stand up to father and Mrs. Cardine for you?"

Gilder's eyes fell before hers.

"Well, you see, darling, your father has forbidden me the house——"

"Even after you had explained that there was no truth in whatever they were saying about you?"

"Even after I had explained everything," he assured her. "I think, and Mrs. Cardine here thinks, that the very best plan will be for you to say nothing when your father tells you to-night, as he will, that our engagement is broken off, and that you must never see me again."

"Oh, but how could I behave like that, when I shall feel so angry and hateful inside?"

"Listen, darling—everything's fair in love and war, and we've got to fight our enemies with their own weapons. Mrs. Cardine has gone behind my back to destroy our happiness for her own ends. Well, we must go behind hers, so to speak."

"And what will happen after father has spoken, and given me my orders? Things can't stand still at that."

"No, they can't. But we must take a little time. What I should like to do is to march boldly into your father's house and take you out of it. But, unfortunately, I can't do that; so we must make plans. It is a great thing having your sister-in-law on our side—isn't it?"

His eyes met Evelyn's, and she, understanding what she saw there, smiled, and said that she would be ready to help them in any way they might decide. Then she departed, leaving them alone.

Nancy ran to her lover, then, and was folded in his arms.

It is not too much to say that Gilder was mightily stirred by this spontaneous act. He honestly cared for her, and had been quite sincere in his protestations that he would live a different life for her sake. Even he would have wiped out the whole varied past, if he could!

"Listen, Nancy—we love one another—don't we?"

"Yes, oh yes, Hugh! And I can't think why all this misery had to come. Just when we were so happy, and everything seemed quite comfortable at home!"

"Neither can I. It is beastly hard luck. But listen, dearest. We can circumvent them yet, if you'll stand to me. I'll make arrangements so that we can be married quietly. Evelyn will help us. So you won't feel quite stranded without any of your own relations approving. Would you think of that?"

"Oh, I might. But I would rather be married properly out of my father's house, and have everybody pleased about it, as they were, until yesterday. I do believe I'll go home and speak to my stepmother, and try to point out to her how hard it is on us, and how much better it would be if she would just leave everything alone."

"I don't think you had better say much to her. You see, she can't be expected to know how you and I feel about things. She has got a hopelessly narrow and plebeian mind."

"But I'm sure she doesn't mean to be actively unkind," maintained Nancy stoutly.

"That may be; but, as I said before, she's got her knife in me. Won't you trust me, darling, and be guided by me? I've lived a good while longer in the world than you, and I know what men and women are, and how difficult life is in parts. If we want to be happy in our way, we've got to keep our own counsel. Do you understand?"

"Yes. Then, you want me to go home and say nothing; and, when father comes home, and begins saying horrid things about you, I'm still to say nothing?"

"It will be better, at least, if you don't protest too much."

"Well, I'll try. Then can I see you sometimes here?"

"Yes, of course. But you must keep that dark, too. And don't even hint that you have been here to-day, or seen me. You had better go home by Charing Cross. Your sisters are still there, aren't they? Then you could just say you had been there all the time. I don't suppose they'll require an account of every minute. It's a great thing to have Evelyn with us, and I'm afraid we must leave ourselves pretty much in her hands. She is so clever and so kind, she'll invent all sorts of ways for us to meet without suspicion."

The dark way of intrigue and secrecy was not natural to Nancy Cardine, and the sweet serenity of her face was clouded. Her lip even quivered as she drew herself away.

"I'll try to remember all you have told me, but, supposing now, if I was just to stand up to father, and tell him I fully intended to marry you in spite of them all—what could happen?"

"Oh, he would send or take you away somewhere. You see you are really not of legal age yet, and he has full jurisdiction over you."

"But we could wait till I am of age."

"We could. But I don't want to do without you much longer, my angel; and I am afraid of the influence they may bring to bear on you. Take my advice, and go quietly home via Charing Cross, but without saying a word to anybody about what has happened. You can look properly surprised and hurt when your father delivers his ultimatum, and seem to acquiesce in his decision; then wait for further developments."

On this understanding they parted, and Nancy, having received her first lesson in deceiving, obediently went to pay a visit to the shop in Charing Cross.

She found Bella, however, very much engaged with a lady who, Jean informed her, might take over the meagre stock at a very low valuation, and there was not a sign of lunch.

"I'm perishing with hunger, and it's a quarter past one. Jean, don't you ever get anything to eat here?"

"We don't have lunch. The funds won't run to it; and we're practising the simple life," answered Jean with a slight dry laugh. "Thank goodness, this will be the last day of it. We're coming home to-night, or to-morrow morning at the latest. Tell Mrs. Cardine we'll be round to dinner anyway, for we can't afford to miss the only decent meal we shall have to-day. But I think we'd better sleep here to-night, and fetch all our belongings away to-morrow. You look well, kid! Being engaged evidently agrees with you."

The flush of inward excitement was still on Nancy's cheek, and her eyes were very conspicuously bright. She laughed, and said she would make tracks for home as fast as she could.

When she got to Huntley Gardens she found her stepmother lunching alone.

"I'm sorry I'm so late," she said apologetically. "I've been to see Jean and Bella. She's got somebody there who is going to buy up the things they have in boxes. I would have stopped to lunch, only they don't get any."

"Don't they?" asked Margaret, looking rather keenly into the girl's face, not quite easy in her mind, yet having no valid reason for doubting her word. "I intended to have gone there myself, but I stopped rather long at your Aunt Mary's, and then I had a good bit of shopping to do. Did the girls say if they were coming back to-night for good?"

"They are coming to dinner; but to-morrow, I think, they are coming back with all their belongings. They seem most awfully glad of it. They haven't given the scheme a very long trial."

"They did it all in too big a hurry. It was ill-digested, and hadn't a chance to succeed. However, it might be worse. Bring the fish up again for Miss Nancy, Barbara, and some hot potatoes."

Nancy thoroughly enjoyed her lunch, and managed to chat quite naturally to her stepmother, who had not the least idea of the plotting that had taken place at Greenbank.

Margaret had heard, over the telephone, from her husband, the result of the interview with Gilder at the office, and he had given her strict injunctions to say nothing to Nancy until he should come home, which he promised to do earlier than usual, and certainly not later than six o'clock.

The moment he entered the house he asked for Nancy, and Margaret herself went to fetch her down.

"That is your father, dear; and he is asking you to come to the smoking-room. I think he has something important to say to you."

"Oh, has he?" asked Nancy, throwing down the blouse in which she had been putting a fresh piece of lace. "I'm just coming. Surely he is home early?"

She spoke with a naturalness which deceived Margaret completely. Her heart ached for the girl as she saw her speed down the broad staircase, but she could not intervene in any way. This was a matter between her husband and his child.

Nancy entered the room demurely, betraying no outward sign of nervousness, though the red was glowing in her cheek, and her eyes were perilously bright.

"Come here, my dear," said Cardine, and his face was both pale and worried. He extended one hand, and would have drawn her to him, but she held back.

"Yes, Father; what is it?" she asked quietly.

"You believe that I love you, Nancy, that every hair of your head is dear to me, and that I would make almost any sacrifice for your happiness, or to save you a moment's pain. Don't you?"

"I don't know, Father. I suppose so," answered Nancy with perfect truth.

"It is true, however; and I hope you will believe me when I say, it is only of your happiness and welfare I think when I tell you I have decided that your engagement to Captain Gilder must come to an end—in fact, has come to an end."

"But why?" asked Nancy, clearly and quietly. "There must be a reason?"

"There are several grave reasons. Since our return home, circumstances and facts have come to my knowledge, which have convinced me that Captain Gilder is not a suitable husband for you, and that you would have very little chance of real happiness with him. The affair has been of such short duration that I hope your feelings are not very deeply involved. I hope you will accept my decision as the best, and, indeed, the only one that can be made in your interests."

"I think that, surely, I am entitled to hear a little more, Father. I am not a child any more."

"You look like one, my dear," said Cardine, and his voice suddenly broke, for she was so like her mother, as he recalled her in the days of her youth, that it almost unmanned him.

"But I'm not one! And I think I should be told what charge has been brought against Hugh; also who has brought it, and whether he has agreed that the engagement is to be broken?"

"I have seen him to-day. He did not deny the facts. They are such as I prefer you should not hear. Again I have to repeat it, Nancy—you must allow your old father to decide for you, here. I'll make it as easy for you as possible. You can either go down to Ardgoil for a time, or I shall arrange that Bella takes you for a little trip abroad."

He was surprised at the calmness with which she received the news, and to his mind she had not the appearance of one who had been stunned by it.

"You won't give Hugh a chance of explaining?"

"He has had his chance. He did not explain, though he tried to justify himself. The facts, as I said, cannot be explained away. Please leave it at that, my dear. You are very, very young; life is all in front of you, and someone else, worthier, will come, I don't doubt, to whom we who love you can give you without qualm."

Nancy's lips slightly curled. Without saying another word, she turned and walked out of the room.

CHAPTER XXVI

GUARDING THE BORDERS

ONCE thoroughly aroused to a sense of duty and danger, James Cardine did nothing by halves. Next morning he spoke a serious word to his elder son.

" You may tell your wife, if she hasn't heard it already, that Nancy's engagement is broken, and I would like to get an undertaking from her or from you, if you can enforce it, that she won't encourage any underhand business, where they are concerned. I think I'd better see Evelyn myself. I'll go round that way to-day, maybe."

The uneasiness and discomfort he felt were writ large on Alexander Cardine's face. He had already heard a highly coloured version of the story at home, together with Evelyn's caustic strictures on it. Now, Alexander had no cause to love the military, to whom he attributed most of the later dispeace in his home, and most of his sympathy was with his own folk.

" I'll tell her, of course," he said slowly. " But you know what Evey is. She doesn't stand much talking to, of any kind, these days."

" You let her get out of hand, my man," said his father dryly. " And there'll never be peace at Greenbank till you get her to understand that you mean to be master in your own house."

Alexander grinned rather dismally.

" That old fetish is exploded, Dad. It's the women who have the upper hand now ! "

" No such thing. Because an insane section of them have flung over the traces is no reason why all the foundations of life should be overthrown. Women are made to be ruled. If you had ruled your household better your wife would respect you more."

Could James Cardine's dead wife, or his living one, have heard this high-handed deliverance, each might have smiled in the innermost recesses of her being ! In his home affairs James Cardine had been under petticoat government all his days, as the best men ever are. Only it is necessary for the good of the nations that the men should not suspect it !

Alexander Cardine took care to inform his wife, over the telephone, that she might expect a visit from his father. At first, she said petulantly that she would go out on purpose to avoid him ; but, on second thoughts, she decided to stop at home and see him. She was rather curious to hear his version, and anxious to get some further information about affairs at Huntley Gardens.

Cardine drove directly out to Greenbank, which he reached about half-past five, to find his daughter-in-law demurely engaged in needlework in the drawing-room. The children were playing about, with that subdued air which indicated that the event was unusual, and not, perhaps, too welcome.

Hamish, the elder child, a beautiful little lad about six, was making his engine run across the smooth tiles of the conservatory floor, when his grandfather came in. He flew to meet him, and immediately sprang on his knee. This little attention mollified Cardine greatly, for he was extremely fond of his grandchildren, and proud of them as well.

" Hulloa, wee chappie ! And where have you been hiding from your granddad, so long—eh ? "

" We haven't been hiding. It's him who never comes to see us any more. And oh, Grandpa! Why can't we go to Ardgoil any more? Me and Wuffles wants to, most awfly! "

Cardine looked slightly uncomfortable.

" I didn't know you wanted to go to Rothesay, my dear."

" It's only because this is the first year since they were born they haven't been at Rothesay in June," said Evelyn sweetly. " They're always going on about it. I tell them perhaps we shall go to a little house at Callander, next month, instead."

" I'm sorry," said Cardine truthfully enough. " But couldn't they go down now? There isn't anybody there except Harry's wife."

Evelyn's expression was a study in careful effect!

" I don't want to be nasty, Grandpa, but, of course, I wouldn't like my nurse to be there, in the circumstances. You know how servants talk."

Cardine did, or imagined he did, and had nothing to say.

" It is unfortunate, but there are other places besides Ardgoil, and the children must have the sea. Take a run down to Millport and see what you can get for them immediately. I'll find the money."

" Thank you, Grandpa, you are always generous, when you are left to yourself," she said, smiling sweetly. " Slip over to the bell, Hamish, and ring for Nannie. It is your tea-time; and Grandpa wants to talk to me, I'm sure."

Nannie came, a very imposing person in spotless white, and her expression was not friendly towards Mr. Cardine. She, too, was missing sunny June in the comfortable island home, with the delightful, easy-going company of Christina Robb, and the prospect of possible flirtations with under gardeners!

The moment the door closed on the children, Cardine said abruptly:

" I've come to tell you, myself, what I've done about Nancy's engagement. She was introduced to Gilder here, and, of course, I take it you did not think there was anything objectionable about the man."

" No, of course not," murmured Evelyn, with her eyes hard on her needlework.

" Alec tells me you know what has happened. May I ask whether Gilder told you, or did Nancy? "

" Captain Gilder, of course. Nancy would hardly be likely to, poor child! "

" You know the story, I suppose."

" Captain Gilder told me the truth. I've never known him to behave other than an honourable gentleman," said Evelyn, with her grandest air. " But, in the circumstances, his tongue is, in a sense, tied. He could not clear himself, without implicating others."

Cardine was rather startled by this quiet, measured statement which coincided exactly with what Gilder had said at Bridgeton.

" But my wife possesses indisputable proof of his behaviour! " he said quickly.

Evelyn maintained a stony silence, which seemed to suggest that it was not possible for her to discuss Mrs. Cardine.

" Well, all the talking in the world won't alter the fact that I have decided that Gilder is an unsuitable match for Nancy. I don't think the child minds much. She took it very quietly; and I may as well say that I came here this afternoon to ask you as a personal favour not to give Gilder and Nancy opportunities of meeting here."

After a second or two Evelyn dropped her work on her silken tea-gown, and looked at him very straightly.

" I don't think there is much likelihood of Captain Gilder doing that. He has got considerable pride, and he is not accustomed to such treatment from people—from people who might be glad to know him," she said deliberately. " He is very angry, and, they say, he has even been considering whether he might not get redress under the law of libel."

Once more Cardine started. The idea was certainly disagreeable.

" Oh, come, Evelyn! Gilder has been bluffing you," he said, on the spur of the moment. " There was none of that kind of braggadocio about him yesterday morning. Of course, I understand that he wants to stand well in with you, as you were his friend to begin with. But we needn't go on discussing this unsavoury story. All I want from you is a promise not to give them any rendezvous here. Not that I expect they will seek it. Nancy, at least, would have more sense and propriety, but Gilder distinctly said he had no intention of giving her up. It is only for a few days I ask it, until I get arrangements made to send Nancy abroad."

"I won't give them rendezvous, as you call it," answered Evelyn. "Of course, I can't prevent them meeting outside, but I should think, after all I've heard, that Nancy has been frightened out of her senses, and that, probably, she'll be a good, obedient, little lamb. Poor child, and she was so happy in London, and at Southsea! I can't help grizzling a little over that."

"She's young," said Cardine as he rose. "And there are other men in the world."

"True," said Evelyn dryly. "But do you think it a good thing to wrap girls in cotton-wool like that? Myself, I think it isn't fair. It doesn't give them a chance in matrimony. It is better to face the facts. I've known one or two other girls who would have run away on their honeymoon if they hadn't been held by conventions. Personally, I wouldn't thank anybody to keep the truth from me."

"Nancy is such a bairn," said Cardine rather stiffly. "Good-bye, Evelyn. I'm glad you have met me half-way, anyhow; for, I assure you, I will never allow her to marry Gilder now, whatever may transpire. It is enough that it was possible to bring such a charge against him. It unfits him, as a husband, for any daughter of mine."

Evelyn's smile was inscrutable as she escorted her father-in-law to the door.

Cardine left the house with an odd sense of defeat. Aware that his son's wife was a very clever woman, he also feared that she was rather an unscrupulous one. He even admitted to himself that Alexander was hardly fitted to cope with her, and that he did not envy him!

Mr. Cardine had been very proud and rather uplifted about the Whitehorn connexion at the beginning, but his wife and family never liked it.

On his way he called in to see Mary Bruar. That busy, cheerful person had fallen a little into the background of late, since Margaret had come to her own. But there was no sense of resentment, or any feeling of being left out in the cold, though she was genuinely pleased to see her brother-in-law.

"It's quite like old times, Jamie! And where are you stravaiging to at this hour of the day, when you ought to be at Bridgeton, earning money to meet your new responsibilities?"

"I can't get attending to my business for these bairns of mine, Mary Bruar," he answered grimly. "I suppose Maggie has told you all about this Gilder chap?"

"She has told me something, and I am glad that you have put your foot down, Jamie; for, apart from anything Margaret has told me, I don't think he was a suitable husband for Nancy. He's very nearly twice her age. It would be a case of Janet Neilson over again—she had an old man sitting by the chimney lug when she was a woman in her prime! What does Nancy want with a man yet? Four or five years hence would be time enough to think of it."

"I agree with you, so far," said Cardine, as he sat down in the familiar room. "I have just come from Greenbank, where I was giving Evelyn a word of warning, not to let Gilder and Nancy meet at her house, because he left me yesterday threatening that he would never give her up."

"What did Evelyn Whitehorn say then?"

"Oh, she was sensible enough. Evey's all right if she's taken the right way. I could manage her well enough. Poor Alec doesn't seem to have the knack of it. The bairns seem terribly disappointed that they are not going to Ardgoil this month, so I bade her go down to Millport, or, indeed, wherever she likes, at the coast, and take a house for them."

Mary smiled.

"You have a good heart, Jamie, and I could wish them all a trifle more grateful. But things are mending at Huntley Gardens, aren't they?"

"They are, and Jean and Bella are coming back to-day, I believe, or to-morrow."

"She's winning them, Jamie! I'm pleased to have this chance of telling you that the more I see of your wife the more I like and respect her."

"I'm glad of it—yet they are trying to blacken her among them," said Cardine grimly. "What do you think Gilder has the impudence to suggest? That Maggie had some underhand reason for getting him pushed out—some personal reason!"

"But you needn't heed what a man like him would say, Jamie. A man in such a rage would say anything."

"I suppose so. I'm glad to tell you that Nancy took it quite well, and that I don't anticipate any further trouble. We'll try to get her away from Glasgow for a while; and surely, by the beginning of the winter, we'll all get a chance of settling down to live peaceably! I've had a time of it just lately. A poor mess Harry has made of his life, after all our pride in him!"

Mary Bruar's face saddened. She could not take Margaret's bright view of Harry's marriage.

"He was Isabel's favourite, Jamie, and I cannot but think that it would have hurt her. But I'm glad you are making the best of it. It is the only thing to do."

On reaching home Cardine found no fresh worry. He laughed a little as he looked keenly into his wife's face.

"Has anything fresh happened? Jean or Bella kicked over the traces?" he asked whimsically.

"Oh, no!" she answered brightly. "They have come home. They are busy now, setting their house in order upstairs, and looking very blithe over it!"

Margaret, after deep consideration had decided to keep her own counsel concerning the Burgess episode. No good could come of it, and it would have upset Cardine very seriously. The best thing was to forget it as soon as possible.

"Where's Nancy?"

"Nancy's up beside her sisters."

"Well, then, come in here till I tell you where I've been."

They entered the parlour together, and he took down his pipe from the mantelpiece.

"I've been to Greenbank and to see Mary Bruar. I thought I'd better see Evey, and warn her not to encourage Nancy about her house unless she forbids it to Gilder. I don't expect she'll do that."

"It is hardly likely from what I know of Mrs. Alexander Cardine."

"She sympathizes with him. Apparently she knows the whole story, and she says precisely what Gilder himself said—that his tongue is tied unless he implicates other folk——"

"I don't know what he means," said Margaret hardly.

"He seemed to imply that there were other folk concerned in the girl's death."

"There was nobody but him," said Margaret rather hotly. "I knew her intimately. She told me everything, and she died of the shame and the heartbreak."

Cardine made no answer, but continued working with the pipe he seemed in no haste to light.

"Are you not believing me, Jamie?" she asked presently in a low, rather strained voice.

"Believe you? Oh, yes, of course. Why not? Of course, I must believe you."

"There isn't any 'must' about it. I'll take you to see Mrs. Semple. She's living at Rutherglen. She'll corroborate every word."

"Oh, no! thank you!" said Cardine hastily. "I don't want to pursue this unsavoury story. I'm only too thankful to be done with it—that is, if we are done. Alec's wife spoke as if Gilder might even bring an action for libel against you."

Margaret laughed.

"That's mere bluff. He'd never do that. He has too much at stake."

"He even had a dig at you in the passing, my dear. He spoke as if you might have had a past yourself, which you were trying to hide, under cover of his!"

Margaret's colour rose a little. Cardine fancied that her eyes shrank from his.

The poison of tongues! How insidious it is! There is hardly a life wholly immune from the curse of it.

"Let Captain Gilder come here, Jamie, and speak out, like a man. I don't think he will. He is afraid of me—and very well he knows why!"

"Well, well! Let's drop the thing at once and for ever. Nancy's upstairs, you say. Has she been cheerful and like herself, to-day?"

"Oh, yes, I think so. Rather quiet and subdued, perhaps. She hasn't spoken much to me, Jamie. Of course, she is blaming me. It was very unfortunate it should have happened as it has. It has rather spoiled my chance."

" Oh, no. Later on when she gets a bit more sense, she'll be grateful, I don't doubt. Well, I think I'll have forty winks, if you don't mind, Maggie. It won't be dinner-time for an hour yet."

She slipped out of the room, conscious for the first time of a subtle something that was not what it should be, between her husband and herself.

She climbed the stairs to her own room. A sudden and overwhelming weariness of all things swept over her, and a longing unspeakable for the old, quiet, self-reliant life, where she was her own mistress, and for her niche in the humbler home where she had reigned supreme.

" Oh, you dears ! " she whispered through her tears. " I wonder are you missing me one quarter as much as I am missing you ? And was it worth it ? Is it worth it now ? "

A few days sufficed to get the family shaken down into something like the old routine ; and, though the elder daughters were most kind and attentive and respectful to Margaret, Nancy held aloof with conspicuous coldness.

And Cardine was not quite the same. Margaret tormented herself with numerous fears. She was not yet acquainted with all the tricks and vagaries of Cardine's moods, and sometimes she was hard put to it to preserve her outward serenity.

A few days later she left the house one morning, after breakfast, saying she was going out to Bearsden to spend a long day with her father and her mother.

Now that the two elder daughters were at home, and Bella knew all the circumstances of the broken engagement, she did not feel that she had any responsibility regarding Nancy. She did not even think it necessary to remind Bella that she had better keep an eye on her sister.

Margaret reached Bearsden to find her mother having a slack day, her father having gone down the Clyde to visit an old seafaring friend who had recently settled at Millport.

" Oh, but I'm glad to see you, my woman ! " said Mrs. Oswald, wiping her eyes. " Though I've nothing to offer you but a slice of boiled beef-ham and a new potato ! "

" Plenty for me, Mother. I didn't come for what I could get to eat ; and I'm rather glad, on the whole, that Father happens to be away. I want a good old crack ! My, I've been on the tenterhooks since I saw you last ! And the woman who marries a man with a lot of grown-up bairns, especially if they're lassies, has not her sorrows to seek, I can tell you ! "

Here in the dear old living-room, with the sunny window where the plants grew and flourished to repay the loving daily care they received, she could throw the whole burden down and lay bare her heart. No fear of misunderstanding or misjudging here, no need to hide or keep back anything ! She threw herself in the old easy-chair with a little gasp of relief, and for one good hour talked hard !

Mrs. Oswald was a good deal shaken by the narration, particularly by the part relating to Captain Gilder ; for she could recall the sleepless nights and anxious days Margaret had spent over that sad affair, and how her heart had been torn over the needless shipwreck of Mollie Semple's life.

" Sometimes, Mother," said Margaret, as she sat forward in her chair, " I've not been sure whether I did right to speak. My husband is not the same to me since it happened."

" My dear, it is always right to speak the truth, even if we've got to suffer for it," said Mrs. Oswald, in her quiet but firm voice.

" Yes—when the truth is demanded of us. But, in this case, you see, it would have been easier and pleasanter for everybody if I had just said nothing."

Mrs. Oswald shook her head.

" My Maggie will never tak' the easy road," she said confidently. " It goes down, aye ! The road up is the one He means us to take."

Margaret gave a little sigh, comforted and strengthened, as she knew she would be, by converse with that beautiful soul. Yet still the cloud hovered on her brow.

" I am nearly certain, Mother, that Gilder said something to Jamie—something about me he ought not to have said."

" And if James Cardine would take that man's word, or any word against yours, after what you have done for him and his, Maggie, God would punish him," said the old lady solemnly. " But I think you are spying ferlies, surely ! All this trouble has gotten on your nerves. I think you'd better leave them to make a kirk or a mill o' it, and come home for a few days, for rest and quiet."

Margaret shook her head.

"I can't do that, Mother. I must stop at home, now I've got the other two back, and try and keep hold of them. A lot of little bairns of one's own would be easier, for with them you could do what you liked!"

Mrs. Oswald leaned forward, and patted the smooth cheek on which one tear lay. She perceived that her daughter's strong, fine soul was a little wearied of the strife and strain; and, presently, was in no way surprised by a burst of weeping.

But it cleared the air and restored the balance, and Margaret, strengthened and heartened, went on her way an hour or two later to take up the daily task.

That it was hardly lightened, however, she speedily proved by the fact that, from the top of an omnibus going along the Great Western Road, she beheld a taxi-cab driving rapidly eastward, in which sat Captain Gilder and Nancy.

CHAPTER XXVII

CHECKMATE

MARGARET, perhaps foolishly, decided not to tell her husband. Her sensitive heart was wounded by his coldness in the last day or two, and pride smarted under it. For what has she to gain by trying to keep Nancy at home? Merely another thorn in the flesh!

Margaret, of course, had not the faintest idea of the anonymous letters and postcards, or the poison innuendoes uttered by Gilder and Bruce Gemmill. The latter she had almost forgotten. Now that she had not to see him he had simply dropped out of her scheme of things.

But she had by no means dropped out of his.

It was just before tea-time when Margaret got home, and she was fortunate in finding Bella up in the old workroom at the top of the house, inspecting sundry parts of her wardrobe.

It was odd how quickly, now that the air had been cleared, these two understood one another. Neither lacked a certain kind of courage; and Bella's smile was one of real welcome when she saw her stepmother's comely figure in the doorway.

"I'm redding up," she said. "I suppose you know Father told us last night we shouldn't get another rag of clothes till all the Charing Cross bills were paid?"

Margaret smiled rather faintly, wondering why Cardine had not told her that himself. She was just in the mood to be wounded by the merest omission of confidence; however, she made no remark that could awaken Bella's suspicions.

"I say, Bella," she said, "I'm fearfully upset. I've just seen Captain Gilder and Nancy in a taxi-cab."

Bella sat back in her chair, the picture of consternation.

"No! Are you quite sure?"

"Oh, quite. Neither of them saw me, and he was talking for all he was worth."

Real vexation and distress expressed themselves on Bella's face.

"Now, that is mean of Nancy! She said she was going out after lunch, and I was most awfully anxious to do something up here, so, as she said she was going to Aunt Mary Bruar's, I thought it would be all right."

"It wasn't anywhere near Aunt Mary Bruar's. I rather expect she met him outside, or at Greenbank. I'm not very easy about your brother's wife, somehow, Bella."

"I'm easy enough. She'll make mischief, or do the wrong thing whenever and wherever she gets the chance! She's a rotter," said Bella, without the faintest hesitation. "I'll just go and ring her up this minute. But I wonder where they could be going?"

Margaret shook her head.

"And Father will be simply furious! He thinks Nancy's all right; and when I said last night I thought we'd better go away quietly, he said perhaps it wouldn't be necessary to go abroad, and wouldn't Ardgoil do, as such a lot of money had been spent. That's Father's way, you know. He makes a tremendous fuss, and then nothing happens. You must tell him you've seen Gilder and Nancy. It'll make him hustle a bit."

Margaret shook her head.

"I don't think I can. I'm going to leave you to look after Nancy, Bella. I'm just afraid your father begins to regard me as a bird of ill-omen."

"Oh, how can you say that?" asked Bella, but came to a pause, struck by the wrung expression of her stepmother's face. For absolutely the first time she had a glimpse of the strain and stress through which Margaret had passed since she entered the family, and both conscience and heart smote her.

She rose and laid her hand very, very softly on Margaret's arm.

"Don't take it like that. I know we've been a lot of first-class beasts, but we're going to be better. I'll tell you what—we'll all clear out, somehow, quite pleasantly and nicely, for a bit, and leave Father and you to settle down again. I see we ought to. Heavens, what a proper pig I've been!"

Margaret swayed just for a moment. Never had she felt so weak, so inclined for tears; but she realized that she must not indulge herself.

"You leave it to me, my dear," said Bella, with quite a motherly, protective air, and herself amazed at the new feelings Margaret's surrender was evoking. "I'll get it all out of the little baggage when she comes home. She's as transparent as the day! Then I'll engineer Father. If we're not going to-morrow or the day after I'll know the reason why, and I'll take good care Captain Hugh Gilder doesn't find out where we've gone, even if I have to act as a first-class wardress! But, I say, isn't it abominable that this sort of thing should be necessary? If Nancy only knew the truth! I can't help thinking that's been the mistake, all along—to keep it from her, I mean. Neither you nor I would like to be legislated for in the dark, so to speak. But I will tell her the moment I think it necessary. I'm afraid that will be the only way to put a stop to Captain Gilder's little game. Now, you go and lie down, there's a dear. I'm sure you're dead tired. And don't worry your head any more about us. I'm going to do what I can. You've had enough dirty work."

Margaret's heart glowed as she slipped down to her own room to throw herself on the bed. She was weary, body and soul, but, after all, something had been gained! To have won Bella's stormy soul was something—nay, it was a great thing! She felt herself already relying on that outspoken young woman's courage and resource. And, of course, Bella knew her father far better than Margaret could possibly do.

To her own infinite amazement, she found herself sinking into a pleasant sleep, drifting out on some full, calm sea, where nothing mattered and even the gales were favouring.

She did not know how long she had lain thus, but was awakened by her husband's voice and presence at her side.

"Are you not feeling well, my dear?" he asked, and his voice had a queer mixture of anxiety and restraint in it.

She sprang up on her elbow.

"Oh, yes, Jamie; I'm quite well. I went out to Bearsden to see Mother, and it was very hot, and I was a bit tired. Why, what o'clock is it?"

"A quarter to seven, and the dressing bell is just going to ring."

"What? Then I've been here two hours! I'm ashamed of myself. Have you been home long?"

"Since six o'clock. I've been talking to Bella in the interval. She is anxious to set off on their little trip, so we've arranged Friday. I don't like you to be tired, my woman. It's not like you."

"Oh, I'm all right. It's just the stress, I suppose. There has been a good deal, you know, Jamie, to contend against, and I'm not so young as I was," said Margaret, as she sat up on her bed, and folded her hands on her knee.

A sudden tenderness swept over James Cardine's heart, and he blamed himself for having given even slight harbourage to doubts of this dear woman, whose face expressed nothing but the sweetness and purity of her soul. The poison of tongues had been working its deadly will with him, and he had that very day decided that he must say something to her about it. But doubt died before the purity of her look.

"Maggie, forgive me! Forgive us all! We've been too hard on you!" he cried, as he bent remorsefully over her. "I haven't deserved all you have done for me and mine!"

So the cloud was swept from Margaret's heart, never more to rest there; and it was a radiant creature who sat at the head of the family dinner-table, where all the daughters were present. Harry had gone down to Ardgoil with his wife.

To the outward eye there was nothing amiss. The talk was gay and unaffected Even Nancy joined in with apparent zest.

When Bella came to say good night to her stepmother she had another little talk.

"I've wormed it out of her. She did see him, and it was that serpent Evey who let them meet at Greenbank! It is quite time we got her away, and if I don't find her amenable in Brussels—that is where we are going first—I'll simply set her down and tell her the whole ghastly story, and point out to her what she's been saved from. At the present moment it's rather like burrowing in the dark without so much as a lantern light! I was all for telling her at the beginning, only you and Father thought it better not."

Margaret was conscious of an immeasurable relief at the prospect of having her responsibility lessened. She had profound faith in Bella's courage, resource, and common sense.

On Friday morning Cardine and Jean went to the station to see them off to London. Margaret did not go. The leave-taking between Bella and Margaret was warm, almost to the point of affection.

"Don't worry. I'll look after the kid," said Bella, with an odd abrupt catch in her voice. "What you have got to do is to sit down and rest. Get Father to take you down to Rothesay, and just sit in the garden or drift about in the boat. I'll write as often as I can, and—and—thank you very much."

She went with that, her eyes wet and her mouth twitching.

In the brougham on the way to the station she did not speak a word. Nancy was neither elated nor depressed at being thus disposed of. She seemed indifferent; though, on reaching the platform, she seemed to be looking out for someone.

About five minutes before the train was due to start Mrs. Alexander Cardine, looking very smart in her fresh morning costume of blue linen and lace, came dashing up the platform.

"If you will go careering off at unholy hours," she said gaily, "your friends must hurry up to say good-bye! So glad I'm in time! But only just. Good morning, Grandpa. I went to Millport yesterday and got quite a nice place. They're going down on Monday. Thanks so much! Lucky Bella and Nancy to be getting out of smoky old Glasgow! Brussels will be simply lovely now! But aren't you afraid to venture abroad just now when what they call the European crisis is on?"

"I don't suppose it will affect us," answered Bella rather dryly.

"Ah, one never knows. I saw the Muirheads yesterday and Professor Muirhead has abandoned the holiday he had arranged for them all in the Black Forest, and I know other people who have cancelled Switzerland tours till they see what is going to happen."

"What do they expect to happen?" asked Bella rather scornfully.

"Well, European war, provided there is sufficient *casus belli*," said Evelyn, with an air of great importance and superior knowledge.

"The newspapers contain many ominous hints of strained relations, and Germany's determination to rush into war," remarked Mr. Cardine thoughtfully. "But I daresay it will blow over as it has so often done before. In any case, you should be safe in Belgium; it's not likely to be in the fighting—unless Germany breaks all her pledges."

"I rather think we'll take the risks," said Bella lightly.

"Well, don't say you weren't warned," remarked Evelyn, "and if you come across any bargains in lace, or get a chance to get some convent-made *lingerie* cheap, don't forget me. Good-bye, then, and good luck."

Nobody noticed, when the good-byes came to be said, that something passed from Evelyn's hand to Nancy's, and was instantly hidden by the girl, with colour slightly heightened.

Bella and Nancy took the journey by easy stages, stopping two days in London, and reached Brussels on the following Tuesday. Their destination was a small, highly recommended, private hotel, on the Avenue Louise, where they expected to be very comfortable.

The weather was glorious, and Bella, who purchased several guide-books, was prepared to put in a most strenuous week. They were going to travel back by way of Ostend and see some of the smaller watering-places, and expected to be out of Scotland for about three weeks. As yet no shadow of the coming war was cast over the fair and famous city.

Nancy might have been a more lively and interesting companion, but, at least, she was not cross, and if she did not betray any enthusiasm over the sights of Brussels, at least she went about obediently at Bella's bidding, and did not occasion her either anxiety or trouble.

Some Glasgow girls they knew were at School in one of the streets off the Avenue Louise, and they arranged to share several excursions with them, one for the first Saturday afternoon. It was a very hot morning, and when the time came for them to set out to the appointed meeting-place, Nancy begged off.

" I've got such a headache, Bella ! Would you mind if I didn't go ? I simply couldn't go in a hot tram or train to-day. Just let me stop at home. I'll sit out in the garden under that big sycamore tree, or, perhaps, I shall go to sleep till tea-time. Madame Lasalle will allow me to have tea with her, I'm sure, and you needn't worry a bit about me."

Bella looked extremely doubtful. She had never left her, but, certainly, the child looked pale, and her eyes were heavy. There seemed not the smallest reason to doubt the truth of her words.

" I'd better send a note round, and say we can't come. Of course, they'll be frightfully disappointed—Elsie especially."

" Oh, couldn't you go ? " asked Nancy, not in the least eagerly, but rather languidly. " It seems rather stupid for us both to stop in, especially as I shall be going to sleep almost directly. I know I shall. Of course, if you insist, I'll go, rather than you should stop at home."

" I shouldn't think of insisting ! That would be brutal, for you certainly don't look well. I daresay we've been doing too much, and Waterloo, yesterday, was the limit. I haven't recovered from it myself yet. Well, I'll pop round and see what they say. If I'm not back inside an hour, you may conclude I've gone with them. But, all the same, it's disappointing. I shan't stop long. Not later than five, anyway. It's a quarter to two, now. Wasn't it two-fifteen we were to meet ? "

" I've forgotten. I haven't felt like thinking all the morning, and isn't it hot ! Don't let us stop another Sunday in Brussels, Bella. It would be much nicer at the sea."

Bella promised to reconsider all their plans after she returned that evening, and, after seeing Nancy safely lying down in the big cool bedroom, overlooking the courtyard, and having carefully closed all the green shutters to exclude the glare of the sun, she took herself off.

When she got to the Château Este she found them waiting with the picnic-basket already packed, and learned that Tervueren was their destination. It was explained to her that it was a lovely tram ride through dense woods which would be cool and delightful on that hot afternoon.

Five of them started, and Bella found the French governess so entertaining that she was kept busy polishing up her French and laughing all the way. They were a very happy crowd, full of high spirits and fun, and Bella regretted very much that Nancy had not been able to join them. The company was such as would have done her good.

The tram ride through the green forest glades Bella decided was the best part of the afternoon. They spread their tea-basket under the shade of an immense chestnut tree in the park, and thoroughly enjoyed themselves. Then they set out to take a stroll about the place, to see whether there was anything worth inspecting.

Half-past four came very quickly, and they were strolling back, feeling pleasantly tired, and glad at the prospect of the return ride through the forest, when suddenly, in a green glade, where Bella was walking with Mademoiselle alone, she stood still and her face went very white.

" Heavens, it can't be ! But yet, it is ! "

She started to run, and the Frenchwoman, surprised at this fresh vagary of the odd English girl, looked after her, and saw her dart up to a couple sitting on chairs under a tree, and presently, when sounds of a rather loud voice reached her, she turned politely away, wondering whether Miss Cardine could, perchance, have discovered a faithless lover !

The couple under the tree were Hugh Gilder and Nancy !

Bella, so angry that she was not, for the moment, mistress of herself, strode up to Nancy and took her by the shoulder.

" You horrid little liar ! " she said, not taking time to pick and choose her words. " And you, Hugh Gilder—how dare you ? You are a wicked, unprincipled man, and I have a very good mind to send for the police ! "

Gilder, furious and crestfallen, pulled his moustache, and faintly smiled in slight derision.

"On what grounds would you send for the police? Your sister, I take it, is a free agent. You can't shut her up. You——"

"Can't I? But it is just what I will do! You know very well why you were forbidden ever to speak to her. Nancy doesn't know. Shall I tell her now?"

Gilder reddened. He had no idea that this determined young woman was in full possession of the facts; and at the moment when they were discovered, he had been discussing with Nancy the advisability of trying to take Bella into their confidence, and enlist her sympathy. But he gathered from Bella's expression, more than from her words even, that it would be a perfectly futile task.

She grasped Nancy's hand, drew it through her arm, and turned away.

"Come, Nancy, back to Brussels, and I will take very good care that you don't get out of my sight again until we get home!"

"Oh, but Bella, you can't! I won't go—at least, not like this. Hugh has come a long way to see me. It was very difficult——"

"I imagine so. Well, he can just go back again, for not a word does he get with you unless I am there to hear it, and, I fancy, he will tire of that."

"I perceive that you have gone over to the enemy, Miss Bella," said Gilder now completely nonplussed. "But Nancy still believes and trusts me; and, moreover, will be true to me until all these foolish obstacles are removed."

Bella looked unutterable things.

"We shan't discuss it, if you please. Good-day, Captain Gilder. Come, Nancy."

"But this is ridiculous, Miss Bella! At least let me have the poor satisfaction of escorting you back to the hotel?"

"No, thank you. I'm with friends who are waiting at the terminus for me now. We can't prevent you riding on the same tram with us, of course, but we needn't speak to you. I was sent here to keep Nancy out of your way, Captain Gilder. Please understand that I'm going to do it."

So saying she marched Nancy off, still protesting audibly, and in less than five minutes the tram started with the augmented party, and Captain Hugh Gilder was left to kick his heels in the forest glades of Tervueren, and to curse his ill-luck and the puritanical narrowness of the Scotch middle-class!

CHAPTER XXVIII

CAUGHT IN THE REBOUND

ALL the brightness had gone out of the little expedition, and the journey back to Brussels was accomplished mainly in silence. The three schoolgirls regarded Nancy with a furtive interest, as one might regard a person courageous enough to essay some high adventure. They had seen the man with her—the cloud was still on Bella's face—imagination supplied the rest!

As for the French governess, her sympathies were entirely with the lovers, and, in her heart, she bemoaned the cruelty of the stern Englishwoman who could nip such a promising affair in the bud.

At the tram terminus the little party broke up, and Bella hurried Nancy back to the hotel. She had not spoken a word to her all the way. She did not speak until they were in their own room where, an hour or two before, she had taken such precautions for the deceiver's comfort.

"Now, sit down there, you little wretch, and tell me whether you think you've played the game!"

Nancy glared at her with bright, defiant eyes.

"There isn't any use talking to me like that, Bella. Of course, you don't understand."

"Understand! What I understand is that you and that man are going to take the law into your own hands if you can. But you won't if I can prevent it! Don't you see for yourself, you stupid child, that a man who would do what he has done—egg you on lying and deceiving people who care about you, and are trying to save you, would never make you happy or even give you a decent time?"

"If it is lies you are talking about," said Nancy sullenly, "there have been enough told about him to fill a book! But, of course, he knew from the beginning that I never believed a word of them. No more did Evey, or anybody who knew him, really."

The mention of Evelyn's name exasperated Bella's temper almost at the breaking point.

"Of course Evey is at the bottom of this! I might have known that! But there, I don't suppose it is of any use talking to you. Let's begin packing."

"What for?"

"To go home, of course. We'll leave by the night train. Do you think I'm going to stand this responsibility any longer?"

"But it's Saturday night, and I don't want to go home," said Nancy blankly. "In fact I won't!"

"Oh, yes, you will—if I've got to carry you," said Bella calmly. "Now, are you going to tell me what that man was saying to you; how he got to know you were here; and what the next move was going to be if I hadn't caught you? In a word, are you going to confess?"

"No," said Nancy, still sullenly. "I'm not. Is it likely when you are in such a rage? You simply wouldn't listen to reason; and, as I said before, you don't understand what—what love is——"

The foolish red dyed her cheek as she murmured the magic word.

"No! I'm mighty thankful I don't understand that kind of love. Are you determined to stick to this man, then, Nancy, though you must see, quite well, that everybody who has common-sense, or right feeling, or who cares for you, is moving heaven and earth to get you separated?"

"Yes, of course! I'm only waiting till I'm of age. Then I'll simply go to him," said Nancy boldly.

"Very well," answered Bella grimly. "Then it's quite time you knew what you may expect. You're a baby in some things, but your eyes will have to be opened. Now, listen to me. About two years ago Captain Gilder enticed a poor girl away from her home. She was only a working girl—a milliner, I believe. She was very sweet and pretty, quite poor, the only support of her mother, who was a widow. He never intended to marry her. Men of that class don't marry milliners, Nancy. But he took her away, all the same, and ruined her young life, and broke her heart, and her mother's heart, and, in the end, she died. That is the reason why Father and all of us who care won't let you marry Hugh Gilder."

Nancy's face alternately flushed and paled at this recital, and her frightened eyes clave to her sister's face. It was as if some gulf had suddenly yawned in front of her, both dreadful and impassable!

"Oh, Bella, that can't be true? Evey told me there was some story, but that every word of it was lies; and that Father's wife had trumped it all up, because Hugh knew something about her, and she was afraid he would tell Father."

"Did Evey say that? Then God forgive her!" cried Bella. "She is a worse woman than I thought. Nancy, every word of that is true! When you come back to Glasgow—and we're going there as straight as we can!—you can prove it. The girl's mother is alive, still, at Rutherglen; and you can see the place where the poor thing was buried. You can prove it to the uttermost. They didn't want to tell you, but, you see, it had to come out. Now, do you wish to marry a man like that, who was so cruel and wicked? He has not got it in him to make any woman happy."

"But I don't believe it," maintained Nancy, though her voice had a faint, trailing note in it, and her face was blanched and drawn. "He never would have dared!"

Bella gave a short, hard laugh.

"That sort of man, my dear, will dare anything to get his own ends carried out. You'll learn that, among other things, when you grow up. You don't believe it, you say? Well, if you know where Captain Gilder is living in Brussels, let me send for him and ask him, point blank."

Nancy shivered.

"I shouldn't dare. Oh, it is too dreadful! Did she die, and do they think he killed her?"

"There is nothing surer, my dear," said Bella solemnly. "It can be proved to you, every word of it! Mrs. Cardine knew the girl intimately. She was one of her club girls, the brightest and best. You ought to go down on your knees to her, Nancy, because she has saved you. Hugh Gilder is not fit to marry you, you poor, little, white thing! Let's go home where you will be safe. Don't you believe it, yet?"

Nancy began to cry forlornly; her castle of dreams and hopes had toppled at her feet! Something awoke in her then which robbed her for ever of her childhood. She was face to face with the sordid reality of life.

She did not doubt her sister's word. Bella, unknown to herself, had never spoken with a more dread and convincing solemnity.

Nancy threw herself, moaning, on the bed. Bella left her there, and without another word went downstairs to see Madame Lasalle, and tell her their visit must come to an end some days sooner than they expected. Circumstances had arisen which necessitated their immediate return to England.

Madame Lasalle was regretful and sympathetic, seeing trouble in Miss Cardine's face.

Bella imagined, even at the moment when she entered the little *salon* on the ground floor where Madame received her guests and took payment of her weekly bills, and was generally to be found ready to give information proper to her bureau, as she called it, that the comely face, with its somewhat elaborately dressed hair and slightly powdered nose, looked gloomy and anxious. Her conscience smote her, because she had come, perhaps, to add to the good woman's care by cutting their visit short.

As it was not possible to explain the circumstances to Madame Lasalle, she must try to get out of it as gracefully and kindly as possible.

"I am very sorry, Mademoiselle, but, as things are, perhaps it will be better that you go quickly—to-morrow, perhaps, or the day after."

"Well, to be quite honest, I was thinking of going to-night," said Bella bluntly. "But perhaps you are right, and I needn't be in such a desperate hurry. Shall we say to-morrow, then, or next day?"

" As you like, Mademoiselle. I do not suppose that now it will make much difference to me, for my business is ruined for the rest of the season."

" Why ? " asked Bella curiously.

" Has Mademoiselle not heard that we are at war ? That the German hordes are marching on our country because the King has refused them permission to go through it to France ? "

" Madame ! " cried Bella shrilly. " It can't be true ! "

" It is quite true, Mademoiselle. The army is mobilized, and my two sons have already gone. Our troops are marching on Liége to keep the invaders back."

" But how awful ! " said Bella. " Why should they do that ? "

It is to be feared that, in common with a goodly portion of her countrymen and women, Bella had not been following closely the current of events in the last few pregnant days. Entirely engrossed by their own personal affairs, Bella had not stopped to grasp the situation, though she had certainly imagined that in the last few hours the atmosphere of the lively city had changed. She had attributed that, however, to the sinister presence in it of her own particular enemy.

" Why should they do that ? " inquired Madame Lasalle with a faint, melancholy smile. " Because it is the German way, Mademoiselle, to ride rough-shod over all ! My Auguste, who looks so gallant in his new uniform, says they have taken the oath to conquer the whole world and make it German. Then Belgium will be no more ! So they think ! But, though we are only a little people, we are brave, Mademoiselle, and for our King all will follow to the death."

" But you don't think there is immediate danger, Madame—for us, I mean ? We needn't rush away, need we ? "

Again Madame shrugged her shoulders.

" That is as you will. Some have already gone, but many will not go at all. They love Brussels, and have confidence the most perfect in our King and our brave soldiers. It is for you to decide. For me—I must stay here and wait on the will of God, who will surely give victory to the right."

" I must go up and see what my sister says," said Bella quickly.

As she left the little *salon*, who should come in by the open front door but Hugh Gilder ! She stiffened at the sight of him, but he paid no heed to her hostile looks.

" You'll have to pack up, Miss Cardine, and travel with me back to England. It isn't safe for you to be here longer."

" Oh ! I think it's quite safe," she answered steadily. " I've just been talking to Madame Lasalle, who does not seem to be very much concerned. It might be interesting to stop and see the fun."

" Fun ! There isn't going to be any fun of the kind you're imagining ! " said Gilder, as he set his jaw. " I've been recalled. They're mobilizing in England, and last night we declared war on Germany."

" Oh ! " said Bella. " Then it's all right if we're in it—it won't last long ! "

Almost Hugh Gilder could have smiled. Whatever his faults, he was an expert at his own business, and was under no illusions regarding the situation.

" We needn't stop to discuss that. I wish you'd go and pack up, and let me see you through at least as far as Ostend. It isn't safe for you to be here. The Germans are actually in the country, and they're in millions, mind you. They'll wipe out this little army as if it were a fly on the pane ! I won't even talk to you, if you like ; but let me take you as far as Ostend."

But Bella, with a singular pig-headedness for which she had occasion later to blame herself, replied :

" We'll go to-morrow. A few hours can't make much difference to the situation, Captain Gilder. Thank you, all the same. It was very kind of you to take this trouble—especially after what I said this afternoon."

He did not smile at that. His handsome face wore an expression Bella had never seen there before—one of awakened gravity, of high responsibility ; and she became vaguely aware that all that was best in this man had responded nobly and swiftly to his country's call.

This little experience added a poignant touch to a situation already bristling with interest, and she thought of all she would have to tell when she got home, how she could thrill her friends and acquaintances with the account of their adventures.

That there was any real menace or peril she did not for a moment believe, being hedged about by the smug complacency of those who think that, because no evil has ever touched them, it is therefore non-existent in the world.

That is a mental attitude commoner in our country, perhaps, than in any other, because its natural advantages make it immune from many dangers—entirely so from those of a frontier nature.

Even yet Gilder seemed unwilling to go.

" I wish I could persuade you. The danger is real. They move in millions, mind—and Belgium will be quickly overrun—is about overrun now! You may find it difficult to get away, even to-morrow."

" I'll risk it, I think, Captain Gilder. Thank you all the same." said Bella, fully convinced that in refusing his escort and protection she was doing the right thing towards her sister and towards her father, who had trusted her.

Such a journey, with Captain Gilder in the new and fascinating rôle of protector, would be full of danger for Nancy's inflamed imagination, and must not be risked on any consideration.

As Gilder turned to go, something in his expression smote her again. Instinctively she stretched out her hand.

" Good-bye, Captain Gilder. I'll always remember this kindness, for you needn't have shown it, you know, and nobody would have blamed you had you left us to sink or swim. We'll be all right, never fear. I hope you will get back to your regiment safely, and I wish you luck——"

" Thanks."

He wrung her hand and went out at the salute.

Something rose in Bella's throat as the unerring prevision came to her that they would never meet again. Although she had, as yet, no intelligent comprehension of the situation, she felt the vague weight of a misgiving.

She knew that Gilder had gone forth to his death.

She ran up the stairs, two steps at a time, deciding not to mention his call to Nancy. Her mind was full of the new situation, and on Nancy's reception of it much would depend.

" I say, Nancy, the most amazing, incredible thing has happened! " she cried, bursting into the room. " I've just been down to Madame Lasalle about our leaving to-night, and what do you think? War has broken out between Germany and France, and the Germans are marching through Belgium to get there, and King Albert won't let them, and has gone out to push them back! What do you think? "

Nancy sprang out of her bed.

" Oh, I say! How exciting! And will they come here? "

" Oh, no; they're pushing through at the other end, trying to get into France," said Bella, with the fine confidence of the uninformed. " But I suppose we'd better get away as quickly as possible—to-morrow at the latest. You see, we're in it, too. We declared war on Germany last night."

" But how tremendously exciting! Don't let us go home yet, Bella. Let's stop here for a bit and see the fun."

" I'd like to, but it might be rather awkward later on if we wanted to get home and couldn't. They "—here her colour rose ever so slightly, but Nancy was too excited to listen—" they seem to think it might be rather serious. If we got shut up here it wouldn't be very nice! "

" Oh, they won't hurt us; we wouldn't be fighting. Let's wait for a day or two at least and see what's going to happen."

This suggestion entirely coincided with Bella's own views, and in a moment the whole aspect of affairs had changed.

Nancy's languor and dour temper had disappeared, and she became the prey of a thousand vivid imaginings which effectually banished all thoughts of her old lover.

They dressed hastily and went out into the streets. In an incredibly short space of time the whole aspect of the city had changed. The peaceful boulevards were alive with marching men, and everywhere there were surging crowds singing the National Anthem and roused to the highest pitch of enthusiasm.

The two Scotch girls felt themselves thrilled to the very core of their being, and as they clung together arm in arm all the friction and discomfort of the past days fell away from them like a useless garment. Here was life! Real, vivid, pulsing life, which lifted the human soul far above everything petty and selfish and ignoble!

The temper of the people was high and hopeful, though the more thoughtful of them were fully aware of the tremendous thing that had been done by Belgium in defying the might of Germany.

It was all so fascinating that when the morrow came they did not even begin to put their things together.

Madame Lasalle did not urge them to leave her house. Why should she? The English were ever a people it was difficult to understand: they were not governed by the laws which rule the conduct of ordinary common-sense folk. They could stay, certainly, as long as they willed. English gold was very good, and perhaps soon there would not be so much of it spent in foreign countries.

At least half the visitors left, but the others, inspired by the confident example set by the Cardines, decided to stop for a short time in the seething capital.

On the morning of the third day, however, a telegram came from Glasgow demanding their instant return. Although disappointed and chagrined, it was a summons they could not set aside.

" I don't want to go, Bella. Couldn't we wire to father and say we're perfectly safe? It's ripping here! I do want to stop, don't you? "

" I do, rather. But perhaps he's right after all. He seems greatly annoyed with us for not having gone off the minute we received the first telegram. I suppose there's nothing for it but to go and make inquiries about trains, etc."

The inquiries made at the station elicited the information that, while it was possible, of course, to leave Brussels, no guarantee could be given that travellers would reach the destination they had chosen. Fighting was now going on fiercely in the north; and, what was more disquieting, enormous squadrons of marauding Uhlans had already begun to scour the adjacent country.

" So we can't get away! " said Nancy gleefully.

But Bella looked at her blankly.

" We can go if we like, but they don't guarantee that we'll reach the coast safely, Nancy. We may be kept here long enough. Heavens! what have I done? Father will never forgive me! "

But Nancy, pleased as a child with a new toy over their now really exciting experiences, tried to cheer her.

" At least we'll score over the others. We'll see a bit of the real thing! "

They did, and it was an experience which would never afterwards be blotted from their remembrance!

CHAPTER XXIX

EXCITING DAYS IN BRUSSELS

GREAT events dwarf the little. From the moment when she had learned from Hugh Gilder that war was declared and that fighting was already begun in Belgium, Bella Cardine did not give another thought to the circumstances that had actually brought them to Brussels. Neither of the girls realized as yet, however, the stupendous nature of the catastrophe in which the whole world was presently to be involved, nor the actual personal danger to themselves.

If they had realized it they would not have lingered those few fatal days in Brussels out of curiosity rather than from any other motive.

For this Nancy was partly to blame. Her eager interest, in which there was not a particle of fear (when is youth afraid ?) communicated itself to Bella, and from day to day they put off going until the day came when, save for a few nurses, they were the only British women left in the capital.

" Ripping, isn't it, Bella ? What things we shall have to tell when we get back to smoky old Glasgow ! I wouldn't have missed this for anything, would you ? "

For the moment Bella had no answer ready. She was not sure. While she was wondering whether she would voice some of the fears which were beginning to possess her, the concierge brought her a telegram.

It was by no means the first that had come from home, and this one, from their father in London, was imperative.

" It's from Dad, Nancy ; and we're to go to Ostend at once. He'll meet us there. I'm glad this has come. We've been wrong, and they told me at the hospital this morning that if we wanted to get away at all we'd better not wait another minute."

Bella had made acquaintance with some of the British nurses at the hospital, where her perfect knowledge of French had been of some use, and had already beheld with her own eyes some of the desperate fruits of war. And that day she had been dismayed by something one of the nurses had said, indicating that those who knew considered the position of Brussels hopeless. This had been even more arresting than the sight of refugees in the streets, wheeling their belongings to the railway station or to one of the various gates of the city.

" We must get out to-day, Nancy, if we can. I'll go and ask Madame Lasalle what she thinks."

Madame Lasalle was a sad woman in these days, for all her men-folk were in the fighting line and her eldest son had fallen at Liége.

The two Scotch girls were now the only inmates of her house, and she had been very glad for them to stay, though she was unable to understand the hardihood which had kept them in the city while they were still free to leave it.

" I wonder where she is," said Bella as she started from her chair.

" I know ; I saw her not long ago in the garden with a big spade. I believe she's digging a hole to bury things in."

Bella's lips blanched a little in spite of Nancy's gleeful tone.

" Let's go and see," she said, and they ran downstairs to the deserted *salon*, which had long windows opening on the garden—one of the principal features of the pretty and well-known house.

And there, sure enough, was the tall, elegant figure in deep mourning, using the spade, in a remote and secluded part of the garden which was not overlooked by a single window.

" Dear Madame, whatever are you doing ? Let me help ! " cried Bella, springing forward.

A huge box, with iron clasps stood by, and the girls understood without asking that it contained household treasures.

" I suppose you are going to hide them. Do you think it necessary ? Madame, do you really believe that they will enter Brussels ? "

" One must be prepared for everything in war time ; and it is the worst that happens," said Madame, with a faint, melancholy smile.

Bella held out the telegram.

" It is from my father. He wants us to start for Ostend at once."

" Ah, he has awakened, then ! But how are you to get to Ostend, Mademoiselle, I do not know."

" Surely the trains will be running still ? "

Madame shook her head.

" There may be one or two ; but, outside, it is no longer safe."

" I must fly to the station and find out. Don't come, Nancy. Help Madame. I shall not be long away."

She spoke these words out of the natural desire to shield Nancy as long as possible, to keep the dire truth from her until it could no longer be hid.

Nancy nodded demurely, and with a little graceful gesture she took the spade from Madame's hands, and essayed to dig.

What a story to tell in Glasgow drawing-rooms next winter ! How she had actually dug the hole in which a Brussels chatelaine buried her treasures from the Germans !

The child's invincibility and gaiety of spirit were amazing ; but Bella flew to the station, in what had become in a moment of time a mortal terror.

She found no cheer there. The station simply swarmed with a seething crowd ; the platforms were covered with little family groups, sitting disconsolately among their belongings, while the more energetic clamoured for information regarding the trains leaving for the coast.

There were none. It did not take Bella long to grasp the fact that, for the time being, they were prisoners in Brussels.

As she made her way back to the comfortable mansion in the Rue Washington, off the Avenue Louise, where, so soon, the German machine guns would be mounted, she felt sick with fear and remorse and apprehension. No longer could the truth be kept from Nancy, whom she found in her own room, adding another exciting entry to her diary.

" Nancy, we can't get away ! " cried Bella, as she dropped into a chair. " There aren't any trains ; and they say the Germans will be in Brussels to-morrow, or the day after ! "

Even then Nancy's cheek did not blanch.

" Oh, what a fool I have been ! I ought to have accepted Captain Gilder's offer to travel with him."

Nancy looked queerly at her sister.

" To travel with Hugh Gilder, Bella ! Did he suggest it ? Why, I never even heard of it ! "

" That is a matter of no consequence," answered Bella feverishly. " He came back later, on that day we met him at Tervueren, to report that he had been recalled, and that they are mobilizing at home."

" Well, we can't help it now. It was very kind of him—don't you think ? " asked Nancy innocently. " But, anyway, we've seen a bit of life, and know what war is like ; and I wouldn't have missed it for anything ! "

" The thing is, what are we to do now ? " asked Bella, with pale lips and tremulous voice. " I heard at the hospital to-day that no quarter is being given to the British. We may be killed, Nancy—shot as spies—or imprisoned in a German fortress ; and it's all my abominable fault, for hanging on here, day after day, just to see what would happen next ! "

The note in her voice was poignant, for with what words should she answer her father for Nancy's life ? The child was so fair and sweet, a sudden wave of unnameable fear swept over her despairing heart. She had heard stories at the hospital—such stories as had made her blood run cold.

" Hadn't we better consult Madame Lasalle again, Bella ? Perhaps she may have some suggestion to make. And we can always hide in her cellars. She showed them to me after you had gone. Ripping places! She's got mattresses and all sorts of things collected already."

But, when they sought Madame, she had no suggestion to make that in any way comforted the heart of Bella Cardine.

"There is always Burgomaster Max," she said presently, with a little fleeting smile.

Bella looked the surprise she felt, for although the name of the intrepid head of the municipal life of Brussels was already in every mouth, he could not, single-handed, stem the German invasion, or prevent their triumphal entry into the city.

"I don't see what he can do, unless he has the power to order a special train to the coast."

"M. Max is a dozen men rolled into one, Mademoiselle. I shall go to him, if you like."

"Thank you, Madame. And we had better go and consult the American Consul. Get your hat, Nancy, and let us go."

When Nancy disappeared, Madame Lasalle came a little nearer to Bella, and her pale, dignified face wore its gravest look.

"It has been a mistake for you to stay, Mademoiselle; but, if you cannot get away, we must make the best of it. You must both pass as my daughters. Your good French will help the illusion. They must not know that you are English, or our sorrows will but begin."

Bella Cardine nodded, her throat too full for speech. But in her heart was the passionate prayer and hope that, even at the eleventh hour, some avenue of escape would be found.

Presently the sisters were out in the sunlit streets.

It was a day of delicious golden sunshine, but over all a strange, indescribable pall seemed to brood. The few smiles encountered on the faces of those hurrying by were suggestive of an April day. Soldiers were everywhere, some standing disconsolately by the few attempts at barricades and defences that had been made within the precincts of the city, but all suggesting by their mien some tensity of feeling, mingled with the active sentiments of apprehension and anxiety.

Suddenly, as the familiar whizz of a motor bicycle smote on their ears, Nancy gave a little cry.

"Look, Bella! Do you see that man on the machine? It's Colin Farquhar! I'm nearly certain—don't you know? I saw him at Cambridge in May. I can't be mistaken! I do believe he has seen us. Yes—he's stopping, and turning round."

They hastened forward, and, presently, met the dismounted cyclist on the edge of the kerb, about a hundred yards farther back.

He was a sorry spectacle, dust-begrimed from head to foot; but, as he pushed his goggles up, and his cap back, the liveliest satisfaction was visible on his handsome, eager face.

"Now, this is an uncommon piece of good luck, and could only happen in war time! They said I'd never get here, or find you even if I did!"

"Who said that? And where have you come from?" cried Bella impetuously.

"My mater and your father. They're both at Ostend. The mater and I arrived only last night. We've been three weeks getting out of Switzerland. Your father was at the hotel—just come over from England, frantic about you, and found the train service stopped. I volunteered to have a run for my money, and a chap obliged me with a bike. The question is, how are we to get back! This thing won't hold us—that's a sure thing!"

"But would it be safe to leave Brussels, even suppose you could take us?"

"Safer than stopping here. The Germans will be inside the town in less than twenty-four hours. We'll have to take the sporting chance. If I can get a car, will you take it?"

The sisters looked at one another, and Nancy's eyes shone.

"Oh, yes, of course we shall! We must! Bella, don't you see it?"

"If I can get a good-going car we'll be as right as rain. I happen to know Belgium from end to end. I've had three cycling holidays in it. We'll keep to the by-roads, and, with luck, should get to Ostend to-night yet. It doesn't matter how late. Will you go to your place and put a few things together—only what you can lift, you know—while I go and see what I can do about a car?"

Standing there, on the edge of the pavement of the Avenue Louise, Bella Cardine had to arrive at what was undoubtedly the most momentous decision of her life.

There is, presumably, a certain amount of safety in crowds, and Colin Farquhar's slim figure was all that stood between them and danger. There was not a hint of hesitation or fear about him, but could she trust him so infinitely far?

"Do you think, honestly, we have a ghost of a chance of getting to Ostend?"

Colin showed his even white teeth in a smile as he shrugged his shoulders.

"I've told you, it's only a sporting chance."

"And will you go alone, if we don't?" asked Nancy.

"I'll have to, for I'll have to join my corps," he answered modestly. "I'm in a mortal funk now, in case they've gone to the front before I get back."

"And you came here, all alone, on a sporting chance of finding us and taking us along!" said Bella in an odd, shaky voice.

"Right-o! But I say, we haven't got time to stand here longer. Where's your place? And am I to commandeer a car, or not? If not, I must be making tracks on this old Sally."

"We'll come," said Bella solemnly. "We're at the Pension Lasalle, 13, Rue Washington—the second on the left."

"Right-o!" said the youth again. "I'll go and get something to eat, and collar a car."

He saluted, started up his bicycle, and rode away as coolly and nonchalantly as if the encounter had taken place in the streets of Glasgow.

"Awfully good of him, isn't it Bella?" asked Nancy, feverishly, slightly awed by the solemn expression on her sister's face.

"It's more than good! It's lovely, Nancy! But I'm afraid—horribly afraid! We shall be alone on country roads, with nobody to protect us but that laddie."

"Oh, but he is very brave; and he has a revolver in his belt!" said Nancy enthusiastically.

Bella smiled somewhat wanly.

"Much good that will do him, if we happen to meet some Uhlans! Well, we can only die once; and as Colin Farquhar says, it is better to take a sporting chance than to be shut up here indefinitely among the Germans. Nobody knows how they will treat the folk in the town; and they'll be here to-morrow. Goodness me, Nancy! I can't believe we are the same girls who set out from Glasgow a week or two back, with hardly a care worth speaking of in our hearts!"

As Bella's courage and resource waned, Nancy's seemed to increase, and it was Nancy who took the lead in getting everything ready for their hazardous ride.

Bella kept on harping on the goodness and the wonder of the thing the lad had done for them; risking his life to discover where they were, and exactly in what plight.

But Nancy knew why!

In London, in the spring, Colin Farquhar had dropped more than one significant sentence into her ears; and she was aware that her engagement to Captain Gilder had disappointed him deeply.

The thought that two men had been equally anxious to save and protect them made her humble, and a little ashamed of herself. For she knew that she was hardly worthy of the sacrifice of either.

"But I will be better!" she whispered to herself, and the tears started in her eyes and fell on the few things she was stuffing at the moment into her blouse-case.

They decided to leave their heavy boxes and the bulk of their clothes with Madame Lasalle, hoping to be able to redeem them at some future time, and if not—well, they were of no great value.

The few articles of jewellery they possessed they secreted on their persons, and with a small case each could carry without the smallest difficulty, they sat down in the courtyard to wait for Colin Farquhar.

Madame Lasalle came and sat by them, under the shade of the chestnut-tree which made the courtyard such a pleasant place, and where it was very peaceful, the pigeons strutting about, cooing softly, as if there could be no such thing in the world as war's alarms.

Madame was not at all sure about the impending journey. While sympathizing with their anxiety to escape, and herself the prey of a thousand fears, yet she felt the safety and comfort of being one of a multitude.

"You are brave children, Mademoiselles! But there! All the English are. To me, it seems incredible, impossible, that you should do it; but, *voila*, doubtless the good God will help to bring you to a safe haven. I will myself pray—but, ah!——"

Here the good soul wept again as if words altogether failed her.

It was almost sundown before the whirr of the motor sounded outside the gate. They ran forward, and admitted Colin Farquhar, who, in the interval, had washed the dust of his hasty ride from his face, and brushed his clothes, and looked the well-groomed, well-set up Britisher once more.

Nancy's eyes proclaimed an almost unwilling admiration.

"I didn't find the chap I was after, for he went yesterday. Yet I've managed to commandeer a car elsewhere—a ripper she is, and if she behaves herself, we'll easily make Ostend before midnight."

The two girls, carried away on the crest of young Farquhar's enthusiasm, failed to notice what would have been clear to a close observer, that he was worked up to a high state of nervous tension. He did not tell them of the warnings he had received, of the assurance from authorities who considered themselves competent that he was simply going to certain destruction.

He had pledged himself to a distracted father that he would get these two girls safely out, and he was going to do it, even if it cost him his life! He had the fine, British bulldog spirit which, while quiet and unobtrusive, imparted confidence to himself and others.

When Bella and Nancy, with their motor veils swathed about their heads, stepped to their seats in the car, her long, grey, torpedo-like bonnet gave them an impression of uncanny speed.

At the last moment, Madame Lasalle, obviously tearful, but trying to smile, bade them God-speed and farewell. She did not forget to stow a little basket of provisions, with a bottle of red wine, in case they should require refreshment by the way. They glided, unchallenged, out of Brussels, and at the obscure gateway by which they left the city, their passports and papers were found in complete order. But again they were warned, and when young Farquhar, in fluent French, explained his purpose, the guard shook their heads and gave him a few words of direction and advice.

As they watched the grey car become a lessening speck on the long, white ribbon of the road, they looked at one another with a strange significant smile.

The Allies, on whom the future salvation of Belgium might now easily depend, were of the right fibre, through and through!

But presently these comrades had something else to distract their attention than the trio of fleeing English, trying to reach the coast.

After sunset the light began to wane quickly, and the car raced on. They passed innumerable refugees, for whom the hearts of the sisters bled. They could have wished to pick them all up and carry them to places of safety, but the seating accommodation of a racing-car is strictly limited, and they were already packed tightly enough for comfort.

But as the devastation of war became increasingly more apparent, and they passed through villages which were now merely a handful of smoking ruins, the horror and fear of it all began to come home.

Nancy, after the first hour, did not speak a word, but, unconsciously, she crept closer to their deliverer who, with set face and steadfast eyes, and hands that did not falter, guided the steering-wheel.

He had been one of the most dare-devil motorists of his year at Cambridge, and had, more than once, been threatened with condign punishment for certain exploits in that direction. But his sunny personality, his winning smile, had got him out.

The car which, in less competent hands, might easily have lured them to destruction, behaved splendidly, and as the distance lessened between them and the coast, their spirits began to rise. But they were not out of the wood yet!

When they were about an hour on the road, the whirr and beat of a motor-bicycle smote on their ears, and presently a scout, smothered in dust from head to foot, slowed down to warn them.

"A whole company of Uhlans, left to right—about three miles farther on. You'd better turn back, or get under cover somewhere, or there'll be nothing left to tell the tale!"

" Right-o ! " sang out young Farquhar cheerily, and waving his hand to the cyclist, who went on as if he were riding to his death.

Cool as a cucumber, Farquhar slowed down, and, standing upright in the car, took his bearings. They were in the middle of an undulating country, and in some of the fields the reaped corn was still standing in sheaves. In three minutes his resolve was taken.

" Sit tight. We must get her across a couple of fields. It'll be bumpy, but we'll get there. I see our cover."

They sat tight, both of them curiously calm, without feeling the slightest desire or temptation to scream out, or in any way disturb or distract their deliverer, upon whose engineering of this appalling situation their very lives depended.

Bella prayed as they drove through the open gateway of the first field, where happily the long drought had made the ground so hard that the tyres made no impression, not even flattening a blade of stubble.

It was getting dark now, and, in the far distance, behind the edge of a little wood, a red moon was coming up.

They crossed one field, Farquhar getting down carefully to close the gates as he had found them, and in the second, where there was some undulating ground, and many sheaves, he sought cover. The car was very low-hung, built on the racing principle, and she was very easy to hide. They grouped some sheaves about her, the girls helping with a will.

" Now she'll do ; and with luck we may get through. We'd better have something to eat while we're waiting."

Bella, marvelling at her own calm, got out Madame Lasalle's basket, and they made their meal.

Young Farquhar, whose face looked very boyish in the weird half-light, while he talked to them in gay whispers, was listening intently all the time. Bella knew it, by the quick, tense look which crossed his face whenever any unusual sound beat the air.

Presently he heard, in the far distance, the sound for which they were waiting—the dull beat of hoofs, on a hard, dust-bound road. " They're coming," he said quietly. " And we can't do any more. Creep in there behind the sheaves, and I'll watch."

Nancy began to cry, but Bella shook her and told her to be quiet.

" There's just one thing," whispered their protector. And now his young face showed very tense and white in the moonlight, as he touched the revolver in his hand. " I've got enough here for both of you, and I promise you shan't fall into their hands. That's all. Creep in, and I'll keep a look out."

CHAPTER XXX

THE ESCAPE

INTO the friendly sheaves the fugitives crept, and the beat of the hoofs drew nearer. Presently other sounds mingled with it—the jingle of accoutrements, the sound of hoarse laughter, scraps of harsh song.

To these hidden refugees the minutes while the troops passed were interminable. They were like centuries! With not a whisper, scarcely a sigh, they clung to each other desperately, while their brave protector kept the necessary watch.

The time of agonizing suspense was really less than twenty minutes, but it seemed an eternity before young Farquhar, shaking himself, crept nearer to them.

"We've had the luck! They've gone on—wanting their dinners, I suppose. That's in our favour. We'll give the road another half-hour, and then we'll scoot again. Gad, isn't it hot?"

The perspiration was rolling down his face, not brought there by the closeness of the night air, but by the terrific mental strain of the moment. No answer came from within the shelter, where the two trembling girls were thanking God for their deliverance.

He warned them presently, when he began to tune up the car again, that it might not be the last of their adventures; but their good fortune had given them a fresh confidence, and presently they were bowling smoothly along the road again, without lights, but needing none, for the moon was nearly as clear as day.

The car behaved like an angel, purring smoothly and softly, as if with a secret satisfaction at the part she had to play.

On, on they went, gathering speed with every mile.

"The sea!" said young Farquhar presently, with a sweep of his arm towards the left. "I think we're safe now, and, with your permission, I'll take a cigarette."

Bella laughed hysterically, but on Nancy's face there came a wonderful look which could only have one meaning.

A heart was caught in the rebound that night, in the danger zone between Brussels and Ostend.

They made the town before midnight, and when they reached the door of the hotel, where a distracted and hardly hopeful father awaited, Bella fainted clean away.

"I've done it, sir," said young Farquhar with a nod. "Near shave! Don't say anything—it meant something to me, too. I'm jolly glad. And now I'll have a wash. But it was a sporting chance!"

When Bella came to herself, she was in a hotel bedroom, with a sweet-faced woman bending over her, whom she had never seen before.

In the background stood Nancy, a little awe-stricken by the sudden collapse of her sister, on whom she had been accustomed to rely for everything.

It is doubtful whether, in these supreme hours, Nancy Cardine had even yet awakened to the realization of the actual danger from which she had been snatched. Full realization would come later, when she, in common with thousands of other women, would find her heart quail before the horrors of the casualty lists, where anguished eyes sought for names familiar and beloved.

"Where am I? And who are you?" asked Bella, wonderingly, as she raised herself on her elbow.

"At Ostend. But, please God, in a few more hours we shall be safe in England. I am Colin's mother, my dear."

"Colin's mother! Why did he do that for us, Lady Farquhar?"

"For two reasons, I think, my dear—because it was an adventure after his own heart——"

Bella did not ask for the second reason. Perhaps, as she observed Lady Farquhar's slight turn of the head towards Nancy, she may have understood.

At the moment Nancy spoke:

"I think I'll go down, and tell father you're all right, Bella," she said, and forthwith disappeared.

"She's the second reason," said Lady Farquhar with an odd little smile. "Your father has told me the whole story while we've been waiting here together. Perhaps the day may come when there will be a closer bond between the families."

Bella closed her eyes. None knew what were her thoughts.

Perhaps she scarcely plumbed them herself. But the largesse of love which had been poured on her careless little sister brought back to her mind certain words of Holy Writ: "To him that hath shall be given."

"It was splendid of him! It won't bear talking of, Lady Farquhar, and we shall never be able to repay it!" she murmured weakly. "And now, you have to let him go out and fight?"

"He will go," answered his mother steadily. "And I wish there were twenty of him! They should go—every one."

Such being the spirit of Britain's motherhood, could there be any doubt of the final issue? Before Bella could make any comment on this, to her, majestic speech, her father knocked at the door.

"She's all right now, Mr. Cardine; and I think I'll go down and see about getting her a light meal of some sort. Yes, you may come in."

When father and daughter were left alone, Bella's eyes became imploring.

"I don't know what I deserve, Father; only don't scold me now; for I don't think I could bear it! To think that you trusted me with Nancy, and that I made such a muddle of it!"

"Scold you, lass! There's no room in my heart, in any of our hearts, for that sort of thing; only for sheer gratitude."

"Tell me about home. It seems such ages since we heard anything! How is dear Margaret?"

"Quite well. She's the most wonderful woman, Bella; and every day I thank God for her. She's mothered them all these days—from Alec and Evelyn, downwards. Both the boys are away, of course; Alec, at Aldershot. It's likely his regiment may be one of the first Territorials to go to the front. Harry's at Bedford; and there's hardly a mother's son of the better sort left in Glasgow. Soon there won't be many of any kind left, if the recruiting goes on as it has been doing. We've reason to be proud of old Glasgow, I can tell you."

"Alec and Harry gone! And the Dempster boys, and the Yuills, I suppose, and Tom Montgomerie?"

"Every man-jack of them! And we stiff old stagers thinking of setting up a Citizen's Battalion, or an Old Sportmen's Brigade, or something, just to keep our hands in and our rifles oiled. Oh, I tell you, we're all in it, Bella, and it's life or death!"

"Before they come back, Father, I must tell you about Nancy, and how we found Hugh Gilder in Brussels, the very day war broke out."

She gave him a brief résumé of the events that had happened at Tervueren, and which she had never had time to write about. For, in war time, there are few, if any, personal affairs, everything being submerged in the one supreme fact.

Even as he listened, Mr. Cardine failed to realize that a final and very treacherous attempt had been made to entrap his girl into a marriage which could never have made her happy.

"Well, it's over, and we'll hear no more of him for a while, as he's safely out of the way. It's just possible he may distinguish himself in France, for that type of man is usually a brave and fearless soldier, and the heat of battle may purge him clean."

Again the look of awe deepened on Bella Cardine's face. Small wonder that she slept but fitfully that night, and was alert, wide-eyed, open-hearted to meet the new dawn.

By eleven o'clock they were on board the Channel boat, all relieved and thankful that, in a few more hours, they would be safe.

It was a crowded boat ; and the scenes among the Belgian refugees were pitiful. Only Nancy seemed wholly undisturbed. Her eyes, full of eager and quite undisguised admiration, dwelt on Colin Farquhar's happy face. The volatile spirit of the child had quickly leaped from one milestone to another, and very probably would never look back.

Perhaps it is the priceless and incommunicable possession of youth, but Bella found herself half-inclined to consider her little sister heartless. Her love affair had been serious enough to occasion a great deal of trouble and anxiety to a considerable number of people, had incidentally given them a taste of the real personal danger inseparable from war ; yet here she was smiling on their deliverer as if he were the only person in the world !

Lady Farquhar caught the expression in Bella's eyes, and fully understood it. As they passed to and fro on the deck together, she alluded to it.

" My dear, you are inclined to judge your little sister, but don't. We are only young once. I love to see her like that."

" To me it seems a bit heartless," said Bella on the spur of the moment. " She doesn't seem to realize what she has cost everybody in the last six months."

" It is merely a phase that will pass—and six months from now none of us will be the same people."

The usually short Channel passage was lengthened by three or four hours, and it was late evening before they reached Folkestone. All the way across the more imaginative passengers were fully conscious of the hidden and unnamed menace of the sea. Nothing was safe or sure any longer ! Sunny waters, sown ruthlessly with mines ; a sky whose brightness and peace might at any moment be darkened by the new and terrible aircraft which had become engines of destruction instead of merely giant birds to wonder at and speculate upon ! All was changed indeed !

Folkestone had taken on a new aspect since that smiling but remote day when the two girls had stepped from the boat-train on to the quay. It was crowded now with a strange and motley throng, largely composed of refugees from poor devastated Belgium, whose capital the invaders were that very day entering in triumph.

In eager haste many pressed forward, forlornly hoping to discover some dear ones among the fresh arrivals. The pathos and the misery everywhere abounding awakened an intolerable pain in Bella Cardine's heart ; and as they hurried to the waiting train, she drew down her veil to hide her tears.

" Oh, God, forgive me ! " she cried in her heart. " I don't know anything, and I've never been of the slightest use in the world ! But oh, I will be, I will be ! We needed something—me and my kind—to wake us up ; only, don't let the punishment be too hard ! "

Such prayer was being wafted daily from every corner of the Empire, of which Bella Cardine was a unit.

They talked but little on the train journey. Mingling with their thankfulness at finding themselves once more enfolded by the safety of their Island Home, was ineffable sadness over the anguish and the terror of which they had seen some small part, and a deep apprehension of the future, which might so easily contain more suffering for innocent people.

There was very little delay at Victoria, for they resembled the refugees in that they had no luggage, save such small parcels as they could take in their hands.

Lady Farquhar smiled bravely as she said good-bye.

" God send we may meet in happier circumstances, my dears. We must not lose sight of one another now ! "

" But, surely, you won't stay in London alone ? " said Mr. Cardine quickly.

" Only until I've helped my boy to get his kit together. Then, most likely, I shall make tracks for Inneshall, to wait for my husband disembarking on the north coast somewhere—port unknown. It's a little like a page out of *Catriona*, but it would interest us all more if we were a little less anxious."

While their elders were exchanging these farewells, Colin and Nancy had withdrawn a little apart, and quite evidently had something of importance to say to one another. The girl's eyes were shining, her cheeks softly flushed; her whole being seemed to respond to what her lover was saying.

Bella, however, viewed the pretty picture with disgust. Her mood was very serious, and she could not understand how her sister could be so volatile, how she could put everything behind her, in a moment, as it were, and find immediate solace in the next that came to hand!

Had her thoughts been put into words, they would probably have voiced the assertion that Nancy's affections were not likely to bring security or happiness to any man on whom she deigned to bestow them!

"Why are you looking so frightfully glum, Bella?" Nancy asked, as they were getting ready for dinner at the Euston Hotel, before taking the night express for Glasgow. "There isn't anything to pull such a long face about now. We're all safe, and as for the boys, it isn't likely they'll be sent to the front. They won't be ready for ever so long!"

"It isn't that, kid," said Bella in a queer, choked voice. "I only wish I were a man, and had my chance! It's the uselessness and selfishness of people like you and me that gets on my nerves. Just see the trouble and anxiety we've given everybody just now! Father looks years older, I think. Margaret will be asking us what we've done to him!"

"Oh, that needn't trouble us. And think of the adventures we've had! We'll score off them at Glasgow over that thrilling night ride to the coast—only, they'll never believe we did it! I say, Bella, wasn't Colin Farquhar splendid? And won't he look a duck in his uniform? He has promised to send me the very first of his photographs—in fact, to have one taken specially if I let him have one of mine."

"Before his mother, even, I suppose," put in Bella dryly.

"Oh, of course, she'll get one, too. I can't think why you are so disagreeable about him, Bella! You don't even seem a bit grateful! Why, if it hadn't been for him we'd be in Brussels to-night, watching the German goose-step—whatever that may be—instead of going back to poor old, smoky Glasgow!"

"I can't make you out, Nancy! Why—forty-eight hours ago you were crying your eyes out about Hugh Gilder, and threatening to elope with him; and now you've no thought for anybody but Colin Farquhar! I've never had a sweetheart, but, if I were a man, I would like something a little more stable!"

Nancy made a delicious little gesture of superior knowledge.

"I seem to be the kind they like," she said—a speech which so thoroughly disgusted Bella that she hastily changed the subject.

She did not sleep soundly in the train; and, when the sweet dawn began to creep over the landscape, she drew the blind of her berth and, leaning her head on her hand, watched the sleeping hamlets as they flew by. Even out there, in the spacious country-side, there were many unusual features—bivouacs, clustering canvas encampments, strange accoutrements, evidence of transport, on a scale undreamed of in time of peace.

A mighty change had passed over her native land—there was even a tenseness in the inanimate air which seemed to grip the heart.

Bella was conscious of a great longing to see her stepmother. She was the kind of woman capable of rising to any emergency; she would never lose her head, but would preserve through all her quiet confidence and serenity of spirit, as well as her big, loving attitude towards humanity.

Bella felt a little thrill of disappointment when Margaret was not on the platform, though, at such an hour, it was unreasonable to expect it.

Great was her surprise, however, to behold Evelyn! Her face hardened a little at sight of her sister-in-law's slim, well-carried figure, for, in her heart, she blamed Evelyn for the whole tragedy of Nancy's love affair.

But, before she had an opportunity of speaking to her, she could not but be arrested by something different in her expression. It was softer and more kindly, even a little wrung, as if she too had already tasted suffering. She was in deep mourning, too, and Bella jumped to the quick conclusion that already war had taken toll from the Whitehorns, who were a military family.

Evelyn, however, smiled bravely as she waved her hand to the little party. Her father-in-law she greeted first, with a nice deference, an affectionate solicitude she had never before shown.

James Cardine was not the man who could refuse or discourage such an advance.

"How are you, my dear?" he said, and touched her sleeve. "I'm sorry to see this—what?—Eh?"

"Willy—and Kitty's husband. Both killed at Mons," she answered, and though her eyelids quivered, she did not cry.

Bella, full of remorse, ran forward to kiss her. She knew what attachment there had been between Evelyn and her youngest brother, a lieutenant in one of the regiments that had suffered most severely in that masterly retreat.

"Oh, I'm so sorry, Evey!"

"It's all right, Bella—fortune of war," said Evelyn, a little unsteadily. "I'm at Huntley Gardens. Mrs. Cardine came and fetched me and the kiddies, directly she heard. She's been so good, Bella! We can't do enough for her. Poor father and mother are shut up in Marienbad, where, I suppose, they won't hear a thing except German or Austrian lies. We haven't heard from them since the last week in July, and nobody knows when they'll get back. Well, Nance, had enough of adventures to last meanwhile?"

Nancy scarcely smiled in response to this little dig.

The sight of Evelyn's black clothing and her subdued air suddenly seemed to bring things home to her, even more acutely than the hasty escape from Belgium. If war had changed Evelyn like that, then surely it must be very terrible in its relentless power!

The carriage was waiting for them. They all got in, and were swiftly borne to the house in Huntley Gardens, where a loving welcome awaited them.

When James Cardine saw his wife standing in the open doorway, her kind, dear face shining with all the light of home, he felt strangely overcome. An overwhelming sense of the goodness of God to him and his swept over him like a resistless sea.

Margaret, observing the tremor of his features, understood, and gave his shoulder a quick little pat.

"It's all right, my dear man. Thank God, I've got you back safe—and the bairns, too! We have indeed much to be thankful for."

Mary Bruar was in the background; and, farther back still, Harry's wife, whom Margaret had been mothering ever since the boy went into training. Evelyn—wonder of wonders!—had neither refused to meet her, nor yet had oppressed her by the condescending Whitehorn manner. She had shed that outstanding family characteristic like a garment no longer needed!

Talk at the well-laden breakfast-table was perhaps a little incoherent. Naturally, the adventures of the two girls were the most interesting topic; and Nancy, at least, was not inclined to let one of them go unchronicled or unembroidered.

Bella had very little to say; and Margaret cast more than one anxious look in her direction, and was glad when an opportunity came for them to have a private word.

"I feel as if I had lived a hundred years since I left Glasgow!" said Bella in a low voice. "I'll never be the same girl again; and I want you to show me how to be a useful woman, like you are, instead of a cumberer of the ground. Do you think I could learn to be a nurse quickly enough to get right out there, to do something for them at the Front?"

"It's what a lot of the lassies are wanting to do, Bella; but there are other ways in which one can help," said Margaret doubtfully.

"I know; and I'm not going to be a trouble. I'll do whatever comes to my hand, and you'll show me how. But, somehow, I think I could be of use out there; for I have no fear, and I can speak fluent French and German. If anything can be done, you'll not stand in my way, I know."

"I, dear lassie! I'll help you all I can. And I wouldn't wonder but that it might be Evelyn that could help you here! She seems to know the army from end to end. Her father would have influence, too. We'll see what she says."

It took several days even for them to make a semblance of settling down; and after Bella had arranged to get a quick course of training at one of the big hospitals, Margaret suggested that they should all go down for a long week-end to Ardgoil, to get a blow from the sea. Mr. Cardine, working single-handed at Bridgeton, welcomed the suggestion joyfully. They were packing up, however, when a long telegram came from Lady Farquhar, at Inneshall, to Margaret—a singular and graceful recognition of her position, which she appreciated to the full.

As it happened there was no one in the house she could consult about it, except Evelyn, who was writing a letter to her husband in the morning-room.

"Look at this, Evelyn. It's from your aunt, Lady Farquhar. She wants Nancy to come up, at once, for the week-end, to Ross-shire, as her son has got leave for forty-eight hours, and is to arrive to-morrow, in time to see his father. She expects him at Lerwick this afternoon."

Evelyn, much surprised, perused the telegram with her brows wrinkled, and her pen held to her lips.

"Well, I think probably that has but one meaning. She'd better go, don't you think? It would solve Nancy's future, and it would absolve me from a good deal that lies rather heavily on my conscience!"

That was a great admission for Evelyn to make. Mrs. Cardine accepted it in silence.

"To make it worth while at all, she would need to go up this afternoon. I see Lady Farquhar says they'll send the car to Inverness to meet her on chance."

"Yes. Where is Nancy?"

"Gone out with Jean."

"And when is the train?"

"Somewhere just after two, I think; but we can soon find out."

"I daresay they'll be back before lunch. If we could pack her things, it would save time. Do you think Grandpa will mind?"

"Oh, no! But, of course, we can ring him up, and ask. He feels the debt he owes to Mr. Farquhar can never be paid."

"He's a dear lad, and Nancy's real mate, I don't doubt," said Evelyn. "Let me ring up Grandpa. I've some things to say that I might find easier over the telephone than face to face. And this gives me the opening."

Nancy, wild with excitement and anticipation, started out for the north, by the two o'clock train, Margaret and Bella seeing her off. As they drove back together Bella said, with an odd little laugh:

"That, I suppose, finally disposes of Nancy! I'm anxious about Jean, dear woman. Don't you think she looks worried and out of sorts?"

"I suppose it's the war."

"It's partly that; but, she's had a small shock of a personal kind, Bella."

"Burgess?" said Bella, with slightly uplifted brows.

Margaret nodded.

"But she never could have married him, though I don't deny there was something likeable about him. He might very easily be made into a gentleman."

"He's got a bit perverted, my dear; but life will teach him. Meanwhile I'm glad he has gone to Australia, though, in the present state of the seas, it's an open question if he ever gets there."

The evening post that night brought a letter for Mr. Cardine which created immense interest in the house. It was brought to him in the library, where he was having his after-dinner smoke.

After he had pondered it a long time, during which his pipe went out, he carried it to his wife's sitting-room, where she was with the girls.

"I've had a letter from Gilder," he said abruptly. "I won't read it to you, because it was a private letter from man to man, written at the base hospital where he died yesterday of his wounds got at Mons. I'll read his colonel's letter, which came with it."

As they listened to the brief, restrained account, written by a soldier's pen, of an act of gallantry which stood out even in a conflict which literally bristled with them, a strange silence, and awe, and grief, not unmingled with pride, held them in thrall.

Hugh Gilder's death had been nobler than his life. The smoke of battle, which smirched and maimed his poor body, had washed his soul clean, and rendered it meet to enter the presence of its Maker.

CHAPTER XXXI

A WAR-TIME WEDDING

On a blustering October day a certain amount of bustle and excitement was visible in the neighbourhood of Huntley Gardens.

Quite early in the day various tradesmen's vans stopped before the Cardines' house at the top of the hill, and by noon a pink and white awning which somebody facetiously dubbed "a flag of distress" was erected from the door to the outside edge of the kerb.

A man in a blue serge suit, and a soft felt hat well drawn over his brows, who entered the gardens from the bottom, observed these signs with a curious contraction of the brows, and something in his face which might easily have been labelled apprehension.

Pausing beside the man who was fixing the last post on the kerb he put a blunt question.

"Somebody getting married here, mate? Who is it?"

"Miss Nancy Cardine to Sir Robert Farquhar's son," answered the man without looking up. He was interested in his job, and had only ten minutes wherein to finish it.

"Where is it to be—in the house?" pursued his questioner.

"No, in Ladyburn Church, half-past two o'clock in the afternune, and if there's onything else ye'd like to ken, jist fire away; but if ye ask me about the brides-maids' frocks I'll be stumped."

He laughed facetiously at his own wit: the man in the blue serge suit smiled responsively, and, turning away, walked rapidly down the hill again as if he had learned all he wished to know.

The man at the head of a rather restive horse in the van looked after him with a mild interest.

"Say, Bill, ken wha that is?"

"No' me, an' I'm no' carin', that's mair. Can ye no' leave that brute's heid a meenit, and come and haud this? That wund's the very deevil."

"I canna, but I micht whustle on Tam Burgess to come back an' earn an honest penny, if he's no abune it noo."

These words were sufficient to arrest the attention of the man on the kerb, and he relaxed his conflict with the wind for a moment.

"Say, it's never Burgess, is't?" he asked, craning a rather thick red neck in the direction of the retreating figure, on whom a few stray snowflakes were beginning to fall.

"It's him, richt enough! Glesca hasna seen him for a while! Somebody telt me he had been sent oot on a labour deputation to Australy."

"Maybe he's come back to jine a crack regiment, an' tak' a pot-shot at the Germans!" observed Bill, with a broad grin at his own pleasantry.

"No him! He was naething but a wundbag. Pit him up to a real fecht, an' he'd flee like a hare. I kent him when he lived in the Garscube Road. Him an' me was thick, an' I never missed a meetin' he was to gas at. But he got ower big for his buits efter a bit. But the war'll maybe settle him an' a few ithers. Haud still, ye vicious brute! If it wasna for that wee aud wifie comin' up the street, I'd gie ye what for! A'thing in petticoats is an inspector o' cruelty noo-a-days—when it's no' votes for weemin.' This wee, auld-fashioned kind is the very warst!"

"Wheest, ye gomeral! That's Miss Mary Bruar, an' if ye get the wrang side o' her face, ye'll wonder whaur ye are! She's Mr. Cardine's sister. This is gaun to be a khaki weddin', they said; but she's in black. Guid-day, mem," he observed as he pulled his forelock. "Stormy, isn't it? But I think the sun'll be oot by half-past twa."

"I think so; and we could have dispensed with the awning, after all," she answered, with her brightest smile.

The sight of it had surprised her, because the wedding, taking place on the briefest notice two days previous to the bridegroom's leaving for the Front with his regiment, was to be of the simplest kind.

But nobody could prevent the church from being crowded to its utmost capacity; for, at that juncture, the Cardines and their affairs were of thrilling interest to their very wide circle of friends.

It is always interesting to the student of human nature to watch the faces of the onlookers. and listen to the chance remarks at a wedding. These were more than usually suggestive that day, because the circumstances were certainly out of the common.

The war itself, and all its dire effects on family life, gave a certain poignant quiet to the occasion, there was a significance in certain of the remarks, which made them worth recording for the benefit of those who have followed the fortunes of the Stepmother so far.

"That's her! See—that one in the amethyst frock and the sables. My! Isn't she sweet-looking? And hasn't she bonnie white hair?"

It was Margaret who was thus being commented on; and her serene face showed how unconscious she was of being an object of interest to anybody.

She had a good deal to say to a burly, smiling, seafaring man and his small, bird-like wife, who wore a sealskin coat—the gift of her own son-in-law—in which she looked very cosy and sweet.

When the bridal procession arrived, there was nothing but standing room in the building, and therefore no one particularly noticed the somewhat striking face and figure of Tom Burgess as he slipped in at the end of a seat near the door opening on the aisle, so that he had an excellent opportunity of studying the procession as it filed down to the chancel. Six bridesmaids followed the two tiny train-bearers, the niece and nephew of the bride, who were in a state of subdued excitement. Their mother, one of the handsomest women there, felt herself, however, slightly out of it, and realized that, beside the second Mrs. Cardine, she was a person of no importance. Everybody was deferential and courteous to her, and all the Farquhars paid her marked attention.

Seldom had a more attractive, well-matched pair stood up to take the vows. Those who looked with discerning eyes saw them young, beautiful, and pure, as the Creator intended man and woman to come together first in Eden. Nancy made a lovely picture, and her gallant soldier bridegroom looked as if he were the happiest man in the world. The ceremony was quickly over, and when the returning procession approached the church door on the way out, Jean suddenly met the earnest eyes of Tom Burgess. She paled visibly, gave him a slight bow, and then seeing that he wished to speak, and as at the moment they were about to disperse in the church porch, she lingered half a moment.

"I want to see you; I must see you," he said very humbly. "May I come to your father's house?"

"I don't know—but, yes, why not? To-morrow morning if you like," answered Jean, and as she passed out the red dyed her cheek. For she knew that he had not forgotten her any more than she had forgotten him.

After all the excitement of the day was over, the guests gone from the family dinner, and the Cardines once more alone, Jean crept up to her stepmother's room. Margaret was very tired, but very, very happy, for the day had been a complete success, and the farewell words the bride and bridegroom had poured into her ears before they left remained like sweet echoes in her heart.

"May I come in just a minute?" asked Jean.

She had taken off her evening gown, and was in her loose wrapper, and Margaret saw that something had happened to disturb her.

"Yes, of course, come in. I quite thought you had both gone to bed. We've had a grand day, haven't we?"

"Oh, glorious, and I never saw anything more beautiful than Nancy and Colin.

That is how people ought to look when they get married. I'm sure it was what God intended."

"Beyond doubt," Margaret agreed. "My heart was just a little overshadowed by memory, Jean. It might have been all so different."

"It would have been, but for you," said Jean significantly. "I wanted to ask whether you saw Tom Burgess in the church this morning?"

"Tom Burgess! No! Was he there?"

"He was close to the door. He spoke to me as we went out after it was all over, and—and he asked me whether he might come here to see me to-morrow."

"Well, and what will that mean, dear? Are you letting him come?"

"Yes."

"You haven't forgotten him, then?"

"No, I haven't," Jean admitted quite frankly. "There isn't any use denying it. I care about him, yet."

"Well, nothing can be said or done till we hear what he has to say for himself to-morrow," said Margaret, but her voice sounded a little heavy. "You will do nothing rashly, Jean, and you'll mind that marriage isn't a thing to be put on or taken off like a garment. With a woman it is for ever. She can't ever be as she was before."

"I understand; but I want him to come. I will hear what he has to say for himself."

"God bless and guide you, my dear," said Margaret, in full tones, and at the moment their little colloquy was interrupted by Cardine coming up to bed.

Margaret said nothing to him, considering with perfect reasonableness that it would be time enough after Jean's interview with Burgess was over. Once or twice in the night she woke up, and it was always of Jean she thought, and for Jean she prayed.

Burgess came next morning about eleven o'clock, and was at once admitted to the library, where Jean came to him.

"I've come to ask you to forgive me," he said quietly and bluntly.

"I do forgive you. I forgave you long since," she answered quietly, and then they stood still, looking at one another.

"I don't deserve that you should speak to me at all, or so kindly," he went on. "Have I your permission to tell you something about myself in the last months?"

"I should like to hear," she answered simply. "But won't you sit down?"

"I haven't earned the right to sit in your presence yet," he said, with his air of proud humility slightly accentuated. "I went to Australia, as perhaps you will remember it was arranged, and on the whole I had a successful trip. It taught me a good many things, especially about myself, I didn't know before. When a man realizes for the first time that the world is wide, and that he is a mere insect on its surface, it is an excellent experience for him. That is what happened to me."

"And what do you intend to do now?" asked Jean.

"Do now! There is nothing for any able-bodied man to do now except to enlist. I've joined the Gordons, and I'm due at Aldershot to-morrow. But I wanted to see you again. I didn't think I could trouble you with words—or even with the sight of me; but when I got here, to the old place, and knew I could see you, I couldn't help myself."

Jean's face flushed softly.

"You're enlisted in the Gordons!"

"Yes—that's good enough for me, meanwhile. If I'm worth anything I'll get my chance with the rest. And, if I ever come back——" he added, and his face took on a look which stirred the listening woman to the depths, "will you let me come and see you again?"

"I will," whispered Jean, very low.

"I haven't the right to say more; but if you would send me a line now and again it would help me to make good."

"Don't speak like that!" cried Jean hastily. "As if you had been some kind of a waster! Of course you'll do well, and come back with a commission, or perhaps a decoration on your breast!"

"Then you do wish me God-speed, my dear?" he said.

" I do more ; bid you come back to me safely, and I will pray that God may speed the day ! "

. . . . .

So, meanwhile, we must leave them all, as it were, in the strangest melting-pot the world has ever seen ! What will be the ultimate end no one knows, save the God who for some wise but inscrutable purpose of His own, has permitted this appalling cataclysm among the forces of the world.

The little group in whom we have become interested are all united in a common bond of sympathy and anxiety ; and human nature, thus purged, must become a finer and nobler thing.

The last news to hand, as I write, is that Bruce Gemmill and Tom Burgess have met in the ranks at the camp of the Gordons at Aldershot.

It was an item of news which, communicated by Jean, sent Margaret Cardine thankfully to her knees. As she wrote to Bella, with the Red Cross in Servia : " God's hand is in all this, dear lassie ; and we must just wait, and thole as best we can, sure that the end, when it comes, will be best for us all."

THE END

Waterlow & Sons Limited, Printers, London, Dunstable & Watford.